WIND FOLLOWER

WIND FOLLOWER

Carole McDonnell

JUNO

Wind Follower

ISBN: 978-0-8095-5779-0
Library of Congress Control Number: 2007925918

Juno Books
Rockville, MD
www.juno-books.com
info@juno-books.com

*T*hese are the words that Loic tyu Taer and Satha tya Monua spoke to our ancestors on the day the Angleni gathered us to this place. How briefly that bright light shone—yet how powerfully! Nevertheless, all is not lost. Tell your children this prophecy, and let your children tell their children, and those children must tell the future generations—because the prophesied time will come. In the last days, the light will shine again with power and permanence. Use these memories as a beacon, my children, for the time will come when the Great Chief will return to us our land and all that is ours.

LOIC
The Reaping Moon–First Harvest Moon

I will tell you first how Krika died.

Okiak, his father and the chief shaman of our clan, brought Krika before the elders at the Spirit Shrine, the sacrificial mound we called Skull Place. My friend was bound, hand and foot, and the skin of his face had been flayed away so that all the muscles and bones beneath his right eye were exposed and glistening. He was weeping and crying out for mercy, choking on his tears. This surprised me, but I forgave it. Who could bear such pain without weeping?

Okiak lifted the shuwa, already reddened with his son's blood, and there—surrounded by bones and burned flesh, remnants of the monthly sacrifices—he shouted, "My son has not obeyed me. I have warned him time and times to pay obeisance to our spirits, but he has refused."

The spirits had ordered his death. I stood far off, struggling with my father and Pantan. Their hands held me fast and kept me from racing to Krika's side.

Nevertheless, I called out, shouted aloud for everyone to hear. "Are the spirits so puny and helpless they must *force* people to worship them?"

All eyes rebuked me, yes, all the elders of the Pagatsu clan, and Father yanked me back by my arm. "Be careful, son," he said, "lest the spirits also demand your life."

I glared at him. "And if they did, would you be so weak as to comply?"

He turned away. "The spirits have not asked for your life. Why ponder a demand that has not been asked?"

I hated him for that. Yes, although I loved him with all my heart, I despised him for those words.

Krika continued pleading for his life. Okiak aimed his vialka and let it fly through the sky toward his son. Krika's wail sounded over the fields and the low-hanging willows and past the Great Salt Desert. But no one spoke for him, not my father, not the other shaman, and not the Creator. He died, battered beneath a hail of stones; all eyes but mine witnessed his last breath. Father had pulled my face into his chest, and I hated my weakness for allowing it. My tears soaked his tunic. He gently stroked my head and played with my braid, and told me that I should forget, forget, forget, for death—however it comes—is the destiny of all men.

They left Krika's body where it fell. Unburied, he was to be devoured by wild wolves and bears. Worse, his lack of a burial meant he could not enter the fields we long for. He could not hunt with the Creator. His father had damned him to everlasting grief.

Krika had been my age-brother, taught with Prince Lihu as I was. While he lived, his presence colored my life as a wolf's continuous howl or a woman's singing might color the night. He seemed to rage against the spirits while yet singing to the Creator. This was a strange thing, for at that time no one in the three tribes sought the Creator; we thought those shadow gods were his servants. Even I, who was suspicious of the spirits from my birth, had never warred against them as Krika had.

That night, as the sun set over my father's Golden House, I escaped to the shrine. There lay Krika, broken on the ground. With many shuwas, I warded off the wolves and lions that had sniffed out my friend's blood. But the spirits fought against me, calling from the east, west, north and south, all creatures of earth and air. How black the field and night sky grew with their descending shadows. In the field, only two men: Krika and I, one living and one dead. All my father's so-called Valiant Men were nowhere to be seen. Although they had battled mightily against the Angleni, on the night of Krika's death they hid in the compound trembling in fear of the spirits.

Then, all at once, I understood the spirits had arrayed themselves in battle against me, that I would always battle them alone, for I had no ally . . . no, not one among my clan.

SATHA
Sowing Moon–First Cool Moon

In those days, I could not sleep, for grief had rolled into grief: a dear cousin slain, a sister kidnapped, our clan destroyed and scattered. The last sorrow—a harrowing journey to a far region where comfort of family and friend could not be found—was the worst of all. My mother changed, growing more sullen than before. She wept continually, crying aloud and begging the Good Maker to roll back time and to bring back her lost youth, her lost fortune, lost clan, and stolen child. So as I paced outside the college courtyard, listening to the songs of the young men inside, I could not help but be overwhelmed with grief.

Many young warriors had died during the forty-year war, and as the songs floated upward and away from me, I imagined their lives also flying away from us. Because of the war, I had not had the privilege of education. I had not studied the dead languages, as one should. Born to wealth but reared in poverty, I did not long for what I did not have. But often I found myself wondering about my lost education. *Which language is being sung?* I wondered now. *Paetan or Seythof? What are the words of the song?* As I pondered this, Mam raced up to me.

"What are you doing here, Satha?" She peered out at the marketplace. "Didn't I tell you to meet me in front of the sword seller's shop? Standing here, listening to men sing the day before the Rose Moon, a day when love is on the minds of all! People will say Monua's daughter is so poor and lonely, she went searching for a man."

The college lay on the western arc, opposite the Rock Gate and a stone's throw from the sword seller's shop. I gestured toward the courtyard wall. "I heard the collegians, so I came closer to hear the song. Do you think Father can tell me what this song means? Do you think they're singing about the Angleni wars?"

"The Angleni!" She spat out the invaders' names with such venom I feared the afternoon would be filled with her recounting of bitter memories. "I don't want to hear about them, even in songs bewailing their cruel deeds. Come, hurry to the sword shop."

"But Father doesn't trade swords. Why should we—"

She glanced back over her shoulder as we sped along. "You're asking too many questions, Satha. Hurry! We have little time."

"Why should not I ask? You ordered me here and then took so long getting here—" I noticed newly applied kohl around her eyes. She had changed her kaba too. The kaba she had changed into was torn and ragged along the hem, far worse than the one she had worn earlier. The gyuilta thrown over it had been relegated to the scrap heap. I understood then that she had determined to appear both lovely and destitute at the same time. This decision provoked even my curiosity—and I was not one who was naturally curious. I tried to ignore this wonder beside me fearing that asking questions would only drag me into affairs I wanted nothing to do with.

Her eyes busily scanned the eastern arcs near the Great Garden, and peered past the children playing tunes on their reed pipes and bamboo drums near the Sun Fountain and the Water Clock. They looked about the wide circle of the marketplace, and down its adobe-bricked streets fanning out from the Sun Fountain. How could I not be curious? Her eyes searched all the arcs and all the radii of the circle all at once.

At last, she took a brief rest from her surveying and said, "I wish you hadn't been standing near the college wall." She tugged my braid hard and her embarrassed eyes shamed me in spite of my innocence. "You're not young or marriageable anymore. People will think you're desperate."

"You put kohl on your eyes—something you never do—and you're accusing *me* of looking for an assignation?"

"Daughter, it's good to have allies."

I could only sigh at this sudden change of subject, so weary was I from sleeplessness. I only thought: *So she's scheming again? And now we're getting around to her plot.*

"Perhaps the shaman can make you something to help you sleep."

She shook her head. "You let life bother you too much. When you get to my age, you can sleep even in the worst disasters, even when family members are stolen from you." She held my right forearm firmly, tightly. Then, clenching my wrist, she dragged me further away from the college courtyard. How I wanted to tie my gyuilta's trailing hem and scale the wall! To lose myself in song and learning and to leave the poor sad world behind!

"Today is the day that changes our lives, Daughter." Yes, she had contrived some mad scheme! What Mam was like before poverty, grief, and the Angleni invasion unhinged her mind I don't know. I suppose she must have been less manipulative, but who can truly know what occurred before one's birth? Like my lost sister, I was born after the war began, after sorrow and repeated Angleni truce breaking and atrocities had embittered my mother.

"Ydalle sent a news runner to our shop this morning," she said.

An image of a stout nervous Theseni woman and a long-haired youth flashed across my mind. "The boy in green leggings?" I asked. "With the butterfly beadwork?"

She nodded. "The Pagatsu markings. The boy was one of Taer's servants." She raised her eyebrows, indicating I should be impressed that Taer's servant had visited us. I shrugged.

A self-satisfied smile spread across her face. "Even though the Angleni destroyed our livelihood, they haven't destroyed your Mam's ability to keep old friends and make new ones. Even here, the Good Maker has blessed us with allies."

She was right, of course. Mam was greatly liked. In our native village, it was even rumored she was to be appointed to the council as a Beloved Woman. She would have sat among the Kluna clan elders of the Theseni tribe. What honor that would have brought her! But we had left the Kluna region and had come to Satilo. I had thought we were merely fleeing the Angleni who now occupied so much of our old region, but I had always wondered why she had chosen Satilo, a town with a population that was mostly Ibeni.

She craned her neck, glancing behind me, then spoke through cracked front teeth as we loitered near the sword seller's shop. "You've heard your father speak of his old friend, Taer, haven't you? The Disa of Scha Menta's army?" Her eyes glowed with scheming.

"The First Captain everyone calls General Treads Lightly? That Taer?"

"Think of it, Daughter! We know the Disa of King Jaguar's army personally!"

I drew in my breath. Partly from sleeplessness, partly from disgust and wariness. Her plot was becoming all too clear, even to my muddled brain. "Mam, Father told you not to communicate with Taer."

"We're not going to 'communicate with' him, foolish girl. We're simply going to accidentally bump into him. Such things happen. Especially in markets. Of course, if one bumps into someone, the law of hospitality declares he must be invited into your father's shop for a meal."

Father's shop was dingier than all the shops in the market. Grief and illness had tied all our hands and we hardly had strength to make it hospitable. "Mam, reconsider this."

"Is it wrong to invite an old friend to a meal?" She scratched her head, something she always did when hatching a plot. "Such things also happen, don't they?"

"And why do you want to invite him to our shop?" I asked, already knowing the answer.

"Why? So he'll see our poverty, of course!"

"Of course." Why one person would want another to see her poverty was beyond me.

"Taer is an honorable man."

I suddenly understood all.

She glanced this way, then that, as if the trees themselves were con-spiring against her. "He has no patience with commerce. No, he was never one to dwell on such earthly matters. Rich men can afford to waste their time studying the gods. Not that I judge the man. Should General Treads Lightly be seen in the streets bartering, selling and buying when he has servants to handle his money? Even so, today . . . ." Her voice trailed off.

"Today?"

"Today, Daughter, he comes to the market. Oh, I've been waiting so long for this."

Her face beamed as if a star of ecstasy surrounded it. "For the first time in eight moons!" She almost danced an Ibeni two-step. "Ydalle says Taer's son wants to buy a sword, and when that boy wants something, well, you know how the Doreni spoil their children. So Taer will be helping him choose."

"Doesn't Taer have military underlings who can—"

"Tsk, tsk, this boy's his only real child! And a sword—"

I could not help myself. "He has an unreal child?"

Her eyes hinted at secrets. "Well, there are other—shall we say—concerns."

"Concerns, uh? Those concerns are no concern of mine. But if he's so close to Our Matchless King, Taer could easily ask the king for a sword for that spoiled brat of his."

"Taer's not one to push himself forward. Ydalle says this boy wants an untested sword, one that doesn't remember old victories."

"Can't he wipe off the old blood like poor warriors do?"

Mam glanced upward at the sun and then at the shadows looming on the ground and waited, pacing. She flung her hand this way and that as if we were discussing some great business. She even lifted my own hand, encouraging me to make the show more believable. Time passed, however, and I suppose she became tired with all that acting. She stood in front of me frowning. Although tears welled in her eyes, a flood of amusement inside me began to overflow. Despite my sleepiness, I laughed at what appeared to be a failing scheme.

"Laugh if you wish!" she shouted, her face betraying her heart's worry. "You're obviously not smart enough to know you're laughing at your own misfortune. Have you so easily forgotten that Kala's parents had to sell her to pay off their debts? And Kala was pretty! Look at you! Twenty-four years old, too dark, and too mouthy! No wonder you're unmarried! My luck was never good."

I had gotten used to the thought of living unmarried. Theseni men valued girls with honey-colored skin. Dark women had little chance of being married and even less chance of being loved. Yet, I had learned to see my dark skin as a blessing from the Good Maker. During the war, many young men from all the three tribes had been killed. Those who had been born in the years before the war ended had been so spoiled by doting mothers they often turned out to be cruel husbands.

"I'm tired of all this poverty." A despairing frown spread across Mam's face. "Tired of creditors and old clothes, tired of eating barley and vegetables, tired. But it's my own fault. I should have listened to my mother. I was in love with Nwaha and I didn't realize how draining a weak man could be. So this is how my own strong will rewarded me." Tears poured from her eyes, which she immediately wiped away with the fringes of her tattered gyuilta.

Then, as if she were tightening her mind, she tightened the gyuilta's loose belt. "If Taer finds out how poor his old friend has become, help won't be long in coming. Who knows—he might even give us some money for your dowry! A massive dowry will make up for that dark skin of yours." She searched the distance as if seeking a lost hope. Then a smile suddenly lit her face and she seemed much younger than her forty-two years. Such joy I hadn't seen in months. I knew without being told that Taer was in sight. "He's come. Look! Over there, near the horse dealer! No, don't look! He's the Doreni in the buckskin leggings and the green tunic. No, no, I told you not to look."

I looked, and saw a muscular well-built man standing beside a slender, almost fragile-looking boy. The boy's unbraided waist-length black hair flew wild behind his back, as if the wind delighted in playing with it. Neither boy nor man cloaked themselves in the finery of the rich. Both wore green tunics and green caps embroidered with their butterfly clan pattern. Their clothes seemed woven from cotton, hemp or other common fabric; neither wore pearl-encrusted gyuiltas, as the rich were wont to do. The older man wore boots, the boy soft leather shoes with the clan markings. Although the cold moons were barely past, their heads, arms and shoulders were uncovered. When I saw how the man's braided silver hair glistened, and how his body exuded strength and quiet power, I spoke without thinking. "Indeed, Mam, even from this distance Taer is good to look at."

"Wait until you meet him!" She smoothed out the kohl around her eyes. "His nose looks like the curve of a bear's back as it turns away to protect its young." She breathed a long wistful sigh. "Beautiful jade-gray eyes. Almond-shaped like all the Doreni—but kind, not fierce like the other slant-eyes. He wasn't one for war when we were young. How he rose so high in the King's ranks, I'll never know. He's too pale, though. Almost as light-colored as an Ibeni. If he had a little more cinnamon in his blood, like most of his people, I would have chosen him when my parents asked me who I wanted to marry. Yes, and our lives would have been much different. But, the Good Maker forgive me, I was foolish and love-struck and I chose Nwaha. Your father had happy, hopeful eyes then. He was a nice brown, too. Dark, but not too dark. He was weak, although I did not know it then. Yes, that was my mistake—"

"Being honorable is no weakness, Mam," I said, interrupting her. Mam's bitterness against Father was like boiling water—always seething over.

"You can call it whatever you want. You're not married to him. The past is gone, though. Taer's married now and even if . . ." Her voice trailed off, then she spoke again. "Yes, he's married. Waihai! Bad luck all three times. Ydalle says his third wife is the worst of his misfortunes." She bent forward and whispered conspiratorially, "An adulteress."

I shrugged, so she added, "The mother of a bastard child."

Gossip against the rich is all the poor have to digest, but gossip always upsets my stomach. When I didn't bite at her tidbit, she said, "I'll tell you that little story later."

"Mam, Doreni women who commit adultery have their noses cut off, or they're stoned or cast out into the marketplace. I've heard no marketplace gossip that Taer has done this, and warriors aren't known for indulging wayward wives. Tell Ydalle to stop spreading false stories."

Mam clutched her chest as if some great disappointment weighed on her heart. "Why the Ancient One gave me a daughter with whom I cannot share my heart—I don't understand!"

"Ask the Ancient One. Surely he knows we would both have been happier if I had been born male."

She winced, but didn't answer me.

"Do not make a fool of yourself with this rich man, Mam. Let me travel across the Lingan Plains to find work. I'll—"

"No! Never! I've lost one daughter. I won't lose another."

"Or you can hire me to an Ibeni farmer across the river."

"Did you not hear me? I said—"

"But, Mam, I have strong hands. I can—"

"Those Ibeni bleed even their own children dry. No, no blood-work for my daughter, and no travelling to parts unknown either. Ydalle says Taer's house is full of servants and former captives. When a woman marries a fool, she learns to create her own destiny. One more servant won't rob him. Maybe he'll hire you as a favor to Nwaha. The Doreni are unlike the Ibeni. They don't worship gold as much. Perhaps Taer will make you his concubine." She grinned and raised her eyebrows.

"I don't want to be a rich man's second-status wife, Mam. I don't even want to marry."

"Stop frowning like that! It makes your forehead look ugly." In those days, unmarried Theseni women wore a sheer full veil that reached from the forehead to below the neck. My mother lifted my veil. With the hem of her gyuilta, she wiped some unseen, unfelt something from my face. "Work with the little charms you have. Learn to smile. A girl as dark as you can't afford to be too high-minded. You want your father sold into slavery for his debts? Is that what you want?"

Her face contorted into the smug triumphant smile she always wore whenever she bested me. "Now, daughter, throw your gyuilta over your shoulders and walk with me, your arm in mine. The Creator will make my old friend recognize me."

LOIC
Encounter

As I walked to the sword trader's shop, a man dressed in a shaman's vest walked past me. He eyed me suspiciously, glowering, as if the spirits had told him some harsh thing about me. As he passed by, I suddenly remembered that all swords were dedicated to one spirit or another. Instantly I resolved not to buy a sword at all, but rather to make one. In that way, no spirits could enter it and I would not be forced into a league with them.

I told my father my intention, but not the reason for it.

He said, "You want to make your own sword? You have no skill in sword-making, and the new swords imported from Ibeniland have such power, grace and—"

"No, Father," I said. "I shall make my own sword."

"How strange your whims have become since Krika . . ."

I shook my head, hinting he should not speak another word.

He stared at me in silence for as long as it takes for a hawk to wing across the sky. At last, he said, "It is I who should tell you when not to speak. Not you who should tell me."

"Why do you insist on speaking about Krika when I do not wish his name to fall from your lips? And don't call my desires 'whims!' Don't presume to think you know my soul so well that you can judge my desires!"

"I knew your soul once," he said wistfully, "and what I didn't know you told me."

"'Once' is a time and times ago. 'Once' no longer exists for me." I pointed at the blacksmith's shop. "As for the sword, will you allow the comrades in our armory to help me make it or not?"

He turned his face toward the ground. Since Krika's death, he had tried often to rekindle our old closeness. I understood his heart, yet I could not forgive him. I chided myself for this because in most matters he was so good a father. Thinking to make the mood between us lighter, yet not wanting to actually apologize, I said, "King Jaguar will smile when he sees the sword I'll make."

Laughter was always ready on Father's lips. "He'll smile when it breaks in your hand. But go ahead. Buy what advice you can from the blacksmith."

In those days, I often knew the thoughts of those around me and I suddenly saw his thoughts. *An eighteen-year-old boy who is petted and worshiped by all the women of his clan: why should he listen to an old man of forty-five? How can he understand that his father is powerless against the spirits?*

It was not "thought-reading" as the Angleni called it. Nor was some demon responsible for it. Knowing another's thoughts seemed nothing more than a natural extension of understanding and insight. What else could Father have been thinking?

When I returned from the blacksmith's shop, he was speaking with a horse dealer. Collecting and breeding horses had become his chief occupation since the war ended. Yes, let me praise my father! He was noble and good and his victories helped stall many Angleni invasions. His vialka broke the backs of many an Angleni general.

He stood examining the back of a painted stallion with red, black, and bay coloring that mirrored the sunset.

When he saw me, he pointed in the direction of two Theseni women some forty paces away near the tent of a seller of exotic vegetables. "The one in the half-veil reminds me of Monua," he said. "The one who lies in the bosom of my old friend Nwaha. She has Monua's fierce stride. A walk I can never forget."

"Perhaps fate has conspired to bring two old friends together again," I said, walking to his side.

"If that is indeed Monua, the other woman—the one in the virgin's full veil—might be her daughter."

He looked past the wagon masters, past the fabric merchants, past the makers of candles and the carvers of wood. "Nwaha should be nearby. Yet I see him nowhere."

"Perhaps your friend is dead, Father. Friends die. Didn't you say he lingered in the old region long after the other townsmen had fled? Didn't the Angleni kill most of the men in the Kluna clan?"

Sorrow swept across his face. "Yes, because of their dark skin. The Angleni killed the Kluna, rather than imprison or enslave them as they did the Ibeni and our people." He wiped a tear from his face. "How I loved my youth spent among the Kluna! How sad it is to think so lovely and kind and good a people are now gone from the world!"

Seeing his grief, I regretted the words I had spoken earlier. "Father, take heart. Look. She doesn't wear the widow's fringe. Perhaps your friend is yet alive."

"What did the blacksmith say?" He asked, his mind obviously on the women.

"That his son could bring all the steel and skill I need to our Golden House."

"He can teach you, this blacksmith's son? How old is he? About Krika's age?"

"He's old enough," I snapped, annoyed that once again he had mentioned Krika. Feeling immediately ashamed, I tugged on his braid, which was so long it reached his waist. "Father, if you're going to stare at the women, you might as well speak to them. But be sure that the woman is indeed your old friend, or be prepared to receive a hard slap for your mistake."

He grinned, and gave me a sidelong glance. "Since when did you become an expert on Theseni women?"

"My aunts have told me that Theseni women don't like strangers speaking to them on the street, as Ibeni women do. Nor are they as joyous or free-thinking as our Doreni women."

He grinned. "They have taught you well. Nevertheless, it is time, perhaps, that men and not your aunts or your Little Mother teach you about women."

"True, I'm smothered daily by women. Yet, it is a good way to learn their habits, don't you think so?"

He took a deep but determined breath and glanced at the women. "Perhaps. But come now. Let's see if my face gets slapped." He raised his right hand and signaled the women.

With that small signal, my life changed.

When the older woman turned to look at us, she nudged the younger one, but the younger one seemed to lack all etiquette and all sense of daughterly submissiveness. She turned, took a brief glimpse at us, then walked in the other direction towards the booksellers' tent. The older woman tugged at the young one's sleeve, but in vain. The young one merely hastened her steps.

Intrigued, I watched her. Her refusal to follow her mother spoke of a fierce beautiful will. *Perhaps,* I thought, *it is this very independence of mind that causes her to wear plain sandals instead of the fashionable shoes Satilo women wear but are always complaining about.*

A wind came from nowhere and blew her veil sideways, revealing her face. Although she was some distance away, I could see how beautiful she was. Then another wind blew—yes, although the day had been as still as summer clouds—and that gust threw her gyuilta from her shoulders, causing me to see how closely her simple cotton kaba hugged her svelte figure.

In the old days, before the Angleni forced their own customs and dress upon us, all tribes and both sexes wore the gyuilta. An unmarried girl could make a gyuilta sing. Whether it was a long one with elaborate fringes and beadwork, or a short one for riding; whether silk, linen, cotton, wool, buckskin, leather, or lowly hemp; whether worn as a scarf to protect against the sand, or as a shawl to shield the face from snow— how that cloak could turn men's gazes!

I must have been handsome in my younger days. Or perhaps it was merely my father's wealth. For many, many girls—oh, girls without number—would let their gyuiltas fall from their shoulders as I passed, allowing them to trail along the ground for me to retrieve. Such flirtations fascinated me, but my heart never leapt for any of those girls, pretty though they were. No, not until I saw Monua's daughter did my heart leap. As an Ibeni poet has said, "My heart leaped then, for love had leaped into my eyes." It was my first taste of love, and after such a small sip I was intoxicated, speechless, wanting nothing more but to devour her.

Father had noticed the girl's behavior too, for he said, "The young one must be her daughter. They share the same fierce walk."

"But the daughter's is gentler," I said. "Less aggressive. She has a better figure too. Thin in the right places. Round in the right places."

Father's turned to me and squinted. He laughed and the laughter momentarily softened the sword scar along his left cheek. "Son, you've found your good mood again. This pleases me. To know how to forget past griefs is to move from childhood to—"

"I'm eighteen, Father," I said, firmly cutting him off. "I've moved past childhood. Or others have pushed me past it."

"Your anger is misplaced, Loic," he said, raising his voice. "Okiak killed Krika, not me. For the past year, you've made yourself my enemy and I suggest you study what it means to have an enemy before—"

"I have not made myself your enemy, Father." I pointed to the approaching woman as another means of silencing him. "No, that was none of my doing."

As the woman was only footsteps away, we put our disagreement away.

She soon stood in front of us, making a great show of studying our faces, craning her neck this way and that. A smile flashed across her face and she bent her head low. "Taer!" she shouted, her voice much too loud. "Is it really you?" Tears streamed down her face. "Has the Good Maker given my Nwaha such joy by causing me to cross paths with his old friend?"

Her joy seemed sincere enough, but I suspected this was no "accidental" meeting, that the woman had planned it somehow. Yet, her deception didn't trouble me. Quite the opposite; for reasons I little understood then, my heart was glad of it.

The flesh on her bony arm sagged as she pointed at me. "So, First Captain of King Jaguar's armies, is this one of your sons? Loic, is it? Your oldest boy?"

I nodded, clasped both my hands together and bowed to her. "This is a day the Creator made," I said, giving her the customary greeting.

"It has certainly brought blessings," she answered. "How tall and handsome you've become, Loic tyu Taer! You have your mother's light eyes! You're thin, though." She tapped my stomach. "The son of a rich man should have more flesh on his bones. I don't know if your father told you, but my precious daughter used to hold you in her arms. Yes, you were her favorite little doll those rare times she saw you. How she used to laugh when you crawled between her feet without so much as a breechcloth!"

"Was that the girl who stood beside you?" Father asked, sparing me further embarrassment.

"Yes, she is the joy of my life. If she had known it was her dear father's dear friend who called me, she would not have left so abruptly. Unfortunately, she had an errand to attend to."

She lowered her eyes and I saw that she was flirting with my father. "I've heard much about the exploits of the First Captain of King Jaguar's armies, the Captain of all the armies of the three tribes! How could we not hear? Oh, and I've seen your beautiful wife many times in the marketplace, walking with your younger son. Unfortunately, I don't know your other little one's name."

Father's eyes widened. "You saw my servants and my wife, and you didn't approach them to send me a message?"

She bent her head low. "Who am I that I should push myself into your life? No, Nwaha and I are unimportant people now. But enough about me. Your wife is a beauty, Taer. But—" she clicked her tongue "—only one wife?"

Father nodded.

"You're being stingy with yourself, Treads Lightly. Most rich men spread themselves around. They don't tread lightly when taking earthly joys. But I'm glad to see you're well, my friend. We've often asked the ancestors to protect you."

The poor are allowed their scheming, I suppose. Especially the poor who once were wealthy. I would have liked the woman better if she hadn't chattered so much.

Father bowed his head. "I've prayed for your family also."

"Waihai!" she said, "The Good Maker obviously heard our prayers, but not yours." She followed this with a laugh so obviously meant to call the market's attention to the fact she was speaking to the King's Captain that if I hadn't wanted to meet her daughter, I might have found an excuse to leave.

Father was always patient with deceptions, however. Or perhaps he was more gracious about them. Or maybe he simply didn't recognize them as often as I did. He said to her, "Give my prayers some credit for your health and happiness."

"You don't want credit for something so small and puny, my friend." Her conniving was relentless.

Wishing to stop it, I asked, "But where is Nwaha? He's wrong not to have told Father you were settled in Satilo."

"Your father knows how proud Nwaha is." She pointed across the marketplace, to the other side of the Sun Fountain where a tattered banner blew before an equally tattered tent. "That's our home. Our shop."

Father began walking towards the shop but—she reminded me of actresses I saw once in King Jaguar's palace—she stopped him, bending low and clutching at her chest. "Don't dishonor us, my friend, by coming into our house. The shame would be too great. I would be doubly shamed to serve a guest the poor food we have."

"To hold my friend in my heart and eyes is all the sweetness I need," Father answered.

That was a common phrase in the old days, intended to free the poor from the oppression of the hospitality laws, and for a moment, I feared the old woman had overplayed her hand. If, out of respect for his friend, father declined to enter Nwaha's house I would be deprived of seeing the girl.

Monua, perhaps suspecting she had played her role too well, lowered her head to the side. Then, crooking her hand, she said, "But if you do not mind poor fare, come and see. I know you're kind and will not be disgusted at our lowly position."

Waihai! My heart leaped! It seemed full of a most profound happiness. I must have been smiling like a fool, for Father gave me a questioning look and gently touched the tiny hairs sprouting on my lip. Perhaps he only smiled at his own happiness at being suddenly reunited with his old friend. Whatever the reason, we both were in good spirits.

Our smiles faded when we entered Nwaha's three-room shop. When I was a young child, my Little Mother taught me an alphabet song:

"If ever you enter a house and find it dirty, dingy or disarrayed,
Don't judge the dwellers of that domain.
For a dirty, disarrayed, and dingy house
Declares its owners are poor, ill, tired, or grieving.
Dinginess doesn't imply defect or dereliction.
Dirty houses do not display dirty hearts.
Decisions decided on disarray should be disregarded.
Your heart would itself be dirty and disarrayed
To determine another's worth on such dealings."

I remembered the little song and restrained my mind from harsh judgment.

The public front room, where Nwaha worked his trade as a tent-maker and where Monua made and sewed dresses, was the most presentable, even though its buckskin walls were crumbling away. I didn't see the inner room where their daughter slept or the third room, which was Nwaha's and Monua's, but the scattered fabric remnants and the abundance of scavenged sundries in first room hinted the unseen rooms hid overwhelming poverty.

Nwaha directed Father to a rickety wooden stool. His tightly curled black hair was turbaned in the northern Theseni style despite the heat of the day. Although he was about Father's age, wrinkles lined his face, making him seem older. "My eyes rejoice to see you," he said. "What victories you've had, Treads Lightly! Your name rings out in many war songs."

"When you hear them, don't sing along with them," Father said, sitting down. "Those victories have cost me deep defeats."

"Even so, I'm as proud of your successes as if they were mine."

"They are yours, Nwaha," Father answered. "I could not have won a quarter of my victories if your spirit had not sustained me."

"So you are Father's childhood friend?" I asked, although as a youth I should have stayed silent in the presence of an older man. "So we meet again? And this time, I'm wearing a breechcloth."

He laughed, and his teeth gleamed white against his dark brown skin.

"But tell me, Nwaha," I began, "is there anything you need?"

Father gave me a reproving look. I silenced myself immediately, realizing to ask such a question was a breach of etiquette that would only shame Nwaha.

However, Monua leaped at the opportunity despite the embarrassment spreading across Nwaha's face. She deftly avoided Nwaha's extended left hand as he tried to prevent her from speaking. "Your father's generosity is known throughout the region," she continued. "And it seems his son shares that same generous nature. But let us not burden your father with our misfortunes."

"How could you burden me, Nwaha?" Father asked. Preserving the honor of another was an art. Father turned to me. "Son, the talk of two old men will not interest you. You know how your Mamya worries when we return late. She dotes too much on her little charge. Now, don't give her any cause to worry. Ride straight home." Yes, he wanted to pay Nwaha's debts, but speaking of such matters in front of me would have been an etiquette breach. That was how things were done in the old days. Subtly, tactfully.

Yet, I wanted one more glimpse of Monua's daughter. "Permit me, Father," I said, "to go to the horse dealer? You wanted the painted stallion, didn't you? The one who looks like a sunset during the cold moons. Shall I buy him?"

"Bargain well," he answered. "Don't let that cheater take advantage of your youth. Instead of riding Cactus home, ride that one. Study how he behaves and tell me all your observations."

I immediately got up and raced out the door. When outside, I searched the arcs and walkways of the marketplace until I saw Monua's daughter. I found her at last, a long way from Nwaha's shop, near the Sun Fountain. She held a water jug in her hand. I hurriedly paid for the stallion after bargaining only enough to assure a fair price, then followed her as she approached two Ibeni beggars sitting beside a hemp plant. The men's faces were tattooed, a sign they had committed treason against the king—probably some conspiracy with the Angleni. None in the marketplace offered them quixa, water, or food. None but Monua's daughter.

I watched to see if she exchanged any words with the beggars. She did not. In those days, an unmarried Theseni woman could not speak to a strange man, but taboos could be worked around. Kneeling beside them, she put fruit and bread in their hands. These they ate greedily and humbly. She fed them then, unspeaking, hurried away. No one in the marketplace reproved her for this, which I considered strange and wonderful indeed. I smiled, seeing her kind, brave heart; seeing it, I loved her more. *Kindness combined with courage is a rare combination,* I said to myself. *Such a wife does not shame or harm her husband, and she is like a warrior by his side.*

Darkness lay over everything like the gentle stroke of a woman's comforting hand. I wondered whether the Wind had sent me one to lie in my bosom, or if—as Father had been saying—grief for Krika had made me whimsical. Even Little Mother, who always gave and forgave me everything, had begun to say I was impetuous. The sun had already rolled away into the far horizon and the vendors were busily packing up their wares. Some had already closed the curtains of their tents. Because the Doreni horse dealer was still present, I decided to open my heart to him.

"Older Brother," I said, greeting him. "This was a day the Creator made."

"It brought many blessings," he answered. "And that horse is one of them. You got a good bargain, there."

"Tell me, Older Brother, if you know . . . what kind of girl is Monua's daughter?"

He glared back at me, his eyes suddenly angry under his clan-cap. "You mean Satha?"

"Is that her name? Satha?"

You who have forgotten the old language cannot understand the joy with which I received her name. You hear our names, you hear the names of people in my narrative and those names mean nothing to you. But before the Angleni destroyed our language, blowing it away as one blew away chaff in the wind, names meant something. "Satha" was a Theseni word which meant "Queen" or, more accurately, "Queenie." It sounded like the Doreni word, "Sithye" which meant "dawn," a name close in meaning to mine.

"Satha," I repeated. "It is a lovely name."

"Aren't there enough women in your father's compound—captive slave girls, servants—you can misuse?" He pointed at the jade bracelet on my right hand that signaled that I was my father's primary heir and the future chieftain of the Pagatsu clan. "Shame on you, Loic tyu Taer." His eyes were like unsheathed daggers, his tone sharp like knives.

In those days every Doreni clan was at odds with every other, and his angry eyes made me wonder if some grudge lay between my clan and his own. I was glad the bracelet gave warning that those who killed a first-born would bring vendettas and clan wars upon their head. "I don't recognize your clan cap, Older Brother," I said. "Is there some fire between your clan and the Pagatsu?"

"It isn't your clan that bothers me."

"Then what fire is there between us?"

"Like a true Doreni, I am a brother to all people. But your rude intentions towards Satha nauseate me. Can you not call any of your slave women to your bed? For all I know, you and your father probably share the same woman despite the taboo. That's the way you rich people are, flaunting the laws. Although you have a herd of women from which you can choose, you want to take a poor man's one little ewe." I watched nervously as his agitated fingers groped about the horseshoes and horseshoe nails on his stand. The knife he suddenly lifted before my eyes glinted in the moonlight.

It was true the Doreni sought to be brothers to all men. Before the Angleni came and colored our perceptions of each other, marriages and love affairs between the different tribes were frequent, but weddings between rich and poor were less common. Although a rich tribe could bring wealth, status, and protection to a poorer tribe, what could a poor tribe give? It was also true that in the Golden House many servant girls and some of my female cousins had shown their desire to couch with me. Although, from what my Little Mother told me, they were more desirous of replacing my father's hated third wife than they were of lying in my hairless bosom.

I pushed the knife away, feeling strangely pleased that my tribesman had defended Satha so vehemently. "Satha tya Monua has nothing to fear from me."

His eyes searched mine, the threat still in them. "Are you being honest?"

"Very honest, Older Brother."

He bent towards me and managed a conciliatory smile. "Well . . . as long as you mean the girl no harm. She's a good girl, that one. Proper. I wanted to marry her myself. But she has no dowry. And, as you can see—" he gestured towards the back of his tent "—I'm a poor man. She's industrious, don't misunderstand me. But when one considers a wife— even if the girl has noble ancestors—one might as well get more than a few quixas to take her off her parents' hands."

"Poor men can't marry poor women," I cited a proverb my Little Mother had told me. I didn't add the end of the proverb however: "Rich men, therefore, have a greater selection."

"Good luck with the girl," he added as he pulled the slatted curtains of his shop together. "And remember me if you wish to buy another horse. Don't tell your father about . . . this little incident between us. I wouldn't want him thinking I tried to murder his son."

"I assure you, Father has met many who wanted to murder me."

He nodded knowingly, "It is always that way with rich men's sons."

I tied the stallion—whom I now called Sunset—to Cactus and to father's horse. How like brothers they looked with their similar sunset coloring, and how like brothers they behaved, nudging each other with their noses. They whinnied as if resuming an old conversation.

I walked to the next vendor. "A lovely day the Creator made, is it not?"

The Ibeni merchant stopped packing away his wares and turned to me. "It brought many blessings."

"The greatest of which was that I met Satha tya Monua and jobara, indeed, she is a beauty."

A lascivious smirk came to his lips. Yes, that one was typical of his tribe—suspicious, lustful, and jealous; hexes, fetishes, and carved idols guarded his shop. He wore the typical Ibeni patchwork leather vest —embroidered spells and chants decorated it but I didn't recognize its clan markings. A Doreni woman in an Ibeni veil appeared behind him but he jealously hurried her away. She fled immediately and I found myself wondering why a Doreni woman—for our women are bold and shrewd—would marry an Ibeni man.

"Yes, Little Doreni," he said after the woman had scurried behind the slatted curtains. "Monua's daughter is a beauty. Even with the veil, one can tell. But she's not one to lay in the fields with a boy, if that's what you're after." He lowered his voice. "Or with a man either. Believe me, Little Doreni, I've tried. Waihai! Who would know? I offered her one thousand quixas for the romp—a lot considering an Ibeni woman could give me far more for far less—but I couldn't convince her. The Uncaused Causer of all things knows her family needs the money."

It is difficult to turn the mind of an Ibeni away from lustful imaginations, but I tried, whistling at his generosity. "A lot of money, that."

"Enough to feed even your household for a month, little rich Doreni." He bent towards me, fingering the porcelain frog fetish dangling from his neck. "I would have married her and made her my ninth wife if she had agreed to play with me." His hands carved a female figure in the air. "That torn-up oversized gyuilta she wears over her kaba can't hide everything, if you know what I mean."

"I think I do." Nine wives. But that was also typical of the richer Ibeni. Their eyes liked whatever they saw, and what they liked they had to have.

"So you want her?"

"I think I do."

He sucked at his teeth. "Good luck! You're Pagatsu, right? That's what those clan markings on your clan cap say?" He too glanced at the jade firstborn bracelet. "You're a chieftain's son?" Knowing the Ibeni love of status and power, I didn't immediately answer. "Come now, little rich Doreni. I know a few things about clan markings and I heard Monua earlier."

"True, I am Pagatsu."

"Taer's son?"

I nodded.

"You're from a noble clan. Unfortunately, that won't win her over. Now, if you were from the Therpa Doreni, let's say. Or the Trabu

Theseni like Queen Butterfly, then . . . perhaps you'd feel no qualms about taking her. After you had her, you could discard her or do with her as you wish. You wouldn't be stuck with her after your lust had cooled, as often happens." If I had fallen into the sewage pit on the outskirts of town, I couldn't have felt dirtier. "How old are you anyway? Fifteen? Sixteen?"

"Old enough."

"Rich enough is more like it. Led by your heart, are you? Believe in a 'destined one' probably?" He chuckled. "Alibayeh! Marry her, then. You might as well start your household now. One young man I know—not Doreni, but very rich—already has four wives."

A Theseni vendor near us interrupted him. A good thing, too, for my anger was already kindled against the Ibeni. "I've been listening to your conversation." He unwrapped his long cotton turban, and scratched his nearly bald skull. "But you've picked the wrong one there. That one is too virtuous to be any fun. And bookish. She's always in the bookseller's shop, looking for writings by the old scribes. That's why she wears that old gyuilta, so men won't take a second look. She doesn't want to marry at all. Sometimes I see her in the cool of the evening, after she's finished her chores, reading. On holy days, she visits the houses of the poor, the old, and the blind, and she reads to them." He grew suddenly silent, and his eyes seemed to be looking at some inner memory. I suddenly knew—in the way I knew many things—he was thinking of his old days. "But few saints have such a body, one obviously made for sin. Try to woo her if you can, but perhaps it's best she grow old unmarried. Who wants a holy one in his bed?"

We Doreni were generally tan-colored, with brown, auburn or black hair. Satha's family, being Theseni, was a rich deep black. I wondered if he thought my mind was like his, for Theseni men judged by such matters.

Both men shared a laugh that turned my stomach. How lucky it was I had decided to make a sword instead of buying one! If the sword had been in my hand, I would have rammed them through. I choked down my anger; they were older than I. One wrong word to either and I would have faced the Council of Elders and Beloved Women as Krika had. Yes, even though I was a rich man's son, the son of the king's First Captain.

I walked from the marketplace towards Nwaha's shop, and my heart ached because such words had been spoken against the girl who had found lodging in my heart. I wanted to clothe her bare arms with jeweled bracelets and give her golden nose-rings and silver anklets and, at the same time, shower her with praise and tell her how beautiful and how good and worthy she was. My heart reasoned that if I bathed her with worshipful love all the snide judgments poured on her would fall like broken chains about her ankles.

Near Nwaha's house, I saw her in the garden, pulling ground tubers.

How, I asked myself, *will I make Monua's daughter speak with me?* I was Doreni, I reasoned; I didn't have to follow Theseni etiquette. Moreover, the law of hospitality triumphed over all customs, as mercy often triumphed over justice. The thought occurred to me that I lived on the edge of the city and could be deemed a stranger. I, therefore, had the right to ask even an unmarried Theseni woman for water from her well.

"Satha! Tya Monua!" I called out.

She looked up in the direction of my voice.

The other vendors had closed their shops and no one would have seen her if she had spoken to me. But she didn't walk toward me. She returned to her work pulling tubers in the dark garden.

I called again. "Satha, are you so aloof you won't talk to the son of your father's friend?"

Again she looked. This time directly at me; again, she didn't approach me. I regretted my casual clothing. Only a tunic, deerskin leggings, undergarment, and breechcloth. Nothing to show my hunting skills, no rich gyuilta, nothing to make her want me. Yet, I reasoned, would I want a girl who accepted me only because I was dressed richly?

What did Sicma the great Ibeni poet say of Queen White Star? "Her beauty illumines the face of all who see her, and in the gates of the city all women shine through her glory." But not for me Queen White Star. Not for me the flamboyant First Queen Butterfly, not for me the gentle Doreni Queen Sweet-as-Jasmine. None were as beautiful as the daughter of Monua. No, none of the three wives of King Jaguar, or any of his eleven daughters could match the girl's beauty, regal bearing and exquisite willfulness.

Her refusal to speak only made me want her more, but before I could call out to her again Father exited the shop.

"Loic?" He raised his hands questioningly. "Why are you harassing Monua's daughter? She's not your servant. I thought you had ridden home."

I pointed at the door to Nwaha's shop and gestured to Father to follow me inside.

When I stood in front of Nwaha, I said, "Father, Monua's daughter pleases me well. Get her for me to wife."

My father's eyes narrowed in surprise, then closed and opened again, angry. But Nwaha said nothing, did nothing. It was Monua who acted. She stood up in such haste the bamboo stool on which she sat fell to the ground. A second later, her hand was gripping the long shaft of a vialka. Jobara! That lance was indeed a graceful weapon. The Angleni have now outlawed it, but Layo, layo—truly, truly—how sharp and graceful that weapon was!

She pointed it at my throat and shouted at my father. "Treads Lightly, have you and this son of yours come here to mock our poverty?"

I had not thought that my sudden request would be considered an insult, but the vialka's blunted edge skating across my flesh—and pressing deep enough to cut—made me realize otherwise.

"I know full well that my daughter is dark and past marriageable age," Monua said. "Unattractive she may be, but I'll not allow the son of a rich man to use her as if she were a slave."

Such a defense of her daughter! More insult than praise, such a champion no woman needs. The anger the vendors had kindled within me still burned and when I heard Monua's words, it burned hotter. Heldek and Pantan had trained the young princes and the dukes as well as me in warfare. Embarrassed though I was that a woman was pushing a vialka into my throat, and able as I was to turn it away, doing so meant insubordination toward an elder. I grasped the vialka's tip with my palm, but restrained myself from turning it on my hostess.

All the while Nwaha continued sitting there, weak and pitiful. Father kept glaring at me, as if I—and not Monua—was in the wrong. *How*, I thought, *can Nwaha sit there and let his wife fight his battles? Even battles she had created in her own mind? How can Father endure a friend such as this?*

When it seemed my neck was about to break from being long held in such an uncomfortable and dangerous position, Father placed his hand on the lance and gently pushed its tip downward. "Loic meant no disrespect, Nwaha," he said. "He's young and easily tossed by the wind's whims. Even so, all in the city of Satilo, all in the Jefra region, and the outlying suburbs of Rega know him to be an honorable youth."

How surprised my heart was that Father defended me!

"His name means 'Full of Light'," he continued. "And he is. If he says he wants to marry your daughter, she has found a place in his heart. He'll treat her well and honor her always as the gatekeeper of his heart."

"As some second-status wife to cover his thighs!" Monua shouted, glowering at me.

Again, Father defended me. "Not so, Monua," he said. "Do not insult my son."

"Should I give my beloved Satha to one who has no manners?" she asked. No, she wasn't one to keep her mouth shut. "Do you want the joy of my life to spend heartbroken nights lying in the women's quarters listening to her husband tumble with other more-beloved wives?" She was a blunt one!

Father answered, "I promise he will marry only one wife, whatever good or evil comes."

In those days, a father's promise would bind his son forever. To break such a promise was to invite death and grief. His insulted soul would return from the dead to haunt or kill the disrespectful child. Yet, his promise seemed a blessing to me. I could not imagine holding any other woman in my bosom.

Monua's suspicious eyes continued staring at me. "How could he want someone he's only just met?" she asked.

I saw her mind then, saw that she was like one standing in the middle of a bridge, not knowing whether to go forward or step back. I searched my heart for the right words to help her cross that bridge.

About that time, her husband found his mouth. "Satha is already twenty-four, my friend. Wouldn't your son rather marry some little girl his age, someone he can grow old with, rather than a woman of unmarriageable age? Consider too that Satha is not of his tribe. Nor is she rich. What can we give you for such—?"

"I don't want some little girl," I shouted, rubbing my neck. Now that I was free from any threat of Monua's weapon I, too, found my mouth. "I want Satha."

"And you rich boys always get what you want, don't you?" Monua said, her eyes scorning me. I saw some ugly thing in her soul, and feared the prospect of such a "New Mother." What if Satha tya Monua turned out to be a "true daughter of her mother?"

Yet, I ached to free Satha from her parents, yearned to caress her in my bed. Already she had begun to fill my future. In my mind, no future event excluded her. No feast, no journey, no riverwalk. How could I live without her if she had so enmeshed herself into my future life?

"A child who receives all he wishes is not a true son," I said to Monua. "I am Taer's true son, the hope of his old age, the honor of my dead mother. Just as Satha is the honor of her mother. I do not waste my time on foolish wishes as others do."

"Mentura—untried boasting," she answered, as if she, a woman, were a warrior or a man my equal. "Your son makes speeches to his elders?"

"Perhaps you should not insult someone you hardly know!" I snapped back. Yes, I did this, even though we were guests in her house. Father lifted his left hand, as if to strike me.

He had struck me only once before, on the day I told him I intended to kill Okiak. Seeing his raised hand again, I feared he would not allow Satha to marry me. Terrified at losing what I had not yet won, I clasped my hands together, and knelt on the floor pleading, "Father, forgive me. I spoke rashly."

Monua shook her head several times. "You're lucky you did this in our house. If the elders knew of this . . . ." Her voice faded with the vague threat. "Before the war, children would have been stoned for less. But the war has made us all tired of bloodshed. The poor have always had to suffer humiliations. Never did I dream I would become one of them." I sensed that three thousand quixas would have suited her "humiliation" quite nicely.

"Your son's mind is mad with love," Nwaha apologized for me. "Young men are rash when they're infatuated."

His words caused his wife's wrath to turn toward him. She removed her wifely half-veil before us and wiped her eyes. "The boy insulted you and here you are wiping his bottom with that weak tongue of yours. Have you no spine? No, I have no husband. Not one worthy of the name."

She retreated through the wooden curtains into a far part of the house. But even hidden from us, she wailed loud enough. Doves in the Eastern Desert could have heard her sobbing. "What a fool I was to marry such a foolish man!"

Nwaha held up his hand. "I frustrate my wife, as you can see." He lowered his head and pushed his dark brown fingers through his hair. "Taer, my friend, you see how it is. Who would have thought that those we love would mar our reunion? Forgive me if I sin against courtesy and ask you to leave, but you will understand that so much shame in one day is more than—"

"Our reunion is not marred," Father said. "Are we not covenant brothers? There is no sorrow or shame, which we cannot endure together. Now, if you honor me, you must allow my son to marry your daughter."

"I've met many rich men in the fifteen years we have been apart. None but you, Taer, have honored the poor. Jobara! Indeed, I've chosen my friends well." He turned to me. "Loic, with a father so honorable, I have no doubt you too are a man of great honor. Forgive me for insulting you. But think about it, lad. You are but—"

"Eighteen and old enough."

Father gave me a quick angry look, then spoke to Nwaha. "Isn't this a surprising thing?" he asked. "My friend, do you not remember our old promise?"

Nwaha squinted, apparently confused. "What old promise, my friend?"

"That our children would marry," Father said, smiling in pretend amazement.

It was the first time I had ever heard of such a promise. I knew immediately that this was one of Father's diplomatic ploys. I kept my head low, my hands clasped, my knees to the ground. "How the fates conspire to bring two covenant brothers together!" Father added.

"Ibye, ibye!" Nwaha said. "Now I remember it!" Yes, Nwaha was as good a diplomat as my father was. "But those promises were made when we were both young and wealthy. Many years have passed and our feet have walked long in different paths."

"Troubles come no matter how well we plan," Father answered. "But the nature of the world is to bring our old promises before our eyes." He raised his right hand towards me, and I stood up. "My friend, let our children marry as we promised each other so long ago. Forgive my son's outburst. Love has its own rules, and a boy's love is often brazen. Nevertheless, the love of one's youth always abides. My first wife, though dead, is ever on my mind. I pray you then, let the boy marry Satha. If he doesn't get his way, it will not go well with me. Loic is strong-willed and will spend all his days hating me—and perhaps you—for refusing him the girl. We would not want that, would we?"

"Waihai," Monua said, wiping her face and returning to the room. "Yes, Taer, children are often like that. They forgive nothing and will hold it over their parents' heads until the day we die. Some even avenge themselves against their elders when they're full-grown. What is this world coming to?"

Nwaha gestured me to a stool opposite him. "So you think you love my daughter?"

"The Wind turned my eyes towards her, and I can see nothing else until she turns her own eyes on me."

"Very poetic, young man," Nwaha said. "But is there a more earthly reason perhaps for your love for my daughter?"

I smiled, feeling a blush across my cheek. "Although Satha wears the Theseni scarfed full veil I can see she is beautiful. And the shape of her body pleases me. I've spoken with vendors in the marketplace and they say she's a good woman. Is there a better woman to be the gatekeeper of my heart?"

Nwaha turned to my father, "So, your son's ypher rules his life?"

"If my ypher rules me, old man," I shouted, "at least it's better than you letting your wife rule you." I stood up, annoyed I had almost begun to like one whose weakness made him unworthy of me. The girl was safely mine. Both Nwaha and Father had opened their mouths to lie about an age-old promise and I would have been a fool not to use it. "I want the girl. Since you promised each other your children, why deny me? Especially since the One Who Holds My Breath in His Hand has brought us together to bless your old promise? Get me the girl for me to wife. Let the half-marriage gathering be tomorrow."

"Tomorrow?" Father looked at me as if I had lost my mind. "A betrothal cannot be arranged by tomorrow."

"In two or three days, then," I demanded. "Enough."

Anger, restraint and shame battled in Father's eyes.

Nwaha's voice trembled. "But won't people say the half marriage was hastily planned because Satha—" He disgusted me by glancing at his wife as if he would topple to the ground without her strength.

"They will say nothing," she assured him. "They know the purity of our Satha."

Unable to stay any more in the presence of such a man, I walked toward the doorway of the tent. "Father," I said, "show them Pagatsu generosity." Then I left. If I had stayed longer, my mouth would have said something my heart would have regretted.

Outside, alone, I paced before the house, wondering what negotiations were going on. For the moment, Satha was nowhere to be seen. Soon, however, she would be mine and I would see her every day.

I knew Father would not demand a dowry. Satha was the old man's only wealth. However, Nwaha, a good Theseni father, would demand a written contract which declared Satha would be my only wife, and I her only husband. But what of that? Father had already promised that I would treat her honorably.

When Father exited the house, I raced toward him. He walked past me, silent, as if I was an unseen spirit. I grabbed him by the right shoulder. Rage flickered in his eyes. I let go.

He took the reins of the horse I had just bought, and silently tied it to the tree beside Nwaha's house. Then, still unspeaking, he mounted his own horse and rode away, with me riding behind him on Cactus like a leaf caught in an eddy.

Silently, we rode to the outskirts of Jefra where our Golden House lay. Nor did he speak when we dismounted at our stables. He walked past me and entered his rooms in the men's quarters while I entered mine. I waited for him to send a servant to me, but none came. When I could bear his silence no longer, I walked to his room and spoke to him through the slatted curtained doorway.

"Father, please! Please speak to me!" I shouted.

There was a long silence.

"Father, please!"

He answered, "My son, who were you trying to impress with your great proud words?"

"I tried to impress no one, Father. I found no one worthy of impressing. I only—"

"You succeeded, then!" he shouted back. "For you impressed no one. When the girl hears of your behavior, your success in not impressing anyone will be complete."

"It's only—I want her so much, Father." I put my hand on the slatted wooden curtain between us but didn't dare push it aside. "Open to me, Father, and let me speak to you face-to-face."

I heard him speaking, not to himself but to the ancestors. Words barely distinct, barely perceptible, I suspected he might be asking them to guide me. I waited long outside his door and then, at last, he directed his words to me. "Perhaps the first error could have been repaired in some way, but you were like a merchant, adding debt to debt. Your shameful behavior has cost me much. And it is not of quixas that I speak."

"What about their shameful behavior?" I asked, annoyed that once again, other people seemed to matter to him more than I did. "Your friend allowed his wife to fight his battle!"

"Shut your mouth or I'll shut it for you! You with your boasting words. You who have not killed so much as a buffalo dare speak against Nwaha? At best, you sound arrogant; at worst, you're a fool. Do you not remember who these people are, or what they have suffered in order to help their people?" He paused and drew a breath.

I remained silent, remembering what he had told me about the Angleni atrocities in the Kluna region.

When he began speaking again, his voice had softened. "We've spoiled you, son. A motherless child is a sorrowful thing. Indulgence would have been wrong in any case, but the Pagatsu clan is large, and I being headman and you my only son, well . . . you received too much petting. A certain amount of arrogance on your part is to be expected, but your illness and the sad fact that you've lived your life surrounded by too many women—aunts, female cousins, doting slave girls, captives—all of whom had duties toward you—"

"My illness has nothing to do with this, and the petting and fawning of worried women might have spoiled other boys, but not me. I am sorry if I did not behave properly toward your friends, but—"

A desert owl moaned and I heard my father's footsteps approaching me. He pushed the slatted wooden curtains aside and stared out at the sparse bushes on the western edge of the complex, apparently searching for the owl. "The past cannot be undone and Nwaha will not nurse a grudge against you. But the girl . . . who knows?" He lowered his voice, softening his tone. "Is it possible, Loicuyo, you're confusing pity with love?"

"But, Father, do you not consider the girl beautiful?"

"I hardly saw her. Nor did you, for that matter. If I know your heart—and I think I do—your love for her is mixed with pity. Jobara! Nevertheless, haven't you seen enough of my life to know that beauty is one thing, and love quite another? You haven't lain with a woman yet—as far as I know—and now you want a guardian for your heart."

My father knew me well. Indeed, I did sense some wound within the girl that echoed with some hurt within my own soul, but Father didn't wholly comprehend that it was I who felt the need of pity and care, that I needed one who would be my true family, an ally like Krika was.

He continued, more practical about my life than he had ever been about his own. "If you had any sense, you would have hired her as a servant. Then you would have had time to woo her. But like an ypher-led love-sick fool, you chose marriage."

"I'll want no other wife as long as I live, Father."

"Good, for that is what you have." He laughed, then tousled my hair. Again his voice became gentle. "Your heart is as soft as mine was once."

"Your heart is still soft, Father."

"But what if you're making the same mistake I did? Will she want you? You're a child still. Have you considered what you'll do if she doesn't love you? What if the year-mark arrives and the time comes for the full marriage and she decides she doesn't want you?"

"I can make her love me. I know this. You were never able to make the Third Wife love you. She scorns those noble qualities you aspire to. That's the difference between your choice and mine, Father. Satha has a noble heart."

"You speak boldly about my heart, my son."

"Only because I see what your heart should have seen ages ago."

He squinted at me, studying my face. "Young men always think themselves strong as they try to prove an old man wrong. But that victorious look on your face won't last long. One day, my son, you'll understand that some victories aren't victories at all, and some apparent weaknesses are really the true victories."

"Gaining Satha is a true victory, Father. Nothing can make me regret that. As for you, look to yourself. Don't judge my actions when you're the one nursing a viper in your breast."

Other fathers in the Pagatsu clan would have publicly scolded me for such a reply. Or they might have killed me as Okiak killed Krika. But Father only re-entered his room and closed the curtains between us. Rebuke enough.

SATHA
Sudden Betrothal
Rose Moon–Second Cool Moon

The next day when a valanku pulled up to our shop and three linen-clad men stepped out of it carrying three silken bolts of fabric—pale green, reddish purple, and ocean blue—our Ibeni neighbor came running into our garden.

"Where did the money come from to buy all this finery?" he asked Mam without even a greeting.

Mam took the silks and said, as if they were nothing new, "My Satha's promised one is always sending lovely gifts to fulfill their age-old marriage vows. These are for her half marriage ceremony, today."

"But this is news!" The Ibeni fingered a small porcelain frog fetish about his neck. "The first day of the Rose Moon is very propitious. Why didn't you tell anyone?"

"To speak of one's good fortune before the blessed day arrives is to invite the evil eye," Mam answered, glancing at me. "I'm not so stupid as to parade my good fortune when there are so many jealous people around. I'm sure you understand what I mean."

The Ibeni nodded knowingly, and Mam waved Taer's servants away, as if she were already their Arhe, the Chief Mistress of the Pagatsu households. As I started following her in, the Ibeni whispered to me, "The valanku bears Taer's markings. That rich little Doreni boy worked quickly! One day he's asking questions, the very next he sends you marriage raiment. Waihai! A boy of such determination will make a good husband."

"Mam," I said when I went inside, "don't tell that lie anymore about Taer's son being my promised one. Our neighbor knew you were lying. Since I've never heard of this promise I had no good answer to—"

"Waihai!" Mam shouted. "Of course there's a promise! But Taer had grown rich and rich men often forget to honor their promises to poor friends. No use giving you false hopes."

It was one altvayu after another. In those days, altvayus—little lies—were an art and they came in all forms: the protective lie, the etiquette lie, the covering lie, and the hospitality lie. By the time I began to wear the scarfed long veil I had heard so many prevarications, ambiguities and ambivalences, I considered every word as veiled as I was. Altvayus were such a necessary virtue that no one believed anything anyone said. My only response was, "I had no hopes, false or otherwise."

Mam studied the fabrics with a seamstress's calculating eye. "The green would probably be the best choice for you," she said. "It will work best against that dark skin of yours. Plus green is their clan color. What do you think of a dress in the style of the Ibeni Kelovet clan? It's the style now, and every woman is wearing it. "

The long puffy sleeves I could accept and I could manage not to trip over a Kelovet veil that trailed along the ground. But I objected to the low square neckline.

"Waihai!" Mam shouted. "Young men, however virtuous, are entrapped by their eyes. You've got two good pillows for his eyes to rest on."

"But," Father added, coming in from the back room, "we don't want her pillows hanging out. We're Theseni, remember."

By nightfall, I was seated in a purification bath of myrrh and aloes trying to accept this sudden engagement as I watched Mam sew a betrothal dress I wanted nothing to do with.

Father spoke through the slatted curtain, which separated my room from my parents. "You've been quiet all day, Satha. Have you accepted the blessing the Creator has given you?"

Mam poured aloe juice on my head. "She's too cynical to see anything as a blessing!"

I tightened my lips against the aloe's bitterness, but the acrid taste crept into my mouth.

"It's good luck to get it on your tongue," Mam said, when I wiped the juice from my mouth. "Bitterness on the lips before the wedding means sweetness in the bed afterward."

"If that's true and everyone takes these stupid baths, why are there so many bitter marriages?"

She grunted, then returned to her sewing.

"I don't want you to think the young man is merely marrying you for the sake of the promise," Father said. "He's quite interested and was very involved in his father's choice."

I squirmed in the large clay wash basin. "Yes, Father, I heard as much last night."

Mam bit off a piece of sewing thread. "Be careful you don't break that basin. I borrowed it from Uda. That hyena never—" She paused, then suddenly started laughing. "Layo-Layo! Yes, yes! Break it, Satha. After you're finished bathing smash it to bits! We can now afford thousands of better basins. We'll give her a gold one to replace it. Can you imagine it, Nwaha? Our daughter is marrying Taer's son! The son of King Jaguar's Chief Warrior."

"Not something I had ever imagined in my wildest dreams!" he answered, and then as if catching himself, he added, "But, of course, when we were young men Taer wasn't a captain. And when you held little Loic in your arms you—"

The trouble with altvayus was they often spun out of the weaver's control. Father was not good at spinning lies. If he continued weaving this one, he would not create a tapestry, but a tangle no one would be deft enough to sort out.

"So, although I'm a woman past marriageable age and without a dowry—"

"Satha," Mam shouted at me, "you don't need to know all our business."

Father added, "Should we not provide for you? Think of Alima. Look what happened when we told her about our money problems."

Tears came to my eyes when they mentioned Alima, my beautiful and lost sister. She had traveled with three women across the Lingan Plains into Theseni territory where they had meant to find work. But women traveling alone are powerless, especially if they left their home regions. Lascivious Ibeni might rape them, patriarchal and pious Theseni could enslave them. Alima's beauty had caught the eye of

Kujhan, a Theseni man from a vicious clan. She found nothing in him worthy of her love. This did not matter to him. On her seventh day in the region, she found Kujhan had "married" her, using proxy. Although Alima hadn't attended her "marriage," the Theseni men considered her to be married. After that, she could not leave that town without her "husband" Kujhan's permission. He never gave it. Starving and alone, she at last relented and went to his bed. She now lived there, an enslaved "wife," held captive by the man whose heart she had inadvertently captured. Worse yet, they followed the old Theseni custom in which a wife was shared among her husband and his brothers until the brothers married. The only mercy she received was death.

"The only power poor men have is their power over women," Father said, shaking his head. "And the cruelty of poor men is worse than the arrogance of the rich."

"Husband! You've spoiled this child by allowing her too much freedom. Her dark skin she can't help, but if she weren't always reading those religious scrolls, she would have been married already. Poor men can't be choosy. But your—"

"Mam, I have no desire to marry this child."

"I can't break my promise to my friend, especially since he's sought to fulfill it after all these years," Father said. "As for his age, custom will be upheld. You will not lie in his bed until the Restraint is over and the year mark arrives. When the full marriage will take place, you'll have become accustomed to one other and you won't mind his age."

"A year? Time enough to prove someone hasn't impregnated me, I suppose," I said, speaking the obvious.

Mam took her eyes off her handiwork and gave me a warning look. "Learn to watch your words, girl. Don't go starting rumors about yourself. The half marriage is the way the Doreni do things. They have their reasons. You don't want a clan war breaking out because someone didn't get the news about such an important occasion. These year-long half marriages ensure that everyone—far and near—gets the chance to approve of you."

"If the Doreni weren't so aware of alliances," Father added, "they would not have conquered our people five centuries ago."

"You'll have to learn to think like a Doreni," Mam said. "Think about things such as enemies and alliances, learn to pretend to like people you don't like, and hate people you don't hate."

I groaned, but she continued. "You can do it. You have to. A person can't live without allies in this world. Certainly not in a great man's house, with people of another tribe. Consider yourself lucky it was a Doreni boy who fancied you. All you have to worry about are slanty-eyed children. Imagine if you had captured some Ibeni boy's heart. He would have kidnapped you to save his greedy family a dowry and I'd be wandering the world looking for you."

"I doubt you'd go searching the world for me. I'm not Alima, after all."

She ignored me although she knew my words had shown my heart. "Remember to size him up. Learn what impresses him. Anticipate what he wants. The important thing is that he like you. If you behave without common sense, your father and I will end up on the streets. If the boy lusts for you, give in. Bend a little. Waihai, look at that pious face of yours! Even the holy ones tasted the joys of the flesh before they locked their yphers away. Think of it! During the Restraint, you'll be living in Taer's compound in the guest women's quarters. Isn't that better than living here? All that food! They'll fatten you up. Skinny women are no good in bed."

"Could we not talk about such things, Mam?"

"All your mother is saying," Father chimed in, "is that if he likes you, the rest of the Pagatsu clan will like you too. Just show yourself to be a woman of good sense and diplomacy. The Doreni like that."

"And take care to watch the women," Mam warned. "Women can make or break you." Her eyes suddenly filled with tears. "Your poor sister, this marriage should have been her destiny."

Her words stabbed my heart. I winced, but if she noticed, she hid it well.

"Daughter," she said, wiping away her tears. "No woman in Satilo would push Loic out of her bed. I've seen the boy's face. His body too. He's a beautiful one. Good to look at. Haven't I seen your eyes light up beneath your veil when a beautiful man walks past you in the marketplace?"

She started dancing—a thing she had not done in many moons—and began singing an old song:

"A rich man's son is a good catch.

He'll be a lord for you to wait upon.

A kind-hearted husband is a good find.

His heart is as generous as any woman's.

If such a husband is found when he's young,

While he wears his youth cap

Teach him to wait upon you.

And he will nurse you when you are old

And in grandmother's leggings."

They both laughed as the song ended. She then held up my betrothal dress for me to see. "Quick! Out of that bath! Let's see how you look!"

I put on the betrothal raiment and before I could stop her, Mam was holding a mirror up to my face. Unprepared for it, I closed my eyes to my reflection.

"Look at her flinching," Mam said. "Even though she looks as beautiful as Queen Butterfly in this dress. What's wrong with your daughter, Nwaha, avoiding mirrors like that?"

"The veil is nearly-transparent," I said, "and it extends only from my forehead to my neck, not covering my breasts as it should. And there's no scarf to cover my head. Am I supposed to behave like an Ibeni whore in order to make my husband love me?"

Mam looked at me, staring wide-eyed. It was clear she thought the answer to my question was obvious. "You need no head-covering now. Doreni women don't wear them. Besides, your husband will cover your head now. But since you're so pious, I'll try to repair it."

The next morning as I took the second purification bath, Mam put the finishing stitches on the dress: she made its neckline even lower. She hid the dress from me until moments before Taer's valanku arrived; I had to enter the carriage in a betrothal dress which exposed so much of my breasts that even the holy ones would have fled.

I had seen many betrothal processions wind through the city. Whether rich or poor, the betrothed women would be driven through the city streets with foreheads and shoulders so weighted with jewelry their heads could hardly be seen. Such spectacles had always offended me, but perhaps I had only been envious all along, thinking such fortune would never be mine.

My parents sat behind me in the open carriage, Mam praising the Good Maker for all our blessings and fingering the long strand of pearls around my forehead and the gold bracelets on my arms. The sunset-colored stallion—a gift from Taer like the jewels, but to the rest of the world a part of my dowry—pulled the cart on which our two goats bleated contentedly. My future husband's male servants rode on black stallions behind us, as if we were royalty.

"Look how glum she is!" Mam said at last. "Sitting there as if she's one of those war criminals she feeds. She isn't the least grateful her New Father has paid all our debts, and covered her with finery."

"Such a dowry!" Father said, shaking his head.

Mam leaned back like a queen resting on a throne. "Not that Taer cares about such things. As far as he's concerned, Satha's now the most valuable jewel in his household."

Small though our betrothal procession was, crowds gathered to watch us pass. Our neighbors at the market and our creditors shouted, "Who would have known Nwaha would have received such sudden blessings?"

Father shouted back, "Sudden blessings come from the Good Maker. May His name be magnified."

Mam, however, seemed to be thinking only of our dead. "Imagine," she kept saying, "how wonderful this procession would be if all our clan—yes, even the lost, kidnapped, and murdered ones—were following behind us! Waihai! Perhaps they are!" She turned and waved to their spirits just in case. "Imagine it! In our younger days, Satha, we had a hundred times such blessings."

We wended our way through the city towards Taer's Golden House, my parents' faces more carefree than I had seen in years. Mam no longer looked like someone who cried every night about the fate HaZatana had brought her. Such were the blessings of selling one's daughter into a wealthy marriage.

"Daughter," she said, suddenly becoming serious, "when you're settled, remember you owe your good fortune to Ydalle. Other servants have gone on with their lives and forgotten the kindness with which I treated them. But Ydalle always had a loyal heart. Treat her well and reward her. You're not as shrewd or as subtle as your elders so it's well to listen to her advice."

"I will, Mam."

"As for other servants in the Golden House, choose for yourself those of the lowest place, the rejected ones, the ones who have little power in the house. They'll be grateful for the kindness, and they'll never abandon you. But choose only the kind-hearted ones. To lift a powerless ungrateful person to power is to create a proud and jealous enemy. Even so, make them know their place. If you befriend them too much, they'll forget they're not your equal."

From within her gyuilta sash, she retrieved a small pouch—a shaman's puha. "I know those pearls around your neck and waist are supposed to ensure fertility, but Old Yoran says I should sprinkle you with this. It's the dust from our ancestral burying place."

"Old Yoran keeps sepulcher dust from our ancestors at hand?"

She inched forward and held the pouch near my neck. "He traveled long last night to get this."

"Mam, do not shower me with dead men's bones." Before I could finish—at the very moment I was telling her not to—she shook the packet. Powdered bones rained down over me. My flesh crawled.

Once again, my wishes didn't matter. It angered me. And too: I was afraid. I felt I had received a curse instead of a blessing, that the sprinkled puha had turned my life towards death. "How many mothers have gone to witch doctors," I shouted at her, "hoping to bless their children with such spells only to open their lives to evil spirits!"

"You're entering a house without our tribal spirits," she said, shouting me down. "You need to bring your ancestors with you. Or else, who will protect you and give you children? You'll be useless to the boy if you don't have children! You don't want him to take a second wife because you're childless, do you? A woman without children can't expect a marriage contract to protect her."

"You should have asked the Good Maker to bless me. He's distant, but even when he destroys, he seeks my good. Unlike these spirits who always want something."

She gave me a playful pinch that hurt more than expected. "When I was younger, my girl, mothers always pinched their daughters on their wedding day. To prepare them just in case their husbands beat them."

I was unsure if this was true or merely something cruel spoken to disturb me. *It would not be beyond Mam to curse me so that she might later be seen as the heroine who cures me,* I thought. I was horrified to hear myself saying, "Mam, what if this boy turns out to be evil and dissolute? If he does beat me, promise you'll help me appeal to the elders for an annulment."

A smirk flickered on her face, as if she was glad her cruel comment had troubled my heart. "It is true that kind-hearted men often breed selfish children. But if the boy is truly evil, wouldn't he use his power to destroy you if you tried to divorce him?"

I stood open-mouthed in front of her, and my obvious worry and distress brought a self-satisfied smile to her face.

"Mam," I said, "I don't want to marry him. Perhaps I'll be lucky and during the half marriage he'll find something distasteful in me and cast me out."

She looked at me as if I had lost my sanity. "If he casts you out, you will be good for nothing except to be a holy woman or to enter an Ibeni brothel."

"But why should I be good for nothing if he rejects me? A half marriage is a trial period, is it not?"

Father took my hand and held it firmly. "For the man, yes. Not for the woman. Daughter, you're old enough to know what the law says is one thing, and real life is another. An annulment after a half marriage is worse than a divorce. People will think he found something unclean in you. At least a divorce after the full marriage means there was some respect and honor in the beginning."

"And you get to keep your marriage gifts," Mam added.

"Daughter," Father said, "all you have is your intelligence and your kind heart. Those aren't good currency in the marriage market. If Loic inherited the traits of his Desai mother, he already loves you deeply for reasons we cannot know. If he is like his father, he will never wrong you. Haven't you washed the feet of poor refugees and cared for the dying? The

Good Maker has blessed you because of this and will continue to bless you with many good things and with virtuous, wise and good children."

Songs floated about the college as we rode by. I leaned forward to listen to them, trying to keep my mind off my fears.

"What are the words of that song, Father?" I asked. "You studied the dead languages. You must know their meaning."

"It's a song about the Good Maker—a Doreni Desai prophecy about a man being wounded in the house of his friends, a warrior whose clan turned against him."

"I've heard that prophecy," I said.

"That is why the Doreni consider inhospitality such a great sin. The traitor against the Savior forgot the laws of hospitality."

Mam interrupted us, "Enough of religion! What good has it done any of us? We've been generous to the poor, and what did we get? Did the Good Maker protect us when the Angleni destroyed our land? Stop thinking about impractical things. You're only getting me angry. Think about your wedding night like a normal girl."

The wheels of the valanku turned smoothly and evenly underneath us, as if a perfect lathe had rounded them. The soothing regularity of the horses' hoofbeats should have pleased me. Yet, the wagon wheels echoed like millstones grinding millet seed to powder; the horses' hooves seemed to be trampling my heart.

As we approached Taer's Golden House on the outskirts of Satilo in the far reaches of Jefra, near the edge of the Great Desert, Father turned to me. "Daughter—" he frowned as if he had sad news to tell "—I have a thing to tell you." He exchanged a quick glance with Mam. "It isn't so very bad . . . ."

"Speak it, Father."

His eyes avoided mine. "Health, my daughter, is a blessing that not many people have."

I studied Mam's face. "Are you sick, Mam?"

"It is someone else who is ill."

"It isn't a fatal illness," Father added, too quickly. "And no, I'm not ill either."

I understood. "Loic? Is he the one?"

They nodded in unison and looked at each other, as if waiting for the other to speak first.

"Is it fatal?"

"Not of itself!" Father said, again too quickly. "Bu—"

"It has its dangers," Mam said.

"Does he have the mosquito illness?"

"Daughter," Father could not help but laugh, "you always think people have the mosquito illness. There are other illnesses in the world."

"What illness is it?"

He spoke the words almost too softly. "The falling sickness."

A long-forgotten memory of a young girl in our old village appeared in my mind. For no reason, she would fall to the ground and foam at the mouth. I saw my future, one filled with sick children, an invalid husband. I did not want to bring healthy children into a world so full of sadness and cruelty, and now I was to bring ill children into it.

"It may not affect your children—" Mam said, knowing me well enough to see my thoughts.

"Did I say I wanted children?" I snapped. "I don't even want to marry! And now I'm— Two days ago I was free to wander as I chose. Now I'm forced to worry about the health of a boy I don't wish to marry, and the safety of children I never intended to bear. Why have you done this to me, Mam? You should never have allowed this rich boy to usurp my life. You would never have done this to Alima—"

Mam looked at me hard; I grew quiet. Shame and grief overwhelmed me. "Forgive me," I said. "I accept what the Good Maker sends me."

"That religious reading of yours has taught you obedience at least!" Mam said. "Alima was naturally good, however. She never needed those scrolls to learn obedience. Listen, Satha, I'm telling you of your future husband's illness because it is a secret. The boy doesn't even look ill, does he, my husband?"

"Not at all," Father agreed.

"Only those within the clan and the household servants know it. Ydalle says, they have their ways of handling it. When he was young, a nurse was always with him. Now that he's older, he doesn't like people hovering about him. His teachers, bodyguards, his father, and the warriors usually find a way to watch him. When the disease comes on him, they prevent him from hurting himself. Then they leave him, right where he has fallen, pretending not to see his shame. When he arises, he is alone. He tidies himself and no one speaks of it. Ydalle says this is what everyone does, and it's best if you learn to do likewise. You'll shame him if you don't, and no matter what you do, do not speak openly to him about it. You don't want to shame one who is mad with love for you."

"Mam, how can he be mad with love for me when he has only just seen me?"

"Perhaps he remembers how you used to tie his breechcloth!" Father said bursting out laughing.

"Obviously his ypher is ruling him," Mam said, winking to Father. "That third leg gets men as well as women in trouble."

Within the golden brick exterior wall of Taer's Golden House, fifty-eight Pagatsu households lived in harmony, or at least as much harmony as was possible for the Pagatsu. As I walked through the entrance gates into the large outer courtyard and surveyed the nearby gardens and the many minor houses that surrounded the Great House where Chief Taer lived, I realized the weight of good fortune the Good Maker had given me. On either side of the marble walkway, servants and noble ladies bowed before me. Their gold, silver and turquoise jewelry glistened in the sunlight.

Ydalle's was the only face I recognized. A dark-skinned Theseni like me, she smiled uneasily and wrung her hands. Other Theseni faces peered out at me from the crowd, along with a few Ibeni and mixed-tribe peoples, but the majority of greeters and onlookers were Doreni. I reminded myself that although the Doreni seemed friendly enough, they were called the Fierce People, and the Pagatsu were the fiercest of all Doreni.

Ydalle seemed to share the same suspicious nature as Mam, and she hovered protectively about me as I took the honored place in the Gathering Room of the longhouse. This longhouse was not like those we live in now. In those days, a great chief's longhouse was a fortress of stone and wood, and the circular gathering room where matters ceremonial and mundane were discussed was like a king's throne room. Clan elders and their wives from near and far were present to examine me, but my prospective bridegroom was nowhere to be seen. Nor was his father.

All around the room, servants busied themselves. Although they all wore the stylized clothing of their respective clans, the edges of their leggings, breechcloths, undergarments, and tunics were embroidered with clan markings indicating they were in the service of the Pagatsu clan. Some were mixed-caste; others were warseed whose mothers had been raped by Angleni soldiers. Many warseed roamed the world in those days. Many begged in the streets, or were enslaved. Those in Taer's Golden House were especially blessed.

Weighted down with jewelry, expectation, and doubt, I sat cross-legged on a pillow, as Taer's clan questioned me about religion, philosophy, history, herbs and medicine, currency, etiquette, farming and agriculture. I answered well, I think, but who can truly judge such things? Loic was the headman's son. Those who questioned me knew that to thwart a Doreni chieftain in his youth was to regret it when he was older. They therefore dealt gently with me.

All but one. The cold eyes of a silent beautiful brown-haired Doreni woman aimed daggers at me. Her gold-threaded dress—she was more richly dressed than all the others—indicated she was a noble in the clan. I realized as I looked at her that she made me tremble.

So rude was she that Mam whispered in my ear—a breach of etiquette, "I'll tell you later why that one hates you. But what does it matter what a ghost thinks? She doesn't even exist."

I looked carefully, perceived. Mam was right. The captive women and servants eyed the noblewoman scornfully, and showed much disdain in their required duties towards her.

"Watch her," Mam whispered. "She might be your future torturer, the one who makes it her goal to destroy you. "

A subtle flicker of her eyelid turned my attention to the slight auburn-haired boy sitting beside the woman. The only child in the room, he appeared to be about twelve or thirteen. He seemed so shy and fearful that I thought, *If not for that red hair of his, he would disappear into thin air.*

"That's your husband's 'brother'." Her tone implied he was no real brother at all. "Even so . . . he's here and not with the other children. Taer is a noble one."

I twisted uncomfortably on my pillow. Suddenly so much needed to be known and understood.

The servants carried the ceremonial food into the room: barley, bala, and pomegranates for fertility, sunflower seed for prosperity, rose-jam for joy. Mukal and distilled pine sap flowed lavishly into goblets large and small; a feast lay on the large mosaic table—a garden of delights my husband and I could not touch until the appointed time.

Suddenly Mam's elbow was digging hard into my side, and her eyes shone as if a bright star had appeared on the horizon. "Ah, your illustrious New Father has just entered."

I looked in the direction she was gazing and saw a tall man about forty, athletic and sturdily built. I had expected the great Treads Lightly to dress in a war bonnet, bone hair-pipe breastplate, furs, and gems for the half marriage ceremony, but he wore a simple green tunic made of common hemp fiber and leather leggings. No dagger hung at his side.

"Not what I'd expect of a warrior celebrating his first son's half marriage," Mam complained in a low whisper. "But look!" She returned to her happier mood. "He honors you by perfuming his hair with carmi oil. That's a month's wages for the likes of you and me. Yes, that's it. He wants you to shine, not himself. " Her eyes roamed his face. "The scar mars his face, but you can see how handsome he used to be." She sounded wistful, but if Father was jealous, he didn't show it.

Mam was right, though. How beautiful Taer was, how masculine compared to Father. The scar only added to his beauty. Father had no scar and it seemed a great pity he had none.

"New Daughter," Taer said as he walked towards me. He almost sang the words, and the soft playful musicality of his voice surprised me. Seductive it was, and it put me at ease. Yet, it seemed strange to me that such a great warrior would speak so gently. He sat on the pillow to my right. "With her dying breath, Loic's mother reminded me of my promise to your father. I have waited many years to keep it."

I smiled beneath my veil, half-hoping the fabric of the altvayu would tear suddenly and bring an end to all pretence.

"Promised One of my son," he said, bending towards me, "what do you think of this proposed marriage? I hope the old promise is not a burden to you."

The question was etiquette, of course, and the right response should have humbly and quickly fallen from my lips. Yet, I didn't immediately answer. A grievous fault, because it made me appear vain and ungrateful. Like armed warriors forcing an unruly enemy into a prison cell, Mam's eyes threatened me if I challenged the marriage.

However, an old man sitting beside Taer nodded kindly in my direction. "Yes, Thesenya, tell him all your heart." I would learn the man was Pantan, Taer's uncle, and he was nicknamed "Thousands" because of the thousands he had killed. "Although the promises of parents bind children, we would not want an old promise to put a burden upon you, especially if your heart already belongs to another."

"My uncle is right," Taer agreed. "He was headman of our clan before he handed his vialka to me. I promise you no curse or vendetta will be laid on you or your children if you refuse my son."

"My heart belongs only to myself, New Father. I hesitated speaking because throughout the land of the three tribes, women younger and more beautiful than I can be found. Good women of higher status and more worthy than I to marry one who wears a jade bracelet."

Pantan grinned. Around me, others smiled. My directness mixed with my diplomacy had clearly impressed the Pagatsu. But Mam and Ydalle both slapped their right hands on their thigh so loudly and in such perfect unison, I almost believed they shared the same soul.

"Daughter," Taer answered, "do not wrong your beauty. But hear me. I know only too well how cruel and bloodthirsty the hearts of women can be." From the corner of my eye, I noticed a smirk flicker across the face of the lavishly dressed woman. "Cold hearts become even colder when wealth and innocent men are involved. What use, then, are beauty and wealth if they hide a cold heart? Were not Salba and Aroun cuckolded and poisoned in their beds by young rich beautiful wives?"

"Old wives can poison too, New Father." I answered. The old man, Pantan, laughed. But Mam squeezed my forearm tightly and an exhalation, like the startled breathing of a bison, flew out of Ydalle's mouth.

Taer turned to Ydalle and, lips in a conspiratorial smile, and took her hand gently. "Ydalle," he said, "you're a good soul, but don't worry so much. Satha and I understand each other." He turned to me again, smiling. His smile honored me greatly, because the Doreni never smile at strangers. "Daughter, it was because your father was so honorable that he lost all his fortune. No one else stayed to feed the poor after the Angleni salted the fields. I can trust my son to the daughter of a poor and honorable man who gave all in his store to feed those who could not repay him."

"New Father," I answered, "I'm relieved you explained this to me. I was beginning to fear, with such talk of cold cruel hearts, you didn't like women very much and that you had chosen me because—"

A sound like that of an eel slipping out of a woman's hand issued from the mouth of the lavishly dressed woman and silenced me.

"I like women well," Taer answered, looking briefly in the woman's direction. "And I find—now that I have spoken to you—that I like you very much." He again glanced at the woman who seemed to have made herself my enemy. "Women who speak their minds don't betray their husbands. Only, only, be gentle with my boy. He's young yet and hasn't enough experience to challenge your wit."

He smiled again, and perhaps I saw too much in it. Perhaps it was only a fatherly gesture, but it troubled me, for already my eyes and heart were finding him too pleasing.

"May I ask you one more question, New Father?" I asked. Behind me, Mam was shaking like a volcano about to release its fury. "Do you truly want a wife for your son? Are you sure you haven't brought me here to be his mother?"

Taer did not hesitate in his response. "Loic has many mothers, New Daughter. He doesn't need another. A guardian of his heart, though— someone who will allow his heart to rest in her bosom—would do nicely."

Many mothers. Orphaned children abounded in our land in those days, and my heart melted at the words. *How sad,* I thought, *to have the falling sickness and to be motherless at the same time!*

A din sounded in the mirrored hallway. All the guests stood up and I, too, prepared to stand. But Mam's hand pushed me back into the pillow. Soon the thin slats of the ebonywood curtains seemed to fold themselves away, and behind them—as if rising up from an unseen realm—was the willful eighteen-year-old who had changed my life. On either side of him near the mosaic-tiled walls, singing servant girls played on tambourines. Leading him was an old woman whose braided white hair flowed out from under a Doreni coif. She wore the cotton leggings of a mamya under a buckskin tunic, and he kept glancing back at her as if asking for her approval. Her response was always a doting smile. She led him toward us as if he were Our Matchless Prince himself.

I should have been happy to marry the son of a great chieftain. Indeed, he was good to look at, nicely proportioned with thick hair tumbling over his shoulders like the waves of a waterfall, not like the little baby I half-remembered. He wore a green clan-cap made of dyed deerskin, with the Pagatsu beadwork. However, no feather or ribbon hung from the two golden loops in his earlobes. The only signs he was a chieftain's son were the flowing embroidered sleeves of his long buckskin gyuilta and the jade Doreni firstborn bracelet.

He walked toward me, and when he arrived at my side, he turned his eyes on me. How silent the room became as he stood there attempting to peer behind my veil. Pale eyes he had, strange eyes, which seemed to mirror everything they looked at. For as they roamed my brown skin, brown they became, and when they rambled over the neckline of my green dress, a forest glade rose in them. Yes, he was good to look at. Except that his nose was a little too long, and one tooth was broken. A dull brown bruise near his chin, and a scar running the length of his forearm made me remember his illness. I thought, *I've married a boy so doted on and spoiled he'll probably end up even more useless than Father. No, he doesn't seem like someone destined to be a warrior at all.*

The moment this thought entered my mind, a hurt look appeared on his face. Surprised, I glanced at Mam. She shot me a threatening glance. I remembered her warning and her fear of ending up on the streets. My eyes stung. But how could I cry when the wounded eyes of a Doreni warrior's son were trying to peer into my soul?

LOIC
Half Marriage

The lace veil didn't entirely conceal my future wife's face. But in those days, veils were made to tease as well as shield. Like a light winter snowfall on a sloping golden hillside, it flowed over her forehead. Beneath the veil, her eyes shone like sunlight and I longed to bask in them. The hem of her dress flowed onto the embroidered carpet like a river flowing into a meadow. Her perfumed skin was a floral garden—that scent alone would make the desert-dweller weep. How my lips longed to kiss hers. My hand wandered under the veil's long hem. I found her fingers and squeezed them. None saw me touch her; none saw how she struggled against my touch, digging her fingernails into the palm of my hand.

"Are you hoping to draw blood?" I whispered. "You've only succeeded in piercing my heart."

She turned her face away as if my whispered yearning was the buzzing of a bee she wished to swat. I thought, *I'll win our private undeclared war.* Sensing she would keep her poise and not betray the struggle between us, I forced my fingers through hers and interlaced them. But her nails dug deeper into my flesh.

I saw a thought floating through her mind. *The Creator has given me a child husband, one who will always be a child.* My heart sank. It was like a boulder crushing my chest. I was seeing the marriage as she saw it. I thought, *How can I prove to the one I love that I will become a true Pagatsu warrior?*

All around us, my clan ate and danced. Although the Kluna clan was absent, scrolls of alliances were made. Wherever the remaining Kluna were, they would be brothers to the Pagatsu.

My heart, however, was on none of this. *What*, I thought, *if I cannot prove myself and she rejects the full marriage when the year mark comes?*

I watched as her gaze fell everywhere—on my father, on her parents, at Ydalle, at my Little Mother—but never at me.

With sunken heart, I sat and listened as New Mother Monua said, "The jewel of my life has now been given to your son—the crown of your life. Taer, your son must now forego wearing the youth cap. He's to be a husband now, after all. Let him wear a marriage cap so all the ladies of Satilo know he's married."

Father laughed and removed my cap. "Layo, layo! Truly, yes! Let's be rid of daughters sending their fathers to me for marriage talks."

Everyone but Satha laughed at this. She looked at me with eyes that clearly said, *I wish some other woman's daughter had married you.*

Little Mother said, "It's time we leave the betrothed couple alone to get acquainted." Then she crept up behind us and threw the red courting blanket that Mad Malana had made over our shoulders. Our families left the gathering room, and as the last foot disappeared behind the curtained entrance, Satha yanked her hand from mine and threw the courting blanket onto the ground. She gave me a warning look, something one would give a child playing too near fire.

"This is a good day the Creator made," I said. My voice cracked, making me feel even younger than I already felt.

"It brings blessings for you and for me," she answered, although she looked as if the day had brought disaster and not blessing.

"It is strange to be at my own betrothal ceremony," I said, trying to look into her eyes. "Last year a cousin of my dead mother married."

She answered with a voice neither inviting nor cold, but patronizing nevertheless. "Is that a fact?"

I pressed on. Oh how lovely she smelled. I can still remember it even now. "I didn't attend. Father received the Desai News Runner and sent gifts but said it was best if I refused the invitation."

She raised her eyebrows. "I thought you people were enslaved to customs."

I thought angrily, *We are not enslaved to customs, Thesenya! As a people, we always do what we consider right in our own hearts, and we change customs more often than you, an outsider, would know.* I was Doreni, however, and not one to argue with the wrong ideas of outsiders.

I only said, "Our dealings with the Desai are always complicated. For some reason, they and my Father don't—"

"Stop trembling. Try to breathe. I'm the one who should be nervous, being dragged into your life and treated as chattel."

I had not realized how my body trembled. I tried to breathe and found myself laughing, immediately liking her again. *How brave and forthright she is!* I thought. Her humor reminded me of Krika's.

"Only rich young men can indulge in that kind of laughter."

I rubbed the indentations her fingernails had pressed into my wrist. "Why are you trying to become my enemy, Satha? Why hurt my heart in the same way you've hurt my hand?"

"Coqulyu—little boy—you're not the kind of person I would think of marrying."

"Coqalya—little girl—and what 'kind' of person do you think I am, exactly?"

"A pretty little boy with too much money."

"I am more than that." My voice cracked again. I did not like defending myself against the woman I so wanted to love me. "Hasn't it been told you that I'm kind and gentle? I've heard as much about you."

"People don't talk about me, little boy, and I doubt they talk about you either."

Remembering the boldness of the Ibeni poets, I approached her and put my arms around her waist. "Satha, since we're to be married and it's too late to turn back now, let's be friends."

She pushed me away. "Would you expect a slave to befriend the master who enslaves her? Rich people and men are used to taking, I suppose I should accept that."

Her anger irked me. "I'm honorably holding up a promise my father made to his old friend. I'll admit when Father told me of it I was nervous, but then I saw you and heard what the townspeople said about you—"

She interrupted me with a scornful laugh. "We will be better friends, Loic, if you're honest with me. You and I know no such promise exists."

I stared at her, amazed. I had encountered Theseni outspokenness before. Ydalle, for instance, needed to learn more about the Doreni habit of silence, but Satha's frankness bordered on rudeness.

She walked toward the curtained doorway, looked through the slats, then turned and studied the gathering room. "No, my father didn't betray your little scheme. But since you have no desire to be honest—"

Although I was Doreni—and the Doreni rarely speak with frankness—I resolved to be Theseni and to speak with an open heart. "Your words are sharp shuwas, Satha, but they're true. No promise exists. I saw you and loved you immediately. How can I prove this to you?"

"I'm not an unpleasant person, Loic." Her voice grew gentler and she sounded almost like Little Mother. "But you can understand how strange it is to find one's self suddenly married. Perhaps, if you'd courted me properly instead of interrupting my life so suddenly—"

Her gaze roamed the gathering room, studying the weapons, the buffalo horns, and pelts. In spite of myself, I found myself hoping my wealth would influence her to like me better. "I've lived by whims, my wife," I said, lowering my voice. "Yet I am not selfish. I understand now that I made a grievous error to marry you so hastily. From my heart now I tell you that in my stupidity, eagerness, and joy, I thought this was the right way to proceed."

"You speak like a poet, Loic. Yet you have much to learn for someone so educated."

I touched her arm. "Jobara! Indeed, I have much to learn. But, can you not forgive my ignorance? Can you not see the blessings in this match? Consider that I'm one who respects your intelligence, your goodness, your beauty and even your anger. I'm Doreni. We Doreni men aren't jealous adulterers like the Ibeni. Nor are we harsh like the men of your people who even go so far as to enslave women in their heaven. We have loving, free hearts and Doreni women freely roam where they please." I paused to catch my breath then spoke again. "I see too you're looking at the wealth which surrounds you. My family—"

"Now I know you're speaking honestly because you're bragging about yourself. Weak men always brag about their wealth. What does your family's wealth mean to me?"

She took a slice of bala from a platter but didn't offer me any. The bala was a fruit with many seeds, often used in wedding feasts to encourage fertility. Custom dictated that she should have put it to my mouth for me to suck on, a symbol that she was offering herself to me. She did not and this was considered selfish in the old days. It meant she considered her body her own and would not willingly share it with her husband.

I saw her mind, however: her ploy was designed to make me reconsider the betrothal. Instead of being offended, I also took a bala slice, chewing it slowly. "How juicy it is!" I shouted. "Flooding at the touch of my lips."

She blushed but her face still retained its hardness.

"Satha," I said, "You want the truth, therefore I'll speak the truth."

She frowned at the bala in my hand. "Say on."

"I'm alone here in my Father's house."

She squinted in disbelief. "How can you say that? It's obvious everyone loves you."

"Perhaps they love me, but I walk on a different path and all here want me to tread lightly."

She smiled at my joke and seemed curious. "And you think I will walk the path with you?"

I was tempted to tell her all my mind, to speak about Krika, about the shadow gods, about my inability to turn Father from the spirits, but I was cautious and I only said, "I sense you will walk with me, Satha. Don't be afraid of marrying me, Satha. We were created for each other, and the Wind has brought us together to heal each other's heart." I stopped speaking when I saw tears rolling down her cheek.

She didn't speak but stood fidgeting near the wooden curtains of the inner court through which our families had disappeared. She wiped her tears and we stood in silence until our fathers and the elders returned.

My father carried the yellow corn mush and Nwaha carried the white. They poured both into one bowl and put the spoon to my mouth. I ate, and after hesitating for a moment, Satha also ate.

Despite my grief at her resistance, I managed to finish the ceremonial oath. "Beloved, in my father's house are many mansions. I have prepared a place for you, that where I am there you may be also. Let not your heart be troubled. You believe in the Creator, believe also in me. Where you go, I will go. If I travel far away, I'll return and bring you to my home."

She bowed and answered, "My beloved is mine, and I am his. Into his hands, I commit my life."

My heart leaped at her words even though I saw how distant her heart was.

As the women of the household prepared to take her to the women's section of the guest quarters, I whispered to her, "Do you think you could love me? Just a little?"

She smiled, but I knew she thought I was like the wind—a force that could blow her wherever it willed, a breeze that could warm and freeze her with a sudden whimsical blast. She considered herself my toy, a thing that I would examine, play with, then throw away when a newer, more exotic plaything was found. Yes, I saw all this, and understood she had steeled her heart against mine.

After the ceremony, I walked to the men's quarters and called out to Father.

"Why are you here, my son?" he asked, his eyes nervously surveying the courtyard. "Now that the Restraint has begun, you know the customs forbid us speaking together."

My father rarely looked nervous, and I understood that he was worried for my sake. "I wanted to share my joy with you, Father."

"I am honored. Tell me then, now that you have finally met the one you love so deeply, what do you think of her? Is she as wonderful as you imagined?"

"We told each other all our hearts, and Father, she pleases me well."

He tousled my hair. "Does she not remind you of Krika?"

"Krika?" He had mentioned my lost friend and had stirred my anger. "Krika was Doreni and a boy. Satha is neither."

"They share the same fire. Can you not see it?"

"If that's true, she's lucky that Nwaha and not Okiak is her father." And then, suddenly, like a silly child I began to cry. On the day of my betrothal! How glad I was that Satha was not nearby to see my childishness!

Father held me tightly, pushing my head into his chest, enveloping me in his arms. "I cried, too, on the day I was betrothed to my first wife. I cried, too, on the day you were born."

I had always understood that Father's dearest love was not my mother, but his first wife, the one his parents had brought to him after Monua rejected him.

"Father," I said, "Your first wife lives happily in the fields we long for. You loved her with all your heart. I loved Krika also. He was my age-brother but much more. He was my other heart. I cannot bear to think of him stumbling about in Gebelda, waiting for a life to be sacrificed for him. Could you bear to think of your first wife, or even of my mother, in such a place? Could we not go to the shrine, secretly, and shed some lamb's blood for Krika? Can I not cut my wrist, hands and palms for him? Should he not be able to sit in the Creator's longhouse? And look, on such a happy day as this, he should . . . he would . . . if Krika were alive now, he would stand by my side in all battles against the Arkhai. Yes, he would stand by me in the full marriage ceremony. He would—"

"Sio will stand by your side," he said, interrupting me. No word about Krika: the deepest heart of my pleading was ignored.

I opened my mouth then closed it again. Clan tradition stated that the son of a warrior's wife is a warrior's true son. The law was made for the children of widows and concubines. Not for the bastards of adulteresses. However, Father had forced his own interpretation on our clan.

My heart closed even more against him. "Although you accept Sio as your son, I don't accept him as my brother."

Ravens winged towards some unseen carcass, cawing as they went.

"Does that matter? The boy has a kind heart and has drawn a circle, which includes you. He'll turn you into his brother soon enough. At least, that is his hope."

"He's young. I hope he'll lose that hope when he grows older."

"When you were younger, you loved him as a brother."

"Yes, when I was young and understood as little as he does. But young minds change when they grow older."

Father started laughing. "Are you one to speak about young people's minds? You who fell in love with a woman you don't know? A woman who is obviously reluctant to marry you? You who hold onto hurt—my hurt—as if it were your own: you dare speak to me about—"

"About Krika, Father!" I said raising my voice. "I was speaking of Krika. My true brother. Not of Sio."

He clasped his hands together in front of his face, a thing he always did when he was losing his patience. "How often have you asked me to order a ceremony for Krika? And how often have I told you that is the one thing I cannot do? The Arkhai stronghold is powerful and they see all. If I—"

I pushed him away, wiping my tears. "They're powerful only because we don't understand the Creator's love."

He stared at me. "And do you know the Creator's love?"

"He's far away," I admitted. "How can I know one who is unlike me and so far above us?"

"True words." He sounded relieved. "In this at least, you're not arrogant. The Creator is high above, yes, and because of this, he cannot tend to small matters or small persons. For this reason, he has given us the Arkhai, the shaman, and the holy ones to teach us how to live holy lives."

"The Arkhai? Those shadow princes? Those posers, deceivers, and boasters? Father, it shames me that you bend to such beggarly and evil spirits! Jobara! Your stupidity in all things—Sio, the Third Wife, Okiak—shames me."

Across the field was the armory where the guns and cannons of the invaders were kept. I pointed at its latched doorway. "You understand the workings of all these weapons, Father. You have conquered many cities. Yet you leave the sharpest weapons unsheathed and out in the open for anyone to fall upon."

"You're speaking of my wife, Loic." He pointed in my face. "Don't let your anger take you into a battle you cannot win."

"Did you see how your wife behaved today? Sitting opposite mine and dressed in costly array and covered in pearls! She's still acting as if she's Arhe here." I clasped my hands together and pleaded with him. "Even now you can divorce her, Father. So, what if the town calls you a cuckold? It's not as if the thing isn't known already outside our clan."

"Perhaps you should remember that as you love Satha so I once loved the Third Wife. Could you repudiate Satha if she wounded you?"

"Satha would never wound me."

"So you say." He touched the fuzzy growth on my chin. "What if after the year-mark she decides not to go ahead with the full marriage?"

His words made my head throb and my heartstrings tighten, but I did not show my fear.

"No answer?"

"Satha will enter the full marriage."

"Kwelku. So you say. Even so. Learn to live with my mistakes as I've learned to live with yours. Your wife will be Arhe over all these households. Is that not enough? There is no need to repudiate my wife. Her lack of status in this household is repudiation enough."

"Kill the whore, Father!" I shouted and suddenly the sting of an open-handed blow silenced me. I had gone too far. Blood streaked from my nose and through my lips. My hand trembled with the urge to return the strike. His scorn-filled eyes dared me to return the blow. I lowered my hand. My head, but not my heart, was bowed, and we stood silently facing each other.

"I should not have hit you, my child," he said at last. "But one so young should not be so unforgiving. Especially if he isn't the wounded one."

I pushed him away, and wiped my bloody nose with the sleeve of my gyuilta. I walked away, throwing my gyuilta to the ground.

When I went to my room, I could not sleep. Love and hate bounced through my mind. I hated the Arkhai most of all because they had caused me to become estranged from father and my clan and were the source of all my distress. As I lay covered in furs, dread began to rise within me, an anticipation of some nameless terror. I began to wonder, *Perhaps Okiak has bound me with a love spell.* Love-spells were charms he did not dabble in, but he liked to control matters. Making me love someone who would betray me as the Third Wife had betrayed Father would not be beyond him. Suddenly unsure of the reason for my abrupt love for a strange woman, I considered dissolving the marriage. At the same time, other thoughts bounced in my mind: perhaps the love I had for Satha was indeed true. Perhaps it was the Arkhai who wished me to doubt it. Perhaps they wanted to be solitary in the world without friend or ally.

If Satha proved to be my true ally, all was safe. But if she did not, what was I to do? My heart had no desire to search the countryside for a priest to free me from the love-spell. Fear of losing her made me conceive a plan. I resolved to ask Father to hasten the full marriage and to allow us to marry within a week instead of at the customary year-mark ceremony. I resolved, too, that I would convince Satha to couch with me. A child would tie her to me and, however unworthy she found me to be, she would not risk losing the child by divorcing me.

My plan conceived, but not birthed, I fell asleep and dreamed of our full marriage. In the dream, I seemed older. The man who took Satha to bed was myself yet not myself. Older he was, and wounds scarred his body. Instead of lying on a bed we lay on a hard jagged rock which slowly, over a long time, softened beneath us into fur.

While I pondered this strange vision, a voice called out to me, "Loic, Loic." I knew it was the Wind, the Creator, the Uncaused Causer of all things.

I said, "Here am I."

All at once, a great sword descended from the sky. Its blade pointing downward, it fluttered like a ribbon of flayed skin in the wind. Of paper the sword was, rather than metal. Words covered its blade, words I could read yet which nonetheless I could not understand.

"Loic," the Wind said, "behold your sword."

"Great Chief," I said, "I shall make my own sword." The sword ascended back into heaven.

But it descended again and the Wind spoke. "Loic, here is your sword."

Again, I refused it and again it was received up into heaven.

Then the voice spoke again. Again the sword descended, but this time it turned itself—its hilt now directly above my hand. "Loic, here is your sword."

Relenting, I agreed to take it. Quickly it descended, and how sharp, straight and powerful it became as it fell from the sky! Its blade seemed alive and the words written on it living words. The sword whirled wildly, smashing Father's armory, and scattered his weapons to the four winds. Finished, it flew towards me, its hilt at last in the palm of my hand.

I awoke from the dream, not understanding it. Nor did I ask Okiak or any of the clan elders to interpret it. I leaned on the window as moonlight shone through, and looked across the fields towards the room where my beloved lay. I could not return to sleep. At last, I put on my soft leather shoes and walked outside, intent on reaching her door and fulfilling my fear-born plan.

SATHA
The Little Taste

Mamya Jontay, Loic's Little Mother, the noblewoman who had raised him since his birth, led me to my rooms in the women's section of the guest quarters. With her were other Pagatsu noblewomen. After greeting me with dancing and singing, they left us alone in my dowry-filled room surrounded by chalcedony, gold, jasper, jade, turquoise and other riches. She gestured toward the bed on which a pearl-encrusted silk quilt rested. I walked in silence toward it.

Glancing around at the furs, fabrics and the objects of wealth, and comparing them to the torn and tattered dinginess of my former home, I regretted my rudeness to Loic and my ungratefulness for such blessings. Although I had lived in poverty, I had not accepted it. Nor had I accepted the loneliness of living in a strange region with no clan to protect me. Now I had both wealth and family.

Mamya Jontay stood near the bed, staring at me, as if waiting for me to speak. I must have looked like a little lost sheep for she suddenly said, "Thesenya, we're a fierce people, but you're one of us now. Despite being in the guest quarters, you're not alone. I know you Thesenyas are close to your mothers. I will bring her here if you wish."

"And my father?"

She frowned as if I had spoken indecent words. "Not your father. Speak to him little during the betrothal feast days, and never in private. During the days of the Restraint, speak no word to him at all."

"Among the Theseni, the betrothed couple—"

"Arhe, you're Doreni now. The Restraint year begins after the six days of the betrothal feast ends. During that time, you and Loic must not see your fathers. Not until the full marriage. Come to know your husband, share each other's sweetness without the interference of men."

"This is a harsh custom you've thrust upon me, Mamya Jontay," I said.

She put her arm around my shoulder and said firmly but with kindness, "You will bear it. The rules are narrow, the Golden House is wide, and you are an obedient girl who wants to show everyone you can restrain yourself from running to your father."

I didn't think I was obedient, but knew well enough to pretend to be.

She indicated the jewelry scattered about the room. "All this is your dowry, girl."

"It is not my dowry. My father's goodness has earned it."

"Layo, layo. True, he has riches now. And if the marriage fails, all this is yours and his to keep." She gave me a warning look. "But the marriage will not fail, will it?"

I shook my head.

She continued. "Such wealth can be intimidating, I know. The love of a passionate young man even more so. But you'll become used to both love and wealth." She smiled, and strange it was to see a Doreni woman smiling at me. I had gotten used to their formidable stares in the marketplace. "Think of all the good this wealth can do. Only, try to love my Loicuyo for himself. He loves you very much and . . ." Her words trailed into silence.

"And what?"

"He'll know if you don't love him. That's all." She walked toward the doorway, pulled the wooden curtain aside, passed through it, then turned and pulled it closed behind her.

I was alone.

Fatigue should have made me sleep, but I missed hearing Mam's snoring from the other room. I worried about not seeing Father. I lay watching the glittering of jewels in the moonlight, wondering what freedoms I had lost and what burdensome duties I had gained. As I lay there, footsteps echoed in the corridor. "Mamya Jontay?" I whispered, rising from the bed. "Is that you? Is that you, Mam?"

No answer came.

I rose and, as was my custom, reached for my veil. I hastily put it on before I pushed the wooden curtain slats of the door aside.

It was Loic, his finger to his lips. "Throw a gyuilta over your nightdress," he whispered and raised his hands to show I had nothing to fear. He gestured toward the dark fields. "Let us walk together alone."

My mother's advice returned to me. *Bend to his will.* I wondered, *If I bend to his will, will he still want me?* "Out there?" I asked. "In the darkness? Without our mothers?"

"I will not hurt you, Satha."

"No," I stammered. "I did not think you would hurt me. But—"

"Ah, I see! I've heard that Theseni women are afraid of the dark and very superstitious, always sprinkling powders and dropping food for the spirits wherever you go. So it's really true?" He grinned, entering the room without invitation, and sat down on the bed.

"I've heard you Doreni men have small yphers and cannot satisfy women. Is that true?"

He raised an eyebrow. "I've heard you Theseni women are so prickly and pious no man's ypher can satisfy you. Is that true?"

We faced each other in silence until he lifted a pair of sandals so exquisitely worked their beauty almost left me breathless. I took them from him and placed them on my feet. How dainty my toes looked in them!

"Don't fear these shadow gods," he said. "They have no real power." He said this with such quiet conviction and with such absolute certitude that I knew it to be the truth. "Let's go, now. While we walk, you must tell me why you don't like mirrors."

I stared at him, then glanced at a gold-edged mirror hanging near the door. "How do you know I don't like mirrors?"

He turned the mirror's face to the wall. "I'll tell the servants to remove them if you wish. But your reason for disliking them is not a valid one. You're not ugly and your dark skin is most becoming."

"How do you know what is in my heart?" I asked, unable to hide my surprise. "Tell me, my husband. Can you truly see inside my heart?"

He seemed almost ashamed. "It is an unpredictable, undependable birth-gift. A trait inherited from my Desai mother. There is no faithfulness in it that I can trust in."

"Nevertheless, Waihai! You're blessed to have such a gift. Jobara!"

A grin spread across his face. "Do you truly think so? Although it's so fickle? When I'm distressed or grieved, it is of no use at all. My confusion thwarts it."

"Even so, my husband. Such a gift breeds fear in others. What warrior would not be unsure of himself when speaking to you? If that is the gift's only purpose, it serves you well. No one can confidently lie to you. And who would dare conspire against you if they think you can see their thoughts?"

His eyes widened as if a new truth had been presented to him. "Jobara! Layo, Layo! Indeed! Yes, truly. Now that you know that secret I will tell you another. I also do not like mirrors. I do not like what I see in them."

"What do you see?"

"I see the other world inside them."

"Is there another world inside them?" I asked, surprised.

"At first, Father said I was imagining things. But then Little Mother recognized many of the mirror people I described."

My eyes must have widened. "Who were these mirror people?"

"Dead ones thrown into the trash heap of Gebelda, or the holy ones taken by the Creator. Or the Arkhai who walk the earth, sky and water." He stopped abruptly. "You do believe me, don't you?"

"Waihai! Such gifts! Perhaps the spirits have marked you to intercede for them. And yet, with all this, your clan did not make you a shaman? Do they think perhaps that the falling sickness has wounded your mind?"

Shame spread across his face. For as long as it takes for a crow to wing across the sky, he stared at me. I realized I had spoken about his illness and stuttered an apology.

"Do you always ask stupid questions of people when they tell you all their heart?" he snapped at last.

"I wasn't . . . it just seemed . . . only shamans and men with sick minds see visions."

"I am neither a shaman nor mad." He breathed deeply, like a child trying to push his angry thoughts away. "Don't doubt me, Satha. I don't doubt you. I've changed my heart. We will not walk tonight." Then, pushing me aside, he walked through the doorway and down the tiled corridor.

As I watched his slender figure disappearing into the darkness, I thought, *Perhaps I am indeed blessed to have such a husband. Even though he's spoiled and not used to someone challenging him, I can see that he longs for the Good Maker as I have longed for goodness. Perhaps the Creator has indeed claimed him as his own.*

The next morning, Mam and Little Mother came to my door. They were like two minds in one head, and each head overflowed with similar plans for me.

"How did you sleep, my married daughter?" Mam asked, pushing the wooden curtain aside.

I was glad to see her. Yet because I was still unsure if such solitary visits were allowed, and because I was a married woman, I told myself that Mam need not know all that occurred between Loic and me.

She set about searching among my gifts for the right dress for me, while Little Mother explained that Okiak had been appointed to tell me about the Doreni food rules.

"In a year when the full marriage is performed, you will be expected to create a great feast for your guests," Little Mother said. "And you're expected to show your skills in Doreni daggerwork, and horsemanship. Horse riding, food knowledge, daggerwork and diplomacy are the four arts a high-born Doreni woman must know. We call them the Four Defenses because they are beneficial in dealing with danger."

The art of Doreni knifework was powerful and graceful. As Mamya Jontay showed me one tactic after another, she seemed no longer an old woman but a young Doreni warrior. "A Doreni woman has a small dagger hidden on her person at all times," she explained, brandishing a dagger. "With all these vendettas, one never knows when one might be carried off."

I couldn't help but laugh. "Mamya Jontay," I said, "My life is protected and safe. I see no use in learning useless traditions."

Mamya Jontay said nothing, only smiled her inscrutable smile, then turned back to her practice.

Later Loic approached us on the field. How happy I was to see him and yet how fearful! I wondered if he was still angry with me.

"I see you've been studying," he said, but his eyes showed neither desire nor anger.

"Mamya Jontay could assassinate even Fiancour, our hardiest Theseni warrior," I replied.

"Fiancour?" He said, whistling. "Jobara!" Then he left. No other words did he speak to me, no emotion did he show.

That night, as moonlight spread across the fields, I paced back and forth in my room waiting for our Love Trespass. That was what they called it in those days. When I heard his footfall sounding along the corridor, my heart leaped.

"You needn't have worried," he said, when I pushed the curtain aside. "I've forgiven you."

I hadn't been thinking that I needed to be forgiven, but I kept my peace. Small twigs can be fodder for great fires, and he was so happy, holding my hand as he danced and leaped along the corridors, I thought it best not to defend myself. He led me from the guest women's quarters to the edge of Taer's marriage quarters where a herb garden of spices bordered a wrought-iron gate.

"This is arvina," he said, plucking a thorny plant with many small purple flowers. "They say it makes lovemaking fierce."

I glanced back at my rooms. "I see."

"When this Restraint is over," he said, "and we have built our own marriage quarters and our own houses and households, we will blanket our bed with it." Without asking, he lifted my veil and pushed aside my scarf. "Haven't we promised we will unveil our hearts to each other?" He kissed my cheek and warmth throbbed through my body. Then he smiled so intimately that even now I'm embarrassed to speak of it.

"Since you asked," I said, "I did not like your coldness to me today."

"Such coldness was necessary," he said. "If I had not been cold you would have seen my anger. My clansmen expect to see wisdom and propriety in our actions. They know we're young and want to couch with each other. They know we will have disagreements. If we display all our emotions and cannot show our restraint, they will think us unwise and deem us people who are easily overthrown by their emotions."

"Jobara?" I asked. "Indeed?"

"Jobara."

"Truly, my husband, living a life of such importance can be both tedious and grievous. I often thought myself unlucky that my parents lost all their wealth, but now—"

"This life is now yours, whether you wish it or not," he answered. "Perhaps it was always yours—from the beginning of time. Perhaps it left you for a while, only to return again. I've found that some people cannot lose their destiny no matter how they fight against it."

"Do the Doreni always speak of destiny and responsibilities?"

He pointed to the east near the longhouse, then to the west near the servants' quarters, the stables and the farm, to the north where the men's quarters and the guest houses were, and at last to the south at the women's quarters and the clan houses. "The Doreni have their moments of light-heartedness, but the son of a chieftain must be serious. And the son of a Pagatsu chieftain who happens to be the king's First Captain . . . well . . ."

In the distance one of our family goats was butting her head against a barrel. "Look at that stubborn Myuhli," I said. "She's a bossy one. She's not hungry at all. She just likes causing trouble."

I opened the gate and ran toward her. When the stubborn creature saw me coming, she sped away another hundred paces. She could not outrun me. I was fleet and fast then, not old and fat as I am now. My two long legs caught up with her four short ones, and I trapped her near one of the squatting places. When I reached her, I tapped her on the nose, then turned to look backward at Loic. He had not moved. I called back to him. "Come, no one will see us. We've broken no taboo if no one sees us." He jumped over the gate. When he reached me, his eyes studied me as if entranced.

"We should not linger too near the Large Path," he said at last. "Remember the taboo."

I burst out laughing. "How can you hate the spirits and say they have no power over us, and yet also speak of taboos? Surely, a freethinker such as you should examine all your customs."

"I have considered many of our customs, my wife. But this is not only a matter of spirits and their demands. These taboos are man-made, sound and proven. They protect us from grief, gossip, and suspicion."

"Do they? Jobara?"

"Consider if we should meet my Father and our guests as we walk on this path. My clansmen would say that because my illness weakened my manhood I went looking for Father's help to bed you. They may consider me a weakling who seeks his father's help in all things. Also, if they see you talking to your father, they'll say your father bedded you before we married and you went searching for him because I didn't satisfy you. Or they will say your father himself had no desire to give you up."

"You've thought all this out, I see."

"Not me, but the ancients. They know how vile and unkind human reasoning can be. The Golden House is large and wide. A hundred towns could be contained within it. Over the next year, we will choose servants from the household for our own household. Then, when the year—" he paused as if pondering the word "—a year seems long, does it not, my wife?"

"It is the custom, my husband. As you say, the ancients know what is best."

"Kwelku." He sounded unconvinced. "In a year, a very long year, when our household is built—"

"My husband, I have thought much about a certain matter. As you probably know, Theseni husbands and wives do not live in separate houses, and at night we sleep in the same bed. I do not wish to live in one house and you in another."

He was silent for a moment. "Theseni customs have fascinated me since my youth. If my wife wishes to live in the Theseni manner, I will do so." He paused and turned his face away for a moment. "I am not sure, however, if you will want to always sleep in the same bed with me."

"Why would I not, my husband?"

He didn't answer, only turned his face away. After a typically long Doreni silence, he said, "Think of it, my heart, when we see our fathers at the end of the year, our lands, houses, servants, allies and property will be established. We will be equals with my father, then, and no longer under his will—"

"To be allied against one's father? How warlike that sounds!"

"Such customs preserve order and create stability."

He led me to a cleft in a small hillside within the prescribed boundaries and far from the Large Path. "Here," he said, "behind these tall dry lingay grasses, and these colrona shrubs—" he pointed to the leaves "—these can hide us."

The shrubs, their immature gourds and wide shady leaves already green and mottled under the fast-approaching heat moons, became our nightly private meeting place after the household had gone to bed. There we would share our hearts, but not all our hearts. If Mam or Mamya Jontay suspected our trysts, they never mentioned it. Such trespasses were expected as long as we did not couch together.

On the fourth night of our betrothal, Loic came running to my room. "Little Mother likes you," he whispered as if this were some great news. "She even likes New Mother Monua."

"Little Mother has always liked me," I answered.

He raised his eyebrow, indicating that perhaps she had not. "When I first saw you, I told Little Mother all my heart. She was angry and shouted at me: "Loicuyo, your whim has destroyed your future." Queen Butterfly, you see, had wanted me to marry her daughter Thira. A pretty girl, yes, but she honors the spirits too much. She's also too ladylike and proper, too obedient to her mother. Waihai, there were too many things wrong with that girl. Jobara! I could not live with one like that, and frankly, who wants Butterfly for a New Mother? Even so, marrying the girl would have ensured my future. If I were joined to Jaguar's family, my clansmen would forget my—" He broke off as if he had caught a thought before it escaped his lips. "But now Little Mother thinks you're a good choice, that you'll mother me as she has done."

"Is that what you want?" I watched his face closely. "A mother?"

A Theseni man would have been insulted by such a question. But Loic —perhaps because the Doreni love their mothers so—only answered, "I can't truly tell what kind of wife I want. My father's marriage is not a good example for me. I hope to love you purely. Nevertheless if there is, in my love for you, something like a son's love for his mother, or a brother's love for his sister, what can be done? We are what we are. I have had many mothers and I have liked them all, although I grieve for my true mother. Yes, although I never knew her." He seemed lost in thought for a moment. "I hope you will not die before me. I hope it is I who will leave you bereft and not the other way around."

"How strange you are!" I said.

"Even so. Promise me this, anyway."

"My husband, I promise I shall not die before you do."

"And I promise I will linger near the gates of the fields we long for and will enjoy none of its pleasures until you arrive."

On the sixth night, hurried footsteps sounded outside my wooden curtains. I raced to them. It was Loic and he held both my shoulders tightly kissing my cheeks through my veil. Then he let me go and leaped in the air, turning about several times.

"I've managed it," he said and finished dancing an Ibeni two-step.

"Managed what?" I asked. "Please stop that dancing! Tell me, what have you done?"

He stretched out his arms to me and smiled a large gap-toothed smile. "I sent word to Father asking him to remove the Restraint." He retrieved a tiny square piece of parchment, showed it to me and, throwing all caution away, shouted, "He has agreed!" His words must have echoed throughout the hillside. "We'll have the full marriage tomorrow." His eyes pleaded with me to share his joy.

I did not dance or leap. I stood silent, trying to understand the full implication of this new event. "What about the year-mark?"

"Father's a traditionalist." His eyes seemed to be trying to see inside my soul. "But he chooses carefully what traditions he'll cling to."

"I see." I began to realize that even a reasoned plea to wait until the year-mark might be seen as rejection. "How did you convince him to set this tradition aside? And why would you want it set aside?"

"I told Father we were young." His voice had grown less excited and more suspicious. "I told him our blood boiled hot for each other, that we were having trouble controlling ourselves. I reminded him that I was whimsical and willful and you were gentle and kind and who knew what would happen? And would it not be a disgrace if you were found with child before the full marriage was celebrated."

Fearful because his face had become more wary and pleading, I phrased my question carefully. "And he believed you?"

My new husband looked at me as if I was suddenly becoming a stranger to him.

I softened my question. "I think only of my honor, Loic. Will Treads Lightly not think I'm as unrestrained as an Ibeni woman? That I forego the Restraint because I myself have none?"

"Father doesn't think like that." The wary pleading look turned to an angry scowl. Anger and fear alternated on his face. "So you don't want me?"

"My husband, you speak often about the wisdom of the ancients. Were they not wise in creating the Restraint and the half marriage? Does it not benefit me? How can I create a household if I have not lived among the servants and understood them? How can I order a household if I have not lived long with the customs of your people? How will you understand how virtuous I am if you have not seen me withstand your advances for a year?"

"Wife, if we marry tomorrow, you will not have to wait a year to see your father."

I grew silent then, not knowing what to make of what was obviously a bribe. I suspect he saw my heart because he hid his face from me as I pondered his words. Mam's advice also returned to my mind: *bend to his will.*

The scowl left Loic's face and suddenly he was carefree again, smiling widely. He put his hands around my waist, then slid them upward to my breasts. "Yes," he said, "a wife should bend to her husband's will." Then, as if I had already agreed to his intentions, he turned about and faced the surrounding field, turning his head to the left then to the right, obviously searching. "But we cannot play here."

He interlaced his fingers in mine and together we ran—How fast! The treetops whizzed by. How breathless we were when we arrived at our private place!

We tumbled onto the grass and he put his hand into the sleeve of his gyuilta. Soon he was holding something up in the moonlight, a nose-ring. "It's a heirloom from my mother, part of her dowry." Of pure intricately wrought gold it was. "This is one of many gifts I inherited from her. When the full marriage is completed tomorrow, all I own and all that she gave me will be yours."

I took the nose-ring and removed my own silver one. Somewhere in the darkness a hornbill sang. I wondered, *Is the male hornbill protectively entombing his mate in a tree even now?* "Perhaps we should wait," I said, shifting on the grass. "Since, you say our wedding night is only a day away, why not wait to consummate it then?"

"Exactly. What is a mere day? Why wait?" While I looked on, surprised, he quickly removed his tunic, leggings, breechcloth and undergarment. "Come now, remove your hand from your eyes. I'm your husband now. Or do you consider my body puny?"

"No," I said, uncovering my eyes and staring at the beautiful slender tan body before me. "It isn't puny. Jobara! Indeed, you're quite good to look at."

"Yes," he said. "My New Mother told me you like slender men. I'll show you, Little Theseni girl, that thinness and muscles aren't what matters. Take your clothes off."

I removed them, but held my nightdress and gyuilta before me to cover my nakedness.

"The top halves of your breasts peek out over your nightdress like dark half-moons," he said, pulling the gyuilta from me and setting it on the soft flowers hidden among the lingay grass. "Dark Half-Moons," he repeated. "Yes, that shall be my love-name for you. Dark Half-Moons."

I burst out laughing, and he asked, "Why do you laugh, Dark Half-Moons?"

I said, "I had never dreamed that one with half-moon eyes would call me Dark Half-Moons."

He pushed my nightdress aside and placed it on the ground. "Nor did I think I would fall in love with a Thesenya." He lifted his face towards mine, kissing me, pushing the singing of the grasshoppers and the pungent smell of the spice garden from my mind. His lips—warm, warm—pressed into mine and I opened my mouth against his softly demanding tongue. The kiss was tentative, and yet, how long, gentle and deep it was!

His lips roamed my neck and shoulders, then he whispered in my ear. "Little Mother taught me many things about giving women pleasure. But you must promise not to scream and not to laugh or weep, or else someone will hear us."

"Half-Moon Eyes, have you spent all your time listening to old Doreni women and reading Ibeni poets?"

As an answer, his hands gently stroked my neck. His tongue then played with my nipples, as his hands slowly traveled down my stomach towards my thighs, pushing them apart. How clumsy it all was, and how stiff my body was! Like an old oak log, unmoving, unmovable. I could feel his heart racing with such life, caressing mine. Surprised at my body's refusal to succumb to joy, I tried to fight my resistance. Perhaps the stories were true. Perhaps we Theseni women could not enjoy ourselves in sex-play. Perhaps I was still grieving for my sister's sorrows. Perhaps I had some foreboding and presentiment. Only the Creator knows our hearts.

"You're lovely," he said, surprising me. Perhaps I expected him to know how far away my mind was. Nevertheless, he must've seen something to suddenly say such healing words. Such good kind words.

I began to believe myself as lovely as he declared. My body relaxed under his hands, and all fears of New Father and worries for my indebted parents fled my mind. All I could think was: *a good and lovely husband loves me.* I breathed freely. His fingers—warm they were— found the softness between my thighs. His lips found my breast again and he entered me. A sensation of warmth passed from his body into mine. It became fire, increased, and raced up my arm and neck. Sudden moisture . . . blood and something else . . . oozed between my legs. Mam had told me there'd be blood. How sticky my legs felt. I saw then what was meant when they said lovemaking was a covenant of blood, a sacrifice. I suppose the child was created on that very night.

After, he laid his head on my heart and his hand relaxed in mine. A ripple of giggles rose from his throat then exploded into laughter. "I never knew such joy existed," he said. Then kissing my stomach he said, "Let's do it again."

We did. This time it lasted longer and was sweeter still.

Then we lay there, eye to eye, knowing our souls had entered into each other. I had heard about the fierceness of Doreni lovemaking. It was said that after couching Doreni women could not walk for hours, often days. Yet, although he embraced me tightly, he had been gentle and I sensed he was afraid to let me go.

He kissed my lips. "How could I ever love another if you own my heart?" He pointed toward a low incline behind Taer's marriage quarters. "There's a tiled pool near there. A hot spring bubbles up from beneath the ground and the pool is carved out of the rock surrounding it."

Wee walked—naked, hand in hand—to the pool.

In the moonlight the glazed tiles shone like blue mother-of-pearl. We descended into it and far off, on the hillside, the women of Taer's household appeared, gathering flowers. I would later learn they were the flowers for my bridal ceremony and that the hasty full marriage had been accepted by all. I thought, *How easy it is to bend to the will of a husband one is beginning to love!* Yes, from that night, I began to love him, and the more I loved him the more unsettled I became.

I was married, not after a year but after a week of my betrothal. On that day we stood in the Pagatsu ancestral arbor watching Okiak and three minor Pagatsu priests kill the sacrificial sheep and draw the bloody circle around Sio, Loic and me to seal our covenant with the Creator. I was sure all the world knew our secret. How could they not? Loic looked like a lover who already knew and enjoyed the secret places of his wife's body. I, for my part, could look no one in the eye. Even when the Ibeni priest watered our hands, and the Theseni shaman blew the wind of life into our faces, I kept my head turned down.

The guests who had come for the seven day feasts extended their stay another seven days. In those days, a wedding feast was a public affair and all came from far and near. Well-wishers joined us in the ring dance. All wore the wedding garments provided for them: tunics which included both the Pagatsu markings and the symbols of my parents' professions—golden tents and silver needles. How wonderful and strange it seemed to me that the household servants had embroidered those wedding garments in so short a time! How honored I felt when my new clansmen danced around me and praised Loic for choosing such a gracious wife. The wedding feast seemed like nothing less than the Great Feast of Heaven! I had once again found a new clan for the lost one. Such love and peace I felt that the past griefs and loneliness that had oppressed me began to dissipate.

When I thought that this joy could bloom no happier, who should arrive at Taer's Golden House with great retinue of horsemen and courtiers but King Jaguar, the three tribal queens, Prince Lihu and all the Matchless Family! I cannot praise the beauty of Our Matchless Prince enough. All the tribes were found in him—the curled black hair of the Theseni; the Doreni eyes, gray and wide; and the high Ibeni cheekbones.

"The people of the land of the three tribes say Jaguar chose the three most beautiful women in the land at his coronation," Loic whispered to me when they entered the Outer Courtyard. "They are wrong. No woman—not even the three queens—is more beautiful than you."

"Truly, any woman would be happy to marry Our Matchless King. But you, my husband, are all I want."

He smiled a bit nervously and stared at me a long time. I suspected he only half-believed me.

From across the room, First Prince Lihu lifted a glass of distilled palm sap and shouted loudly. "Little Thesenya," he said. "Lift your veil and let me glory in your presence."

"The Thesenya will no longer wear her veil," Loic shouted back. "I have told her repeatedly she is Doreni now. Even though she wears the Theseni marriage veil now, it still hides too much. My wife, let my guests see how beautiful you are. Indulge me by removing your veil."

At this Lihu added, "Wait, brother, tonight she'll remove everything."

Everyone except Queen Butterfly laughed. She seemed to be trying to make me feel like an intruder at my own wedding.

Lihu must have seen this, because he turned to his mother and said, "Loic has found a beautiful Theseni woman to rest his heart and head and ypher on, has he not, Mother? You and Thira will have to wait for Sio to grow up."

Queen Butterfly was the only one who didn't laugh at her son's joke. Lihu's first-born status had made her Chief Queen and she relished her position over Second Queen Sweet-as-Jasmine and Third Queen White

Star. The Trabu Theseni were like that. Willful and arrogant, power-hungry, and lacking in humor. Not fun-loving like we Kluna. However, her strong will made her a good advocate for all the Theseni in the land even if her flamboyance and arrogance had earned her the nickname Butterfly.

She tossed the too-long sleeves of her brightly-colored gyuilta over her knees and clapped her hands together. Immediately, wooden, metal, reed, and skin instruments sounded throughout the Golden House, in the outer and inner courts, and in the longhouse. Dancers rose at her bidding to perform traditional and contemporary songs. This silenced her son. Then rising, and giving me a disdainful look, she gestured that Sio and Thira should also dance. They rose immediately. Together their feet skimmed across the floor as lightly as a feather floating on water. When the dance ended, they were giggling in a corner together.

The Third Wife had spent the wedding glaring at me but when she saw her son dancing, she smiled. I had been sorry for her. The servants —even the half-Angleni ones—had been ignoring her all day, even while they filled her platters and bowls with honeyed sweets and fat meats.

"How good those dainties look," I said to Loic.

I wanted to pile my plate high, but Loic had only touched the rich foods when the ritual required he "taste a little sweetness."

His Mamya hovered near him, offering only vegetables, fruit, and buffalo meat. If at any time, she saw him put any cake or bread to his mouth, she slapped his hand. This he endured long into the night until at last he pleaded with her to leave him alone.

About sunset, the entrance curtains of Taer's Golden House were pulled aside and several Doreni men in blue clan caps marked with patterns I didn't recognize walked through the doorway. Their leader, one who wore a jade bracelet, seemed only a few years older than I, but I would later learn he was above thirty-five years. Although he had the slanted Doreni eyes, his dark red hair showed that his clan had intermarried with one of the northern Ibeni clans, or possibly with the Angleni. The beauty of his face shone like one of Ywa's messengers, yet it seemed strangely familiar.

The gathering room grew silent when he entered, and the pipes and drums slowly halted. He strolled toward Our Matchless Family, who greeted him warmly. The eyes of the Pagatsu clan all turned from Taer to the stranger and then to Taer again. But Taer's gaze turned toward the Third Wife and her son Sio. The young boy's apparent joy at the stranger's presence was evidenced by an admiring smile. I understood suddenly why the stranger seemed so familiar. I thought, *Sio is the stranger's son.*

Loic turned to me and whispered, "Yes, he is. This is Noam, my father's captain and former friend, now his dearest enemy."

"If he's your father's enemy, why is he here?"

"Because my father has designated Sio as the Bridegroom's Friend. Because Noam is one of my Father's Valiant Men. Because of Father's actions, I must now endure him for the next seven days and must feast with—"

He stopped speaking when Theseni Queen Butterfly loudly greeted the newcomer. "Of all Taer's Great Ones, only you, Noam, could come to the full-wedding? What has happened to the famous camaraderie of the Valiant Men?" She looked at me as if the absence of the other Great Ones was my fault.

Noam answered her, "Are Heldek and Ganti are not here?" How gentle his voice was. He called out to Taer, "But it is understandable. A wedding hall cannot be filled when a boy and his betrothed dare not wait."

A groan of disapproval arose, and the room became silent. Noam's words were purposely lacking in etiquette.

Taer did not answer him, but Our Matchless King said, "Jobara! Indeed most of Taer's Valiant Men are here. The Seventy Warriors, the Thirty Masters. But, know that Heldek is away on a mission to the Angleni King. As for Ganti, well, you know the Desai."

Noam nodded. "Ah, yes! The well-known Desai reclusiveness. Even so, any who wished to attend still would have had a hard time of it. The event was so hastily—"

King Jaguar raised his hand and his voice. "Enough, Noam! I excused your rudeness before, but you insist on straining etiquette by pushing your point. The girl is honorable, and what if the marriage was hastened? They have been betrothed to each other since their youth. Why should they wait another year?"

Noam immediately stopped speaking, but resentment marred the beauty of his face. He walked towards the Matchless Family and bowed low before the king. After that, he whispered something I could not hear but which set the queens to arguing. Third Queen White Star, the Ibeni Queen, suddenly began gesticulating at Butterfly, who seemed relentless in pressing some point. Sweet-as-Jasmine, the Doreni queen, tried to make peace but after several attempts sat silent.

After a while, the king lifted his hands and pointed to Noam. "With a simple phrase, Seared Conscience," he said, "you have returned my Queens to their old quarrel."

None of the queens paid attention to their husband, and White Star seemed at the point of tears. "Husband King," she said, "will you allow that woman to insult my people as she's doing?"

"White Star," the King answered, "you are well able to defend yourself against Butterfly." He called out to Loic, "How wise you are in choosing to marry only one wife, my boy! Do you see what I suffer? Only my dear Sweet-as-Jasmine understands my need for peace. Nevertheless, at my coronation, these were the women I chose. What a lovely week I had bedding them all. Now they disrupt the loveliness of your wedding."

"Don't speak so ill against your wife, Jaguar," Loic answered. "All in our land bless you for your wisdom in choosing such honorable wives."

Then I added, "Matchless King, I am honored to have arguing queens at my wedding. We Theseni say it is not a true Doreni wedding if no fight breaks out."

Everyone laughed at this, and Our Matchless King shouted, "Taer, your son has found a Thesenya with a Doreni sense of humor. A hard thing, that."

Loic smiled but whispered to me, "Consider carefully what Noam has done. Jaguar rebuked him publicly just now. This is not something we Doreni often do because a shamed friend becomes a harsh enemy. Even so, Jaguar is king and he can do what he wishes. Notice how Noam responded to the king's rebuke. To avenge himself, he started a disagreement between the queens."

I eyed him askance. "Come now, husband. You are finding machinations where none exist."

"You do not know Noam as I do, my wife. In everything he's too easily offended and when offended he must win. His name among our people used to be 'Slippery as Oil' because he was so shrewd, but now everyone calls him 'Seared Conscience' because he is often cruel in avenging himself. Especially in small slights."

"If he is so dishonorable, why hasn't anyone killed him yet?"

Loic pointed to the jade bracelet on Noam's arm. "We Doreni are warlike, but—it's a paradox, but it's true—because we are involved in so many blood-feuds, we do everything to avoid vendettas. Like me, Noam is a first-born son. The son of the Therpa clan chief. To kill him would cause clan warfare with a great and powerful clan, a clan with many alliances. Who would want to start warfare now, considering the Angleni are still scheming to take our land?"

As he spoke, I noticed that several warriors were slapping Seared Conscience's shoulder amiably.

"He seems very loved," I said.

Loic nodded. "That he is. It is quite difficult to dislike Noam. Even when one distrusts him."

"Cuyo!" Noam greeted us from across the room. "May the Wind blow good things toward you, and evil things far away!" He strode toward us and extended his arm to stroke Loic's shoulder. My husband recoiled as if Loic's hand carried a taint or poison. In response Noam smiled, as if my husband's reaction amused him. He turned his green eyes toward me and my half-moons. His eyes roamed over the landscape of my body as if I was a new land he had discovered, a land that was all his heart had ever wanted. Ashamed of being the object of a lust so freely shown, I turned my eyes toward the ground.

"Cuyo." Noam still kept his eyes on me, although he was speaking to my husband. "Is it true the year mark was eliminated because your father fears for your health? A healthy son would surely preserve the headship for you. Yes, considering your health, your father was right thing to forego the Restraint."

Loic squeezed my hand so hard my fingers hurt. I looked at his hands. They were trembling and his veins were taut against his skin.

"Hasn't the king told you to cease all talk on this topic?"

Noam grinned, obviously amused at my husband's words. I clutched my husband's agitated hand and gently rubbed it tight.

Loic's shoulders relaxed and he closed his eyes. Like shut doors they were, refusing to be opened. *Loic, you must learn to be a good warrior,* I thought. *Put bravery on your face and steady your hand.* He looked at me as if he had seen my mind, and smiled.

Like a child stalking a pet, or a favorite uncle, Mad Malana was creeping up behind Noam. She held something behind her back. She touched Noam's arm and he swung round wildly, his dagger immediately drawn. She jumped back, spilling the berry mukal glass on the carpet. "Noyu," she screamed, "it's me, your little Malana. Do you not recognize me?"

He slipped his dagger back into the sleeve of his tunic and shouted at her, red-faced. "Malana! Never do that again!" He shook her hard. "I could have killed you. You don't want to be killed, do you?" Although his voice was raised loudly, his love for her was evident. He held her tightly and wiped terrified tears from her eyes.

She opened his arms wide and closed them around her, snuggled inside them, "No, Noyu, you would not kill me. Come and see, come and see what beautiful things I've made for Loic. But really, really, you should not bring a dagger to Cuyo's wedding." In her madness and innocence, she had said what Jaguar and the other warriors had not said, that it was poor taste for a man to carry a concealed weapon to a feast.

Noam walked away and continued teasing Malana. Then he turned around and his gaze caught mine. He smiled, a smile full of sweetness.

Is this how he seduced the Third Wife? I wondered. But why is he harassing Loic? Or is he badgering Loic in order to make Taer angry? And how his eyes roamed my body!

The moment I thought this, Loic turned his eyes from Noam to me. I knew he had heard my thoughts and had been thinking the same thing.

LOIC
Dove's Eyes

Waiting in the marriage chamber for the one who would lie in my bosom, I tried to push Noam's insults from my mind. My unstable gift was known to him and I knew he knew I had seen his intentions towards Satha. I reminded myself, *To plan a thing is not to succeed in it.* Satha was nothing like the Third Wife. Noam's seductive schemes against her would all fail. I keened my ear, listening for the drumming of the women and the gift they would bring me—my wife.

Little Mother stood beside me, holding the hem of the long silk gyuilta which covered my naked body. "My boy," she said, "did I not forbid you to eat the grains? The last time you ate barley bread, the seizures came for three days straight."

"The day's joy pushed my fears away," I answered. "Besides, eating the fertility grain is part of the ceremony. I tasted only a little. Should I not eat even a little of my wedding feast?"

"You could have touched the dainties to your lip and not eaten them, my boy. Frown and look at me in anger all you want, but you know my words are true."

I looked away. Her words were indeed true. If I assented to my wife's desire and made our household in the Theseni manner, a woman, even a good woman who loved me, would not want to wake in the mornings to a sick, shaking husband in a urine-soaked bed.

"Remember now," Little Mother said, calling me from my thoughts. "Be fierce and powerful in your lovemaking and Satha will be satisfied. You don't want her to be like Jura, after all. Even a good woman will seek a new lover if she finds no satisfaction with a fool."

"Little Mother," I said, an inner trembling within me, "your words add fear to fear. Give me no more advice or my heart will fail from worry."

She put her hand to her lips. "Do mere words make your heart tremble? My boy, you must be more fierce than that."

Outside, the howling of the wild dogs and the hoot of desert owls joined the voices of the servant girls and the household noblewomen. I knew where the women were: they were crossing the inner courtyard and advancing to our marriage room.

"They're teasing her about your age and about the size of your ypher," Little Mother said, laughing.

"Are they teasing Satha also?"

She thought for a moment. "A little. The size of her breasts, or the roundness of her Theseni buttocks—big pillows, those! My boy, you've got good taste. Don't worry, the women are being gentle with her. If you had waited a year, you would have had your own house and household by now and everyone would know her better, flaws and virtues, but no one knows this girl well. Perhaps she cannot survive our fierce Doreni teasing?"

"From what I've seen she is good-humored enough."

"Let's hope so," she answered. "These Theseni are often too serious for my taste."

Soon, it sounded like a thousand bare feet were standing outside my doorway. Little Mother's eyes grew wet with tears. While I stood, paralyzed with fear, she approached the doorway and pulled the curtain aside. There stood my gift—my wife—before me in a woven gold silk gyuilta surrounded by all the household women, noblewomen, female servants, captives.

New Mother, who was beaming with joy, was standing beside Satha. She removed her daughter's gyuilta while Little Mother undressed me. We stood before each other "unveiled." How beautiful my wife was! During our nights in the field, I could not see how her brown skin glowed or how radiant the gold nose-ring in her right nostril, but as she stood before me I stumbled backwards, overwhelmed by her beauty. She, on the other hand, raced past me across the room and jumped into the bed, her right hand covering her breast and her left attempting to hide the lush hair-covered mound between her legs. My ypher rose immediately.

"Waihai, boy!" Little Mother shouted. "You've been growing!"

My ypher fell as my embarrassment rose, and another round of laughter ensued from the servant girls and noblewomen.

Little Mother tapped the wedding gyuilta, both now in Satha's hand, and the noblewomen and servants shook their tambourines and blew into their love flutes as they were now in Satha's permanent keeping. "Keep these safely, my child," she said, "because you cannot enter the Creator's fields without them." This she said because in those days our wedding garments were also our death shrouds, and an unmarried woman could not enter the fields we longed for. Little Mother raised her hands and the servants pulled the doorway slats close behind them. Satha, New Mother Monua, Little Mother and I were alone in the room. Outside the sounds of drums and flutes continued.

New Mother put her hands over her ears. "Are they going to keep that up all night?"

"They must," Little Mother explained. "What if this girl has a spirit admirer or a vengeful ancestor who tries to prevent consummation of the marriage? We have to play our clan music so the spirit will know our own ancestral spirits are nearby. Then he'll give up his claim against your daughter."

New Mother nodded, understanding. "Among our people we take weeds and dust from our ancestors' graves and burn them. The smoke and ashes protect the girl. We don't go deafening people. You Doreni must really reconsider some of your ostentatious ways. Indeed—" she looked about her "—I find this particular custom somewhat distasteful. You don't really expect my daughter to couch with her husband in front of us, do you?"

"Theseni Sister," Little Mother said, "the young couple must be instructed in the ways of lovemaking. Even you flexible Theseni must admit there are some customs that cannot be bypassed."

"True, we're not as rigid as you Doreni, but 'instructed'? We Theseni trust young couples to discover things for themselves."

"Perhaps your daughter is not as prudish as you are, Mam Monua," Little Mother said, glancing up at Satha.

I looked at Satha. She was holding the blanket in front of her. I reminded myself that she had seemed to enjoy our play. Indeed, she had laughed as we lay there among the lingay grasses. Nevertheless I remembered that the Ibeni poets had written of wild lovemaking, and the Doreni always said lovemaking was as fierce as warfare. If the Theseni wrote love poetry, I had never read it.

"Such matters cannot be entrusted to chance," Little Mother was saying. "We Pagatsu are contentious. Our women often divorce men who do not satisfy them, or they find themselves lovers. All this can lead to warfare. A fierce people must do what they can to avoid warfare."

"I doubt the Kluna will be fighting the Pagatsu anytime soon," New Mother answered. "There are none of us left."

"Kwelku, but this will protect your daughter. In the past, certain ignoble men have broken alliances by claiming that when they married their wives, they found the girls were not virgins. To prevent this dishonorable behavior, our custom demands that both New Mothers be present on the wedding night. Or would you rather we behave as the southern Doreni do and call a priest to 'break her'?"

New Mother shuddered. "Those hymen-breakers are more lascivious than holy."

"Well then, Sister, you and I understand each other well. Together we will examine the bloodstained bed sheet; together will show the tokens of the girl's virginity. Are you not honored you are here to witness the Pagatsu alliance to the Kluna clan?"

New Mother breathed deeply. "Why do you insist on speaking of a Kluna-Pagatsu alliance when the Kluna are no more?" She shook her head as if shaking away a sorrowful thought, then glanced at the bed and sucked at her teeth.

"Dark Half-Moons—" I said, sitting beside my wife and quickly joining her under the blanket.

"Dark Half-Moons!" Little Mother interrupted me, laughing. "Already he's nicknamed her. My boy has lost his mind for your daughter!"

She removed a wooden ypher hanging on the wall. "When men love—" she moved it up and down in the air "—they take. When women love, they fight, then they yield. Girl, those downcast eyes of yours should look at his thing. That little worm will bring you pleasure soon enough. Hurry and touch it before it gets too hard and hot to handle." She laughed harder, but New Mother seemed about to die of embarrassment.

"Satha," I said, touching her thigh under the blanket. How I wanted to couch with her!

She screwed up her face and stilled my roving hand, then glanced at her mother, who was seated at a pillow at the end of our bed with her head turned toward away the doorway.

I looked at my wife, and whispered. "You're beautiful, my wife. The kohl about your eyes . . . you have dove's eyes."

She smiled but showed no sign of following the traditional Doreni marriage customs.

"Tomorrow night we can play," I finally whispered. "This custom is only for the first night. Then they'll leave us alone."

"Good," she said. Then, holding my ypher in her hand under the blanket and ignoring the nervous look on our mothers' faces, she fell asleep.

SATHA
Tokens of Virginity

The morning after my wedding I woke to feel the bed trembling beneath me. The sickness had come upon my husband during the night. The sheets on which we lay were wet with sweat and urine. His entire body shook. How frail he looked. I feared for his life and grew sad, knowing I had begun to love him and that love often brings so much grief.

I put my hand on his forehead. When I did this, his body relaxed and the seizures stopped. Our mothers lay snoring on pillow mats at the foot of our bed. My hand rested on his face until dawn came and Mamya Jontay rose from her pillow.

She stretched, then rubbed her face, and immediately as if remembering something, ran to our bed. "This is a day the Creator made," she said, apparently not bothered by the stench of urine rising from the bed.

"It will bring blessings for you and for me, Mamya Jontay," I answered.

She groaned when she saw the dried mucus on my husband tear-stained face. "You must prevent him from eating the wrong things, Satha. You're his wife now. Hasn't Ydalle warned you about these things? Teach him to be careful."

I nodded, hiding the shame I felt at being rebuked on the morning after my wedding.

Gently pushing both Loic and me aside, her eyes searched the furs and fabrics on which we lay. "Nothing," she said at last, obviously disappointed. "No matter," she continued. "Everyone knows you were a virgin when you came to the young chief's bed. That's how you Theseni women are. But for Loic's sake—"

"Ah, I see," Mam said, interrupting her, "That's why you saved it?"

Mamya Jontay dropped the fur she had been examining. "Yes, Theseni Sister. Loic's headship will not be jeopardized because others consider him too weak to bed his wife. We must go and get it."

I already sensed that a child grew inside me. Tokens of my virginity or not, the child would be proof my husband was indeed a virile warrior. Yet, I found myself wondering what "it" was. Our mothers disappeared from the room, and quickly returned with a bowl of blood hidden under Mam's gyuilta.

"Sister," Mam said with a smile of approval, "you have foresight indeed!"

Mamya Jontay bowed. "Lamb's blood comes in quite handy, in less honorable marriages. Loic's illness, your daughter's propriety—well, it is not unwise to expect something might go wrong."

They began wiping the blood on the bed until their agitated movements woke my husband.

"So you're up at last?" Mamya Jontay said when he lifted his head from the bed. "Boy, you've proven yourself a man!" She pointed to a portion of the sheet which Mam had already smeared with blood.

He lifted himself up in the bed, and for several moments looked at me strangely as if trying to find his memory. "What?" he asked, confused. "Proven myself a man? What—?" He lifted the wet blanket that lay between us. A whiff of urine wafted towards us and he turned his face from me. I smiled, thinking to reassure him but he continued avoiding my gaze.

"I'll go tell Okiak to prepare your first bath together," Mamya Jontay said. "And perhaps you should speak to Satha about—"

Like desert storm clouds suddenly transforming a clear sky, Loic's face changed from confused calm to stormy anger. "Don't tell me what I should and should not do. I'm the chief's son. It is I who gives orders and commands and it is you who must listen and obey. Do not go to Okiak. I do not want his charms and spells in my marriage bed! If you allow any of his foul spirits to touch my wedding bath I'll never forgive you."

Mam shook her head. "So you're one of those, are you, young chief? All sweetness before the wedding night, but bitterness after you've entrapped your bride?"

Mamya Jontay waved her blood-covered fingers at him. "Discover the true root of your anger, Little Chief" she retorted. "Whether it be Okiak, or your shame at this illness. But don't threaten me with your unforgiveness!"

Humiliation and anger mingled on his face, but he was silent, staring at her for several seconds. After glancing shame-faced in my direction, he shouted, "I don't need old women telling me what to do. Both of you . . . get out!"

My heart hurt when I heard this. Mamya Jontay had asked a little thing. Such a little thing. It should not have caused so much anger. Moreover, the sound of voices raised in anger had always terrified me, ever since I was a child. I sat trembling, fearful his anger would now be aimed at me. Never in my life had I dreamed of a marriage morning scented with urine, covered with lamb's blood and filled with angry voices.

I tried to understand what had provoked his rage. In my days of poverty, I had moments when sudden anger rose from my heart and tumbled over my tongue. Moments when shame and grief made me feel powerless and forgotten by the Good Maker. I wondered if these were the emotions at work in him.

"Forgive me, Mamya Jontay," I said. "I do not wish to meddle in this disagreement between my husband and his mother. I'm still a stranger here and lacking in wisdom and knowledge of the cause of my husband's outburst. I know, however, that my husband loves his Little Mother with a love equal to the love of many mothers. As for Okiak, we need neither his protection nor blessings. Let there be peace on my wedding day."

Mamya Jontay approached me and stroked my face tenderly. "You were raised in poverty, Arhe. But your tact shows your breeding. My heart has some peace now because my son has found a good wife. *Some* peace, I say, because your husband has found someone as foolhardy as himself, someone who also ignores the spirits. I warn you, daughter. Don't spend your nights being converted to the young chief's way of thinking. Keep to the old ways and let Okiak bless you. Learn to attend to more carnal matters like other people."

She grasped Mam's hand and together they pulled the bloody blanket from our bed. Then they walked through the curtains, mumbling to each other as if we were fishermen using a leaky boat to cross dangerous waters.

When I could hear their footfalls no more, I turned to Loic, "My husband," I said. "I, too, understand shame. When my sister was forcibly married, after my clan was destroyed, poverty mixed with grief. Pain and sleeplessness descended upon me. Remember the dinginess of my house? Grief made the smallest matter seem like a great burden. I could not work; I could not clean our house properly. You were kind when you saw our dirty house. Others were not as kind as you or your father. So, my husband, I, too, understand shame. Do not fear to speak to me about your illness. I—"

Although his face had softened while I spoke, anger returned to his face and, glaring, he rose from the bed. Wrapping a silken blanket about his body, he shouted, "Illness? What illness? I have no illness!"

"But, husband, of course you do—"

"Silence," he shouted. He seemed like a madman, not the husband I had begun to love.

"Loicuyo," I said, "Husband. Am I not to be your ally? If so, we must speak honestly of your—"

"One more word, Satha." He waved a warning finger. "One more and I'll divorce you."

My mouth fell open. To my astonishment, I realized I did not wish to be divorced.

"I will say that when I came to your bed, I found you were not a virgin." He turned his face away after he had spoken. I imagined my parents cast out into the streets, and my heart pining for the husband I had only just met yet had begun to love.

"Would you use cruelty to hide your shame?" I asked, my voice trembling.

"I have nothing to be ashamed about," he shouted and stormed out of the room.

The bloody token of my virginity was displayed in the family arbor and I was taken to the far end of Taer's compound to the tiled pool where we had bathed when I had truly lost my virginity. Loic appeared, now showing no signs of his earlier displeasure. He joined me, as was proper, and we stood together next to the pool.

Mam and Mamya Jontay had become like twins, always together. They ordered the servants to pour jasmine, attar of roses and other perfumes from alabaster bottles into the pool. All the while, my husband and I stood silent, avoiding each other's eyes.

After our mothers and the servants left, my husband stepped into the hot water, throwing his tunic and gyuilta on the hot rocks behind him. He closed his eyes and descended knee-deep into the water, then inhaled deeply, pulling the aromas into his nostrils. "How lovely this water is." He gestured for me to finish undressing. His gaze never left me as I did.

"Little Mother can be subtle," he said when I undressed, as if our earlier disagreement had not occurred. "I've warned her not to betray me by slipping potions and spells—"

"Mam, too, is to be distrusted in such things," I agreed, quickly. "But I have no doubt the bath is safe." But I found myself thinking, *So, this is how a spoiled chief handles unpleasantness. He shouts, ignores the feelings of others, and expects others to do the same also.* Remembering his gift, I feared he had seen my thoughts. However, he appeared not to. I relaxed slightly, but only slightly, wondering what kind of life my marriage would bring.

When Mam and Mamya Jontay returned, Ydalle and Malana were with them. Ydalle showed me a Doreni coif the household seamstresses had prepared for me. Green linen, it contained both the Pagatsu Doreni and the Kluna Theseni markings with dark green Pagatsu butterfly beadwork and the black and red Kluna stripes.

"What wonderful workmanship!" Mam wept when she held it out for me to see. "This is now the mark of your household, my son," she said. "All will know you are Pagatsu but they will also know you are allied to my lost and destroyed clan."

Ydalle then showed me a linen Theseni kaba in the Kluna style— newly woven and embroidered in silks.

But Mamya Jontay shook her head. "She must wear the short tunic and leggings of the Pagatsu," she said.

"A true Doreni woman must learn how to ride," Malana added in a sing-song voice, as if she had learned the words by rote. "What use is a woman who cannot ride beside her husband? The short tunic and leggings help a woman to ride."

Mam raised her eyebrows. Clapping her hands—as if she was Doreni-born and accustomed to ordering Doreni servants about—she waited until two servants appeared. One held a long gyuilta and the other a short one. The long gyuilta was of woven-gold encrusted with pearls. The sash of its fringes seemed woven from silver moonbeams. The short riding gyuilta was made of leather. Both had the distinctive green butterfly beadwork.

"You'll wear the Doreni clothing, girl," she said. "Not the kaba. The long gyuilta you'll wear when you walk through the households and the riding gyuilta when you learn daggerwork, riding and all those things Doreni women must learn to do. This hasty marriage has left you with the title of Arhe, but not the skills. That must all be remedied as soon as possible."

Ydalle threw the long gyuilta over my naked shoulders. "Look, Arhe Monua, it falls across her shoulders like a queen's robe."

"It does, it does!" Mamya Jontay said.

Ydalle looked at the Doreni coif and began weeping. "Do you remember, Arhe Monua, how it was in the old days? Do you remember all the cattle and land your father had! Do you remember his Great House? Do you remember it? How many of our clansmen lived there? A hundred households?"

"More than that, Ydalle," Mam said sighing. "More than that. Taer's Golden House cannot compare with what I had before HaZatana took all my blessings away. Tears flow from my eyes like the remnants of my old life. The Creator, however, has seen our suffering and has restored to us much of what we lost. My daughter is Taer's New Daughter now. She has a wise husband. Unlike me, she will live as a queen all her life and never know suffering."

Never know suffering? Even the Matchless Family knew suffering, but during that first week of my marriage—Jobara! I did feel like a queen!

In addition to the daily feasts, the servants were continually bringing figs, raisin cakes, pomegranates, berry juices, exotic and local fruits to us and laying them outside the marriage quarters. Mam's commanding finger made my life easy. She ordered people about effortlessly. The servants seemed more hers than mine. My only responsibilities were to couch with my husband at night, feast and spend my days with mentors whose sole duties were to teach me how to be the wife of a chieftain.

The duties of a chieftain's wife were burdensome. Already I longed for a secret place far from rules and duty. Like a continual heavy rain dripping on a nomad's tent, Doreni culture was poured over me in an unceasing stream from sunrise to sunset. I felt as if I would drown. Perhaps if my wedding week had not arrived with such haste, I would not have found myself so often on the verge of tears. I would have danced and talked with the guests at all those feasts instead of being sullen, diplomatic though I was at hiding my general annoyance.

On the fifth day of my wedding week—a mere twelve days after the betrothal ceremony—I felt I could bear the duties of a Doreni chief's wife no longer. Abruptly, I dismissed the noblewoman who was my riding teacher. She looked at me with disapproval, her slanted eyes growing even narrower, as if I had no heart for learning or hard work. I told myself that for one day, I did not want to seek to please everyone. Whatever happened, I would walk alone without care or responsibility.

And walk I did. I soon found myself in a meadow of tall grasses hidden behind a sloping hillside near the guest quarters. The journey there had been long but worthwhile. I could see the spice garden in the outer courtyard of the Great House and the fifty minor households surrounding it, yet no one could see me. A small boulder hidden among the brush hid me well. I sat behind it and breathed the fragrant air deeply, glad that I had found a haven from my duties.

As I sat there, finding my own heart and soul again, I did not notice the sound of someone approaching, not until Noam stood staring down at me. His soft voice greeted me.

"This is a day the Creator made, Arhe Satha," he said, smiling awkwardly. How gently his voice rolled from his tongue.

"It will bring blessings for you and for me," I answered, wondering if I should wish for a passerby to happen upon us.

Theseni married women did not walk alone with strangers, but this was not taboo among the Doreni. My heart was still Theseni. Worse yet, the stranger looking down upon me was none other than the enemy of my New Father. To be seen speaking with such a person could cause gossip among both Theseni and Doreni. I rose from the rock, nodded to him and quickly began walking toward the family quarters.

Orange mukal floated on his breath and raspberry mukal stained his blue Therpa tunic. His long red hair blew wild about his waist. I kept my eyes on the far columns of the outer courtyard, determined to pass him without speaking.

"Your husband is talking with your mother at the other end of the compound," he said. "Shall we walk together to meet him?"

I declined and began to hasten away from him.

A gentle ripple of laughter crossed his lips. "Arhe Satha, are you still following the Theseni custom of not speaking to strange men when you walk alone? You're Doreni now. Speak your mind. We Doreni believe it's the mind that charms men."

Even so, I thought, *I don't want my husband thinking I'm out here charming you with my mind.*

"I've heard Theseni women are among the most beautiful in the world," he continued. "I might believe it, but they hide their beauty with silence or behind a veil. Did I not see you in the Doreni coif yesterday? Are you Theseni one day and Doreni the next? You are Arhe here, wife of Loic. All bow to your will. Arhe Thesenya, your piety is protection enough. Throw your veil away."

Such refined educated flattery, I thought. *So is this how he seduces his friends' wives?*

Angry with myself for walking through the fields alone, I became even more nervous after he called me Arhe. I was Arhe over a world I did not understand and I had no desire to risk offending against the Doreni hospitality laws.

"Arhe Satha," he continued, "if you do not speak to your guest you're no Doreni Arhe at all." He smiled a smile both paternal and flirtatious.

"We'll have to teach you our ways. Do I see a frown on your face? An Arhe should not frown." He pushed a stray hair from my forehead. "Yet, I suppose I would frown too if strangers were hedging me in with rules. Rules weigh down the heart, don't they?" It seemed he understood the turmoils of my heart.

How like my dear slain cousin he seemed! How like my lost sister! His eyes sparkled with delight as he spoke. Yet a strange sorrow edged his conversation, a sorrow that almost made me like him because my heart was knitted easily with the heartbroken.

He came closer and whispered in my ear. "Let me tell you a secret, Arhe Satha. The Pagatsu, and even the Therpas, allow for many mistakes. You must not worry yourself trying to be perfect. Taer and the Pagatsu, I and the Therpas, will forgive you."

I feared his words would find a place in my heart, I feared liking him. I sensed that would be a dangerous thing to do, and hastened my step.

"How blessed Loic is to have such a good wife!" He matched his steps with mine. "A prophet should have a good wife."

In those days, the three tribes called those who spoke to spirits "shamans," but if God spoke to a man, that man was called a "prophet" or a "seer." I stopped and looked at him. "You think my husband is a prophet?"

"A shaman, maybe. A prophet more likely." He smiled. "Thank you for speaking with me, Arhe."

"Why do you call my husband a prophet?"

"Because I believe he is. Some say the falling sickness has wounded his mind. Others say he inherited spirit gifts from his mother's people, the Desai. The Desai themselves have odd ideas about your husband." He shrugged. "But the Desai have odd ideas about everything."

As I thought on this, he suddenly said, "Have you ever heard the saying, 'To conquer a dark woman is like the moon trying to conquer the bright sun'? Loic has conquered the sun. Suitable for a prophet, I think. Jobara! If I had found you before he did, I would have been your husband and not Loic."

I returned to my senses, and answered him rudely, "Noam, have you not read in the Scriptures that a man should not compliment a married woman? I'm sure you did not mean to insult me with such flattery."

His eyes narrowed, and an angry flush rose to his cheeks. "Forgive me for flattering you, Arhe. I had no intention of insulting you. Although Loic's lovemaking was not fierce, and we believe he satisfied you among the lingay grasses, certainly you have married a good man!"

I swallowed hard, trembled. Were we seen? And by Noam and someone else? Taken aback at the double surprise, I stared at him, my mouth not daring to speak the question in my mind.

His fingers touched my lips, gently closing them. His hands lingered on my face. "Yes, your secret is known. We were surprised to see a virtuous Thesenya behaving in such a manner, but the Ibeni influence is everywhere."

The columns of the outer courtyard were near and I hastened my steps, anxious to flee my embarrassment. Again, he followed hard at my heels. When I reached the main marble corridor, he grabbed my wrist, and leaned into me. He burst out laughing and brought his face nearer to mine. His hips pushed against mine and pinned me to a nearby wall. Standing in front of me, his fingers played upon my lips.

Angry, I bit his middle finger. He pulled his hand away and looked at the finger, then sucked on it as if I had kissed it instead. "You bite deeply, Satha. Like a snake in the western desert. But you draw no blood. If you were truly angry, you would have drawn blood."

"Some people are so thick-skinned only the Good Maker can draw their blood!" I said, fighting to keep from raising my voice. "Only someone with a seared conscience would use the hospitality laws to enter a house where he betrayed his friend. Your presence shames you and it betrays the Third Wife! A woman you loved!"

He rubbed his bitten hand, stepped backward, and laughed again. "How presumptive and innocent you are, Arhe. My tainted cousin is Therpa like myself. I know our clan too well to fall in love with any of our women."

I pushed him away and searched the corridor. I saw no one. "When Taer hears how you've insulted me—"

"What will you tell him? That Noam and someone else saw you and Loic playing in the grasses on the night before the full marriage? Our world is built on altvayus, would you shame yourself so?"

Freed from his arms, I hurried down the corridor but he caught up to me and grabbed my veil, ripping it from my face. I raised my arm and slapped him across the face and neck.

"Yes, Thesenya. There's passion in you. Like the passion in your bite, and yes, there'll be passion when I take you in Loic's bed. More passion than your night in the grasses."

"Mentura!" I shouted. "I'm not like the women you've had. Those women you encountered were open doors. I am a reinforced wall."

"Kwelku—so you say."

When I entered the women's quarters, the servants greeted me with worried frowns. How nervous they looked, as if they thought I had disappeared into some well or swamp somewhere.

"Arhe, we could not find you," Ydalle said. "Okiak awaits you in the cooking rooms. It is he who will teach you about Doreni food taboos."

Nothing about Okiak made me fear him. He was good to look at, with green Doreni eyes and waist-long black hair tumbling over his Pagatsu beadwork shaman's vest. He seemed regal, but approachable, like a king who walked every day among his people. When our eyes met during the wedding, he had seemed friendly enough. But my encounter with Noam made me suspicious of friendliness.

The area around the cooking pit was redolent with herbs and the odor of broiled buffalo, but I had no appetite as I walked towards it. My only thoughts were of finishing the day and escaping to bed.

Mam approached, but as she was about to speak, Okiak rebuked me. "Arhe, the riding mistress said your heart is faint."

"My heart is not faint," I answered and bowed before him. "It is as fierce and as strong as any Doreni warrior. I wished to walk by myself. Do the Doreni not say that love of solitude is a great virtue?"

Mam and several of the servants smiled; I had answered in a true Doreni manner. Fierce, but diplomatic at the same time.

"Well said, Arhe," Okiak said. He came closer and gently touched my shoulder. A strange heat shot through my body. Suddenly, he seemed no longer a stranger but a good dear father in whom I wished to confide.

I resisted this emotional pull. I was not about to be charmed—whether by spell or seduction—into friendship with another of my husband's enemies.

Okiak stroked my shoulder again. Again, a warm flush flowed through my body. It seemed as if all the ancestors were pleading with me to confide in him, but this time Mam was promptly at my side. She firmly removed Okiak's hand from my shoulder, then stroked my arm several times, using a wiping motion as if she were pushing rainwater from my shoulder.

"My daughter is well enough, shaman," she said, but her eyes warned, *Do not touch my daughter.*

Okiak was scowling. "Mam Monua." He pushed her aside. "Satha is Arhe here. Not you."

Mam stepped backward.

Once again the shaman put his hand on my shoulder, but this time—perhaps Mam had some protective magic of her own—the urge to confide in him was gone. The angry glare he shot in Mam's direction made my blood run cold. I realized a war was being waged over me. Then Mam, who was never one to walk from a fight, surprised me by abruptly leaving the room.

Ignoring Mam's retreat, Okiak began. "Because passion and youthful impatience hastened the year mark, you must learn many things quickly." Several servants chuckled at the mention of youthful impatience, but their humor seemed good-natured.

He continued. "You understand, Arhe, that during the week of the full marriage, the Bride must create a Feast, do you not?"

I nodded.

"In your particular situation, this feast is even more important because you are to become Arhe of the entire Pagatsu clan. Your feast, then, must show your wisdom. Your guests must not be offended. Offense, as you are wise enough to know, often occurs when food is involved."

I nodded.

He pointed at two large cooking pots and some skinned buffalo meat soaking in a pot of water. "Unlike the Theseni, we Doreni eat neither fish nor fowl because anything that lives in two worlds is an abomination to us. What lies under the earth belongs to the spirits. What is above belongs to the Creator. Prophet Koloq said humans cannot eat food given to the spirits and to the Creator at the same time. We must choose one or the other. In practical terms, this means when you prepare your feast you will not cook tubers, root vegetables, reptiles, insects, or even four-legged animals that go underground . . . and, of course, no fish or birds. You will therefore have to restrain yourself from cooking the Theseni fish soup or the curry and pepper fish fritters."

Already the food offenses terrified me. I could imagine all the taboos I would trip over. "Of course."

"The most important rule," an imperious female voice suddenly joined in, "is that a woman doesn't handle food during her moonweek."

Silence, gasps, and whispers followed. I turned and looked behind me. The Third Wife was standing in the doorway.

"Ignore the nameless one," Okiak said. "She's a ghost here, like fish and birds lost between two worlds."

"Jobara!" Edi a servant girl, muttered, "Ghosts always seek to return to the haunts they've been cast out of." She pointed to the gold butterfly brooch pinned on my coif. "Okiak! Exorcise this ghost. Tell it that Arhe Satha is Arhe here."

"I am quite free to travel the compound," the Third Wife said, raising a scornful brow. "With all this feasting, and with so many of my husband's clansmen visiting, someone might decide it's a good time to poison me. It's only prudent that I investigate."

She turned her arrogant eyes on me and I bowed to her, not knowing how far I should go in my politeness. When I did this, the servants ignored her or mumbled against her under their breaths.

About the time it takes a hawk to fly across the sky, my husband rode up to the kitchen, Taer at his side.

"My husband," I said, bowing low.

"Dark Half-Moons," he said.

It was a Doreni habit to have a love-name for everyone, love-names they felt no qualms in speaking in public. The Theseni were not like that and my cheeks warmed with embarrassment when he spoke my name so openly.

"'Dark Half-Moons?'" the Third Wife repeated. "Is that what he calls you? Is that all he sees in you?"

I smiled, not knowing how to respond, but a scowl came to my husband's face. Tears of frustration welled up in my eyes. So many rules and expectations!

The Third Wife turned her dagger eyes towards me. "Or are you only half a moon because he has counted your worth among all his other lovers and found you wanting?"

Okiak took my hand. "Loic has worshiped under no other moons, Arhe. Whether they be rich or poor, noble or ordinary, girls will tell the sun and stars all about their moon's conquest. If he had lain under other moons, all the household would have lit up with the news."

Everyone laughed at Okiak's poetic phrasing. Everyone except Loic, the Third Wife and me.

My husband yanked my hand from Okiak's. "I must speak to you, Wife. Now."

Angry, I pulled my hands from him. This was neither time nor place for such a show. "I will speak to you when I can, my husband. Jobara—indeed—I am quite busy, as you can see."

His eyes narrowed and he flinched, but he did not force me. "Tonight, then," he said with a quick nod. He left me to my cooking lesson and the watching hate-filled eyes of the Third Wife.

Later that night, we walked silently in darkness through the fields and along the Large Path. Mam was approaching us from the far fields, her gyuilta splattered with wet dirt as if dipped in mud. She came towards us, smiled nervously, but did not stop to speak.

"It is all too much," I said at last. "My mind is bursting."

He did not answer. Again, we walked in silence.

After a while, I asked, "Are you angry with me, my husband?"

He didn't answer.

Soon Malana appeared on the path. As she neared us, she turned to the left and to the right as if searching for an escape. Her hands were behind her back.

"What do you hide behind your back?" Loic asked her when she stood before us.

A guilty grin played on her face. "Nothing, Cuyo." She looked in the far distance as if something in the distance interested her.

"Maliya, you're lying to me." Although she was gray-haired and much older than he was, his tone was as gentle as a father's with a child.

"No, Cuyo. Your little Malana is not lying to you."

He extended his arm. "Let me see what you're hiding behind your back."

"Let her go on her way," I said, pushing his hand downward. "It can't be that important."

Scowling at me, she pushed my arm from Loic's and showed him the gyuilta I had worn on the day I met him.

Her obvious jealousy only added to my discomfort. "It's not a very pretty gyuilta, Malana," I stammered. "Mamya Jontay or Mam can make you a new one. Would not you want a new one?"

"I dig it up from the ground, Cuyo," she handed the gyuilta to Loic and pointedly ignoring me.

Loic turned the mud-covered gyuilta over in his hands. "She likes your Mam," he said to me. "That's why she follows her everywhere. She's just curious."

"She's more than curious, Loic," I murmured. "She's jealous of me."

Both he and Malana stared at me.

"Her jealousy is harmless," he said. "Despite those gray hairs on her head, Maliya was one of my favorite playmates." He looked about the fields. "I spent many hours in these fields with her and Krika. It was only as I grew older that I realized the shadow gods had stolen her mind and her destiny from her." He held the gyuilta before her. "Did you see who buried this, Malana? Was it Okiak?"

"No, not Okiak," she said, shaking her head. "New Mother bury it."

He lifted one of the cords binding the gyuilta. "Does she not trust your love?"

His question shamed me. The day seemed to add sorrow to sorrow. "Mam loves me. She doesn't have to bind me to her. Those spell cords are Old Yoran's work. Mam's probably trying to protect me from Okiak's spirits."

"Spirits don't protect from other spirits. They conspire and work together. Even when they seem not to." He waved Malana homeward. "Maliya, tell Little Mother and New Mother Monua to make some pretty clothes for you."

She clapped her hands and broke into joyous laughter. After one more scowl in my direction ran down the Path.

"Not only do you have the Third Wife and Okiak to worry about," Loic said, "but now your mother's spirits."

"Not you?" I asked, taking the opportunity to speak my heart.

"Me?" He asked the question as if challenging me to continue.

I did. "Why do you not say that you're angry with me? Speak honestly, earlier did you not wish to kill me? You looked as if you did."

He shrugged. "Perhaps I did want to kill you, but I'm not likely to. The Third Wife and Okiak probably would, however. The adulteress is a schemer if ever there was one."

"I was not speaking of the Third Wife or Okiak. I was speaking of you, and you have changed the topic."

He lifted his hand and stroked my face. "Dear Dark Half-Moons, stop frowning like that. I was angry with you when you acknowledged her, and angry when you did not obey and follow me but . . . I love you. If you—"

Suddenly his hand grasped mine tightly, so tightly pain raced up my arm. I felt myself being yanked downward toward the ground. Suddenly my hand was freed and my husband had fallen to the ground. Foaming spittle flowed from the corners of his mouth as his body revolted against itself and the seizure tossed him about. His open eyes gazed nowhere, everywhere.

Although the servants and noblewomen had told me what to do in case the illness attacked him when we were together, I stood paralyzed. His head thrashed wildly against the sharp long thorns, causing pinpricks of blood to appear on his cheek. I knelt beside him, wanting to prevent him from hurting himself but fearful that any aid I would give would only cause further hurt.

Footsteps raced towards me. I turned and saw Sio, the Third Wife's son. His hair was cropped shoulder length in the Therpa tradition, but all else—his extreme reticence, the deliberate way in which he spoke and behaved, declared him to be Pagatsu and a true son of Treads Lightly.

"I can help him, Sister," he said, removing his gyuilta. His shyness made my heart ache a little for him, for he bowed low and avoided my eyes as if he were a lowly servant in the compound and not one of Taer's heirs.

After making a soft pillow for Loic from his gyuilta and tunic, he said, "We should not move him, but we must make sure he doesn't hurt himself."

"I'm glad you're here, Younger Brother," I said. "Yet, I find myself wondering. Have you been following us all this time?"

His eyes nervously searched the dark landscape, and he seemed to be strengthening himself to speak. "Arhe, it is my duty as the Groom's Friend to create a feast in Loic's honor. Such a feast—one need not remind you—should be attended by the groom. But I know my brother's anger against our clan and I have been following him along this dark path trying to encourage myself to plead with him."

"Younger Brother, don't wring your hands so, and turn your eyes toward me. I mean you no harm. Now, say on."

He seemed to force himself to look into my eyes. "The Therpa chief's son and your husband's father are enemies, Arhe. All are aware of that, but there is an old covenant between them, a covenant which declared that Taer's first son and Noam's first son would be allies—battered but nevertheless unbroken. The Therpa Great Chief still honors our house's old covenant with Taer. He remembers their friendship. The old man is kind and for the sake of the old covenant he wants to repair the breach between your husband and me."

How strangely these matters unfold! I thought. *The sons of the fathers' covenant were brothers indeed!* "Jobara! Indeed, Mamya Jontay showed me the many wedding gifts the Therpas gave to Loic."

"Jewels, fabric, horses and cattle are nothing compared to a restored covenant."

I nodded.

"I'm glad you see the wisdom of the alliance," he said. "I was surprised and honored when Taer told me your husband had chosen me to stand by his side at his marriage. I half-expected him to choose Lihu or one of Pantan's sons. When he attends the feast I will give in his honor, he will see that all the Therpas still love him, I especially."

"I will tell your brother all your heart."

His face radiated a bright warm smile. "I am honored to have so noble a sister, Arhe. I know your people, the Kluna, are no more and that the Bride's feast will be sad. Jobara! The Kluna still remaining, although once a powerful clan, are now worthless as allies to the Pagatsu."

"You speak of my heart's sorrow as if it were no more than a strategy of war."

He bit his lip as if struggling to find the right words to excuse himself. "Forgive me, my sister. Forgive me. I speak only an inconvenient but necessary truth. Understand, the Groom's Mother is dead, and her clan, the Desai, have not attended this marriage. As always, they distance themselves from your husband. You can see then, that Loic's household will have few allies. Perhaps that is his secret wish, I cannot say. Nevertheless, I would advise him that renewing his friendship with the Therpas would serve him."

As my husband's seizures slowed, then halted, Sio skillfully attended to him. He seemed a mature child, a boy whom Taer and my husband would have loved, if circumstances had been otherwise.

We sat silently together. Like Taer and Loic, he seemed to dislike speaking. But he also seemed constricted somehow, as if he was all too aware that I was Arhe over the household and he should not overstep his bounds. After some time, when my husband had settled into a quiet sleep, he stood up and bowed to me.

"Are you leaving, Younger Brother?" I asked.

He nodded. "The young chief would not want to find me here when he wakes up." He paused. "Perhaps you should leave also." He walked away.

I kept remembering my husband's plea: *I hope you will not die before me. I hope it is I who will leave you bereft and not the other way around.* I suspected that in the past he had often awakened to find himself alone in the fields, yet I did not want him to wake in that darkness alone.

I held my heart tightly, reminded it that it should not love such a sick one too deeply. He woke at last and looked up at me. Long, long, he lay there looking up at me, his mind and eyes seemingly lost. At last, shame darkened his face and I knew his senses had returned to him.

"Do you know where you are?" I asked. "Can you walk?"

He raised himself from the ground, picked up Sio's gyuilta and tunic and silently walked away. I followed behind him, unspeaking, wishing I had done as Sio suggested.

He did not sleep in the marriage room that night. Later that week, I urged him to attend Sio's feast in the Pagatsu gathering room. He denied my request—even when I told him the Theseni believed a husband should grant all his wife's wishes during the bridal week. I went to bed weeping. Partly because the trials of the week had fatigued and burdened me, and partly because peace with my new husband was so hard to find.

I fell asleep and dreamed.

In the dream, I stood near the Sun Fountain watching the Water Clock. The clock changed form and became a seething pot roiling and stirring with dead men's bones and the blood of women and children. Its top leaned toward the north, and everything in it bubbled out and flooded our land. After the flooding, flowers and weeds sprang up. Very beautiful flowers, good for healing the spirit, soul and body, but also very bad weeds used for poisoning. Both growing together. The contents of the pot flowed until it reached a valley where Loic and I stood. We held each other while the blood came up to our ankles, and then to our thighs, our waists, our necks, and then knocked us over. Flowing over our heads, it swept us away from each other, then toward each together again.

Then the waters spoke to me, a trickle rising to a thundering. I knew it was Y'wa, the Good Maker, he who was wind and water, rock, fire and light, he who made everything.

"Satha," he asked, "do you see the seething pot?"

"Yes, Good Maker."

"What do you think it is?"

"You know better than I what it is."

"Soon you will also know."

LOIC
Lihu's Death
Reaping Moon–First Harvest Moon

Several days before my nineteenth birthday, six moons before the year mark celebration of the full marriage, my wife came to the fields where the builders were constructing our new house.

"How beautiful our house is!" she said. "Even while incomplete!" She bowed to the workmen. "A Theseni house with Doreni stylings and decoration is a wondrous thing."

I crooked my finger and led her to an inner room of the unfinished house. Pregnancy had made her more round and I often laughed loudly to see how she walked, waddling like a mother duck. "This will be the child's room," I said, putting my hand around her waist. "As you wished, it's beside our bedroom."

She placed my hand on a spot on her belly where the child kicked. "He's active today," she said. "The room is good, and the windows are many. I'm hoping you will change your mind and allow him to continue living with us after his seventh birthday."

I shook my head. "That I will not concede. If he does not move into a household with his age brothers, he'll have no allies."

"Jobara?" she asked.

"Jobara," I answered. "There are many ways of establishing kinship and alliance. Krika, my age-brother, was closer to me than a blood bro—"

She interrupted me with a gentle wave of her hand. I stopped speaking and stood silent before her. She would, if I continued, use the opportunity to try to repair the breach between me and young Sio. Being Theseni, she often did not see the world as I did.

My silence allowed her to introduce a topic she wished to address.

"Speaking of blood kin, my husband, although you have honored my father by putting him in charge of all this work, he is tired of workmen coming to him to complain about your decisions."

"Has he told you all this? Or is this your assumption?"

"It is my assumption, but I know Father well enough. He is at peace when speaking with your father's warriors, but he has never cared for dispute and quarreling. What is he to do when you allow Theseni carvers to work on our house, yet forbid the Therpas and the Pagatsu from adding their skills? You do not reason rightly concerning this, Half-Moon Eyes. Jobara! The Pagatsu could work on the gardens and those of the Therpa clan could create the courtyard. Why make enemies of those who are not your enemies?"

Instead of replying, I touched the interwoven strands of her hair. It was now styled differently, braided and intertwined, like serpents in a snake pit. My fingers moved lightly over their soft woolly thickness. "This new hair style is intricate," I said.

"My husband, do not avoid the conversation."

"There is little chance of that with you, my wife. I sought to assure peace rather than disrupt it when I ordered the separation work. But I will discuss it with your father and, perhaps, your suggestion will work." I tugged a braid and smiled. "Is this some new style Ydalle or Little Mother devised to impress me?"

She smiled, now satisfied she had made her point. "Do you still need impressing?"

"It's only that Theseni women seem to use strange hairstyles to impress their husbands. Now, if you would commit to knifework and to horseman—"

She interrupted me with a shake of her head. "How insistent you Doreni are about your customs!" she said, with a laugh.

I held my hands up in mock dismay, "But have I not studied the ways of the Theseni with the dedication of a true scholar?"

"If you, great scholar, think you know so much about Theseni customs, then what feast day begins tomorrow?"

"The Theseni have thousands of celebrations. How am I to remember them all?"

"Any scholar would know it is the celebration of HaZatana!"

"Ah yes, the Light Bringer; the Serpent who supposedly brought the illumination of Good Maker's Law to enlighten your ancestors. He likes braided hair?"

"The braids are serpentine, can't you see? This hairstyle honors the Light Bringer."

"How can you honor such a god?" I asked. "First he tells you what the Creator demands—tasks any human is hard put to perform—then the reptile runs back to the Creator and accuses us when we fail to keep to those tasks. Who wants such an adversary and troublemaker for a god?"

"He's Y'wa's other self, the shadow of the Good Maker. All your studies and you know nothing about this?" She sounded like my old instructors, and I bowed my head like an obedient student. "Y'wa, the Good Maker heals and forgives. HaZatana blights, and punishes. 'One they both are and they do all for our good.'"

I yanked her longest braid, the one that trailed down her back. "We Doreni believe the Good Maker is always good, that he does no evil. He gives the blessed rain to all farmers, both good and evil, and sends sunshine to them both. To worship HaZatana would be offensive to a Doreni because we do not befriend our adversaries."

"Kwelku. But I will not give up a family tradition." She turned just so and the golden morning sunlight highlighted her face.

Pregnancy had made her breasts fuller and their roundness intoxicated me. I grasped her and held her tightly against an untiled wall. "Dark Half-Moons, those half-moons are like full moons now. Come, let us go to the lingay fields and let them shine down on me."

She started laughing. "Those Ibeni poets thought more of couching than of their children. Put their poetry away, my husband!" Her hand touched her stomach protectively. I remembered the pain and cramping she endured the last time we couched. The midwives and noblewomen had cautioned us against our youthful fire and we had not listened. My ypher shrank when I remembered the women's rebuke.

I rested my hand on her belly, weaving my fingers and hers together. "I care for this child more than you know. This child will give me the love and loyalty my father did not. He will be the beginning of my own clan because I have determined I will no longer be Pagatsu." Outside the raised voices of the workmen called to me. I said to my wife, "Now return to your rooms and rest. You don't want the women rebuking you again."

Smiling, she suddenly placed her right hand between her breasts and swift as sorrow, removed a small dagger and held it at my throat. Suddenly I wanted to couch with her again. Waihai, her knifework had truly impressed me. And the dagger—such a masterpiece of deadly workmanship I had never seen. Its blade was no larger than the forefinger of a man's hand. Its steel gleamed in the half-light of that unfinished room. She handed the knife to me and I pressed its blade against my thumb: the brief touch drew blood.

"It's an assassin's weapon," I said. "So easily hidden and so deadly. Where did you get it?"

"A traveler from Ibeniland, a seller of foreign knives, traded it to my father. As your birthday approached, I remembered it and asked Father for it. You were looking for a sword on the day you met me, weren't you? And you never did make a sword, did you?"

"The Creator promised me a different kind of sword, then he gave me you," I said.

"Yet you say the Good Maker doesn't have a destructive side!" She pulled the dagger's sheath from between her breasts.

"There's nothing destructive about you," I said, taking the sheath, and again my ypher rose. "You are like one of the holy ones. No poor or weak one, no traveler who visits Arhe Dark Half-Moons at the Golden House goes away with empty arms."

As I was speaking, Ydalle's voice called from beyond the courtyard. "Loicuyo! Arhe! A horseman approaches. He whips at his horse like Heldek does and rides with a madman's fire. Your father and Pantan are standing near the gates waiting for him."

The news carrier was indeed Heldek. He brought grievous news: Lihu, the First Prince of our land, Butterfly's son, had died. Sorrow welled up in my chest. I hid my face after Heldek related the news and fled to my room lest the household see tears rolling down my face. There, I fell onto my bed and poured out my heart to a Creator whose love I was unsure of.

The funeral would be a day's ride away in Chyar, the chief of the royal cities, in the region near Colebru, the spirit-field where many of our great warriors were buried. The mourning period would be twenty-one days, a day for each year of Lihu's life. Twenty-one days away from Satha. At the time I most needed to speak to her about life, death, the Good Maker, and the spirits, we would be separated.

It was believed, then, that women, especially pregnant women outside the departed's family, should not attend funerals because the ancestors in their fearful jealousy of the living might damage the child. The custom could nowhere be found in our Scriptures, but the Arkhai had built up the tradition. Clans that challenged the spirits' power would find themselves overwhelmed with death, famine and disease. Worse, they would lose all their allies because no clan will ally itself against the Arkhai. The Arkhai were, in truth, the largest and strongest of all clans.

As I lay in the marriage room we shared, grieving for Lihu, I saw my wife's sandaled feet below my doorway curtain. How long she had stood there, I didn't know. "Come in, Dark Half-Moons," I said, wiping my tears. "The Creator has given you to me for times such as this."

She entered and I held her tight and rested my head against her belly. "My mind swarms with fears," I continued. "I fear Lihu, the spirits, death. I fear for the child. I fear for the unhappy spirit of Krika."

"Death brings many fears, my husband," she said, wiping the tears from my face. "We Theseni say weeping washes fears away. I noticed Heldek also fought back tears. If such a great warrior can weep, so, too, can you."

"How can I not weep when my mind dwells on Krika? Often I wonder if the Creator has allowed him to enter the fields we long for."

"My husband, these things we cannot know. Perhaps the Good Maker, although distant, is merciful."

I lifted the dagger she had given me and put it in my right boot. "Would that someone's dagger had struck Okiak—before he struck his son!"

That afternoon, she painted two broad black mourning stripes across my cheeks and across my chin. I kissed her hand and belly as she did so.

The tenderness we shared then would not be felt again for years to come.

SATHA
Seared Conscience

Atop the Arhe's Rampart, the cool winds blew wild about me. Once, twice, three times my husband turned to look back at me as he, Taer and the minor household heads prepared to ride through the outer gates. My beloved had recently killed a buffalo, and braided ribbons hung from his ear-loops. A ceremonial dagger made from the spine of a stingray protruded from the sheath on his right thigh. He carried my dagger also. Yes, he was a warrior at last, yet I worried for him.

Mamya Jontay and the household noblewomen had dressed him in the Pagatsu ceremonial tunic, leather leggings and riding boots. He was perhaps overdressed because we had given him a woolen gyuilta and a quilted Ibeni vest. As he exited the gates and rode towards Chyar, the cool desert wind blasted the fringes of his gyuilta and his waist-length hair fluttered like weeds shivering in the wind.

I descended the rampart steps and was met by Ydalle, Jival, Gala, Edi and Jival. Jival, the Ibeni-Angleni warseed whom everyone called The Emigrant, spoke first. "Arhe, tell Ydalle and Gala to stop calling me a traitor. I am not."

"Jival has a kind and innocent heart," I said, catching my breath. "She pities the Third Wife. Come now, Loic's sudden absence has made these once-bearable pains harder to bear. Your suspicions and disagreements pull at my heart." I took the wolf fur coif from my head and removed my gyuilta. I asked, "What does the Third Wife want to do?"

Light-hearted plump Gala and flirty thin Edi—both fierce Doreni girls—glanced at Ydalle.

"The Third Wife wishes to use one of the valankus to enter the city," Ydalle said. "Now tell me, why should she want to do such a thing? On today of all days?"

"She's allowed to do what she wishes," I answered.

"But why today?" Gala repeated. "When Taer and the warriors have gone? When all in the region are mourning for Lihu? Do you not see something evil in it?"

Jival pushed Ydalle aside. "There is no evil in it. Taer has forbidden Sio, Lihu's friend and cousin, to sit with the Pagatsu at Lihu's funeral, and he has also forbidden the poor boy to travel with them to the Therpa encampment. This is a double dishonor. Any mother would grieve for her son. Is it not human for her to wish to escape a place that continually dishonors her? Taer should have—"

"Learn your place, Jival!" Gala shouted at her. "Who are you to say what Chief Treads Lightly should do? The Arhe—Arhe Satha, not that other pretender you're always advocating—might be fooled by your pretended innocence, but not me. When you return from the marketplace with foreign sweets for Sio I see nothing more than a schemer, plotting future trouble."

"Giving sweets to Sio is acceptable, Gala," I said.

"The boy is likeable enough, Arhe!" she said, "but not the Third Wife. Emigrant, can you not see how you wrong Arhe Satha by befriending this—?"

I leaned against the column, wincing from the pain in my womb.

"You should be in bed, Arhe," Edi said.

Ydalle extended a steadying hand. "Arhe, go to your bed and rest and tell Jival not to help the Third Wife destroy you."

"The Third Wife does not destroy me by entering the town. The vendors have all shut their shops and grief has made the marketplace silent. But if she wishes to enter the city, let her."

Gala sniffed, sounding more outraged and protective of my status than I was. "She probably has a lover there."

Edi added her protest, grumbling also.

I was not as innocent as my female servants thought. Mam had taught me: *Those who gossip with you will often gossip about you.* There was also an old Theseni proverb: *Befriend the one who has befriended your enemy.* For these reasons I thought it best to take Jival from the general household and make her one of my personal servants. Her lips were loose enough.

"Come now," I urged, "let us not see evil where none is. The Harvest Moon has arrived and gone. The harvests of barley, corn and spices have been reaped. The baby goats and horses are all weaned, or sold or bartered away. We should be rejoicing, not sitting here imagining evil things." I turned to Jival. "Emigrant, tell the Third Wife she can enter the town. Let her use the Arhe's valanku if she wishes. There are more important things to ponder."

Jival beamed. She bowed and raced towards the Third Wife's household.

Edi was rubbing my too-large belly. "Let the silly one go. The Third Wife will deceive even her in time. Now, Arhe, you must rest. You proved yourself a capable Arhe ever since your triumph with the Bride's Feast. Let Mam Monua and Mamya Jontay do the work of Arhe while you rest."

"True," Gala said. "We Doreni say, 'rest now for trouble later.'"

"Interesting saying," I said.

"In a Doreni Great House," she continued, "the smallest slight is cause for vendetta and trouble tends to rise up suddenly. It's best to rest when peace rules. When war is thrust upon you—"

"Yes, yes," I cut her off impatiently. "You Doreni are a fierce people."

Ydalle was rolling her eyes at me. "It's obvious, Arhe, that you mock this tribe. You think they see themselves as fierce when they aren't. I also used to think that way, but learned long ago how wrong I was. Everyone, from stable boys to the highest nobility—craftsmen, old soldiers, indigent relatives with letters of introduction and mistresses of the minor households are all ready to be insulted. Accept Gala's warning and stop your childish mocking."

Although the Theseni in the Great House loved me dearly, they treated me like a child. They considered Mam the household head, Doreni household or not. Pregnant and still new to my status, I bristled at the continuous rebukes from servants who thought they were my mentors. Yet, how could I argue? It was evident that all—Ydalle, Yiko, and the few others—loved and cared about me. Shouldn't a child drink up authority like water?

"Lihu's death has numbed us all," Ydalle continued. "Rest while the numbness lasts. Twenty-one days are a long time and soon enough some squabbling or contention will start. This peace will not last long."

Peace did not last even one day. The next day Mam, Yiko and Ydalle ran into my rooms with Malana following close behind them. Being Theseni, they did not ask permission to enter my rooms as the Doreni servants did, but boldly walked in.

"The Third Wife is claiming to be sick," Yiko said, sucking at his teeth. "And that bastard son of hers is pleading for Mamya Jontay to attend to her."

"The old woman will have nothing to do with her," Ydalle chimed in. "None of the noblewomen will taint their reputation by being seen with her, and Taer is not here to order the servants to help her."

"Rightly so!" Mam added, breathing indignantly. Malana also breathed indignantly. It had become her habit to imitate Mother in everything.

"If the whore is sick," Ydalle continued, "sick people have been known to get well. If she does not get well, then she will be free from our disdain. Improvement or death, things will turn out well for her."

I slowly rose from my bed. How my belly hurt as I turned on the bed, and how all three looked at me in angry disbelief. "Despite what my husband thinks, he needs Sio as an ally. So does this child I bear him. Sio will be much displeased if his brother's wife refuses to help."

I pointed to my gyuilta. "The morning is cold and the walk to the Third Wife's household is far. Let me lean upon your arm. It must not be said that the Arhe of the Golden House allowed the wife of Treads Lightly to suffer. Believe me, Mam, such things will be said. Remember, too, that her son is my husband's brother."

The walk from the lingay-covered hill near the marriage room past the field where Loic's house was being built to the far hill where the Third Wife's household was a long journey I did not wish to make. In addition, I had misjudged the length of the journey and the hardness of the hillside. Mam and Ydalle held my hands tightly as we walked, and Yiko and Malana followed nearby. Waihai, how my womb shuddered and cramped as I walked. So great was the pain, I squeezed Mam's hand.

"The Creator made this day, Sister," I called from outside the curtained door of the Third Wife's room.

"It brings no blessings," she answered, her voice weak. "Unless it brings my death. Sio should not have called you. Leave me alone."

"Sister," I said, "with or without your permission, I will help you." I pulled her ebony doorway curtain aside, but did not enter.

How rich and luxurious the room was! Jobara! Indeed she was a high-born lady accustomed to wealth! Gold and silver, silks and linens, many jeweled trinkets surrounded her. I thought, *I have forgotten how the rich are supposed to live. It is Taer and Loic who behave abnormally, and I too because I have sold so much of my dowry to feed the poor.*

Sio sat at his mother's bedside, worry lining his young face. I had seen death many times. In our old region, dying soldiers and peasants with sunken eyes and gaunt sagging skin were like the dust of the earth. The Third Wife lay listless and pale under an embroidered silk blanket, and the acrid odor of vomit assaulted my nostrils. Yiko pulled me backward, putting his hand before his nose. I pushed his hands away from me, although my chest tightened with fear as I walked across the room to her bedside.

"All the households in the Golden House are yours to rule, Arhe!" she retorted. "Do as you will."

Together Mam, Ydalle, Yiko, Malana, and I entered the Third Wife's quarters.

"Third Wife," I greeted her as I approached her bed. I found myself fearing for her, for myself and for the unborn child. *Some terrible disease,* I thought, *has attacked her body.* "How long is it since you've fallen ill?"

But she didn't answer me. Instead, she suddenly bolted upright and vomited violently. A foul-smelling clear liquid spewed from her mouth onto the silken sheets, narrowly missing me. Sio screamed aloud and tears rolled down his face.

Mam rushed to the bedside and placed herself between the Third Wife and me. "Daughter, do you not remember Milvia?" she asked, holding her nose. "Did she not lose a child because she nursed Orla during that plague the Angleni brought to our shores? Did she not die years later because of the blood disease? Who knows but this sickness might latch onto you and—"

My heart and eyes studied the Third Wife's drawn but still youthful face. "Mam, I've nursed many sick folk. Never have their diseases latched onto me."

Gently pushing Mam aside, I knelt beside the Third Wife's bed. Her hair, luxuriant and red, fell into a pool of vomit near her pillow. She closed her eyes as if pain itself was trying to close them. I wiped her mouth with the sleeve of my gyuilta, and pulled the strands of her hair away from the foul-smelling liquid.

"I'm saddened," I said, "to see Taer's beautiful wife reduced by such sickness. But soon, Sister, you will be well."

Sick though she appeared to be, she managed to glare at me.

"Truly, Sister," I said, stroking her forehead and indicating to Yiko that he should make a fire in the hearth, "my words are from my heart. I mean you well. When your health improves—and yes, you will improve—you must stop imagining evil schemes in everything I do."

Her green eyes studied me a long time. Then, her voice shaking, she said, "I will try, Satha—"

"Arhe Satha," Mam interrupted her. "Remember that."

"Arhe Satha," Malana repeated. "Remember that."

"Arhe Satha," the Third Wife corrected herself.

"Arhe," Sio pleaded, "forgive my mother. She has insulted you all these months, while you have been kind and good to her. She should not have done so, but you can understand—"

Yiko raised a warning finger to Sio. "In this situation, Sio, the Arhe understands only what her husband wishes her to understand."

"Many here," Sio continued despite Yiko's warning, "have not forgiven her sin. They're like their master in that way."

"If we are to be friends, Younger Brother," I answered, "you must not speak harshly of my New Father, who is—jobara!—your own father as well. Perhaps when you are older and you also understand the strength of love, you will understand that lovers often find it hard to forgive a loved one who proves treacherous."

Mam sighed. A long exasperated sigh. But Malana repeated my words. "Yes, Sio. Perhaps you will understand love."

I continued. "Perhaps, he'll forgive her one day. A man with a good heart cannot hold his anger forever."

"Daughter," Mam screamed at me and both Yiko and Ydalle looked as if they wanted to shake some sense into me. "The man has held his anger for at least twelve years now. Forget those stupid proverbs you've read in the holy books and open your eyes. Their love is over. Now, do what you must. Order one of the healers to come to see her, and get yourself back to your own bed."

The Third Wife's gaze flickered from me to Mam, to Yiko who was building a fire in the hearth from his tinderbox, and to her son. She groaned suddenly, and her body shivered. Sweat rolled down her face.

"Arhe!" How weak she sounded! "Thank you for allowing me to venture into town. I should not have. I was grieved in my heart and in need of medicine."

"Jobara, Sister?" I tried not to become ill from the foul smell of sickness permeating the room. "You could have sent one of the servant girls."

"I could only trust Jival to do such a thing, and Jival—you know as well as I—is innocent and somewhat stupid. She would not have gotten the right herbs."

Ydalle and Mam exchanged glances. "What do you mean 'the right herbs'?" Mam asked.

"I walked through the empty marketplace," the Third Wife said, "and found one small apothecary shop that opened to me. Its grieving owner, an Ibeni, searched among his goods, but could not mix the herb to make me well. I had ventured into town for nothing. And then I thought, *It is better for me to die than to live.* I asked him to give me poison instead."

"Older Sister!" I was suddenly terrified for her. "Would you kill yourself and leave your child alone in the world without a mother?"

But Mam said, "Just like a selfish woman to do such a thing!" She turned to me. "See how this evil one's mind works. She plans to kill herself while you're here alone. She wants all the world to blame you for poisoning her."

"I had no such thought in my heart!" the Third Wife weakly defended herself. "Why should I not want to die? Death, even if I were to walk unshrouded outside the fields we long for, is better than *this* Gebelda. Arhe Satha, I want to die. My death is not a scheme aimed at you. Oh, let me die, for I can no longer live in shame."

Sio began wailing, as if his heart would break. His hands grasped mine as if they were cords binding his mother to life. "Make her live, Older Sister," he cried. "Make her live."

"I cannot make her live, Younger Brother, if she does not want to live."

"Make her want to live!"

Muffled whispering behind me made me turn around. Mamya Jontay had entered the room. She stood near the doorway talking softly to Mam, their eyes looking at the Third Wife suspiciously.

"Older Sister," I said, stroking the Third Wife's forehead and pulling the vomit-soaked blanket from under her sweat-covered head, "you've endured suffering and rejection long. And perhaps you deserved it for betraying such a good and noble husband who loved you. But I will not reject you. Hold on to life a bit more, for even though earthly joys are as yet unseen, perhaps they are just outside your door."

"Do you truly think so, Arhe Satha?" the Third Wife asked, lifting sad eyes to me.

"Truly I do, Older Sister. Think how wonderful it is that the Ibeni poisoner gave you poison and yet you are still alive. Could it be that the Creator has appointed you to life?"

"To such a life? It cannot be."

"Life often calls us to endure great things. If we endure well we are rewarded."

I continued wiping the Third Wife's brow. "You need to eat, Older Sister. I'll command Yiko to bring you food. Good country food, not the rich fare you rich Therpas tend to poison yourselves with, and I'll ask Jival, your great defender, to attend you."

Fear flashed across her face. "Arhe Satha, please! Let no one here cook for me. Many here want to poison me. Jontay, especially"—she eyed the old woman suspiciously—"would like to see my corpse on the

Therpa grief tree. It may even be this is not caused by the poison I've ingested but by some herb placed in my food to poison me."

"But I thought you wanted to poison yourself," Ydalle said, coldly.

Mam was also impatient. "Tyungkyra—don't be a silly fool!" she said. "How long have you lived in the Golden House since you sinned against its owner? No one has murdered you yet. Satha, her evil heart makes her imagine what is in no one's heart. And you? You swallow her words like a bird swallowing a worm caught in a fowler's snare!"

"I'll eat nothing made by Yiko or any of these servants," the Third Wife shouted before vomit choked her words. Her trembling hands gripped my fingers.

"I will not allow myself to be insulted by a whore," Yiko shouted. I would have rebuked him but I remembered that he was Taer's servant, and had befriended my father. He was also part of Mam's little wolf pack. I kept quiet but, with a withering look, hinted that he keep quiet.

"What if Sio watches the cooks as they prepare your meal?" I asked the Third Wife.

"What does a child know of poisons?" she asked as a trail of vomit slid down her cheek onto the bed.

"What about Jival?" I asked. "She likes you, and she won't allow anyone to harm you."

"Jival is an innocent! Even more so than Sio." Her eyes pleaded with me. "Arhe Satha, if you cook for me—here in my rooms—I'll eat. Look, see, there's wood in the hearth; bring fire, flour, oil and a pot and your herbs. Fry bread here for me to eat. I trust you. You're not my enemy."

"Let me call Okiak," I said. "He knows healing foods that will—"

"No, Not Okiak!" Her face reddened with terror. "Those shamans terrify me. I hate to think their spirits might be looking into my mind. No, Arhe Satha, you and only you must attend me. The Good Maker will bless you for all your mercies."

"The journey from my quarters to yours is a long one, Sister," I answered. "It's one I cannot easily make. Yiko, go to the kitchen now. Ydalle, you too. Older Sister doesn't need your frowns. Tell the cooks to prepare some food for me but tell Jival—privately—to bring the food here." I turned to the Third Wife. "In the next days, I will try to visit you."

While Yiko and Ydalle left, Mam dragged me outside into the marble corridor with Jontay and Malana following. "Remember your child!" Mam whispered, looking backward at the slats of the Third Wife's doorway curtain. "Your journey here caused you great pain. Do you not want to protect your child, your husband's legacy?"

Then Jontay took up Mam's song. "Arhe, you don't understand the Doreni concept of *kribatsu*—reflected honor. If a wife is found to be stupid, or disgraced, or . . . well . . . then her husband's honor—Loic's honor, Taer's honor, all the household, the entire Pagatsu clan—"

"The entire world falls, my daughter!" Mam interjected. "The entire world!"

"If you overtax yourself and the child dies," Jontay sad, "the elders of the clan will think the ancestors have lost patience with Taer. You must—"

I wanted to lie down. My thighs and lower stomach tensed with pain. I saw the gleaming roof of my almost-finished house shining far away in the distance. "Mothers," I whispered, "I cannot consider all you say right now. I'm tired. Mam, you've filled me with fears all my life, always, always causing me to worry about some possible evil that never arrives. Don't continue to hound me with your fears!"

Tears rolled down my mother's cheeks, and she choked and gasped on her sobs.

I hardened my heart against her weeping because it seemed necessary to protect my own heart. "Do you know what Loic calls you, Yiko, and Ydalle when we're alone?"

She wiped her eyes. "Your bed talk doesn't concern me, Daughter."

"He calls you the Thesenkuyu."

Mam gave Jontay a questioning look.

A smile spread across Jontay's face. "It means 'the little Theseni wolf-pack.'"

I added, "Mam's the she-wolf to whom the little cubs cling."

Malana looked worried. "What does Cuyo call me?" she asked.

"He calls you the Thesenkuyu's wild cub."

She grinned, obviously happy Loic had named her among the pack.

"Wolf-pack, uh?" Mam said, smiling also. "I like that husband of yours. A she-wolf, uh?"

Jontay nodded. "Jobara, he must respect you greatly to give you such a name. The wolf pack has great earth puha. All the households know to bow low to a wolf-pack."

"Even when they look silly walking around whispering together?" I asked.

Ydalle's unmistakable nervous footsteps came racing up the tiled corridor. When I turned to look at her, she was wringing her hands and frowning in her typically agitated manner. She pointed in the direction of the outer courtyard. "Arhe Monua, Noam just rode into the outer courtyard."

Malana leaped high into the sky, as if some inner joy overwhelmed her and in a flash her tiny feet were flying toward the outer courtyard.

Mamya Jontay and Mam, however, didn't look so joyful.

"How strange that he should come now!" Mamya Jontay exclaimed. "Should he not be flying to the king's side?" She extended her hand. "Hold on to me, Arhe. If Noam is here, no good can come of it."

Noam passed through the entrance gate of the outer courtyard, through the inner courtyard. He entered the longhouse, and the servants and several noblewomen—including Jura, Pantan's daughter—seated in the longhouse showed him the honor due him by bowing low. But Malana jumped into his arms. He lifted her by the waist above his shoulders and wheeled about several times then, together, they danced around the gathering room.

"The Creator made this day, Wise Sisters," he said, greeting us all.

"It is a day full of blessings," Jura, Pantan's daughter answered. As formidable as her father, she smiled that inscrutable Doreni smile and seemed amused both at his presence and my obvious discomfort.

She and the other noblewomen were exchanging glances. Above all the noblewomen and female servants in the longhouse, Jura was the one whose judgement I most feared. Noam's unexpected visit had caused me to become an unwitting and unskilled player in a diplomatic game. I resolved not to appear weak and uncomfortable before her.

I turned my eyes to Noam. Although he stood several paces away from me, the odor of sweat and mukal exuded from him. Trouble too.

"Seared Conscience," I said, "the warriors and elders of the Golden House have all journeyed to the Royal City for Prince Lihu's funeral. Was not Lihu your friend and cousin? Should you not be at Chyar?"

He turned toward me, his gaze on my breasts. "Lihu was a friend who held my heart in his hand," Noam answered me. "I often bounced him on my knee when—"

He stopped speaking suddenly and stepped forward, looking steadily at my bulging belly. "I had not heard, Arhe, that Loic was having a child."

I nodded, and rubbed my cramping belly to quiet the child who seemed suddenly disturbed.

At my answer, he glanced backward through the doorway he had just entered. Long, long he stood there, peering through the corridor at the entrance gate until Mamya Jontay challenged him.

"Seared Conscience, you seem to be deciding if you should stay or leave," she said. "Surely rushing quickly to the king's side would honor the king's son, your cousin."

As if some hard-won inner battle had been won, he turned and walked towards her. Jura gave me a warning glance when he joined the women near the large gathering table, but the other women grinned among themselves, not caring to hide their interest in the outcome of this sudden diplomatic skirmish. I, too, was wondering what I would do with my New Father's great enemy.

"Ydalle, my sweet!" Noam waved in her direction. "Some wildberry mukal!"

She didn't move, only sucked at her teeth in the Theseni way. Then she threw me a challenging look.

"Get it for him," I ordered.

My command was obviously not worth much, and she looked at Mam. Mam gave her a wary but approving nod and she left, turning back several times to glare at Noam.

"You haven't answered Mamya Jontay," Mam said to Noam. "Why are you here? Quench your thirst and leave. If you have some important matter to discuss with my daughter's New Father, speak to him after the funeral or when he returns."

"I see the Theseni influence has come to Taer's house," Noam answered. "Indeed I had heard Loic was now the head of a Theseni household. Are the Pagatsu no longer Doreni, then?"

Giggling, the Doreni noblewomen covered their mouths with their hands. How their eyes twinkled at my discomfort! Yes, what was a trial to me delighted them! In those days a Doreni proverb existed: A true Doreni woman needs no defender. Noam's insult was subtle, but the hospitality law and the covenant of friendship between him and Taer were matters I could not easily navigate. Yes, the rules, responsibilities, and laws of those days were complex indeed.

Mam, being Theseni, didn't waste time on Doreni niceties. Nor did she care about laws she neither understood nor respected. "Noam," she said, "I hope you're intelligent enough to know that not everything your spies tell you are true. This is a Doreni household. There! One of their lies is destroyed."

"Let us not argue, Mam Monua," he answered. "I speak only because I know the Theseni reputation for . . . gentleness." He turned to face me. "Arhe, I know that you understand loss. I have heard you have lost a sister. I am overwhelmed by loss. My lost cousin, my lost friendship with Taer. This new sorrow revived old griefs. Perhaps the proverb is true: Mukal and wita both revive the guilt and memories they're meant to destroy."

I nodded, remembering the poor men who also sought to hide from grief with mukal.

Mam, however, was never easily deceived. "Don't fall for this ploy, Daughter. I've learned much about this demon."

"Loic has chosen for himself a mouthy New Mother," Noam answered, not hiding his anger at Mam. "Men, not doting women, raised me. Perhaps Loic likes all this female tayu. I, myself, am perplexed by it."

When Ydalle returned with the mukal, Yiko, Taer's chief steward, followed close behind her. When she handed the mukal to Noam, she almost threw it. Verbal sparring between servants and honored guests would have been unheard of in a Theseni household. My chest tightened.

I expected Noam to demand she be whipped, but he only winked at her. This added to my confusion. I frowned and the noblewomen roared with laughter at my distress.

I will tell you truly, I never liked certain Doreni traits: their impenetrable silences when angered, their formidable stares and cold attitude toward strangers, their teasing. Such behavior only angered and confused the openhearted Theseni. As Arhe and a foreigner to the clan, I had learned to endure them, but at that moment if a vialka had been close at hand, I would have pierced all those giggling women through the heart.

Noam was leaning against the gathering table. He uncorked the mukal bottle and turned his attention to Yiko. "Yiko, I've often heard 'Theseni women feign weakness but strike hard with their tongues.' More and more I find this to be true."

"Theseni women only strike what needs striking, Captain," Yiko answered.

"Even if I need striking, tell Ydalle not to strike me with food." He took a long sip from the bottle, then stood up and winked at me. "I'll stay in my usual rooms."

Yiko's eyes widened. "Young Chieftain, you push all boundaries! All the clan nobles are absent. Only male servants and old warriors remain. We are unimportant people. Perhaps you should push the hospitality laws when more worthy opponents are here."

Noam drained the mukal bottle. "Consider the state I'm in. I smell of mukal, sweat and brothel sex. Would it not disrespect the king's son if I entered Chyar as I am? Moreover I'm tired. I can journey no more today." He smiled at someone behind me and I turned to look. Sio had appeared behind me in an open doorway. Jival was by his side.

"Younger Brother," I said, "you've left your mother's bedside?"

"My mother and I were told the Therpa chief's son had arrived. My mother gave me permission to leave."

Although Sio had spoken in his usual restrained manner, his joy at seeing his father was evident. My heart went out to him. His noble spirit was evident, as was the rejection it had borne so patiently. I did not understand why Noam had not acknowledged him. Nor did I understand why Taer had accepted Sio as his second son. Perhaps both clans had implicitly agreed to protect the reputation of the adulteress and her son—despite the fact that Sio was Noam's firstborn son and should have worn the jade bracelet.

I spoke to Sio. "We cannot have it said that Taer was inhospitable to the Therpa chief's son. Let Noam have his 'usual' quarters."

Noam gestured toward his son. His pride in his son was also evident as he watched Sio enter the room and slowly approach him. "Arhe Satha, Loic has chosen well. If I had found a good woman such as you, I would not have ended up as I am now."

Sio turned his eyes downward when his father spoke and Ydalle could only have added to his shame when she said, "Obviously, you weren't looking in the right brothel or, perhaps, good women didn't attract you as much as the bad ones did."

Noam laughed, the noblewomen too. Only Mam, Sio and I seemed to find the situation uncomfortable. Noam closed his dark-ringed eyes, then opened them again as if willing them to see. He leaned his head against the table. "The mukal has made me sick, Ydalle." He pushed his hands through his flowing shoulder-length red hair. "I cannot spar with you today. Tomorrow, perhaps."

"Spar when you will," she answered, "your schemes and parries will not help your child rule the Golden House."

The noblewomen tittered and at that moment it seemed to me that Ydalle seemed more Arhe than I was.

Noam winked at Ydalle, then rising and holding Sio by the shoulder, he left the gathering room.

After he had gone, Yiko called me outside into the inner courtyard. His voice was like that of a Theseni father berating an unworthy daughter. "You have married into a Doreni clan and you want to behave like a true Doreni," he began. "I understand this. The hospitality custom and all those other burdensome rules can weigh on anyone's mind. May I say, however, that I have been steward here for three decades, and although I am not an expert in Pagatsu matters, I will say the Doreni do not follow any of their customs to extremes. In all their rigidity, they are most pliable. Remember, too, that though you are Arhe here,

Loic's household is not yet established. He might declare one action acceptable and Taer then decry it. And, of course, the opposite can happen. Therefore, while Noam is here—and with any luck he will not be here long—perhaps it would be best for you to avoid him, pass him by and, in general, give no commands to anyone concerning him."

The pain in my belly made me impatient with the finger he wagged in my face. "Tell me, Yiko, are you Arhe here? Are you married to the one who wears the jade bracelet?"

He looked me up and down, surprised at my harsh reply.

"Keep your mouth shut," I continued. "Noam and the Therpas will not leave the Golden House feeling slighted. Not again." I remembered all too well how my husband had refused to attend the Groom's Friend Feast the Therpas had made in his honor. "And Yiko . . . in the future, do not shake your finger at me. Taer might be chief, and you may be his steward, but I am Arhe here."

The trembling and cramping in my womb lessened, as did my impatience with the Thesenkuyu. I understood they meant me well, and I even found myself agreeing with Yiko's suggestions. I worried for the child, asking it to forgive me for my journey to the Third Wife's house. I longed for my husband to return. How I wished he lay by my side. Although our common house was not complete, we had begun sleeping together in my room in the guest women's quarters or in Taer's forsaken marriage quarters. During the night I slept fitfully and my hands reached out for him but did not find him. How empty my arms and hollow my heart felt without him.

During this uneasy rest, between sleep and waking, I heard what seemed to be spirit voices raised in angry dispute. The holy prophets on the one side; Okiak and the spirits on the other. I remembered what the midwives had told me—pregnancy brings strange dreams—and I forced myself to sleep. Nevertheless, I wondered if the spirits had indeed been arguing about my bed.

I was determined to spend the next day in bed, but when I woke, I saw sandals below my threshold curtain. I recognized them as Sio's.

"The Creator made this day, Sio," I said loudly enough for him to hear.

"It brings blessings for you and for me, Older Sister," he called back.

"It's strange to hear you at my door, Younger Brother." I sat up in my bed and the child kicked inside me. "Enter and speak all your heart."

"Wife of my Brother, I request that Ydalle not attend to the Therpa chief's son. She shames him continually, and in shaming him, she shames me."

"Your words don't sound like your own, Younger Brother. From what I saw yesterday, Noam and Ydalle understand each other. He didn't seem offended—"

"I'm offended! When I told my mother of Ydalle's actions, she suggested I ask you to remove Ydalle."

"Why should this matter, Younger Brother? Isn't Noam prepared to leave today?"

"The effects of the mukal have not left him."

"No?" I began to dread the day.

"He might stay another day."

"This is a hard request, Sio. Few of the servants are willing to attend him. If your father—Taer, I mean—were here, he could command any man, noblewoman, warrior, servant to obey him. I can't command those not directly in Loic's household."

"You are Arhe, Older Sister. Do whatever you wish. Take the power, no one will challenge you."

"Power is not something I like to 'take.' Nor do I wish to overstep boundaries even if I have power to do so. I will not force my household servants to attend the Therpa chief's son. Jival is tending to your mother." I squirmed on the bed, tired already. "I can't put any additional burden on her."

"Older Sister, Jival won't mind caring for those I love. Free the girl from all other duties except those concerning my mother and the Therpa chief's son."

The worry in his voice touched me. "Let it be as you say. Go and tell her your wishes."

"One more thing, Older Sister."

"What is that?"

"Among the many duties of an Arhe is the duty to greet guests. Such a duty can be put aside if the Arhe is ill, but Noam is the son of a great chief, a chief your husband insulted." He said no more leaving me to draw whatever conclusion I wished to.

Sio was a noble and good youth, but he was also a warrior's son. "I'll come and see the Therpa chief's son," I said. "Have no fear, I will not dishonor him. Go and call Ydalle. I need her to help me dress."

The sickeningly sweet smell of mukal and stomach juices greeted me as I—and the Thesenkuyu—stood outside the chieftain's son "usual rooms."

"Over-indulgence as usual," Yiko sniffed. "That he should corrupt himself by such—"

"Noam," I called, interrupting Yiko's complaint, "this is a day the Creator has made. I am told you did not eat with my clansmen at the longhouse this morning. Do you wish the servants to carry your meal here?"

A weak voice answered, "Enter, Arhe."

When we entered, I was surprised to see Malana lying beside Noam and stroking his forehead. In a moment, Mam had raced toward Malana and dragged her from the bed. "Come here, girl! Don't you know this man could violate you?"

Mukal bottles surrounded the bed, and Noam seemed half in the grip of a mukal stupor. Yiko made a great show of opening the windows to drive out the stale air.

I bent over Noam. "Are you not well, Young Therpa Chief?"

"Wife of Loic," he said, his voice a weak whisper, "it's been long since a woman's voice showed such concern for me."

Mam's voice was cold as the night wind. "Perhaps you wouldn't be feeling so ill if you hadn't asked Malana to bring you mukal."

"Malana and I are old friends, Mam Monua," he said. "The mukal demands. I listen to its demands. I cannot resist. I asked Malana for more mukal and she brought it."

Mam tightened the belt of her gyuilta as if it were a noose being tied around a murderer's neck. "You make yourself guiltless in all things.

The mukal demands, or Malana listens to the mukal's demand. Your evil heart takes no blame for anything."

"Ydalle," I said, "go now. Bring Jival here."

Ydalle screwed up her face. "I suppose The Emigrant is useful for something. Best to have her tend to these things rather than walk about staring into space as if she's looking for her home country." She then held a piece of folded parchment before me.

"What's this?" I asked.

"It's a message from the whore to Noam. Sio had it."

Noam's eyes pleaded with me not to read the parchment.

"We mustn't read messages that don't concern us," I said. "Give it back to Sio."

Instead of returning it, she opened the parchment and held it before my eyes. When she did this, Noam seemed to hold his breath.

He need not have worried. The writings on the parchment were strange, the alphabet foreign. "It's in one of the old languages," I said. "None of which I ever learned. Return the note to Sio."

When I said this, Noam relaxed.

Ydalle held the note to her chest, obviously unwilling to let it go. "Well then, I'll take it to one of the noblewomen. They can translate it."

"I said to return it to Sio! Where is he?"

"I sent him to his mother."

"Go find him. Return the note and let him finish his task in peace. We must stop suspecting plots and further complicating our lives. Sometimes it is best not to know certain things."

"Well spoken, Arhe!" Noam said from the bed.

I patted my belly. "Today, I've promised the child I will rest. Mam and Mamya Jontay will be glad to hear this. Your clan honored me with a great feasting during my bridal week. I cannot but attend to the Therpa chief's son. Nevertheless, this pregnancy is a difficult one. I cannot fulfill all my duties toward you. I trust you understand this and will not consider it a slight if I absent myself."

Ydalle mumbled something. In response, Noam winked and kissed his hands to her.

Wagging her finger at him, she said, "You fox. The Thesenkuyu know how to trap little foxes like you."

I spent the morning in my rooms, free from all care. How idle and immoral I felt! The morning passed as if in a dream. The servants kept arriving with soups and herbs the midwives had prescribed for me. Foul and bitter brew most of it. I drank it nevertheless and was happy to be my only company. In the afternoon, however, Jival came to my room.

"Chief Noam has visited the Third wife," she said, her face shining with joy.

"That was likely to happen," I answered her, rising up in my bed. "But perhaps you should not show such joy over an adulterous liaison."

"There is nothing new in this. He visits her often."

"Does he? And what does Taer think of all this?"

"Yes. He does, and Treads Lightly turns his eye from seeing their meetings." She sat on the bed beside me, and nibbled some of the fig cakes Gala had brought for me. "But I rejoice because the romance between Chief Noam and the Third Wife is quite dead."

"Jobara? A good thing for Chief Taer and the Golden House to rejoice at."

"Jobara." I sensed her happiness was more for herself than for Taer. She continued, betraying her own heart. "The more Noam sees of her, the more he despises her. No, she is not worthy of him at all."

"Jobara?" I raised my eyebrows.

"The Third Wife is quite grieved that his heart seems to lie elsewhere," she rattled on. "But what can be done?"

"Perhaps she should try to win back her husband."

"That's what I told her. But she told me just now that you've convinced her to try to win Taer's love."

"Has she?" I found this sudden change unbelievable but I kept silent.

"This," she continued, "and Noam's rejection, have turned her heart to virtue again. She says she will try to urge her cousin to desist in his insolence toward Taer. Yes, Arhe Satha, many breaches are being repaired."

I sucked at my teeth. "Jobara, this is news indeed!"

"You are very persuasive, Arhe Satha."

I leaned back on the bed. "I'm not that persuasive."

"Ah, but you are! And now the Third Wife has freed her heart from Chief Noam, and Chief Noam is freed from her, then . . ."

"Then?"

She smiled to herself. "Nothing, Arhe. But now, you must come. The Third Wife wants you to witness her last words to Noam. The very last ones."

"Let another witness her words. I've promised the child—"

"But, Arhe!" She turned her innocent eyes to me. "You must come. Sio is at her side even now. Rise, rise, and leave your bed. A new era has surely begun for the Golden House. You have put hope into the heart of the Third Wife. She honors you by asking for your attendance. Will you dishonor Sio and the Therpas by denying her request?"

There was such wisdom in what she said, I wondered if the words were her own. I slowly rose from the bed. "Well said, Jival. I will come. The Third Wife has made a wise choice. Chief Noam is charming, but he is nothing compared to Taer."

"So you say, Arhe, but others would disagree."

"Perhaps. Yet, I trust that with your help, good Jival, she can fulfill her determination and not fall again into Noam's bed."

When I rose from the bed, my womb did not hurt. But as we walked across the large expanse of the compound to the Third Wife's rooms, the pains returned.

When I stepped inside the Third Wife's curtain, Noam was already there. He was wearing a riding gyuilta and riding boots and sitting on the edge of her bed. He turned to face me when I entered.

"Arhe Satha," he said, "I see you've affected my cousin for the better. She tells me she will try to win Taer's forgiveness."

"I'm surprised to see you so well, Noam. This morning, it seemed the mukal had overpowered you."

"I am well." He looked out a near window. "So well, in fact, I came to say farewell to my cousin. After, I'll ride to the side of Our Matchless King."

I answered, "I trust he will understand why you could not arrive at Lihu's memorial on time."

"King Jaguar is loving enough," Jival said. "He'll understand Chief Noam was ill. Especially if Mamya Jontay sends a message to him."

Noam's face lit up. "A good idea, Jival! How smart you are! I would not have thought of asking Jontay. Jaguar respects her greatly. Her husband served him well. Do you think she will indeed write in my behalf?"

"Jobara! Of course she will!" Jival answered, nodding in my direction. "If Arhe Satha asks her."

"Ask her," I agreed.

"It's already past midday," Noam said. "Isn't she sleeping? Age has caught up with her, I hear."

"I'll wake her." Jival raced to the doorway, almost leaping with joy. "I'll wake her." She bit her bottom lip. "But, Arhe, her room is on the other side of the compound. I'm afraid I'll be long."

I shrugged and Noam added, "I'll wait."

Jival stood in the doorway watching Noam, her eyes full of admiration. "Chief Noam is a good one to look at, isn't he, Arhe?" she asked, beaming.

I blushed for her, and even Noam seemed shamed by her compliment. "My stallion is in the stables, Jival," he said. "When I retrieved my tunic, I forgot to ask the stablemen to bring him to the Guest Gate."

"I'll tell them," she answered, fawning. "Shall I give them some quixas from your pouch?"

"If you wish."

She giggled flirtatiously, then raced to the Third Wife's bed. She hugged the Third Wife. Then she disappeared through the wooden doorway curtain, her footsteps scampering down the tile corridor.

"She's an innocent one," I said, as her footsteps faded away.

"The innocent are rarely as innocent as they seem," Noam answered. He put his arm around my waist and led me to a chair beside the Third Wife's bed. "Arhe, you're holding onto the wall as if your life depended on it. Perhaps you should not have come."

"The walk here was a bit arduous." I removed his arm and turned to the Third Wife, who was dressed in the Evod Ibeni manner. The

Evod Ibeni were an anomaly among all Ibeni clans, their women often dressed in pure white linen. There was even a proverb which went, *A good woman is as pure as an Evod Ibeni or a Theseni nun*. Although she appeared in better health, when I saw how severely dressed she was, I worried for her. "And you, my sister? Are you well?"

"I too am well," she answered, and surprised me by rising from her bed. "Better than I have been all these years."

"Even in so unflattering a dress, Sister," I said, "you manage to look ravishing."

She exchanged a glance with her cousin. "I have always liked the holiness of the Evod Ibeni, Younger Sister. To strive for holiness among that tribe is determination indeed. I dressed in this manner to show the change in my soul. With perseverance my soul will be as austere as this dress."

Such a conversion was suspicious at worst and premature at best. "Older Sister, we all strive to be perfect. Strive for goodness, but do not strive overmuch, nor risk your sanity or your own vivaciousness. This is what the holy ones have written, and I've lived long enough to know their words are true."

She walked to her doorway and pushed the curtain aside, "Tell me, is the world outside as lovely as it feels?"

"The day is fresh and full of dreams, Older Sister."

"I must see it," she said. "How I've missed the sun!" Nodding to Noam, she added, "I'm sorry, my cousin, that our private conversations have now come to an end, but all our passions have been played out, and this day brings an end to that part of our lives. Perhaps Jival will suit you better."

With those words, she disappeared through the wooden curtain. Realizing I was alone with Noam, I rose to follow her through the door but Noam's hands grasped me. He quickly covered my mouth.

"You must promise not to call out, Arhe," he whispered in my ear.

I nodded.

He removed his hand, but something sharp pressed into my skin. I looked down; a blade gleamed.

I called out to the Third Wife, pleaded, "Older Sister, help me." She did not answer. I stared at the doorway. She did not return.

"You promised you'd be quiet," Noam said. He didn't cover my mouth, but he pressed the blade closer to my stomach. "She will not answer you call, Arhe. Do you understand what I want from you?"

I shook my head slowly.

"I want you to lie with me, Satha."

I winced. Such a soft voice, such harsh words.

"Arhe," he continued, speaking as if I was Malana or a small child. "You must be silent. You don't want to be killed, do you?"

I glanced at the doorway. "Older Sister!"

"Do you still believe she will help you? It is she who has plotted your shame."

"Older Sister!" I screamed. "Will you return cruelty for kindness?"

He put his hand to his lips. "She wanted to stay and watch your ruin, but I gave her the safer task of watching the corridors. We wouldn't want anyone to happen upon us, would we?"

"Jival will come! Jival knows I'm here."

"Ah," he said, "Jival. I would not depend on her." He removed the dagger's blade from my belly and using it gestured that I remove my clothing. "You must understand that I truly like you, Arhe," he said.

"You like me, 'but'? What subtlety is this?"

"My cousin is jealous and rejected," he continued. "You are praised everywhere. Her son—my son—has no heritage among the Therpas because Taer claimed him as his son. But neither does he have a heritage among the Pagatsu because he is not truly Pagatsu. My cousin is not one to endure such a thing. I love my son and I see the wisdom in her plan."

He glided the dagger upward towards my breasts. "Arhe, undress. Stop waiting for that fool Jival to return. If she returns, the Third Wife will send her on another errand! Do you not think so?"

"Noam, can you not foresee the outcome of this crime? Do you want vendetta declared between our two great clans?"

He glanced outside the window and his eyes surveyed the outlying fields. "Taer's patience insults me." He gestured again that I remove my clothing. "His ignoring of me offends me."

"But you don't reason rightly concerning this—"

"I reason as a Doreni," he shouted. "I reason as a man who refuses to be tolerated." He slowly slid the edge of the dagger across my right cheek, neck and shoulders, then slowly brought it down, circling my right breast and pressing the blade deeper and deeper into my skin. After lingering on my right breast, the knife slipped downward and rested on my stomach. "Your husband's clansman, Perik, raped his enemy's pregnant wife in an open field while her distraught husband looked on. Then he cut her stomach and removed the living child, lifting it high."

"Would you rape a pregnant woman in her own house?" I glanced at the doorway behind him, wondering how I could escape. Steeling myself, I tried to push past him.

"Enough!" He threw me against a wall.

I shrieked in pain as I fell backward into a large ebony table, crashing into a large mirror and sending its shards across the room and into my skin. My back burned from the assault. I feared for my unborn child.

"Arhe Satha," he said, "if you had taken the studies of daggerwork to heart, you would not be in this position."

Painfully, I raised myself from the floor and lurched toward him. Angrier than I had ever dreamed I could be, I slapped him hard against the cheek.

A smile flickered across his face. "You didn't like my joke?" My anger seemed to excite him. He dragged me onto the bed and, knocking my breath from me, he stood by the bed looking down at me. I struggled to regain my breath and covered my belly with my hands. He lowered himself atop me. Holding the knife to my stomach and pressing on my leg with his right elbow, he used his left hand to remove his leggings and undergarments, then ripped my clothing from me.

How difficult it is to speak of this! Even now! The full force of his weight pressed down upon my belly, and although I had worked my hand free, hitting him hard, digging my nails into his back and yanking at his hair, I could not stop him. I could only plead for him to stop. My screams filled his ears. My tears soaked his hair and covered his skin, but he continued pushing and thrusting inside me. Pain pulsed down my legs and along my hips. Wetness gushed between my legs; my heart leaped into my mouth. The thought occurred to me: *He did not kill my child with his dagger, yet my child has died nevertheless.*

His breathing raced, his body shuddered then slumped. Finished, he lay on me unmoving, and breathing hard. He was not a heavy man, and yet it seemed that all the heaviness of the world lay crushing my heart and preventing me from breathing.

I managed to push him from my body, sliding out from under him.

He stood up, and avoiding my eyes, wiped the tears from my face. "I'm sorry, Arhe," he said. "This is no personal hatred. You were a small means to a greater end."

I lay curled up in the Third Wife's bed. Blood smeared everything— the silken sheets, the carpet near the bed, the shards of broken mirror— and still more blood flowed down my legs.

"The child is dying," he said, avoiding my eyes.

"The child is not dead!" I shouted.

"No, Arhe," he responded. "It is dead. If not dead, dying. Its grave is your womb. You probably want to tell Loic how you lost the child. Don't. Let Taer avenge your honor. If you do not wish the Third Wife's complete plan to come to fruition, don't let Loic know of your degradation."

He lifted a pitcher from the table. He stood before me, smeared with my blood, his buttocks bare and his leggings around his ankles. He had been right about Doreni knifework. A woman should always have a dagger wedged in a sheath between her breasts or in the sleeve of her gyuilta. I had gone into my enemy's territory unprepared. If a knife been close at hand, I would have killed both Noam and myself.

From the Third Wife's table he took a small blue bottle and mixed its contents in the water in the pitcher. Then he splashed the combination on his ypher, washing off the blood. The Third Wife entered then. Her gaze lingered triumphantly upon me. Shamefaced, he closed the curtain behind him and was gone. Jobara! Her conscience was more seared than his.

While the Third Wife's scornful eyes now revealed her disdain for me, a tremor arose in my womb. My abdominal muscles began to tighten, like the belt of a gyuilta being pulled tight, as if the child within were struggling to hold onto life. A cold shiver ran along my waist. A warm sensation followed it. My heart fluttered wildly. The convulsions continued knocking me to my feet. I kneeled on the ground beside the bed, unmoving, fearing my womb would tremble again. It did. A series of cramping waves followed, then my womb heaved. I clutched my stomach. More blood suddenly flowed from me, gushed, poured out. Slowly, as burning pain flashed through my body, I crawled past the hateful Third Wife toward the curtain. I tried to call out, but my voice was a whimper.

"Jival!" I shouted, my voice more like a gasp than a human voice.

The Third Wife grinned. "If I know the Emigrant," she said, "she's probably gossiping with Noam even now. You can see how fascinated she is with him."

I slumped to the bloodied tile.

"No one's coming," she said.

As she said this, a pressure, an urgency in my abdomen made me squat. The child was emerging from my body. I squatted and pushed. Pain wracked my body. I shivered and shook, went cold and hot. At last, a tiny perfectly formed girl slid from my body. No sound, only an oozing; no purposeful movement, only a quivering. She opened her eyes and turned those pleading orbs upon me. And then she died.

How I needed the Creator then! But he was far away! And what could he do even if he were near? Could he bring the child back? Long, long, I sat there and prayed, pleaded, bewailing my child and my marriage, begging the Good Maker to remake my child and to turn back time. And all the while the Third Wife stood there smirking.

How long I sat there, I do not remember. The Third Wife walked past the dead child and me, unmoved, singing to herself as she removed her white robes and dressed in her usual rich attire. Soon Jival's voice sounded at the door, asking permission to enter.

"Enter." The Third Wife's voice was cold but triumphant.

I saw Jival's sandals as she entered and heard her footsteps in the richly embellished room. I did not turn to look at her and no human voice spoke. Then I heard her footsteps speeding away and her shout, "Help, help! Noam has raped my mistress and killed her child."

"Satha!" Ydalle's voice called out as she ran into the Third Wife's room. Mam and Mamya Jontay followed after, Malana holding onto Mam's arm. When I turned to look at Ydalle, she was striking the Third Wife and knocking her to the ground.

At first, Mam's gaze was fastened on me, but perhaps because she could not bear the shame on my face, because she turned her face toward the bloodstained carpet and the dead child lying in my arms.

"Ydalle," Mam shouted, "send one of the old warriors to ride after Noam." She screamed louder. "Tell them to bring him back or to die trying. Tell them to send word to Taer at Chyar."

Ydalle began to move toward the doorway but Mamya Jontay grabbed the edge of her kaba. Rubbing the fist with which she had struck the Third Wife, Ydalle seemed confused as to whether to rush through the wooden curtains or to stay at my side.

"Loic must not hear of this," Mamya Jontay said, slowly sitting on the bed. She put her hand on my head, and gently stroked my forehead. "No," she repeated, "Taer must not know now."

Mam took the child from me and, without speaking, held it in her arms. I half-hoped she knew some hidden wisdom that would bring the child back to life, but she only hid the child within the folds of her gyuilta, as if I had not been holding the dead child all along. Her arms swayed as she slowly caressed it and begged the Creator to return its life.

"My life will always be filled with sorrow," she said. Her shoulders heaved and fell. Weeping shook her whole body.

Ydalle, too, fell to weeping, and Mamya Jontay also. They cried for Mam, for the child, for me, for Loic. Only Malana and I remained silent. Malana was staring at the child as if trying to understand what a small bloody infant was doing in the Third Wife's room.

Then Mamya Jontay stood up, wiping her tears away. She walked over to the Third Wife who was rubbing her cheek. "How you have used our customs against us, Therpa whore!" she shouted.

Mam, too, attacked the Third Wife. "What are you smiling about, Evil One? You've just forfeited your life! At first, you were a living ghost. Soon, you'll be a dead one."

Mamya pushed the bloody sheets aside. "Don't weep, little daughter. This matter is not the same as it was with the Third Wife. Loic will understand, I think. Or perhaps he will not. But the Pagatsu . . . they'll say Noam conquered both the chieftain and the young chief in their beds. Moreover, you've lost a child. Already they were whispering, saying that Loic's seed was too weak and the ground it was planted in was frail also. They forget I also lost my first child in the womb and then brought forth three noble warriors." She sighed. "Would that all the others had died as that first one, instead of in war!"

All around us was quiet except for the howling of wolves in the distance.

"Jival was never wise," Mamya Jontay spoke up again. "She should have remained silent instead of shouting this news throughout the compound. This is a truth that can cause Loic his life. Or his heritage. Or his love for Satha."

"My husband won't kill me," I said, looking at the small dead infant in Mam's arm. So small it was.

Ydalle shook her head as if I had no sense. "Are you so sure, Satha?"

A heaviness crushed my chest when she said this. My breath seemed incapable of rising past my throat.

Mam pointed at the Third Wife. "What prevents me from killing her? She who has made my daughter a wife who is no wife, and me the mother of a wife who is no wife?"

Mamya Jontay removed a dagger from her leggings and waved it before the Third Wife's face. "Her death should be a lingering one with much pain, but Taer insists on honoring the blood covenant of the full marriage. Even though she dishonored it, he won't harm her."

The Third wife drew a breath. "Doreni custom," she said, "prevents Loic from lying with the Arhe if she has lain with another man. Loic will surely do what his father has done."

"So this was your plan?" I asked.

Footsteps appeared below the wooden curtains of the Third Wife's rooms. Moments later, Jura's voice pleaded to come in. Mam and I exchanged a quick glance but no one spoke.

Jura entered despite our silence and surprised me by kneeling before me and bowing low. "Your grief is hard for to bear, Arhe. It is my grief also."

"Bad news spreads quickly," Mam said. Her observation was so weighed down with futility and despair, I feared for Loic's future and my own.

But Jura's actions and words surprised me. She rose from her kneeling position and squeezed my hand, then walked to Mam's side.

"Mam Monua," she said, tears streaming down her face as she looked on the baby, "if Loic rejects Satha—for that young man is unpredictable and I cannot guess what his reaction to this sorrow will be—the noblewomen will defend her. I myself will make sure of it."

Surprised to find I had an ally, I nodded but did not answer. Yet the thought that Loic might reject me only added grief to grief.

Jura slammed the walls angrily. She repeated what Jontay had said. "Jival has no sense of propriety! She should have known to keep quiet. She has caused you great harm by speaking this news."

"An Arhe should not have one so tactless and ignorant among her personal servants," the Third Wife said, smirking.

"Depart, whore!" Jura removed a tiny dagger from her gyuilta belt and held it before the Third Wife's face. "Go now! If you wish to live, hide yourself away in your son's rooms. You wished to create a childless future for Satha, but perhaps it is you who have created a childless future for yourself. Loic may not consider himself bound by the covenant his father made with Noam. Consider that your son's days here in the land of the living might be coming to a close. "

The Third Wife's eyes widened. "You would not . . . you would not kill Sio?"

Jura sneered, "Did you not consider all aspects of your plan?"

The Third Wife raced through the doors, her gyuilta flying behind her. When taunts on the other side of the door greeted her, I trembled. It seemed that all the world was waiting outside that door.

Mamya Jontay stood staring at the wooden doorway curtain. "We cannot kill the boy. Vendetta would break out. At least we cannot kill him openly."

"Taer's scruples have allowed this foolishness to continue for too long," Jura said. "We should have destroyed this viper long before her venom had a chance to strike. Now Loic's heritage is in danger of being taken away. The boy has a battle whether he wishes to fight it or—"

"And yet—" Mamya Jontay interrupted her.

"And yet?" Mam asked.

"Noam's battle is not with Loic but with Taer. When elephants battle the little ants are trampled. Loic, poor boy, knows little of battles. He is no warrior, but Noam is. Taer will have to avenge—"

Malana's wailing interrupted. "I don't want Loic to battle Noam." She shook both her hands agitatedly. "And Taer must, must, must, must not battle Noam." She stamped her sandaled feet angrily against the tiles. "No one, no one, no one is to battle no one. I don't want no one to die."

Mam turned her tear-drenched eyes on Malana. "The world is not made up of our wishes, Little Daughter."

"Arhe," Jura said, taking my hand, "rise from the ground. Stand on your feet, Arhe. All in the household have heard of this by now. They await you. Wipe your tears. Let all the Great House know that a true Arhe walks among them."

We were a sad slow procession as we walked through the field toward the inner courtyard. Servants and old warriors silently watched us. Jival had indeed told all the world.

She came running up to Mam. "Arhe Monua, is that the little one you're holding in your arms? Why do you hide it?"

"Be quiet, girl," Mamya Jontay said. "You talk too much."

Jival buried her hands in her face. "Forgive me, forgive me. I should have known. But I was so . . . I didn't think."

"In that you speak truly," Mamya Jontay said, "You never think."

Yet, there was no hiding the dead child. All could see the little hands peeking out from under Mam's gyuilta. All looked on in silence and the silence rolled towards the fields, silencing all it encountered. Grief descended upon the Pagatsu outer courtyard as rain descends upon a mountain peak. Only Mam, Malana and Gala wept. The noblewomen and servants, true Doreni, kept their emotions hidden. Malana's wailing echoed through the garden. Perhaps she wept for Loic. Perhaps for Taer. Perhaps for Noam. Perhaps for the child. I could not tell.

"These things happen, Arhe," Edi said at last. "Don't grieve. Loic is honorable. He will not repudiate you."

Father slowly loosened his turban and walked down the corridor towards the curtained doorway of the longhouse. Then, kneeling in the sand and throwing dust on his head, he sang a lament:

"Many have lost children,

But I have lost my grandchild.

The child would have been a new birth for my people,

But now she is gone unnamed to the land of the dead."

Many have lost children,

But I have lost my grandchild."

While he sang, Ydalle came running to me with a small blue bottle. I recognized it as the bottle Noam had thrown to the ground.

The servants whispered among themselves, "What is that bottle?"

"This is Terbur," Ydalle answered, and all about us groaned loudly.

"Terbur?" Malana asked.

"Terbur," Jura answered, "is a potion used to make one sick unto death, and yet one does not die. This is what the accursed wife used to deceive you, Arhe Satha."

Hearing this, Mam angrily pushed Jival with one hand and continued walking toward the Pagatsu ancestral arbor. When night began to fall, they took the child and hung its little body upon the ancestral grief tree. In its tiny netting, it swung as the ravens devoured and clawed on it. I could not bear to watch, but it was the Doreni way. Soon my eyes closed and I fell asleep out there on the grass.

LOIC
The Desai Counselor

By the fifth day of the mourning period Heldek and the other News Carriers had returned to Chyar from the four directions. The headmen, villagers, and elders of the far-flung clans turned the royal city into a mourning-field as each clan pitched their tents throughout the yellowing fields. On the seventh day, the bleating of the sacrificial lamb echoed through the royal family's ancestral burial field. With thirty-nine spiked thorns made from the memorial tree, they pierced its head, feet, and heart. With hands reddened by the lamb's blood, they smeared Lihu's body. After this they brought a cobra's crushed head and put it under Lihu's feet, then lifted Lihu to the top of the grief tree.

We chanted the words given to us by our prophets: "Lift him, let him draw all creatures to himself." Soon, the birds and all the flying powers of the air alighted upon his corpse and devoured it. What they didn't eat, what fell to the ground or stained the tree, the crawling creatures of the earth gnawed. What those creatures did not consume, the earth swallowed up. Because of the lamb's sacrifice, Lihu's soul would not be in danger of being eaten by the undying worms of Gebelda. He would be able to enter the fields we long for and hunt with the Creator.

Of course I thought of Krika whose soul was unwashed by lamb's blood and whose body burned continually in the eternal trash heap of Gebelda. How my mind lingered on him and my heart grieved about this. I would see Okiak sitting silently among us and even the loveliness of the Kelovet Ibeni mourning ritual could not push hatred from my heart.

"Father," I whispered as we sat in the Pagatsu encampment that made up such a tiny part of the large circle surrounding the Matchless Family's ancestral tree. "Within my heart a deep grief holds sway. I cannot—"

"Lihu's death is strange and unexpected," he interrupted me. "Such deaths often create great grief."

"It is not Lihu's death that makes me mourn."

"Perhaps you're lonely for your wife." He shaded his eyes from the mid-afternoon sun. "Separation and death are very much alike. I myself often experienced separation from my wife as a kind of death." The yellowed grass and the faded flowers surrounding us only added to my feeling that all the earth was dying. "Or perhaps you grieve for our land. A prince's death—one so young!—often causes one to think of greater things. Moreover, you haven't eaten. The grain-eating rite lasts this week only. Jaguar understands your illness and has excused you from eating but he can offer you no substitute."

"I need no substitute, Father. I am a warrior and can endure many things."

"Even so, fasting is difficult and often causes the mind to turn in on itself." He tapped my stomach. "In a week, when vegetables can be taken, perhaps this grief will leave you."

I looked about at the thousand clans of all the three tribes. "I hope so, Father. Now there is such a dread within my soul—I sense destruction, as if something greater than Lihu's life has come to an end. But perhaps you're right. A prince's death and a nation's collective grief cuts deep."

Father gestured across the campsite. "Look around you. Not one eye is dry."

"The cold blue eyes of the Angleni ambassadors are," I said, indicating a tall pink-faced man with long yellow hair. "That courtier over there. He feigns tears. I can see his heart, Father. He thinks our lives and our deaths of no importance. Strange, then, that they eat continually at Jaguar's communal table and travel here and there with the Matchless Family yet can remain so unmoved—"

Father tilted his head towards a dark-haired Angleni man whose clothing was like ours and yet not. "That one cries."

I almost laughed. The man's clothing was badly coordinated. A native inhabitant of our land would have known how to wear apparel from any tribe without accidentally aligning himself with any clan. The stranger wore feathers like the southern Doreni clans, tattoos like those the Ibeni mountain clans wore, an embroidered vest that wrongfully proclaimed him to be a member of the Salt Sea Ibeni and a gyuilta with Theseni fringe. Yet, ridiculous though his hodge-podge clothing was, he wept. I saw his heart then, and indeed it was a kind and sorrowful heart.

"True, Father," I said. "Yesterday when Butterfly was removed from being First Queen, and the hereditary pearl necklace from Lihu's neck was put around the neck of Sweet-as-Jasmine's older son, he alone—of all the Angleni courtiers—wept."

"Butterfly has been First Queen for these twenty years. It will be difficult for one so used to preeminence to accept her new position, but removal is necessary. Her son is dead and no longer First Prince. Sad it was to see High Counselor Noni remove the pelu from his sister's head. Doubtless this is another cause of your dread. Grief added to grief." He leaned low and whispered to me. "Yet I find myself wondering: Did you see how the Angleni courtiers showed such great deference to Sweet-as-Jasmine? They did not do so with Butterfly. Apparently, they find a Doreni queen's skin color more palatable."

"I, too, observed that. Moreover, my heart sees the Angleni would much prefer having White Star as Queen, for she is Ibeni and lacks the Doreni eyes."

We spoke no more of the Angleni, however, because our heart was on greater matters: Lihu's very sudden death.

As the sun set on the tenth day, as the official mourners of the Kaythra clan danced and wailed, their embroidered clan colors swirling about them, the captains of fifties, hundreds and thousands presented themselves to the king. Noam was present among them. He bowed low before Jaguar, who extended his arm to him.

Noam approached the king's high seat and the king leaned his head on Noam's shoulder. They stood afar off, speaking words I could not hear. After they finished speaking, instead of returning to the Therpa encampment, Noam walked towards the Pagatsu clan formation.

I assumed the king had sent him to my father with a message. When he came face-to-face with Father, he indicated with a military gesture that he had something private to say to him.

Father walked with him to the edge of the Pagatsu formation. They spoke long, and although I tried to see into their minds, my gift failed me. I saw only that the attitude of my father's body changed and that his hand grasped the hilt of his sword. Noam laid his hand on Father's as if to say, *not here.*

When my father returned, his countenance had changed.

"What news is it, Father?" I asked. "I had not seen Noam among this vast multitude of people. Has he just arrived?"

"He was late in arriving," he said. "But that is nothing that concerns you."

My heart sensed falseness in those words. "Are you telling me the truth, Father?" I asked. "I cannot see your mind."

He only answered, "I speak the truth, my son."

After the nightly ritual was finished, Father sat cross-legged for hours, saying nothing to me.

At nightfall I returned from speaking to Pantan just as an unknown Ibeni clan began singing a mourning song for Lihu:

"Brown and black bands
Striped against the sky.
Has the prince died?
Turn back, oh Time.
Oh Time, roll backward,
So we can dance again with our lost prince."

"How true it is, Father, that we cannot roll time backwards!" I sat beside him in our tent. "Yet, although I grieve, I don't want time to turn back at all. Except, perhaps, to bring Krika back again. But if Krika had been alive, would I have journeyed to the market that day and met my wife? What do you think, Father? Perhaps we were destined for each other and would have met soon enough, but—" I noticed his quietness and became ashamed of my selfish conversation. "Forgive me, Father. Something oppresses your mind, and here I sit—"

"It is nothing, my son."

"What troubles your heart, Father? Did Noam say something to you?"

"Noam spoke only of . . . a broken truce."

"The Angleni break all truces, I hear." I eyed him warily. "Is that why he was late arriving? A broken truce?"

"That is what he told the king."

He seemed so lost in thought that I found myself asking, "Father, I think you must grieve for the Third Wife as I grieve for Satha. How sad and strange it must be for you, to need to touch such an unworthy woman."

"Taer!" A female voice shouted outside our tent. "I want a word with you."

"It's Puhlya," Father said. But he didn't immediately rise.

"Puhlya? The woman who sits on the king's council and is always in his presence? The woman who kept staring at me? Why is she even here? A woman? And such an unpleasant one."

"She's a Beloved Woman of the Desai. As for her being here, customs don't apply to her."

"I'm waiting," the woman's grating voice sounded again. "Taer!"

I almost laughed. "For a diplomat, she's very bossy, isn't she?"

He stood up, but still he lingered. "I suppose such power can make any woman bossy."

"Ask her why she kept staring at me. Does she always stare at people like that? Tell her I'm not interested in her dragging me off to an assignation. Tell her I'm married to one prettier and better-behaved than she."

"Puhlya's not one for assignations. Contrary to the stories Jontay has filled your heart with, not every woman stares at a man to lust after him in her heart." He tousled my hair and yanked my braid. "Besides, who are you to talk? You yourself have often stared at others in much the same way she stared at you."

His words surprised me. "I have?"

"More often than I can say." He picked up his riding gyuilta and flung it about his shoulders.

"I must work on not staring, then," I said.

He was about to answer when Puhlya called his name again. Father closed his eyes tightly. This time her voice boomed against the buckskin doors of our tent, shaking it. "Before you come to meet me, return your son's dagger to him. It isn't yours, nor is its enemy your enemy."

Surprised, I glanced at Father. "You have my dagger? Why? Why would Satha's gift interest you? And how did this hag know you had it?"

Unspeaking, he removed the dagger from his boot and handed it to me without an explanation.

He left the tent without answering. In the darkness, Father and Puhlya spoke long and gestured passionately, angrily. Father's agitated movements only disturbed me even more. Dread piled onto more dread. She left quickly but not before ordering seven of Jaguar's guards to surround Father's tent. They remained with us until the twenty-one days were ended and sat among us during the feast. During that time, Father and Pantan whispered together with worried faces, yet never once did they tell me their hearts.

SATHA
Grief Upon Grief
The Selling and Storing Moon
Second Harvest Moon

A week after my child died, I dreamed of a large wicker cage. Shaped like a human body, it was long and wide but broken and shattered. Inside a fiery bird fluttered and pushed against its walls trying to escape. At last, the cage broke and the bird flew free.

When I awoke, I thought the dream spoke about the dead child. Indeed, I hoped it did because among our people there was a saying:

"Troubles often follow each other
Traveling hand in hand in hand
Like careless children
Mindful only of their own journey
They skip and hop along the road
Never caring for the grass they trample."

I woke that morning, the dream on my mind, hoping this last sorrow had walked a solitary road, that the death of my child was a friendless grief with no companions. Nevertheless, I was afraid and filled with some nameless dread. I dragged myself from my bed and peered toward the bright sun with trepidation, fearing some looming, terrifying, unknown thing.

On that morning, news came from afar that my sister had died. My father, perhaps hoping to alleviate our family's grief, had sent gold quixas to my sister's husband's clan. He had offered to buy Alima back from her husband. Too late we discovered she had died. Surprisingly, my heart grieved. I had thought my heart had grown cold, but I wept.

I comforted my parents: "This is what the dream spoke of: Alima's freedom. This is our family's last sorrow and it has come and gone.

Surely, only good can follow our steps now." But Mam ran weeping to her rooms.

The next day Father woke to find Mam's cold lifeless body in their bed. My heart ripped, from the top to the bottom. Some said Mam died of grief, but others said Okiak's spirits killed her. Whatever the reason, she was dead. Father, too, seemed to die. Yes, although he lived, breathed, and walked among the living, all could see that death had already marked him. In time, he too would die.

Our prophets often said that one dream can have many meanings. In the case of that dream, it spoke to me of my own future but it was also my family's parting communication to me. I became sickly after that—sick in mind as well as body—because I no longer had Mam to guard and to protect me.

LOIC
Hard News
The Selling and Storing Moon
Second Harvest Moon

On the twenty-second day the funeral ended. Father and I prepared to leave. Puhlya approached us, barefoot.

"Son of the Wind," she shouted to me, as she drew near. Stout she was, with a body as thick as an Ibeni totem pole. Her long black hair trailed along the ground. She lifted her right hand and with one movement, the dust our horses' hooves kicked up separated before her. "Are you Desai, younger brother?"

"My mother was Desai." I looked at my father, wondering what the strange woman wanted from me.

"You don't behave like Desai!" she shouted back.

"How can I behave like them if I don't walk with them? For reasons I don't know, the two clans to which I belong avoid each other. I therefore 'behave' like a Pagatsu, and it is the Pagatsu who will honor, teach or avenge me."

She approached me and her hand grasped Cactus's reins. "Pagatsu you may seem. But you are Desai." She squinted into the sun. "But perhaps I am wrong. If you were Desai, you would not haste homeward when you have unfinished matters here to attend to." She whirled around and shook her hand at Father. "And you, Treads Lightly, remember what I've told you. Keep out of this matter. Although this grief began with you, it's no longer yours to repair."

"What matters, Father?" I asked.

"Waihai!" Puhlya shouted before I could answer. "The Desai are deeply divided about you, Younger Brother! I have taken your side, but if you continue to ask Treads Lightly what you should already know . . . I can't continue to speak up for you!"

"Older Sister, I don't need defending. Nor do I concern myself with the opinions others may have about me."

"Don't you?"

"From what I've heard you people are prophets and shamans and it is your ignoble occupation to walk the world saying cryptic things to people. You, woman, seem to be a typical example of that type. Go somewhere else and mutter your puzzles to people who care about such things. I have my life to attend to."

"Younger Brother," Jura's youngest son called out to me, "do you answer the king's counselor in such a rude manner?"

"I answer all who mutter and peep and read stones in this manner."

"Ah! An arrogant one!" Puhlya cried. "It is as the prophecies declare. But be careful, Younger Brother, who you are arrogant toward. The cause of your deep grief is here, although he flees before you even now. He is the one you should hate, not me. Grief will meet you soon. When it meets you, be strong."

"Older Sister, I am always strong."

Her laughter sounded like thunder rolling over many waters. "Be loving then."

"That I also am."

"Kwelku. Worship, lust and duty will do no good for Satha."

She was the king's counselor and older than I was, yet I could not help but dismiss her rudely. But Father's attitude puzzled me. He neither rebuked me nor hastened our horses in our homeward journey. He sat on his stallion, as still and silent as a hushed sea.

"Puhlya, I have a new wife waiting for me to return. I don't want my mind preoccupied with enigmas when I see her. Why don't you spirit-mutterers ever speak plainly?"

"I do not speak to the spirits, I speak to the Creator. Don't you know the Scriptures of your people? I mean the words recorded by the Desai clan, not the tainted Scriptures the other Doreni—like you Pagatsu—use."

I shrugged. Such shrugging was impolite in those days.

She disregarded it. "In past times, the Wind told our people—the Doreni—that he had made three types of people in the earth. To one tribe, and one tribe alone, he gave his True Law and his Great Book. He gave it to them, to show them how difficult it was to worship him. He hoped to show them the uselessness of their own righteousness that they might seek him with a humble heart."

"This I know. Tell me what I don't know."

"The other tribes he allowed to create their own laws. But the foolish hearts of these tribes were darkened and they worshiped mere spirits and shadow gods, and forgot him entirely. Yet, he loved them and winked at their errors, for he knew they often tried to do what was right in their hearts. Many truths from the Lost Book are found in the beliefs, sayings, and songs of many tribes, but the uncorrupted truth is found in the Lost Book and there is no error in it. Our prophets state that the Wind has appointed a fierce and greedy people to bring it to us."

"This, too, I know. We Doreni belong to one of these tribes. As do the Theseni, the Ibeni and all nations we war or bargain with."

"But there is a third people—"

"This, too, I know . . . the Called-Out Ones."

"Yes. The Called-Out Ones belong to all tribes and to no tribes. They are a tribe and clan unto themselves, the Creator's own people, people he created to be loved by him, people to whom he has imputed lamb's blood. When the Called-Out Ones read the book, they will plainly hear the words of He Who is the Desire of All Nations."

From the corner of my eye, I spied Okiak riding hastily up to my side. "Curious as always, old man?" I asked. "Even about things that are none of your business."

"None of her words will miss my ears," he said. "Yes, Loic knows of this tribe. Blessed are they to be so favored by the Creator. But what are they to him?"

She answered his words but looked directly at me. "Loayiq is his name. Not Loic. Not 'The Light is coming' but 'The Light has come.' Loayiq is Called-Out. He and Satha are fated to bring the Lost Book to our people. They and they alone will be trusted with interpreting it. The Bringers of the Book are destined to rule and to destroy our people, yet after they fade, we will shine at last, because our light will have come."

"Many in your clan don't believe that Loic is the true interpreter," Okiak challenged her. "They believe instead he will destroy us."

"Their interpretation is wrong. They're not as wise as I am."

Okiak exchanged a quick knowing glance with Father, but I could only laugh. "Do you think I am so stupid as to see myself as a destined prophet? Woman, fools who believe themselves favored of the Wind often fall into evil and presumption."

"Is that something your Mamya told you?"

"Mamya's plain-speaking is better than your cryptic prophecies!"

"Perhaps I am indeed wrong," she said, then turned and walked away, her scarlet gyuilta blowing about her in the wind. Glad I was of that, for she had begun to make me angry. Our Lost Book. What did it have to do with me?

The sun had begun to set as we rode toward the Golden House. Many times had I ridden homeward—from the Nadam games, from travels to outlying Pagatsu households—but never had such joy stirred in my heart upon returning, nor such dread. I galloped fast, outpacing my father and the minor heads of our household, about ten horse-lengths. The unfurled standards upon the ramparts were like gracious hands urging me home. Tired though I was from the long ride, I longed for Satha's smile to wipe away all the sorrows and confusions of the past weeks.

I reached the entrance gates of the outer courtyard and Malana came out to greet me. She ran swiftly, yet I could sense that some grief caused her heels to stumble because she didn't leap as high as she was wont to.

"Have you been weeping, Malana?" I asked, reining in Cactus and looking at Father behind me. "What? None of the silly songs you always sing at my return?"

She lifted my hand from the reins and touched it to her eyes that were drowning in tears.

"Little Mother rebuked you again, has she?" I asked. "I warned you to be careful with her. But hasn't Satha protected you in my absence?"

Before she could answer, Yiko and Little Mother came running through the gates of the inner courtyard, followed by the servants and the noblewomen. I searched for Satha but she was not among them.

Doubt nagged at my heart because Father lingered so purposely behind me. I dismounted Cactus and called Yiko to take his reins. He took them but instead of leading Cactus to the stables, he didn't move.

"Is all well?" I asked, and without knowing why I dreaded his answer. "Is it well with my wife? Is it well with the child? Are you yourself well?"

He didn't answer and the servants and noblewomen stood silent. Little Mother stood among them, her face buried in her hands, and Ydalle was wringing her hands—unusually silent.

I called out to Father, "How strangely they all behave!"

Father glanced at Okiak, who began to approach me. How could I not feel that some disaster had befallen the Golden House, or Satha, or my life? Okiak was a man to whom the spirits told secrets, and if some disaster had occurred, he would have known it. But as he rode toward me, his face was a spy's face, giving no information to me.

"Where's Satha?" I grabbed Little Mother's hand so tightly, she winced and pushed me away.

"The Arhe is in her rooms," Okiak said. "The spirits say she's well."

Ydalle, tears streaming down her face, added, "She's locked herself away."

"Locked herself away? Why?" For some reason, I thought to search the crowd for New Mother. "Where's New Mother Monua?"

At this Ydalle and Malana held each other's hands and the female servants and noblewomen all began weeping.

Chills like the fingers of ghosts crawled along my arms.

Okiak questioned them, as if he already knew the answer to his question. "Has New Mother died?"

His question was met with increased wailing. Surprise flickered on Father's face. Yet, I could see in his mind that more grievous news awaited me. I thought, *How can he seem both surprised and unsurprised at once?*

"This death is sudden," I said, looking about the grieving faces for anyone who seemed inclined to speak to me. I found none. "New Mother was not old. Has her body been placed in one of the shrines? Or has she been taken to her ancestral lands?"

"Yoran brought dust from their old place to help her ancestors claim her," Little Mother answered. "Arhe New Mother lies in the higher hills of our compound, buried in the Theseni way."

"We will mourn her in the Theseni way then," Okiak said.

I had not expected to be so overcome with grief, but I hardly knew what to do. I put one arm around Ydalle, and the other held both Little Mother's hand and Malana's. "Hurry and take me to my wife. I must comfort her." No one moved. I turned to Little Mother. "Little Mother, all this weeping, all this grief—it's too much for me. I know that New Mother was your true friend. You had, at last, a companion, one who would worry with you about small and great things. But why weep like this? Haven't you told me that death is always unexpected? That death is common to all? This was how you comforted me when Krika died and when you spoke to me about my mother. I know that New Mother's death follows hard upon Lihu's, but for that very reason—" Tears stung my eyes. "Look how much we loved her! How can such a one not enter the fields we long for? Show me now, where Satha is. Is she in the marriage quarters? Or has she covered herself in the mourning tent? Lead me to her."

Still no one moved. No foot stirred. "I am losing my patience!" I shouted, leaving the group huddled together in the outer courtyard and walking into the inner courtyard of the longhouse.

The group ran after me but did not disperse. They stood looking at Father and at Okiak and at me.

"Soon the balconies and balustrade will overflow with ribbons," I shouted, but I sensed I was shouting not to comfort them but to push my own growing dread away. "The house will be filled with mandrake, oyster shells, and pomegranates to celebrate our child. It's sad the child will not know New Mother, but the birth will be some comfort to us in our time of sorrow. Little Mother, you too will be especially happy. Because a healthy child will put the clan's doubts about me to rest."

I had not finished before the curtained doorways were pushed aside and my dear wife entered. My heart leaped with joy to see her, but the servants surprised me by forming a half-circle protective barrier between her and me.

The servants' strange behavior dampened my joy. I pushed through them towards my wife and wiped away the tears streaming down her sunken cheek. How lovely she looked even in grief! "Don't sorrow," I began, but then I noticed her stomach. It was flatter than it had been. "Is the child . . . ?"

"She was born dead," Little Mother answered, racing up to my side.

"She? I asked. "The child was a girl?" Many children I have now, but that first unseen one will always have a special place in my heart. I grieve even now.

As I stood there, I could only think, *Those vengeful spirits are behind this. But how?* I tried to search the hearts of those around me, but the undependable gift betrayed me. "Has she been placed in the ancestral tree?" I asked my wife, hungering for her voice.

Ydalle started wailing again, mucus falling all over her face. "How sadly that little bundle hung!"

Little Mother added, "The death of New Mother caused Satha to lose the child. It is often that way. I, too, lost a child because of grief. When the news runner came to tell us my husband had been killed."

Although the gift had failed me earlier, it did not fail me then. It was all too clear that Little Mother was lying. And when Yiko added, "Yes, yes, these things happen," the sense that I was being lied to was too strong.

"Yiko," I said, "You were never good at lying."

Little Mother's eyes signaled Father as they often did whenever she desired to speak to him in private.

I put my arms on the stomach of my dear wife and again wiped the tears from her face.

Then Satha spoke. "Seared Conscience has been here," she said, her voice a mere whisper, anxious and muffled.

I looked at Father, remembered Puhlya's words. My chest tightened.

"He's promoted himself from shame to shame," Yiko began, but before he finished speaking, Jival had thrown herself on the ground in front of me.

"It was all my fault, Young Chief," she shouted, tears streaming down her face. "Forgive me! Seared Conscience deceived me. Forgive me, Young Chief. Forgive me. If you must, destroy me, rather than Satha. I was the fool who should have known better."

The hands and fingers I had scarred in Lihu's ceremony were still unhealed, but that fleshly pain was nothing compared to the stinging grief I endured as the truth slowly unfolded itself before me. "Seared Conscience was here?" I asked, growing increasingly more impatient at the nods, sobs and wails.

"What . . . why . . . ? But . . . Jival! Stop clawing the ground like that. What—" I was stumbling over my words. I was like water frozen during the cold moons, stagnant like lowland lakes after the leaves have fallen into them. The future I had built in my mind fell like a tower overwhelmed by siege. The flowing blue silk gyuilta of the Third Wife appeared through the entranceway. How triumphant her smile was! The servants seemed to be even more disdainful of her, as if she was to be blamed for Satha's distress. All the while, the Third Wife smirked until her cruel grin transformed itself into spiteful laughter.

Satha's gift still lodged in my bootleg. I wanted to make its new sheath the Third Wife's evil heart, but like a ruined peasant watching his fields being plundered by invaders, I was too stunned to move or think. Satha turned her eyes away towards the interior corridor. Nwaha who was hiding behind the door seemed too grief-stricken to speak. Father was also silent.

My heart tried to calm itself. Even with Satha standing there silent and the weeping Jival clinging to my feet. I turned to Father. "What was it the Desai counselor told you when she came to our tent? What broken truce did Noam tell you about?"

Father's eyes avoided mine, then glanced piteously at Satha. They seemed unable to find a resting place. At last they turned toward the ground where Jival knelt, head bowed, on the tile. My feet were heavy; unable to move however much I tried to lift them. I stood frozen until my wife turned away and ran from the room, her brown cotton gyuilta falling from her shoulder.

At last, my feet stumbling, I followed after my wife. Outside her chamber, I laid my hand on the curtain of the door. "My wife, open to me."

Slowly, she pushed the threshold curtain aside, but her eyes avoided mine.

My own eyes also wished to avoid hers and the sorrow in them but I forced them to look at her. "My wife of the blood covenant," I said. "Please. Remember there is a full marriage and a blood covenant between us. I will never leave you."

She stood trembling before me, wet brown eyes studying me. She did not seek my touch, nor did my hands seek her hands and her face, so fearful was I of touching one so deep in grief. Long we stood facing each other and then I lifted my hand to stroke her hair, which was unbraided and hung unkempt around her face.

"My husband," she said, pushing my hands away, "I don't have a Doreni mind. Nor is my mind like my mother's was, always seeing schemes. I did not understand how subtle your people are. My stupidity has brought us much grief."

I found myself answering—and I regret it even now but I could not stop my mouth from speaking my heart, "Didn't I tell you to be wise and careful when dealing with Noam or the Third Wife? Did I not say to you, 'do not speak to her,' and 'do not trust him'?"

My heart burned against Noam and the Third Wife only, but my words were aimed at Satha. She pushed my hand away as if my words were daggers. All at once, I stopped speaking although my mouth was as yet unemptied of bitter words. Afraid I could not control the angry flood that threatened to pour out, I hastened away to my rooms.

That night Jival appeared at the threshold of my room. How happy I was to see her, for I believed my dear wife had sent her to call me. But Satha had not sent her to me.

"Jival?" I said, stepping aside to allow her to enter. "Is all well with my wife? Did she send you here?"

"All is well, Young Chief," she said. "The Arhe has not sent me here. I have come begging forgiveness for the evil I've allowed to come to you."

"The innocent should not bear the guilt of evil people. You didn't know Noam's plans. My wife didn't know either. Tell my wife this. My bitterness made me sin against her, but my anger was not directed at her. I'm afraid all the words in my heart should not have been spoken. Speak to her for me."

She pushed aside her long unbraided hair and began unlacing her tunic. Her breasts, pale and bare, lay before me. How lifeless and lacking in life they looked compared to the rich brown of Satha's skin!

I brought the edges of her tunic together. "Jival, I've seen the kindness of your heart and the generosity you have shown my brother. There is no need to ask forgiveness from me. Perhaps from my wife, but not from me. I thank you also for your desire to comfort me. But I have no power over my body, my love, or my heart. Through the covenant, they all belong to my wife. And I have no wish that it be otherwise. Go now, lest the other servants see you here, and tell Satha of this." My words seemed to me like the words of one who had read too many Ibeni poets and not the words of one who truly knew how to respond to all that was happening around me, and yet there was truth in them.

That night my dreams were filled with Noam's blood. Hatred dirtied my heart. Only Satha's love could wash it clean. I awoke and went to her rooms, passing through her curtains without asking for permission to enter. She was lying in bed and looked up when I entered. Then, as if my father or Little Mother had seen my journey to my wife's rooms and had ordered it, Gala appeared with sweetened mint tea and pressed figcakes for us.

"All the sweetness is gone out of my life now," I said, after Gala had left. "All future sweetness is gone also unless your happiness returns. Remember that I have promised our fathers that I would take neither second wife nor concubine, that I would have one wife only. Do not fear that I will ever leave you."

She said nothing, but picked up one of the figcakes. My hand found her arms, and gently stroked upward, hugging her tightly about the shoulder and neck and the small of her back. Suddenly, she rose from the bed, turned and glared at me, her face stern and hard.

"The servant girls can give you all the sweetness you need," she said, throwing the flatcake at me. Then she removed my mother's nose-ring and tossed it at me.

I remembered Monua's fierceness and all I had heard about the temper of Theseni women.

"Has someone told you about Jival?" I asked. "Why would I want Jival or any of the servant girls? I never wanted them before. Why would I want them now? If it weren't for you and your love I would have lived here alone and friendless with no ally or true friend."

She looked past me at the doorway. "When I was told that Jival had left your rooms unlaced, at first I did not believe it. But I had all night to think about it. Jival is so weak and in need of love and affection you would not worry about allowing her into your bed. You knew she would not judge you."

I held my breath, unsure where bitterness and her thoughts were leading her. Already, her words were like a mallet and my heart a cracked tile beneath it. "Why should I need a woman to praise my lovemaking?" I managed to ask. "Were there not wild nights enough for you when we were first married? Did we not agree with Little Mother that softer play would be necessary when she said your womb was weak and would not keep the child if we were not careful?"

"I'm not speaking of that." She approached me, walking around the end of the bed to do so. "Have you not asked me 'why should you want me? A mere boy? One who forced his love upon you? A boy who falls sick and wets himself?'" She pointed to the curtain. "You have always asked this, although I assured you that I loved you. But you have never believed me. I suspected you thought I married you to free my parents from their debt. Or because I myself hated poverty. But you have never loved me. How could you? You never trusted me to love you or trusted yourself to be loved! Marriage to me was torment and now, you are able to free yourself from this torment by ridding yourself of an ugly and poor woman who was the only woman you thought you could have."

Words—great verses from the Ibeni poets—failed me. I thought, *Many poems have I read, but now I understand with my truest heart what those love songs were truly about. That one can love and love and yet not be understood by the woman who holds one's heart. That words cannot show the truth or depth of any love.*

Again, the words that I spoke were not the ones that lay in the deepest part of my heart. Rising, I crushed the tossed flatcake, grinding it into the tile. I picked up my mother's nose-ring and held it before Satha's face. "In the future, your servant girls will supersede you."

I left her room, angry and bitter. Hanging my head in sorrow, but burning within from rage. How could she speak of me as someone bound by my illness? How could she not see my love? Why did she see me as a shamed little boy no one else could love?

From that day, I began roaming the inner and outer courtyards like a lost soul forbidden to enter the fields we long for. Whenever Satha stepped outside her room, how my body shook when I saw her in the family courtyard! But we always stood far apart, neither of us walking toward each other.

At mealtime in the longhouse, we sat together but did not speak. She lifted a figcake to my lips and served me, and I ate what she placed before me. But no words escaped our mouths. When I realized how Satha avoided the ancestral arbor, I began to spend my time there. I would sit staring at the little netting of bones as it swung. I would haunt myself with worries about that unborn unnamed one who—because she had not breathed the breath of life—could not be named. This was our belief in those days. Those who had died without breathing the earth's air had no human soul.

Father approached me one day as I sat there. "Loic," he said, "go to your wife."

"I'm grieving," I said. "I can't go to her."

"The child did not attain its first year. One day of mourning is more than enough and the Theseni mourning period is also finished. You're grieving as if it will become your lifelong occupation. Accept the sorrows of life. You will go to join the child, but she cannot return here to be with you."

"I will not disturb Satha, Father. And who are you to speak about the sorrows of life? Have you ever lost a child and a mother at the same time?"

"True, it is a hard thing to lose a mother but the old always die and you and Satha can create another child."

I searched my heart for another excuse. "Father, are you asking me to lie with a woman knowing she's tainted? Have you—who should know better—forgotten that custom forbids couching with one whom another has touched? Such a coupling—unless the woman is an honorable widow, a captive servant or a whore—is shameful. Or do you think I have less honor than you do?"

He put his hand on my shoulder and didn't hide his impatience. "Since birth, you've discarded one taboo after another. But now you're making yourself out to be a follower of old customs? Surely, this cannot be the reason you've put such distance between you and your wife? I don't believe it."

I lied, "It is the reason, Father."

He knelt beside me and his eyes, full of worry and questions, peered into mine. "My son, don't wrong Satha. She's not like the Third Wife. This evil pounced on her as a tiger does its prey. Satha didn't know she was Noam's quarry." He stood up and looked toward the barracks where the old comrades lived. "As for this custom of ours, it's time it was done away with. The war has made such doctrines questionable at best and cruel at worst. Many broken-hearted husbands would gladly return to erring wives and their wives would gladly have them. I'll speak to Jaguar about modifying it."

"Jaguar may change the doctrine if he wishes, but the Pagatsu—"

"What do the Pagatsu matter? You, my son, *are* the Pagatsu. What you decree they will accept. If Jaguar and I uphold your decision, what can they do?"

I saw then how much my father loved me. Despite the many lovelorn widows and grieving comrades who would have been glad to see the custom go, he had never petitioned Jaguar to change it. But because of me, he was ready to bury that age-old tradition. I sat beside him, my arms aching to hold him and to tell him about my argument with Satha. Yet, how could I admit to him that he had been right? That the woman I had so hastily married had not learned to love me? That she had not understood my heart?

I turned my face again toward my daughter's bones. "Father, why didn't you fight Noam when he betrayed you?" My hair was wet with tears and I pushed it from my face. "Even if Jaguar is war-weary, even if you feared a clan war. Jaguar might have forgiven you. You could have killed Noam by stealth if you wished. Then my daughter would be alive, and my life would not be as it is now."

He sighed. "Blood-weariness is something few can understand."

"Perik has seen blood flowing like rivers and corpses raised like mountains and he's not wearied by it. Are you so weak that bloodshed has wearied you?"

He half-smiled. "Perhaps."

"Even so. You seemed ready to kill him before councilor Puhlya warned you. Why didn't you tell me about the cruelty Noam had prepared for me? I would have followed after him and killed him. My shame among my clan would not now be doubled. The falling sickness and now this! Father, it is hard to bear! Oh that Noam had killed me! I would not know the sorrow of the death of my firstborn, or the death of love."

"Your love has not died. You're—"

"Don't tell me what I'm thinking, Father!" I could hardly hold back my tears. "You don't know my heart."

His face had grown red with anger. "Go to your wife, Loic. This self-pity of yours will allow Noam's ploy—a war strategy used when war was not declared—to tear your heart and take the headship from you. You do understand that if—"

"Be silent, Father! You're telling me nothing new."

He began walking away. "Since you're so knowledgeable, you know what you must do. Sio is not my son, but often he acts with more honor, with more maturity, with more fierceness than you do."

He continued toward the family quarters, leaving me alone to my tears. When he was a long way off, and my tears had begun to freely flow, he turned suddenly towards me and shouted, "Don't sit there like a petulant woman! Go to your wife. But first, take a bath."

I disobeyed him. Indeed, I continued avoiding Satha. Soon I began to notice that all in the Golden House—the servants, the retainers, the old soldiers, the noble women, and the elders—avoided me or trembled if forced to be in my presence. I sensed they thought I was like Muran Volcano, always ready to erupt. One day the eruption came.

Yiko had brought mukal—it had become my sole comfort—to my room. As he poured it, I grew angry with him.

"You should have known what would happen," I shouted. "Why did you allow Noam to wander the house as he pleased?"

Satha's dagger was by my bed. Suddenly I took hold of Yiko, pushed him to the ground, and cut off his right ear. He howled in pain, startling me from my anger. When I saw his blood on my hands, I remembered again why the servants long ago had given me the love-name of Loicuyo. *Wildfire.* The memories of my childhood anger were hard to bear.

Father heard what I had done to Yiko and called me into the courtyard. After tying me naked to the ancestral totem, he whipped me fiercely, not heeding Little Mother's cries. Seven times, with reeds from the Precious River, he struck me. When he had finished, I picked up my clothes and walked to my room. I hardly cared. Such a whipping was necessary to restore order, to show he honored his servants. However, he had stoked the wildfire within me and it could not be quenched. It burned against Satha and my Father, against Noam and the Third Wife, against Little Mother and the servants, against myself.

The next day Father came to my door and rebuked me harshly. His words I will not repeat, for even now they stab my heart, but he ordered me to follow him to my wife's rooms. I did, and when we arrived, he called Satha to the entrance.

She pulled the curtain aside, avoiding my eyes. "Yes, New Father." Her voice sounded as distant as the hooting of a forest owl. She glanced at me but her eyes kept their secret. As for me, I felt neither pity nor love for her.

"I'm war-weary," Father said, shaking his head. "As you both know, old soldiers hate losing battles. These strategies used by the Third Wife to destroy my legacy will succeed if you avoid each other. Loic has promised not to marry another. If you do not befriend each other, you will remain childless."

He waited for us to answer him, but we didn't answer.

"Loic," he said, at last and how slowly he spoke. "Can you not see what will happen? My son, you know the elders love you but consider you weak. Since your youth when the falling illness struck you, they have wanted you to show yourself as a true warrior. It is not the disaster that they will question, but your reaction to it. Although you've never prized the headship, I have reserved it for you. I don't want you to lose what is rightfully yours. Appear strong and the Pagatsu will follow you to the ends of the earth. As for your honor, it is not lost. Satha's virtue and Noam's cruelty are both well known. If you think your honor is lost, do some great exploit and find your honor again, but stop weeping. Stop walking about the house wailing like an Ibeni from some ignoble clan. Do you wish the servants to speak of your weakness in the streets?"

At this, Satha burst out laughing. "Obviously, New Father, you don't know our servants well. They've probably sounded all this business throughout all of Jefra." Bitter words, but I almost smiled because she had challenged Father.

"I know my servants well enough, Satha," Father said. It was the first time he had ever sounded annoyed with her. "They also know me, and they know what griefs they'll endure if they speak evil against my daughter."

"Kwelku," she said, shrugging. "So you say."

"I do say!" Father answered. "Noam is not one to brag about his deeds—be they good or evil. He still has something of a warrior's heart. Your secret is safe." He held her tear-stained face in his hand. "Your secret is safer than Loic's headship. So then, walk together, be heard playing in the marriage quarters, create more children. If you must pretend, then pretend. Only, do not let the Third Wife win this battle against me."

"Say nothing about the Third Wife!" Satha shouted. "In my dreams I imagine her skinned, scarred, peeled and defiled, lying before base men in the marketplace. No, New Father, I don't care about your wishes or your love for the woman. Well I know my husband cannot harm her because to harm a father's wife means certain death. But her lover defiled me and killed my child; their son could inherit my heritage. Is there nothing you can do about it?"

He walked away without answering her. She and I looked at each other but said nothing. Neither did we couch together.

The next day as I walked across the compound, I saw Satha in the distance beside the rose trellis wall. A shuwa was in my hand. I let it fly. It flew wildly, missing her throat and getting its tip stuck in the latticework of the trellis. I raced toward her, expecting her to flee. She did not. She watched me unflinching, unmoving as I yanked the shuwa from the thorn-covered wall.

"Some man you are!" she said, scorn in her voice. "Yesterday, when I challenged your father to kill the Third Wife, why did you stand there silent?"

"My father will not kill the Third Wife," I answered, beginning to walk away. "Why ask for the impossible?"

"I ask for the impossible if the impossible is the only thing that will satisfy me."

"I don't ask for what I will never get."

"My poor Mam was made to develop a man's will after she married my father. Now it appears as if I must do the same. Is this how a warrior answers Noam's violation? By threatening women? By sleeping with servant girls? By whining and weeping? By not challenging his father? I thought you Doreni were warriors, but the Golden House is ruled by confused men who allow their enemies to trample them."

"Thesenya, you've found your tongue!" I brandished the shuwa before her face. "Be quiet and lose it again! Or my dagger will cut it from you!"

"Why should I fear you? You who cut off the ears of faithful servants and cry and weep like an Ibeni brothel owner who has lost his favorite whore?"

I lunged at her. I was so angry I grabbed her and squeezed her cheek tightly, digging my fingers into her flesh. "You should fear me, Satha, because I am not like my father. I do not tread lightly. Nor will I spend my life pining over a woman so stupid she allows a known villain to rape her? There are ways of getting rid of stupid women."

She raised her hands to strike me but I pushed her hand away.

"Sick and puny thoughts from a sick mind in a puny body. So this is why you sit here like a slave, not venturing forth to avenge me?"

Anger had made her cruel as it had made me cruel. I thought, *Are we on a path with no returning? Will we only become more hardened against each other?*

But although I thought this, I heard myself asking, "Should I wage a clan war because my wife is stupid? Should I fight Noam because of a woman who never really loved me?"

She disdained my tears. "Doreni custom demands you do something to avenge me, despite Jaguar's wishes. Do you remember Archer's Armlet, the great Theseni warrior? He started a clan war over a stupid woman. He was honorable. He wasn't one who wore a jade bracelet either. Just a lowly musician. If my honor is nothing to you, your honor must mean something to you. Or are you as weak as your clansmen think?" Then after giving me a scornful look from head to toe, she turned and walked slowly away.

The next day she rose like one who had risen from the dead and called all the Golden House, including the Third Wife and her son, into the longhouse. I had no desire to go, but in such a matter an Arhe's orders must be obeyed.

SATHA
The Arhe's Challenge

"Are you coming now?" Jival asked, as I prepared to leave my rooms for the longhouse.

I nodded. "Yes. Go and tell the households to assemble in the gathering room. I will arrive soon."

She bowed low—almost too low—and lingered in the doorway.

"Is something keeping you, Jival?" I asked.

"Nothing, Arhe." She glanced at Ydalle, Gala, and Edi, who stood nearby helping me to dress. "It's just that—well, the household will want to know what you wish to speak about."

"They'll find out soon enough, Jival," Ydalle said. "Now go."

Still she did not go, but when Gala asked angrily, "Why do you linger, Jival?" she disappeared through the curtains.

"She's afraid for her neck, Arhe," Edi observed. "Afraid you'll dismiss her and leave her alone in the marketplace. No one around here will hire an Angleni warseed. No woman at least."

"An Ibeni brothel owner might take her in," Gala said.

"Not that one," Ydalle said. "An Ibeni would be the first to see how deceptive she is." She turned to me and finished putting the brooch on my Doreni coif. "I still think it's a bad idea to keep her around. Yes, she might prove to be vindictive and might speak our business in the streets, but who believes warseed?"

I looked wistfully at my flat stomach and pulled the gyuilta over my empty childless arms. "I forgave her because she says she was stupid to believe the Third Wife, but I do not forgive her for going into my husband's rooms unclothed."

"Arhe!" Edi said, chiding me. "I have told you already. The young chief would not betray you."

"Kwelku, Edi," I answered, "but if he has couched with her, do you not think it a sensible idea for me to keep my eye on his favorite?"

"Loic wouldn't couch with that thing, Satha," Ydalle said, sucking at her teeth.

"The boy is mad with love for you, Arhe," Gala answered. Then she added, "I cannot endure this disagreement between you. Can you not see the love he bears you?"

I heard Ydalle groan, and turned to look at her. "Do you not believe he loves me, Ydalle?"

"I believe he loves you. But, like you, I believe he should have defended you. Who cares about Jaguar's war-weariness? I have seen my people, the Kluna, destroyed by the Angleni. I have seen blood and mayhem. If King Jaguar thinks a war between two great clans will cause the Angleni to renew their warfare against us, he should not have made a truce with them in the first place." She tiptoed to the doorway and carefully pulled the curtain aside. "Jival wished to stay with us because she suspects we hide secrets from her, but—"

"Soon she will stop suspecting secrets and conspiracies." I pulled the hood of my gyuilta over my head. "When she wakes or sleeps, whether in the town or in the field, she will not be alone. How can we have secrets against her if she is always with us? Let us keep those we distrust close to us, and let us see if Jival is as innocent as she pretends to be. In the future, she must prove her loyalty to me. Are you ready, then?"

"It is you who must be ready," Ydalle answered. "Can you do it? Can you challenge Loic, Taer and the Third Wife?"

"I can."

Together we left my rooms and entered the longhouse where all the household, including Jival, were assembled to hear my words.

When I entered the longhouse, all eyes turned to look at me. All sat silent, noblewomen and warriors, retainers and servants. My eye fixed on Taer's sword hanging on the wall. I walked to the Third Wife and grabbed her by the hair, pulling her deceitful head backwards. I called out to Loic. "Your dagger, Loic? The one I gave you? Where is it?"

He seemed startled for a moment, then bowed silently, and said it was in his room.

I looked at him, saying nothing.

Silent, he nodded to Yiko, giving him permission to retrieve it. Yiko left and all time stood still as I waited for him to return, holding the Third Wife's hair. She did not struggle. When Yiko returned to the gathering room, he started to approach my husband with the dagger in his hand.

I shouted to him, "I was the one who demanded it. Give it to me!" He did and I held the dagger to the Third Wife's throat. No one approached.

"This woman," I yanked her hair again, "betrayed me. Despite my kindness to her, she searched out my weakness and showed my enemy how to breach my walls. Treads Lightly, you've been patient with her long enough. The punishment for adultery is death. But you have allowed this dead woman to live all these years among you, allowing her corpse to contaminate your house. Have done with it now and kill her!"

My husband's father drew his breath, shook his head. "New Daughter," he said, "I cannot kill her."

"I can," I shouted back. "Let me kill her. Am I not Arhe here?"

"Daughter," my father shouted, his voice hoarse from prolonged weeping. "Although the crime done against you was cruel, don't harm your soul by murdering one whose soul is already dead. Y'wa, the Good Maker—"

"Y'wa be damned," I shouted. "What has he ever done for us? Let me kill her."

"You're too kind-hearted to kill anyone, Daughter."

"You're wrong, Father. I'm not kind-hearted. How can I be kind-hearted when I have no heart, when it's broken to pieces and shattered on the ground? So if I can't kill her, what can I do?" I pulled the sheathed blade across her neck. "Tell me, Treads Lightly, that I might do it. What am I allowed to do? What can I do to her?"

I burst into tears then, and I suppose they expected me to collapse but I didn't. I removed the dagger's sheath and pressed the dagger into the Third Wife's throat. At the same time, Sio's terrified eyes pleaded with me.

"The Arhe is right," Pantan said. "The Third Wife must suffer. But be careful that you avoid war with the Therpas. The Therpas will not fight for this whore's honor, but Noam wears the jade bracelet of his chieftain father. Taer, let the nose of this wicked one be cut off—as is the custom for adulterous wives in some of the western regions. Or let her be placed in the far off edges of Jefra and Rega—"

"No, no, farther than that!" I interrupted him. "As far as Gebelda and farther!"

"The Northern Ibeni clans have a custom," Pantan continued. "Sell her into whoredom and let her whore for her living."

My New Father buried his face in his hands. "Satha . . . Arhe . . . this is not what—"

"New Father!" I shouted back. "You have tolerated and loved this woman long enough. Why do you falter and sit there wavering? The woman does not love you! She has never loved you. She will never love you. Kill her and have done with her."

He raised his hand to silence me, but I would not be silenced. "New Father," I said, "if you are going to speak, you are going to speak only to affirm what I say. Or else, keep silent! I am Arhe here, and even you must listen to me."

"Loic," he said, "let your most faithful servants—those who hate the Third Wife and who cannot be deceived into betraying you—let them take her to the far regions. Leave her only with the rich clothes on her back. Then the people of that place will see that not only was she an adulteress but a stupid woman who didn't prize the fortune of being married to a rich—"

"You have chosen well, New Father," I answered, raising the dagger against the Third Wife's nose. I lowered it, splitting the Third Wife's nose vertically in two pieces. A blood-curdling scream echoed through the longhouse. Another horizontal slice finished the job. Two pieces of tan-colored flesh lay on the ground. The bloodied hands of the Third Wife covered her face. Sio stood beside his mother, his body shaking as he wept. Jival began to walk her hands outstretched to comfort, but I halted her with a pointed finger. Sio's wail had turned my attention toward him.

"As for this son of hers," I concluded, "cast him out too. Let them never set eyes upon each other or on this place again. If you place her in the north, place him in the south. Let him roam the streets begging for his living also. He was not altogether innocent in my downfall."

"He's my son, New Daughter," Father began protesting. "The laws and customs—"

"Your son?" I said, laughing. My voice must have echoed throughout all the courtyards. "Do you really love him? I've seen no such love. If you loved him, you kept it well hidden. And as for him being your son, he is not your son. You have pushed Doreni customs altogether too far. The boy betrayed the wife of your real son! And you want to spare him? How weak you are!"

I turned to my husband. "You're heir to New Father's headship. You can plead for mercy for Sio. Do you plead it?"

Loic seemed to swallow. His eyes darted at his father, at Sio, then at the Third Wife.

"Speak up, coward!" I cried at the top of my voice. "Do you plead for this bastard?"

He bowed his head. "I do not. Let the Third Wife know what her victory over you has cost her son."

Sio clutched his mother's silken gyuilta, and then mine, trembling. But I held the dagger aloft. In one deft move, the only skill I learned in knifework, I had grabbed the child and cut off his right ear. The ear landed in a pool of blood at my feet. "I am not Doreni now. Nor am I Theseni. I am myself and, like all others, I will use the power I have to harm as I have been harmed." I grabbed Sio again and cut off the other ear.

Blood continued flowing from the wound above the Third Wife's sneering lips. Her hands dropped to reveal the mutilated nose. "Taer," she said, "You've long lived married-and-yet-not-married. Now you will be free. I know you and this woman well enough. When I am gone, you will lie with your son's wife because you have always wanted her and because your son has rejected her. "

A gasp arose from everyone in the room. Loic's eyes roamed my New Father's face. It was clear he was wondering if the Third Wife's words were true. New Father, however, looked as if he was only beginning to see how evil the Third Wife was. He shook his head. "The wounded snake can still poison the well before she leaves it."

"Haven't I seen the way you look at her?" she shouted back. "How foul and perverse your own heart is!"

Little Mother stepped into the circle beside me then began walking towards my husband. When she stood near him, she slapped him hard across the face. "Why are you standing there staring out into nothingness as if you believe this whore? My son, don't allow her lies to take root in your heart. Your father doesn't seek your wife for his bed."

"No, I don't believe the Third Wife," he said weakly, but his distrust of his father and distrust of himself was all too apparent.

"Husband," I said, calling to him, "I've seen the way you look at me. You want me. You think I don't want you. How can I accept your love if you do not trust mine? If you think only a poor ugly woman like myself would choose you, what does that imply I am?"

"Satha!" he shouted. "That is not true."

I stretched the bloody dagger toward him. "Kwelku, but if you will avenge me, and return to me, you will prove yourself my true lover indeed. But will a true warrior return to me?"

He took the dagger from my hands and turned to his father. "The world is wide and long, but I will return to you. I will find Noam wherever he hides. Whether in a sanctuary city or in his father's house."

"The Therpas are a powerful clan," New Father said, "and war against Noam, a firstborn, would create war between them and the Pagatsu." He turned angry hurt eyes on the Third Wife. "Nevertheless, let a war council be convened."

The next day, New Father sent runners to the four winds to the dispersed Pagatsu. He also commanded four of his trusted warriors to take the Third Wife and Sio to the streets of a far southeastern city. When they got there, the warriors pushed Sio from the valanku, forcing his mother to watch. Then they rode to the northwestern region where they threw the Third Wife into the streets. Then they returned to the Golden House in Satilo. By then, we had received word from Okiak's spirits that Noam had returned to his homeland.

LOIC
War Council

As Satha spoke to the household elders in the longhouse, a people not her people, I listened with awe and admiration. *What an Arhe is this!* I thought. A woman to send warriors across far seas! The elders, too, seemed to admire her fierceness. Before, they had whispered that she was a Thesenya, an innocent who could not recognize a scheme or an evil plot, but when she spoke—ah yes!—they saw that she was a Doreni Arhe indeed. Here was a woman who could create wars and who was relentless against her enemies.

To see so many warriors, their standards flying in the breeze, arriving at the Golden House emboldened me. A noble and large group, they were. A mighty band that could destroy whole armies. Because I had warred against the spirits since my childhood, they had feared for me, but they had also secretly admired the ferocity of my fight. Yet, because I suffered from the falling sickness, they had also deemed me unworthy of inheriting the clan headship.

While the hundred elders agreed that the Therpas should not be allowed to gloat over their insult to the Pagatsu, there was one question: How could I, who was already at war with the Arkhai and with the falling sickness, avenge myself against Noam without causing war between two such large clans and their allies?

Darkened flecks of blood fell from my dagger's blade as Pantan plunged it into a totem post, signaling the beginning of the war council. The dried blood—the Third Wife's and Sio's—sprinkled to the mosaic tile. He removed the dagger from the totem, and all turned hard eyes to me. I took the weapon, making sure I did not glance at Father or at Satha, who was sitting with the household women beside the walls of the inner court.

Pantan spoke in this manner. "My clansmen, my brothers, many of your wives have given their opinion on this. But their opinions only lead to more confusion. They all agree that Noam should not have raped the wife of one who was not his enemy. They say also that Loic wears the jade bracelet and should be avenged, but here is where the confusion begins. Rape, cruel as it is, is not murder. Should Noam be killed for a rape? Why invite Therpa vengeance—?"

Near the wall, angry women's voices interrupted him "Noam killed the child! Isn't that murder?"

Others shouted, "The child was not yet alive!"

To which the first group responded, "The child would have been alive if Noam had not killed it."

Such a great argument ensued among the women that Pantan raised his hands to silence them. "Aren't you all tired of war and death? I am. Aren't you afraid—as Jaguar is—that while we war among ourselves the Angleni will prey upon us? Let us also remember that Jaguar is grieving for his son. Is there no way of rebuking Noam without causing bloodshed?"

Father answered, "Jaguar is no fool. His spies, no doubt, already know what has occurred here. Even if they are unaware of it, Puhlya knows when the smallest breadcrumb falls on our floors. If this was someone other than Noam who had done this, that rapist would have been exiled to one of the cities of refuge, but Noam is allied both to Third Queen White Star and to Second Queen Sweet-as-Jasmine. Our Matchless King cannot easily rebuke him."

"Are we not also allied to the king?" Razo asked. Razo was the uncle of my cousin's fourth wife and Jura's husband. He was a fat man devoid of scars, a man no warrior would want at his funeral, and yet he always dared to speak at clan assemblies.

"Pantan's third daughter is married to Jaguar's brother," he continued in that self-important way he had. "My brother's half marriage to White Star's daughter has just been accomplished. Are not such alliances worthy of note? Brothers, we have power enough to ask—at least—that the king exile Noam to a sanctuary town. Although it would be taboo for Loic to kill Noam in any of the refuge cities, if Noam were to leave the gates of the city, Loic could kill him without fear of the Therpa vengeance."

"Noam's not like you," Little Mother said. "He's not one to avoid warfare. He would not accept the king's exile, and if Loic killed him the Therpas would not easily accept the death of a firstborn."

Razo sat glumly on his pillow, staring hard at Little Mother. No, those two never liked each other, and although Little Mother should not have been speaking at a war council, she was so greatly honored among our people—and Razo so hated—that no one rebuked her for speaking out so boldly.

"Taer!" she called out to Father. "If we cannot kill Noam, perhaps he could be enslaved. You have friends in far-off Ibeniland. Let one of them kidnap and imprison him. Let them demand a ransom fit for a king, and let them make the years roll by. The Ibeni prisons are evil places. Before his redemption Noam would learn much about being raped. And who could prove to the Therpas that you had hatched the plan?"

"A fit punishment!" several noblewomen shouted.

Father answered, "Fit only if it can be accomplished. Noam is not so stupid as to ride without warriors. Not now, when he knows our blood has begun to boil."

Cyor, the third brother of my father's first wife, a man we called "Skinny," spoke up. "As I walked through the streets yesterday, I heard a rumor that you had sent your younger son off to foreign lands because he displeased you. Noam has probably heard such rumors."

Razo clapped his hands together. "Perhaps the Therpas will consider Sio's exile your response to Noam's crime. Perhaps they won't seek revenge. Perhaps no further vendetta is needed. Loic lost a child. Now Noam has lost a child. Lost, I say, but not murdered." He turned and smiled at the noblewomen. "Fit punishment, I think."

The noblewomen returned a scornful stare, and Satha's eyes were challenging me.

"Sio's removal might satisfy Razo," I said, holding the dagger aloft. "It doesn't satisfy me. It doesn't return my life to me."

Little Mother entered the center circle of elders and threw her coif to the ground. Her unbraided white hair fell like a rivulet down past her waist. "Loicuyo is right. He must have his revenge. I know you Pagatsu men too well. If Loic doesn't kill Seared Conscience, you'll create mocking fest songs about him. You'll sing, 'Taer's boy was so weak, the king had to avenge him.' You'll say, 'Loic's ypher was so weak, he allowed another man to take his wife.' You'll sing, 'He allowed someone to take his wife and did nothing, let us take his headship away.'"

Razo rose to his feet. "Do you think so little of us, woman? Why would we steal the headship from Taer's son?"

"Sit down, Apple-Face!" she shouted. "You talk too much for someone who only wars against women. Lose all that fat by doing some actual fighting, and when you've slit a throat or two then come back and question me!"

Razo returned glumly to his seat and Little Mother continued. "Loic's been taught how to murder silently and secretly. If he avenges himself, and if our spirits are with him, the Therpas will have no proof he killed Noam." She turned to the rest of the group. "Taer was a war-weary fool who allowed a snake who violated his nest to continue burrowing into it. Loic is not war-weary. Let him find that snake and kill it. Should he allow the one who killed his first child to roam the world free?"

"The child was a daughter," Perik said. His nickname was "Knows His Enemies" and he was much honored among our people for his ferocity. "The child could hardly be called a true firstborn, created as she was during the time when there should have been restraint."

As a child I had admired his cold-bloodedness in raping his enemy's pregnant wife, but as I listened to his words against my daughter, that lauded feat suddenly seemed worthier of shame than of glory. I raced toward him and lunged, slicing his cheek with my dagger.

"Loic!" Father shouted, rising to his feet.

But Perik laughed, and wiped the blood from his face. "Perhaps you are a warrior, young chief. Well then, do what your heart wishes. Prove yourself destined to be our headman. Yet, young warrior"—he licked the blood from his fingers—"you should have aimed for my neck. There was too much tentative mercy in that stroke. When you strike, aim to kill. Leave nothing and no one behind, and leave no eye open to weep for the dead."

"I'll leave nothing of Noam," I said. "Not blood of his own or of his descendant."

"Do you intend to kill your brother?" Father asked, angrily. "No! If you find him again, you will not touch him."

I looked at my clansmen then turned to look at Okiak. "Okiak killed his own son, Father, and yet you cannot kill your wife's bastard?"

The room became silent when I mentioned Sio and Krika. Both of them, like me, had been greatly loved.

Pantan broke the silence by asking, "If we're sending a boy to kill Noam in foreign regions—and we do not want it to be suicide—should we not prepare him?"

I answered, "The Creator will teach me how to war. Even against Noam. If weeks and moons must fly by, let them. I will not return here until I've washed my hands in Noam's blood."

Father walked toward me, but I pushed him away. I grieve when I remember this. Even now. How often I've longed to turn back time so those hands could touch me again!

"Treads Lightly!" Galil, a noble old warrior, shouted, "why do you tolerate this?" He slapped me hard across the face. "Is it because Loic has the falling sickness? Is that why you baby him? Such insubordination would have earned him an early grave if he were my son!"

Galil alone among all our clansmen could have rebuked my Father in such a manner, but Razo felt compelled to add his opinion. "Loic has always been a good child. If anyone is to blame, Taer is. Yes, yes, goodness is praiseworthy, but Treads Lightly has always been extreme in his spirituality. Since the war, he has gotten decidedly worse." Then, with great flourish, he added, "Foolish kindness is always rewarded with betrayal. If it had been my well that Noam drank from, both he and my wife would have been dead by now. My son would not have had to suffer because of my stupidity."

Several women tried to hide their knowing smiles but others burst out laughing. Jura, too, could not stop herself from laughing at her husband's stupidity. Only one of Razo's five children bore his features, and both his older sons—on whom he doted—bore a startling resemblance to his Ibeni friend, Longstick who was so named because, although he was a great warrior, he detracted from his greatness by his intemperate boasting, his overbearing swagger and his tendency to couch with his friends' wives.

"You've been living too long among your Carpo friends, Razo," I said. "You philosophize about other people's lives too much, and you know too little of your own."

His response was a bewildered look. All eyes rebuked me. I had come close to breaching etiquette by telling him that long married though he was, his wives had betrayed him and his pretty and flirtatious concubine had fallen backwards before many of the warriors of our clan.

"Young Chief," Ilem began. Ilem was one of Perik's sons. "Killing kills the killer." He looked at his father. "Perhaps it's time he learn a few things from Ganti. Not the theological silliness his mother's clan indulges in, but practical help on warfare. The kind of help only Ganti can offer him."

A face loomed in my memory; I was unsure if it belonged to Ganti. A thought came to my mind: *Ganti's nickname is: "Beloved by the Spirits."* Where this knowledge came from and why, I didn't know, but I knew the words were true, and the nickname made me wary.

"In the past," Perik said, still rubbing his cheek, "Ganti was like a crouching bear always ready to attack. Now he's gone weak, studying theology and living in peace so near to the Therpas, a clan he detests."

"Perik!" Father shouted. "Stop speaking as if all men tell you their plans. In your younger days, you were like Loic—obstinate, yet fragile. You wept at the sight of a dead animal. Ganti taught you how to kill without killing your soul. After he did, you could cut a young child in two and eat a feast with the child's blood on your hands. Now you dishonor him?"

Perik stepped backward and bowed low. "I meant no dishonor—"

"Often, hatred is the best gift we can give to an insightful teacher," Father answered, forgiving him. "He searched into your soul, challenged and changed you. Because of him, your life and mind are spared. How could someone as proud as you not hate him for all you owe him? Perhaps Loic will despise Ganti as much as you do in the future, but I hope this won't be so."

"Yes," Little Mother chimed in, "Ganti will teach him how to die, if he has to die."

"As long as he doesn't teach Loic to murmur and chant and call upon useless spirits," Razo said, and although I disliked his pomposity, his disdain for the spirits made me smile.

In the outer courtyard the next day, as the cool winds blew all around us, the elders surrounded me. Father placed his long vialka and double-edged coulba in my hands, then held my arms aloft. How strange it felt to be holding my father's long lance and battle-axe! "Go and make war, my son. But as we have warned, avenge yourself secretly."

I placed the coulba near my feet and held the long vialka in my hands, one hand on either end. My hands could not span its length.

Father was looking at me, worry and awe on his face. "I have one thing to ask you," he said. "Allow me to ride by your side in this quest."

"That I cannot do, Father. You know what our clansmen will say if I do."

"Then I have another question."

"Say on, Father."

"If I can't fight with you, I beg you to let Okiak's spirits travel with you."

Okiak strolled towards me. Nauseated for reasons I could not understand, I closed my eyes and breathed deeply.

"He's my right hand and my helmet," Father continued. "The spirits who ride with him know the weird haunts of the Therpas. They will help you."

Okiak's face appeared patient and full of good will. But I knew him too well.

"Loic," he said, "let the spirits help you travel safely through the deserts and woodlands. Our ancestral spirits will bargain for your life with the spirits of those woods."

"If the Creator is with me, a passage will be made for me."

Okiak burst out laughing, his face wrinkling as he spoke. "What if the Creator knows nothing about you? Or do you think you really are one of the Called-Out? Do you think you are one of the special sons of the Creator, created to be blessed and favored by him?"

"You spirit-speakers can discuss that among yourselves. As for me, if the Ancient One doesn't help me, my own right hand will suffice. Either way, I want no help from your shadow gods. So, stop speaking to me. Go elsewhere and do what you do best: murder young boys and terrify old women."

The words had hardly left my mouth when I felt a hard slap across my cheek. My face stung; Pantan's wrist burned red from striking me. "You're talking to our high shaman, Loic," he said. "Do you want the spirits to strike back at our clan?"

I lowered my eyes, ashamed of the rebuke and knowing how true his assessment of the spirits was, but when Okiak laid his hands on me, my flesh crawled. I pushed him away. "I don't wish to insult you, old man," I said. "But keep your blessings far from me."

"Loic." Again his voice was sweet and cloying as honey. "You loved my son, yes, but I was his father and loved him even more than you could ever love him. The ancestors and the spirits demanded his death. I couldn't refuse their command to kill him."

"You know how adamant the boy is," Perik said. "Let the matter rest and let him leave without the blessing. If the spirits go with him, good. If not, perhaps the Creator, far away though he is, will look down on him." He turned to me. "Remember, little warrior. When you find Noam, if there's anyone with him, kill him. Horse or dog, mistress or friend. Destroy them utterly. If he has begotten any children other than Sio, kill them too. Yes, leave no eye open to mourn for the dead or to tell where ravens eat Noam's flesh."

I bowed to Perik, rejoicing that one who had drunk the blood of so many of his dying enemies believed that I, too, could be a warrior.

"Drink his blood at the moment death takes him," he said, "and his life and puha will become yours. In dying, he will give you life."

I nodded.

Pantan lifted my travel pouch. "Loic, Ganti's compound is called Blade Castle. Go there, do what you have to do, and return alive."

He raised his hand and my clansmen removed their daggers from their waists. Slowly, they—not Razo, he was too much of a coward—pierced their palms until blood flowed. Then they wiped my arms and face with Pagatsu blood. After covering my bare skin with their blood, they wiped their bloody hands also on my unweeping wife who stood silent in the cold courtyard, staring at me, her face expressionless. Yes, she looked like a warrior's wife.

I held her dagger to my lips and kissed it. Such was the custom in the old days and how I trembled when my lips felt the steel blade. I longed to have my father at my side. I wanted to cry out, *I am only a child*. But I could not. Instead, I encouraged my heart. War had been declared against me. Youth or not, I could not decline it. I lifted the dagger high. "My father, my wife, my Little Mother!" I shouted. Then I took Cactus by the reins and led him from the stable.

I climbed onto his back and listened as the weeping of my little mothers punctuated the silence. No drumming and dancing sent me on my way, only the tears of fearful old women.

When I was ready to go, I spoke to the four winds, "Elder brothers and beloved sisters, if I do not return, may we all meet again in the same fields we long for."

That was when Little Mother began weeping. She wept until her frail body shook. I had not spoken the common farewell: "May the Creator be with you." I had used the prayer Doreni priests spoke over the bodies of dying warriors from other clans. Disregarding Little Mother's sobs, I gathered Father's vialka, shuwas, Satha's dagger and a handful of arrowheads and rode eastward, traveling across the sands of the Salt Desert toward Noam's region.

Satha
Year Mark
Sowing Moon–The First Cool Moon

The year mark of my betrothal came and went. As I looked through the window of my room, I was like an old woman whose every thought was of regret. *We should have waited to marry. I should not have demanded vengeance. I should not have visited the Third Wife's room.* All this and more.

I found it hard to move. My body ached. If I had looked into a mirror, I would have seen the face of an old woman. I understood then that women are made old by remorse and by the consequences of a mistake made in a single unthinking moment. Although he had been gone but a few days, I began to long for Loic's return, not caring if he returned with a dagger unstained by Noam's blood. Many mornings, many nights, my heart told me to climb the Arhe's rampart, but when I had reached its heights and searched the far horizons, I always found my heart had deceived me. Loic was never anywhere to be seen.

One morning, footsteps echoed outside my doorway; I placed my feet on the cold mosaic tile floor.

"Arhe!" Gala called, "We've hung green fern from the wooden lamps in celebration of the Sowing Moon."

"Come in, Gala."

She entered, and together we sat on my bed looking through the window. The sun hung lower than it should have, tempting me to retreat to my bed.

"I wonder how Arhe Monua would have comforted you," she said, looking out at the morning sky.

Gala was not that much older than I, and yet the worried, motherly way she looked at me made me smile.

"Why do you think I need comforting?" I asked.

"Because your heart is broken, Arhe," she said, absent-mindedly braiding and unbraiding her hair. "So many sorrows all in one year, and if we add the sorrows that came before that—when almost all the Kluna were killed—how can you not be brokenhearted?"

"Am I brokenhearted?" I asked, rising to my feet. "I thought my heart was saddened but I thought it whole."

"You're brokenhearted," she answered. "Sometimes we don't know when our own hearts are broken. A good friend has to tell us."

I reached for my gyuilta. "I'm glad you're my good friend."

"I'm worried for you, Arhe. You need to cry more."

"I've cried, Gala."

"Not enough." She stood up and looked through the window. "Perhaps we should ask Yoran or Okiak to open the gates of death for us! Do you want them to call Monua up from the grave? It might comfort you to speak to her."

I shook my head. "Ask Okiak? You know what the young chief thinks about such things."

"He isn't here, he won't know, will he?"

"My husband thinks the Arkhai play tricks upon the living and pretend to be our departed ones."

"But—"

"There are no buts, Gala. Should I disobey my husband and speak with the spirits against his will? No, I will never break covenant with him by doing such a thing."

"But the dead in Gebelda and the dead in the fields we long for know many things, Arhe. They could tell you how the young chief fares." She looked at me, eagerly. "Spirits and shamans know these things. They are always busy talking. I'm sure some spirit has seen him in his journey."

"So they might say, but like my husband I don't trust anything these spirits say."

She frowned and returned to braiding her hair. "I think the young chief is wrong to trust his life to the Creator. Arhe, do you really believe the Creator—the Great and Supreme Spirit—cares about such small human matters as a broken heart? Certainly, we are not so important as to come into his presence?"

I didn't answer, and she looked through the window. "Last Sowing Moon was much warmer, wasn't it?" she asked, changing the subject.

I smiled, remembering. "When I met Loic the Rose Moon was just passing. He roamed the market bare-shouldered only in a tunic. When we danced at our marriage feast, the vines were already draping the walls of the courtyard." I tossed the fur-lined bed coverings over my shoulder and touched my flat stomach.

I joined Gala at the window. Mamya Jontay, Edi and Jival were approaching. "Jontay walks so much slower now, since Loic is gone," I said.

In the distance past the outer court and the large rock at the far end of the compound, Taer sat with his head bowed. Gala directed my attention to him. "We've all grown old since the young chief left. What will we do if—"

I put my finger to my mouth, signaling that she say nothing more. "Loic will return. He cannot not return. How will I live with this broken heart of mine if he doesn't return?"

She burst into tears, and we waited without speaking until Jontay and the others joined us.

"Poor Taer," Jontay said when she and the two girls entered my doorway. "How sad it all is!" She joined me under the fur-lined covering. As we stood shoulder to shoulder, she seemed more aged and frail than ever. Placing her hands around my waist, she said half as a prayer and half as a demand, "Loic, may the Wind keep you safe."

The feel of her aged hands around my waist and the weight of her stooped shoulders brought tears to my eyes. An inner trembling made my whole body shake. "Mamya Jontay," I asked, "what have I done to you? Forgive me. What have I done to myself? What if Loic doesn't return? What a fool I was to send a young sickly boy out into the world to avenge someone like myself? Who am I that someone should avenge me?"

Jival held my hands tightly, "Arhe, don't cry like that. Stop it, you will make me weep! If you lose your strength, what will happen to the rest of us? Why are you assuming Loic will die? He'll live, of course, and return to us in triumph. Today is the year mark, a time to celebrate. Loic has not died. Loic will not die. He has lived long enough to be married and now he will prove himself a great warrior. Should we not anticipate his future glory and celebrate such a life?"

She picked up a coral comb from my table and gently pulled it through my thick hair. "Arhe," she continued, "let us all go to the market and show the world our happiness. Our journey there will help put all those rumors aside."

"True words, Emigrant," I said, finding my courage again. "Call Ydalle. Tell her to order the stables to prepare a valanku."

I dressed. Then, while preparations for our trip was being made, I walked across the compound to our unfinished house. Arriving at the doorway, I heard the sound of boots against stone and looked toward the inner courtyard. Taer stood at the far end of the colonnade. He smiled at me, and long, long we stood there silently watching each other. Then I remembered what the Third Wife had publicly accused me of and turned toward the gathering room, hurrying to meet my servants.

The day grew warmer as morning turned to noon. How warm the sun fell on my neck and arms! The sights and smells of the market lightened my heart. Sweet, tart and sour fruits; leafy green and yellow vegetables; brown and red tubers, long and round—all promised a feast that would push sorrow and guilt far from my mind—at least for a little while. How easy it was to quell the rumors and deceive the merchants, to tell them that Loic was in the north studying for a year with the king's children.

Edi, Jival and Gala followed me around the marketplace with their baskets, which continually overflowed with merchandise. They raced back and forth to the horsemen waiting near the valanku, filling it and refilling it with candles, fabrics, and a bounty of foreign fruits and sweets.

As we traveled around the market, I began to notice that two red-haired men followed us. They were cinnamon-skinned with slanted eyes—Doreni—but they wore no clan caps and were poorly dressed.

When the younger of the two saw me looking at them, he came near and bowed to the ground before me. "Wife of Loic," he pleaded, "have pity on us. Your clan markings are well known to the poor and we have followed you wondering and hoping."

"Please, don't beg," I said and turned to my waiting women. "Girls, our baskets are full and we have yet more to buy. Carry your full baskets back to our valanku and come back with the two empty ones. Before you go, however, let these men choose whatever they wish from our goods."

The men eagerly chose all they wanted and my serving girls left to go to the valanku at the far side of the market. The men lingered near me, ravenously eating some fruit they had taken. Although Theseni women never talk to male strangers, I was no longer Theseni but Doreni. The men weren't Ibeni or Theseni and I had no fear of being sold into a brothel or into slavery. We spoke easily and they told me stories of how poverty had come upon them in a region far from their clan lands. How sad their stories were!

I removed two five-hundred quixa gold coins from the sleeve of my gyuilta. "Take this money," I said. "I know you probably have debts. If you need more, come to Taer's compound and I'll give you more."

I noticed a third man approaching us. Although he was a fat fellow, he, too, looked like a beggar. The Therpa markings on his cap troubled me, however, and I wondered if I could show generosity to one whose clan had wounded me so cruelly.

"Satha, wife of Loic," the third man said. He was not only the fattest of the three but also the oldest and his hair was like Noam's, a coppery red. "We have business with you."

I bowed my head, hoped anxiously that my servants would return soon. I looked towards the far side of the market where I knew Taer's valanku was. Neither the vehicle nor my servants could be seen. But Jival was approaching, and I breathed a sigh of relief.

"What is the business?" I asked, keeping my eye on Jival.

He retrieved a dagger from his boot and held it close to my neck. The other two men stood close around us, binding my hands. "Speak or shout one word," the fat one said, "and you're dead."

Jival was at my side by that time, but she avoided my gaze. "Hurry," she said to the fat man, and handed one of the men a signed parchment. "The others are in the valanku on the other side of the Sun Fountain. Take the woman and leave."

The man who had taken the parchment placed it in the sleeve of the fat man's gyuilta. My heart tightened. Had I been betrayed again? The two men who had pretended to be beggars held my hand fast and threatened to kill me if I shouted for help. How I wanted to wipe the grins off their faces.

"Tell Noam that I love him," Jival said. "And that he must remain faithful to me because I gave him all my love in the lingay fields."

The fat one shook his head. "That's a hard promise for Noam to keep. I have never known him to love any woman who willingly gave herself to him."

"I have never known him to love any woman," one of his fellow kidnapers said.

Jival frowned, but nevertheless turned and glared triumphantly at me. There was no trace of guilt on that evil woman's face.

"One thing more," the fat man said.

She gave him a questioning look. "What?"

Suddenly, he slapped her hard against the face. She lurched backwards, surprised. Blood flowed from her nose. Weeping from the pain, she said, "Did you have to strike me?"

"I've just saved your life, little warseed," he said. "If you were to return to Taer without any wound or grief, Taer would suspect your story. Now I've given him a reason to believe you."

She nodded as if she understood. "Tell Noam I will stand on the Mistress Ramparts, just as the Third Wife did, and await his messenger." Then running and holding her nose, she disappeared into the crowd.

The abductor in the Therpa clan cap turned his full attention to me. "That one is as deceitful as her ancestors. Still, Noam is grateful to her. She's watched over his boy, and she did find out from Taer's warriors where Sio was taken. But . . ."

"But what?"

"Small satisfaction this may be to you, Arhe Satha, but this war is not against you. It's not even against Loic. As you Theseni say, 'When elephants fight, the tiny grass gets trampled.' Tiny grass, you were caught up in a war you had nothing to do with. But then, you laid your hand on Noam's son. Not a good thing to do." Without warning, his right hand clamped over my mouth. Something acrid stung my nostrils. Sudden sleep and darkness overcame me.

LOIC
The Battle With the Desert Spirit
Thanksgiving Moon–Third Harvest Moon

On the edge of Jefra, the Salt Desert loomed large and wide. Long ago, the Salt Desert had been a sea flowing between two deserts. It had dried up, leaving only its saltiness and a bleak whiteness that melded into gold as it merged into the eastern and western deserts on either side of it. No obvious border separated Jefra from that sea of white sand, that treeless expanse. Yet I knew when I had passed into the desert which the Theseni called Gulacan-Gulnayacun, a name which meant: *You go in, but you won't come out*. With great foreboding, I entered the desert of deserts where only Time roamed without fear, where only the changing color of the sand would mark my way.

Pantan, my father, and my mentors had told me many stories of their journeys through the Salt Desert into the Great Desert. It was best, they had said, to sleep during the heat of the day and to ride only at night. This I did, and all the while I searched the skies for desert owls and the sands for angha burrows, since both creatures often led travelers to oases. Thirsty and weary though we were, Cactus and I never failed to find those oases. How could we not when the Creator was our advance guard and scout?

I had not been riding long when I realized I had rarely been alone. Growing up surrounded by cousins and little mothers, I was not accustomed to solitude and I certainly didn't like it. I was not afraid, but to hear no human voice, to feel no loving hand, to smell no human odors—I found it hard to bear. Although I did not know the Creator, I hoped he traveled with me.

During the days, I slept under oases-watered bulba trees or I dug a burrow inside the grassy areas and slept there. Drifting off to sleep, I always remembered Krika, Satha and my dead daughter. At nights, I rode as the wind willed, and used my shuwa and vialka to trap food. Monkeys, rats and angha baked, smoked or steamed inside in tura leaves on hot stones. This I did for many days. The Thanksgiving moon turned toward the snow moons although I could not fully know when one season became another.

One night as I unpacked my travel pouch and rested my head on my gyuilta, a tiny bright speck flew toward me. One moment it flickered above the faraway sands; the next, it flickered at my side, hovering. It slowly transformed and became a light no longer but a creature in a fire-colored tunic and leggings like a salamander's skin. Its mottled arms shimmered in the moonlight.

"Stranger," it called as it approached. "Who are you? Where are you going and why?"

"What are you that I should tell you?" I asked, standing up.

"I'm the head spirit of this place. I've noticed that no spirit walks with you to mediate and battle for you. I ask you then, who are you that I should let you pass?"

How deceitful these spirits were! And how ignorant and gullible they thought we living were! I wished to destroy the thing. Five shuwas and my vialka nested in my saddle, but they were no use against spirit folk.

"The One Who Holds My Breath in His Hand owns this place," I said. "He is greater than you and if he is for me, none can be against me. Therefore I need no spirit to make a way for me. The Creator will let me pass."

"The Creator is high above all things and cares little for humans. Are you truly saying he knows you're here?"

"The One Who Holds My Breath in His Hand knows who and where I am."

"Kwelku, but pay homage to me nevertheless, for I am close at hand. I'll let you pass and protect you as you journey through my domain."

"You think quite highly of yourself, Spirit," I answered. "But you are a creature as I am. No closer to the Creator than I am. Why should I worship anyone but the Creator?"

"Ah, but the Creator has created a hierarchy which must be followed. He is distant and holy. Sinful humans cannot hope to reach him. He has therefore appointed us spirits to help him by helping you. And for the good we do you—bringing humans food, protecting them from danger—it's only proper you bow to us, for he has given us authority over you. Be humble, then, and respect us and don't forsake the spirits who have helped your father."

I didn't know at that time what power this particular spirit had, or how strong the spirits' alliance was, but desolation suddenly crept into my soul. Not mere desolation but a loneliness I had never encountered before. I felt as unloved and as forgotten as the desert. I came to believe with a strange clarity there were none who loved me, none who understood. Only death seemed to bring escape from that alienation and isolation. Satha's dagger lodged in my mind as the key to my freedom.

The spirit came closer to me, standing directly in front of me. Its features became clearer and seemed male. His face was burnt by the sun, wrinkled, yet ageless and eternal. What I had first thought was a cloth tunic I now realized was a suit of discarded bird feathers. The leggings, too, weren't made of fabric but of salamander skin. Seeing him in such borrowed clothing, I regained some lightness of heart and picked up my vialka, placing its sharp tip on his shoulder.

"How poor and beggarly you are, Spirit!" I said, laughing. "You're even bereft of a body. Why should I respect a minor spirit who uses nature's cast-offs to dress himself? You don't even have a body to clothe yourself in!"

The spirit put his hand under the feathers of his tunic and removed one small feather. "So you think I own nothing?" He laughed and made a small movement of his hand.

The wind, which had been calm, now rushed past my cheek, sounding in my ears like thunder as it passed. I looked to the east and west. Great sandstorms swirled toward me. They poured themselves into the little lake in the middle of the oasis. Dust, like smoke, clouded my eyes and smothered my breath.

"I tell you, Loic," he said, finally calling me by my name, "you will thirst for water and hunger for palm dates, but food and water will escape you. Yet if you only worship me and—"

Although dust choked my throat, I coughed out, "I'll worship no one less than the One who holds my breath in his hand, even if it causes my death." The now muddied oasis was useless to me and I mounted Cactus. "I am young yet, and I know very little about spiritual matters, but I have found you spirits to be deceitful and cruel. I don't know the Creator but I doubt you serve him. I have come to believe that if I fight against you, the Creator will fight with me."

I rode away, and the dust-clouds continued to swirl in eddies around me, never relenting. How thirsty and tired Cactus and I were, how choked with sand! The gyuilta provided little help against that unnatural storm, but when I thought we were past all hope and the thirst was about to kill us, a great rain began to pour from the sky. Sweet pure sky water covered me and I no longer had need for earthly oases. The Wind also sent ravens to feed us. They brought bread from heaven, honeyed and crunchy, which filled both our stomachs.

I rested, sat down and rejoiced at this sudden reprieve. Soon a mizca—a running snake—appeared. It was about as long and thin as an uprooted vine. In those days, running snakes were revered among the Doreni because, like us, they never fled from their enemies but pursued them until death came for one or the other.

I leaped to my feet and tried to run away from it. It followed hard at my heels, skating along the sand as if it ruled the wind. Now I laugh at the memory, but I was young then, and afraid. I ran long and in circles but it didn't relent. At last, angry and having taken all I wished to take, I lost my temper and turned toward it. Grabbing my father's vialka, I hacked it into six little pieces. Its blood seeped into the sand. Then to my surprise the pieces of its body found each other. In the sand, piece called out to piece, sought each other, and interlocked again. I realized I had been battling a spirit—probably a brother of the same desert spirit I had encountered earlier.

That made me angry. I called out that it could neither harm nor intimidate me. It slunk away and fled.

SATHA
Enslavement

A sharp painful slap across my cheek, and I was at last fully awake. The bulky man in the Therpa clan cap then squeezed both my cheeks tightly. "So you're with us now, Satha?"

Nauseated and confused, I didn't immediately answer. The right hand of my Therpa captor once again threatened to strike. I held my hand up to my face to forestall another blow, and through a mist of tears, saw the back wheels of a wagon directly in front of me. I realized I was lying on the ground.

"I gave you a bit too much, uh?" the Therpa clansman said, smirking. "You been sleeping a long time." He smirked and pointed at an old man in the distance whose pale skin was as white as boiled fish. An Angleni. The pale old man seemed to be putting some coins into the hands of one of my captors.

"Thirty pieces of silver for you," the fat Therpa man said. "Not a bad pay for an easy day's work."

"For me?" I stammered, still not quite awake. "Am I a slave, then? Have I been sold? To that man?" I struggled to rise from the dirt mat which encased me like a shroud, but my body ached all over. "Do you think you'll get away with this? Loic will hear of this."

"If Loic lives, where will he search for you in this vast land of the three tribes?"

Twisting about, I realized my hands were tied behind my back. Shedding the heavy blanket that covered me, I managed to rise to my knees and to pull myself up from the damp sandy ground. About me, on auction blocks, children of all tribes and clans—most of them Angleni warseed—cried and wailed. Some begged to be bought, some cried for their mothers, others clung to their Theseni owners. Theseni chieftains were bidding for them. Indeed, most of the crowd was Theseni. I was at a Theseni slave market.

Disgusted that many in my tribe continued to sell and buy people despite Our Matchless King's orders, I said to the Therpa clansman holding me. "Our Matchless King has outlawed slavery except in the cases of thieves, prisoners and debtors. I'm freeborn and guilty of no crime. Nor am I in debt. Neither I nor those orphans should be here."

"You owe my clan chief a great debt, Satha. You sent his son into the far regions. Alone, with no one. How can you say you're not a debtor?"

The old Angleni man walked toward us with my two other abductors beside him. He proceeded to look me up and down, studying me as if I were damaged goods he had been forced to buy.

"My husband is the son of a great warrior," I pleaded. "I'm not supposed to be here. I am no slave. Do you come here to enslave freeborn people? Kidnapping of freeborn people in order to enslave them is illegal in the land of the three tribes."

"Illegal or not," one of my other abductors answered, "it's done everywhere."

The Angleni gave my fat abductor a questioning look and asked him something in a language I didn't understand. One of my captors answered him with unknown words that seemed to reassure the old man.

I spoke in the Doreni language. "Angleni Brother, whatever he just said to you is not true. "

The Angleni smiled patronizingly as if he knew better than to trust the words of a Theseni. "Open your mouth," he said.

When I didn't comply, the old man—whose age belied his strength— put his hand on my cheeks and pried my mouth open.

"I'm Talub," he said in the Doreni language. "A sojourner here in your land. You belong to me now. I bought you as a handmaid for my wife. She's getting old and we need a woman in our caravan to care for her."

I couldn't answer him immediately. His fingers were pushing at my gums and teeth as if he were a horse trader checking a mare. "She seems healthy enough. She seems young, but one can never tell with these Theseni. They're often older than they appear. Do you know if she's had any children?"

"One," my abductor answered. "A healthy child who nonetheless died early. The mosquito illness. But she can still have other children if you want to buy her as a breeder."

"The mosquito illness is prevalent in these parts," the Angleni agreed. "A shame. It is a painful way to suffer. But, other than that, there's nothing else wrong with her? And you're sure she's young and strong?"

"Yes. This woman was born a slave and well-treated, even though the Therpa warrior who sold her to me told she lies and thieves."

The Angleni nodded again. "Yes," he said as if he was the fount of all wisdom, "I've heard how lying these Theseni are. But what can one expect from people whose skin reflect the darkness of their souls?"

"Are you, a lying truce-breaking Angleni, calling me a liar?" I asked, struggling unsuccessfully against the chains on my wrists. "My husband is a rich chief, the only son of a great family. You have no right to enslave me!"

The Angleni gave me a dismissive superior glance and quickly turned his gaze toward a covered wagon. "If you were a chief's wife, you would not be here. I've learned much about your people and I know that the wife of a chief doesn't travel alone."

"I was not alone and I am not a Theseni chief's wife. The wives of Doreni headmen often walk alone . . . if there is no vendetta against them. But I was captured because this man's clan has a vendetta against me."

The old man sucked at his teeth as if he were speaking to a child who was telling lies. "Now, woman," he said, "See how you twist yourself up in lies. First you say you were free to walk but now you say you were not free to walk because there was a vendetta against you. Look at your clothes. A chieftain's wife wouldn't wear clothes as simple as that. And where is your headdress and all the trinkets you people use to show your status?"

"They took my headdress away from me, and those who captured me stole me when my servants were away."

"My wife and I were told you were taken captive in one of the tribal wars," the Angleni answered. "We have no reason to doubt that."

The Therpa abductor was shaking his head as if he too was stunned by my supposed lies. "Don't accuse us to this man. We Therpas are not so stupid as to steal a warrior's wife and sell her at an illegal market."

The Angleni began walking back to the covered wagon. "You should meet my wife. After all, it is she who owns you now."

He left and the Therpa warrior whispered to me, his lips curled into a contemptuous sneer. "Thesenya, you do not fully understand that we Doreni are a fierce people and the fiercest of us are the Therpas."

In the distance a yellow-haired woman stepped out of the covered wagon. "That's Voora, Talub's wife. She will rule over you as cruelly as you ruled over your servants."

Voora approached and looked me up and down, then turned to her husband who was at her side. "Talub, are you sure this one is clean and has no fleas?" she asked in the Doreni language. "You know how unclean these dark ones are."

I said nothing. It would have been no use.

LOIC
The Fall Into Gebelda

The golden sands of the desert slowly gave way to strange unpredictable landscape of the Patchwork Prairie. When I entered the prairie, I hesitated, wondering whether to ride into Colebru or toward the Pine Forest. Both ways led to Therpa regions, but Colebru was a land dedicated to the spirits and the ancestors, a place of beauty but also of peril. The Pine Forest, however, was more easily navigated and led to many villages. I traveled through the Pine Forest, then, for I preferred human company rather than the haunts of spirits. A cold rain had fallen over the trees—how bright and beautiful the color green is, after rain and after such a long journey! I dismounted Cactus and stood a long time on the edge of the forest smiling, lost in admiration of the green lushness before me.

As I stood there, a green man in mottled leggings stepped out of a wooded grove into the clearing. "Loic tyu Taer," he called out. His voice sounded like the rustling of autumn wind among fallen leaves, and his short green hair blew about his head like eddying leaves. "You owe much to the spirits who have helped your father. If you persist in your journey, you will destroy your own house and our nation."

I wanted nothing to do with this forest spirit or with any of his brothers. I turned from him and urged Cactus to ride away. Although he had been forty or more paces away, he suddenly stood before us.

"Krika was a rover," he said, putting his green spirit hand on Cactus's mane. "His body roamed, his mind too. He traveled forbidden paths. It was good his father killed him at our behest, because the young man had no desire to follow in the footsteps of his father."

"Even so," I answered him, "you and your brothers should not have forbidden the lamb sacrifice. Why prevent the Creator from taking

Krika to the fields we long for?" I pulled on Cactus's reins, but he reared, afraid of that menacing spirit.

"Cactus," I prodded, "don't fear these spirits. Look closely. See how weak and beggarly he is. His clothing is nothing but ivy and bark." I turned to the spirit. "Poor Spirit! You're bereft of power, as well as proper clothing. Yet you promise great things and threaten harsh punishments. How foolish I would be to be deceived by you!"

Scowling, he pointed to the forest, where a rumbling suddenly began to echo through the trees. It sounded like many axes laid into the roots of many trees and like the roars of lions and the hissing of snakes. Yet I saw nothing. I peered into the forest waiting for some great unknown thing to appear and maul me, but, although the sound grew louder and more furious, nothing appeared. Then, a sudden pain, a harsh wounding to my head. I touched the top of my scalp, brought my hand down, saw blood. Then saw nothing else in the world I knew as this world gave way to another.

I was suddenly in a dark place where breathing was difficult. I was crawling out of a cramped moist cell where cruel mocking laughter echoed around me. Although all about me was black and nothing could be seen, yet in that darkness beyond all darkness, I still saw. Three beings—fanged and horned—shared my cramped quarters. Their faces were of such beauty, yet from within their eye sockets a fire of hate and anger burned, turning all their beauty to monstrosity. The fire seemed born from within them and outside of them. Although we were fellow-prisoners, they grasped and clutched at me as if their collective purpose and their only remaining joy—for they seemed incapable of no other joy but the joy of being cruel—was to torment me.

Wishing to tell them there was no conflict between us, I managed to raise my head—how tired and wearying! There was no air. The weight of all the human world was heavy upon that place. When I looked up, I saw a bright light—a lake of fire that seemed to be continually enlarging itself. Naked people from all tribes and clans—and I knew them to be the souls of those who had died—hastened away from the fiery lake's fast-encroaching edges. But as fast as the dead ran, so fast the lake grew, and everywhere there was weeping, hopelessness and grief. The shadow gods lunged at them and shouted all their sins at them. A strange thing it was to be in a place where the luxury of hope was not present. Yes, everyone in that place knew there was no escape and they would be in that domain of suffering forever.

I, too, had no hope, for I had died and was in Gebelda, the great garbage dump of souls. There was no one who could enter that place and free me. I wanted to cry out but who was there to cry to? Neither human spirit nor shadow god could save me. Many friends and ancestors stood nearby—I seemed to know the names and lives of all present—yet all of us in the clan of the dead were alone. In that dank place, clan and affection could not save.

I had heard of Gebelda, and had seen glimpses of it in mirrors and in night-visions. I even understood in my heart's deepest place that I truly deserved to be there. Yet I had never truly understood the horror of the place. Nor had I, in spite of all the living had said about the place, truly believed such a place of eternal suffering truly existed. I looked all about me, dumbfounded that Gebelda actually existed.

"Why did I not believe in the dangers of this place?" I asked myself. Koloq and the prophets had warned us. All the Scriptures of all the clans and tribes had described some eternal place of punishment . . . yet we had lived as if—forgive me and my tears, the memory of this place still grieves and terrifies me—as if that place was not the common destination of all but the Called-Out Ones.

I saw then the lake was widening toward me. Too late, I thought to run. But where to? And how? No strength remained in my spirit body and the air was so oppressive, so foul, so hot and so thin. I crawled backwards but the lake rushed toward me and, like quicksand, the ground below me gave way. Fire seared through my spirit flesh as the roaring lake enveloped me. Yes, dead flesh can burn and evil sensations await the spirit body. My spirit flesh singed like flayed pig flesh, and I knew that forever I would burn and there would be no end of the burning.

I realized I was falling. Forever falling, with no hope of a restful landing on any ground. About me, all manner of foul things also fell. Unclean animals, human and animal waste, all manner of refuse. *If I had known there was truly such a place as this,* I repeated to myself, *I would have done all in my power not to come here. I would do all in my power to prevent even Noam and Okiak from coming here.*

Suddenly a strong hand lifted me up and set me on my feet in the air above the lake. The hand turned me about and I found myself looking into the face of One who seemed unconquered by the fire and the darkness. Strange to see such a loving face in such a horrifying place. Spikes protruded from his bloody hands, from his head, feet, and from a grievous wound in his side, and he reminded me of the lambs we slew whenever a death occurred.

"By my mercy I will free you from this place," he said. "But your life will be a prey to you from now on."

The weight of my sins fell from me as he spoke, and the demons that had taunted me fled. I could breathe easily. Oh, how lovely and wonderful it is to breathe! Freed from torment, I studied the faces of the grieving dead around me. Many faces I recognized—chieftain and beggar, servants and noblewomen, shamans and sinners. But not Krika. Not Lihu. Not Monua. Not my child. Nor did I see anyone who might have been my mother. I wondered if the one who had freed me was preventing me from seeing them. Fearing the answer to my question, I did not ask it.

"I will show you a Way which will prevent you from returning here," he said. "But there are predators and plunderers who wish to send you permanently here."

When he said this, I opened my eyes and woke from death. I realized my head rested beside a heavy boulder. Thick congealed blood smeared my face. I sat up and feared to move, feared to travel, lest another spirit attempt to take my life again.

I comforted myself. My vialka was lodged in my saddle; my quivers were full of arrows and shuwas. They would protect me from animals, stray Angleni and even Noam. But what could protect me from spirits?

But then I began to reason to myself. "If the Creator has told me to continue," I said, "then I must trust him to keep me safe." How difficult it was to hope and believe this! In those days it was considered foolish to trust the Creator because he was so far off.

I was grateful to be alive. The grass seemed greener, the sky bluer. The freshness of the air removed from my memory, although not entirely, the stench of death that had permeated the land of tormented souls. The singing of the birds was joyous music to me, as were the summer breezes blowing across my face and arms. The damp mincemeal of fallen leaves was like a luxurious blanket under my feet.

I resolved then that I must walk through that dense dark forest, even if death lay within its the thick overgrowth. I had to find the Way that would prevent me from returning to Gebelda. Loyal Cactus had stayed beside my body even though my soul had sunk into the lowest reaches. We walked together through the thicket until we came to a weed-choked river. I knew then that a city lay nearby. Stopping at the river's edge, I watered Cactus, and washed the blood from my face and hair. As his reins trailed along the muddy riverbed, I thought how happy those dead souls would be to put even that dirty water to their lips.

A woman soon rose from the water. Blue-skinned and green-veined she was, with green-gray hair. Her long silver tunic reflected the sunlight, and she was beautiful to look at. In the distance, a forest spirit scowled, unspeaking. I feared he was the same spirit I had encountered earlier. I noticed he didn't set his foot in water and the female spirit didn't touch the land.

"Loic!" Her voice rippled like water rolling over pebbles. She beckoned toward me with a regal hand. "Come and tell me why you still intend to veer from the path of your ancestors."

"Lady," I shouted to be heard above the roaring of the waters. "Although you're beautiful, I have no desire to approach you. I've heard stories about you water seductresses. I refuse to be one who loses his life because he is charmed by you. I have other things to do than to be bound to some seductive spirit until she tires of me."

"I'll not harm you, Loic. Approach."

Such spirits could not be trusted. They build lies upon lies! Nevertheless I took hold of Cactus's reins and walked through the canopy of waters, my hands shaking. The waters stood up on either side of me and as they parted I walked through them, trembling, to the middle of the river.

As I neared the spirit, I saw her clothing was made of fish scales and her hair of coral and small fish bones. I soon stood before her and she pushed my wet hair from my face.

"My brother spirit met you in the desert." She smiled like an Ibeni woman intent on an assignation. "How rude you were to him!"

"He was rude to me first. He blew sand in my face." I pointed to the forest spirit. "And that one over there . . . that one killed me."

"If it's necessary for you to die to save your people, Loic, then you must die."

The unquenchable fires of Gebelda burned in my mind. It was not a place I wanted to return to, not even in my thoughts.

"A true Doreni must avenge himself," the spirit said. "We understand that Noam must be murdered, but let me be honest with you about—"

"What concern is my concern to you? And honesty would be a new thing for you spirits. Look at you, smiling at me, yet your brother spirit killed me—"

"How beautiful you are to look at, Loic!" she said, interrupting me. "I had heard about your beauty. Many a spirit has longed to couch with you."

"Cease your flattery and speak what you have to speak that I might travel on."

"Jobara! How faithful you are to your wife! Do I not tempt you? Satha is indeed lucky." She preened her weed-green hair, showing me the curls in her hair as if inviting me to touch them. "Young human," she continued, "my love for you makes me want to preserve you. I tell you honestly, you can either preserve your country or destroy it. To preserve it, you must turn aside and return home."

"If this is what you wish to say, I have already—"

"Noam is an excellent warrior, Loic. You cannot defeat him. We could kill him for you. A wind could blow him off a cliff; a fire could descend from heaven and consume him. If we killed him, you would not be risking your life. And the Therpas would not war against you. You would be safe and alive . . . not risking Gebelda and most important of all, not risking our nation."

"If you helped me, there'd be a covenant between us—I make no bargains with spirits. As for Noam, I'll kill him with my own fire."

"You wish to serve the Angleni god even if it means destroying your country and your clan?"

Surprised and insulted at what seemed a strange question, I protested. "I said nothing about the Angleni god. I spoke only about the Creator. Nor do I see why serving the Creator would mean the destruction of our nation."

"Has it not been told you you're appointed to save our land from the Angleni and from the Angleni god?"

"Spirit, truly, if you knew how distressed I am about what I've seen today, you would not seek to discuss these unimportant matters that are none of my concern. Jaguar has made a truce with the Angleni. They're bothersome but they have eaten the nuchunga reconciliation meal with us. We have already conquered them. Now, cease from making me seem more important than I am. My main concern is to slay my enemy and return to my wife. After that, I will do all I can to prevent myself and all those I love from eternal torment in Gebelda. Now, let me pass."

She sighed—like wind playing on water. "Dorenyu, believe me. I often wish you weren't as important as you are. Unfortunately, the future of our land depends on choices you must make. Let me now show all that is in our power, and all that you may choose to have . . . and think no more of Gebelda."

She did not move. Not her hand, not her lips. Yet suddenly the shells, scales and weeds in the river swirled around me, like sand paintings made by a shaman or by court artisans. They formed pictures that moved from left to right. In this moving picture, all the clans of the three kingdoms, as they were then and as they would be in the future, flowed in a story before my eyes. All manner of women, of jewels, of power. "All this can be yours, Loic. But to receive it, you must defy the Angleni god when he seeks you."

"Spirit, you obviously don't know me. Nor does the Angleni god. He certainly has better things to do than to seek one whose father has warred against him. If he's a god, he should know I seek only the Creator."

"The Angleni god thinks he is the Creator," she said.

This surprised me. "He's bold, this god from across the seas," I answered, unsure if she was speaking honestly.

"Jealous and powerful, the Angleni god allows no other gods in his presence. So jealous is he that he declares those who worship him must worship him alone. He's at war with all the spirits of our land, and he has sought you to be his warrior."

I shrugged, although shrugging was considered rude in those days, but what did I care for the feelings of spirits? "Spirit," I said, "like you, the Angleni god has only limited power. I have nothing to fear from him."

She shrugged in turn—in the way spirits often did, implying she knew so much more than humans did and if any words were to be dismissed, they would have to be mine. "The Angleni god is subtle and scheming, as are the people who worship him. He's a pretender, and it's prophesied in the Desai scriptures, Little Doreni, you and Satha will be deceived by him and will teach your people to worship him. There is much you do not know and yet you flaunt this ignorance of yours."

"Everyone seems to have read this Desai prophecy," I countered. "And everyone keeps telling me about myself."

"We spirits know all things. We have every right to tell you about yourself." She sounded angry and I could see she was about to lose her patience with a mere human like myself. "However, it's not my fault your father and Okiak hid certain truths from you."

"Wise of them," I said, deciding that it was best to leave the side of one who was obviously losing patience with me. Pulling Cactus's reins, I directed his gaze toward the other side of the river. As we were turning away from her, she lifted her arms, and the waters suddenly crushed in on me from all sides.

Many times had Pantan and Heldek told me that a warrior's life was one of struggle, beatings and injury, but never had I imagined the waves of the sea would lash me, their crests tossing me to and fro. I floated like broken shells, being sifted in that watery sieve, surrounded by cold water. I feared returning to the fires of Gebelda. At last with a triumphant toss, the waves threw me upon the land. When I stood on my feet, I looked about for Cactus. But he was nowhere to be seen.

SATHA
Voora
The Rose Moon–Second Cool Moon

For weeks the wagon passed through towns I had heard of but never seen. I saw clans I had heard of but never known. But after much traveling, I entered a town whose name my tongue could not pronounce, with houses built in ways I had not dreamed. The houses sheltered pale-skinned people whose eyes were full of hatred and superiority. How disheartening it was to see how hateful, greedy, and selfish those people were. How they hogged everything that was lovely and fertile, pitching their tents and building their houses on the fertile plains!

But Talub's wagon didn't rest long in this town. Although I wondered why he preferred to leave, I was glad to be far from the hateful people in that place.

While the caravan moved, my time was my own. I rode in the wagon and watched the world pass by me. But the day came when the caravan came to rest and I understood I was a slave. It had already become apparent that Voora considered me less than human and another of her beasts of burden. She laid heavy tasks upon me, ordering me about from morning until night. She had no heart and I had no rest.

At first I thought it best to submit to the destiny HaZatana had given me. Who knew what sins my ancestors had committed that I was called to pay for? If I did not submit to this grief and rebelled against my fate would HaZatana cause greater sorrow to come upon me? Try as I might, I could not please Voora. We argued constantly. At last, I revolted and told her I would not work until she realized that I was a woman as she was. For two days I did nothing—I neither cooked nor fetched water.

On the morning of the third day, she leaned against the wagon she had given me, the third in line from the lead wagon, and wagged her finger at me. "We have treated you, slave, better than our people treat their servants," she said. "Yet you insist on challenging me. You have not behaved yourself with humility towards those who are obviously your superiors, those whom the Creator has appointed to rule over you. I am old, and you are the only other woman—yes, see, I agree you are a woman—in this caravan other than myself. But you are not my equal and you must accept that. Simple work for simple minds. Why are you not grateful and obedient?"

So this is how life is? I thought. *I was kind to my servants and the Creator rewards me by enslaving me.* I stood up and walked from the wagon.

"You walk away like a queen, Hajra," she shouted to me. "Try to remember you aren't. Nor have I given you permission to leave my presence."

"My name is Satha. It isn't Hajra. Hajra means 'footwasher' in the Ibeni language. I am not a footwasher. I *am* a queen. That is what my name means."

"We believe the Creator made you dark because you are supposed to be the slaves of whiteskins like myself. You are not a queen."

"The Creator would not enslave my people, let alone to a people as pale as you."

"To the Creator, we pale-skinned people are the most beautiful tribe in the world." She lifted the ends of her hair and pointed a lock at me.

"If that is true, the Creator does not understand beauty."

"Look at my hair and look at yours. Mine is silken like the moon, yellow like the sun. But your black hair and black skin speak only of the darkness from which your people spring."

"Who are you to come here, to a land not your own, and—"

"The land is ours!" Her voice dripped with disdain. "The One Who Loves Us Alone has appointed it for us and it is our destiny to inhabit it until our descendants own all of it."

If I had had a dagger, I would have plunged it into her heart. Indeed, I had stolen a small one from the armament wagons lest one of Talub's herdsmen tried to force himself on me, but it lay hidden under my sleeping mat. I had forgotten that a woman could also be an enemy.

We traveled until the Thunder Moon came. We came to rest in Colebru, the burial place of our ancestors, a land whose yield was dedicated to the poor. Every year the king's shaman would bless that fertile region and give all its yield to the poor. I wondered what Jaguar would say if he heard that Talub had settled there, disregarding our sacred things and eating from a land that only the poor had a right to eat from.

I had not seriously questioned the Creator's character before this. How the faces of the poor used to light up when they saw me! But the Creator had forgotten all that. I had not been vain. I had not been cruel. I had not forgotten the Creator. Yet he had allowed so much turmoil to come into my life. I could only think I didn't belong to myself, but that my life was a thing the Creator could play with, something he used to benefit others, but I myself was of no importance.

While I pondered all this in my heart, a night came when I dreamed of Loic.

He entered a field but stayed near the sandy path. I walked beside him, unseen. He came upon a sand clock rising out of a grassy mound. Near it, a three-headed totem marked the village's holy place.

At last he spoke, as if to me. "The topmost head," he said, "reminds me of a forest spirit, the middle of the spirit I had met in the desert, and the bottom is the water spirit. All of them concerned with my quest, and now I've come to the place that honors them."

I sensed then the water spirit was the leader of the other three, that if she fell all the others would fall because they derived their power from her. I seemed to draw closer to my husband. What he saw, I too saw.

Written on the edges of the sand clock in an Ibeni dialect I didn't understand in waking life but which I understood in the dream were the words: *To the Unknown God*. My husband eyed the sign, squinting. He seemed unsure if the message was written out of superstition or genuine awe.

I whispered to him, "Knowing the Ibeni, fear caused them to write this."

He didn't seem to hear me, but passed the totems without paying the spirits any honor. The anger that had burned against him dissipated and a loving pride welled up in my heart for my young husband when he did this.

He continued walking about a stone's throw, when an old Ibeni shaman came running up to him. My husband examined the man, as if he were wondering if the stranger was human or not. But as the man came closer, my husband relaxed. His eyes studied the man's tattered short Ibeni vest and dirty headband. "I can see by your clothing you're human," my husband said.

"Why didn't you honor the spirits?" the old man asked, scowling. Sensing the man's anger, I feared for Loic's life.

"Why should I pray to spirits I don't like?" my husband answered the shaman.

"Foolish boy!" The man opened his fetish pouch. "What's liking the spirits got to do with worshiping them? These are great and powerful gods. They came to me in a dream a long time ago and told me to carve their likenesses on this totem. I have carved them exactly as they appeared to me."

I laughed as I slept because I was dreaming of man who spoke of dreams.

Loic didn't hear my laughter, but he pushed past the man. "Old man," he said, "my only concern is finding my horse. You Ibeni are, at best, unfriendly and greedy and, at worst, clannish and thieving. If I don't find my horse, someone will steal him and I'll be tricked into buying back my own horse."

"A young man's goods aren't his own property," the man said. "The thief who steals from a young man cannot steal much. If a thief steals from you, he'll be giving you a priceless lesson."

"Very witty," my husband said, "And what lesson might that be, Ibeni?"

"You're a proud one, aren't you?" The man waved his finger spitefully in Loic's face. "You think you walk in light now, but the day will come when you will be surrounded by darkness. You think yourself free to disobey the spirits, but these spirits will hedge you in one day, and only when you plead and humble yourself will they allow you to walk free."

"Kwelku, old man. Now, let me go."

The old man's face wrinkled with worry, so much so that I said to Loic, "He's worrying more for himself than for you." But Loic didn't seem to hear.

The old man was speaking. "Little Doreni, why cause the demons to war against you?"

I saw someone else approaching in the distance, an Ibeni boy about my husband's age. Loic saw the boy too. He turned to the old shaman. "Old man," he said, "try to serve gods who dress you better than these spirits do."

I burst out laughing and Loic walked toward the boy. When I turned to look at the man again, he was shaking some dust from his fetish bag in Loic's direction.

"Foolish man!" I said, believing he would not hear me because what was passing before me was clearly a vision.

But he turned hateful eyes at me and spoke angrily. "Yes, Satha," he said. "I see you. Neither you nor your young man will escape."

I woke up terrified, screaming until my throat ached. I didn't stop until Sena, Talub's chief steward, rushed into my tent to comfort me. His dark eyes peered out from his dark face and he anxiously searched the shadows of my tent. Relaxing his shoulders, he shook his head at me, then finished wrapping his turban about his head.

"Now girl," he said, "what's the matter? I thought one of the men had—"

Trembling from the cold and from the memory of the shaman's words, I tried to push the dream from my mind. "Had what?"

"Forced himself upon you, of course." He looked around the darkness of my wagon for an intruder. "You're a beautiful woman with no male to protect her. Who knows what could happen?"

"I'm safe from violation," I said pulling the knife from under the mat.

"Put that thing away. It's a best thing to avoid weapons if you're not an expert with them."

I waved it before his face, flicking it in the way my mentors had taught me. "Do you want to know if I know how to use it?"

He looked at me in silence for a while. "Stop or you'll hurt yourself trying to show off." He edged beside me and put his arm about my shoulder. He was about thirty years older than I was, yet his touch was not fatherly.

I removed his hand. "Any man who dares to touch me will fall."

Perhaps emboldened by the darkness, he allowed his eyes to linger over my nightdress and to show his desire for me. "True, there are things a man cannot own, but he can woo and win them."

My heart did not want Sena, although I knew that if I accepted protection under his mantle I would have been free from the advances of other men. I knew the Theseni customs well enough and would have found ways to delay the marriage indefinitely.

"Sena," I said, pointing at the door, "you should leave." I wanted to lie alone in my wagon and revisit the dream. I found myself wondering if Loic or even the Creator had sent me the vision.

"I could give you much if you married me," Sena said, not leaving.

"What could a slave give me?" I asked. "Not freedom. You would be making me a breeder of more slaves. Keep your wooing to yourself. I love and wait for my husband." Through the doors of my wagon, I saw the gray dawn pushing back the dark of the night. "No use me trying to fall back to sleep."

"You still haven't told me why you cried out."

How intrusive that man was! "I had a bad dream."

He nodded knowingly. "Yes, it's very hard to return to sleep after a bad dream." He lifted my gyuilta from the end of the wagon. "Come with me. I know a high rock near the edges of the homestead. When the sun rises the view makes your heart sing."

I remembered Noam and how he had deceived me. Yet, I trusted Sena. "I'll greet the morning with you," I said, showing him the dagger. "But keep your hands to yourself and speak no more of wooing."

How far and long the walk was I do not now remember. I am old now and even a short walk strains me. I remember we passed a river, meadows and totems sacred to our three peoples and as we walked I looked up at the constellations and at the promises written in them. The promise of a hunter who would chase the scorpion across the sky, the water bearer who would give us living water, the virgin-with-child whose son would rule the world and the uneven scales that would be balanced at last by the Southern cross. I longed for this savior to come and to free me from my life.

"You're quiet," Sena said suddenly. "I get nervous when you become quiet."

"We're trampling the holy ground of our ancestors underfoot," I said. "We should be quiet."

He shrugged. "Talub says we should not worship our ancestors. He says they don't live near us at all. He says everything our prophets have ever taught us is false, and that when we worship the Good Maker, we're not worshiping the Creator at all, only a demon pretending to be."

My heart burned against him and I defended my god. "Y'wa is the Good Maker, the Wind, the Creator, the One Above All. The Doreni have taught us that we all worship the same Creator and the only difference is in how he is worshiped."

The first rays of the sun gave the early dawn a dark blue cast. "The Creator has blessed my master. Because of this, I know his words are true. His descendants and his kind are destined to be the chief tribe of this land."

Great Chief, I prayed in my heart, and my body shook with grief. *You have seen and heard what these pale-skinned Angleni say. I know you speak only to witch doctors and to shamans, but you must understand how much I have loved you, and how deeply I have worshiped you and followed you. I am far away from those you usually speak to. Forgive me if I am bold to speak to you. Unless you are a heartless and distant God, you will answer me. Tell me, Great Chief, why those who serve you destroy their own lives. Look what happened to my mother! Look what happened to me! You do not lift my head from sorrow or deliver from afflictions, and you cause my enemies to trample me. Why?* No answer came, but I had not expected any.

We arrived at a large rock and Sena helped me climb to the top. "Look, Satha," he said, pointing down at the meadow beneath us. "Are we not kings? The earth is beautiful and lovely. Isn't that enough to ask for? Look all about you. Do we not have all that our master Talub has? Without the worry or the care. Look! The Colebru prairie is yours to see and to enjoy as much as if you owned it."

"I don't care to own it. All I wish is to own myself!" I spat and watched my spittle descend and disappear far below the rock. "So this is what being a slave does? It teaches men to accept small joys. Look at Talub's herds tearing at our holy ground as if they knew the land was already theirs." I turned to Sena. "Perhaps the king will hear how these foreigners desecrate the Colebru fields. Hospitable though he is, he will not allow such sacrilege."

Sena answered, "Jaguar is war-weary. A war-weary king often betrays his people. Anything for peace. I have heard it said also the death of his son has taken away his joy in life."

"I will still hope," I said. I did not understand then that grief could change the soul of even a king.

LOIC
Trumpa
The Weed Moon–First Heat Moon

"The One Above All be with you, Doreni," an Ibeni dialect greeted me.

When I looked up I saw a young man whose right arm was a twisted stump. This he seemed to continually scratch.

"The Creator has made this day, Ibeni," I answered.

"Blessings will come to you and to me," he said. Then, looking me up and down he added, "Oh, but you are wealthily-dressed! Or are you a thief who stole those fine goods?" He perused me further. "No, a thief you are not. A thief has not got such kind eyes."

He pointed to a house across the fields. "There is the rich man's house. But you ain't gonna get no help there. They got wooden doors there! Real wooden doors! With locks and latches. Best you stay at my house." His rough breechcloth and leggings were so patchy I almost refused his offer, but his adherence to the laws of hospitality impressed me.

"Locked doors?" I asked. "Have I reached a town so dangerous that locked doors are necessary? Jobara! Do people indeed walk into each other's houses and steal?" I looked around for Cactus, but he was nowhere to be seen. I imagined some Ibeni stealing Father's vialka and my shuwas from my unguarded stirrup.

"Everybody has them. People here keep learning and mimicking Angleni ways." He raised his stump of a hand. "You looking at this, right?"

I was. Although I had seen many wounded and maimed warriors, I had not seen a hand so badly mangled. Mud and dirt had collected inside folds of skin and crevices.

"Everybody looks at it first time they meet me," he continued. "Some mad Angleni soldier didn't want the war to be over. He got hold of me in the forest when I was a boy. Right back there somewhere . . . cut my hand off." He shook his stump in front of my face. "I can work well enough with it, though."

I grinned and, to please him, made a show of studying his hacked-off wrist. I suspected he thought of it as a badge of honor, and perhaps it was.

"I'll show you Ibeni hospitality," he said, taking a quick look at my travel pouch. "It ain't such fare as you're probably accustomed to eating. Being rich, you probably dine on meat three times a day. It's nothing but barley and beans around here. Not exactly enjoyable, but it puts the fat on you." His stump slapped his thin chest. "At least it puts the fat on most people."

To eat barley would be to invite the illness, and yet I was so hungry. Barley would be a feast to one who had spent the past moons eating wild berries and anything that would not eat him. I answered, "Indeed barley sounds good, but let me not take all your food. Give me only some of your beans."

"Waihai, you sound like you were taught to be grateful. You don't see that often. But you'll have to wait until I finish my work. Gotta be finished by nightfall or I'll lose the entire day's wages."

Behind him, the bare rain-wet fields lay red and bleak. "I can't take a poor man's food without doing some work for it. Tell me what is your work exactly. The field—"

"I make bricks."

"Bricks?"

"The Palefaces live in a village just past those two hills. They like bricks for their houses. Houses they're always building." *Palefaces?* That was the first time I had heard the word. "They're pals with the Therpas and seeing the Therpas are the largest clan around here, well they kinda make it impossible for folks not to make bricks."

"Bricks?" I asked. "Nothing else?"

He made a wide sweeping gesture that covered everything from the river to the plains ahead. "This used to be all ancestral lands. During the

Thunder Moon, everyone in Ulia used to plant jalak tubers and mukal berries near the river. In the Campfire Moon when prickly quinchea hung from hanging vines, we'd mix them with Carmi and make many different kinds of Carmi oil. My father would sell the oil in the market. Our specialty was an oil flavored with blossoms from the percusa trees—our own special formula. Our Matchless King did wrong when he made a truce with these enemies. He should have destroyed them and cleared them from our land. But even kings and their counselors can make stupid mistakes, I suppose."

I had never heard anyone speak disrespectfully of Jaguar, and I didn't know how to respond. Luckily, he gave me no chance to speak but rattled on. I had gotten so used to silence that his constant chatter annoyed me. Several times I felt the urge to shout at him, to tell him not to talk so much, but I kept my peace. He led me to a patch of ground where dried reeds rested on the reddish-brown clay.

"The name's Trumpa," he said kneeling down.

I knelt down too and watched as he used his stump to knead the reeds and clay together.

"It's a nickname," he continued. "Everyone says I can't stop talking when I start. *Trumpa, trumpa, trumpa, trumpa.* That's me. Like galloping horses." Self-mocking laughter rose from his throat. "But what else is there to do when you got no girl to talk to? You know how Ibeni women are . . . they want a man with a lotta money. They don't want no one-armed man. Especially someone from the poor Delco clan."

I had never met an Ibeni so indiscreet, so quick to talk about himself and anything on his mind. A friendly Ibeni was quite a paradox. Nevertheless, his concern for money and women showed he was a true Ibeni. "Your words are true," I said. "Ibeni women do not marry a man who has no chance of becoming rich."

"Which reminds me," he continued, "My sister thinks some rich man'll marry her and take away from all this." He made an exaggerated and sweeping gesture that encompassed all the mud and weed around us and laughed awkwardly. "Watch out for her. Tell me, though, when are you going to introduce yourself?"

I resisted the urge to say he would have known my name sooner if he hadn't been talking so much. "My name's Loic."

"Loic." He repeated the name several times. "A good name that. We had a Loic in my family back a ways. A good man too. Least that's what the family stories say. Nice meeting you, Loic."

We talked and made bricks until the sun set.

When I entered the little hut that Trumpa called home, a woman who I later learned was Trumpa's father's second wife—Trumpa's Little Mother, Unira—was sitting beside the hearth warming herself. She was a woman so thin I thought, *Perhaps it is only poverty, but she seems to me like one whom the demons are eating.*

The family ate in the twilight by a small lamp. Trumpa's father, Barro, seemed to begrudge me even the smallest bean I placed in my mouth. His eyes glared at me as if I had stolen the food from the mouths of his young children who played on the ground near Unira's feet. I took only a few spoonfuls, avoiding the barley carefully, then pushed the bowl away as if sated.

"You have fed me much too much." I slapped my stomach.

Trumpa's sister, Arlis, edged toward me. "You should eat more. This'll be the only thing you have to eat if you stay in this village which the One Above All has forsaken!"

But Unira added in a sickly whisper. "Hush, Daughter! The One Above All doesn't forsake. Don't blaspheme."

Arlis began flirting with me through her veil. "Chief Loic—"

"Don't call me Chief Loic," I interrupted her. "No one does."

"So you're not rich?" Her eyes examined the jade chain bracelet. "You're the first-born son of a poor clan?"

Offended at her obvious greed, I rose from the table. "I am in your debt, good family. May the One Above All bless you for your kindness in helping me. I was wrong to take what little food you have, but I will do as our laws command and repay the poor for their hospitality."

A guttural laugh rumbled up Barro's throat. "Kwelku, young Doreni. But I will not waste years waiting in my field for your repayment. In Ulia, the poor help each other and the rich forget any help the poor give them." He lifted the bowl with my leftovers and placed it in front of one of the younger children, a dirty little boy in tattered leggings who quickly gobbled them up. The child's obvious hunger shamed me even more.

"I will repay you," I insisted, but I did not explain that Doreni warriors did not travel with gold when they rode out on vendettas.

"What I'd like to know is this: Trumpa tells me you did not bow to the village totem. Why not?"

"I don't like being bullied by gods who are not gods. Nor will I worship them."

"Mentura. But don't let your disregard of the spirits fall upon us. The shaman you spoke to will no doubt tell the village elders about your actions. The spirits, of course, already know. As yet, they have not avenged themselves against us for helping you. They know that even though the Good Maker is afar off he still watches over the affairs of men. The Creator's curse flies through the earth ready to destroy the inhospitable and those who are unjust to their hosts. Even so, I've done my duty. You must leave at daybreak. Past dawn and the spirits will think I've betrayed them." He pointed to a spot near the fireplace. "Sleep there." He gave Arlis a warning look. "And only there."

My traveling gyuilta was lost now, tied to my wandering horse. I lay my head on the warm stone floor beside the hearth thinking of home. Home thoughts led to Satha and to Sio.

Sio and I had grown up together as brothers until I came to understand the truth. Even if the servants' resentment whirled about him, he had worn my father's name like a shield against harm and poverty. Now, however, I thought, *He is alone and unshielded and poor. I wondered how he fared in the bleak streets of some far-off city.* I tried to comfort myself with the thought that if our positions were exchanged Sio would not have been lying awake pitying me. But I knew this to be untrue—the boy had a kind heart— and such self-comfort was small indeed.

Barro threw a tattered horse blanket at me. Catching it, I folded it under my head. Anger against my father had journeyed with me, but now, it melted away. I thought of his kindness toward the poor, the weary or the foreigner. The rich in the Satilo region had followed

Father's example and strictly obeyed the ancestors' hospitality laws. Their obedience had probably saved the lives of many people, even though Father's continued hospitality toward Noam had brought ruin to my own life.

I had not lain there long when I heard footsteps approaching. At first I thought it was Trumpa, coming to afflict me with more stories about his life. The footsteps came softly and stealthily and stopped near my head. I pretended to be asleep, but soon felt warm female hands stroking my face. I opened my eyes. Arlis was looking down at me, her unlaced tunic revealing her breasts and her face unveiled.

I did not speak, only stared into her eyes. I was no fool. I knew she wanted me to couch with her. I opened my mouth to speak but she put one hand across my lips. With the other she held my right hand, once stroking my first-born bracelet.

"How much will you inherit of your father's wealth?" she asked. "All? Is it much? And how much is that? A lot of horses and houses and land, right?" She edged closer, causing me to scoot backwards.

"I have nothing and I don't know what I will inherit on my father's death."

"He wouldn't leave you penniless, would he? Or do you have a younger brother he loves better?" She bent lower, almost pushing her large pale breasts into my face. "What's the use of wearing the jade chain if it doesn't matter in the long run."

"If I, a first-born Doreni son, is killed, the entire clan must avenge me."

"So that's all it means, uh?" She sounded disappointed. She tossed her loosely-hanging hair over her shoulder pushing it out of my face but at the same time giving me an unblocked view of her breasts.

I wondered if I should say the obvious, she was squatting over me with bare breasts in spite of her father's warning. But to speak so clearly might have made her lace her tunic and I found myself wanting to see even more of those breasts.

"Chief Loic, my married friends say you Doreni men are a real catch." She glanced quickly at my breechcloth, then at my marriage cap. "But unfortunately, you're married? That's what the cap is for, right?"

I nodded.

"But your wife's far away. She won't know if—?"

"I'll know." It took some strength to say this because my ypher consented to her seduction even if my mind didn't.

"Does it matter if you know?" she asked. "All guilt is forgotten soon enough. If not, how could we humans live with the memory of our sins?"

This was how the Ibeni always thought about things. Always ready to indulge in some sexual sin, yet always guilt-ridden. I studied her face and liked her. The rawness of her unperfumed body was like mukal to all my senses. Warmth in my veins turned to heat. I burned with a passion that threatened to overtake me. It was a strange thing, this passion, more like a need than pure desire.

I lifted my hands to stroke her breasts, but then Little Mother's warnings came into my mind. Lust, she had always said, could rationalize itself. I knew then the woman was not right for me. Even so, I longed to kiss her. My fingers played with her hair and pushed her face toward mine.

Suddenly, my eyes were opened. By the firelight, but also by some inner and greater light, I saw something dark and sluglike oozing from the girl's neck. At first it seemed nothing more than a wound, a seeping pustule. Such diseases were common among the Ibeni, especially those who cavorted with Angleni soldiers. But the dark slug grew before my eyes. No wound ever did that. Although rooted in one spot, it snailed and stretched from her neck towards the top of her head. Slowly, it transmuted itself into a face with eyes, ears and a mouth. As the last lash of its eyelid formed, the eyes turned to look at me. Fire and hatred blazed in them. The face glared at me. A beautiful face full of hatred, fire and lust! Fear gripped my chest and I could not breathe. I lurched backwards, but not having eyes in the back of my head, I hit the back of my head against the hearth.

Arlis started to laugh. "Now look, your guilt made you hurt yourself."

She extended her hands toward me but I cried out, "No, don't touch me. I am perfectly all right."

She stood up, managing to look both flirtatious and motherly as she did so. "You're a strange one. You should allow your desires to overtake you. Life is short and such joys are all we have." Ibeni foolishness, yet again. But now I had seen the source of her philosophy.

"I-I . . ." I stuttered. What else was there to do but stutter? I could not say a demon lived within her and would have contaminated me if I had lain with her. I managed to mutter, "I must be faithful to my wife."

"Ah yes, Doreni faithfulness!" She squatted on the floor, her legs wide open. "Does she sing for you at the Nadam games? 'Thrown down, fallen, unable to rise! Thrown down, fallen, never to rise!' Is that the song she sings when you triumph in the horse races and archery tournaments? Does she sing: 'A thousand women want this warrior, but he is mine. Ten thousand women seek this warrior, but he is mine'?"

"She sings both those songs, and more," I answered and scooted backwards, careful not to let her touch me, careful to avert my eyes from the hairy moist place between her legs.

She sighed, and her breasts glowed gold in the firelight. "Loic, I wanted you the instant I saw you. I've never felt anything like that before. The others were only a little fun . . . but you . . ."

I winced and continued crawling backwards. The demon in her neck grimaced wretchedly, then vanished. Yes, he was angry that I had seen him.

"Well, if we can't play, I suppose I'll have to sleep," Arlis said and walked slowly back to an inner room. Wary lest she return and lie unasked at my side, I tried to put off sleep. I fell asleep at last, but even in sleep the spirit's face haunted me.

I woke early and lay on the floor with my eyes closed, confused about where I was. My head ached. Then, the dampness of the blanket beneath me and the smell of urine made me realize my sickness had come upon me while I slept. *The barley,* I told myself. *I should have known that I would not be safe from it.* Around me sounded footsteps—heavy and light—and pots, pans and metal tubs clanged. I opened my eyes slowly to see a veiled Arlis looking at her father and holding her nose. She wore a Kelovet-styled dress and obviously knew how to wear it well.

"You rich boys sleep late," she said when she noticed I was looking at her. "I suppose we should have told you where the squatting place is."

She lacks etiquette, I said to myself. *She should have pretended not to notice.*

Barro said to his daughter. "A fine dress you're wearing only to go to the market." Unlike his daughter, he was gracious and polite. He did not force me to acknowledge my shame, although my situation was obvious.

Arlis chuckled and pointed to something outside the door. "That horse of yours is as faithful to you as you are to that wife of yours."

"Is Cactus outside?" I asked, rising quickly in spite of my shame, or rather because of it.

My hair had unraveled while I slept and it hung limp and dirty about my waist. It too smelled of urine.

"You rich can afford to wear your hair long and oiled," Barro said. "No machinery to grab it. No clay to dirty it."

"It'd take a year's worth of a poor man's wages to oil and perfume it, would not it, Father?" Arlis agreed. "I bet you do have servants to wake you, Chief Loic. You probably wear them long fancy gyuiltas too." She picked up the horse blanket on which I slept and, holding it gingerly between her fingertips, walked outside the door with it.

"When I return home," I said to Barro, "my father will repay you for your kindness to me. Fool that I am, I carried no quixas with me."

"I've heard the Doreni do not carry money when they go on vendettas. Is that true?" Barro asked. "Because they do not venture into cities or villages. They stay in fields and meadows plotting their schemes. Have you traveled here seeking revenge?"

"How could I be on a vendetta?" I asked. "I have ventured into a village."

"True," he said, but I saw in his mind he did not believe me.

Arlis re-entered the door, holding up my travel pouch which she had removed from Cactus's saddle. She lifted my gyuilta from the pouch and examined it with a vendor's eye. "This is the kind used by travelers. I bet it has a lot of hidden pouches. "Maybe you've got some quixas in here?" She stroked it as I approached and seemed loath to part with it. "Oh, this is real warm. Well-made. Good protection from the desert sand and the cold snows. Look at the hood, Father. Is it not well-made?"

"Too well-made for the likes of us," Barro answered, giving me a steaming cup of barley-grass tea, which I refused. "To wear something like that around here is to invite our neighbor's envy. I don't want them sending spirits to trouble us for a cloak."

"True," she said, nodding and continued searching my bag. Finding the golden nose-ring I had given Satha, she squealed, "Ah, you are rich! Your wife's?"

"Arlis," Barro shouted. "Are you going to the market or not?"

She stood in the door and held the ring to the morning light. "It's a pretty one! The work of a talented goldsmith. That marriage cap of yours is nice-looking too. Your wife made it, didn't she? She's a good maker! Is she pretty? A rich and beautiful Doreni girl?"

"Very pretty, but she's Theseni and yes, she's a good maker like all Theseni girls."

She gave me a pitying look, and shook her head. "I suppose she must be pious. Only a dutiful Theseni girl would take you. Even money can't make up for your little problem."

I had no time to answer her before the loud slap of Barro's open hand hit hard against her face. She recoiled, rubbing her cheek and pouting.

Barro returned the nose-ring to me. "I recognize the markings on your cap. Pagatsu. This nose-ring has Desai crafting, but here you are in the Therpa homeland? Not much of a homebody, are you?"

"I've come to see a cousin from my mother's clan. A former captain of my father's. A teacher of religion."

He eyed me suspiciously. "Ganti?"

Arlis clucked her tongue, then found her voice again. "That old preacher? First you marry a Thesenya and then you study religion. I suppose the sick need religion."

"Girl, you don't know when to keep your mouth," her father warned. He turned to me. "Does your father know Ganti is a zealot, with a vendetta against the Therpas?"

"Noam Therpa was my Father's captain, his good friend. The Therpas will not harm me. Jobara! They gave me many gifts at my wedding. If Ganti has a vendetta against them, it is his alone. Not mine or my father's."

Barro almost smiled, almost, and yet he seemed profoundly relieved for my sake. "This warring among you Doreni used to amuse me. Now, the Angleni are creeping into our land, and your infighting fills me with fear. Only sure kingdoms can waste time fighting small internal battles." He looked at the door for a long while as if pondering some deep thought. "You Doreni have never been conquered, so you cannot imagine being conquered. You value fairness and honor and so you imagine others do the same. When you Doreni conquered this land you tried to make all live together in harmony, so you cannot imagine a religion whose believers behead those who do not convert to their beliefs. I fear for our land. One hundred years from now will most of its inhabitants bear Angleni features and speak the coarse Angleni language? Will any of the three tribes still exist? I often think—"

"Them earrings in your ears?" Arlis interrupted him. "They're awfully pretty, aren't they?"

I stared long at her, hoping to shame her. In those days, custom dictated that if a stranger admired something you owned, you should present it to her as it a gift. The nose-ring was my wife's and I could not have offered it to her. The marriage cap would have been useless to her. The earrings, however, could be offered to her, but even an Ibeni would consider it shameful to ask a warrior for his ear-loops. I started to remove them but Barro stopped me with a slow shake of his head.

"Warriors need to look like warriors. Even if they are young. Hurry now and prepare to leave. Your helping my boy with the bricks yesterday was payment enough. A little piece of advice, however. Around here, it's best not to give anyone anything that you wear." He nodded towards the door. "I suspect there's more to your journey than you're willing to say. I also suspect it's best for me if I know as little as possible about it. The spirits of this region love Ganti and he might intercede for you against the villagers, but trouble from the spirits is one thing, trouble from the Therpas quite another. For your own sake, and because the Therpa chief's son is your father's friend, pay them a visit to the Blue Fortress while you're at Ganti's. Such etiquette has been known to save lives."

———————

Outside, the beauty of the dawning sky was only made more beautiful when Cactus came trotting towards me. I threw up a quick praise to the One Who Holds My Breath in His Hand. Together Cactus and I strolled toward the river. "I need to bathe," I whispered as I rubbed his nose. "The illness came upon me last night. I smell as if I've been wading in a squatting place. Do you think the water-spirit will pull me under the waves?"

He shook his long mane as if to say, "When did you begin fearing spirits?"

I did not tell him that the fall into Gebelda had made begin to fear many things. Instead, I plunged into the serene water. If the spirits were there, they left me alone. How cool the river's waves felt as they flowed over my body! So warm and languid was the day, so free from care!

Trumpa soon came shouting across the fields. "The Creator made this day, Loic."

"It brings blessings to you and to me!" I shouted back, throwing water on my head.

When he reached the river's edge, he turned and looked in the direction from which he had come. "Now that morning has come, the hospitality law can no longer protect you—or us."

Worried as much for him as for myself, I walked onto the shore. "How far away is Ganti's place?" My wet tunic lay dripping from the large rock on which I had laid it.

"Haven't you told my father you would be visiting the Therpas?"

"I made no such promise, but—"

"We have two large cities in these parts. Both are about two days hard ride. One is in that direction." He pointed with his good hand. "That's mostly Ibeni people. A few Theseni slave-traders, some Doreni from scattered clans—mostly Therpa, but you might find some of your own clan there."

I hastily pulled on the tunic. My leggings, although moist and cold, comforted me like an old friend. "And Ganti's school?"

"That's the other direction. Near the other city. Mostly Therpa

Doreni there. Small villages and of course, the Therpa Great House. Some other scattered clans. Several Angleni settlements. One or two good towns, but for the most part they're pretty hateful. Be careful when you pass those. Them Angleni prefer to live by themselves and if they find you alone, who knows? I've heard stories that some of our people have disappeared when they got too near Angleni settlements. If you follow the river, and don't turn aside, you'll arrive safely to Ganti's place. You'll hear them rich boys singing. About war, devotion, honor, the spirits, and the Wind God. Stuff we normal people are to busy to care much about."

I whistled for Cactus. He galloped toward me, but he shook his mane so vigorously, I thought some insect had bitten him and searched his mane and forelock. It was no insect that bothered him but spellwork. Many threads there were, looped and braided in intricate knots. I quickly unwound them. Other threads, too, were craftily interwoven in the fringes of the sleeves of the gyuilta on my saddle and through the loops of the beadwork in my travel pouch. Them I could not unwind, and so I cut them with Satha's dagger and broke the spell.

As I did this, Trumpa watched me, a guilty look on his face. "Was your sister up all night holding my future captive in her magic needlework?" I asked, annoyed that she had tried to bind me.

He looked at me, shamefaced; yet how I feared Arlis' spellwork! *What,* I asked myself, *if I am already bound? If in spite of myself I soon am overcome with longing for this Ibeni whore?*

Little Mother used to say: "A curse causeless will not come." So I thought hard and searched myself and hoped there was no sin in me in which a curse could root itself.

I threw the binding cords into the river and bade farewell to Trumpa. Then I mounted Cactus and rode far from that field. When I had ridden a great distance, I stopped and dismounted beside a large boulder. Most Pagatsu clansmen only cut their hair to acknowledge the great changes of life. I sensed that I was facing a change in my life and my hair should be cut.

Removing Satha's dagger from my boot, I sliced through my scalplock like the Creator's words shining through darkness. The

Doreni holy books had taught us that the Creator God was a rock who shields from the storms of life. I called out to the Creator and reminded him that he was my rock and my shield from the evil winds. Then, as a covenant between him and me, I put my hair under the rock. "Let me hide myself in you!" I shouted. "Cover me."

A vast sandy bay spread ahead of me. The river's tide receded and disappeared over the horizon. I followed the river to Ganti's compound. *Father trusted him,* I told myself. *If Father trusted him, I would trust him also.*

SATHA
A *Lost Child*
Thanksgiving Moon–Third Harvest Moon

A wave of cold air enveloped me, and Voora's wagon closed in around me like a grave. *To lose a child in the Thanksgiving Moon,* I thought. *If our positions had been reversed would she be helping me?* Her faint breathing made me compassionate in spite of myself. The curtain of her wagon flung itself outward as if some invisible wind was calling me from her side and back to my sense. I could see outside where the sun's beams bounced off the golden fields the Angleni already claimed as their own.

The image of my dead daughter returned to my mind, and memory of that first grief made it difficult not to feel sympathy for a woman whose child had died. I thought, L*oic is right. I am not a true Doreni. Once again, I'm having compassion for an enemy. What harm will this new mercy cause me?*

As a slave-midwife, you had opportunity to increase your mistress's suffering. You could even cause childbirth to kill her if you wished. The thought seemed not my own, but it persisted and grew stronger in my mind.

"The child will survive, Voora," I lied, gently massaging her stomach and trying to push the murderous thoughts from my mind. "The herdsmen are praying to your god. I am praying to mine."

Sweat glistened on her wrinkled face. "Your superstitions can't help—" A shriek cut her venom short.

Talub stood outside the wagon, peering through the curtain, his eyes pleading and questioning me.

"There's much blood," I said, glancing up at him. The mat on which she lay was soaked with blood, and yet the dead child had not emerged from her body. I touched her stomach gently. Hard, Tight. No sign of life within. "When I lost my child, there was much blood also."

A disdainful look spread across Voora's face. "The death of your dark child, a child of sin, should not be compared to the death of my child."

Again the wagon in which she lay closed in on me like a tomb, like the tomb of my people. Tears brimmed in my eyes as I considered what HaZatana had called me to submit to. I rose quickly and hurried towards the wagon's door, not wanting her to see my tears.

"I will return with more tea for you," I said, keeping my voice steady. "It is a tea our midwives use."

Outside in front of the fire, I made more andarda tea, until Talub approached and hovered above me, silent.

"I won't leave her for long," I said. "The tea must be made. It helps to push the child and the afterbirth out."

As I spoke, a voice interrupted me. *Satha.* It sounded like a voice of many voices. *Make the tea stronger. Add some anley to it. We, the ancestors, demand you save the land of our people.*

I looked into Talub's eyes and saw that he hadn't heard the voice of my ancestors. Nor had he sensed the authority with which they had ordered me to kill his wife. All about the encampment, the fields glinted wet from the cold rains. Near my feet, a patch of purple anley wildflowers gleamed. In the distance, fog and frost mingled on the herdsmen praying for Voora as they tended Talub's cattle.

The voices spoke again, *Satha, this woman's child is destined to create a law which will destroy your people. Kill her now or your children's children will be gathered to barren places and removed from their land forever.*

Talub's features still showed only worry for his wife. *No, I thought, he has not heard the voice. Am I mad? Has grief made me mad?*

I remembered the madmen who used to stroll the market, wild-eyed and raving. Had I seen so much sorrow that my mind had turned on itself? Was grief about to make me a murderer? An inner trembling arose in my body, throbbed until my whole body shook.

Talub put his hand on my shoulder. "Although you are often disobedient to those superior to you, you have been helpful to my wife . . . and to me."

His touch only agitated me; I gently pushed it away.

He thinks himself your superior, the voice of voices said. *We, the Arkhai, are the ones who are your superiors. You must hearken to us.*

The andarda seethed, boiled, until the surrounding air was redolent with it. The floral scent of the anley seemed to merge with it. I struggled to catch my breath, and hoped the voice wouldn't speak again.

But it did. Again, the voice seemed to comprise many dialects, many clans, all three tribes. *We, your ancestors and the spirits of this land, demand you kill this woman who is fated to bear a son who will rule our lands.*

The air about me crackled cold, but my heart burned within me as if a fiery shuwa had pierced it. *Are the Arkhai indeed speaking to me?* I asked myself. I should have felt honored, that they knew of me. But how could I? They had asked me to murder, and I was no murderer.

I had always thought Voora's insistence on having a child was an Angleni female madness, but the Arkhai's words made me wonder. *Was Voora so important? Who was she that I should kill her? And who was I to be placed with such an important woman?*

Behind me a long moan escaped, fled Voora's wagon.

"If Loic were here—" I began, then realized I was talking aloud to myself.

"Loic?" Talub echoed, then searching his mind, "Ah yes, the one you say you're married to."

The Arkhai spoke again. *What is Loic to you? A husband who never trusted your love? A husband who chose you because you were the best he thought he could do? You have allowed your life to be destroyed by silly pious teachings—and what has all that pious reading done for you? But you can still redeem your life from meaninglessness. Kill the Anglenya.*

Silently, I poured the tea into a bowl and a small cup. Slowly, I rose and walked past the patch of anley toward the wagon. The nearer I came to the wagon, the frostier the air became. A wall of ice seemed to descend all around me. My feet felt encased in snow, but I pushed through, my teeth chattering, my feet aching, and climbed into the wagon.

Voora's terrified, grieving eyes stared at me, as I knelt on the mat beside her. She glanced weakly at me when I lifted her head into my lap.

Tears full of questions flowed from the corners of her eyes. "This is not the way it should be," she said. "I am destined to have a child who will rule this nation."

The voices grew angry then, sounding like thunders bouncing and echoing off each other. *Will you betray your people and your husband's people, Satha?* they screeched. My spirit ear tried to close itself against them.

I do not want to betray my people to the Angleni, my thoughts answered *the ancestors. But neither do I want you Arkhai warring against me.*

I stroked Voora's hot moist forehead and held the bowl of tea to her lips.

Satha, have you ever warred against spirits intent on avenging themselves against you? they asked. Terrified and shaking, I spilled the bowl of tea on the floor of the wagon.

"Fool!" Voora whispered, her voice weak but her venomous hatred as strong as ever.

The voices of the Arkhai, although unheard with human ears, raged loudly, *Make this invader more tea, and this time, steep anley with it.*

My physical ear burned and I clutched it to push the pain away. Suddenly Voora howled, a moan like that of a buffalo speared through the heart. The dead child oozed out of her womb. Cold daggers pricked at my collarbone.

I pulled my gyuilta closer around my shoulders to stave off the cold, and lifted the perfectly-formed small thing that lay between Voora's legs. It had gone gray. Covered with blood it was, and I lifted it to her face that she might see her dead child for the first and last time. She wept then, as I did. Not for her grief, but for my own remembered loss, and because now in addition to being separated from my clan and family, the Arkhai had begun their war against me.

Talub entered. I gave the child into his arms and ran outside to fetch water and to clean the blood from Voora's legs. When I returned, Talub sat holding his dead child. He did this until sunset, reminding me of Loic's vigil in front of the ancestral arbor.

When the moon rose to its height, Talub ordered the herdsmen to dig into the ground. How surprised I was that their burial rituals were so much like the Theseni rituals! And how grieved I was when he changed the name of that place—a place so holy to our people— to the name of his lost child.

The next morning, Sena strolled up to me when I sat grinding corn. All my muscles ached as if I had been on a long journey. Yet the action of pestle against mortar soothed me into a rhythmic numbness, and I had no desire to speak to Sena.

"It's good for Voora to have a woman here," he said, throwing a wool gyuilta over my shoulders and leaning on my wagon.

I shrugged, not wanting to think, not being able to think.

He bent down and brushed some dried corn from my bare feet. "I've always liked the kindness and wisdom of our Theseni women. A Doreni woman would have killed her when she had the chance."

When he said this a sudden burning pain seared through my body. My stomach heaved as if some living thing had been put inside me, something that wrestled to escape.

"Perhaps Voora will remember your kindness to her," he continued, looking over at Voora's wagon. "I doubt it, though. Maybe if you helped her to conceive a child—"

"And why should I help bring another Angleni into the world?" I shouted, trying not to bend over from the pain in my stomach.

He stared at me, offended. "Such anger!" He waved his finger in my face. "This is not the way proper Theseni women behave. The Doreni fierceness has influenced you badly. Did not the Good Maker teach us to be kind to our enemies and to bring water to them in their thirst?"

"How I hate to hear Theseni men speaking platitudes!" I said, rising. "Even now—even with the Doreni laws against it—we Theseni sell each other to the highest bidder. So stop binding me to laws and morals that others feel free to discard. Especially since you don't seem to be following them."

I held my stomach, trying to push the pain from my body.

"How beautiful you are when you're angry!" he said, gushing. "How righteous and full of strength and wisdom! Satha, you must marry me."

"Have I not told you to stop speaking of these things?" I shouted, trying to quell the pain in my stomach. "Do you really think I would couch with a man who cares for livestock?"

"Oh yes, I forgot," Sena said, looking hurt. "You're a Doreni Chieftain's wife. Supposedly. But there is no talk of this in any of the towns? If the son of Captain Treads Lightly had lost his wife, would everyone not be out searching for her?"

"Why should the Doreni tell Angleni strangers any of their business? If they were searching for me and planning a vendetta, why would they tell anyone? You obviously don't know the Doreni as I do."

He sucked at his teeth. "All the same, you should think of a better lie. Consider also that having a man in your life will make your lot easier." He looked nervously in the direction of Talub's wagon, then quickly slipped his arm around my waist. "When a man's day's work is done, he helps his wife with her chores." Then, taking another quick look around the campsite, he suddenly kissed my cheek.

"Does the death of an unborn child excite you with thoughts of couching with married women, Sena?" I asked, intending to shame him.

Shame did indeed spread across his face like dark clouds spreading across the sky.

"Satha"—his pitiful wooing was pale compared to Loic's youthful passion—"will you not consider me for a husband? I know I'm an old man, but can't you see how much I love you?"

I pushed the pestle and mortar away and scooped the crushed corn into a bucket. All the time the fiery pain in my stomach burned hotter. "This talk of yours comes at the wrong time, Sena!"

Near us the ravens cawed. The ancestors' messengers. Sena crushed the dried blossom of a meadow flower in his hand, as I had crushed the corn, and as memory, slavery and the Arkhai's whispers in my mind were crushing me.

LOIC
Ganti
Mackerel Moon–First Snow Moon

"Approach, Loayiq." Ganti looked away from his target, turning his arrow to the ground. "This is a day the Creator made."

"It will bring blessings for you and for me, Older Brother."

"I'm honored to see you, Younger Brother."

"Older Brother, you treat me with too much honor, especially since I've forgotten you."

His eyes, gray like the waters of the Great Sea and seemingly as moody, studied me while falling leaves and twigs swirled around him. "Young children only remember what's important to them." He laughed and pointed to the surrounding high walls and columns of Blade Castle.

So this is Ganti? I thought. Like many of the old soldiers in my father's compound, he was bent, walked slowly and his body seemed gnarled with pain. Like theirs his face was handsome and stoic. Besides his large straight and too narrow nose—which Little Mother always reassured me was a Desai trait—he had one distinguishing mark—on his right cheek, a dark red stain like congealed blood bulged under his tanned skin.

In the distance behind him, a girl disembarked from a boat in the river bordering his property and began walking towards us. She wore leggings like Puhlya's, with Desai markings. But instead of a buckskin dress, she wore an Ibeni vest—a garment worn only by men. Although etiquette demanded that I speak to my host, the girl fascinated me because even though the air blew cold, she wore a female Ibeni vest without a tunic. Its laces were clasped over her bare breasts, something no Doreni woman—not even our greatest female warriors—would have done.

"Jobara!" Ganti said, as if he could see my thoughts. "My daughter is indeed beautiful to look at!"

As the girl approached us, her dark hair, curly and thick, blew wild about her head. The fierceness of her walk fascinated me, and although a freezing wind blew from the river, her barely covered breasts peeked over her vest.

She stood before me, a girl about my age or younger, and gave me a searching look. Then, after giving Ganti a playful squeeze on his shoulder, she said, "He doesn't look like one of our people."

Bold words, I thought. *She doesn't have Doreni eyes and her skin is as pale as any Ibeni's yet she says I don't look like a Desai.*

A knowing smile spread across her face and she raised her hands, perusing them for a moment. "True, I lack the deep dark brown color of the Theseni, but should you judge me on skin color alone?"

"Alla, my child," Ganti said, "this is Loayiq tyu Taer. You've heard me speak of him."

Her eyes widened. "I thought this was the one the spirits told us to expect today, but I was not sure at first."

"The spirits told you I would be coming?" I almost turned on my heels and left. Perhaps I should have, but then I might never have met my destiny.

She lowered her eyes, flirting. "Loayiq tyu Taer, I hadn't thought you would be so lovely to look at."

She was not like Satha. Satha weighed each of her words and kept half her thoughts hidden. Alla spoke all that came to her mind. Intrigued, I realized I was now faced with a woman who would have no qualms about trying to take me to her bed.

She continued. "Just now, the spirits told me to return to shore because you had finally arrived. I had expected you to arrive sometime in the afternoon." Her eyes studied my clothes and my cut hair as if I were a strange creature washed up from the sea. "I've heard that you didn't care much about your mother's clan, and I don't remember seeing you at any of our Desai feasts. Layo, layo! I would've remembered seeing you, memorable as you are."

"Both clans have been in the wrong concerning restoring alliances," I said, growing more uncomfortable. Fear of her directness, fear of her beauty, fear of the spirits and their influence over her—all combined to make me worry for my future. "The Desai as well as the Pagatsu. But all that is past. Lost time no longer matters now that my father has sent me here to study with you."

"Well answered, young chief," Ganti answered, smiling slyly as if he had seen the other thoughts strolling in my mind. "But haven't I seen you lately? At Lihu's memorial?"

I searched my mind. "I don't remember seeing you, Older Brother."

"You had other things on your mind."

His words only agitated me further. He seemed to be playing with me, hinting that he could see my thoughts and studying me to see what my response to such a challenge would be.

"I haven't come to study long, Older Brother. A few things only. Those truths a warrior needs to know. I'll stay seven days, maybe less. As long as it takes for me to understand and accept death."

A playful grimace flowed over Alla's face. A chuckle followed. "Do you, who cry so easily, and who see spirits at every turn, think you will so easily learn to accept killing another?"

But Ganti said, "The funeral of our dear Prince Lihu was lesson enough!"

I had not thought of myself as one who cried easily. Her words shamed me. I thought, *Even if her words are true and I don't have a warrior's heart, should she have been so rude to tell me about myself? Should she not have shown etiquette by hiding this truth from me?*

She shrugged then and rolled her eyes. "For a Desai, you're not very tough-skinned. If you had lived among us and seen how easily we knew each other's hearts, you would not be behaving like those stiff closed Pagatsu—"

"I heard you married." Ganti interrupted her, and gestured towards a long series of steps by a nearby colonnade.

"Yes—" I glanced at Alla "—a kind-hearted Theseni woman."

"I'll tell Kaynu that this cousin of ours has arrived," she said, walking toward the steps.

"Tell him Loayiq will lodge with Twin."

She frowned and I immediately began to fear this unknown Twin. She left, swinging her bare arms in the cold breeze.

I walked with Ganti toward the steps. He removed the bow from his shoulder and hefted it in his hand. "It's a good weapon," he said. "A graceful weapon. Little use, though, against the Angleni fire—hand cannons and guns. Have you studied it?"

"I prefer the vialka."

He raised his eyebrows, then began to laugh at me. "Young Chief, warriors don't 'prefer' weapons. A warrior might use one weapon more capably than another, but the battle chooses the weapon, not the warrior." He gave me the bow. "Your father likes the vialka also. It sails from his hand like the wind."

He smiled, perhaps at his thoughts, but for a fleeting moment an image presented itself to my mind: my father stood in a field facing his enemies, the vialka flying from his hand. "Was he not a good warrior?" Ganti asked.

I knew then, that he had placed his memory in my mind. *How strange*, I thought, *that Father should keep me from perfecting this Desai gift!*

"You Pagatsu are a silent clan," Ganti said. "Alla is right. You're closemouthed in order to be kind, closemouthed because of etiquette. But if you wish to kill and not be haunted by killing as your father is—"

My mouth fell open. I wondered, *Has Puhlya or a messenger from my father been here? Or is this the Desai gift yet again?*

I waited for him to put his foot on the landing of the first step. He lingered. "Noam was my fellow captain during the war," he said. "I never disliked him. He had a spirit that might have been truly noble if he had been born in another clan. He was reckless and wild—good traits—but he did not commit himself either to the spirits or to the ancestors. Such a man is bound to find trouble." He gestured for me to extend my hand. "Although I hate the Therpas as I hate all clans who have befriended the Angleni, I was grieved the friendship between Noam and your father was destroyed by the Therpa wife. Your father's heart is too kind; he sees evil but excuses it."

I nodded. I saw the Therpa great house in his mind, suddenly. Images of the Blue Fortress colored his mind as coorat tea leaves colored brewed water.

He continued, resting his hand on my shoulder as we climbed the stairs. "My only warning is this. If you intend to kill my old compatriot, don't kill him while so near the Therpa region. It complicates my own plans."

"What plans?" I asked.

"If you were truly Desai, you would already know my plans."

"Are the Desai all of one mind, then?" I asked.

"We are not all one mind, and there are ways of protecting one's mind. Trouble is, Young Chief, your mind is easily seen because you have had no practice living among your own people."

At the top of the stairs, he turned and peered triumphantly down the steps. "In my younger days, I wouldn't consider climbing stairs such a feat." He turned to me. "Consider what I say. It's sad to kill an enemy but even more devastating to kill a good friend. Are you prepared to do this? I remember days when you crawled about our legs." He touched my earloops. "By the time I had reached your age, many ribbons and feathers dangled from both my ears—and not from killing only buffaloes. I had killed eighteen men. Or maybe nineteen, I don't remember. Most were Angleni. But some were friends. Former friends. Again, I adjure you to think carefully, young man. Perhaps you do not want to kill a friend."

"I want to kill a former friend," I answered.

He pointed to a door in a nearby wall. "We shall see. Now, if you will pardon an old and busy teacher, there are student writings I must read —some of which aren't worth the parchment they're written on."

"To write a love poem is difficult enough," I answered. "One can hardly blame students for not knowing how love and war work together."

He looked long at me, then threw his head back, laughing. "So you are truly Desai! I was wondering when you would prove yourself. Perhaps you are indeed the prophesied one. Those who can reliably see the thoughts of another are often trained for years by mentors. But, young man, you have great skill. And yet no Desai has taught you."

"I am not the prophesied one, Older Brother. Prophecies are not my concern. Nor is this skill reliable."

He pushed aside the doorway curtain. "Kwelku. Even so, my people have argued about you throughout the years. Some say you follow the Wind. Some say otherwise. Tell me, did your Pagatsu clansmen give you a nickname?"

"My Little Mother called me Loicuyo."

"Wildfire, a fiery wind."

"I had a bad temper when I was younger."

"Not now?" He grinned as if he knew the answer already. "And did your wife give you a nickname?"

"She called me Loic," I lied, "no other name."

"So the half-moon I see coloring your mind means nothing to you?"

Caught in a lie, I turned my face away.

"Remember, you're among Desai now. Why lie? Now tell me, why do you dislike the true pronunciation of your name? Loayiq is the name your mother called you. When I was younger and not curious about the workings of the minds around me, I thought the Pagatsu called you Loic simply because they couldn't pronounce the 'oay' vowel as those from the Desai region did. I got older, however. There is more to this than simple dialect. Your father—"

"I do not dislike the name, but the last person—the first person—who used it irritated me."

"Puhlya?" He nodded, and gazed wistfully over the slowly-flowing river. "Our Desai women are like that, unfortunately. I suspect if your mother had lived, you would have liked Puhlya. They were very similar."

A grin spread across his face, softening but not blurring his distinguished features. "We humans are strange, indeed. You will avoid the truth of your name simply because you dislike the one who used it?" Again, he seemed to be thinking of the past. "When Chula my concubine was killed by an Angleni during the war, he shouted one of our war cries across the field. It had been ours but I grew to hate it because the Angleni used it. When my beloved chief wife died of grief because our sons were killed, she too uttered that cry. With that she returned the word to me and to my people."

As he spoke I saw, more vividly than I could if I myself had remembered it, the scene of his children's death. "Older Brother!" I gasped, suddenly fearful that being Desai would mean understanding the griefs and sorrows of all those around me. "The death of sons! The death of a beloved wife. The death of a concubine! My grief is nothing compared to those you've experienced."

He looked past me, past the fields and toward the river. "Who can compare griefs? Nevertheless, I will not use a name that offends you, even though the name was yours before Puhlya spoke it."

Still overcome with the images of the death of his concubine and sons, I wiped my eyes with my sleeve.

"Don't be ashamed of your tears," he said, pulling my head toward his chest. "Death is what we live for, is it not? We want to enter the fields we long for, and all our life is a journey towards it. My children are hunting with the Creator. And the others—well, they are here to welcome you into the family."

"Not all your children died, then?" I asked.

"I have some children left to me. A married daughter living in the north. Married into the Dicco Ibeni clan."

"A noble clan indeed!" I said.

He nodded. "Jobara. Nobility is rare among the Ibeni. My other children are Alla, my adopted daughter. And Kaynu, an adopted son, the only son of my cousin—his first and only child."

"You adopted your cousin's only son?" Although Doreni clans were always adopting strangers, such an adoption was unheard of in my time.

"Kaynu is the warseed of an Angleni soldier who raped my cousin's wife during an incursion. My cousin still loved his wife, but wanted nothing to do with the boy."

"Even though custom dictates the son of a warrior's wife is a warrior's son?"

"Yes. That custom he could not obey. But he did bow to the custom which dictated he could not couch with his wife after another had tainted her." He sucked at his teeth. "Strange the customs we hold to, and those we discard. Would he not have suffered less if his choice had been the other way around? To couch with a beloved wife and have children instead of continuing childless forever?" A shadow fell across his face. "As for Alla, I found her when she was about four in an Ibeni brothel. She had been cast about from one family in her clan to another. She was originally from the Xodos clan."

I took a deep breath. The Xodos were known as the worst of the Ibeni clans.

"I need not tell you what might have become of her if I had not taken her under my care. Or what they might have already done when I found her. Although they would have made more selling her in the brothels, they were willing enough to hand her over to me for a few thousand quixas. Your sorrows and griefs, Younger Brother, will be in our heart, as the griefs and sorrows of your father's clan are in your heart. You have found your family again."

He studied my face again. "But you need to be named, Young Chief. What do you think of the name 'Wind Follower'?" His eyes searched my face—and probably my mind—to see my reaction to the name.

"I neither like nor dislike it," I answered.

"Do you not? I am told that when you were young you roamed from place to place as the wind blew you. Now you're older, you may still travel or rest as the wind wills."

I shrugged. "Kwelku."

"Kwelku jobara! Indeed, I do say. You will come to own the name, Wind Follower, because it is already yours."

When I entered the Blade Castle schoolhouse, Alla was waiting for me. A boy about my age with skin as pink as a pig's and light brown hair stood beside her. He wore a clan cap with Desai markings and a beige Ibeni vest made of hemp fabric.

"So this is Loayiq?" he asked her when I approached. "Layo, Layo, Jobara? Truly, truly, indeed?"

"Jobara," she said slowly. Their eyes looked me up and down in such a startling manner, I grew ashamed, receiving unearned, undeserved glory.

"This is a day the Creator made!" he declared, with the excitement of a child meeting a renowned warrior.

"It will bring blessings for you and for me," I answered. Nevertheless, my heart glanced backward toward the door, toward the mountainside outside Blade Castle.

"I'm Kaynu," he said and touched my right shoulder. "I've longed to meet you, Brother. May I call you 'brother'?"

"Why should you not call me 'brother'? Are you not Doreni, adopted by a Desai father? We are brothers, indeed."

Alla started laughing. "Loayiq, you don't think Kaynu's your brother at all. You think his skin is pale and washed-out like a scroll left in the sun too long."

She was right. I had met many full-blooded Angleni in Jaguar's palace and the paleness of their skin had always made me wonder if they were ill. Kaynu, however, was born of a Doreni mother. Even so, his skin color troubled me.

Alla spoke all that came to her mind. Strangely, I felt safe in her presence, knowing there would be no secrets between us. Kaynu's pale skin troubled me. I imagined the worst: that he had the Desai mind-reading trait combined with the Angleni shrewd secretiveness.

"Don't judge my father's clan by my lack of politeness, Brother," I said. "My father tells me I stare at everyone. Nevertheless Alla should learn etiquette and not speak her mind so easily. I'm afraid she has hurt you more than my unspoken thoughts ever could."

"You should not worry about being impolite, Brother. So bright is the honor of the Pagatsu that none can dim their kribatsu. Nevertheless, I must tell you that Alla is not wrong. She saw what was truly in your mind. Blade Castle, you will find, is a place where few thoughts are hidden."

"I must learn to hide my thoughts, then."

"If you wish, but I already know the hatred our people, the Doreni, bear for the Angleni. When someone from one of the three tribes meets me, he often finds friendship with me distasteful. But soon, we learn to understand each other and my brother learns I am a true Doreni. A true brother to all people. A true Desai."

After an uncomfortable meal with all eyes staring at me, he led me to a doorway at the end of the hallway. We walked until we reached a small room at the end of a hallway. He pushed the wooden curtains aside. "This will be your home while you're with us."

He left me, walking into the room immediately to the right of the one he had directed me to. I entered the cluttered little room where a tall bare-chested fellow of about seventeen years dressed in red leggings was sitting on a large hemp blanket. He quickly rose to his feet. His face showed both Ibeni and Doreni features and he eyed me as if scrutinizing me. I wondered what clan or clans he belonged to. Certain clans were known for their rudeness.

"Another student of warfare, uh?" He touched my right shoulder in greeting. "This is a day the Creator made."

"It brings blessings—" I began but he quickly interrupted me.

"I wondered how long I'd be in this room by myself," he said. "The last student quickly lost patience with me." Without asking, he removed my marriage cap from my head and began studying it. "You're married, uh? And rich too. From the looks of your clothing. What clan do you belong to? How many wives?"

I reached for my cap. "One."

"More wives will come in time. It's good to spread one's marriages out over time." He gave the cap to me and returned to his blanket. "So you have an enemy to destroy? Oh, don't look so nervous. Avengers abound around here. Except, of course, for me. I have no personal enemy, myself. What's your name, anyway? Your real name and the one the Master gave you?"

I put my travel pouch on the flat bed beside him. "So you are here only to learn theol—?"

"Ah!" He laughed, patronizing. "You are a secretive one. Come now; tell me the name Ganti has given you. My name—the name Master Ganti calls me—is Twin."

"Why does he call you—?"

"He says I have one mind one moment and another mind the next."

"Is that why you lack manners when you speak to strangers? Because you're so accustomed to talking to yourself?"

He started to laugh. "Waihai! How rude you are! I was only trying to be friendly, but obviously your clan is one of those priggish moral ones—what clan do you belong to anyway? I suppose I should recognize your clan markings, but honestly, clan markings never interested me."

The name *Carpo* floated in my mind. The Carpos had a reputation for disdaining clans and were considered arrogant and lacking in good sense. "I'm tired, Twin, and it's been a long journ—"

"Ah, so you plead tiredness when you don't want to speak about yourself?"

"My name is Loic," I said, thinking it best to answer one who seemed to have no ability to relent. "I'm from the Pagatsu clan."

He made a show of visibly sizing me up. "Now I'm really impressed. General Taer's clan?"

I nodded.

"I'm from the Carpo Ibenis! I'm sure you've heard of us. Your clan is about as famous as mine."

In Chyar, the King's Seat, mention of the Carpos only brought amused scorn. The warriors and courtiers considered them self-satisfied intellectuals with paper hearts. "No, I can't say I've heard of the Carp—"

He stared at me, eyes wide in unbelief. "How strange. We Carpos are well-known. Are you from the country, then? Jobara, someone from General Treads Lightly's clan should know about us. Our clan is very important. Not that it matters, I suppose. Whether we are Carpo, Pagatsu, Trabu, Chianu, Desai or any number of the ten thousand clans, the important thing is that we should not fight among ourselves. That is all Our Matchless King requires. Especially since the Angleni still connive. It's them we must fight and we mustn't get caught up in silly vendettas."

An annoyed voice shouted from an adjoining room. "Twin, be quiet."

"Kaynu is very sensitive to my chattering," Twin explained, although he did not change the tone or loudness of his voice. "All he does is study those Scriptures. You ought to see his room, covered from end to end. Like father, like son."

Kaynu spoke up again, this time louder. "Twin, we have prepared a banquet in Wind Follower's honor. When the sun sets, lead him to the gathering room where we can praise the spirits for the arrival of the prophesied one."

Kaynu looked at me, mouth open. "Wind Follower?" He whistled, impressed. "Kaynu...did he just call you....Is that great one you? Waihai! Well, it's...it's...we were told by the spirits...and Alla said....but it was really the spirits...she and they said to expect a great one. And now...Wind Follower is a sky name of great puha and power, my friend! The Desai Scriptures declare he will follow the Wind God, gently or brutally, clearing large and small paths. And here you are—"

"If it is a name of great power, I should not have such a name. And as for clearing paths, I have no desire or power to clear any—"

"Master thinks you do, obviously," Kaynu called from inside his room."

"Layo, layo," Twin answered, still looking at me in amazement. "Or else he wouldn't have called you by such a powerful name." He stopped speaking and studied my face. It was one of the rare moments I saw him silent.

"Aren't you going to ask why Ganti walks like he does?" Twin asked me as we walked toward the feast in my honor in the Blade Castle gathering room.

"Many old soldiers walk like that," I answered. "They're ruined inside."

"Do you know," he glanced about the plain brick walls, "he can't hold his water?"

I kept my eyes on the doorway to the longhouse ahead of me. "I suppose I know it now."

"He's castrated too. The Angleni did it. Two days before the truce. Can you believe it? Bad timing, uh?" He motioned to the curtained doorway. "But he's not just ruined physically, but...well, hatred controls him. One would think a soldier could handle such things."

"Do you enjoy speaking about the weaknesses of old soldiers? I do not."

"Wind Follower, forgive my rattling on." We continued walking and he managed to be silent, if only for a short while. "Pardon my nervousness and cynicism, Wind Follower, but you don't look at all like the one I pictured."

"Perhaps because I'm not this prophesied one," I answered, "and it must be very hard for someone from the great Carpo clan to be both nervous and cynical at the same time."

"I suppose it's because I believe you are indeed the one, and at the same time I don't quite believe it."

"Let me at least free you from your nervousness, " I said. "I'm not the one."

I hastened toward the door, intent on asking Ganti to free me from both Twin's room and from the rumors that abounded about me.

Inside, the students sat in a circle in the gathering room, their eyes on Ganti. He was speaking about the shadow gods. "My students," he was saying, "you must know yourselves, for the shadow gods know you all too well. They know your failings, your flaws and your willfulness." He glanced up at me. "And it's one's own willfulness that often brings defeat. Those of you who are lustful, the spirits will use your lust to conquer you. Those who are easily angered, the spirits will destroy you by your anger. Those of you who are proud and righteous, the devils will destroy you with your own righteousness." He beckoned to me. "Come in, Younger Brother."

The expectant look in the eyes of Ganti's students almost made me laugh. I had never seen anything so ridiculous, and I was embarrassed to be the unwilling center of that farce.

"This is my cousin's son," Ganti continued. "He lives with his father's clan. His father is the great General Treads Lightly of the Pagatsu. For this reason, honor him not only as your fellow student and as an honored member of my family, but the son of a warrior who has saved our empire. Honor him also as Wind Follower."

All eyes stared at me as I walked into the center of the circle. I was like a spirit materialized before them. I searched all the faces in the room. Of the two hundred students, about a half were women. Most of that number wore Desai clan markings.

"Speak, Wind Follower," a Doreni girl mumbled.

"Friends and brothers," I said, "Older Brother is allowing me to stay here a week to rest with you. I am honored to be in your presence. I sense, however, that you all seem to think I am someone I am not. I am a student like yourselves. Nothing more, nothing less."

I sat down and they kept staring at me. Ganti's eyes seemed full of both worry and worship for me. Never had I felt so uncomfortable. I kept looking at the door, hoping for courage to escape. But to leave a feast in one's honor would have shown a lack of etiquette, and the table was a garden of edible delights—such sweets I had never seen. The students seemed to be waiting for me to eat, and when I lifted a bowl of curdled sweet milk to my mouth, they seemed amazed a living prophet could actually eat. Although I was hungry after my travels, I was careful about eating all that was placed before me. I carefully avoided all grains; nevertheless halfway through the meal the room began to darken. Even now I don't know what food hid the grains, but I had been careless. The falling sickness had come upon me. When I awoke, Kaynu and Alla were kneeling beside me as I lay on the floor of the gathering room.

"So you have the falling sickness?" Alla asked. She pushed her long curly black hair behind her ears, but some stray strands fell on her bosom. "The spirits didn't tell us this, and neither did I see this sickness in your mind. Kaynu, do you remember reading anything about this in the prophecies?"

He was silent for a moment, keeping his eyes on me. In that moment, something about him reminded me of Krika. Krika often had those pensive silences. But there was something else. Like Krika, he seemed to be weighing his father's words and examining how they applied to certain situations. At last he spoke up. "Alla, isn't there a verse that says, 'The one who falls will rise again'?"

"Layo, layo—Truly, truly!" she answered, nodding vehemently. "I had thought it referred to his falling from power and rising up again in the hearts and mind of his people."

Falling in the Golden House, in the woodlands, deserts, prairies or fields had not grieved me. None saw or admitted they saw my shame, but the seizures in Barro's house and in Ganti's Blade Castle were not unseen. The illness of Taer's son had not been hidden; worse, I was shamed in full view of strangers. I understood suddenly how lovingly my clansmen had shielded me, how they had loved me in spite of their disagreements with me.

Kaynu's hands—pink and white—soothed my forehead. I thought of my mother, and my Little Mother, and Satha and all the mothers who had taken care of me since my birth. I thought, *It should be Alla, a woman, who should be trying to comfort me.*

Alla answered my thoughts. "Little Pagatsu, if you wish to be a true Desai, you must learn to cover your mind."

I rose from the floor, and pushed past them towards the door, my heart burning with embarrassment. "Tell Ganti I had to leave."

"This illness is a great mercy sent to you by the Creator," Alla said, ignoring my shame, and therefore shaming me even more. "It has taught a chief's son how to understand sickness and humility." For a moment, she seemed like an old alchemist who considered me nothing more than a collection of emotional and physical elements she could combine and recombine as she willed. "If you understand these, then you will not quickly humiliate others. A great hero must learn all this."

Advice from strangers who presumed to teach me had always annoyed me, but she was the daughter of my host. I thought, *She speaks to me of humiliation in a humiliating manner. I will be gone from Blade Castle soon and I will leave this humiliation behind me,* but I answered, "The Creator does not give illness. This sickness has not made me merciful."

Kaynu squeezed my forehead, but kept his head low. "Perhaps, you are young yet."

"I would not recommend leaving," Alla said. "Everyone in the village is talking about the rich boy who didn't respect the gods' totem. I assume it's you the headmen of the clans and the village headman are searching for."

I don't care what the headmen are doing! I thought, but said, "I have to leave."

"So you'll fight the villagers, the spirits, and Noam Therpa alone?" she asked. "You have no skill in battles and Noam will find out that you're here. If Noam thinks the Pagatsu and Ganti of the Desai are your allies he'll think twice about hurting you." She laughed as if something amused her. "The spirits are protecting you, Wind Follower. At least that's what they tell me. Don't let your wrong-headedness leave you without allies."

My head, which still ached from the fall, throbbed. "Stop discussing me with the spirits."

"Are you really at war with them?" Kaynu asked, sounding amazed. He exchanged a quick glance with Alla. "The prophets wrote about such a war, didn't they, Sister?"

"I leave the spirits to themselves, but they refuse to pay me the same courtesy," I answered and began walking toward the door, hoping to leave both Blade Castle and my humiliation far behind me.

"All here know your heart, Brother," Kaynu said. Again, he reminded me of Krika. "How can we humiliate one whose heart we know?"

Yes, I thought, *very like Krika*. But then he said, "Wind Follower, reconsider leaving. The spirits don't hate you. They only want you to see the truth. The Arkhai hate the Angleni as much as we do. Perhaps the Arkhai hope you'll turn your heart to the right path. It is often that way with spirits. They're willful and one cannot live without them. At least one cannot live safely."

I said to myself then, *Would that he was like Krika! Krika examined all his father's words and only those words which proved themselves worthy were allowed to enter his heart. But Kaynu, he parrots everything his father believes. Is this why Father sent me to visit Ganti? To improve my fighting skills? To learn how to bend to a father's will? Or to turn my allegiance back to the spirits?*

That night as I bathed in the river—not in the school's baths because I was ashamed to face my fellow students—I found myself becoming angry at Father. Why had he sent me to such a place? A freezing rain fell all about me. Light it was and airy, cold too. It should have soothed me, but as the drops fell on me, I kept looking at the longhouse, the archery fields, stables and schoolhouse. I resolved to finish bathing and to quickly leave Blade Castle.

Telling no one of my plans, I saddled Cactus and rode fast through the outer courtyard toward the entrance gates. I took one last look behind me, then urged Cactus onward, preparing to leap through the gates and never return, but as his hooves touched the river's edge, we—horse and rider—were bounced backwards, like leaves thrown by a violent wind.

Surprised, I looked all about me. No leaf stirred. Except for the gently falling rain, nothing else moved. I prodded Cactus again. Again, we tried to pass through the gates, but this time more slowly. Now, we were not blown back, but we could not move. Cactus's head seemed crushed against something. I extended my hand; it met an unseen but firm wall.

Then I heard a voice saying, "The Arkhai have ordained it. You will not leave Blade Castle."

I looked about the fields and the courtyard, searching for who had spoken. I saw no one. Realizing the speaker was a spirit, I disregarded the voice and urged Cactus to push against the unseen wall. The wall seemed to push back at him, like winds bearing down against the winds of a sail.

"Let me out," I shouted.

"You have no guide to tell you where to turn," the voice taunted. "No guide to tell you how to defeat us. If there's a way out, you'll never find it."

I whistled to Cactus. He turned his head toward me. Together we backed away from the wall and toward the river. *The river doesn't seem deep*, I said to myself, *and if the land spirits have created this wall to bound me in, I will pass over the river.* Several paces away from the river's edge, we gathered speed and plunged forward toward its shore. Faster and faster we went, louder and louder the spirit voices laughed. When we came to the shore Cactus flew through the invisible wall and stood in the middle of the river, whinnying, but I was suddenly unhorsed, my skin crashing into a wall of icy daggers. Driven by a furious wind, they pierced my flesh one by one. I sat half in the river and half out, my forehead and chest burning, my skin flayed and bloody as if a shaman had tried to skin me alive. Three times I tried to escape; three times bloodied and defeated I was pushed back.

Beaten, I returned to my room. When Twin saw me, his mouth fell open and he exclaimed in his excited yet analytical Carpo way,

"Jobara! There is indeed warfare between you and the spirits." He yelled for Kaynu in the next room. Kaynu entered and when he saw me, he brought me limping and bleeding to Alla's rooms.

My wounds healed slowly, but after that—many times—I tried to pass through the invisible wall and battled the spirits again. My skin became covered with wounds upon wounds, scars upon scars. Many of these were grievous and long in healing, but I cared little for that. I had been suddenly and cruelly caged and I wanted my freedom.

But whether I walked to the east or to the west, to the north or to the south, I could not escape. Always and everywhere, there were walls of icy daggers to rip my flesh and blast my spirit. Always, day by day and night by night, a thousand spirits assailed me with hail shuwas, ice vialkas and a wall through which only I could not pass.

Every morning, I woke with a mixture of futility and dread. You who were born enslaved by the Angleni cannot truly understand how freedom feels. You cannot imagine how difficult it was when the Angleni first conquered us. And you surely cannot understand how I felt being trapped by the Arkhai. Human bondage is cruel and selfish, but the cruelty of the spirits is relentless. Before my imprisonment, I would often ignore them, only challenging their schemes if they crossed my path. In Blade Castle, however, I would grow to hate them—whether or not their schemes concerned me.

At night I wished for sleep because in dreams I could roam the Golden House with Satha, couch with her in the lingay grasses and near the arvina plants. But at nights, in my sleep, the Arkhai also visited and gloated about their triumph over me. Instead of sleeping, I began rising from my bed. I would walk to the far fields and watch the night sky beyond the borders of Blade Castle. This I did many nights until the Mackerel Moon came and fled.

SATHA
A *Proposition*
Scavenger's Moon–Second Snow Moon

It is a strange thing to live a life that is no life, a life in which one's life is comprised of waiting for one's life to begin or end, but this had become my life. I forgot how to hope. And even that hope was not really hope. I lived, hoping only to endure the day until night came and brought me sleep. Yet, I could not sleep. Once, however, hope did rise in my heart for one brief moment, but the end result of that particular hope was to renew my despair and hopelessness.

It happened upon a day when I looked up from my cooking pot and saw three riders in Doreni garb atop a high mountain overlooking Talub's site. They camped there and I often saw them standing and looking across the plain from the crag. They continued there many days, and although Talub armed his herdsmen, he did not seem to fear them. I suppose he trusted the Doreni to keep their part of the truce although he himself had broken it. Every day I would look toward the mountain, wondering what the horsemen were doing there. *Are they King Jaguar's spies?* I asked myself. *Perhaps Our Matchless King is aware of these arrogant invaders.* But I secretly hoped the riders were Pagatsu warriors sent to rescue me.

But one day they descended the hill and rode into the campsite. My heart sank when I saw that their clothes were not dark green Pagatsu but Therpa blue. As they neared me, I recognized Noam.

Hate and anger, regret and despair, powerlessness and betrayal all assaulted me as Talub greeted my oppressor, and my oppressor—full of his power—eyed me.

I was ordered to bake bread for our guests and prepare a small lamb. As the fire burned and the flatbread browned and the lamb seethed on the spit, I gazed at the wild anley growing on the ground. Perhaps Noam had also seen those poisonous flowers, because when I placed a platter of bread and meat before him, he did not touch it but ate only from the common pot.

Later as Noam's warriors busied themselves with turning Talub's attention to small unimportant things, Noam walked to my tent and whispered in my ear. His hands stroked my back as he did so. "I've seen that you journey frequently to the far fields to walk alone there. Tonight meet me there, among the wildflowers."

"Why should I meet you there, Seared Conscience?" I asked.

He bowed his head. "I have something to tell you about your husband."

I pushed his hand away. "Tell me now."

"Do you wish to grieve and cry here in front of your owner? An Angleni?"

His words made me afraid. Why would his tidings make me grieve? There was only one answer. I agreed to meet him. That night, after the sun had set, I hid my dagger in the sleeve of my gyuilta and asked Sena and two of the herdsmen to accompany me to the meadow. *I have not killed anyone,* I said to myself, *but tonight I can learn. If I cannot kill one who has raped me and killed my child, I am no true Arhe.*

When Noam appeared below a small cliff wearing a buckskin fur-lined riding gyuilta, Sena and the herdsmen exchanged glances but kept their silence. As we walked, my hand squeezed the hidden dagger. I said to myself, *Noam's body will tumble down the side of this boulder tonight. And mine will follow it.*

"Satha," Noam greeted me when he saw me. His voice was soft and musical and the wind ruffled his hair, but I was wiser then. I understood I could not judge a Doreni warrior by the gentle musicality of his voice. Nor did the beauty of his auburn hair prove the beauty of a heart.

"I find myself unable to stop thinking of you," he whispered when I stood in front of him. He extended his hands to greet me but I pushed his arms away.

"You had a thing to tell me?" I asked. "About my husband?"

He covered his face with his hands and blew on his fingers. "When my warriors told me to whom they'd sold you, and that this Talub was now sojourning in Colebru—which is so near to my home—I told myself—"

"My husband!" I insisted, raising my voice calmly. "Your conversations with yourself are none of my concern."

"Satha." His voice was sad, slow, and full of regret. "If you're willing . . . if you can allow me to redress the harm I've done to you and care for you in my household, I will cover you in diamonds and—"

"I grow tired of hearing sorrow in the voice of one who has cost many so much grief. Speak plainly. Why would I want to go into your house?" I realized I feared the answer as much as I desired it.

He bowed to his knees, like a penitent in a Theseni temple. "I have caused you harm, double-harm, and now added a third trouble. If you would allow me to bring you to my house and give all I can to you as a recompense . . ."

"My life knew trouble before you came into it, Noam. Surely, you were not responsible for that." Tears stung my eyes, but to prevent them from falling I told myself to remember the dagger I would soon plunge into his heart. "Evil is everywhere and I have learned to be satisfied in whatever state I find myself. Therefore do not trouble yourself about recompensing me for anything. Therefore, speak plainly, and tell me what your soul so desires to tell me."

"Satha, the Pagatsu blame you for Loic's death."

"Loic's death?" The world reeled about me and I held myself to prevent myself from falling to the ground.

"They also believe—because Jival has told them so—that your shame caused you to flee the Golden House. They believe you are spending your life as a Theseni holy woman." He looked toward the horizon where the moon shone brightly. "I have wronged you, Satha."

My fingers slid along the edge of the hidden dagger, and I forced myself to breathe. "You said that Loic had died. Why do you say that?"

"I've killed him and I killed my own soul when I killed him."

I withheld my tears, and thought, I *can kill him now. Surely.* But my trembling hands seemed incapable of gripping the dagger with the required amount of murderous rage.

"We met on the plains," he said. "I had expected Taer, not Loic. I did not wish to kill Loic. But there he was. Satha, your husband was fierce. He fought valiantly. He was young, an unskilled but determined warrior. You would be proud of him."

"And so you killed him?"

He bowed his head. "I had to."

"Yes," I said, trying to quell the throbbing in my head, "Loic was unskilled."

"Can you not," he asked, "let me find redemption by removing you from this enslavement? As Loic lay dying, I told him I had sold you to a foreigner—an Angleni—and I promised him I would take you from this lonely place. The sight of the young chief lying bloodied on the ground . . . No, the vengeance did not satisfy me. I suddenly grew sick of bloodshed."

I put my hand inside the sleeve of my gyuilta and my fingers lingered on the handle of the dagger. "If indeed you have promised to free me from this Angleni, why did you not tell the Pagatsu that I am here? Even if they think I have forsaken them, they would not leave me here alone."

"Do you think the Doreni will receive you as one of their own after you have brought them such grief? Do you think me foolish enough to tell my enemy that I have killed his son? Although I desire to kill Taer and would destroy him if I found him alone, I will not walk into his lair. Satha, your clan, the Kluna, is destroyed. Your mother is dead. How else can I keep my promise to your young husband except by bringing you to my home?"

My strength and rage returned. At last, I was ready to kill and to suffer the consequence of my action, even if it meant death for me, the herdsmen, Voora and Talub. "Break your promise to my husband, Noam . . . if indeed you made a promise . . . if indeed Loic is dead. I would rather be a slave in an Angleni campsite than live in the house of the man who raped me and killed my child and my husband."

Slowly, I removed the dagger; slowly I raised my hand. But Noam quickly grabbed my arm. Twisting it gently but firmly, he wrenched the dagger from me. "The Noam you met," he said, kissing me, "the

Noam who harmed you, is dead. This Noam who lives remembers the old Noam's ways and grieves at the old Noam's sins."

Tired, I pulled my hand from his and stood still, gazing out into the distance, while he kissed my cheek and neck.

He returned the dagger to me. "Perhaps if you did not lack the skill and the heart to kill me, we both would be free from our grief, free from ourselves."

His words and voice startled me with their tenderness. "Are you teaching me how to fight, Noam? Are you teaching me the best way to murder you?"

"If you could murder me, I would allow it." He knelt before me. All around us the air was redolent with the fragrance of the sweet-smelling deadly anley. "Can you not see that I love you, Satha? My mind turns always on you. It cannot stop. I regret that I . . . Perhaps, if the course of our lives had run differently . . ."

"Seared Conscience, you love no one but yourself. You have nothing but disdain for women."

He burst out laughing and pushed his wildly-flying hair from his face. "You speak as if most women are worthy of my love or even my respect. They aren't. Only you, only you have touched my heart."

"Noam, again, you flatter a married woman. Yes, you say my husband is dead, but I do not think so. If he were dead, he would have come to me in a dream. As a married woman, I will not allow you to praise me."

He whistled and turned to look at me. "Even in his death, Loic is a man to be envied. Few men have the love of women as noble and kind as you." The cold wind blew his hair behind him and he pulled his gyuilta close about his shoulders. His voice mingled with the buzzing of the bees. "Could you not love me, Satha, even a little? Could you not forgive me? If I am as evil as you say, can you not trust your love and kindness to save me from myself? I have heard it said that you Theseni believe evil men can change."

I saw his heart then: dried like a thirsty husk in need of water, shriveled like a seed cast on hard ground. Such a pitiful man I could not hate; such a hateful man, I could not pity. Nor could I love such a one either. "Noam, I am no longer Theseni. I belong to the Doreni, a fierce unforgiving people."

Those were the last words I spoke to him. I left him standing alone in the meadow.

"Waihai!" Sena said, when I returned to them, "Jobara! You are someone of importance! Perhaps you are a chief's wife indeed. Or was that your lover? You Theseni women are often so lacking in morals."

"If I was a chief's wife," I answered, "I am no more. And I was never that man's lover."

He sucked at his teeth as if I was lying. "Did I not see him kiss you passionately about the neck?" He nodded to the other herdsmen. "And you play at being so innocent."

"He kissed me. I did not kiss him."

"Perhaps," one of the other herdsmen said, "he saw her at Talub's fire and wanted to buy her?"

"It is often that way," the third herdsman said. "Why didn't you allow him to buy you?"

"Yes," Sena added, "a Doreni slaveowner is often much kinder than—"

How he disgusted me! How they all disgusted me! "Unlike you, Sena," I said, "I do not spend my days wishing for better, kinder masters."

For days after that, Sena and the herdsmen waited to see if the horsemen would return in force and steal me from Talub. Such things were done in the old days. But no one came.

My life continued as it did. I carried water buckets from the Colebru stream, I cooked, I hoed and I cared for the old woman. But after Noam's visit, hope left me. I half-believed my husband was dead and that I would be a slave forever.

One day as I thought on these things, Talub called to me. "Put down the bucket, Satha," he said. "I have something to ask you."

I turned about and saw him following after me. He appeared so serious I could only think that either his god had told him how close I had come to murdering Voora, or Sena had told him about Noam's night visit. "I can carry water as we speak, Talub."

He took the bucket from me and helped me carry it as if I was indeed a woman. His eyes seemed to be avoiding mine, yet at the same time they seemed to be trying to plead with me. Suddenly, almost shamefacedly, he said, "All this land will be mine and my descendant's." He said many words in between, but at last ended with, "Voora cannot have children, and I need a son."

If I had accepted Sena's offer of marriage, I would not have been in such a situation. "And if I allow you to lie with me," I asked, "what will I gain?"

His right hand stroked my neck and snaked towards my breast. "The truth is, Satha, if you don't allow me, I'll take you anyway. But if you are a playful understanding girl, you'll profit. I can give you many gifts and I'll free you after I die."

Voora had returned to her ways after she had recovered and my anger against her burned. My anger against myself burned even worse. If I had killed her, I would have been better off, but my kind heart had made me a prey to all the predators in the world. I saw in Talub's offer a kind of freedom and power. "Am I to be like an Ibeni whore and couch with a rich man for money? Or like a Theseni slavewoman who breeds children for her owner? No, Talub, if you're going to force me to couch with you, you'll have to marry me. If you take me in any other way, I'll find a way to kill you in your bed."

He guffawed, showing yellowed teeth "You're not the murdering type, Satha."

"True, but there is always time to learn."

His eyes gleamed with lust. I wondered why I had never seen that before. "You're hot-blooded under that cold demeanor!"

For a moment, I considered quenching his lust with the water in the bucket. "Have I spent the past moons commiserating with an old woman's childlessness only to be pulled into your obsession to have a child? There are Ibeni villages nearby with fair-skinned Ibeni women. They can bear you children who will be better accepted by your people."

"Ibeni women are an untrustworthy, jealous, whorish lot. To be bound to such a woman doesn't suit me. I'd rather have you. But . . . Voora will not like it if I marry you."

"The woman spits my name whenever she speaks to me and you want me to couch with you? If you want me, marry me. Make me a second-status wife, a concubine who has some rights. In that way laws will protect me."

I hoped he would not agree to my demands. But he followed beside me, obviously thinking. I thought of my sister and my mother. Both Mother and Alima were good, and yet, look how they died. Certainly the Good Maker was not on my side but neither, it seemed, were the ancestors. I was alone in the land of the living and I had to do my best to make my life better.

When Talub turned to me and said, "I'll do it, Satha. You'll become my secondary wife," I was surprised.

He walked to Voora's wagon and I waited to see what she would say. When Voora came out of her wagon, both hate and superiority dripped from her eyes. Later when Talub told his herdsmen of the intended marriage, Sena came up to me. "So you're marrying the master? Like all high-minded Theseni women, your seeming virtue is just a game way of playing with men's hearts!"

"Your words show your own heart, Sena. Be silent. You're speaking to Talub's concubine." Seven days later, Talub and I were married.

On that marriage night, Talub's breath smelled of undigested garlic and onions. The Thunder Moon turned its face away from the Theseni blanket on which the old man and I lay in my tent. Even so, I could still see all I desired not to see. Because she was chief wife, she was present at the coupling. The rustling of her white dress outside my tent as she paced irritated me and made the old man feel so guilty his ypher shriveled and he could not enjoy his prize. I lay underneath him, and watched Voora's sandaled feet circling the wagon, glad of the old man's near impotence, hoping he would relent. But, after many attempts to enter me had yielded no result—perhaps the Creator loved the old man more than he did me—he gained enough stiffness to push into me. I shrieked. The boundless prairie echoed back my shout but sent no one to help me.

Even now the memory of the old man's rancid breath and deteriorating body ploughing into me makes me queasy. I shut my mind away as he pumped and thrust. A liquid oozed between my legs. The old man dragged his body out of mine and signaled Voora. When she came near, she smiled down at me as if she herself had just raped me.

I had thought my heart had died and that all my sorrows concerning my lost child were gone forever. But as Talub entered me, the fears returned in terrifying strength and my body trembled as I considered the sorrows that having a child might bring me. "Good Maker!" my heart pleaded silently, "you know that even in my youth my heart feared the thought of children. You know these fears were proven true with the death of Loic's daughter. Good Maker, don't give me another child. For my life is doomed to sorrow."

Three weeks later I discovered I was pregnant.

LOIC
The Desai Scriptures
Fever Moons—Third Snow Moon

Kaynu entered my room and dropped several scrolls onto the pillow to my right. I looked up from the wounds I had received from my latest battle with the boundary spirits. He was leaning on the wall near the doorway, studying me.

"Will you not change your mind, Wind Follower?"

"No, Kaynu. I will not change my mind. I intend to leave this place."

He shook his head as if I was a fool. "Do you not wish to understand why rumors abound about you?" He pointed to the scrolls. "All the Desai have wondered about your destiny and—"

Twin rose from his mat, interrupting us as he always did. "It is about time you read those things. It might help you prove you really aren't who they think you are."

I slammed my hands on the window facing the river. "Why have you all conspired to keep me here?"

Twin picked up the parchments and pushed them in my face. "Your father was the conspirator. He prevented you from seeing the Scriptures. Now, you add to the conspiracy by conspiring against yourself and preventing yourself from looking at what may be the truth."

I pushed him aside and began walking through the doorway, but he grasped me by the wrist and prevented me from passing.

"Wind Follower, you're battling the Arkhai. How long do you think your body will last? Your skin is so scarred from those unseen daggers that—"

"Come," Twin interrupted him. Unrolling the Scriptures on the floor, he crooked his finger. "Let us understand what all these others are thinking."

Only a Carpo would be interested in what others are thinking about him, I thought, but to Kaynu I said, "Are we Doreni not men of free will? You're a smart man, Brother. Should the spirits be so relentless? Should they force people to worship them? We Doreni do not believe people should believe what they do not wish to believe. Why do the spirits wish to prevent people from seeking the Creator?"

An apologetic smile came to his lips.

"See," I said, "you know what I say is true."

He changed the subject. "Alla wants a word with you. She is better at understanding the spirits than I am."

Although Alla's beauty made me glad, it also confused my heart. I did not want to betray my heart and I was convinced that if I spoke often to her, I would be unfaithful to my vows to the Creator. In those days, marriages were vows made to the Creator and only the foolhardy would dare to break such a vow. Therefore I avoided Alla and spoke with her only when she tended to my wounds.

"She has important news to tell you," Kaynu said. "News that concerns you."

"The last time we spoke, all she did was talk about my destined war against the Angleni. Hasn't she heard about the nuchunga last year? Did they not eat the bread of reconciliation with us?"

"Who believes in these communal confessions?" Twin chimed in. His eyes were still on the Scriptures but, like two people, he was able to concentrate on two things at the same time. "Even if our people believe in confessing our evils against the land, these 'forgiven' Angleni do not and are not worthy of the earth's forgiveness." He sighed. "I don't know whether to laugh or cry when I think of it. The Theseni they have killed are not here to accept Angleni confessions. But perhaps the dead Theseni don't care, eh, Wind Follower? Perhaps they submitted to the destiny HaZatana created for them. Although at this rate, soon HaZatana will have no one to worship him. Strange thing for a god to destroy the only ones who believe in him."

Kaynu pointed to the small window in my room. We walked to it and together we surveyed the landscape. "Do you think, Wind Follower, this land will indeed be ours in the centuries to come? I think not.

These Angleni are unable to keep a treaty and should be killed quickly before their evil plans succeed."

I looked into his eyes. "Truly, truly, indeed! You're a true Doreni, Kaynu! You hate your enemies without relenting."

He bowed low—so low that he embarrassed me. "I'm honored the son of Taer should think me a true Doreni. Even more honored that Loayiq, the Wind Follower, should say so. But, please Brother, speak to my sister. She awaits you in her room."

"Come with me," I pleaded.

"Why should I? It's not as if we're in Pagatsu territories. Here, if you enter an unmarried woman's room and linger, people will not assume you're courting." He started to laugh and raised one eyebrow. "Unless, you wish to court her, of course."

"I do not."

"Then go to her. It is said among us that she is a Called-Out One. If you are indeed the appointed interpreter of the Lost Book, you and she will have much to talk about."

Jobara? I said to myself. *I had not dreamed of ever meeting a Called-Out One.*

Alla's room seemed a storehouse for all Ganti's wealth, surrounded as she was by gold, silver, pearls and precious gems. She, herself, was dressed in a simple Theseni kaba, not the kind of dress I ever imagined an Ibeni girl wearing.

She met me at the door and kissed my forehead and cheek. "Brother, how battered, bruised and beaten you look!" She led me to a richly-decorated pillow on the floor, large enough for two people. Such pillows were called love pillows in my youth. I decided to sit on the carpet. However, she joined me there and took my hand in hers. "Wind Follower, the Uncaused Causer of all things has told me wonders about you."

"Has he?" I thought, *He has been quite silent to me.*

"Jobara!" she said, throwing her hands in the air. "Why do you not believe me?"

"I hardly know what or who to believe." The scent of jasmine in her hair almost seduced me and I found myself longing to touch her. I began to rise.

She held onto my arm and pulled me back to the floor. "Your wife was sold into slavery, Wind Follower. She is dead now. Future news will prove my words true. You will soon discover that the light of your Dark Half-Moons is utterly extinguished. What use, then, is rushing to her side?"

I stared at her, speechless. Was Satha dead? I could not allow my heart to believe such a thing. I had grown used to Alla's frankness, but now her words seemed cruel. "Sister, do you expect me to believe this? I do not."

"Why should you doubt me, Wind Follower? It is not I who speak but the spirits. The One Who Holds Your Breath in His Hand has shown me this."

"You speak as if the spirits and the Creator are one. They aren't."

"Let us not get into that disagreement again, Loayiq."

I nodded. "Well then, let us find another matter to disagree about. First, you tell me that my wife is stolen and sold into slavery. Then, before my heart has time to understand that, you tell me my wife is dead. Is this not cold and cruel? If it is the truth, there is no etiquette or kindness in it."

"If the truth is the truth, why dress it up in etiquette?"

"Because the heart aches when it hears such news," I shouted at her. "If my wife is indeed stolen and dead, tell me where she is that I might find her. Tell the spirits to free me from this place that I might go and free my wife's soul in death. No, Sister, I do not believe you. The spirits are telling you lies, and you believe them all too easily."

"Why would the spirits lie to me?"

"Why should my wife's death concern you?"

"It is important that I, too, should know these things, Wind Follower. Our lives are bound together. The Creator told me this so I might know how much you loved her and that—knowing this—I could heal your heart."

I stared at her, my mind reeling and my chest tightening. A sharp pain, like the edge of a knife, sliced through my heart. I knew the spirits were liars, yet in spite of that knowledge I found myself half-believing Alla.

"The Creator tells me your beloved wife was very like Krika, your age brother. Satha was holy and innocent, too, like all Theseni women." Tears pooled in her eyes. "My heart breaks as yours breaks, Wind Follower. Perhaps I have been too frank and should learn how to speak with those who do not understand the Desai way. Perhaps this is something you will have to teach me. I promise you, however, that you will have your revenge against Seared Conscience and your heart will be healed at last. Forgive yourself and shake off your guilt. When you hurled the lance at her, you did so in grief and not in anger. You were grieved because your wife did not believe you loved her. Forgive yourself. Satha now understands how deeply you loved her."

Jobara! My mouth fell open. I asked myself, *Why have the Arkhai told her about my life?*

"I am to marry you, Wind Follower," Alla continued. "It is appointed that you shall conquer the Therpas and destroy the Angleni and their god, and I will be at your side when you do it."

I rose hastily from the carpet and pushed her away. "I don't believe you, Alla," I yelled. "I don't believe you or the spirits."

She stood up and her hand stroked my face. She lifted the hem of her kaba and wiped the tears from my face. "Wind Follower, I do not lie."

I hastened to the door. "It is an easy thing for spirits to know past events and human interactions. They gossip among themselves. Information— truth and lies intermixed—is their currency. They use such reports about the past and the far-away present to fool us into believing untruths. But I will not believe anything unless the Creator himself tells me."

"You speak boldly, Wind Follower. But your heart is not so bold. Your heart says one thing, your words another."

"You can't see my heart," I mumbled, angry that the Desai's gift was so intrusive.

"You're angry," she said, patronizingly, "only because you wish to weep."

"Why should I weep for what may not be true?" I asked, biting my lips to prevent my tears from flowing.

She gave me a pitying look. The Desai seemed to look upon everything with pitying patronizing looks. "I won't break your heart by telling you any more truths you cannot now bear. Rest, my destined one. I only wished to prepare you. Soon, one will ride here to meet you and he will tell you all I have just said. My love, all I can say is . . . prepare yourself."

She began stroking my arms and shoulders, but I could bear her words no longer. I raced from the room and out of her presence.

Later that night, Kaynu visited me in my room. "Go and grieve for your wife, Wind Follower. Weep silently in the far fields."

I did not believe my wife was dead. Nevertheless I rose up and walked the fields, listless. Soon, I saw a rider in the distance. His seat upon his mount was familiar. Stately, unswerving and steady, he easily passed through the invisible wall that barred me in. I knew the rider was Yiko, yet I trembled, remembering Alla's words.

"Yiko!" I called out, running to him. "Is it well with you? Is all well with my wife?" I hoped Alla's words would fall to the ground, conquered by some joyous truth.

He bowed, and a cold wind lifted the hood of his gyuilta. The wound I had given him was apparent. Ashamed, I avoided his eyes while he spoke. "Young Chief," he said, "The Good Creator made this day but he had made better, happier ones. I have ridden long and hard to find you. Okiak said you were still here, therefore—"

"Okiak knows everything, unfortunately," I responded.

Absent-mindedly, he scratched at the earless space on his head. I resisted an urge to ask his forgiveness and tried to calm my shaking hands. "I have bad news, my boy."

"Is it Satha?"

He seemed surprised. "Have the ancestral spirits already told you of these things? If so, your clansmen will be glad to hear the spirits have forgiven you."

"The spirits have told me nothing. Nor do I want their—or anyone's—forgiveness."

He pulled at the horse's reins, steadying its head. "Young Chief, Oh that they had told you! I would be spared from saying it."

A wildfire rose in my heart—I always found myself losing my patience with Yiko—but I resisted the anger. "Speak, Yiko," I said, "I'm ready to hear."

"Young Chief, the Arhe and her handmaids went to the marketplace to celebrate the year-mark of your full marriage. She was stolen from us. Only Jival saw the perpetrators, but the poor thing didn't recognize the clan markings." He tilted his head and whispered although no one was near us. "Your clansmen believe the Therpas are behind it. They think Seared Conscience sold her into slavery or, that—because of spite or lust—he has made her one of the many comfort women in his household."

How madmen understand the world, I do not rightly now. And yet, upon hearing those words, I felt as if the world had gone off-kilter. Or perhaps, I had veered from it. Or that both I and the world were off course. My hands trembled and my heart jumped into my throat. "Does Okiak not know where she is?" I asked, shaking him. "Haven't the spirits told them where she is?"

"If they have, he has not told us."

"Yet he knows I'm here?" I asked. "Is that not strange?"

He did not answer. That was how the Theseni were. Fearful of the spirits, and not wanting to challenge them or those who spoke to them. He removed a yellowed parchment from his travel pouch.

I unscrolled it but could not read it in the surrounding darkness. I directed him to the stables, then together we walked to one of the small guest houses in the compound. "We will read this inside."

Father had written a note to me but in one of the ancient languages.

The calligraphic swirls read: *I have been called to secret business. Some of the clans consider Our Matchless Prince too conciliatory towards the Angleni. Others do not want to rise against the Matchless Family. I go to defend Jaguar. I'm sending this missive with Yiko whom I trust with my life and yours. My Son, I hope we will meet again soon, perhaps in battle against a common enemy. But if we do not meet again in this world, may we meet again in the same fields we long for.*

I trembled. For the first time, I was worried I would never see my father again. Even in peace, the Angleni troubled our land. Now they were the cause of a secret conspiracy.

"Stay here until tomorrow morning. I will return with food and blankets for you. Ganti loves my father and he respects those who speak to the spirits. If anyone sees you and asks what your business is, tell them the Pagatsu shaman sent you here to speak to me. But say nothing else. That answer should suffice."

We ate and spoke together all that night. How glad my heart was to see one from my distant home. He was a true Theseni, open-hearted but discreet, and I appreciated his carefulness toward me. He told me nothing that would add grief to grief. I had never liked Yiko. Yet as we sat in the candlelight speaking of Razo's continued stupidity, of Jura's many lovers, and of Little Mother's dealing with vendors, I found myself admiring him.

When sleep began to steal upon us, I constrained him to lie on the guest bed. Wrapping my gyuilta about me, I fell asleep on the floor. The next morning I awoke to find myself covered with the bed furs, and the old man lying on the carpet beside me.

As he prepared to pass through the invisible wall, I longed to pass with him into the fields outside Blade Castle. Indeed, they were earthly fields but they were fields I longed for. I could not bear to see him go and I turned my face from him as he left. "Tell my father I love him, Yiko."

He did not answer me, but I did not hear him ride off.

"Do you delay because my words seem desperate, Yiko? Do you consider me weak?"

"Young Chief—you know me well enough to know what I think."

"I love you, Yiko," I answered, turning to look into his face. "Forgive me for my cruelty to you." I approached and hugged his face, covering his earless right cheek with my hand.

"What a man you've become, Young Chief," he said, obviously marveling.

"I have not become anything, Yiko. I am still myself. I have not changed."

"I did not say that you had changed, Cuyo. I said you had become a man."

He passed through the gates, and I—like an unredeemed prisoner watching the release of the last companion of his captivity—was alone again. I said aloud, "I will do anything to be free." And immediately, the Desai Scriptures and Angleni parchments appeared in my mind.

I returned to my room where Kaynu greeted me. "I'm sorry for your great loss, Brother."

"Are you?" I asked. "Don't be."

"But did this visit not prove Alla is right?"

"It proves nothing. Satha is stolen, yes, but she is not dead."

His face grew pensive again, and again it had that cold, analytical Desai detachment. "Yet it should comfort you to know that this was determined from before the beginning of time? Jobara! The Creator and the spirits often confuse me. The events they ordain—"

"If the Creator ordains heartbreak," I interrupted him, "I will not serve him. I'd rather serve the spirits."

"They are all one, Brother," he said, rebuking me.

"I don't believe so," I said. "If the Creator could ordain Krika's death—and Satha's—then I will not serve him." I walked toward him and held his hands in mine. "Where is your heart, Kaynu? Have you not seen how much I love my wife? Have you not loved anyone? Can you not leave all this thought of theology behind and hear only my heart? I want to leave this place, Brother. I want to leave. I weep with the desire to leave. And yet, you . . ." I burst into tears, more a woman than a man, more an Ibeni than a true Doreni warrior.

He picked up the prophetic scrolls and carried them to me. "Ganti told me to give you the Desai scriptures and I have done so. I can't force you to read them."

Angry, I took the parchments and attempted to rip them down the middle. They did not tear. "Am I to be here forever friendless and alone?" I asked. "Why can you not see me? I am Loic. Not Loayiq, not Wind Follower. But you don't see my heart. You don't want to see my heart. You have spent your days reading stories and verses about some appointed leader and all your responses to me are responses to your speculation and your indoctrination. But as for me—Loic—you do not see me."

He studied me closely. For a moment, he even seemed a little ashamed of himself. But then he seemed to find his Desai indoctrination again. "It is you, Wind Follower," he answered, "who do not see who you are. The Desai saw the coming of pale-skinned people destined to overrun our country. It is evident they spoke of the Angleni. The Scriptures warn us that this land of three tribes is to become the land of only one tribe, the Angleni. Our prophets say, however, the Angleni would bring with them the Lost Book of the Creator. We must hearken to do everything written in that book. We must believe the Angleni Scriptures, yet distrust the Angleni themselves. You must read the Scriptures and allow Ganti to interpret them for you. If you do not do this, you will betray our land."

I could no longer restrain my anger. "Do the prophecies speak of my wife?" I asked. "Do they speak of my heart? If the prophecies concern me, should they not address this grief and anger and loss I feel in my heart? Should they not have given you gracious and kind words to help me in my grief? Instead, you mention my wife as if she . . . as if I—" I stopped short, suddenly remembering a day long ago when Sio knelt at my feet and pleaded for me to love him as a brother. I stood still, trapped by the memory.

"One Scripture," Kaynu was saying, "declares that after a great loss, you will marry a woman not of your tribe. Ganti interprets that as Alla. She is neither Desai nor Pagatsu and she is not Doreni. It is evident when one studies the verses that —"

I held my right hand with my left. The urge to slap him across the face was so strong. "I will forgive your cold-heartedness," I said, "because it is 'evident' you have been trained by these cold and hard-headed Desai."

"Read the parchments yourself, Wind Follower. And let my father teach you how to interpret them." He walked towards the curtained exit. "I cannot stand here any longer in your presence."

"Yes," I yelled as he walked from the room. Looking around I picked up a quiver and threw it at him, "Leave my presence. Your cold hard heart might melt if you stand too close to real humans."

I paced back and forth and still angry raced to Alla's room. When she pushed her curtain aside, I grasped her shoulders tightly. "Sister, if your words are true—"

"They are," she answered calmly.

"All your words," I emphasized. "Then why not let me leave? Will your prophecy not fulfill itself in spite of my will? Sister, I plead with you. You must have a woman's heart locked within that cold Desai heart. Tell the spirits who have hedged me in to let me go. I beg you. Plead with them for me. Tell them to part the curtain of daggers and let me seek the dead body of my stolen wife. They must know that without her wedding dress my Pagatsu ancestors will not receive her into the fields we long for."

"Let her go to the Theseni heaven," she answered coldly. "She is still Theseni, is she not?"

"In the Theseni heaven, women are enslaved to men forever. She would be married to one man and he himself will have many virgin wives. She would not want that, Younger Sister. Please, let me go. And after I have buried her in the proper way, I will return to you."

"No, Wind Follower," she answered, and for these words I long hated the Desai, "I cannot help you. You look at the world with too much emotion. Such weakness is not worthy of a Desai. We who know all are not easily perturbed by dead wives."

"How grievous it is," I said, "to be among those who do not care about the griefs of our hearts. But do not deceive yourself about your noble and great heart. It is not that you cannot help me, but that you will not. There is more evil in your lack of emotion, than there is weakness in my perturbedness."

I turned on my heel and left her room, raging. A short time later Ganti arrived in my room, carrying parchments—Desai prophetic writings and Angleni Scriptures. He held the parchments toward me. "Wisdom often causes grief when we are unprepared for it."

"Leave me!" I shouted. "If I had been caught in a trap with friends, that would have been bearable, but I am trapped in a cage and surrounded by ravenous enemies."

"I know that Treads Lightly and Pantan taught you the invaders' language. Read and you will see we are indeed your friends. Jobara! We love you more than you could ever know."

I pushed the scrolls away and squatted on the floor, crying like a child.

He exited the room, leaving my heart raging. Angry, I pushed the Scriptures to the bottom of a basket and lay on the floor, weeping and fearing I would go mad. I thought of the warriors who had been trapped in Angleni prisons before the truce. I remembered rodents I caught in cages and the buffalo I had killed while hunting. I thought of those the spirits had trapped in sickness, in their minds and in Gebelda. I was no better off than they were. How I wished for a powerful one to walk beside me! One who could lay one of his hands on my shoulder and the other on the shoulder of the Creator. Grieving and trapped, I curled up on my side and lay weeping and defeated on the ground.

I fell asleep at last, and dreamed the sky opened. There, outside the gates of the fields we long for, I saw my beloved wife's spirit languishing, unable to enter because no man had claimed her. Waihai! How I wept for her! When she saw me, she pleaded with me. "Half-Moon Eyes, let my soul rest peacefully in death. Live a happy life without me, love another, and at the end of time, perhaps we will meet again."

I woke to find Twin's hands shaking me. "Wind Follower," he asked, "why are you weeping in your dreams?"

"Because my wife is dead," I said. "Because my father is far away, because I'm alone, and because I do not understand the Creator's heart."

"I can't say anything about the Creator or his heart," he said, "or even if he has a heart. For reasons I don't understand, he's distant. As for your father, I think if you bend to the spirits' will, they will allow you to leave and your father will love you again because all fathers love obedient sons. No need to challenge ideas the whole world believes in. Give up challenging the spirits. As for this wife of yours . . . if she is dead, what can be done? Some things, like death, simply cannot be undone. Life, as they say, is for the living . . . and who knows what truly comes after we leave this place? But, tell me, who told you your wife was dead? Certainly this is news to me! Yesterday morning, you were speaking of returning home to her and now you say she is dead."

"I saw her dead in my dream, and Alla has told me my wife has died."

He wrinkled his face into a frown. "Dreams I know little about. Some come from the Creator, some from the spirits, some from our own minds, some from eating too much. So puzzle your dream out for yourself. Bu . . ." his voice trailed away as he grew pensive.

"But?"

He winked. "Well, I'll tell you what I know about women. Alla's words—"

"What about them?" I grew strangely hopeful and wiped my tears from my face.

"Just this, my friend. Alla is obviously in love with you. Everyone sees it. Even before you arrived, there was all this talk about Loayiq. You may not know it, but yours is a body that is good to look at. Your face is not half-bad either. Alla cannot help but look at you. And, because of her earlier life, let's just say she's perhaps a little desperate. Do you know what my mother told me?"

I shook my head, and I could feel joy rising in my heart.

"She said, 'When a woman loves a man, she is apt to be dishonest in order to win him.' Some of my ancestors were Doreni, but my mother is Carpo Ibeni. Carpo women are wise women, more shrewd than the women of your tribe. I believe everything my mother says. Therefore, ignorant and sheltered possible prophet, if I were you I would not believe anything that a woman says about her rival. If a woman says her rival is dead, go and look for the corpse with your own eyes. If you find the corpse, make sure the living woman had nothing to do with the death."

All this was news to me. I must have looked dumbfounded because he suddenly burst out laughing. Nevertheless, I believed him. I began to like him after that, despite his talkativeness and arrogance. He did not quite believe I was the appointed Bringer of the Lost Book, and because of this he accepted me for who I was.

Several days later, Alla came to me and wagged her finger in my face as if I had done her great wrong. "Wind Follower, I've been waiting for you to tell me about your visitor. You didn't bring him to Father. Father is the headman of this place, and I am its Arhe. You've made us seem mean and inhospitable in your visitor's eyes by not allowing us to greet him as we should."

"Forgive me, Sister," I said. "It didn't seem necessary that you should meet a servant who only stayed one night."

"My future husband," she answered, "I did not wish to rebuke you. But you must understand that customs exist for well-proven reasons. Are you not aware that my Father has many enemies? I don't know how you Pagatsu treat the hospitality laws, but we Desai greet all visitors. Rich or poor, a visitor to a noble house must be greeted by the headman."

As I was determined to believe that Satha still lived, I resolved in my mind to judge all of Alla's actions as lacking. I smiled at her, knowing she was not helping her cause. "We Pagatsu," I said, "follow the same precept. But, Sister, we Pagatsu trust our guests not to bring enemies within our gates. And surely, the spirits must have told who it was who passed through their curtain."

After a momentary giggle, she broke into triumphant laughter. "Loayiq, you made your steward flee early because if I had spoken to him you would have had to admit that I was right. That's all that needs to be said. I was wrong in that matter, I will be proven right in all the others."

No, I did not like her. Unlike Satha, she was selfish and like Noam, she liked triumphing over those who slighted her. She stood before me, studying my thoughts. She well knew how much I despised her. Yet, she lifted her face to mine and kissed me again on the lips. This kiss was longer, and I surprised myself by not pushing her away.

"How strange it must be for you, Wind Follower," she said, pushing my hair from my face, "that you are grieving for your dead wife and at the same time falling in love with me! I have no fear of your present anger. I will triumph over your heart in the end."

Disgusted at her arrogance and her easy dismissal of my wife, I left her standing there. She was laughing, but I hoped her words would not prove true. I did not wish my heart to yearn uncontrolled for one like her.

SATHA
Temptation
Weed Moon–First Heat Moon

*S*laves own nothing, not even their own wombs. Those were the words I kept hearing. Morning, noon, night. *You don't want a child,* the voices said. *Who would want to bring more slaves into the world?*

I see clearly now which voice was mine and which belonged to the Arkhai, but back then I could not sort their voices from my own thoughts and my heart sank into despair as the child grew within me. I retreated to the rock Sena had taken me to when we first arrived and remembered my smooth, flat belly. *Your belly is no longer flat, the voices said. Your body is marked by childbirth, and the child is not Loic's. The young Pagatsu chief is young. He will not desire you.*

I pushed their words from my mind. The cold moons were waning. I stroked my stomach. *Spring, then summer,* I thought, *and soon Talub's son—my son—will be born. Talub's son. Talub's son.*

What if you are unlucky enough to have a daughter? the voices asked. *It would not secure your future.*

Talub's son. Loic's daughter. Satha's son. Yes, the thing Talub has planted within me, will also be Satha's son. The boy I bear will be mine.

If it is a boy. If it lives. And it probably will not live. The ground it is planted in is weak.

I remembered the Doreni law: *The son of a warrior's wife was a warrior's son.* Yes, Talub's son would be Loic's son. Just as Sio was Taer's son.

The air bristled with an angry cold. The winds seemed like knives, cutting my flesh. I listened to the lowing of Talub's cattle. *In time, my son—Loic's son—will own all Talub's herd.*

How you dream, Satha! Have any of your dreams ever been fulfilled? This dream will be fulfilled.

I climbed down from the rock and ran to some of Talub's Theseni herdsmen. "Good Sirs," I said, "when you visit the towns, bring me funeral clothes to wrap the baby in."

This they did, returning several days with the swaddling cloths they had bought.

When Voora saw the cloths, she asked what they were and I told her.

"Funeral cloths?" she asked. "Why would you wrap a new born baby in funeral cloths?"

"We Theseni believe that a great savior will come to us, a savior born to die. So we shroud our children in death to remind us of the savior born to die. We also place a child in the stables, among the excrement, to show that the loving savior, the desire of all nations, will pitch his tent among humans. We lay down with him in our birth, and after that we live forever."

She looked at Talub as if my words troubled her. But Talub said, "Let her swaddle the child. It is their custom."

Voora's jealousy made her even uglier than she was. "Such pagan customs are not mine. Have you decided to treat her as Chief Wife because she is bearing this dark child?"

"And why should he not?" I asked. "I am the mother of Talub's future heir. And aren't you too old to bear our husband a child? Be quiet then! I'll give birth to a boy who will own all of Talub's treasures, lands, and cattle. When Talub is dead, my son—and I—will determine where you live and how long . . . what you eat and drink, and how much."

Slowly, with cold determination, she walked away and entered her wagon. I heard rustling in the wagon and soon she reappeared again, a large whip in her hand. She walked toward me, holding it high above her head. Then—with surprising strength—she lashed it across my left shoulder. The whip cracked the sky, the air echoed like thunder. Then with another swift and powerful movement she brought the whip down across my right shoulder. Hotter than the Satilo sun, the sharp lash burned into my skin. "I am Chief Wife," she said.

From that day, she treated me even more harshly. No longer could I draw water for her from nearby wells, no longer could any of the herdsmen help me. I had to bring water from streams more than a half-day's journey away. I had to hew wood, and carry coal—men's jobs.

She wants your baby to die, the voices said. *There is no hope for you, no hope to escape her. Loic will not find you. And even if he does, he is a weak man, weaker than your father. There is no help for you. Go to the large rock near the far side of Talub's encampment and jump down. It is better for you to die than to live.*

"No," I said aloud. "I should not think such things. HaZatana destroys whatever and whoever he wishes. We must submit and hope until he turns his face toward us and becomes Y'wa again. Therefore I will wait until my change comes."

This plan of yours—bearing Talub's child— is bound to fail. As all your plans tend to fail. You are alone in the world and your husband has either died or has forgotten you. In all your life, have you ever seen Y'wa's mercies? Even your blessed marriage was a way to bring you to disaster. Only HaZatana knows of you. Perhaps only HaZatana exists, and you humans create Y'wa to make sense of your sorrows.

Like a continual heavy dripping rain, every day their words soaked into my heart—until one night after sunset, I walked alone to the large rock. A long walk it was, and although my heart was weary, strength returned to me and helped me scale the smooth sides of the slanting boulder. I forced my bare feet into a crack in the rock and climbed it as easily as if I was a goat on a rocky hill. Atop the rock's narrow top, I peered down the cliff. The shrubs below looked like tiny ants.

Jump, Satha, the voices said.

I closed my eyes, and tried to prepare myself to jump. But when I closed my eyes they opened into the unseen world and I saw what was hidden from eyes of flesh.

A sea of blood flowed before my eyes, an ocean of unformed lifeless children killed in the wombs of their mothers, children sent by the Creator to women who had not wanted them.

"Why are you showing me this?" I asked, half-aware that this harsh sight before me was the Creator's doing.

A voice more loving than comfort answered me. "For this crime and others, your land rebels against you. Centuries ago, I sent the Doreni here to change the ways of the people of this land. But they turned their eyes from seeing the slave shops of the Theseni and the brothels of the Ibeni. Now I have sent the Angleni to cleanse the land."

"Even more reason for me to kill myself," I said, remembering my dream of the seething pot.

"My decree against the three tribes is not yet inscribed in stone. This future can yet be changed. Whatever future unfolds, you, Loic and your descendants are destined to teach the three tribes all I have written in the Lost Book. Do not let the Arkhai weary you, Satha. You have six great works to accomplish."

"I care nothing about the three tribes or about this land. I want to die and to go to the fields we long for."

"Remember this, Satha: The Theseni heaven is harsh to women. One man becomes the husband of many virginal wives. If you cannot enter the Doreni fields, the Theseni heaven is your only option."

"I'm Doreni now. It is that field I will enter."

"According to the spiritual covenant between the Doreni and me, a Doreni woman cannot enter the blessed fields without a husband. Will you linger outside the gates until Loic dies?"

"Is he still alive?"

"He is, and he will find you soon enough."

"Y'wa, your 'soon' is not my 'soon.'"

"No, Beloved Daughter, it is not. But endure. Read the Lost Book and enter the best of heavens. Now, search among the faces of the children here and see."

I searched, and from the sea of faces, a little girl with a smiling half-Theseni half-Doreni face looked lovingly up at me. I knew she was the nameless one, my daughter who had died.

"Does she indeed exist even though she did not breathe air before she died?" I asked.

"She lives with me in the best of heavens. What name will you give your daughter?"

"I may still name her?" The only name that came to me was Monua.

"Her name will be Monua, then," the Wind answered my thoughts. "Now, Daughter, give up your thoughts of self-slaughter and live the life you have found yourself in. I have appointed you to care for Voora. The time will come when she will need you, for you are to cradle this new generation."

From that day, the Arkhai's words had no power to cause me to despair. I named that rock, Ne'Adbo-Y'wa which meant "Here I met the Good Creator." And I named the Good Maker, Y'waGulTuyat, which in our old tongue means, "Creator God, you see me."

LOIC
Blade Castle
Traveling Moon–Third Heat Moon

The Snow Moons rolled past the Cool Moons into the Heat Moons. All attempts to escape from Blade Castle had failed. Any lightheartedness I had—which had never been much—left me; grim despair seeped into my soul. I no longer laughed, but neither did I weep. I became distant, even from my own anger. During the first weeks of my imprisonment I had fought with everyone, wildfire flared up at incidents great and small, but now the wildfire had quenched. I was like a forgotten prisoner in a distant land who realized he had no hope of amnesty or being redeemed out of the hand of an all-powerful captor.

It soon became evident—as the Desai were proud of saying—that my escape depended on bowing to the Arkhai and on the Scriptures. I had begun to read them.

As I did, I grew to understand many Doreni rituals better. *How wonderful these writings are!* I thought. *I've lived with these rituals all my life and yet never understood them fully.*

Other scrolls, however, only confused me, especially those which spoke about the Wind Follower. They were so cryptic they made me angry. In one Scripture, the prophet Eleo said, "Wind Follower, be at peace with the enemies of your people." But in another, Prophet Koloq exhorted, "Wildfire, destroy the plunderers! Show the Called-Out Ones the nearly-too-good-to-be-true-news."

If the prophets speak to me or of me, I thought, *I can make no sense of their words. It seemed a waste of my time to try to interpret them, for what should I do if one prophecy declared the Wind Follower's first child would die, yet another stated his first child would not be his? Satha had come to me a virgin; the child who died had indeed been mine.* Confusion made me desperate and hopeless, and hopelessness made me grieve. Nothing in the Scriptures was of any immediate help to me. All I could think was that the Creator had made himself distant and cryptic, and I returned the prophecies to the basket.

This was the state of my heart when Alla came to my room. "Wind Follower," she said, lifting her hand and lecturing me. "The time for grieving must come to an end. Life is to be lived by those who are fully alive." She pulled the curtains closed behind her.

Outside in the fields, other inhabitants of Blade Castle practiced in the archery fields, entered and exited the invisible curtains. "Let me die, then," I said, turning my back to her, "because I am not fully alive."

"Wind Follower," she said in a superior tone I had grown to dislike, "you lack a warrior's heart. How many of Father's former students have survived imprisonment in Angleni dungeons less pleasant than this! Yet you complain because you have wide fields to roam in? You have not joyfully endured the test the spirits have imposed upon you. How will you endure when you war against the Angleni?" She stood behind me and encircled my waist with her arms. "If you continue your petulance, I will not give you the surprise I had planned for you."

She lifted the strands of my hair and began playing with them. At first, I cared little that she wove and interwove them through her fingers but then, again remembering Arlis, I pushed her away. "I want no surprise. In my life, surprises are generally disagreeable."

She smiled. "Is freedom disagreeable, Wind Follower?"

"Freedom?" My heart leaped.

"At least for a while."

My heart sank.

"The spirits think you need respite from this place. They also want you to understand what the Angleni have done to our land."

I thought. *If the Arkhai allow me to pass the invisible wall, I will owe them no allegiance, and I will most assuredly never return to this place.*

She took both my hands in hers and squeezed them. How warm and soft her hands felt in mine! "We will see about that, Wind Follower. When the villagers become acquainted with you—and you with them— you will begin to form your army against the Therpas and the Angleni.

The villagers will forgive your slighting their local spirits when they realize you're the one the Arkhai prophesied about."

"The Arkhai made no prophecies," I said firmly. "The holy prophets did. And the holy prophets made no prophecies about me."

"Yes, Wind Follower." She dismissed my words as if I was an ignorant child. "The Arkhai made those prophecies. They work with the Creator and they and the Creator spoke through the mouths of those holy prophets. And yes, they created you for this very time." She kissed my cheek. "Now, get yourself ready. I'll meet you at the stable."

After she left, I searched my travel pouch for my marriage cap, and finding the cap I put it on my head. I hid the travel pouch inside my woolen gyuilta, then I raced to the stables where Alla was waiting for me. She glanced at my clan cap, but said nothing. I mounted Cactus and determined in my heart that I would never again return to Blade Castle.

In her short leather gyuilta, Alla seemed like a woman warrior from the northern Doreni clans. When she spurred her horse onward, I had to steel my heart against itself, so lovely and so fierce did Alla seem. *Oh that my Satha could ride like that!* When I thought this, I feared that spellwork had been laid on me.

"Come," she said, "while you fall in love with me, I will show you all the evil the Angleni have done."

I followed her, not caring about the Angleni and only wishing to be free. My mind listened carefully for any spell she might use; my eyes studied the gestures of her arms. But she did nothing out of the ordinary. Nor did she speak strange words of power. She only asked the spirits to let me pass, and at her words the wall of shuwas parted and we rode through.

We traveled far until the sun rose high in the sky. All the while, my eyes looked right and left, searching for the right time to escape. We passed a totem and I began to believe the spirits in Ganti's house had reached their boundary. But even then, I did not immediately try to flee. *Surely,* I thought, *if Alla can see what is in my mind she knows what I'm planning.*

Whenever she turned around to look at me, I would study her eyes. She gave no hint that she knew my intentions. She spoke only of the

Angleni, told me to look upon the fields the Angleni had salted, or at the skeleton mounds the Angleni had left when they massacred our people.

We reached an intersection where brick walls hemmed in a long narrow road. This road led to a nearby village, but another road diverged from the intersection. I decided the time had come to leave. I led Cactus toward the road that turned aside, riding away from Alla. "I'm leaving," I said. "I have a vendetta to fulfill. I can stay no longer at Blade Castle."

Her face reddened with rage. "The spirits were right! You are a deceiver. If you would deceive me in this manner, you will also deceive our people."

"I did not deceive you. Did I make you or the spirits any promises? No, I would be a deceiver if I stayed here and deceived my wife who needs me."

"If she is dead, you cannot deceive her, Wind Follower."

"You're wrong. One can indeed deceive the dead. I would deceive Krika's search for the Creator if I followed the Arkhai. And I would deceive my wife if I don't try to find her. If you loved and understood me as much as you say you do, then you would know I cannot stay here while she is stolen. If she's dead, I will have no happiness until I find her body and shroud it in our wedding garments. How can I stay here when she lingers outside the fields we long for, unable to walk proudly with the Creator? And if she's alive and married, lying in the arms of another, I must still kill Noam because I am bound by a vendetta. Are you so unworthy a woman that you could love a warrior who so easily forgets his promises to his wife?"

She pulled her horse aside, and yanked angrily on its reins. "Leave then! Leave!" Her words were strong and defiant, yet tears flowed down her face. "Go and couch with your dead wife! Betray us to the Angleni!"

I hesitated, my heart troubled. "Let us not part as enemies, Alla. Can you not see the honor in this? If we are . . . if you are to be my wife—if the prophecies are true—if the Angleni god is worse than the Arkhai . . . I will return to you."

"Go!" She sat still, scowling and sulking on her horse.

I turned Cactus toward the river, toward the direction of the Therpa household. Alla's gaze followed me. I spurred Cactus onward. He didn't move.

"Come, Cactus," I urged. "Don't make a fool of me. We're escaping the world that held us captive these many moons."

Again he didn't move. Angry, I raged, "Cactus! If these reins in my hands were daggers, I would kill you right now."

I heard a voice speaking within my mind. *Am I not your very own horse?* it asked. *Your companion whom you have ridden since your youth? Would I harm you?*

I trembled, fearful the spirits were playing some maddening trick on me. The prophets of old often spoke to birds and beasts. As I pondered this, my eyes suddenly opened to an unseen world. All about us fire encircled. Invisible to the human eye though they were, the flames would have scorched me had I entered them.

"Cactus has saved your life," Alla shouted, her face red and angry. "Even though you wished to disobey the spirits. Why can you not understand? The Arkhai will be merciful if you change your ways and obey Ganti."

I dismounted Cactus and approached the fire, intending to walk through it. I advanced toward the ring of flames. My face flushed with heat, the smell of smoke permeated my clothes as fire singed them. I continued onward, determined to push past my fear. I stepped into the flames. Fire engulfed my body. Heat, like the heat I'd experienced in Gebelda, went through my body. Unable to bear the burning fire, I leapt backward, beaten.

With a sweeping motion of her right hand, Alla approached and quelled the flames around me. "Follow me," she ordered, and the cold winds blew her hair about her head. "Fool! Never again try to leave my side."

Together we rode silently until we entered the village. The poor lined its streets like dirty snow; they flowed past the riverside like refuse and sewage. Open sores, dark-ringed eyes, foul stenches, distended bellies. Unshed tears caused my eyes to sting. My heart sank and I hated myself for this. Warriors should not weep for swooning children and starving babies. They should walk through salted towns and destroyed cities and not be overwhelmed by crawling children waiting for spoiled meat to fall from the mouth of a mangy cur. They should see skin flapping on bodies like brittle paper and should count the bones of those deformed by hunger without swerving from their course. They should couch with Doreni and Theseni harlots—girls who must sell their bodies for a stale crumb—without feeling the girls' shame.

Are the Therpas—indeed, are all the rich Doreni in these parts—so unlike my noble father? I asked myself. *What a useless warrior I am! I'm supposed to be an avenger, yet I desire to heal and feed these oppressed people. How can I restore to these people all the Angleni and the Arkhai have stolen? Their arms, their legs, their health, their husbands, their homes?*

Now, here is a thing I have not seen again, although I know that even now such things still exist. From the moment Cactus had spoken to my mind, the Creator had not closed my eyes. I still did not see the world in the way ordinary eyes saw it. I saw the world as it truly is, as perhaps the Creator sees it. The arcs and streets and columns of the marketplace, the shore of the river, the burned and salted grasslands were still before my eyes, but other things floated before me as well.

At first I hardly knew what I was seeing. Every vendor shop seemed covered, as if draped with ivy, moss, or a living veil of lice. On every corner, walkway and column people stood or sat, but these were not humans. They did not walk like humans. It was not ivy or moss draping the buildings. They did not move like natural things. Spirits, of all hues, textures, sizes and shapes abounded in that place. What an infestation it was. An odor of putresce, similar to that of corpses I had encountered decaying under the ancestral tree, assaulted me and made it hard for me to breathe. Like green mold, white leprosy or black mildew, the mottled almost-transparent skin of a demon draped—through, outside and above—the walls of a brothel.

The mottled transparent demon snarled at me as I passed by, and shouted—what a foul breath he had!—"You cannot conquer us, Loayiq!" But then he turned his attention to a young man lingering near its doors, saying, "Enter and fulfill all your desires."

All the demons of that place glared at me as I passed by, triumphing over me and making mockery of me. Jobara! They knew everything that had ever befallen me and took pleasure in relating all the sorrows they had caused me.

Strangely, the villagers seemed unaware of the spirits all about them. Alla, too. The town's inhabitants ran toward her, giving her fruits, grain and flowers and asking her to entreat the spirits on their behalf, calling her Beloved Woman. And she, as if the spirits were so very far away, promised them her intercession.

She's young to be a Beloved Woman, I thought. *But this is the way the spirits bribe her, letting her bathe in their glory and allowing her to do insubstantial tricks among the people.*

She glared at me, but said nothing. We journeyed deeper into the village. More women, mostly old and some with young children, greeted her. They all wore long black skirts made of hemp and red woolen gyuiltas about their shoulders.

Towards the center of the village, totems seemed to sprout in every intersection or corner. At the base of each totem plants, fruits, foods of all kinds, were wrapped in parchment covered with petitions and promises.

"Can these spirits not feed themselves?" I asked Alla. "Why do they take what little food these poor women have?"

The air bristled like crisp parchment being crumpled in a scribe's hand. I fully expected to see the sky flaking away and sizzling into nothing. It did not. The sky remained as it was, but a spirit squatting beside an Ibeni desert totem rose up and suddenly flew towards me. I cannot say how he hit me or with what, but a searing pain sliced through my neck, knocking me off my horse.

Angry, I picked myself up from the ground and shouted at him. "Since my youth I've seen that you spirits rule towns only to deplete them. Poverty and the worship of shadow gods always work together. You pretenders delight in—"

Alla's raised voice interrupted me. Her eyes challenged me. "Be careful, Wind Follower. My presence won't save you if you continue insulting our ancestors. If you say the Arkhai are evil, you're also saying that I am evil." She slowed her horse and waited for me to mount Cactus. "The Angleni have killed their husbands and clansmen. Or their husbands have destroyed their own minds with strong Angleni drink. And you argue with our spirits? It is not the Arkhai who have brought this trouble upon us!"

I looked about at the devastation around me. *How stricken this place is! How cruel this war is between humans and the Arkhai!*

She held her horse's reins high. "No! There is no war between humans and the Arkhai. No wonder the Scriptures warn you against helping the Angleni god!"

I gritted my teeth, angry that she could not see what I saw. *The Angleni were cruel indeed, but who could stand against the cruelty of the Arkhai?*

When I thought that I had seen all and no more was left to be seen, the Desai mind-seeing gift assaulted me. Now the minds of all those around me opened to me. Within my heart, I heard all their prayers to the heartless spirits. Within my soul, I heard all their longing for the Creator and the longed-for savior of humans. I saw all their sicknesses, sins, lusts, weaknesses and cruelties. They weighed down my heart and I could not bear the burden of them. My powerlessness in the face of the poverty and helplessness all about me made tears flow from my eyes. *I do not like this Desai gift,* I thought. *Who can bear this burden of feeling everyone's griefs? The spirits are unkind. Disease is relentless. Poverty is cruel. Shame and sorrow are all these people own.* I hid my face in my gyuilta, and for a moment glanced at Alla. *How indifferent she was! How could she—a Desai—not be overcome by all the misery which surrounded us?*

"Perhaps you are evil," I shouted to Alla. A startled look came to her face, and on the face of those who had surrounded us. "What I've seen is this. The poor give you of their goods and ask you to intercede for them against the Arkhai. Yet, how have your prayers helped them? How has your heart cared for them? Your heart doesn't see these poor people. Nor did you bring any of Blade Castle's bounty to these people outside its walls! Your heart doesn't bind itself to the poor as the heart of my dear wife does."

Anger and hatred flashed in her eyes. Not only had I challenged her—my host— but I had done so in front of the villagers. She hastened from the village with me following behind her. For many days after that, she didn't speak to me. Yet she lost her anger and after a while began to court me again, returning frequently to my room. She often lifted my hands to her breasts, inviting me to touch them. But I could not.

SATHA
Ewi
Reaping Moon–First Harvest Moon

I gave birth to my son alone in a field surrounded by lingay grasses. When I returned to the campsite with the child in my arms, Voora didn't help me as I had helped her. But I knew already that was the way she was. She had no heart. Or perhaps she had a heart only for those who were Angleni. If she had been cruel to me before I became her husband's second wife, despising me for my black skin, now she found me even more intolerable for bearing a child when she could not.

I named my son Ewi, which in our old language means "heart question." (We use Angleni words now. Sad, because in many ways, the Angleni tongue is not as rich as our old words.) When I gave birth to Ewi, my heart question was "Should I try to live or allow myself to die? Should I strangle the child and kill myself or should I submit to the life I now have to live?" All that was bound up in Ewi's name.

During my enslavement, I did not care for myself. If an insect bit me, I didn't worry if it was poisonous. If a splinter entered my foot, I didn't care if it came from a befouled twig. I half-wished it did. Life was such a hard thing, so full of grief. I could not kill myself, but I could not gladly fight for life.

There is an old Doreni word: *skortuka*—allowing oneself to give up the fight.

But when Ewi was born, I decided to live. I continued to hope. I told myself I would wait until he "passed the worst of childhood." This was a Theseni saying. It meant I would allow myself to live until Ewi was grown and settled into a family that loved him. It is grievous to live unloved and without family or clan. So I lived, and watched the child grow, and tried to love my life.

The child was a joy, darker than his father but cinnamon-colored like most of the Doreni, with curly hair like the Ibeni. Yes, he looked like someone from the Matchless Family. The Creator seemed to have favored him with strength, power, wisdom and even protection. I say this because often the spirits sent snakes, spiders and hawks into his sleeping net to kill him. There were diseases too and accidents. Once, as he stood near a fire, the spirits sent a wind from nowhere to pick him up and throw him into it. At other times, he would be thrown into the river by unseen hands or down a mountainside. But he always emerged alive. After a while, it seemed the spirits gave up on trying to murder him.

LOIC
The Therpa Feast
Fever Moon–Third Snow Moon

The snow was knee-deep as we trudged toward the Blue Fortress, the Great House of the Therpa clan. It was there, between its walls gleaming blue like the inside of an oyster shell, the old Therpa chieftain had lavished me with sweets and gifts. As a child I had run through its courtyard as a favored guest. Now I was entering my former playground disguised with camel hair and a mustache and beard that weren't my own. We were there, Ganti had told me, for my sake. I was to listen, discover and understand. What I was to learn, he did not exactly say, but he often spoke as if my vendetta against Noam only complicated his larger plans against the entire Therpa clan.

Ahead of us on the large field outside the Blue Fortress, farmers in ragged woolen gyuiltas ambled home, their bodies slumped from hard work, their clothes tattered and hanging from their bodies. Yet how I envied them their freedom because I could leave Blade Castle only if Alla or Ganti were at my side.

"When you arrive at the Therpa feast," Ganti said, smoothing out a smudge of dye on Twin's face, "try to resist the urge to make eye signals to each other or to make secret gestures with your hands. This is no game. Know that you are in the house of wise warriors who are even more knowledgeable in warfare than you are. Even so, when there, behave as if you are in the house of friends."

"And," Kaynu added, "although they resist helping the poor on most days, on feast days they try to be honorable."

"But," I wondered aloud, "will the Therpa spirits allow me to enter? They know I wish to kill Noam and I have none of my ancestral spirits with me to bargain for me."

"The spirits who guard this house will not harm you," Ganti assured me. "They know you will not kill a man in his own house. Besides, they have greater concerns than your vendetta against Noam."

Irritated and angry, I stared at him. The Desai were inclined to belittle and humiliate all those they did not consider wise or enlightened. I had suffered much because of Noam, suffered even more because of the spirits and their invisible wall. Yet, none in Blade Castle considered me enlightened until I surrendered my will and mind to Ganti's view.

"Enjoy yourselves," he reminded us, ignoring the anger he knew was seething in my mind. "Enjoy the music, the food and the festivities. Flirt with the young women. There are many there, even a few as beautiful as our Alla. But do not flirt with the Therpa sins, do not allow yourself to be convinced, as these Therpas are, that friendship with our former enemies is a good thing. It isn't."

Ganti uncovered his head. The skin dye made him look like a swarthy Ibeni. Even the shape of his eyes had been transformed. He stepped more briskly than I toward the Therpa House.

"Master," Twin's surprised voice echoed across the bleak stubbled field. "Your limp is gone!"

"What limp?" Ganti asked, laughing. "Ganti has a limp, but I have no limp." He tousled Twin's hair. "Talker, keep control of your mouth. Forget your Carpo greatness for a moment. Can you do that?"

Twin nodded apologetically.

"Now," Ganti continued, "we must not enter the Blue Fortress together. Kaynu, you will go ahead of us. Twin and I'll arrive later. Unfortunately, I have to stay close to him. How sad it is, Twin, that I can't trust you wholeheartedly! And Wind Follower, you walk into the town, then turn back and enter. Don't mind being alone, do you?"

"You know I will not be alone, Master Ganti," I answered as politely as I could. "Even if I walked to the end of the town, at my first thought of escaping the Arkhai will create a barrier to entrap me."

He smiled and tapped the eight-stringed plika in my hand. "Although your dagger is locked tightly in the back of this instrument, you must not use it. Know it's there, but forget it's there."

Twin repeated one of the school's proverbs: "A good assassin knows how to bring his instrument before the eyes of his prey and yet keep it invisible."

"When we are all present in the house," Ganti continued, "we must not speak to each other immediately. If you wish to speak to each other, seem to meet as guests at a feast meet. Seem to speak your heart, but remember we're here to find information, not to give it. Wind Follower, make sure the edge of your tunic drags along the ground. A messy and poor minstrel easily disarms his prey. Now . . . get going. And—one thing more."

"What one thing more?" I asked.

He lifted a warning finger. "You've gotten careless with your food lately. Perhaps purposely so. Now, however, consider carefully if you truly want to die. Sio knows your sickness only too well. If you're tempted to pile grains on your plate and eat them, you will be giving yourself away."

"It is a feast," I reminded him. "I suspect the Therpas know how to treat their guests. Perhaps they will even teach you Desai a lesson or two." I left them and walked silently into the town.

How full of life and beauty the night was. Fireflies flitted across the barley fields like fallen stars. In the distance, near the river, a man kissed a woman. I thought of Satha and longed for her and for my own freedom. By the time I arrived at the Blue Fortress, I wanted to plunge my dagger into Noam's heart as much as I wanted to kill Alla and Ganti for denying me my freedom.

At the feast, dancers danced, whores whored—their transparent and shortened tunics swinging wild about their hips. The Feast Table, unlike those in most Doreni great houses, was not a perfect circle but was oval-shaped. I began to understand that those who sat at either end of the table were considered highly honored. Such an offensive thing I had never seen before, but it was the Angleni influence. Mukal spiced, warm, iced, twice fermented, flowed like river water, as did the potent 'fermented ale' of the Angleni.

I had not been there long when Noam came stumbling into the gathering room calling for Angleni fermented ale. The Therpa great chief's disappointment with his son was obvious. A servant girl brought the fermented ale to Noam, and he leaned in the doorway half-listening to the talk of politics and half flirting with an Ibeni whore. Noam had never been one for politics. He left the room and walked through a doorway.

I hoped he was not going to the family quarters. A stranger could travel through the outer court to the inner court but not into the family quarters, nor into the guest quarters, unless invited. I sat nervously shaking my feet and waiting for Noam to return. A wildfire was burning within my soul and I wanted to set Noam and everything else outside of me aflame. I wondered if I could sin against the hospitality decreed by the holy ones and actually kill a man who was my host.

After Noam left, the Therpa great chief lifted a glass of fermented ale aloft in his hand. "How clear this poison looks!" he said. "Can something so simple destroy a kingdom?"

One Angleni answered, "It is recommended as an elixir to soothe the grieving soul."

"Is this why your people gave it to our king? Too soothe his soul after his son died? To numb his mind after Butterfly also died?"

I had not heard of Butterfly's death, and hearing about it now—so suddenly—made me wonder if those deaths were accidental, spirit-caused or the effects of poison.

The Therpa chief turned the glass of fermented ale over and spilled the liquid onto the carpet. "How healthy Jaguar would be, and how much better a king, if you had not given him such medicines to cure him!"

A Theseni answered, "Alas, now Our Matchless King needs cures to cure him of your cure."

The mood of the feast changed slightly. Drinking persisted but now few touched the fermented ale.

"For the Doreni, feasts are created to help build alliances," the Therpa chief said. "The poor meet the rich, the outcast is welcomed as family. I do not wish to insult our guests by suspecting them of evil, but their fermented ale is dangerous. See how it has enslaved my son. Although the Angleni have brought this poison to our shores, they are people like ourselves. Some of them are good, some very bad. They have signed a treaty with the Therpas. They will not break faith with us, but do not touch their poison."

I fingered the secret compartment in the plika where my dagger lay, but as I clenched the instrument's neck, a guest sitting to my right touched my hand. A man dressed in gold silk, obviously a man of much importance, sat up and beckoned me towards the center of the room. "Let us hear you, singer." He shouted to the Therpa chief. "Here is a musician! The one sitting beside the Angleni warseed. Musician, let's hear your plika."

I rose to my feet and walked past a lower-clan Doreni house-girl who was allowing a guest to touch her breasts for all to see.

"My guest wishes to hear you, singer," the Therpa clan chief said. "Poor you may be, with poor clothes, but you can enrich us with your voice."

"I can't sing," I answered with a faked hoarse whisper. "Too much mukal, too much food, has affected my voice."

"Yes, yes," the Therpa chief said laughing. "Eat while you can, poor man! But sing nevertheless, bad voice or not."

I played a song for him, one created by my heart on the spot. I don't remember it well now, but it went something like this:

"All that was mine
All that I loved
All that my father taught me to love
Is gone.
Who will return what is mine when another has soiled it?
Who will return what is mine when another claims her as his own?"

I heard Ganti's thoughts: *Jobara, the prophets said you were a singer, Wind Follower.*

Some of the feasters declared the song an honorable one that honored those who had died in the war. Others were more wary, looking toward the Therpa chief to see how he responded.

"You sing for our country, singer," the Therpa chief said. "What clan do you belong to? Why no clan cap? Tell me where you live so you may come here and sing again."

"I am called Wind Follower," I answered.

"Wind Follower?" the Therpa chief said. "Are you Desai? Or did your mother study theology?"

"Aha!" a Theseni guest shouted. "That's why he's so poor and hungry."

The Therpa chief nodded. "Sad but true. These priests see invisible and immaterial things which they value more than food and money. Yet they need to eat." Everyone laughed. "I think I've heard your name mentioned in one of the towns. Aren't you a member of Ganti's school?"

"I have heard of Ganti," I answered, "and I have hopes of meeting him. Indeed, I have come from afar to visit my father's friend in the hope of studying theology at Blade Castle."

"Study theology somewhere else," the Therpa chief said. "Ganti and the Desai will turn you into an unfeeling, uncaring ascetic."

"I will remember your advice," I began to say.

But a boy rushed into the room. His hair—a bright shock of red, bright curls loosely flew about his head—covered his ears. Or rather, it covered the place where ears should have been. Jobara! It was Sio—my brother—safe and at his family home. He wore a buckskin tunic with fringes and was fuller than he had been when last I saw him. Joy at seeing him turned to fear when I noticed the jade bracelet around his wrist. He searched the faces of those in the room and, in turn, the Therpa chief searched his face!

"My boy," the Therpa chief said, "I see you've decided to join us after all. Taer's austerity is leaving you. Tell your father to desist from drinking the fermented ale and come and enjoy our company."

"I will, Father of my Father."

"Promise me you will not ruin yourself as your father has."

"Taer taught me well to avoid such things," Sio answered, looking out across the room. "Tell me, who was singing just now?"

The Therpa chief pointed at me. "That's the singer. Do you know him?" He seemed even more suspicious now, and my heart raced. I hoped with all my heart that the disguise and the long separation between us would make it impossible for the old man to recognize me. But what of Sio?

My brother walked toward me and stood in front of me, his face close to mine. He studied my face, touched my hair, and looked at my broken tooth and the scar on my chin. His eyes gazed into mine for a long while. "No," he said, "it isn't anyone I know."

The Therpa clan chief still seemed suspicious. "Who did you think this man was, my boy?"

"I thought he was a singer I knew in Taer's house, Great Chief, but he is not."

The Therpa chief rose to his feet. "Are you sure? Are you telling me—and all here—your heart?"

"I am."

"Call your father. He knows Taer's musicians and servants well. Perhaps your father will recognize him."

"My father doesn't know him," Sio said too quickly. "How can he recognize someone he doesn't know?"

I listened with wonder. Why hadn't he given me away?

Sio left the room after taking a sidelong glance at me. The Therpa chief's voice took on a threatening tone. "Perhaps the boy does recognize you, musician."

I tried to see within his mind but could not. "Perhaps."

"And you say you do not yet know Ganti?"

"My theology teacher is a Theseni who lives in the far highlands."

"Are there still Theseni left in the far highlands?" an Ibeni in a blue vest said. He shook his head sadly. "The Angleni killed so many during the war. It is good to know that a Theseni theologian still thrives."

"And what is the name of this Theseni teacher?" the chief prodded. "What does he teach?"

"Great Chief," I said, "why should I tell you my teacher's name if you will not know it? Are you acquainted with all the theologians and their schools?"

"Good answer," the Therpa chief said and relaxed into his tapestried pillow. He clapped his hand. "And you're arrogant enough to use it." This brought a roar of approving laughter which only made me more uncomfortable. "You dress like a poor theologian but you have a warrior's heart, singer. I'll remember you, Wind Follower."

I plucked at my plika. "Good Chief, I would rather you did not. The thought of a Therpa warrior remembering my name fills me with fear."

The Therpa chief laughed again, yet suspicion and worry shone from his eyes. "Yes, yes, you must come again to my house, and if your studies prevent us meeting again, may we meet again in the same fields we long for."

I nodded and moved towards the back of the room as he continued looking in my direction. After a while, he seemed to turn his mind back to his other guests. I felt sufficiently forgotten. With much stealth, I managed to remove Satha's dagger from my plika and to leave the gathering room. Outside in the inner courtyard guards and soldiers, lovers and their betrothed, warriors and harlots wandered in the gardens of the outer courtyard. Pretending to be drunk, I clutched my breechcloth and staggered as I walked.

A warrior came up to me. I suspected Sio or the Therpa chief had told him to follow me. "No pissing on the walls, musician," he said.

"Where's a squatting place, then?" I asked.

He pointed to a corridor near the end of the outer courtyard. "Over there. A long walk, for one who's in a hurry, but if you're a real man, you won't dampen your breechcloth."

I suspected other squatting places were close by but that the soldier liked cruel jesting. Although I had no need for a squatting place, I disliked him for such cruelty. I pretended to stagger toward the squatting place. It lay in darkness far from the main house and was hidden by a terraced wall out of which many large hemp plants grew on several levels. As I approached it, the stench of vomit and mukal, the dark stains on the swinging bamboo curtain made my stomach heave. I didn't have to pretend to stagger then.

I pushed its bamboo curtains aside, being careful to avoid the dark stains, and entered the chamber holding my breath. Excrement surrounded me, but I did not leave. I suspected the warrior was in the shadows watching me. I waited long inside it, and moaned and made such noises as he might have expected. After some time, I heard laughing and looked through a crack in the wall. The soldier had left off following me.

Seeing him leave, I slipped out of the squatting place and walked toward the Therpa family quarters. Red-headed Therpa warriors, their wives, children, and concubines passed by. I hid myself, crouching in the dark. How like my own home it seemed, and how it made me long for the joys and busyness of the Golden House.

Soon I heard Noam's voice. "In two moons, perhaps," he was saying.

"Not sooner?" Sio's troubled voice answer. "What if he finds you alone? With no one to protect you?"

Noam's drunken laughter was tender, reminding me of his gentleness to me in my youth. "Are you so worried about me, my son? I'm honored. I'm not much of a father. Not compared to Taer."

I saw them then. Father and son, the younger supporting the older. How my heart raced when I saw him! My hand trembled for the dagger in my boot.

"Jobara! Taer was honorable indeed," Sio said, "But you are my father. Honorable or not."

Noam laughed again. "You're an honest boy, Sio. A good trait, that."

"Don't go on this journey alone, Father. Let warriors ride with you. I know that the musician was Loic, I'm sure of it. If he is so bold as to come here—"

"He will not kill me in my house." He grasped a column for support, the fermented ale making his feet unsteady. "I can't kill him here either. It's the law of hospitality. And now they've named him 'Wind Follower.' How strange it would be if I unintentionally fulfill the prophecy and kill the savior-guest? Remember, my son? That is what Koloq says the evil one did to the savior of the world."

"Kill him after he leaves, then." Sio's voice wobbled. "I know him, Father. He was my brother for a long while. 'Wind Follower' he may be, but there's a reason they call him 'Wildfire.'"

"Do you truly want me to kill your friend, Sio? Your brother?"

"I do, Father. Or he will kill you."

"He will not kill me. The boy is no warrior."

"The Therpa chief said he left the gathering room." He looked around. "Do you think he's left the compound? Or is he still here?"

Noam shook his mane of red hair and looked about the courtyard. "He's still here." He gazed out across the landscape. "He's watching us." His voice rose as if he were speaking to me. "Perhaps he is even behind the hemp plant there." I trembled, and chided myself for having chosen such an obvious spot. "But what is that to us, my son?"

"Father, Father!" Sio shouted, his voice breaking with fear. "Why didn't you restrain yourself? Women in our household and all through the land of the three tribes have desired your love. Yet, you took Taer's wife. And after that, you climbed into my brother's couch. Satha! Father, she was my friend, always kind and just to me. Why didn't you consider?"

Noam answered, and as he spoke I saw names in his mind. Voora, Talub. I sensed Satha lived with them. "There are matters I cannot speak of, that I will tell him when we meet. To you I will only say: Loic's illness has always made him a bad choice for the Pagatsu. Because of their love for Taer and perhaps because of whisperings about Loic's destiny, they kept their peace. But your mother felt they would not endure a boy who could not breed sons to lead the clan. If Loic had refused to war against me, he would have been considered weak as Pantan's sons were considered weak. The Pagatsu would refuse him as headman in the same way they refused Pantan's son because of the mosquito illness."

"But Loic *has* gone to war against you, Father," Sio challenged.

"Your mother considered this also. She knew that if Loic warred against me, I would kill him, and again he would not be headman. Moreover Taer has adopted you as his son, and because of Jaguar's edict against clan warfare, your mother thought that as a way of creating peace between the Therpas and the Pagatsu, the Pagatsu would turn to you."

At this Sio burst into scornful laughter. "The Pagatsu are true Doreni, Father. They are fierce in their loyalties."

"True, but your mother's scheme seemed good in my sight."

"Why?" his son asked, and his words dripped disapproval.

"Because Taer insulted me by refusing to avenge himself against me and —"

"And," Sio interrupted his father, "you used a woman to avenge yourself in the only way you know how."

Noam was silent for a long while. "My son," he said at last, "another father—not Taer, and not me—but another father would kill you for such an insult." He walked towards the Therpa family quarters.

Sio didn't follow him but stood staring out in the darkness sobbing, his body trembling. He wiped his face with his gyuilta and after staring long through the leaves of the hemp plant, he turned around and walked away.

I hurried toward the gathering room but the same warrior who had guided me earlier approached me. "I was worried you had fallen into the pit."

"And if I had?" I asked.

"I wasn't going to dig you out."

"Jobara?" I asked. "If I had fallen in, I would have preferred to stay there than to let one such as you dig me out!"

He roared in laughter and slapped me hard but good-naturedly on the back. "You look weak, little musician, and your long stay in the squatting place made me think you have weak entrails. But I like you. You've got heart."

I didn't think I had heart. If I had had heart, I would have found a way to kill my enemy—even in his own house. And I would have decided, whether I lived or not, to destroy all those who conspired to keep me trapped in Blade Castle.

SATHA
Another Child
Thunder Moon–Third Cool Moon

The day came when Voora announced she was pregnant.

"Expect another lost child," Sena said. "Why can't this old woman simply stop trying? I suppose she can't stop now since she's in a battle with you."

"I thought you believed the Creator was blessing them."

"True." He shrugged and squatted beside my tent, speaking to me as if I were his equal, although I was Talub's concubine. "She keeps saying the Creator has promised her—an old woman—a child. But you know how mad these childless old women can be?"

"I do know how mad they can be, and yet," I looked at Ewi playing with his father in the distance, "I know she will have a child. Yes, I fear for Ewi when that child of hers is born."

He stroked my shoulder. "You're the only woman here. Be good to her. Help her with the child. She's so old and fat now she can hardly move, and I doubt she'll be able to run after a little child. If you help her with her son, she might be merciful."

The day came and Voora's baby was born. This was Nyal—he whom the Angleni regard as the first king of this land, the one who warred against our people and gathered the remnants of us to this desert place.

Everyone was so surprised the child and Voora had lived there was much feasting. Voora lay weak and tired in her bed for many days, but I tended both baby and mother. Yes, even my Ewi waited on her. How I killed my soul trying to gain that woman's favor. As long as the child was young and needed someone to play with it, to wipe it, to feed it, she was kind to me and there was a truce. Ewi loved his little brother, and his brother loved him. But one day when Voora saw our sons tickling and teasing each other, she shouted to me. "Your son needs to know his place."

"He is his father's eldest son. That's his place."

Her pale face reddened. "Is that what you think? Call Talub to me."

When I brought him to her, she pointed to me disdainfully. "I don't want my son to be heir with this slave woman. Divorce her."

I trembled then, and raced to pick up Ewi.

"But Voora," he began. How weak that man was! "You know that I love you and you are my first wife. But although I don't love Satha as I love you, I find no fault in her. If I divorce her, where should she go?"

She pointed towards the Patchwork Prairie on the outskirts of Colebru. Beyond it was the Great Salt Desert and beyond that Taer's Golden House. "The desert."

I fell to the ground and clutched his leg.

"They'll die in the desert, Voora," he said. "The cold season is hardly over and desert plants are hard to find. Can your heart be so—"

"Divorce her!" she shouted again, and her voice echoed through that field and far into the desert. "In a hundred years, my descendants will cover this land like the stars in the sky, like gnats across a field. And, what does this dark one matter?"

So Talub packed a travel pouch with seven days worth of bread and water and put it on my shoulders. He kissed his son on the cheek and gave me my divorce parchment. I walked toward the Patchwork Prairie, toward the only home I knew, Taer's Golden House.

Most of the herdsmen didn't turn aside from their work to look at me. What could they have done? After Ewi and I had traveled far, Sena was a lone and grieving speck in the green distance.

LOIC
Theological Disagreements
Weed Moon–First Harvest Moon

After I had seen Noam at the Blue Fortress, I returned determined to escape Blade Castle. It seemed to me that the answer to my freedom lay in reading the Desai Scriptures earnestly. I began to discern the truths our prophets had spoken and to separate them from the lies the Arkhai had sprinkled among our rituals. I realized that Koloq, Eleo, Warki, Khumna and all our prophets had warned against the shadow gods. Koloq prophesied the day would come when we would be called upon to be hospitable to the foreigners who would bring the Lost Book to us. He told us the foreigners would destroy us but we would realize that our true enemies were the Arkhai.

"A wildfire will come from a noble clan," he wrote. "He will be Desai and yet not Desai. A great warrior he will be, a weak warrior he will be. This wildfire will pass through the land, destroying."

"Is this is one of the prophecies which have troubled the Desai?" I asked Ganti one day as we practiced in the archery fields.

"It is one which causes disruption, yes." He eyed his mark closely, holding his bow steady. "Have you also read the Angleni book?"

I nodded.

"What did you think when you read it?"

"My mind questioned and my heart leaped."

He let the arrow fly. It reached its mark. Beside the river, a twig on a small tree bowed, then snapped back into place, split in two. "Your heart recognized something in it?"

"It mirrors much in our culture. Koloq, for instance, says the burial tree must be a tree with three trunks and the Angleni believe their god is threefold—a god far above us all, a god within us and a god who

314

was the word come alive. The Angleni also have a sacrificed man who was pierced as our sacrificial lamb is. Yes, I see much goodness in the book."

"Much goodness, yes," he said. "But what do you think of their Creator?"

I walked into the river whose shores marked the limit of my freedom. "I can believe that all the words the Creator ever spoke—of his love, of his laws, of his truth, his kindness and his responsibility towards us—became a living person. We also believe that words are living things. Yes, it is possible for that living word of the Creator to be made alive on earth. I also believe the Creator showed his seal to that teacher's message by raising him and him alone from death. I can believe their god is the one Koloq speaks of as the 'Inviter to the Great Feast' who is wounded in the house of his friends. Yet I cannot believe the Creator wants to be the blood-brother of imperfect humans, or make covenants with them."

"But don't the Ibeni also have an incarnating god who sometimes lives among humans?" Kaynu's voice spoke up behind me. I had not heard him approach.

I retrieved Ganti's arrow, "Qwisna takes on a human body only to pursue the wicked, not to save evil humans from their sins or from their own hearts," I answered him, but I thought, *And is this not what I need? A god who saves me from myself?*

"Wind Follower," Ganti said, "if you think the Angleni Good Book is truly the Lost Book, what will you do? This is what our prophets have argued over for many centuries."

"I wondered too," Kaynu answered, "how similar their ideas are to the Desai! Even when they diverge, they are similar."

He laughed at his own words, but I understood what he meant. "Yes," I said, "the Theseni worship HaZatana and speak of submitting to evil as a way of overcoming evil. But the Angleni god speaks of destroying evil. He says that evil is already destroyed, one must only believe it."

Kaynu stroked my shoulder. "Strange, is it not? That evil should be conquered and all the world not know it? Is this why the Arkhai hate the book so much, because they have hidden many truths from humans and the book shows how defeated they already are?"

"And yet," Ganti prodded, "that such a lying and cruel people should have such a loving and near god!"

Kaynu pointed to a boat floating toward the river. "Perhaps it is because their god is so near, so giving, and so forgiving that the Angleni are so selfish. Like spoiled children who know their parents love them, they know all things are theirs. They take without asking."

"Wind Follower," Ganti said, "you haven't answered my question. What will you do if you are indeed our prophet?"

"I'm not this warrior-prophet Koloq speaks of. I'm not cut out for warring against people. How can I lead our people against the spirits?"

Ganti looked at me strangely, a look of disappointment on his face. "Koloq's prophecy doesn't say you war against the spirits, Wind Follower."

"That is how I interpret it," I said. I could see that the one guiding the boat on the choppy waves and white crested waves was Alla. I thought of her beauty, of her passionate hatred of the Angleni, of her horsemanship. All virtues worthy of admiration, yet I could not love her.

Ganti had fallen into a sullen silence. His anger seemed ready to boil out at me. Then, as if giving me another chance he asked, "Why do you think the Creator would want you to war against the spirits? Haven't the spirits helped us all this time?"

"The Angleni Creator is a god who saves from self," I said. "The spirits save no one. They make our own sins worse. You yourself have said this."

"What is the sin you need to be saved from?" Kaynu asked.

"Too many to count, Brother. But these two oppress me more than all the others. I treated my wife shamefully and I treated my father with disrespect. When I remember the harm I've done to them, my guilt is greater than I can bear."

Ganti raised his hand, waving to Alla on the water. "Yes, regret is a grievous thing. Especially when the one whom one has harmed is no longer alive."

I turned to him. "Satha is indeed alive, Ganti. I don't care what Alla says."

He laughed. "Alla is never wrong. The spirits have proven that countless times."

"Kwelku," I answered. "So you say. But when I looked into Noam's mind, I sensed he knew she was alive."

"Do you remember," Ganti asked, "where Koloq writes:

The evil ones are subtle and they know us well.

They cannot make me steal: for quixas are less than dung to me.

They cannot make me run from battle:

Because my heart is not paper but iron and steel.

But when I think I stand, I must be prepared to fall.

If I pity the poor, the spirits can use my pity to bring about my downfall.

If I righteously avoid sinful women or loutish men,

The spirits make me lose my compassion for the fallen.'"

"Do you think the spirits are deceiving me?" I asked.

He smiled slyly. "You have never liked the spirits, therefore you are interpreting the Scriptures in such a way to preserve your enmity against them. Be careful, or you will destroy both yourself and your people."

I bit my lip to prevent myself from speaking rude words to my host.

He continued. "Do you not wonder why your mother asked Taer to keep the secret of your clan from you? It was to keep you safe, young man. To protect you from yourself."

To avoid an argument, I turned my eyes from him toward the river and Alla whose boat was approaching us.

"If you were truly your mother's child," he continued, "you would not destroy your people by forsaking her for strange gods."

"Enough!" I said, cutting him short. "I do not wish to speak to one whose hatred against the Angleni is so great he cannot see what is so clearly written in his own Scriptures."

He was not surprised at my words. He never was. He always knew what I would say—sometimes even before I knew it. We walked into the silty water to greet Alla as she disembarked. At last he said to me, "Wind Follower, you aren't following the Wind. You don't breathe our god or walk the Wind's Way. You continue to offend the Arkhai, and now you misread the Desai Scriptures. Do you expect to live long if you do such a thing?" I could sense his worry for me.

He turned and limped away, but Kaynu gently pulled on my braid, surprising me. Alla walked toward us wearing an Ibeni dress which seemed to be created only to seduce. Certainly it was useless as clothing as it left breasts and stomach bare.

She extended her hand; I didn't reach for it. It seemed safest not to. I took a lingering look at Alla and her dress which trailed along the water. Then turned about and left her by the river.

I had begun to believe that the Angleni god and the Creator were one and the same. If he proved himself capable of protecting me from the Arkhai and from Alla, I would cast my life on him.

That night as I read the Angleni Book, a shadow hovered over me. I looked up and saw one who looked like Krika. He had not visited me since his death, and this had worried me, for we had been age brothers, and other living friends had been visited by their dead friends. My heart leaped to see him, alive and healthy before me, the twinkling eyes, and the swarthy cheeks. "Krika!" I shouted, rushing over to hug him.

But lips that were wont to smile did not smile on me. Rather, he stood near my door weeping. "It has been a long time," he said, sounding like himself and yet not like himself. "Do you know what you're reading?"

"You've come to me after all these years, and you're asking me what I'm reading? Come now, my friend! Tell me, do you run with the Creator? Are you happy in that land? How do you spend your days? Are the days there like days here?"

He didn't answer. He only stood looking at me, his lips curled in a frown. His silence put fear in my heart. "Are you in Gebelda?" I asked. "Has the Creator allowed you to roam the fields we long for even though you were not covered with the blood of the sacrificed lamb?"

"The spirits sent me to you," he said.

"The spirits? What do they have to do with you? We rejected them long ago."

"Even so, they sent me here."

My heart sank. "Why did they send you?"

"To warn you against betraying our people."

I turned from him. "No, you aren't Krika."

He did not answer me. All I heard were the voices of my fellow students in the surrounding rooms. Joyous memories of my old days with Krika passed before my eyes, but I hardened my heart. "You are not my friend, and you cannot convince me that you are."

The beautiful lost face now became distorted, the eyes became flames. "Do you really want to know who I am? Do you want to see me as I really am?"

Suddenly, a living corpse stood before me, his face pale-green and drawn, his breath foul and stinking like the garbage heap of Satilo. Others appeared behind him, equally grotesque, all the Arkhai. All turned hateful sunken eyes on me.

I understood their unvoiced threat, but I didn't put the Book away. Instead, I put on my gyuilta and walked out into the fields, the parchments in my hand. My heart ached for my freedom and for Satha. I lay on the grass and pleaded with the Creator to free me from Blade Castle.

I parted with my ancestors that night. I told myself that if the Angleni god could free me from Blade Castle, then I would believe he was the Creator and I would serve him forever. This I did many days. Then one night, although the windows were locked because of the cold, a small breeze blew into my room and awakened me. I walked past my sleeping roommate and out into the fields near the river. *If a spirit is calling me,* I vowed to myself, *I will not run from it.*

I stood alone under that dark midnight sky, and soon something took human form and stood before me, bloodied with lamb's blood. It was the same being who had pulled me from Gebelda. "Loic," he said, and love enveloped me. "I am the Wind. The Savior of Angleni and of all men. The desire of the nations."

"Kwelku. So you say. But perhaps you were sent from the Arkhai to deceive me. I've seen the way you spirits put on and remove faces. How can you prove yourself to be who you say you are?" I turned to leave, but thought for a moment. "You say you are the Angleni Savior?"

"I am."

I stared at the being, who had the form of a man, and basked in the great love and kindness that shone from his eyes. "The Angleni Book states the Wind came in human flesh to save humans from the power of evil, the powers of the Arkhai, the powers of death, and the power of self. Is this true?"

"It is true."

No spirit of the Arkhai would have admitted such a thing. I bowed before the Creator. "What would you have me to do?"

"Be not afraid, Loic. Be not ashamed of me. Do not forsake me."

"No, Great Chief, never! Never would I be ashamed of you. And if you protect me from the Arkhai and keep me forever safe from Gebelda and return my wife to me, I will never forsake you."

He smiled, as if I had answered too eagerly. "Today," he said, "I have called you out from your tribe and your clan. You are my son."

"Are you saying . . . that . . . that I'm a Called-Out One?"

"Even though all creatures in the world are my children, the Called-Out are more like me than all others. You and Satha and your children have I called, and because of you all the people in this land will learn that I love them as much as I love you."

"Tell me, Great Chief," I said. "Where is Satha? Where is this Talub I saw in Noam's mind?"

"You will be reunited with her soon enough, Beloved Son. I have come to give you a full life, both here and in the world to come. You will meet your wife again in this life and your joy will be complete. Look now"—he touched me gently—"I give you power over all sickness, all disease, all demons. Speak and trust me and even the mountains will obey you. They will jump up and skip at your command."

As I stood there wondering at this strange too-good-to-be-believed news, the river water became clear as pure glass and a sweet-faced sweet-smiled Theseni woman looked up out of the watery reflection at me, smiling: Satha. I watched as she danced, smiled, reached towards a dark-haired man whose naked body rose above hers. The man's features reminded me of my father's and I remembered the Third Wife's accusation. A sense of being doubly betrayed rushed into my soul, but from within, something pushed the rising anger away, compelling me to continue looking. I forced myself to gaze at the vision, and the male image turned to look at me. Although the image looked like Father, it was not Father. Father had a strong muscular body, but this man was lithe and slender, with a broken tooth. It was myself in the future, enjoying Satha's body as a man enjoys his beloved wife's. Around us, the sky glowed like mother-of-pearl. How beautiful she looked! My anger melted away and turned to puzzlement.

I looked up again and saw three signs in the sky: a fountain overflowing, a fishing net breaking with an overload of fish and a ram's horn filled with a bounty of all manner of blessings.

The Creator directed me towards the overflowing ram's horn. Houses, sheep, land, healing, peacefulness, joy and so much more lay inside it. He said to me: "I am your reward, your shelter, your provider, your refuge, your healer, your dear friend, your Creator, your God. Take all you need."

"What shall I take?" I asked.

"Take everything."

"All is mine?"

"All that is mine is yours," he answered.

I clearly saw the Creator was, is, and will always be the one who gives wonderful gifts to those unworthy of his gifts. I saw too that I was a bad Guest in the Great Chief's House, yet he had not refrained from giving all things to me. From that moment I began to worship the Angleni god because he was none other than the god I had always worshiped: the Wind.

The next day Sio came to visit me at Blade Castle. I so wanted to tell him all my heart, but he had other matter on his mind.

"At the feast, you said you were Wind Follower and you didn't know Ganti." He pointed to the jade bracelet on my wrist. "You should be more careful with that. It's nothing to you, a mark of honor you hardly notice." He lifted his hand and showed me the jade bracelet on his arm. "But its meaning is apparent to others. That was a stupid mistake and one Ganti should have noticed."

I burst out laughing. Yes, the jade bracelet had been there all the while for everyone to see. The Chieftain would have recognized its markings. What a man Sio is becoming—his demeanor proud and his bearing so like a warrior.

"After you left, the Therpa Great Chief asked me why I lied for you," he continued. "I told him you were my brother and I owed you protection."

I bowed. "I am honored." Love for him warmed my heart, surprising me. "I have loved you also, Brother. Often I have thought about you, wishing you safety."

"I remember how we played together and how well you treated me in your father's house. I don't want you killed. Nor does my father, although be sure he will kill you in battle should the two of you meet. Do you not wonder how, even though he was drunk, he knew you were nearby?"

So, I thought, *Noam did speak to me as I hid there.*

"Your tracks in the muddy ground," he said.

"Jobara!" I said, choking on laughter and shame. "I am truly no warrior."

Sio didn't laugh. "You laugh too easily, Brother. Do you take your life so lightly?"

"I laugh only to prevent myself from crying at my inexperience. I laugh at some inner joy. At seeing you, at feeling that somehow all is right with the world. But you're right. I should not laugh. I visited the great house of an old man who used to hold me on his knee and I hid myself. I was seen too, even though I tried to behave like a stealthy warrior. But, if we are to be honest, I am now speaking with someone who brought terbur and a dagger to his father to rape my wife. Jobara! I am indeed a fool, not one for this world."

Shame reddened his face. "I was not a party to that plan."

I shrugged. "Kwelku. Whether you were or not, I cannot hate you. I am sorry you were turned into the streets, but you were shown mercy and you returned it with betrayal. You may have been an outcast in our house but you were treated as the son of the clan chief. How could you then harden your heart against my wife?"

He showed me the wounds on the sides of his head, where his ears should have been. "To be earless brands me as a traitor. Isn't this justice enough? I came to tell you you must not kill or battle my father. That is all. Now that I've said what I needed to say, I will leave you."

"How can I promise not to kill your father when his murder is all that is in my heart?"

"Then cleanse your heart of it!" he snapped.

"How can I cleanse my heart of it when I have promised my wife to kill the one who violated her?"

"You are wise. Find a way. Or—"

Alla rushed into the room. Two female servants and two warriors followed her in, the burlier of whom eyed me with suspicion. "What is the matter, Young Chief?" she asked.

"You've helped me understand the musician's craft much better, musician," Sio said, walking toward the doorway.

"Let me kiss you farewell, Young Chief. Who knows if we will ever meet again?" I extended my hand, but the burly guard immediately stepped between Sio and me and drew his weapon. Sio extended his hand and I touched his shoulder. Immediately, before my eyes and before the eyes of all gathered near me, his ears returned.

"Look!" the thin guard said, "The Young Chief has ears again!"

Alla's eyes widened with surprise as she looked at my hands.

So? It is true? I thought. *The Good Maker, the Creator, The One Above All has not lied to me.*

My brother slowly lifted his hands to his ears and touched them. He stared back at me, startled. "Perhaps it is true that you are one of the Called-Out."

"I am."

He narrowed his eyes. "The Creator speaks to you?"

"He speaks to all who will listen."

"Ask the Creator to help me find my mother."

"I will try, and if the Creator does not help, I myself will send the household to search all the land for her."

He took his leave and after all had left, Alla held my hands in hers and turned them over and over. She looked at me several times. "You healed Sio's ears?" she kept repeating.

Angry, I pulled my hand from hers. We had journeyed to the Blue Fortress for reasons other than the ones Ganti had shared with me. "You knew I wore the jade bracelet," I shouted. "Yet you did not tell me?

And why did I not think of something so obvious? Did you blind my mind that I did not remember I was wearing it?"

Smiling triumphantly, she answered, "Why should I not allow our enemies to know who our allies are? Even the Therpas believe you to be the prophesied one! And now—now that Sio's ears—"

"I will not be used by you and Ganti in your war against the Therpas and the Angleni," I said.

She slapped my face with an open hand. "Whether or not you wish to help us, you will. The spirits have appointed you." She walked out of the room singing to herself.

When she left I put on my gyuilta and walked to the river's edge. If the Creator was with me, he could help me leave. But when I tried to leave, the Arkhai boundary still held me firm. "How can this be?" I shouted. "You should not be powerful against me now the One who has given me breath has given me all things? Doesn't 'all things' include my freedom?"

I continued pushing against the empty space. Again, a wall of wind pushed against me. "Show yourself!" I shouted. "Show yourself!"

A cold mist gathered, made itself denser and formed a female face. "Wind Follower," she said. How beautiful she was. Dark like Theseni women, yet having Ibeni features and Doreni eyes. "Many of us are gathered here. But I only will show myself." She sighed and her cold breath perfumed the air. "I suppose because you are such a handsome boy."

"I don't couch with spirits, so keep your compliments to yourself."

"My sister-spirit tempted you in the river." Her misty face flirted and she winked like a true Ibeni female. "Couching with me would be a memorable experience. You'd remember it all your life. If you hadn't married such a moral girl, Wind Follower, Seared Conscience would have had to find another way to unseat Taer. And you would have been happily at home enjoying yourself with your wife. But Satha was raped, you left the Golden House. And when you left the Golden House, you met your destiny." As she spoke, an odor like that of decaying corpses filled the air. "We even tried to use Ganti to teach you how to interpret the truth. Yet even that turned against us. Still, we have not surrendered. We have more ways of thwarting the Creator's plan."

"You aren't more powerful than the Creator." I shouted.

"Kwelku. But you're the one who is trapped here."

Fish scales dropped from her hair. Laughter like stagnant waters flowing into sludge bubbled up her throat. Her laughing mouth was like a cavern full of darkness and which emitted the odor of decaying corpses. She waved her hand across the sky and faces appeared before me. The faces of thousands of spirits, all aligned against me.

"Am I so hated?" I asked. "With so many enemies?"

"You are hated more than you know, Wind Follower. Do you expect to fight against us?"

She and the faces of the spirits behind her dissolved into the night sky, but I knew they were still there—unseen, but watching.

I returned to the house and prepared my travel pouch but lingered there seven more days in discomfort and fear. I still did not fully trust the Creator's ability to protect me.

Worried, I opened a parchment written by one of the Desai prophets. I read: "Fly to the queen. The Light Has Come. Return the gift you gave to the dawn on the night you played in the lingay grasses."

Wasn't Satha also Sithye? The Dawn? The Queen? Was not Loayiq also The Light Has Come? Did I not have within my pouch the nose-ring I had given Satha the night we couched in the grasses?

My heart leaped with joy. My trust in the Creator grew. So joyous was I that Twin looked up at me. "Wind Follower, you've become a happy prisoner at last!" he said. "Much has changed with you."

"Why do you say so?"

"Well, you're smiling, aren't you? And a day ago, we walked through the barley fields. In the old days you would have fallen to the ground. Yet you have had no seizures. Not when you're awake, not when you're asleep. Is that not strange?"

"Indeed you're right," Kaynu said, coming in from the hall. "I, myself, have heard no sound through the walls these past nights." His eyes lit up. "Wind Follower, surely if the One Who Holds My Breath in His Hand can heal you of the falling sickness, he can free you from the spirits which have imprisoned you here!"

I stared at Kaynu. His words surprised me. He had often seemed so cold. But now his heart had softened. Instead of being the cold, analytical and dismissive Desai, he had become a noble open-hearted Pagatsu.

I gathered my travel bags, tucking the Angleni Scripture inside it. "I believe I will be freed from this place today," I said.

"Why today and not another?" Twin asked.

"I believe the Creator now," I answered. "I truly trust his power and his love."

Twin started to laugh. "Because of the illness? Such a small thing?"

"Small it may be to you, but it was a powerful thing to me. I believe the Creator, my friends. And in the future I will see greater things than this small thing. But this small thing will always be remembered by me."

Kaynu laughed, almost as excited as I was. "Then I, too, will forsake these spirits and go with you."

I stared at him. "Has the Creator been speaking to you also?"

He nodded. "Perhaps." He lowered his head. "You were right. Living here under the Desai theology, I had trained my heart not to feel. But when you came, I grew to like you. And yet, I could not truly like you because you were not what you were supposed to be. But you helped me to find my heart. Forgive me, my friend, I was so cold and hard to you."

Although my heart leaped to have a new friend, a replacement for Krika, I feared for Kaynu. "Kaynu, you speak of forsaking your father. Blade Castle is the only home you've ever known. The Desai clan have accepted you because of Ganti's love for you, but will others of our people accept an Angleni riding in their midst?"

"Don't tell me not to follow you. Where you go, I will go. Your people will be my people, and your god, my God."

"Kaynu," I held his shoulder. "You are also forsaking the Arkhai. My friend Krika forsook the Arkhai and his father killed him."

"I doubt Ganti would do that," Twin said, interrupting.

And Kaynu said, "If the Creator has brought us the Lost Book, what else can I do?"

Twin stepped back even further, growing suddenly silent. He watched sullenly as Kaynu and I gathered our belongings together.

"It is good," he said, joking nervously. "Wind Follower will leave this place, and be free from Alla. Personally, I think he'd rather have a woman with less anger and aggression in her soul than Alla."

Kaynu smiled at me, "Was Satha so submissive, then?"

I shook my head. "Satha was Satha."

"Waihai." Twin sucked in his breath. "If you are leaving, hurry. Perhaps the spirits are telling Alla your plans even now."

"Will you come with us?" I asked.

A grin spread across his face. "I would like to come and see if you conquer the Arkhai's wall, but you know how they are—a proud and vengeful lot. They wouldn't want me seeing your victory against them. They know I talk a lot. Farewell, my friends. If I don't see you again, I'll know you have succeeded and that the Angleni god is the true god."

"And we will meet in the same heaven," I answered him.

Outside I called for Cactus, saddled him and found my shuwa, quiver and vialka. Kaynu called for Blue Sky, his blue roan. Together we rode toward the edges of the compound. How nervous we were! It soon became clear that the spirits knew our plans. Their power made the air like a thick bamboo curtain. When we reached the river's edge, the barrier held fast: like a sheet of glass through which we could not pass.

They showed themselves to me, a large army spreading upward and downward; eastward, northward, westward, southward; behind and before. All around me the sky glittered, so bright were the sand vests, the dew tunics, the scaly gyuiltas, and the leafy caps of these spirits. Their faces, too, were hard against me. If power had been given to them, they would have killed me.

"So you've come again?" a watery spirit voice finally asked from the sea of faces.

"I have." I studied them carefully. True, they were a tattered lot. But now I saw them even more clearly. They were worms, nothing more. They wriggled among themselves, no longer or wider than an earthworm. They had tails with stingers, and their heads were shrunken and lacking in any beauty. I realized that all that time I could have crushed them with a single step. I was so surprised at this that I stood for a moment unable to move.

"What is it, Wind Follower?" Kaynu asked. He was staring at me with terrified eyes. "What do you see?"

"Don't you see them?" I asked.

He shook his head. "I see nothing at all."

"It is no matter. Perhaps one should not strive to see them. They're not worth it."

I called to the spirit who had wanted to seduce me earlier. "Seductress! You taunted me loudly enough the other day, but now you have no courage to show what you really are."

I saw movement from the left, a rumbling among the worms like the movement of water in sand. The spirit approached, shrunken and destroyed. How spoiled she looked, like a conquered enemy! I burst out laughing. "You're the spirit who wanted to seduce me?"

I whispered to the Wind. Removing my gyuilta I stood at the river's edge and looked towards the four winds. "I am not truly alone, if you are with me. I am tired of false gods, tired of the very action of believing. I will follow you to the far ends of the earth. Aid me now—"

A wonder appeared in the sky. A lamb at the moment of slaughter. Shuwas pierced its head, shining out like the rays of the sun; from its mouth hung a sword. It was the same parchment sword I had seen in my dream. Again, words were written on all sides, on its hilt and on its blade, words I could now see were from the Angleni Scriptures. Silent, I stared at it, not knowing if Kaynu could also see it. From the mouth of this slain lamb, the sword began to descend. Down, down through the constellation our people called the Scales, past the cross that balanced the Unequal Scales. Down, down it came, until at last it thrust at my lips, forcing itself into my mouth and throat. How sweet it tasted to my mouth. But when its blade arrived in my stomach, how bitter and sharp it was!

Kaynu stood staring at me. Only later did I learn he had not heard the voice. Nor had he seen the sword. All he heard was the thunder speaking to me.

"Loic," the Creator said. "Although your people conquered this continent, you have tainted yourself by taking upon you the habits of those who lived in the land before I gave it to you. The Theseni spirit worship has turned your veneration of the ancestors into blasphemy. You even treat the ancestors as mediators. You worship the Ibeni demons who are nothing more than shadow gods. The Ibeni sojourners have also tainted you with their greed, their clannishness and their jealousies. But worst of all, your people have allowed them to continue killing their unborn children. This is hateful to me. The blood of my children screams out of the ground at me. You have violated the laws of hospitality and now I will give the land to a new nation. Go now, Wind Follower, and meet your destiny!"

"Let not the Great Chief be angry if I question him," I said. "Are we truly destined to be destroyed? Is there no way we can save ourselves?"

"You are neither destined to be destroyed nor to lose against the Angleni. Nevertheless, you will be destroyed and you will lose your land to the Angleni."

"Great Chief, your words confuse me. Are we free from destiny or bound by it?"

"You're bound only by your character, but you are a fierce people. You love to worship, but you not wish to speak directly to your Creator. These traits will create your destiny."

I turned to look back at Blade Castle; its whitewashed walls gleamed in the moonlight. "But what about the wisdom of my people, Great Chief? We have long studied the words of Koloq and all our great teachers. Are we to forsake them?"

"Those teachings were shadows. Shadows give way when the True Light appears. As for Ganti, I had surrounded him with a hedge of protection but now I will remove it and allow the spirits to kill him. I know he has a place in your heart, but if he lives he will be a thorn in your side. He would cause many to turn from the true way and continue to walk the way of the shadows."

"Great Chief," I said, and I glanced at Kaynu but he seemed not to hear the Great Chief's voice. "Don't allow the spirits to kill him."

"He cannot live." The thunder of the voice stopped, then rumbled forth again: "But Noam must not die."

My heart burned hot within me. "Great Chief, I read in the Lost Book a cowardly philosophy that we should befriend our enemies and forgive them. For Sio's sake, I do not wish to kill Noam, but neither do I want to befriend him."

"Vengeance is mine, Loicuyo, therefore let me repay it. Do not kill Noam. Leave him unharmed and hasten to Satha's side in the Gulacan. Destroy the Arkhai. Those shadow gods are invaders who come only to kill, steal and destroy. But I have given you and all who believe the words of the Lost Book power over all those serpents. Go and tell this too-good-to-be-believed news to all you meet."

With that, the thunderous voice ceased. I raised the gyuilta high, holding it by its sleeves. I struck the water with the gyuilta. "I command the spirits to leave me." Immediately the boundary fell away. The river opened up, water rising up on both sides. I passed through between the walls of water, dying to my old life and being born again into my new one. Yes, the spirits groaned and hissed behind me, but I no longer feared them. I knew now, that not only was the Creator more powerful than they, I was more powerful than they.

Kaynu took one last wistful glance at Blade Castle, and galloped with me across the river on dry land, the last snows of the cold moons falling around us.

We rode for many days, and no harm could the shadow gods do to us, although many times they tried.

On the night before we were to pass through Trumpa's village, Trumpa's Little Mother came to me in a vision. "Come and help me, Loic." How sick she was!

So we rode until we came to Ulia, Trumpa's village. But the whole town had gathered to meet us, and they stood near the boulder where my hair lay buried. Arlis stood with them, looking disgusted that her spell had not entrapped me.

The old shaman who had previously challenged me came walking up.

"May I enter your village?" I asked him.

"No, you can't! Traitor! The spirits have told me about you. They've told all of us. You're destined to destroy our town and to help the Angleni conquer our land."

"I know nothing about that," I answered him and, turning to Arlis, who seemed paler and thinner than I remembered, I said, "May I enter your house, Arlis?"

"Don't give him permission!" the shaman shouted.

"Why not?" I asked.

But the whole village took up the chant. They had made a pact with the Arkhai. The spirits promised to protect them from all evil and sickness."

"Bind yourself to the Creator with a greater covenant," I said, "a covenant of blood that cannot be broken. How have they helped you? Have they not made you poor and sickly?"

As Arlis glared at me I wondered what she was thinking. That was when I realized the gift of seeing into minds had left me.

"Why has this gift, a thing from my childhood and my mother's heritage, left me?" I asked the Creator.

"Because it is not a gift from me," He answered. "Fear not, you will receive greater, truer gifts than that."

Behind the shaman, Trumpa's mother leaned on the boulder. Ten spirits like worms crawled through her stomach and along her spine. It was an infestation that made me turn my eyes away from the village that had turned us away. Saddened, I realized I could never repay my debt to Trumpa's family.

We rode on.

We soon arrived at another village, a strange and blighted place. All fertility had ceased and the ground was parched and without life. As we approached, I saw its inhabitants racing across the dry fields toward us. Armless warriors, bent and bruised old women, sickly children from all tribes and clans raced toward us.

A shaman, running among them, greeted us. "This is a day the Creator made."

"It will bring blessings for you and for me," I answered.

He came nearer and said, "My name is Luda. Are you the one who brings us the Great Light? The wolves and owls of the field have told us of a scarred one who would bring the Lost Book to us, a Light to lighten us who live in darkness."

I was surprised at their words and, seeing their plight, I pitied them because they were like stray and sick sheep without a shepherd, so desperate to know the truth about the Creator.

"I am," I answered. "And I have the Lost Book."

A frail gray-haired Ibeni woman in the crowd called out, "Our fetele and history songs told us the Creator was near and cared for us. Even though the spirits declared war on us, we rejoiced anyway because we knew the book was coming. After long waiting, we had almost lost hope. But now you've arrived."

Tears came to my eyes and a heavy weight seemed to roll from my shoulders. From every eye, love poured forth in my direction. Every arm reached out to touch me. Every heart understood me. All about that dreary landscape the air suddenly bristled with joy. It seemed as if the stones themselves were singing. Overwhelmed and surprised, I put my hand into my travel bag and removed the Angleni Scriptures.

"Do you have scribes and writers in this village?" I asked, pushing back unbidden sobs of joy.

"We do." Luda's eyes widened as he looked at the bound sheets of parchment. "Is that it? Is this the Lost Book?" He, too, was weeping and his trembling hand reached out for it. "May I touch it?"

All about us, the villagers began to fall to their knees. Some wept for joy and in awe that the Creator had not forgotten them and the prophecy had been fulfilled at last. Indeed, although I did not need it, their joy at my presence was further proof to me that I had not followed the Creator in vain.

Yes, they were like sheep who had found one who would lead them to the Shepherd. To prove the Creator's love for them, I laid my hands on them and, with the authority given to me by the Creator, I commanded their bodies to be healed. Immediately arms sprouted where formerly there had been none, lame feet walked, deaf ears opened, blind eyes saw. Singing erupted from their throats, and the tinkle of dancing ankle bells sounded everywhere. Seeing this additional proof of the Creator's love for us, I rejoiced greatly that soon the entire land would be saved and freed from the oppression of the shadow gods.

And yet, I had a more pressing, more immediate quest.

When I had managed to quiet the people, I gravely handed the book to Luda. "Gather all the scribes you can," I told him. "A faraway task calls me, and it must be done. I cannot abide here now, but I will return. Kaynu, here, is my faithful friend. He will teach you all you need to know."

Luda eyed Kaynu warily. "But the prophecy speaks of you," he said.

"Look again in the prophecies, my friend," I answered. "You will find that they speak of a companion who will help me."

Luda nodded. "I think I remember such a prophecy. Yet, his features—"

I glanced at Kaynu. Frowning, he, too, seemed to resist my departure. "Kaynu's features may appear to be Angleni—and yes, his demeanor is unpleasant at present—but his heart is Doreni. I will return again when my task is done. Meanwhile, Kaynu will translate the words of the Lost Book from the Angleni language into our language. He will show you all the Creator has given to humans—his dear and near love, and power over all that seek to hurt you."

"Yes, yes," a Doreni woman agreed. She wore a coif which displayed the markings of the Sahod clan. "Let our own scribes translate the Lost Book into our own language!"

"But which one?" a handsome Theseni asked. "One of the old languages? Paetan? Seythof? Of all languages, they—the ancient languages of the scribe—are the most beautiful."

"Use the common language," I answered. "So that all may readily understand what they read. No longer will we need scribes or shamans to tell us about the Creator. We will discover him for ourselves."

I took my leave of Kaynu. The villagers gave me food enough for a week's journey and also bade me farewell.

I journeyed as the Wind willed and joy remained with me. Soon, however, I heard something like a loud hissing across the prairie. I searched all about me, towards the Gulacan, backward toward Blade Castle. I saw nothing.

Then a spirit, a woman's head on the body of a snake, slowly became visible. She slithered near the ground and then rose and twined herself around Cactus's neck. She had only one eye in her head. The eye seemed made of living tiles, linked but floating together on a dark sea. That eye was full of evil, and never once turned its gaze from me.

"Loic," she said, her voice soothing and gentle, "you have already begun your work against us. From the beginning, it has been recorded that you will succeed. How much you succeed, however, is still in our very capable hands."

"Spirit, you speak of capable hands when you have none. And even if you had them, the Lost Book and I would cut them off."

"Bold words, Loic." She drew closer, and the tip of her forked snake tongue licked my face. "Yet, my brothers and I are giving you a chance to make a truce. Why do you insist on making yourself an enemy of all other gods? You insult us by calling the Angleni god the true god and us usurpers. What harm is there if we continue to mediate between humans and the Creator?"

"Great harm," I murmured, remembering the sickness, grief, hunger and poverty they had inflicted on the inhabitants of the village of Ulia and the village of the Called Out Ones.

She gently coiled and uncoiled her snake-body and I found myself fearing for Cactus. "I'm not at war with you, why war against me? Are not all gods equal? Therefore, let there be a truce between those who follow the Creator and those who follow us."

"You're our enemies. Can two walk together and not be agreed? Why should I walk with a murderer whose sole purpose is to kill, steal, and destroy me?"

She spoke again—and her breath suddenly grew foul, as if something lay dead inside her mouth. "I have two things to tell you. The first is that Ganti has died. He died in great distress. He should have turned your heart back to your ancestors but he did not. He allowed you to leave his compound alive, which was not what we demanded."

Grief struck my heart and guilt too because Ganti had died because of me. I managed to utter, "You spirits are relentless indeed, even turning against their friends."

"Jobara," she hissed. "We forbade Alla to cover Ganti with lamb's blood. Can you imagine how brutal your own death will be?"

"I can imagine it, yes. Yet I have met One who has demanded much of me and I cannot turn aside from following Him."

"Kwelku. I must warn you that even now, your father lies at home in death-sleep. If you refrain from spreading this news about the Creator, your father will live. If not, well . . . are you prepared to send your father to Gebelda? Now, young Wind Follower, what will you do?"

Stunned, I stood speechless. No real proof existed that her words were true. I could neither believe nor disbelieve her. I could only hope the Creator would protect my father—and Satha. But would the Creator protect those who were not serving him? I answered, weakly, "The Creator can make my father live in spite of your magic."

"Are you sure of this?"

"I am not sure of anything you say, spirit," I admitted. "But whether or not the Creator allows my father to live or to die . . . I'll follow him."

"Mentura," she said. "You boast of victories you have not yet achieved."

Insulted at her mockery, I waved my hand at her, making a coiling motion. "I must find my wife. Go your way, and let me go mine."

She began to slowly unwind herself. "Do you still refuse our offer to kill Noam for you?"

"Let the Good Maker unmake Noam. My wife alone concerns me."

"But kill Noam you must."

"Why must I? And why do you seek Noam's death?"

"I do not seek it. But, even a paper heart knows that if he does not kill his enemy, his enemy will kill him. Surely, you will not leave your enemy free to wander and do as he wills?"

Vile though Noam was, I did not want to disobey the Creator, and yet it seemed viler to be a paper heart. I remembered apple-faced Razo whose mouth was always filled with boasts, and in spite of myself I found myself agreeing with the spirit.

"Loayiq," she said, laughing. "Wind Follower, Loic, whoever you are—you are certainly no warrior, no true Doreni, and certainly no Pagatsu. A false god who calls himself the Creator has told you not to avenge yourself and you believe him. Jobara! Indeed, you have a paper heart. Have you forgotten how Noam humiliated your wife and dishonored your clan? How badly will your honor reflect on the Pagatsu when all the world hears that you did not destroy your enemy?"

Spirits, living from age to age, create schemes that humans can never puzzle out. I answered tiredly, "First you told me to hasten home and now you want me to linger and fight Noam. The Creator has ordered me not to fight Noam. That is enough."

She shrugged, a snaky kind of shiver all along the length of her serpentine body, and her wide eye looked into mine as if she spoke an obvious truth. "Orders can be disobeyed, can they not? And if this god is as understanding and as forgiving as you think, will he not forgive you for disobeying him?" And having challenged me, she faded from Cactus's neck leaving him relieved and me in confusion.

Several leagues outside the town, a wolf howled on a hillside. As I approached it, it howled louder. Whether the animal was a true animal of flesh or a spirit guide, I didn't know. But since it was clear the creature had called out to me, I thought it best to follow him. *Perhaps,* I said to myself, *he will guide me on the path I must go.*

Riding like a blizzard in the snow moons, I journeyed for a day and a half in a direction I somehow knew would lead me to Noam. At last, in the distance, I saw one riding whom I immediately recognized. He wore the Therpa color and his red hair flew wildly under his blue clan cap. Noam. I remembered what the Creator had said: *Do not kill Noam.* Yet I rode toward him.

He stood still, his horse moving neither forward nor backward and called out. "So you've found me, my enemy? At the Blue Fortress I sought to save your life. Turn aside and return to the Golden House. For now that Taer is dead, if you die, another must be raised up to rule the Pagatsu clan. Taer would not want that."

My body weakened and my heart tightened within my chest. "Is my father dead?" My mind tried to understand that the one I had known all my life was now no more.

Noam stared at me long and hard. "I'm sorry I'm the one who brought you this news." Tears welled in his eyes. "He has been dead for almost a moon."

His pity irked me. I found myself, sounding like a callow youth, repeating, "Moon?"

"I loved him, Loicuyo." His sincerity, although an offense, was real enough. "Taer was a good warrior. Faithful and just."

"Don't let your evil lips speak my father's name," I screamed, finally finding my Pagatsu heart. Yet, my tears were building within me. How like a child I felt!

He turned his face away from me towards the sun. "You're right, Loic. My lips should not speak that honorable name." Then, his back to me, he began singing a dirge for my father:

"Taer lifted his shuwa

And bodies piled like mountains

He aimed his vialka

And blood flowed like rivers

Noble and brave was Taer

And his bravery encouraged both men and women.

The poor never were turned away from his door.

Open the great fields to him

And grant him entrance to the fields we long for."

Tears streamed down my face as I listened to Noam's dirge for my father. I found myself wishing I had not turned aside to confront him. I realized I was indeed a paper heart. I could destroy my enemies, even the spirits, if called on. Yet I could not kill a former friend.

A deep sigh escaped his throat and he added, "In a world of honorable men, your father was the most honorable of all."

He paused, then said, "Death should not bring tears. But, Younger Brother, you were never a warrior. Not that you have a paper heart, but—"

"Don't tell me what I am," I snapped at him. "You neither know nor understand me."

"I understand more than you know, confused child. You have also promised your brother you would not kill me. Yet that is your only desire. It is a strange predicament to find yourself in." His eyes narrowed and then they opened wide as if an inner light had opened them. "Still, Little Brother, the time has come." He dismounted and began walking away from me. After several steps, he turned. "Do you know about Walking the Ritual?" He sounded like Pantan or even Little Mother, a voice kind and caring.

"Pantan taught me."

"But you've never practiced it?"

I clasped my hands together over my face. "Only once," I half-whispered.

His eyes seemed to pity me. "Once is not enough. Yet . . . it will have to be enough. As one life is enough."

Do you doubt that my adversary would treat me so kindly? This was our way then, a way we have lost since the Angleni conquered our land. "Are you ready to walk the ritual with me? Let us see if you have learned how warriors prepare themselves for their final battle."

There was nothing else for me to do. I began to Walk with my enemy. All day, alone with our thoughts, we walked beside each other silently through the wakening prairie, through blossoming woods, and through thawing streams as we prepared our hearts to kill or die. Coldly, dispassionately, we took what we believed would be our last look at the world we knew, at a world that soon would know us no longer. We were hoping the Creator would see the courage of the loser, whoever it turned out to be, and because of that courage, bring the fallen to the fields we longed for. We feared too. Feared being mortally wounded and left to linger alone in the plains unburied with no lamb to be sacrificed for us. If the Creator was not merciful, we would suffer for all eternity in Gebelda.

Slowly, I began to understand the value of Walking the Ritual. Although I had trembled when we first began, coldness at last seeped into my heart. I understood clearly that passion had to leave—because passion impedes a warrior's prowess. All day we walked. Sometimes we spoke, sometimes we fell silent. And soon all emotion left us and only cold indifference remained. I often wished to turn back, to run to the Creator and confess that I should not have disobeyed him.

But I did not. We ate and drank together and often during that afternoon and night, he turned towards me and spoke encouragingly to me. Once he said, "Death is perhaps not as bad as we fear. For don't we have many companions already in Gebelda? How lonely can the afterlife be if we have so many loving friends awaiting us?" I did not answer him; I had not forgotten Gebelda.

Night came; the sky went red and black. I removed my vest as he built a fire from his tinderbox. The evening breeze blew cool through my tunic, but my hands were hot and moist with fear and sweat. I tried to remember that my destiny was great, that I was not destined to die at Noam's hand.

"Loic," he said, calling me from my thoughts, "I grieve that I raped Satha. Even now."

"Is this part of the ritual?" I asked.

He nodded. "Yes, truth-telling is part of the ritual. Didn't your father or Pantan tell you that? If I die, the truth should not die with me."

"What use is the truth if your clan does not hear you tell it? Would it not be best if all men knew—all Doreni and all Therpa—knew the truth?"

"And what is that truth?"

"That you are no better than Razo," I said coolly, "that you fight men by fighting their wives? That you were dishonorable, and nothing more than a paper heart who destroys women because they are easy prey?"

He burst out laughing. "How proud Taer would be to hear you speak such brave words! Even if those words are untrue."

"I speak the truth, Noam. But you do not." Angry, I found myself shaking. "Noam, if I kill you, our clans must wage war against each other."

"Are you so young and yet so tired of death?" he asked. "Yet, I'll admit Sio also would find it hard to war against one whom he loves so much. What a useless father Taer was to you both!"

His words knocked my heart. Jobara! Taer was indeed the father of both of us. And having just learned of the death of my own father, I did not wish to deprive my brother of his true father. I hated Noam but I did not wish him to fall into Gebelda. I could not forgive him—how I hated that word!—and yet I did not wish to kill him and leave him unburied on the plains.

"The king does not wish clans as large as ours to war against each other." I realized I was half begging. "Not with the Angleni conniving against us."

He burst into laughter and tousled my hair as he used to do when I was a child. "The spirits, too, connive," he said.

I remembered why I had once loved him, how often our hearts had been knitted together in mutual understanding.

"Perhaps," he continued, "the spirits led you here to be killed."

I answered, "To kill you would be to please the Arkhai whom I hate even more than I hate you. For now, they are our true enemies. If only, if only you had not . . . why did you . . . you should not have raped my wife, Noam." I buried my head in my hands. "No, you should not."

"The woman—the Third Wife— deceived me twice, Loic. The mukal also—"

The indifference that had crept into my heart left and immediately a new anger burned against him. "Your words are as false as your heart, Noam," I interrupted him. "Is this a time for excuses? The Ritual is a time for truth, a time when we see our very nature before we meet the Creator? And yet you lie, and even now you defeat yourself? Truly, if the ancients had not declared that the battle should begin at daybreak, I would cut out both your heart and your tongue right now."

"I pity you that you cannot."

"Jobara," I answered and, realizing I was biting my bottom lip, I turned and gazed back at the wolf lingering in the distance.

He rose from the fire and walked past me, blocking my view of the wolf. "Be of good courage, Cuyo. I promise you, your death will be merciful and quick, and your body will not lie unburied on these plains. Promise me you will do the same if I die. Not that I will die."

"Nor will I speak of your tears if you die," I answered. "And if I cry, you must not speak of mine."

While imprisoned in Blade Castle, despite my resentment, I had honed my skills in daggerwork. But this was Noam, one of General Taer's Valiant Men, a warrior more skilled than I, a man who had been my friend. I hated him, feared him and loved him.

As I waited for sleep to come, I grew afraid again. The nearness of my own death, my disobedience of the Creator's commands, the memory of Gebelda, and the newfound knowledge that my father had died filled my mind, Lying on the hard ground, I called out in my thoughts to

Father. I begged him to visit me in a dream, to tell me he now walked with the Creator, to tell me he had forgiven me my cruelty toward him. In time, sleep came but my father did not.

In the morning, Noam awakened me calling loudly as he stood over me, his dark red hair blowing behind him. "Had any dreams, Loicuyo?" he asked.

"The heavens were metal. You?"

"One dream." His face seemed troubled, but he seemed to shake the troublesome thought away. "Only one."

Gray dawn turned to blue sky and the time had come for one of us to die. I sat cross-legged on the ground watching him as we undressed. Together we removed our short gyuiltas and together we removed our riding boots. At last, he walked toward me, gestured at the same time for me to stand up. I did and saw suddenly that his dagger gleamed in his hand. A true warrior, he had been thinking of the battle all along.

Seeing the glint of the blade, I understood how true panic felt. How many times had Pantan and Heldek told me that a warrior's enemy was often himself? Now I comprehended. My hands had grown moist; my stomach heaved. I lurched backward, falling on my back. He stood above me, then—being more prepared to kill me than I to kill him—he hit me hard with his left hand. I pulled myself to my feet but another blow caught me on the side of my throat knocking the wind out of me. Coughing, gurgling and choking, I grabbed my throat. Blood—salty, bright red—trickled from my mouth. Anger made me fierce. I knew now that he was my enemy. I, who had once been called Wildfire, was tamed during those moons at Blade Castle. Now I returned to myself. Boiling anger made me shrewd, fear made me desperate. Ferocious, I kicked him in his crotch. He sank to the ground. Yanking his hair I jerked him close to me, raging. I removed Satha's dagger from my boot. He dodged away, but not quickly enough.

Within seconds—how it happened I cannot tell, because I myself do not know—Satha's dagger was no longer in my hand, but lodged in his chest. His eyes—surprised that death had come—stared up, seeing past me into that fearful place. He seemed to fade into the grass. Still numb, and unsure what to do, my hand hovered over my fallen enemy. I could hardly breathe, and the fierce blow he had struck at my neck had not yet waned. I slumped on the grass beside him.

"I can feel death working in me," he said.

Blood seeped from his mouth and from the wounds on his stomach. Still clutching for my own breath, I watched him, hating him, not desiring to help. At last, he clutched my hand and squeezed. His hand relaxed. He was dead.

Then dark swirls arose like smoke from his body—fleeing spirits, eight in all. Their fiery eyes glared at me, as if searching for some entry into my own body. I held my breath until the dark cloud dispersed. Long long, I knelt by his side, yet I could not pray to the Creator to bring him into the great fields.

There was no joy at the death of my enemy. Only tears as I cradled his head on my knees and as his horse tramped along the edges of the prairie, dragging its reins. I was supposed to wash my hand in his blood, but I only stroked his face and looked into his open eyes until grief made me close them.

I found my heart again at last. Throughout the night, weeping, I used my father's vialka to dig his grave. To prevent the wild creatures from tearing his body apart, I buried him in the Theseni way.

Soon, the anger had dissipated. One cannot long hate the dead. What good does it serve? They die and our anger dies with them. I remembered both his kindness and his cruelty and for the kindness' sake, I managed to pray to the Creator, begging him to allow Noam to enter the place of peace and rest.

All night the ravens flew overhead, attempting to steal his body. But I would not allow them to come near him. At last a wild goat appeared, its horns trapped in a thicket. With my shuwa I aimed and hit its heart. After I had washed my hands in its blood, I wiped Noam's face and body. Then, I laid my dagger across my finger—yes, he had been my friend!—and drew blood. I grieved for him as I had not been allowed to grieve for Krika.

After I buried him, the wolf howled among the tall grasses. Willows newly-leafing and leafless bushes blossomed in all directions, but the wolf beckoned me to follow. Noam's horse stood above his grave guarding it. As I neared her, she reared. I stopped and we examined each other for as long as it takes a raven to wing across the sky, then I approached her again. This time she shook her forequarters and shoulders. At the edges of the meadow, the wolf still lingered.

I sat down on the grass and the sun rose high in the sky. At last she relented enough to allow me to catch a hold of her trailing rein, a leather braid painted with the Therpa pattern. Then with a long wistful look, she glanced at Noam's solitary tomb and hung her head. Soon she was following me as Cactus and I trailed the wolf.

While I rode, my hands looked strange to me. Although bloodless, they still seemed stained with Noam's blood. Again, I thought of Father. I prayed aloud, "Father, I've killed an enemy just as you did. But this killing doesn't satisfy. I was no warrior, I grieved like a child."

I waited for him to answer but no answer came. "Father," I said again, "I called out to you when I learned of your death, yet you did not come to me in dreams. Has the Creator ruled against dream-gatherings between the living and the dead?" How sad that thought made me. How sad the whole land would be! To be guided by the ancestors, to speak daily with those long dead, those were customs that gave our hearts joy and encouraged us. If the Creator had ruled against them, and if he proved to be unapproachable and unloving, our days would be grievous indeed.

I rode on, at once hopeful about reaching Satha and desperate about the changes that would come to the land of the three tribes. Night came again, and the wolf stopped. I stopped also and fell asleep. That night, I dreamed.

"Great Chief," I said, "I am no warrior and the least of the least of my people. I see now that many changes must occur in the hearts and minds of my people. Not only must we separate from what harms us, but we must separate ourselves from what comforts us. How can I wage war against the spirits if my heart still clings to many of our customs? How can I war against the Angleni if one killing alone has undone me?"

"Knowing me and the words of the Lost Book is joy and peace enough. And although you claim you are no warrior, I have called you a warrior. Noam's death will be the cause of many deaths. Ready yourself for all the battles you will face after you find Satha in the Gulacan. Now, take a shuwa from your quiver and aim it towards the caves of Gulacan. "

"The caves of Gulacan are leagues away, Great Chief. The shuwa will not reach it."

"I will guide its flight. But you must cause it to sail through the air."

The Great Chief left off speaking and as the day dawned, I dreamed again. In the dream, an aged and cruel Angleni woman stood beside Satha while Satha held a young child in her arms. The old woman held a whip high and pointed toward the Patchwork Prairie. Satha began to walk into the wilderness. I awoke suddenly from the dream and lay under the sky while the wind blew across my face. Then I remembered what the Great Chief had commanded and I took a shuwa from my quiver. I let if fly across the bright yellow prairie sky.

SATHA
Memories of Other Endings
The Selling and Storing Moon
Second Harvest Moon

For days the sun rose and set and the green pastures of Colebru gave way to the Patchwork Prairie and the Gulacan. I had eaten little, saving my food for Ewi, and my throat was as parched and dry as the stubbles of the desert. But the day came when food and drink were gone.

Ewi and I traveled long after that. I wasn't afraid because I believed The-God-Who-Sees-Me was with me. I didn't fear hunger or thirst. Nor did I consider myself lost. Although I didn't know the way, I felt the God-Who-Sees-Me would lead me home. During the day, the desert was slowly regaining its heat, but the snow moons still hovered over the nights.

The little gyuilta I had woven for Ewi hung from his thin body. I lifted it and the tunic below it. His belly was sunken; I could count all his bones. His eyes stared into mine, and his cries tore my heart. Ravens flying overhead streamed several times across the sky as if waiting for his life to ebb away under the hot sun.

Lifting my fists toward the sky, I shouted, "Did I tell you I wanted a son? Didn't I tell you not to give me children?"

I looked in the four directions. The sky looked the same as it did on other days. The Creator didn't answer me.

"You cannot die, my son."

I could not cry, no moisture was left within me. I begged for his life until night fell. The purple petals of the poisonous anley flowers glowed in the dark as if beckoning to me.

I plucked several flowers and held them in my hand, crushing them until their deadly sap smeared my fingers. "My son," I said, although he was asleep, "forgive me when you enter the afterlife. Why should I allow you to die here in lingering anger? The anley will bring you sweet sleep from which you will never awaken."

Sometimes a woman thinks that all her tears have been shed, only to discover that her heart still lives. Memories of other endings entered my mind. I looked about for the twigs, stones and large branches I would gather to bury him within the cave.

He turned in his sleep and a little wail escaped his mouth. Just then, a loud whizzing sound cracked the sky. I looked up in time to see a shuwa flying toward me. It fell to the ground beside my arm. I studied it closely: it bore the Pagatsu clan markings. My eyes looked in the four directions to see if Loic was nearby. I saw no one. Nevertheless, I understood its meanings: I should endure and do nothing desperate; Loic would find us in time.

Hastily, I threw the crushed flowers onto the ground and rubbed my hand in the sand, rolling the poison away.

A strange speckled bird the size of an eagle flew toward me: his cry echoed across the prairie, awakening Ewi. The bird's eyes, wet and piercing, caught mine, then he suddenly flew upwards again. Then about a stone's throw from me, he descended again and lighted onto a barren branch lying on a stretch of sand. He perched looking at us expectantly. How strange that bird was, and yet Ewi looked hopefully on it, wriggling his little fingers as if to say he wanted me to follow it.

"The bird awaits our death," I said, knowing he could not understand.

He scratched his small head, very much like my mother used to do, and his eyes brimmed with tears.

The bird came closer. This time it rested on a leafless bush in front of me. I studied its feathers, which shimmered black and red, the Theseni colors. It extended its talons and clutched my hand, almost piercing my flesh.

"I'm not dead yet," I shouted angrily. But Ewi pointed at it and it flew up to the sky again and landed several paces ahead of me. I wondered if I should follow it, and decided to do so, my feet sinking into the sands. As soon as I neared it, it flew off again. My heart burned with anger.

"Are you bird or spirit?" I asked, calling out to it as it perched again, further off.

"I won't follow you this time!" I said, turning away. But Ewi pointed at it again.

"I won't follow!" I told him. "These spirits have nothing better to do than to play tricks on us. I'm tired of their deceptions."

"Maaam," he pleaded, urging me to follow it.

The bird turned towards me, hovered for a moment, then purposely settled on my hand. Its claws grasped at me, pulling me onwards, digging deeper. Ewi grinned and laughed but the bird didn't relax its grip. I relented and followed. When I reached the place where the bird had landed, I could smell moisture on the wind. I watched the bird fly skyward, as if it had finished with its task. Two steps ahead, near a stubbled bush, I saw what looked like the cover of a well. A rope lay near it. I pulled on the rope, and a bucketful of clear water was attached to it. Racing with the bucket, I raced to Ewi, whose little dimpled face broke out into a smile. We sat down to drink, and soon I heard the bird cawing again. I looked in the direction of her voice and saw that she had returned with several of her friends, ravens and a covey of quails. They carried bread and meat in their mouths and laid a table for us in the wilderness.

"Jobara. Y'wa! Indeed you are the God Who Sees Me!"

Ewi and I traveled on the strength of that food until we found a cave, one of many in the Gulacan.

Despite the heat of the desert, the cave walls were moist, seeming to weep tears. I found myself surrounded by Doreni pottery, the swords and daggers of great Theseni warriors and Ibeni fetishes. I realized we were in a burial cave.

When Ewi fell asleep, I rose from his side and, my hands guiding me along the damp corridors, I ventured through that dark dreary place. The ravens roosted outside and on top of it and I sensed I was to wait there. The cavern provided us with water from its streams and lakes. The ravens brought us bread and meat.

For many days, when Ewi slept, I walked, crawled, and stumbled through the cave, waiting. Many winding compartments lay within it, and even though I would not journey far from my son, I lost my way several times. Some inner caverns held half-frozen lakes, some had rivers descending under or ascending up from the earth. It had many exits but they opened upon cliffs, or snake pits, or onto rushing rapids, or descended farther into the earth. I ached to leave it. But the ravens continued to prevent me. Every day Ewi and I sat silent among the dead bones, staring out into the distance, towards the north. And strange it was, after all those moons, to trust that the Creator and my husband had not abandoned me.

LOIC
Morning Dream

The Wind led me to a cave. As I approached it, my heart burned within me. Anger, worry, fear. I advanced, and entered it. I reminded himself that I was young still, although gray hairs were on my head. I understood grief, vendettas and madness, but I was still no warrior and I should not enter a cave alone and carelessly.

Walking stealthily past the entrance, because I did not wish to be heard, I stood in a dark corner just within the cave. A young child sat in the dirt among woven baskets, playing and laughing to himself. Amazed to find a young child, I continued watching until I heard footsteps approaching from deep inside the cave.

There she was. My Satha. Seeing her again, I saw how beautiful she was. Indeed, I had forgotten how good she was to look at. Dark brown like the earth. Tall and graceful, beautiful despite her torn gyuilta. Her hair was cut short like the hair of Angleni women but she wore the beaded leather shoes of my people. She seemed lost in thought and at first didn't sense my presence, but then she glanced in my direction and I was brought from my reverie.

My mind swam and I called out her name. My Satha.

SATHA
Reunion

I turned to see Loic, although in the darkness I was not sure it was truly Loic. He didn't look like the youth who had ridden off years before to avenge a woman he hardly loved. In the darkness, my eyes strained to recognize the slender Doreni warrior standing before me in high riding boots. His hair was shorter than before, parted in the middle around the scalplock and braided on the sides. Two broad black stripes ran across his forehead and lower face. The face startled me. Bruises and scars covered it, extending across his neck and shoulders. I knew the scarred stranger before me was Loic, yet my heart could not quite own him. I thought, *Can one encounter such battles as this man has obviously encountered and still be sane?* I was so fearful I was trapped with a madman, I instinctively ran to pick up my son and searched about for a dagger.

The warrior stared at me, lifted his hands as if to show me he meant no harm. That moment, the lifting of his arms, convinced me that it was my lost husband. I burst into tears, slumped against the cave wall and then fell to the ground.

His face had lost much of its lightness and been darkened by suffering and grief. A forelock of his hair was lightly threaded with gray. The spoiled young man who had wooed and then rejected me was no longer present in that face. Tears flooded from my eyes.

In the first year of our marriage, Loic had taken me to the forest for a night-picnic. We had sung and danced under the night stars. Now it seemed like a dream. But those days of childhood and its innocent joys were long gone. Life and all its griefs had come to both of us.

LOIC
A Changed Wife

Tears stained her dust-covered face and my heart melted with pity for her. Taking her hand, I held it tight. We stayed in the cave until morning came, when we would see each other's faces in the full light.

In the morning, a warm wind blew across my face carrying the scent of cedars and willows. The dawning sun, bright and searing, spread its heat across the plains. Kneeling, I retrieved my knife from the leather pouch hanging at my side and stabbed at the ground. I found kindling and, taking my tinder-box, I created a fire, all the time watching this half-Angleni boy who was now my son.

We sat silent together as he removed fruits and bread from my travel pouch.

"My son likes fruits, I see," I said, amazed at the love I already felt for the child. I wanted to hold him and caress him in my arms. "Satha, Wife, our lives have come together to build grief upon grief. But what do past griefs matter if the Creator has restored our love for each other?" I lifted my hands and showed her the cuttings I had made for the dead. Markings for my mother, Krika, Lihu, Noam. For my father.

"New Father Taer is dead?" she asked, staring at the ground. When she looked up, her face reflected my own grief. "Even this new joy adds new grief."

We did not speak many words. They seemed, somehow, to be inadequate. And yet, the Lost Book had taught me that words were not weak things at all, but a strong force.

Instead, we lay on the ground, on the dried sandy desert, and slept —Ewi between us. Peace itself seemed to blanket us. When we woke, I placed Satha on Noam's horse and, after putting the jade bracelet on Ewi's small wrist, I put him on Cactus with me.

We traveled on in silence until we arrived at a region where a few scattered Angleni settlements dotted the hillside.

"I passed through this area as a boy," I said to Ewi. "The Ibeni lived here then. It was a big city then, with many markets and fruit shops. Now it is destroyed."

He grinned, not understanding.

"They did this to the Kluna region also," Satha said. "It's the Angleni way."

We journeyed on and came upon some bedraggled Angleni children playing in a thicket. In the distance, dark smoke rose to the sky and the odor of roasting buffalo filled the air. But I knew the Angleni well. Instead of obeying the law of hospitality, they would have killed us instead. I resolved to hasten from that region.

But several children saw us and began singing,

"The Slant-eyes and the darkies will soon leave this land.

Their land has been given to us.

Yes, yes, their land is ours now.

Yes, yes, the Creator loves us so much.

He has given us their land."

I hated the Angleni for what they would do to our land. My anger was like a fire seeking something else to devour. I looked toward the Angleni village with its strange houses and smoke rising from their roofs. How I wanted to call fire down from the sky to destroy those children.

I remembered Noam's death, how his blood flowed into the ground and wondered, would I be willing to wage war and cause the blood of my enemies—even Angleni blood—to run like rivers of blood?

SATHA
Return to the Golden House
Scavenging Moon–Third Snow Moon

When we entered the gates of the outer courtyard of the Golden House we were like weary sleepers waking from a dream. We looked at each other in silence until Mamya Jontay came running toward us with Mad Malana at her side.

"Malana was sitting atop the Mistress Ramparts," Jontay shouted to us as she ran. "And when she said you were coming, I didn't believe her at first. Not until I had seen you with my own eyes."

Tears came from her eyes and she turned and shouted to others who also came running from the inner courtyards and the main house.

When Malana reached us she started jumping up and down, and began pulling Loic from his horse. "Cuyo, Cuyo, you're here," she kept repeating. The whole outer courtyard echoed with her joyful sobs.

She kept her eyes on Loic as he dismounted and after lifting her hands to touch his scars. She stroked his hair and watched as the loosely-hanging gray strands flowed through her aged fingers. Tears welled in her eyes as she said, "My boy, war was not made for the likes of you." Then she held him tight and kissed his face, cheek and hands.

After this, he lifted Ewi from Cactus's back, handing him down to her. She took Ewi from his arms and closely examined him. Then, comparing Loic's features to Ewi's and touching their noses alternately, then touching their lips, she said, "This is your son? He's not like you."

"He is my son," Loic answered. "The son of my wife, therefore my own son and the first-born son of Taer's first-born. His name is Ewi."

She then kissed Ewi. "Child, your father has killed his enemy." She turned to look at Loic. "If you are alive, Noam must be dead." She turned to me. "Am I right?"

I nodded.

"And Satha?" she continued. "How silent you are! The spirits have brought you two together! Rejoice now that you're home. We were distressed, all of us, when Jival told us the Therpas had stolen you away."

The sound of Jival's hated name was like a dagger piercing my heart.

"So bruised and beaten was she," Jontay continued. "She told us how valiantly she fought against them. But they overpowered her."

I marveled at how coldly my blood ran. Enslavement and powerlessness had taught me how to disguise hatred, to appear not to hate even while I planned murder. Among the growing crowd of rejoicing clanfolk, I saw Jival holding a small red-haired boy. "And the child in her arms?" I asked so coolly only Loic would know my heart.

"Noam's son," Jontay said, again without emotion. "We will talk about that later. Now, it's time to celebrate your return. You both left us in tears, but now joy has returned to our hearts."

With Ewi in her arms, she brought us into the longhouse and then to a wonderful newly-built house. Yes, in our absence, the servants had perfected our house. I whispered to Loic, "Their hope in our return, indeed their love for you and me, reminded me of how loved I was."

He squeezed my hand. "Your words speak all that is in my heart."

I will not speak of the mourning that took place in the days of our return. The bones of Treads Lightly hung from the ancestral grief tree. My own father was buried beside my mother. Nor will I speak of the dancing and feasting, or tell how the minor households rejoiced to see us, how clansmen and noblewomen came from long distances to greet us.

In the midst of the celebrations, following the performance of the Elcari which formally brought Ewi into the Pagatsu clan, Loic turned to me. "It's good to be here," he said. "Nevertheless my greatest desire is to free my clan from the Arkhai."

"Do what you wish, my husband," I answered. "Truly, I too have seen the evil done in this land by the Arkhai. Your wishes and desires are mine also. You have killed a man for me. Whatever grief and war come, I will be your ally forever."

He embraced me tightly, but said nothing.

"There is one mercy I wish to ask you," I continued.

"Speak, Dark Half-Moons."

"Ydalle tells me that Jival often was mediator between the Third Wife and Noam. In course of time, Jival grew to love Noam. But Noam forsook her."

He nodded, "Yes, that is the story I too have heard."

"That she loved him? Or that he loved her?" I burst out laughing. "The girl is not as innocent as she pretends. Noam could neither trust nor love a woman, much less one who betrayed both an Arhe and an Arhe's betrayer."

He looked at me a long while, his eyes wary. Then said at last, "Yes. Such double unfaithfulness, what use is it to anyone? Snakes rarely charm each other."

The singing and rejoicing went on into the night. During that time, I watched Jival roam the longhouse. Always on the edge of my sight, she seemed always to be whispering to someone. At last, I could bear it no longer. I leaned close and spoke softly to my husband, "She must die. I can bear this no longer. She has done me great evil and even now, she wastes no time in plotting against me."

"You mean Jival?" he asked.

"Who else?"

"Why should she die? She is not who-she-once-was."

"Who-she-once-was affected my life greatly, husband. The-woman-she-once-was threw my life into an earthly Gebelda. As we journeyed homeward, did I not tell you all the things I suffered because of her?"

"Indeed, but the past—"

"The past is not finished," I said, gritting my teeth. In my youth, I had read much about the lives of the prophets. *How sad,* I thought, *that no one ever thought to write about the harsh lives of prophets' wives and of the foolishness those women endured because of idealistic husbands.*

"My husband," I said, pushing my point, "You lived long among good and wise women whose goodness caused you to believe only in the kindness of women. But I have lived long enough to know that of all cruelty, female cruelty is the worst. And of all living creatures beneath the sky, women are the most treacherous. This thing I know: I cannot love you fully if you forgive someone you have no right to forgive."

His eyes narrowed and a long deep sigh escaped his lips. "My husband, my ally. Do you not see how she walks through the Golden House just as the Third Wife did? Can you not see she's conspiring against you? She thinks her child protects her, that her position as the mother of Noam's son protects her."

He looked past the dancers and past all the guests gathered in the outer court. "The child is Sio's brother. For Sio's sake, I will not kill the mother of Sio's brother." He gently placed his hand on my right shoulder. "It is hard to win a brother's heart when a mountain of bodies lies between us."

"What do warriors care about bodies?" I whispered, standing up. "Is this not the very thing your father did with the Third Wife? And did it not cause Taer and his son much grief to have spies and traitors in his tent? Don't you worry for Ewi and for your future children?"

"Even so, I have learned to tread lightly. I know that many will turn from me because of the spirits. Sio has won the hearts of many of our clan. I will not—"

Angry, I began walking away. "You left a man and you return fearing to lose allies? You have never cared about allies."

He seemed to be seeing across the ages. "My true allies will come."

How exasperating, I thought, *to be married to a prophet! Is this the life I am fated to live?* "I demand her death," I said, bringing him back to the mundane. "Or, if you cannot kill her, send her away."

"She is in your hands. Do what you wish to her, only spare her life."

I rose up angrily. "Why do you repeat the very words Talub used when he allowed Voora to send me away?"

"Because revenge does not satisfy." He took my hand and drew me closer to him. "If your heart is still the heart I once loved, it will only grieve to find itself grown so cruel. The girl is harmless. If you forgive her, you will find a grateful ally."

I kissed his forehead. "Unfortunately, Loic, I am no prophet like you."

That night, I ordered several warriors to take Jival and her son to the Blue Fortress. Malana stood beside us, crying, as she bade the little boy goodbye.

When Loic stroked her face and pushed her tear-wet hair from her face, she slapped him so hard against the cheek the sound echoed through the courtyard. "Why did you send them away?" she asked. "And why didn't you perform the Elcari ceremony in the right manner? Okiak says—"

"Malana, the household will bend to the new customs I bring. I will not dedicate my son to the spirits. It is enough to dedicate him to the Creator." Then he reached out and touched her.

Her face brightened suddenly and she blinked several times. Called suddenly from mental darkness into a wonderful light, she shouted in a voice higher than a hawk's, "Loicuyo, I understand all. The bindings around my mind have fallen away. What did you do when you touched me? I no longer see through a veil."

"The Creator has given all humans power to heal and he has also given me power over the spirits that have bound your mind."

"But how can it be?" Malana asked, looking at me for the first time with loving eyes.

"I've found the Creator's Lost Book," Loic answered. "But we will discuss such matters later before the elders. Now, go and find Yiko. Bring him here quickly."

She did, and when Yiko stood in front of us, Loic touched the place where his ear had been. Immediately the ear returned. The next day all the Golden House blazed with the news of Malana and Yiko's healing.

Loic began expounding to all his clansmen all the great things written in the Lost Book. Okiak and the other shamans and holy men warned that those who believed the Lost Book were forsaking the spirits of their fathers.

When elders and warriors of the Pagatsu clan arrived from the four winds. Loic eagerly told about the Lost Book.

Okiak's anger raged. "You speak arrogantly against the Arkhai, Loic," he said, his tanned faced growing red. "Are you saying the Creator has spoken to you? Who are you that he should speak to you?"

"The Creator is close to us all, Okiak. As for sickness, evil and poverty, the Arkhai are the ones who plunder us. Then they pretend they mediate for us. The Creator brought us the Lost Book with its too-good-to-be-believed-news in order that we may know our true heritage as his children. When we know what power he has given us because of the one who was sacrificed for us, we will war against the Arkhai and conquer them."

Okiak smiled in amusement. "I am not convinced the Creator is so very near us. At least, not all of us. Some people are nearer to him than others. As for this war against the spirits—you speak as if such a war is easy. People do not leave their old ways so easily. Are you prepared for blood rivers and corpse mountains?"

"You speak as if you believe me, Okiak."

Although I was still angry with my husband for the words he had used, his courage filled me with pride. I thought, *This new Loic is hard for me to understand. Truly, I have suffered many sorrows because I married him. Even so, I also suffered before our marriage. Even if we lose allies and our clan forsakes us, we will survive.*

"It is not a matter of belief, Young Chief," Okiak was saying. His body shook as he raged and paced the longhouse. "We must preserve the old ways. Since your return, I've watched you. You have allowed drumming, but forbidden drummers to call upon the spirits. You allow us the old songs but only those which praise the Creator. You change the Elcari ritual. We can dance and chant in memory of our ancestors, but we can no longer entreat them to mediate for us. All this grieves me because you're rejecting the Arkhai who have been our protectors and providers." He turned to me and bent low. "Arhe Satha, if your husband continues with these changes, the spirits and the shamans of all the clans will war against him, against you and your children. Are you prepared for this?"

"Okiak," I answered, "don't speak to me about these matters. Once I befriended my husband's enemy and I lost much because of that. I am no friend of the spirits. Speak to Loic yourself."

"In their anger," Okiak warned the gathered warriors, "the spirits will declare war against the Pagatsu clan and bring all the tribes and clans against him if we forsake them."

I answered, "Many people in all the tribes have wished to be freed from the pettiness of the spirits. If war comes, let it come. My husband believes that if the people of the three tribes will trust in the Creator's power, our people will not only conquer the Arkhai but we will destroy the Angleni from our land."

Okiak burst into scornful laughter. "If Loic had wanted to join the clans and tribes together, he should not have killed Noam. The Therpas will war against him, and if the Therpas do so, the holy men and the Matchless Family will also defy him."

Loic answered him. "I do not want to die, my brothers. If I die, this new way will die with me. My destiny is not to create a religion that dies. I do not want my wife to die either. But I will not return to worshiping the Arkhai. In order to make peace with the Therpas, I will not war against you. Know only this: I will not serve the Arkhai."

The next day the king arrived with his retinue and with Puhlya at his side. No longer was he our noble and handsome king. Instead he was bloated and his skin blotchy. As we sat in the gathering room of the longhouse, the warriors whispered among themselves that grief for Butterfly and his dead son had caused him to become enslaved to the Angleni fermented ale.

His words slurring, our besotted king said, "News has come to me that a vendetta has been declared against the Pagatsu clan. The Therpas are the most loathsome of clans, but I can't join hands with you on this, Loic—even for your father's sake."

Respectfully and firmly, Loic challenged him. "My father's stupidity almost destroyed my life, just as your stupidity, Matchless King, will destroy our nation."

The room broke into an angry uproar. Several of the warriors, and even Razo, reminded the king of Loic's wrong behavior toward the spirits when Krika was killed. I had heard Loic speak many times about that incident, yet never had I felt his isolation as I did at that moment when they reminded the king of it.

With a raised hand, Jaguar calmed the warriors whose voices were raised in anger against my husband. "True, Loic," he said, "I am often too diplomatic in dealing with my enemies. I was stupid because I thought the Angleni were honorable. However, I am not ignorant of the power of the Arkhai. You're alone, Loic, whether you recognize it or not. The Creator is far away." He called Okiak to stand before him.

Okiak approached, carrying Taer's axe. He lifted it over his head, then to the east and to the west. He called for his fetish bag, which Razo immediately gave to him. He took from it two desiccated fingers and declared them as his, sacrificed to the spirits when he vowed his obedience to them and his ancestors. Then he removed a bear claw and a small stone cup which had been dipped in the blood of a recently deceased elder. "The spirits will be merciful to you, Loic, if you allow them to be. Repent therefore, turn aside from your foolish arrogance. Bend down before me and let the spirits help you."

Loic slapped Okiak's hands hard, knocking the claw, the fingers and the cup onto the floor. At this all the elders arose as one.

Razo rose to his feet, "Younger Brother," he said, "you fill me with disgust! You could have worshiped any God you wished. The world is full of Gods and yet you chose the Angleni God."

Okiak put his hand over his ears and spat on the ground. "Jobara! Your Little Mother spoiled you indeed!"

I did not see a spoiled child. I saw a great a warrior who had fought Noam and who was fighting the spirits, his clan and King Jaguar himself.

"Beware, Loic," Jaguar said, clasping his hands. "Don't resist the help of those who aided me so powerfully during the war."

Loic rose. "How strange it is, Jaguar; when you speak with earthly countries, you demand an audience with their kings and highest rulers, yet when you speak with the country of the spirit, you are satisfied to speak only with pretenders and usurpers."

He did not answer. Instead, Puhlya stood up. "Matchless King," she began, and although she had been silent she sounded as fatigued as if this conversation had gone on for days. "Why do you believe the Creator could not help us win against the Angleni? Or even against the shadow gods? Is it such a hard thing to believe the Creator's life and power are near, even in our very human hands? Is it so hard to believe he loves us?"

The king answered, drooling as he spoke. All who were present looked at him, unable to understand his incoherent answer. Then, realizing we had not understood his words, he managed to speak more clearly. "Yes, Puhlya. It is a hard thing to believe."

"Matchless King," Loic addressed him, but his gaze was on Okiak and the other shamans. "You are wise and worthy. Yet I have always heard that if a wise man listens to a fool he will be deemed a fool."

Jaguar breathed long and deep but said nothing. It was Okiak who grew angry. He slung his fetish bag around his shoulder. "Am I a fool?" he asked. Then, as all the elders watched, he left the room and walked toward the stables. There, he mounted his horse and rode through the outer courtyard gates of the Golden House. Pausing beyond it, he brandished a threat, "Loic, you will see if I'm a fool soon enough."

My husband replied. "What you intend to do, do quickly."

After Okiak left, Our Matchless King rose from the gathering table. "Your father has always been faithful to me, Loic. Therefore consider my words: I will return to Chyar now, but when Okiak returns, send a news-runner to tell me if you've changed your mind. The spirits and your brother are already at war with you. Make no more enemies."

"My brother?"

Jaguar nodded. "When he heard of Noam's death—yes, the spirits are everywhere and they tell all—Sio sent his warriors far and wide to find his mother. They found her. Dead. She had been living in a brothel."

The news of the Third Wife's death made my heart smile. I thought, *A strange whore indeed. Not a face one would choose to look at while couching.* Loic looked at me at that moment, compassion for me—and possibly for her—in his eyes.

But I had no compassion for her.

The king continued the grim details. He spoke of how the brothel owner had led the Therpa warriors to her grave and how Sio had buried her in the Therpa ancestral arbor. How, because of family alliances, he had attended that evil one's funeral.

Jaguar warned Loic, "You would not have wanted to see that young man's face. He hates you. If the shamans and spirits rise against you, he will look for a chance to destroy you."

I walked toward Jaguar and knelt before him. "Jaguar, as long as you are king over the lands of the three tribes, you have power to forbid vendettas."

"Perhaps," he answered, "perhaps I can prevent war between man and man and clan and clan. But who can prevent the spirits from warring against a man?"

LOIC
The Great Decision
Sowing Moon–First Cool Moon

With Okiak absent from the Golden House, I could breathe easier. I taught my clan brothers the many lessons I had learned from the Lost Book. My wife, too, listened to me, although she often declared that though she trusted the Creator, she was not sure she could quite believe that such a good god would give the Angleni the Lost Book. "Certainly," she would often say, "it doesn't seem to have touched their hearts."

One morning, I followed her as she went to the pool to bathe. Standing nearby, I watched her as she disrobed and entered the water. Childbirth had made her body rounder. When I saw her naked body, passion reawakened. She had not, as yet, wished to couch with me. *Perhaps,* I said to myself, *holding each other will repair her heart and restore some of the joy we once shared.*

I began to remove my boots, tunic, breechcloth and leggings. As I stood almost naked among the moonseed, she looked up at me with love and pity. I had been feeling like a dove that has lost its mate and I was hoping she still considered me good to look at. There among the lingay grasses and the moonseed hope began to rise in my heart. I left her at the pool and walked down to the meadow near the henna bushes. Many willows grew there and many types of grasses. I found a bamboo stalk, broke a blade and began to carve a courtship flute for my wife. I had not wooed her in our youth and it seemed right to court her now.

I gazed back toward the pool. Naked, she was retrieving her clothes. I remembered my mother's nose-ring still in my travel pouch. My wife put on her tunic and I imagined it clinging to her wet skin, imagined her breasts and body beneath it. How beautiful she looked, how radiant and joyful.

I thought, *Why should I not couch with Satha? Is she not my wife? Is her heart not only good but noble? Is sorrow so powerful that it has left us with a duty-bound love, a mere alliance, that does not satisfy?*

I remembered when I first met her in my father's house, the day my Little Mother wrapped us in our courtship blanket.

"Satha," I called out when I saw her arising from the pool. "I long for your heart. Open it to me."

She raised her eyebrows. "Do not fear, my husband. My heart is opening to you, even as it opens to life. However, you must admit that our sorrows and worries are not finished. Perhaps my heart is steeling itself against future sorrows."

She made to pass by me, but I said, "Home and family await us. My home and your home, my family and your family. Our home, our marriage bed. If one waits for all sorrows to end before one learns to rejoice, one may never find joy until one enters the fields we long for. Too long a time, I think, for me to wait to couch with you."

"I thought customs declared you cannot couch with your wife once she is tainted." She smiled, half-joking.

I answered, "Customs mean nothing to me."

She sucked at her teeth. "My husband, although the Angleni carry the book with them, they don't carry it within their hearts. But you, you are worthy of the book."

"And our people are worthy of it also." My fingers touched her skin. "Dark Half-Moons, you've never left my mind." I stroked her shoulders and she allowed my hand to linger near her breasts.

We parted then, she to her duties, I to mine. But I found time to retrieve the nose-ring.

That night after Ewi fell asleep, she allowed me to take her into my arms. I gave her what I had given her once before, the gold nose-ring, as a pledge of my devotion. How awkward our lovemaking was, and how full of grief as we strove to rediscover each other's bodies and hearts! From that moment hope began to build a home in my heart.

On the fortieth day after Okiak left, I awoke and walked outside my house. The air bristled and crackled and yet there was no wind. Biting cold it was, and yet no snow fell from the sun-white sky. I recognized the presence of the Arkhai and shouted: "Show yourselves, spirits! I know you're here."

They answered my request slowly. The air and dust clouds of the outer courtyard began to take on humanlike form. Faces and contorted limbs appeared. A mighty band they seemed, all the ranks that made up the Arkhai of the land of the three tribes. Clothed in Ibeni, Doreni or Theseni garb, they stood around the Golden House, in all manner of dress—warriors with vialkas, household spirits in gyuiltas of many patterns, spirits of various crafts and regions. They were beautiful or terrifying, tall or short, fat or thin. They stood side to side, head to foot, reaching in all directions. Dense, dark and thick they were, like vines intertwined in overgrowth.

From inside the Golden House, the faces of my clansmen and my servants peeked out, their faces horrified. But although brave warriors trembled in their saddles, and the highborn women and the female servants of our clan all told me to be careful, I knew the Arkhai's powerlessness too well to be afraid.

"Loicuyo!" Jura called out, "Don't persist in this madness. Don't fight against the Arkhai."

But Satha, my Little Mother, and Malana clung tightly to each other and Little Mother encouraged me, "Loicuyo, fight. The Creator is with you!"

A sand-funnel arose from within the ranks of the spirits. The air grew heavy, hard to see through, hard to breathe. The sand assaulted both those inside and outside the Golden House. The warriors of my clan trembled, choked on the sandy air.

Little Mother's voice dwindled to nothing. I challenged the spirits. "You cannot murder me. I do not follow you now!"

Six figures stepped out of the spirit crowd. Ganti, Noam, Krika, my father—and two women. I recognized Alla as one of the women. She was wounded in the chest and I seemed to understand the wound was self-inflicted. But who was the other spirit-woman supposed to be? The answer came to me suddenly: my mother.

"Father," I said, trembling. "Is this really you?"

"It is." Hearing his voice—a voice I had not heard in so long—I trembled even more. Here was my father, dead yet standing before me. Yet, how weak that voice sounded, how full of despair.

"Are you grieving, Father?" I approached, wondering if I could touch him. "I have brought freedom to our land. I've killed your enemy and mine." I knelt on the ground and bowed low before him. "Forgive my harshness and disrespect towards you." Weeping stopped my voice and I stuttered, "Yes, Father, what a cruel and harsh son I was to you."

"That is forgiven, my son. The young do such things. But—"

"But?"

"What you've done now, since our parting, that is what grieves me. Even now, I cannot rest because of it."

His upheld hand prevented me from touching him. "You've left the old ways, Loic. Now, what is there left for me? How can I continue to live if your children refuse to honor my spirit or leave food for me in the fields? Even worse, because you war with the spirits, they now bar my way into the fields we long for. I have no home either on earth or in that wonderful place."

A wail escaped his mouth and I remembered the screaming and anguish I had heard and seen in Gebelda. I grieved for my father, remembering how the Arkhai had prevented me from leaving Blade Castle.

"Do the Arkhai have power even now, Father, to prevent you from reaching the Creator? The Creator is powerful and kind. Ask him to help you and he will command the spirits to stop their vengeance and resistance against you."

"I'll not speak to the Creator," Father answered. "He's too far from humans, living or dead, and nothing brings him near. Nor does the Creator care for those the spirits have rejected."

When he said this, something like scales fell from my eyes. I stepped backward, suddenly seeing my error. This was not my father. My grief had deceived me. "Go away and stop deceiving me!" I cried out. It was difficult to say even that, because the spirit looked so much like my beloved father. But the lies were the old lies of the Arkhai.

The spirit's face contorted into its true gruesome form and I slumped to the ground. I thought, *If this is not my father, where is my father?* I told myself to hope in the Creator's mercy. My father worshiped those deceiving spirits in ignorance. He had been taught by blind teachers, how could to know the truth?

All was silent around me. Such a silence I had never heard before or since; then suddenly there came a rumbling of hoofbeats over the far horizon. Afar, Therpa standards blew wildly. I watched and waited until I saw Sio—Taer's son and Noam's son—leading an army of warriors against me. Okiak and a great shaman army rode with him. Jival, too, was at his side with Noam's small son also in her saddle.

Okiak's horse raced towards me. The beast seemed as glutted with arrogance as its master. "As you see," the shaman said, "I have been busy."

"Quite busy," I answered. "But evil is always busy."

Forcefully, he reined his horse because it pranced merrily before me as if it was no ordinary horse but a disguised spirit. "My brother shamans and I have studied the old prophecies and nowhere does it say you are to be our leader. Therefore Loic, who made you a prince and leader over us?"

I shrugged, not caring about leadership or rank, and turned to my brother. As I looked on his face, my heart melted for him. A strange thing it was to look at him and to discover too late how much I loved him. How proud I was of him! Indeed, he was always more of a warrior than I was. Jobara! He seemed more Taer's son than I.

He sat astride his horse looking into the distance. "Loic, the prophecies say the shamans are to teach this new religion to the people."

I laughed. "They'll merely teach the old religion in new dress. New wine in old wine bottles."

"That's the way you interpret it, but the prophecies warned us against your wrong interpretations. This new religion will be under the shamans' control and the king will appoint teachers who will teach it. Moreover, we have made peace with the Arkhai through the shamans, and the Therpa and Pagatsu clans are now joined together under one headship."

Seeing the subtlety of the spirits, I found myself smiling. Sio, Taer's son, was also Noam's son. He was now heir to both the Therpa and Pagatsu clans. They had won a battle, indeed. Yet I was determined that they would not conquer me nor continue their devastations against our peoples. "I understand."

All about me the spirits laughed and their laughter echoed across the plains. I remembered the day I had declared war against them, the day Krika died. *I'm alone again,* I thought, *yet I am not alone because the Creator is with me. And my soul has not bowed to the Arkhai.*

Hoofbeats sounded in the distance and a multitude of people rode over the horizon towards the Golden House. As they neared, I saw Kaynu riding in front of them and my heart lifted; I thought the Creator had sent me allies. But then the crowd parted and I could see a group of riders, all in shaman leggings, riding among them. The Creator opened my eyes and I understood, then, what had happened among my people, the Called-Out Ones.

The Arkhai had indeed been busy. Their aim was to separate the people from the Creator, their talent was to confuse. This they did marvelously. Although the scribes had translated the book faithfully, they had added their own personal idiosyncrasies to their teaching of it. Some of them had included the ancestors and spirits in their worship, some had made their own clan important and other clans less so, some believed the Creator could be reached by mere humans, but that priests and shamans had more power to be heard. Some clans, like the Carpos, thought the book too moralistic and rigid. Others concerned themselves with small matters, such as what happened to the dead, what day and where to worship, what food to eat. There were some clans who created new books to "explain" or supplement the Lost Book. There were others who removed portions which didn't suit them. There were teachings based on wrong translations of the old Seythof or Paetan languages. There were teachings that said the Lost Book required a great deal of education to understand. An Ibeni prophet also, angry that his ancient enemies—and not his own people—had been given a book from God, created a version which he called *The Ibeni Recitation*, professing it was the true uncorrupted version of the Lost Book. This self-styled prophet gathered followers to himself, declaring he was the Creator's only prophet. All these united themselves under the power of Okiak and came against me.

How saddened my heart was! "If you taint the new way with the old ways," I shouted, "the Creator will allow the Angleni to conquer us."

Kaynu and a few—a small few—of the Called-Out Ones rode to my side. But what were we among so many? Even if we triumphed against the Angleni, the Arkhai, our true enemies, would triumph.

I grew silent, pondering the evil error the three tribes had fallen into. Long, long I stood there with Kaynu and our tiny band until a vialka flew past my head. Sailing through the air from Sio's hand, it had not aimed for my death.

"No, my brother," he said, "I will not kill you. But neither will we hearken to you. The shamans who have gathered here have all agreed against you. They and the Arkhai will interpret the Lost Book. Together we will fight against the Angleni and win."

I answered him: "How strange that the Therpas—former friends of the Angleni—should pose as the saviors of our land! But if you think the Angleni are your real enemies, you deceive yourselves. The Creator has told me we cannot win against the Angleni if we cling to the old spirits. The Angleni are evil, but they have one thing that brings them victory: they serve the Creator."

Just then I heard Sio's voice calling out to me. It was a voice full of rage and hurt. "Silence!" he shouted. "Murderer, you have neither status nor place in this clan."

Jival added, "Loic, know that you stand in the presence of the headman of your clan."

I held back my tears and prevented my heart from grieving about my exile. But as I searched my heart, I remembered the love the village of Called-Out Ones had showered on me. Yet now, most stood against me. The hurt in my heart seemed new and yet somehow ancient, as if the hurt my heart felt was somehow akin to the hurt the Wounded Rejected Savior must have felt. It grieved me that during my own lifetime, the truth and power of the Lost Book would again be "lost." The three tribes had chosen to ally themselves with the Arkhai and against the Creator.

Not long after that, the Angleni defeated us, and the Arkhai managed to reign despite the teachings of the Lost Book. Our land was now doubly enslaved.

In time, a few would learn to follow the unmixed teachings of the Lost Book, accepting me, Kaynu, Satha and our children as their true teachers.

Now we are only a remnant. One day we will be a great multitude.

Epilogue: Satha's Call to the Descendants

My children, you know the truth. The Therpas and Pagatsu had formed a truce but the Angleni conquered us anyway. The Arkhai too, for they continued as they always had—except they used so-called teachers of the Lost Book. The true way was still tainted. As for our Golden House, it was taken from Pagatsu hands and given over to Sio. But Sio's rule did not last long. Nor Jaguar's. The Angleni overturned all.

Even now, I can still hear the spirits laughing. I know they will not laugh forever. In those ancient days our people failed to enter into the joy the Lost Book called us to. But the time will come again—Jobara! it is almost at your doorsteps!—when all will see the true riches of the Lost Book. Yes, even in the land of the four tribes. In that day, when you have shaken off the shamans' teachings and have learned how to hear the Great Chief speak directly to you, Oh my children, how free and how fearless and how powerful you will be!

Ω

Glossary

The Four Tribes

The Doreni

A race with a rich variation in skin color, they are primarily tan to light brown and have almond-shaped eyes. A fierce people whose clans and sub-clans often fight among themselves, they have a pragmatic respect for all tribes and consider inter-clan and inter-tribal alliances important. They conquered the dark-skinned curly-haired Theseni five hundred years before the time of this story when they invaded the continent. They believe in a good, but distant, "Creator." Originally, they had no belief in mediating spirits and honored their ancestors but did not worship them. Over the centuries they were tainted by the ancestor-worship of the Theseni and the animistic spirituality of the Ibeni.

The Theseni

Original natives of the land of the three tribes, they are a dark-skinned people of high moral standard whose women wear veils and are taught to be submissive. They have learned to live with the other tribes who share their land. Although the king has outlawed slave-trading except in certain specific instances, many still continue to engage in slave-trading. They believe in a god who manifests himself either as "The Good Maker," a creative and good force, or as HaZatana, the destructive force. Hence, they are often submissive to evil.

The Ibeni

Sojourners in the land, they have tan skins with high cheekbones. They tend to be insular, clannish, superstitious, greedy, immoral, and fearful of spirits. They call the Creator "The One Above All," but seek to appease all spirits and gods, especially Qwisna.

The Angleni

A pale-skinned and hateful tribe, who invaded the land of the three tribes decades before. Although the war is over, the defeated Angleni, who call their god "The Good One," believe the land was promised to them by their god. They intend to be not the fourth tribe but the land's only tribe because they believe "The Good One" loves only their tribe and has created all other tribes to serve them. Although they consider the Ibeni immoral, they prefer the Ibeni above the Theseni and the Doreni because the Ibeni skin color is almost as pale as theirs.

GLOSSARY

Tribal Commonalities

Clothing Styles

The tribes dress differently, although they all wear gyuiltas, a cloak that can be either useful or ceremonial and often displays the caste and wealth of the wearer. A short riding gyuilta is worn like a jacket. A long gyuilta is worn in colder weather or by the rich. Doreni warriors wear earrings and women from all the tribes wear nose-rings. Men and women both wear soft moccasin-like leather shoes and sandals. Warriors wear boots. A multicultural society, it is common to see people wearing clothing made for other tribes. Generally, however, Doreni men and women wear leggings, short tunics and gyuiltas; Doreni women wear a coif or cap. Theseni women wear a tight-fitting calf-length dress called a kaba. Married Theseni women wear a half veil and unmarried virgins wear a full-veil. Theseni men wear a cloth turban and knee-length cotton tunics or robes. Ibeni men wear waist-length tunics, leggings, and vests. Ibeni women wear tight-fitting dresses of various styles, and are always veiled.

Language

The three tribes (and all the characters in the book) all speak the common Doreni language in addition to languages and dialects peculiar to their tribes and clans. Theologians and scholars study the old dead languages of Seythof and Paetan.

Households

The Golden House: Abode of the Pagatsu Doreni clan chief

Pagatsu [Pa-GAT-su]: The Doreni clan to which Loic belongs. The noblest of Doreni clans.

- Cyor [KYUR]: One of Loic's kinsmen.
- Edi [EE-di]: Personal handmaid to Satha.
- Gala [GAHL-a]: Personal handmaid to Satha.
- Galil [GAHL-eel]—Loic's kinsman.
- Ilem [EEL-im]: Perik's son, Loic's kinsman.
- Jival [Ji-VAHL]: A female servant, chosen by Satha as a personal handmaid, child of an unknown Angleni soldier and an Ibeni mother; mother of one of Noam's sons.
- Jontay [JON-ty]: Loic's primary caretaker; called Little Mother and Mamya Jontay.
- Jura [JOO-ra]: Razo's chief wife.
- Kluna: A Theseni clan.

- Krika [KREEK-a]: Okiak's son, killed at the spirits' behest.
- Loic [LO-eck]: Taer's son, born of Taer's deceased second wife; husband of Satha tya Monua. Nicknames: Wind Follower, Loicuyo, Cuyo and, by his wife, Half-Moon Eyes. Referred to as Loayiq in the Desai Scriptures.
- Malana [ma-LAH-na]: a mentally disabled girl in the Pagatsu household.
- Monua [MON-u-a]: Satha's mother, daughter of the chief of the large Kluna Theseni clan. Impoverished by the war, she is a dressmaker.
- Nwaha [EN-wah-ah]: Satha's father.
- Okiak [OK-i-ak]: Chief shaman of the Pagatsu clan.
- Pantan [PAN-tan]: Former headman of the Pagatsu clan, Taer's uncle.
- Perik [PAY-rik]: Loic's kinsman, a respected warrior known for his fierceness.
- Razo [RAH-zo]: Loic's kinsman, a coward, glutton and braggart.
- Satha [SATH-a]: Wife of Loic, daughter of Monua and Nwaha; nicknamed Dark Half Moons by her husband, Loic.
- Sio [SEE-o]: Taer's adopted son, child of the adulterous Third Wife and her cousin Noam; a member of both the Pagatsu and Therpa clans.
- Taer [tare]: Headman of the Pagatsu clan; nicknamed "General Treads Lightly."
- The Third Wife: Taer's adulterous third wife; member of the Therpa clan.
- Ydalle [EE-dal-le]: Taer's servant, and Monua's friend, from the Theseni Kluna clan.
- Yiko [YEE-ko]: Taer's steward; Theseni from an unspecified clan.
- Yoran [YOH-ran]: a shaman of the Kluna clan.

Trumpa's family: Family abiding near the Ibeni town of Ulia

- Arlis [AHR-lis]: Trumpa's sister.
- Barro [BAR-ro]: Trumpa's father.
- Trumpa [TRUM-pa]: A young man Loic meets on his journey.
- Unira [YOO-nee-ra]: Trumpa's stepmother, Barro's wife.
  (and younger children in the family)

Blade Castle: Seminary & School for warfare, Desai Doreni clan

- Alla [AHL-a]: Ganti's adopted daughter, born Ibeni but adopted into the Desai clan.
- Ganti [GAHN-ti]: One of Taer's Valiant Men.
- Kaynu [KAY-nyoo]: Ganti's adopted son, child of a Desai mother who was raped by an Angleni soldier.
- Twin : A student, from the Carpo clan.

GLOSSARY

Talub's (Angleni) Encampment

- Ewi [HUE-y]: Talub's firstborn son.
- Nyal [Ny-ul]: Talub's second son.
- Sena [SEHN-na]: One of Talub's chief herdsmen, an enslaved Theseni.
- Talub [TAH-lub]: An Angleni sojourner.
- Voora [VOOH-ra]: His wife.

The Blue Fortress: Abode of the Therpa Doreni clan chief

- Noam [NOH-am]: Firstborn son of the Therpa headman and chief; Taer's former friend, the Third Wife's cousin. Also called "Seared Conscience."
- The Therpa Chief: Clan headman and Noam's father.

The Palace at Chyar: The "King's Seat"

When the Doreni conquered the land, they set up a kingdom and instituted a system wherein the king marries three wives—one from each tribe—on the day he ascends the throne. The first queen to have a son becomes Chief Queen and her son becomes heir to the throne. The royal family always considers itself Doreni but they are called "The Matchless Family" because their racial characteristics and status among their people are without match.

- (Queen) Butterfly: The Theseni Queen, also called First Queen because she gave birth to the king's oldest son and heir.
- Heldek [HELD-ik]: One of Taer's Valiant Men, who are also the king's messengers (news-carriers).
- (Prince) Lihu [LEE-ooh]: The Crown Prince, firstborn son of Butterfly and Jaguar.
- (Scha) Menta [SHAW MEN-ta]: King Jaguar, also called Our Matchless King.
- Noni [NON-ee]: One of the king's counselors, from the Trabu Theseni clan; Butterfly is his sister.
- Puhlya [POOL-ya]: The king's chief counselor, from the Desai Doreni clan.
- (Queen) Sweet-as-Jasmine: The Doreni Queen, also called Second Queen.
- (Princess) Thira [THEE-ra]: Butterfly's daughter, the princess Loic might have married.
- (Queen) White Star: The Ibeni Queen, also called Third Queen.

Clans

• Carpo [CAR-po]: A mixed Doreni-Ibeni clan known for being intellectual, smug, and generally useless.
• Chianu [CHA-nyoo]: A clan, unspecified tribe.
• Desai [do-SI]: A mystical Doreni clan to which Loic's mother belonged.
• Delco [DEL-co]: A poor Ibeni clan.
• Dicco [DIC-co]: An Ibeni clan.
• Kathyra [KATH-ra]: a clan.
• Kelovet [KEL-oh-vit]: An Ibeni clan known for its fashionable and sexually sophisticated clothing style.
• Kluna [KLU-na]: The noble Theseni clan to which Satha belongs, destroyed by the Angleni.
• Lotoupi [Loh-TOUP-ee]: a Doreni clan.
• Therpa [THER-pa]: A fierce, unruly, immoral Doreni clan.
• Trabu [TRA-bu]: A Theseni clan, somewhat power-hungry and ruthless. Queen Butterfly's clan.
• Xodos [SOD-os]: One of the worst Ibeni clans.

Miscellaneous People

• Alima [ah-LEE-ma]: Satha's "lost" sister.
• Eleo [El-ay-ho]: A Doreni Prophet.
• Koloq [KOHL-ok]: A Doreni prophet.
• Luda [LOO-da]: Shaman, tribe and clan unspecified, of the "Village of Called-Out Ones."

Places

• Colebru [KOHL-eh-bru]: A fertile region, the burial place of the great warriors, traditionally dedicated to the ancestors. The Angleni, however, have disregarded the tribal customs and have several settlements there.
• Eastern Desert: The desert on the eastern side of the Salt Sea.
• Gulacan-Gulnayacun [GOOL-ah-can-GOOL-nay-ah-koon] The Theseni name for the Great Desert which comprises the Western Desert, the Eastern Desert and the Salt Desert. It is also the symbolic place where all the deserts merge. The literal meaning is "You go in, but you don't come out."
• Jefra [JEF-ra]: The region where Loic and Satha live. It comprises the primarily Ibeni city of Satilo, the suburbs of Rega and borders the Great Desert.

GLOSSARY

(Places, continued)

• Lingan [LIN-gan] Plain: Area between Ibeni and Theseni territories.
• Patchwork Prairie: A region with a variety of geographical features bordering the Great Desert near Colebru.
• Rega [REE-ga]: The suburbs surrounding the city of Satilo.
• Salt Desert: A now-dried-up inland sea which formerly flowed between two desert shores. A white desert of salty sand, it flows like a white river through the Great Desert.
• Satilo [sa-TI-lo]: The seaport city in the region of Jefra where Satha lives.
• Ulia [OOL-ya]: A city near Blade Castle, primarily made up of Ibeni.
• Village of the Called-Out Ones: An otherwise unnamed village faithful to the Creator, later the center of the Lost Book's translation.
• Western Desert: Desert on the western side of the Salt Desert.

Customs

• Altvayu [Alt-VAY-u]: A lie spoken to prevent hurt feelings.
• Elcari [Elk-AH-ri]: a birth ritual for children in which they are dedicated to the spirits and claimed by the clan.
• Etiquette: the practice of being careful in speech and behavior, especially when dealing with those with whom one has nothing in common.
• Greetings:
  ◎ Bowing low: A bow made from the waist while clasping both hands in front of the face. Generally used when great deference is due.
  ◎ "The Creator made this day": Typical greeting to strangers, family, and friend alike.
  ◎ "The day brings blessings for you and me": Typical response to such a greeting.
  ◎ "May we meet again in the same fields we long for": The form of farewell used to those whom one may never see again.
  ◎ Touching the shoulder: Warriors greet each other by touching each other on the shoulders.
• Half marriage (also, The Restraint): The year between the official engagement and the consummation of the marriage. During this time, the betrothed girl lives as a virgin with her husband's family. At the end of the year, if the engaged couple still consider each other worthy, the *full marriage* is performed and the girl shows her household skills by giving a feast.
• Kribatsu [KRIB-aht-su]: Literally, "reflected honor"; how a person's actions reflects on his clan's honor.

• The Law of Hospitality: Primarily a spiritual ordinance, it rules all social customs. It is especially important to the Doreni who, because they are so fierce, do everything to avoid war. Closely linked to the Doreni principle of etiquette.

• Nadam games [Na-DAM]: an annual national sports competition.

• Nuchunga [Noo-CHUNG-ah]: A reconciliation ceremony.

• Skortuka [skor-TOOK-ah]: A term which means "to allow one's self to give up the fight." Akin to suicide.

Spiritual

• Arkhai [ARK-eye] (also, spirits): The system of demons who rule over a nation.

• The Creator: The Doreni god, positive but distant.

• The fields we long for: The Doreni term for heaven. The Doreni heaven is a fertile land where warriors are joined by their wives. An unmarried woman cannot enter it. The Theseni heaven is primarily a masculine place where a woman serves her husband and the many virgins who await him. The Ibeni are vague about their heaven and don't know what awaits them.

• Gebelda [geh-BELD-a]: The underworld where the evil or unlucky dead go. The name also means "garbage heap." Although all the tribes have different heavens, they all believe in a common hell.

• The Good Maker: In Theseni belief, god made manifest as a creative and good force.

• HaZatana [HA-za-tan-ah]: The destructive aspect of the Good Maker who gives humanity cruel trials. Worshiped only by the Theseni.

• Lost Book: The Creator's book which Doreni prophets declared would be brought to the land of the three tribes.

• The One Above All: Ibeni name for the Creator.

• The One Who Holds My Breath in His Hand: A name of the Creator.

• Puha [POO-ha]: Spiritual power.

• Qwisna [KWIZ-na]: An Ibeni incarnating god who sometimes takes on a human body and lives among humans in order to pursue the wicked.

• Tayu [TAH-yu]: Energy or essence.

• Wind: The Creator.

• Y'waGulTuyat [E-wa-GUL-tyat]: "Creator God, you see me." The name Satha gave to the Creator God when he helped her in her distress.

• Y'wa [E-wa]: the name the Theseni give to their God.

GLOSSARY

The Seasons

- Cool Moons (Spring): Sowing Moon, Rose Moon, Thunder Moon.
- Heat Moons (Summer): Weed Moon, Campfire Moon, Traveling Moon.
- Harvest Moons (Autumn): Reaping Moon, Selling and Storing Moon, Thanksgiving Moon.
- Snow Moons (Winter): Mackerel Moon, Scavenger's Moon, Fever Moon.

Abstract

- Arhe [AR-hay]: The female ruler of a clan, usually (but not always) the wife of the headman.
- Beloved Woman: A woman on a village's council of elders.
- Coqulyu [ko-KUHL-yoo]: Little boy, of any clan or tribe.
- Coqalya [ko-KAHL-ya]: Little girl, of any clan or tribe.
- Disa [DEE-sa]: a title which means commander-in-chief of the King's army. Taer is First Disa, of the king's armies.
- Dorenyu [doh-REN-yu]: Little Doreni boy.
- Fetele [fet-AYL-eh]: History song, a traditional song which preserves a clan's history.
- Ibye [e-BI]: A word meaning "Now I remember it!"
- Jobara [jo-BAR-a]: An exclamation which means "Indeed!"
- Kwelku [KWEL-koo]: A word that can mean "So you say" or "That's what you think."
- Layo [LAY-o]: A word that means "truly." Often said to add emphasis to an assertion.
- Little Mother: Mamya (see below).
- Mam: Mother.
- Mamya [MAM-ya]: Little Mother, a term often used for nannies or foster and adoptive mothers.
- Mentura [Men-TUR-ah]: "Untried boasting," used when someone has bragged about something as yet not accomplished or unknown.
- Moon: The seasons of the year, also a term used for a woman's breasts.
- Moonweek: A woman's menstral period.
- New Mother: Mother-in-law.
- New Father: Father-in-law.
- One who wears a jade bracelet: A firstborn son and presumptive heir. Among the Doreni, to kill one who wears a jade bracelet is to declare war.
- One who holds my heart: A spouse or affianced.

(Abstract, continued)

- Plika [PLEEK-a]: A musical instrument, something like a lute and a mandolin.
- Scha [SHAW]: King.
- Shaman: One appointed by a village, clan or community to communicate with the spirits.
- Thesenya [thay-SEN-ya]: Little Theseni girl.
- Tya [Tyah]: A term which means "daughter of." A woman is always referred to as the daughter of her mother. Satha's full name is *Satha tya Monua Kluna.*
- Tyu [Tyoo]: A term which means "son of." A man is always referred to as the son of his father. Loic's full name is *Loic tyu Taer Pagatsu.*
- Tyungkyra [Tyoong-KI-ra]: Literally "son of stupidity," but generally used to mean "Don't be stupid" or "You're being silly."
- Valanku [Val-an-KOO]: A horse-drawn carriage—either open or enclosed—used by the rich.
- Waihai [WHY-hi or Wah-YAY]: Theseni exclamation of joy, also used by the Doreni.
- Warseed: A child descended from an invading Angleni soldier.
- -ya, -yu: Female and male suffix, diminutive, means "little." Often added to names or titles.
- Ypher [IF-ur]: The male sexual organ.

Organic

- Andarda [An-DARD-a]: A tea used to ease child-bearing.
- Angha [An-GA]: A desert rodent.
- Anley [AN-lay]: A flower than can be made into poison.
- Arvina [Ar-VI-nah]: A thorny plant with small purple flowers; considered to be an aphrodisiac.
- Bala [BAAH-la]: A juicy fruit, often eaten in betrothal ceremonies because its many seeds symbolize fertility.
- Bulba [BUL-ba]: A tree that grows in sparse areas such as a desert,
- Carmi [CAR-me]: A flower made into expensive oil.
- Colrona [Col-RO-nah]: A shrub.
- Coorat [KU-rat]: A kind of tea.
- Falling Sickness: Epilepsy, Loic's illness. Treated primarily through dietary restrictions.
- Jalak [JAH-lak]: A tuber, a staple of the Ibeni people.
- Kuthara [Koo-THAR-ah]: A poisonous plant.
- Lingay [LIN-gay]: A tall meadow grass.

(Organic, continued)

• Mosquito Illness: Malaria.

• Mizca [MIZ-ca]: An aggressive snake honored among the Doreni because it pursues its enemies relentlessly.

• Mukal [MOO-kal]: A fermented drink made from various berries.

• Percusa [PER-coos-a]: A plant.

• Quinchea [KWIN-cha] : A type of melon that is often preserved in salt and used as a relish.

• Terbur [TER-bur]: An herbal potion which causes painful but not fatal symptoms.

• Tura [TOO-ra]: A desert plant.

• Wita [WEET-a]: An addictive weed, an intoxicant.

Inorganic

• Clan marking: The geometric designs and embroideries that symbolically represent each clan.

• Coulba [KOOL-ba]: Double-edged battle-axe often carried by warriors.

• Gyuilta [Gyoo-IL-ta]: A hooded cloak worn by all classes and by both sexes.

• Kaba [KAH-ba]: A close-fitting dress worn by Theseni women. Its seductiveness is offset by the transparent veil.

• Pelu [PAY-loo]: A metallic head-covering, something like a crown, worn by queens.

• Quixa [KWIX-a]: Metallic coins that can be gold or silver.

• Shuwa [SHOO-wa]: A short lance, somewhat like a bolt or an arrow. Made from wood or iron. Because they are dispensable, they are often left in the field in warfare.

• Vialka [VYAL-ka]: A long lance, the symbol of a warrior's prowess. A warrior owns only one vialka during his lifetime, then it is passed on to his son at his death. A triumphant warrior takes his enemy's vialka and displays it for all to see.

Music

IN THE LIFE OF

Albert Schweitzer

WITH SELECTIONS FROM HIS WRITINGS

BY Charles R. Joy

ILLUSTRATED

Harper & Brothers . *New York*
The Beacon Press . *Boston*

TO THE MEMORY OF

LATHAM TRUE

The music of his spirit
by distance made more sweet

MUSIC IN THE LIFE OF ALBERT SCHWEITZER

Copyright, 1951, by Charles R. Joy

Printed in the United States of America

FIRST EDITION

B-A

Contents

v

List of Illustrations

The Hands of Albert Schweitzer (*Frontispiece*)
(*Following page 140*)

A Tribute to Albert Schweitzer

FROM THE DIRECTOR OF THE BOSTON SYMPHONY ORCHESTRA

THE name of Albert Schweitzer is linked with my childhood. It brings back recollections of wonderful evenings, when I heard him passionately discussing with my father every little detail in a score by Bach, after they had worked together performing it. At that time Albert Schweitzer played the organ for the concerts my father conducted at the church of St. William in Strassburg. He had studied previously with my uncle Eugène Munch.

Schweitzer had also studied with the great French organist, Charles Marie Widor. At that time Widor was very much perplexed by some of the Bach movements, and Schweitzer, who knew the texts of the old German chorales by heart, showed Widor how the words explained the music. Then they played through the chorale preludes one after the other, and a new Bach, that Widor had never known before, was revealed to him. At Widor's suggestion Schweitzer undertook to write a book on Bach. The book, which was begun in 1899, took him six years to complete, and brought forth a new interpretation of Bach's music, and of art in general.

Schweitzer's capacity for work is incredible. I have often seen him, after a full and strenuous day of activity, sit down with students and take time to correct their work and to guide them through new problems.

His talents and abilities are manifold. Through his great professional knowledge he has made an enormous contribution to the art of organ construction in France. His simple philosophy of reverence for life is the expression of a great man's faith in God and of his own humility. His work is an example of self-sacrifice and dedication to humanity.

There is another link that has brought us nearer together. In the Strassburg days my sister married Albert's brother.

As for me, his example and his advice have been present all through my life of work and strife. During the disaster of the last war and the

German occupation, it was his book, *Out of My Life and Thought*, which gave me courage and patience to endure the trial. It was this book which kept alive my hope, my belief in victory. It inspired my work and helped me to fulfill my duty. By a secret channel this same book was sent to our common nephew, Pierre Paul Schweitzer, who was arrested and imprisoned by the Germans at Fresnes, Paris, and then afterwards deported to the horror camp of Buchenwald. When he was released the precious book was lost.

On December 8, 1949, Albert Schweitzer wrote me from Lambarene:

"How curious is destiny! Who could have foreseen, when I used to take you out for a walk along the River Ill, near the Garnison church, you a small boy, that one day you would be helping me, working for me in the United States? Who could have told us that a day would come when we should both be known in America?

"I have been profoundly moved by what you and the Boston Orchestra have done for my work and myself. When I came back here on November 18th I was obliged to face a series of unavoidable expenses which I had not expected. I was depressed, overwhelmed by the prospect. And behold, you in Boston, a few days before, without my knowing it, had already relieved me of many material cares. Nobody knows what a burden of responsibility this hospital, grown so big, represents to me. It is terrible not to belong to oneself. But you have helped me to carry this responsibility at one of the critical moments of my life, at a time when I was really wandering in a dark valley.

"I wish I could have heard the orchestra, the organ, the compositions included in the program. The composition that would have interested me most was the *Concerto for Organ and Orchestra* by Poulenc. I try to imagine the Haydn *Concerto*, but without success, since the art of organ playing was not far advanced in Austria at this epoch.

"I am much moved by what you tell me of the place I occupy in your life. I have not forgotten that day after the first war in Strassburg, when you told me about that, and said, 'I have kept it all in my heart.'

"I have the great privilege of seeing my thought winning hearts in the world, a thing I should never have hoped for. I knew it had an importance, because it is elementary, and the result of reflection; it goes to the bottom of things, and establishes immovable values. But I never thought to see it already on the march. I accept it as a grace given me, as I accept the sympathy you have for me."

This, then, is Albert Schweitzer, a man who has devoted his life to music and his fellow men, a man near to my family and dear to my heart.

It is with deep emotion that I bid godspeed to this book.

CHARLES MUNCH

Boston, Massachusetts
January, 1951

Foreword

THERE are no sidewalks in the little Alsatian town of Gunsbach. Some of the houses are set back from the road, but not the house of Albert Schweitzer. Behind the house broad meadows stretch down to the banks of the little river Fecht. There is no physical reason for it, but the house of Albert Schweitzer crowds on to the street. The man himself is not there often, but when he is there he wants to be as close as possible to his people. He wants to be able to look out through the ivy-edged window and see the passers-by, wave a friendly greeting and call out in his loved Alsatian dialect "Boshour." And if a visitor sets his feet directly from the running board of his car onto the steps that lead to his front door, Monsieur Albert can be there in a trice to meet him, for of all the rooms of the house his study-bedroom is closest to the main entrance, only a few feet away.

He sometimes calls this house the house that Goethe built, and in a sense this is literally true, for it was built with the money Schweitzer received from the City of Frankfort when he delivered at its invitation the Goethe Prize Address in 1928. To one of his friends who came to see him he told the story, and then said, standing on the threshold, *"Tu vois, celui qui te reçoit ici véritablement, c'est M. Goethe!"* There was no pride in his heart, and there was a twinkle in his eye when he said this, but there was a truth in the words, which Schweitzer himself would quickly and humbly disclaim, but which all his friends know to be so. There is no great man in this modern day whose life more closely resembles that of Johann Wolfgang von Goethe than Albert Schweitzer. Dr. Schweitzer himself once said to me: "Goethe is the personality with which I have been most deeply concerned." [1]

If, however, Goethe greets you from the house he built beside the road, it is Bach that greets you when this same man sits down on the

[1] For the striking parallelism between the lives of Goethe and Schweitzer, and for Schweitzer's acknowledged indebtedness to Goethe, see my introduction to *Goethe. Four Studies,* by Albert Schweitzer. Boston: The Beacon Press, 1949. C. R. J.

bench of the lovely little organ in the village church. The church is set back from the square on a knoll above the town, a bit remote from the community, as the beauty and the majesty of God must needs be from our human striving, but when Albert Schweitzer sits at that organ in the high balcony at the rear of the church, he becomes a mediator between God and man, and the words of mediation are usually found in the cantatas and choral preludes and Passions of Bach. Here is Bach reborn for our day.

Goethe had no close personal meaning for Schweitzer during the first half of his life. It was not until that Good Friday afternoon of 1913, when the bells were sweetly ringing from beneath the slender spire of the church, and the little train came clattering down from Munster trailing in the late sunlight its bright pennant of smoke, and Albert Schweitzer climbed up the steep steps into the third-class carriage on his way to Africa, that Goethe began to have a very intimate significance for him. But from that moment a clear-eyed sibyl might have seen the two lives going on into the future side by side like the converging tracks of the valley railway leading down to the plains of the Rhine.

Bach, however, took possession of him from his boyhood on. To Eugène Munch, his music teacher at Mulhouse, the Well-Tempered Clavichord had been in childhood a kind of daily food, and the flame of his ardor spread to his impressionable pupil, who felt in Bach that deep, religious fervor which was his own inheritance. He recognized the Leipzig cantor as a symbol of something very deep within his own soul, something that was perhaps more spiritual than musical. So Bach became to him "the Master," and he became from that time on a Minister of Music, trying to interpret to the world the religious significance of the cantatas and the Passions, himself more and more an embodiment of the man whose works he reproduced.

The life of Albert Schweitzer has been strung on a continuous, golden chain of music, which will not be broken until his fingers are silenced beneath the waving, sun-drenched palms of the hilltop cemetery at Lambarene, or within the lot beside the wall of the Friedhof at Gunsbach, where his mother and father and little sister already lie.

Albert Schweitzer has become one of the greatest living interpreters of the music of Bach; but the reverse is also true—that the music of

Bach is the only adequate interpretation of the life of Schweitzer. So
one of his recent biographers states, "The St. Matthew Passion is
alone adequate to cover the African venture, the joy of the journey
and the disappointments, the magnificence of the aim, the apparent
failure and eventual triumph." [1] The same writer in a later passage
likens Schweitzer's life to another of Bach's magnificent writings, the
B minor Mass. In that Mass the Kyrie Eleison would be his early
theological controversy, strife and victory; the Gratias Agimus his
musical triumphs, cheerfulness, and tranquillity; the Et Incarnatus
his work in Africa, sacrifice and redemption; the Crucifixus his war
experience." [2]

The purpose of the present book is twofold: first, to recount in
simple human terms the story of this man as a minister of music, a
story too little known outside of Europe; and second, to bring to the
English-speaking world all of Albert Schweitzer's writings on music
which have been hitherto unavailable in English. These writings, biographical and autobiographical, historical and critical and technical,
have an importance which will be quickly recognized. Most of them
are as timely today as when they were first written, and the few that
are not have a value in tracing the development of music in the past
half-century which should not be underestimated. For Albert Schweitzer is in large part responsible for the finer ideals in modern organ
building and for our new understanding of the immortal Bach.

I am greatly indebted to William King Covell, of Newport, Rhode
Island, for suggestions concerning the translation of technical terms
in organ construction; to Harold Schwab of the New England Conservatory of Music, who has read with great care the organ section of
the book, and has given invaluable counsel; and to Professor Archibald Thompson Davison of the Department of Music in Harvard
University, who has gone over the entire manuscript with me to my
great profit. Without the generous aid of these friends this book
would have been impossible. To them I extend my heartfelt thanks.

Acknowledgments are due to the following publishers and authors

[1] Albert Schweitzer: Life and Message, by Magnus Ratter. Boston: The Beacon
Press, 1950, p. 43.
[2] Ibid., p. 54 f.

for permission to translate and include in this book copyrighted material controlled by them:

A. & C. Black, Ltd., London, and Harper & Brothers, New York, for quotations from *Albert Schweitzer, the Man and His Mind,* by George Seaver.

Breitkopf & Härtel, Leipzig, Germany, for several chapters from *J. S. Bach, Musicien-Poète; Deutsche und französische Orgelbaukunst und Orgelkunst;* and "Die Reform unseres Orgelbaues auf Grund einer allgemeinen Umfrage bei Orgelspielern und Orgelbauern in deutschen und romanischen Ländern," in *III Kongress der Internationalen Musikgesellschaft,* 1909.

The Deutscher Musikliteratur-Verlag, Berlin-Halensee, for "Warum es so schwer ist in Paris einen guten Chor zusammenzubringen," which appeared as an article in *Die Musik,* volume IX, no. 19.

The Dial Press, New York, for the quotation from *That Day Alone,* by Pierre van Paassen.

Editions F.-X. Le Roux & Cie, Strassburg, France, for the chapter "Souvenirs et Appreciations," by Albert Schweitzer, from *Un Grand Musicien Francais: Marie-Joseph Erb.*

P. H. Heitz, Strassburg, France, for "Souvenirs d'Ernest Munch" and "Zur Geschichte des Kirchenchors zu St. Wilhelm" from *Le Choeur de St. Guillaume de Strasbourg, un Chapitre de l'Histoire de la Musique en Alsace,* compiled by Erik Jung.

Imprimerie J. Brinkmann, Mulhouse, France, for *Eugene Munch, 1857-1898.*

L'Alsace Francaise, Strassburg, France, for the article "Mes Souvenirs sur Cosima Wagner" which appeared in volume XXV, no. 7, February 12, 1933.

Les Dernieres Nouvelles d'Alsace, Strassburg, France, and the author, Mr. Louis-Edouard Schaeffer, Strassburg, for "Das verschwiegene Bachkonzert für die weite Welt," which appeared on November 7, 1936.

The Macmillan Company, New York, for a brief passage from *The Prophet in the Wilderness,* copyright, 1947, by Hermann Hagedorn.

Musikzeitung, Zürich, Switzerland, for "Der runde Violinbogen," no. 6, 1933.

Mr. A. A. Roback, of Cambridge, Massachusetts, for quotations from *The Albert Schweitzer Jubilee Book*, Sci-Art Publishers.

Vandenhoeck & Ruprecht, of Göttingen, Germany, for "Zur Reform des Orgelbaues," in *Monatschrift für Gottesdienst und kirchliche Kunst*, volume XXXII, no. 6, June, 1927.

To all of these for their gracious co-operation my most sincere gratitude.

CHARLES R. JOY

Music

IN THE LIFE OF

Albert Schweitzer

PUBLISHER'S NOTE

The text of this book is set in Electra type. The introductory and explanatory material by Charles R. Joy is set in *italic*. The writing of Albert Schweitzer is set in roman.

Early Raptures

THE old presbytery at Gunsbach was built in 1771. It was over a hundred years old when Louis Schweitzer, the new pastor, arrived there, bringing with him a frail little baby who had been born in another valley to the northeast, and it had all the friendly charm of an Alsatian home. Between the tiny stream, which the Alsatians called the Bachle, or little river, and the vine-clad Rebberg, which rose above the town, it stood in the midst of the village, not crowded among the other houses yet intimate with them. In this pleasant home the sickly baby grew well and strong in the health-giving air of the lovely Munster Valley, and there his earliest recollections were filled with music.

Perhaps time has made the notes more sweet, perhaps memory has filled the music with the faint, exquisite beauty of a dream, but Albert Schweitzer recalls the late afternoons of those earliest years, when he sat quietly in a big chair and listened to his father improvise on the piano, keeping time with hands and feet, while his little heart beat for joy. But even before the recollections begin, this music was molding the young life.

The square piano, on which his father played with no great technical skill, but with a gift for improvising, had come down the Munster Valley from Mühlbach, where Grandfather J. J. Schillinger, his mother's father, had been the pastor. The first World War left only a single house standing of all the buildings of Mühlbach—the Schillinger parsonage and the church went with the rest of the town; but the grave of Pastor Schillinger, behind the new church, is still a place of pilgrimage to Albert Schweitzer, and to others for whom the old truth-loving pastor is still a vibrant memory. He had a passion for

1

organs, and was a brilliant musical rhapsodist. He used to travel about for the sole purpose of visiting new organs, particularly while they were being constructed, for then he could talk with the builder, and be one of the first to make the new pipes speak.

Perhaps it was from him, as Dr. Schweitzer states, that the passion for the organ was inherited, along with the square piano; but surely not from him alone. For his paternal grandfather was also an organist, as well as this grandfather's two brothers, and music had blossomed on many other branches of the family tree. It was a tradition in Germany and Alsace that the schoolmaster should study music, and usually he played two instruments, the organ (piano) and the violin. The long line of Schweitzer ancestors is full of schoolmasters and organists. It was as natural for Albert Schweitzer to become an organist as it was for Bach, with his ancestry, to become an organist.

Of course that was not Schweitzer's idea at first. When he was asked as a child what he wanted to be when he grew up, he replied that he wanted to be a swineherd. And anyone who has seen a swineherd in the smiling valleys of the Vosges, or has wandered with the cowherd in the lonely solitudes of the high alps, will understand the poetic appeal of that kind of occupation. But the family had other ideas. At five years old he was practising his scales on the old piano under his father's tutelage; at six he was overwhelmed by the voluptuous beauty of some duets which by chance he heard the big boys of the singing class give; a little later the harmony of brass instruments filled him with such rapturous ecstasy that the strings of his heart almost snapped within him; at seven he was showing his singing teacher, who played with one finger, how a hymn tune should be properly harmonized; at nine he was playing at times for the regular organist in the service, and playing also in Pastor Schillinger's old church at Mühlbach, where his grandfather had had a fine organ built under the direction of the organ builder Stier.

His father was not a very systematic teacher, and from the point of view of a thorough musician the boy's training was rather sketchy. He paid very little attention to notes. He liked to harmonize the familiar hymn tunes, but was in no way a promising youngster.

During the vacation periods he used to visit his godmother in Colmar, Madame Julie Fellner–Barth, and every day while he was there her daughter used to give him a piano lesson, so that he would not get out of practice and forget what he had already learned. His teacher, who is still living in Colmar, reports that in these brief ten-minute lessons he held his fingers rather awkwardly, and showed no particular aptitude for music. He was a rather placid, dreamy boy. Not many years afterwards he played the organ at his teacher's wedding, but by that time the awkward fingers had become supple and gifted, and the boy who showed no particular aptitude had become a brilliant organist.

In the seventh century the Benedictine monks had established themselves in the Munster Valley, for what reason no one knows, and there four kilometers above Gunsbach they had built a monastery in honor of their patron saint Gregory. From this Monasterium Sancti Gregorii the name Munster was derived, and Munster became in the course of the next twelve hundred years a considerable community dominating the valley. To Munster the boy Albert was sent, when he was nine, for a year at the Realschule,[1] and it was characteristic of the "placid, dreamy boy" that he preferred to walk to and fro between Gunsbach and Munster, not in the company of the other boys, but alone, that he might enjoy the changing seasons in the valley and indulge his own fantasies. It was for him the Happy Valley; and when next year the family judgment was passed down that he should go to Mulhouse to study, he was heartbroken. He was only ten, and going to Mulhouse meant leaving his home.

The bridge is short that leads from joy to sorrow, the German proverb says. But the bridge is just as short in the other direction. It was a fortunate fate that brought Albert Schweitzer to Mulhouse, for there he met Eugène Munch, and through Eugène Munch he met Bach, and through Bach he became the musician that he was. Mulhouse made a great organist out of Albert Schweitzer.

It is doubtful if he knew much about Bach when he went to Mulhouse. His father, his first teacher, did not care for Bach. Perhaps the boy did not even know that almost two hundred years before, June 15, 1707, Johann Sebastian Bach had received an appointment to the organ of this free imperial city, and had agreed to

[1] The Realschule was the nonclassical secondary school in German education. C. R. J.

take in payment 85 gulden, 3 coombs of corn, 2 cords of wood, 6 trusses of brushwood, and 3 pounds of fish per annum. Bach had not been happy there, and had stayed for only a year. Two weeks before he came, a large part of the town had been destroyed by fire, the pietists and the orthodox were quarreling in the church, and music had been frightfully neglected. So Bach became discouraged, and a year later resigned to go to Weimar with his young wife. His connection with Mulhouse had been very brief.

Still it is significant that it was in a Bach city that Albert Schweitzer first became acquainted with Bach, almost immediately after his arrival there.

The boy of ten found himself transplanted from a little country town to an industrial city, whose cotton thread was known to the ends of the earth, even in the heart of the jungle to which he was later to go. Except for the magnificent Hotel de Ville, however, there was very little of beauty in the city. The old church of St. Stephen, erected in the twelfth century, with choir and steeple of the fourteenth century, had been demolished in 1858, and a huge building of doubtful artistic taste had taken its place.

It was also an austere and rather gloomy home to which the impressionable lad went, under the kindly but rigid discipline of Uncle Louis and Aunt Sophie. As elementary school director for the city, Louis Schweitzer, the half-brother of Albert's paternal grandfather, had an official apartment in the École Centrale, and there for eight years the boy lived while attending the Gymnasium.[1] He was a poor scholar at first, but the good teaching he received gradually aroused him. He had no great enthusiasm for the piano either, but Aunt Sophie insisted upon regular practising after the noonday meal, and, when the home lessons were completed, after school at night.

Then, one day, something memorable happened. Uncle Louis and Aunt Sophie took him to a concert, the first he had ever attended. The concert was by a young Alsatian musician, Marie-Joseph Erb, who had been born at Strassburg in 1858, had studied in Paris at the Niedermeyer School of Classical and Religious Music, and then, refusing an appointment to the school as professor, had returned to

[1] The Gymnasium was the classical secondary school in German education. C. R. J.

his native land. He began to give brilliant piano recitals and to publish his first compositions. In 1883 he accepted a post as organist at St. George's in Selestat, and had private pupils there and in Strassburg. He remained at Selestat until 1890, when he moved to Strassburg. The years from 1884 to 1890 were fertile years, when his musical genius found expression in highly personal works of rare loveliness and pure style. It was during this period that he came to Mulhouse to give the concert attended by Albert Schweitzer, the boy of eleven or twelve, to whom the piano was still drudgery. Sixty years later the memory of that concert was still so vivid that every impression was fresh in his mind.

This is his account of it.

※

MY FIRST CONCERT [1]

MY first memory of Marie–Joseph Erb is all mixed up with my memory of the first concert I attended. It must have been about 1887; I was then eleven or twelve years old.

The concert was held in the hall of the stock exchange in Mulhouse, where I had been living since 1885 with my great-uncle, Louis Schweitzer, the director of the Écoles Communales, who had taken me in to permit me to go to school in that city. My uncle and aunt took me to this concert. I was astonished to see all the people in evening clothes, and I wondered what kind of figure I was cutting in my Sunday suit, which had become too small. The women were sucking bonbons. And now suddenly the hubbub which had been reigning subsided. A gentleman who seemed to me to be very tall and thin, in an evening suit, went onto the platform, and was immediately greeted by applause.

This, then, was Mr. Erb, who had recently come from Paris, after having had a brilliant success in his musical studies. He sat down at the piano, played a prelude until there was complete silence, and then

[1] From *Un Grand Musicien Français: Marie–Joseph Erb*. Strassburg–Paris: Editions F.-X. Le Roux & Cie, pp. 83 f.

attacked with spirit the first number on the program. I then realized what a *virtuoso* was. I was stunned to see his hands whirling around on the keyboard. And all by heart, without hesitation, without a mistake! I was lost in astonishment. With my modest knowledge of piano-playing, I tried to figure out how he went to work to launch those cascades of arpeggios and those bursts of shooting stars, to make the melody come out so clearly, to achieve those *pianissimi* in which, nonetheless, not a single note was lost. . . .

After the first piano pieces, which had kept me in a state of rapture, the artist rose, bowed as the entire assembly applauded, disappeared behind a door, came back when the applause did not die down, disappeared again, came back, disappeared. Finally there was silence. People studied the rest of the program. The women offered each other bonbons. I could not understand why all these people, after having applauded so heartily, did not remain like me, under the spell of what they had heard, and how they could resume their chatter.

But here was Mr. Erb back again, smiling, and mounting the platform beside the singer. The latter had curls like those that young girls wore for their first communion, and carried long white gloves. She put a big bouquet of flowers on a chair, made a curtsy, opened her sheet of music, which trembled a bit in her hands, coughed lightly, looked at the pianist and made a slight sign with her head, to which he replied by beginning immediately the first measures of the accompaniment. I was very much aware of the beauty of the singing, but still my attention was especially attracted to the accompanist, who followed the singer so well when she accelerated or decreased the tempo, when she passed from *pianissimo* to *fortissimo* or returned from *fortissimo* to *pianissimo*. Never could I have imagined such flexibility. The display of virtuosity at the end took my breath away. It was for me a sudden revelation of the possibilities of the piano. On the way home I walked as in a dream.

The following days I worked on my scales and finger exercises and struggled with the Czerny studies with an unprecedented ardor, even when they were starred with sharps and double sharps, which I had so detested theretofore.

Afterwards I heard the most celebrated piano *virtuosi*. But none of them ever agitated me and stirred me as Erb did, when as a little student in the collège I heard him for the first time.

⚜

*B*ESIDE the church of St. Stephen stands a plain three-story stucco house, on the second floor of which the organist of the church used to live. There, from the age of ten on, Albert had been going regularly to take piano lessons from Eugène Munch. It was not a pleasant experience for either master or pupil. For the master, Albert was the worst of all pupils, his "thorn in the flesh." His playing was expressionless and faulty. No wonder, for Albert preferred to harmonize, to improvise, to play at sight; and he disliked the drudgery involved in the thorough mastery of the pieces given him by his teacher. Even the wholesome effect of that first concert wore away; and when he played for his teacher there were few signs of either technical excellence or personal appreciation. Again and again his teacher fumed and scolded, but to no effect. Then one day something he said stung the boy to the quick; and when he came back a week later he played the Mendelssohn Lied ohne Worte which had been assigned to him in such a way that the teacher felt at last that the boy had been won. A few weeks later Albert began on Bach, which was this teacher's perfect tribute of praise.[1]

Albert Schweitzer never fully approved of the great new church of St. Stephen, because it had no chancel. A chancel, he thought, was a necessary part of the perfect church—an aid to devotion, a spur to the imagination. But he did approve of the organ, one of the several lovely instruments which it was his good fortune to know as a youth. It was a Walcker organ of sixty-two stops and three manuals, built when that concern was constructing wonderful organs in the sixties and seventies; and when, on Palm Sunday, 1890, Eugène Munch played as a processional the stirring "Lift up your heads, O ye gates!" from Händel's Messiah, and Albert marched in with the other

---

[1] For a delightful account of Albert Schweitzer's early life, see *Memoirs of Childhood and Youth*, by Albert Schweitzer. New York: The Macmillan Company, 1949. C. R. J.

boys to be confirmed, his own heart was lifted up like the everlasting portals through which the King of Glory passed. Two things moved him deeply: one was the holiness of the spiritual experience, an experience he felt much more profoundly than old Pastor Wennagel, who thought him indifferent, had ever suspected; and the other was the promise of his music teacher that after his confirmation he himself would be permitted to have lessons on that marvelous instrument pouring out its heavenly harmonies from the gallery above his head.

He was already familiar with the organ. For Dr. Munch had been in the habit of taking him every Saturday evening to listen in the organ loft, while he practised for the Sunday service. There at ten years of age he had first become acquainted with the chorales of Bach, and there he had been strangely stirred as he listened to the mysterious sounds losing themselves in the dark nave of the great church. And now he himself was to learn to make music from the manuals and pedal keyboard, from the levers and stops and soaring pipes of this magnificent instrument.

He had played an organ before, for Daddy Iltis, the organist at Gunsbach, and in Grandfather Schillinger's church at Mühlbach; but this was a great organ, and he was to study under a great organist. Now at last music became to him a serious business, and into it he poured all the resources of his gifted mind, all the riches of his sensitive soul. In another year he was occasionally taking the place of his teacher at the organ console, and soon after he was playing the organ accompaniment of Brahms' Requiem, while Eugène Munch conducted the choir and orchestra.

Another stirring incident from these days of plastic adolescence occurred when for the first time, at the age of sixteen, he was permitted to attend the theatre, and heard the overpowering music of Richard Wagner's Tannhäuser. For days afterwards he went about in a trance, reliving the rapture of that evening, unable to attend to his work at school.

So the Mulhouse years came to an end. Much of what was musically significant there are only memories to Albert Schweitzer now. On September 4, 1898, Eugène Munch died prematurely, forty-one years old, and about the same time the wonderful Walcker organ was "modernized," by the same firm that built it, and its lovely tone disappeared. "How are the mighty fallen!"

Immediately after the death of his beloved teacher, Albert Schweitzer wrote a little brochure in French, for the family and friends of Eugène Munch. This tribute to the great teacher who gave direction to his musical life was Schweitzer's first published writing. In the Avant-Propos of his J. S. Bach. Le Musicien-Poète, unfortunately omitted from the later English version, he says:

"When I undertook to write the chapter on the chorales, memories of these first, profound, artistic emotions came flooding back to me. Certain phrases came to the point of my pen all formed, and then I realized that I was only repeating the words and using once more the imagery by which my first organ teacher had opened my understanding for the music of Bach." [1]

※

MY FIRST ORGAN TEACHER [2]

> Blessed are the dead which die in the Lord from henceforth: Yea, saith the Spirit, that they may rest from their labors; and their works do follow them.
>
> REVELATION 14: 13

EUGÈNE Munch was born on April 3, 1857, at Dorlisheim, where his father held the posts of teacher and organist.

The year after his birth his parents moved to Niederbronn. It was in this pretty little village of our Alsace that Eugène Munch spent the years of his youth. After the loss of an elder sister, who was taken from her loving parents in her ninth year, death for a long period spared this household, where six children were growing up under the strict guidance of a father esteemed by all who knew him. Very early Eugène Munch showed a great talent for music. The father

---

[1] J. S. Bach. Le Musicien–Poète, by Albert Schweitzer. Paris: Costallat, 1905, p. v.

[2] Eugène Munch, 1857–1898, by Albert Schweitzer. Mulhouse: J. Brinkmann, Publisher, 1898.

himself directed the musical education of his children, and he laid the foundation for the musical career of his oldest son by introducing him to the works of Bach. Eugène Munch delighted later in saying that Bach's *Well-Tempered Clavichord* had been from infancy his daily bread. On Sundays, when his father played the organ for the church service, he stood at his side. Soon he was in a position to substitute for him. When he was sixteen he entered the normal school at Strassburg. After having passed the final examinations he remained for seven years at Niederbronn, as assistant and colleague for his father. In 1883 a dream came true: he went to Berlin with his brother Ernest to study music there. Mr. Haupt, the teacher of organ in the *Musikhochschule*, became greatly interested in the two young Alsatians, whom he numbered among his best pupils, and never did he fail to ask for them after he had lost sight of them.

Upon his return to Niederbronn, Eugène Munch resumed his work as teacher, and established a church choir, which continued for only a few months after his departure.

In 1885 he was called as organist to the Protestant Temple at Mulhouse, and it was in this city that he was thenceforth to pursue his artistic career and establish his home. In February, 1886, he married Miss Bockenhaupt of Wissembourg. The young household was plunged into profound grief by the death of their first child, a little daughter. With the birth of their son, Ernest, happiness again brightened their home. Six children were born in succession, and filled the house with gaiety. In 1889, Eugène Munch suffered the great sorrow of losing his father. A heart ailment proved fatal before he was able to see his son reach the highest steps in that artistic career whose beginnings had filled him with happiness.

When Eugène Munch came to Mulhouse he was primarily an organist. His talent was revealed to the public at the outset through the fine instrument that was entrusted to him. At that time he was not yet the great organist which we knew in his last years. He was just leaving the Conservatory; he was still a pupil. At Mulhouse he found the one organ of all the imaginable organs which best suited his personality. We can say that this instrument completed his education as an organist, and led him to heights where we marvelled at him. The remarkable sonorousness, the delicacy of tone, in this organ invited those refinements in registration in which he excelled. The faulty mechanism of the instrument made clear and precise playing difficult, and imposed upon him that tranquillity which gave his playing an imposing and majestic quality. The instrument demanded delicacy and serenity, and his nature responded to it. However, this harmony between the character of the instrument and the personality of the organist would not of itself alone have produced the great artist, if Eugène Munch had not had the perseverence and the indefatigable energy that are the essential conditions of all artistic achievement. More than any other instrument the organ exacts these qualities of those who come to it as slaves, before recognizing them later as masters and rendering obedience to them.

By ceaseless toil Eugène Munch had developed himself into a remarkable mechanism. His hands and his feet obeyed him admirably. At the same time he had a touch that many better known organists might have envied. This touch had an extraordinary suppleness; it was quite inimitable. The quality of his playing impressed all the organists who heard him, and gave a strange stamp to his interpretations. One day he insisted laughingly that a good organist playing *fortissimo* ought to be able to create in the listener by his touch alone the illusion of *crescendi* and *diminuendi*. These words made clear the great importance he attached to touch in organ playing. This, however, escaped the novice. Another thing fascinated them more because the ear caught it more easily, namely the registration. Through constant experimentation he had come to know all the sonorous combinations of his rich instrument. For some time he kept at his organ a piece of paper on which he noted all the combinations to try, from the simplest to the most exotic. Audacities which at first thought seemed impossible succeeded admirably with him, thanks to his experience. For every theme in the Bach fugues he sought tirelessly the sonorous quality which it required. He was not content, however, to seek the sonorities suitable for the portions; what he wanted most of all was harmony among the sonorities, so that the piece would produce the impression of unity. This effect never ended for him: he corrected, noted, eliminated, only to begin again. One can get some idea of this work by casting an eye on his notebooks. Often one finds five or six registrations indicated for a single piece, and each registration is the result of long reflection and many trials. For years he worked on the registration of Bach's *Toccata*.[1] Twice he played this majestic work in organ concerts, as well as the *Passacaglia in C minor*. In private auditions he sometimes played the same thing ten times in succession, always working it over, forever changing and correcting, only to take it up another time afresh. The effects of registration he produced while accompanying solo instruments (I am thinking of the organ concerts given with Adolph Stiehle as soloist) were amazing. One day at one of these auditions, when Stiehle's marvelous violin blended with Monsieur Munch's exquisite playing, one of those present could not refrain from saying: "What a happy marriage!" How true! But in spite of these gifts of touch and registration, Eugène Munch would not have been this marvelous organist had he not added to his performance a taste for simple and exact phrasing, which was the connecting link between the two qualities we have just emphasized. In phrasing he was infallible. The component parts of it were simplicity, truth, and good taste. These things he never sacrificed to get registration effects. First of all he tried to bring out the great lines, which he called "the plastic art of organ playing." He delighted in comparing this effort with that of the artist who brings to birth from a block of marble the harmonious forms of human beauty. This quality made him majestic as an organ player, and, added to his talent as an accompanist, produced surprising effects. The last time he played at Strassburg—he took his place at the organ to play Bach's great *Mass*—his manner of bringing out the plastic structure of the first chorus surprised everyone who was able to appreciate this artistic feat at its true worth. It was like a revelation. His playing was fine and simple, or, rather, it was fine because it was simple. All effects which could prevent the unfolding of the beautiful forms in a work were odious to him, all those sonorities which obscured it were proscribed. "One must be a miser with organ *fortissimi*," he said one day. "The audience ought to feel the *fortissimo* before it comes; it should await it, watch for it, even hear it, before it is overwhelmed by it."

What delicacy, and at the same time what emotional veracity!

---

[1] Schweitzer does not indicate to which *Toccata* he is referring. C. R. J.

Refinement and simplicity, art and nature were happily wedded in this gifted organist, and gave to all his performances the classic beauty which everyone admired in his playing. He knew how to take advantage of everything, and detested nothing but pedantry; but that he detested profoundly. These were the characteristics which this organ virtuoso displayed in his playing; he was the equal of all his confrères, many of them he surpassed.

I have often asked myself why Munch did not travel, why he did not try by giving organ concerts in the great cities to make a name for himself which would have reverberated far beyond the frontiers of our Alsace. If anyone had asked him that question he would have certainly replied: I do not want to be a virtuoso, I want to be an organist. Those who heard him only in concerts never knew the real organist Munch, but those who heard him every Sunday in the church service understood him. The organ in a concert hall left him cold, the organ in a church concert interested him; the organ played for the service—that was his life and his happiness. It was then that he poured out his soul, bestowing all that was best within him as man and as artist. With exquisite feeling he knew how to select the pieces that best suited the nature of each service. He never permitted himself to be carried away into playing something that had no place within the frame of Protestant organ music. Nevertheless he was not narrow. I have heard him play in the service some of Beethoven's sonata adagios and some of the *courantes* [1] from Bach's clavier suites. With the organ, however, the deep emotions of Beethoven's adagios took on through his interpretation of them a severe and religious character, and the gaiety of Bach's *courantes* took on a majestic dignity. In preparation for his part in the service he used to play the chorale preludes from Bach's fifth volume. [2] He liked to use them in the service, and many people whose musical understanding did not at first appreciate the reverent beauty of these pieces learned to love them through hearing them over and over again in a receptive mood, and, thanks to the interpretation which Munch gave to them,

[1] The *courante* was one of the four traditional movements of the *suite*. C. R. J.
[2] Bach did not collect his organ works in numbered volumes. The final collection of choral preludes in the famous Bach *Gesellschaft* edition appeared in 1890, and was numbered Volume Four. C. R. J.

came to comprehend the spirit which the great Leipzig master had embodied in them. "When I am tired of all kinds of music," he said one day, "I turn to these chorale preludes and recover the inspiration of the art which I was vainly seeking." The inspiration of religious art: he knew how to transmit it to those who listened to it receptively. The consciousness of contributing to the beauty of the religious service, of translating religious ideas into music, of "preaching with the organ," as he used to say, was a more genuine satisfaction for the organist than long newspaper articles and the applause of concert goers would have been for the *virtuoso*. By virtue of his being an organist he was indeed a *virtuoso*, worthy of that title. The concert public forgets quickly; but a congregation edified by its organist cherishes an ineffaceable remembrance of him—it is as if the spirit of his life clung to the instrument and ennobled it.

If one may say that the Mulhouse organs educated the organist, it is not less true to say that the *Chant Sacré* molded the musician, the director. Between him and the *Chant Sacré* existed a relationship that was mutually instructive. Without this society he would never have had the opportunity to direct Bach's *St. Matthew Passion* or the *Requiem* of Berlioz. He would have continued to be a remarkable organist, but he would not have become the universal musician that he was. Without him the music lovers of Mulhouse would not have had this artistic center, where the beauty of religious music, both classical and modern, was revealed to a public which was accustomed to look elsewhere for entertainment of this kind. This development was the result of serious application over a period of many years, on the part of the director and on the part of members of the society. What a difference between the day when Monsieur Munch had a modest choir located in the corner to the left of the organ sing Bach's chorale "*Jesu meine Freude*" [Jesus, my joy], and the moment when, filled with noble pride, he nervously gave the signal for the attack upon the *Requiem* of Berlioz to a choir which was entirely equal to its high and difficult task.

It would be false to say that Eugène Munch had any special talent as director or orchestra leader. On the contrary, he had more difficulties to overcome than many another. This type of musical performance was completely unknown to him when he went to Mulhouse.

If he became the able director that our listening to the Bach's *St. Matthew Passion* or Berlioz' *Requiem* revealed to us, he reached this goal only by an enormous amount of work. He knew by heart the score he was to direct. Even during his last illness, when the *St. Matthew Passion* and the *Requiem* of Berlioz occupied his mind, his memory never played him false in regard to an *entrée* or a *recitatif*. He had moreover two qualities which were of great help to him in his development as a director, his modesty and his patience. He did not ask too much of the choir, and did not suddenly set before them tasks that were too difficult. He let them go on slowly and progressively to arrive the more surely at the ideal end he had planned: the rendition of the masterpieces of religious music. How many times before he felt it possible to put on the *St. Matthew Passion* did he not go over this admirable score by himself at the piano; how many times did he not beat out, as in a dream, the generous measure of the first chorus—then he closed the book: not yet, too soon. Concerning another of Bach's monumental works that he dreamed of doing one day, the great *Mass*, we say sadly: too late, alas. The performance of the *St. Matthew Passion* was one of the most beautiful days of his life. The evening following the rendition we were with him; his face shone like the face of a happy child. Then, suddenly, turning to his brother, he said: "If only my father were still with us to share my joy!" Certainly his father was the only one who could have completely understood his rapture.

One moment for rest, for rejoicing, then on again. It was often hard and sad, that onward march. The hall for rehearsals was not always a happy place for him. The elements of which the choir was composed often arrived before him untrained. He had to clothe himself with patience, begin again the work that he thought was already done. The false notes, the bad tones—his ear suffered from them after the weariness of the day. His remarks often had a nervous accent, a note of entreaty which betrayed his suffering, especially during the last winter, when he had fallen into a state of prostration that was realized only by his intimates. By patient endeavor he succeeded in giving cohesion to this choir with all its different elements. Its members did not come for the *Chant Sacré*; they supped in haste, they braved the bad weather—for Monsieur Munch. He knew it and was grateful, though his words did not interpret his feelings as he wished. He was not an orator, especially not one before the singers. His discourses at the first rehearsal of the season or after a concert were recitatifs punctuated by chords struck on the harmonium. Though not an orator, he had a very special gift for making himself understood in a few words, of painting the idea as it lived in him. "Ladies, weep!" he said one day at a rehearsal of Mozart's *Requiem*, when the choir did not get the intonation of the "Lacrimosa" as he wanted it. This was said with so much earnestness that they were impressed by it. The ironic imitations he often used were not always flattering, but he was excused for them because the final result pleased everyone.

The concerts given by the *Chant Sacré* were all successful, for nothing was neglected, and everything thoroughly prepared. Each concert showed progress. In these performances, as in his organ playing, the delicacy of his intonation and the brilliancy of his phrasing gave a special charm to the works he was directing. One felt that the personality of the director had entered into the choir. There was an interesting unity which gave an original stamp to the performance. The "Hallellujah Chorus" of the *Messiah* had more of nobility than of crushing grandeur. These constantly repeated successes formed a bond between the choir and its director which grew closer from day to day. The society saw in him not only its director, but also the artist whose needs it knew and understood. It knew that one cannot always produce without having from time to time some stimulation from without to give new ideas and to enlarge the horizon. They arranged for him to have this joy of seeing and hearing something new, of escaping from the isolation of his artistic life at Mulhouse, by sending him to Bayreuth.

The society certainly believed that they were giving him a great pleasure; but it was impossible for them to imagine the exuberant joy with which this journey filled him, for he was not the kind of man to reveal his intimate feeling in public. This journey to Bayreuth was the luminous point of his closing years. He went there already knowing by heart the scores; and there he lived through moments sublime. The orchestra, the singers, *Parsifal*, the *Twilight of the Gods*—he used to dream of them and speak of them often. It is impossible to see the Bayreuth letters without being moved by the happiness they breathe forth. I saw him a little while afterwards in the Munster Valley. We were sitting at the edge of the road; it was a beautiful day in September; the mists which softened the lines of the mountains announced already the coming of autumn. In our conversation we were exchanging our memories of Bayreuth. "Oh! those last pages in the *Twilight of the Gods* when all the themes of the trilogy are massed together and engulfed, when the world falls into ruins!" he said. "And *Parsifal*—such music, such chimes; they thrill you, they exalt you, they lead you upward, ever higher; you are no longer conscious of the earth, it disappears. . . . I must go back, I must see it again, I must hear it again." A year later, on that very day the solemn tolling of the bells of Niederbronn were announcing that the soul of an artist was rising ever higher and higher . . . and had left the earth. . . .

The journey to Bayreuth marked the beginning of a new epoch in the artistic life of Eugène Munch; he came back resolved to devote his talents not only to the masterpieces of religious music, but also to the great works of secular music. At Bayreuth he became aware of the close kinship between them. He felt keenly how much of religious character the masterpieces of tragic music had in themselves by virtue of their beauty. He foresaw already the possibility of giving the *Ninth Symphony* of Beethoven some day at Mulhouse. It was not by chance that during his last winter he was primarily occupied with Beethoven and Berlioz, the two representatives of secular music who have grafted the style of this music on religious music, one in his *Requiem* and the other in the *Missa Solemnis*. The forms and effects are borrowed from secular music; the subject and the sublime character make them religious. The speech that Monsieur Munch made at the first rehearsal of the *Chant Sacré* after his return from Bayreuth clearly reveals the new direction which from that moment his activity was to take. Then it was that he resumed the direction of the *Sainte-Cécile*, the members of which assisted him greatly in the performance of the *Requiem* of Berlioz. In his mind this change, or rather this development, had been in preparation for a long time, from the day when he began to study the esthetics of art. It was Lessing who first attracted him. He studied him with pleasure and often returned to him. The study of this great theoretician of the arts had a lasting and enormous influence upon his development. Here he caught a glimpse of the close bond between the law of beauty and the law of truth, which bring together the most widely diverse arts. Later, in his last years, the theoretical works of the French school particularly interested him. He read many of them, and his delight in them reconciled him to the modern art of France, with the recent musical compositions of which he had very little sympathy. The study of the works of Wagner before his journey to Bayreuth led him still farther into this kind of work. He took great satisfaction in studying the purely musical questions, and in setting them against a vaster background—that of art in general. There again he came into touch with Beethoven, who had tried to include the total literary and intellectual movement of his time in his musical interpretation. The score of the *Missa Solemnis* thrilled him, followed him—he did not study this work, he lived it. His last wish to direct it in its entirety with an orchestra, even if only at a rehearsal, was realized. This was pure delight for him. He did not hear the work as the choir and the orchestra gave it, he paid no attention in this rehearsal to faults—he heard Beethoven's *Mass* in its perfection. As he closed the score after the last rehearsal he said with great happiness: "It is not completely beautiful, but I have heard the work; now I know it." This was his last moment of artistic delight.

If he did not exercise upon the totality of the artistic life of Mulhouse the influence of which he had dreamed, if he departed too soon, not only for his own people but also for the task which was left for him to do in Mulhouse, it still remains true that what he created in this sphere cannot be lost, what he planted will bear its fruit some day. It is strange! On the last page of the score of Beethoven's *Missa Solemnis* he wrote in pencil the following quotation: "It is enough that the wave should drive the wave, and that the result should remain nameless." [1]

This was the public side of his artistic activity. It was happy. The great vexations, the sense of working without seeing results, were spared him. Alongside this ideal part of his artistic activity, he had to cultivate, like most of his colleagues, the prosaic side of the musi-

---

[1] *Genug, wenn Welle Welle trieb, und ohne Namen Wirkung blieb.*

cian's life. He gave lessons. He gave them all day long. His pedagogical talent, developed in the Strassburg normal school, assured
him of an incontestable superiority in teaching music. He used to
say laughingly that in order to give good lessons in music one had to
be first of all called to the profession of schoolmaster. The calm and
friendly manner in which he made his remarks quickly dissipated the
embarrassment and the timidity of his pupils, and tempered the
irony with which he was accustomed to season his criticism. His judgment was severe, but a word of praise from his mouth had all the
more value because of it. His lessons were always interesting. He was
in the habit of playing himself the pieces he gave pupils to study,
adding his appreciation and his historic and artistic comments. All
this made comprehension easier and invited reflection. In this way
the piece became familiar before one had studied it. Sometimes he
told what impression such and such compositions—especially the
preludes of the *Well–Tempered Clavichord*—had made on him
when he played them for the first time. His teaching bore the stamp
of his personality. His ambition was not to form violoncellists or
pianists; he wanted to make of his pupils musicians capable of loving, comprehending, and interpreting with good taste all kinds of
beautiful musical works. But he did not neglect to teach them musical structure. Each lesson began with a quarter of an hour of exercises; but the intellectual and artistic development outdistanced the
progress in technique. He often gave his pupil pieces to play that
exceeded his capacity, and then permitted him to leave them before
all the details had been perfectly mastered. "You will take them up
again later." It was a comfort to the pupil. In this way he avoided
excessive toil and weariness, and gave with every new piece new
courage. The end of the lesson was devoted to pleasant things. They
played at sight, four hands, a symphony. They turned the pages of a
score. What lovely memories! Sometimes during the closing period
—though very seldom—he would take his violoncello and have his
pupils accompany him, to initiate them in the art of accompaniment,
which he himself possessed in a remarkable degree. His pupils left
him regretfully. During the last years he was so overburdened with
care that the musical education of his own children became difficult.

He was compelled to select the early morning hours to give them their lessons. He witnessed only their first efforts. His children will not even have the memory of the charm which characterized the musical instruction of their father, they will not have enjoyed the quarter hours of delightful talk on the seat of his pedal piano, which the more advanced of his pupils will forever remember.

In spite of the unconstraint he sometimes displayed, he never became intimate with his pupils. This was one of the most striking traits in his character. He knew no true intimacy beyond the circle of his family, at least he never sought it. He had many friends at Mulhouse, but no comrades. The members of the *Sainte-Cécile*, which he directed at the beginning and at the end of his career, appreciated him, and on his side he greatly valued the sympathy and regard for him shown by the members of the society; but the frank comradeship between the director and the singers one finds in other societies did not exist. The nature of Monsieur Munch did not at all lend itself to this. In conversation he permitted himself to go up to a certain point, and then it was as if something prevented him from unveiling his ideas and his private opinions, as if he were afraid to reveal himself as he was. Certainly he did not lack interest in the questions discussed. One could talk with him about anything except politics. But he never knew the joy of debating with friends the topics of the hour. Only when he met again his former classmates did he let himself go completely. In his last years he narrowed even more the circle of his close friends. Except for the pupils he had known when they were young, he never used the intimate form of address.

This characteristic, this impossibility of giving himself, of letting himself be intimately known, was regrettable. Our friend missed that interchange of ideas of which he often felt the need. He was plunged into an isolation that led him to judge badly those who were outside the group of his intimates, and among whom he ran the risk of not being well understood. Must one attribute to this isolation the gloomy ideas that sometimes obsessed him, especially during the last winter, ideas that seemed to presage his untimely end?

To understand the reason for this we must return to the period of

his childhood. He had caught a cold which resulted in a permanent
ear trouble. Every illness, even every disturbance, was felt in this
weak spot in his constitution. The moral suffering which came with
the physical suffering weighed even more heavily upon him. In vain
he sought the treatment of a specialist. Each year the pains returned,
always with greater intensity. The thought of becoming deaf, of no
longer hearing his organ, of no longer being able to direct his society,
tortured him. During his last winter the pains became particularly
alarming. His lugubrious premonitions attracted him to Beethoven:
in the accents of Beethoven's music he found again his own anguish.
Might he also have shared the fate of the great composer, might he
have had to lay down with tearful eyes the director's baton, if premature death had not snatched it away from him? This idea may be a
feeble consolation for those who lament him.

He said little about his apprehensions. The allusions he made
during the rehearsals of Beethoven's *Mass* were incomprehensible to
those who did not know what it was all about. He sought and often
found forgetfulness in his work and in the life of his family. In the
midst of his loved ones, with his children on his knee, he was happy.
His home breathed calm, and a gracious simplicity idealized by music.
It reminded one of the home of J. S. Bach, his ideal. In 1891, at
Christmas, the *Chant Sacré* gave him as a gift the fine picture
"Family Worship in the Home of Bach." He used to show it to
everyone who came to visit him, and evinced his pleasure; which arose
not simply from the artistic conception of the picture, but also from
the remarkable resemblance between his own family ideal and the
scene pictured by the artist.

In Mulhouse his seriousness and his work gave a kind of austere
character to his family life. But what a happy moment was the departure for the vacations! They talked of it the whole summer. Finally the day arrived when the train transported the happy family to
Wissembourg, and later to Niederbronn. The vacation had a special
charm. The days usually passed gaily in perfect relaxation—the severe
father remained behind at Mulhouse.

During these vacations he became the joyous companion of his
children in their pleasures and excursions. Thanks to his camera, he

has preserved some of these charming scenes: the children on the grass, or harnessed to the baby carriage, and many others. His children will look at them some day, and with the memory of a happiness not yet understood will mingle a feeling of regret. The second half of his vacation was passed at Niederbronn; in the beautiful forests there he regained his strength. In the midst of his brothers and sisters, surrounded by memories of his youth, he gave himself over to the gaiety that one hardly ever saw at Mulhouse. This summer as well, we hoped that he would come back restored to health, but he did not himself have that confidence. He was very tired when he left Mulhouse. The last time he touched his organ, on a Sunday afternoon, he was so exhausted he could hardly finish the service. At Wissembourg he seemed to recover. He even recovered his gaiety on a Sunday he spent with his brother at Strassburg.

Upon his return to Wissembourg, the terrible illness which was to be fatal became slowly evident in an inexplicable weariness. As usual, he left Wissembourg at the end of August to pass the second half of his vacation in his mother's home. He arrived there on Saturday evening, the twentieth of August. Even his brother's children noticed the change in his features, and spoke about it to their father. The following Sunday he tried to take a walk with one of his sisters. He carried his little sister in his arm, but the burden became too heavy for him and he had to return. It was the last time that he saw the mountains of Niederbronn. In the evening they called the doctor; it was too late. He went to bed, never to get up again; to die surrounded by his own family in his dear Niederbronn. The sickness developed rapidly; fever seized him. He remained gentle and patient. The smallest service done for him touched him. The physician soon saw the dangerous turn which the sickness took, and which he diagnosed as typhoid. He ordered that his wife and his children, who had caught the same illness, should be separated from him. A moving exchange of words and news took place from one chamber to another.

He was resigned. Only his eyes betrayed his suffering and his anxiety. The Wednesday before his death he had a completely lucid evening. Seeing the end draw near, he requested his younger brother, the vicar at Strassburg, to administer holy communion to him. He asked that his family gather around his bed. He looked about to see if everyone was present. One of his sisters was missing; they had to look for her. Then he raised himself a little in his bed and began to speak to them—as if it were a dream, in short phrases, interrupted by long silences.

"My life has been short, but lovely through the art which I have cultivated. It will be more beautiful in heaven." These words set the mood for this touching meeting. He said farewell to each member of his family in turn, and for each he found an affectionate word. But he could not see his wife and his children. "I commend my wife and my children to you," he said. "Bring the children up simply; let a place be found for each of them suitable to his ability." The *Chant Sacré* was much on his mind, this choir he had created, and to which he had given the best of his strength. "You will be able to bring up my children," he said to those who surrounded him, "but it is the *Chant Sacré* that I leave with the greatest regret. Say farewell to them for me. There is no one at Mulhouse who will be able to continue my work in accordance with my ideas."

Then he passed into a state of delirium. Art glorified his last moments. Secular music did not enter the shadow of oblivion; he no longer knew anything but religious music. Even the Beethoven *Mass* did not have a place in his delirium. He directed the Berlioz *Requiem* and the *St. Matthew Passion*. The recitatifs, which he sang until his dry throat could no longer utter a sound, were present with him note by note. He wished to hear the chorales. "Find the children for me," he said, "so that they can sing the chorale." His sister and brother had to begin singing "When some day I must part." [1] This calmed him. And always he kept thinking of his choir. In his delirium he sat up suddenly and said, thinking that he was addressing the society: "I bid you farewell. Be happy. I can do no more." One morning when the regimental band, which was on manoeuvres at Niederbronn, was passing, he listened attentively. "How beautiful it was," he said, "when the chords lost themselves in the distance." When he heard the retreat, he remarked, "That is the signal for me to prepare." He spoke a great deal about his organ. "What will be-

[1] *Wenn ich einmal soll scheiden.*

come of my organ?" This question recurred ceaselessly. He consoled himself with the words: "I shall be an organist in heaven."

On Sunday, the fourth of September, about two o'clock in the afternoon, while the church bells were sounding, he gave up the spirit.

II

Widor's Pupil

ON June 18, 1893, Albert passed his final examinations at the Gymnasium and prepared to enter the University. He had already made up his mind that he would study philosophy, theology, and music. But before he went up to the University it was decided that he should spend a few weeks in Paris with Uncle Charles, his father's brother, and Aunt Mathilde. It was hoped that he might take a few lessons from the great organist of St. Sulpice, for whom Eugène Munch thought he was now ready. So this handsome young man, with the small moustache, the well-trimmed eyebrows, and the luxuriant dark hair set off for the great metropolis to visit Uncle Charles and to see Charles Marie Widor.

Widor had been born in Lyon in 1845, and at the age of twenty-five had been called to succeed César Franck as professor at the Conservatory of Music and to play at the great Church of St. Sulpice with its wonderful organs, which had been completely rebuilt and enlarged by Aristide Cavaillé–Coll. Widor was then at the height of his fame, known everywhere as a great composer. But he thought of himself first of all as an organist. Organ music was to him "a special kind of music, the music of the eternal, awakening thoughts of immortality." To play the organ, he said, was "to manifest a will filled with the view of eternity." That meant, therefore, to play Bach, for Bach had this mystic sense of the eternal. When Widor was not improvising or playing his own compositions he played Bach almost exclusively. He could not imagine any organ playing as sacred which was not somehow hallowed by certain preludes and fugues of Bach.

Armed with an introduction from Aunt Mathilde, Albert went at once to the great seventeenth-century church on the left bank of the

Seine, almost as large as the cathedral on the Ile de la Cité, in which the architects sought to replace the traditional Gothic elegance by a Greco–Roman majesty. Seeking out Widor, he asked if he might play for him. "Play what?" Widor asked. "Bach, of course," was the young Alsatian's reply. And suddenly Albert found himself sitting before the five manuals and the hundred speaking stops of what was universally regarded as the greatest organ in Europe, and probably the most beautiful in the whole world, the masterpiece of Europe's greatest organ builder.

It is needless to ask how well he played, for Widor, who seldom took any pupils outside the organ class of the Conservatory, not only consented to give him instruction, but to give it without charge.

By the end of October, Schweitzer was in Strassburg to begin his work at the University, where his student days continued until 1899. Strassburg was the administrative, military, and intellectual capital of Alsace. It was a fascinating place, with its old quais on the River Ill, its quaint bridges and square towers, its old palaces and timbered houses, its ancient fishermen's quarter called "la petite France." And above it all towered the glorious spire of the cathedral, when built the tallest structure erected by man since the time of the great pyramid. At once gigantic and delicate, fantastic and exquisite, the whole fabric was one magnificent upthrust of man's aspiration. And at sunset the rosy gray of the stone took on new and startling colors, so that it seemed like "petrified fireworks."

The University, with its faculties of medicine, law, letters, and Protestant theology was recognized on both sides of the Rhine as a great institution of learning, and students flocked to it from every land. It had a little of what has sometimes been considered the profound but confused thinking of German scholarship, illustrated by the remark of a Württemberg metaphysician to an Alsatian critic, "Now that you are no longer analyzing my books, I no longer know exactly what I think." Nonetheless it was a truly great university.

These student years were devoted to theological and philosophical studies, but with one exception all the interludes were musical. The exception was his year as a soldier in the army. He studied piano under Gustav Jacobsthal, professor of music at Strassburg, who had been a pupil of the musical theorist and composer Bellerman of

Berlin. Jacobsthal, Schweitzer said, "refused to acknowledge as art any music later than Beethoven's," but to him Schweitzer was indebted for excellent instruction in counterpoint.

His acquaintance with Wagner had begun with that memorable performance of Tannhäuser at Mulhouse, but at Strassburg all the operas except Parsifal were given under the direction of Otto Lohse; and as he witnessed them one by one his admiration for Wagner grew apace, until he began to venerate him as he did Bach. His knowledge of the operas was completed with a visit to Bayreuth in 1896, made possible by tickets presented to him by friends in Paris, and by his own self-abnegation. To make ends meet he ate but one meal a day.

It was worth it. Richard Wagner's great tetralogy, Der Ring der Nibelungen, with his last and crowning work, Parsifal, had been performed for the first time in 1876 in a building specially erected for the purpose. And then for a score of years it was not repeated. When in 1896 it was once more performed at Bayreuth, Wagner was dead, but Hans Richter, who had conducted the 1876 orchestra, was still there, and Heinrich Vogl, who had played Loki, and Lilli Lehmann, who had been one of the Rhine daughters, but who now played Brunnhilda. And Cosima Wagner was there—the daughter of Liszt and Wagner's second wife, whom he had married in 1870—imperiously directing the performances. Schweitzer was deeply moved by the opera, and particularly by the singing and acting of Loki, the god of fire, restlessly swinging his red cloak from one shoulder to the other, symbol perhaps of the flaming destruction of Valhalla, when the gods who have broken the moral law pass and give way to a new era of truth and love.[1]

On his way back from Bayreuth in the fall of 1896, Schweitzer stopped at Stuttgart to see the new organ which had been installed in the Liederhalle of the city. The instrument had been much praised; but when the organist of the Stiftskirche played a Bach fugue on it, and Schweitzer could not follow the separate voices, he was filled

[1] See Out of My Life and Thought, by Albert Schweitzer. New York: Henry Holt and Company, 1949, pp. 11 f. This book is Schweitzer's own account of his life up to 1929, and is supplemented by a postscript by Everett Skillings, which brings the story down to 1949. C. R. J.

with dismay about the modern organ. This he called his "Damascus at Stuttgart," and his experience led him to a careful study of organs and organ building, which bore fruit at the end of the following decade.

On May 6, 1898, Schweitzer passed his first theological examination, set by the government, and then spent the summer in the study of philosophy. In October he returned to Paris, to continue his philosophical studies at the Sorbonne, to write a thesis on the religious philosophy of Kant, and to study organ again under Widor.

At the same time he continued with his piano, studying under two teachers, J. Philipp, afterwards of the Conservatory, and Marie Jaëll–Trautmann, a fellow Alsatian and a pupil of Franz Liszt. The former was a capable but conventional teacher; the latter was developing her theory of touch, working from a physiological foundation, and educating the hand to feel and know. As teachers they did not think highly of each other but Schweitzer gained much from both.

With Widor, however, a collaboration soon began which far transcended the usual teacher-pupil relationship. It all came from a chance conversation. This is the way Widor reports it: "As Schweitzer knew very well the old Lutheran texts, I explained to him my uncertainty in the presence of certain works of Bach, my inability to comprehend certain chorales which passed abruptly from one order of ideas to another, from the chromatic to the diatonic scale, from slow movements to rapid ones, without any apparent logical reason. What can the composer's thought be, what did he want to say? If he breaks the thread of his discourse in this way, he must have another purpose than that of pure music, he must want to emphasize some literary idea . . . but how are we to know this idea?

" 'Simply by the words of the hymn,' replied Schweitzer, and then he recited the words of the chorale in question, which completely justified the musician, and showed the flexibility of his descriptive powers when dealing with the text, word by word; it had been impossible to appreciate the composition without understanding the significance of the assumed words.

"And so we began to run through the three collections to get at the exact meaning of things. Everything was explained and clarified, not only the great lines of the composition but even the slightest detail. Music and poetry were tightly clasped together, every musical design corresponding to a literary idea. In this way the works which I had admired up to that time as models of pure counterpoint became for me a series of poems with a matchless eloquence and emotional intensity.

"The first result of our analysis was our recognition of the necessity for an edition of the chorales carrying the literary text above the music which interprets it, an edition which would respect the order desired by the composer and follow the festivals of the church year.

"The second result was the recognition that a study of the symbolism of these three books was just as necessary, and that if any person was indicated to undertake this task it was Schweitzer himself because of his theological, philosophical, and musical gifts." [1]

Thus Schweitzer was launched by this chance conversation on a new and important enterprise. The little study at first contemplated grew into an important and laborious enterprise. Merely to assemble the texts was difficult, since many of them were no longer used in the Lutheran liturgy. The study of the chorales became inseparably involved with the study of the cantatas; a chapter had to be written upon the history of religious music in Germany; the biography of Bach was necessary for the interpretation of the work. And when Schweitzer expressed to Widor his consternation, confronted by the constantly growing proportions of this subject, and knowing full well the obligations of his diverse undertakings and his university career, Widor simply replied: "You are right, but what can one not do with order and the will?"

So began a work which was to consume much of Schweitzer's time for the next half dozen years, one of the fruitful undertakings of a rich life. Schweitzer "grasped the skirts of happy chance," and by a strictly ordered life and an inflexible will produced a masterpiece in the literature of music.

The rôles of teacher and pupil were reversed in this interpretation of Bach, but in other respects Widor remained the incomparable master, helping the young man to improve his technique, to achieve

[1] From *J. S. Bach. Le Musicien-Poète*, by Albert Schweitzer. Leipzig: Breitkopf & Härtel, 1908, pp. vii–ix.

plasticity in his playing, and to catch a vision of the architectonic, which is perhaps the greatest gift to the world of French music. Schweitzer gratefully remembers also Widor's solicitude for his health, and how at times, when he feared that his young Alsatian friend was hungry, he took him to the Restaurant Foyot near the Luxembourg and let him eat the kind of meal his means did not usually permit.

The spring of 1899 found him back in Gunsbach for a month. The family had moved into the new presbytery in 1890. Then in April he was in Berlin for four months to study philosophy and the organ. He was not impressed by the Berlin organists, who lacked, he thought, the plasticity which Widor emphasized. Neither was he impressed by the Berlin organs, which lacked the rich and beautiful tones of the masterpieces of Cavaillé–Coll in Paris or the Silbermann organs in Strassburg. But he liked the intellectual life of Berlin and its social freedom. In July he was back again at Strassburg.

At the end of July he took his degree in philosophy, and a few months later published his thesis on the religious philosophy of Kant. He then began to study for his licentiate in theology.

The work which Albert Schweitzer had promised Widor to do on the interpretation of Bach had become possible because of Schweitzer's association with the Strassburg brother of his first organ teacher. Ernest Munch had been a student of music in Berlin with his brother Eugène, and then had settled in Strassburg as organist of the church of St. William. Schweitzer became acquainted with him immediately after his arrival in Strassburg in 1893, and remained closely associated with him until he (Schweitzer) left for Africa in 1913. Ernest Munch was a passionate admirer of Bach, and had undertaken the task of having, one after the other, all the vocal works of Bach rendered by his small but excellent church choir. Schweitzer a few years later wrote a tribute to this choir: "Every great work of art, like every great idea, needs an atmosphere of enthusiasm for the revelation of its perfect beauty: the singers in the St. William choir, with their fine director, so devoted to the cult of Bach, created this atmosphere around me." [1]

[1] From *J. S. Bach. Le Musicien-Poète*, by Albert Schweitzer. Leipzig: Breitkopf & Härtel, 1908, p. v.

A special program was issued for the twentieth anniversary concert of this choir, on January 15, 1905, and for this program Albert Schweitzer wrote a brief unsigned history of the organization. A longer tribute to its director was written many years afterwards. The story of Ernest Munch and his choir, as told in these two articles, forms an important chapter in the musical life of Albert Schweitzer.

❦

THE STORY OF THE CHURCH CHOIR AT ST. WILLIAM [1]

THE St. William church choir was founded in December, 1884, by the organist of the church, Mr. Ernest Munch, who had returned from Berlin a short time before. The establishment of the choir was the first step in the practical realization of the vision he had caught from his teachers.

In his petition to the presbytery he gives as the purpose of the newly organized choir the presentation of music in the service of worship. Bach's works are written for the service of worship. As his cantatas and passions have no place in our order of service, and yet are essentially and unchangeably ecclesiastical in character, there is nothing to do except to arrange services of worship with the works of Bach, if they are to be rendered in the atmosphere in which they arose.

So the program of the new choir was outlined. The choir has been faithful to it up to the present day. At the same time its special character and justification in relation to the choirs already in existence were determined: the Chant Sacré, Stern's Oratorio Society, which first brought honor to the great church music in Strassburg, and the church choirs of Old St. Peter under the direction of G. A. Merkling and Young St. Peter under the direction of Professor von Jan.

The new choir performed for the first time during the Passion Week of 1885. Its beginnings were modest. It numbered about forty

[1] Zur Geschichte des Kirchenchors zu St. Wilhelm, from Le Choeur de St. Guillaume de Strasbourg, un Chapitre de l'Histoire de la Musique en Alsace, compiled by Erik Jung. Strassburg: P. H. Heitz, 1947, pp. 13–17.

members, who had been gathered from the parish of St. William and from elsewhere in Strassburg and vicinity. At present there are from 100 to 120 members.

The performances of the choral and orchestral pieces took place at first under the bell tower, as there was no room in the organ loft. So in 1894 the *St. Matthew Passion* was performed in two separate locations: the big chorus stood under the bell tower, the little antiphonal chorus with its soloists and its orchestra beside the great organ. But in the long run this arrangement was impossible, since it was acoustically bad to have the choir singing behind the congregation with very limited assistance from the organ. In 1896 the church council, which has always had the warmest regard for the choir, decided to have the great organ, one of Silbermann's creations, renovated by the organ builders, the Brothers Walcker, and at the same time moved back to the rear of the choir loft, in order to provide space in front of it for the choir and orchestra. The city contributed generously to the costs, so that since 1898 the St. William choir has had a place in the organ loft that is ideal in every respect, in the sight of the congregation and under the best imaginable acoustical conditions. Widely traveled artists have declared that they have hardly ever seen another place as perfectly adapted for the performance of church music as St. William Church.

The performances in the church of St. William have been conceived as concerts for the people, and therefore in principle free. Until the middle of the nineties there was no charge for admission to any place, and to defray the costs the choir had only the freewill offerings left by people going out. That meant, however, that no distinguished soloists could ever be called in; and the lack of them became all the more noticeable as the work of the choir became more perfect. It seemed, therefore, to the leaders of the choir, President Küss, the General Secretary of the Board of Directors of the churches of the Augsburg Confession, and the director, an unavoidable necessity to reserve places in a part of the nave of the church at one mark each, and so to assure the choir of a fixed income. This measure turned out well, and did not injure the popular character of the performances. Nonetheless, for many concerts the costs were not covered. To meet this deficit the *Statthalter* Prinz zu Hohenlohe-

Langenburg made goodly contributions. The cost of giving a cantata runs each time to 600 to 700 marks, a Passion 900 to 1000.

The choir at St. William has a special significance for ecclesiastical music in Alsace–Lorraine, in that its leader is at the same time the teacher of Protestant church music at the Conservatory. A number of excellent young organists have learned to direct and accompany Bach's works in the choir of St. William, and choirs have been founded in a number of Alsatian cities, whose leaders got their inspiration from the St. William choir. The choir always offered its assistance to all projects for the rendering of church music. From 1889 to 1899 many of its members assisted in the concerts of the *Chant Sacré*, which at that time was being conducted by Mr. Munch, and produced the *C major Mass* of Beethoven, the *Creation* of Haydn, the *Samson* of Händel, the *Paul* and *The Hymn of Praise* of Mendelssohn, the *Deluge* of Saint–Saëns and the *Manasseh* of Hegar.

Together with the academic church choir the St. William choir gave in the presence of the composers the first performance of the *Passion* and the *Harvest Festival* of Heinrich von Herzogenberg and the oratorio *Through Darkness to Light* by Rauchenecker. It shared also in the perfomance of the sixteen-part *Mass* by Grell, given by all the church choirs of the city, seven hundred voices, under the direction of Mr. Munch at St. Thomas on July 27, 1902.

And now the choir of St. William looks back upon half a generation of work. Only a few of those who helped to found the society are still among its members; many of them who shared with joy in their early successes, advising and encouraging the director, have gone to their rest. The choir suffered a particularly heavy loss in the death of the organist, Eugène Munch of Mulhouse, who had played the organ part for the more important concerts from the beginning. He died in 1898. His successor as organist for the choir was Doctor Schweitzer, his pupil.[1]

Among the regular soloists of the choir at St. William may be named the following ladies: Miss Perrin, Mrs. Adels von Münch-hausen, Miss Ast, Miss Kohlrausch, Miss Marais, Mrs. Hirn–Wolf, Mrs. Altmann–Kuntz, Miss Hedwig Mayer, Mrs. Geist, Miss Han-

[1] This article, written by Dr. Schweitzer himself, was unsigned, and so he speaks of himself in the third person. C. R. J.

nig, Miss Hackenschmidt; and the following gentlemen: Georges Boeswillwald, Wolfgang Geist, Theodor Gerold, Ricard Fischer, Robert Kaufmann, Epitalbra, Fritz Haas, Karl Weckauff, Anton Sistermans, Kalweit, Adolf Walter.

Special thanks are due the members of the municipal orchestra who have participated with artistic devotion in the Bach concerts at St. William, many of them since the organization of the choir.

Special thanks are due also to Mr. Frick, the member of the church council who assumed responsibility for the arrangements and oversight of the concerts.

The church choir gave each year four or five rather important concerts. A Bach Passion was always given every Passion Week. Sixty of Bach's two hundred cantatas have been given, a number reached in very few cities. Besides the works of Bach, the choir has performed pieces by Mendelssohn, the *Psalms* by Schütz, *The Death of Jesus* by Graun, the *Reformation Cantatas* by Becker, the *Dettingen Te Deum* and the *Messiah* by Händel, the *Requiem* by Mozart, and the *German Requiem* by Brahms.

Thus it has been granted to the choir to give itself by its earnest devotion to the popularizing of the noblest in church music. A devout congregation always fills the church at its concerts, the press supports the project with warm recognition, and the leader of the choir has won honorable distinction by being appointed director of music, and by being given the title of professor.

May it be granted to him and his faithful singers to continue in the future with their great task, working incessantly upon our generation with the ennobling influence of pure art, with constant self-criticism and selfless striving.

❦

ERNEST MUNCH, AS I REMEMBER HIM [1]

WHILE I was Eugène Munch's pupil at Mulhouse, I often heard him speak of his brother Ernest at St. William. I met the latter for the first time about 1892, when he came to a concert Eugène was giving at Mulhouse, where Eugène was an organist. The two brothers were very different. The Mulhouse brother [Eugène] was far from possessing the temperament of the Strassburg brother, but in his own way he was just as great an artist. His interpretation of music was based upon extensive and comprehensive study.

In the autumn of 1893 I came to Strassburg to study theology, after having been before that the pupil of the Parisian organist Widor. Ernest Munch received me with great kindness. In a very short time we were addressing each other familiarly. He was living at that time on the quai St. Thomas. I often went in the evening to visit him with his brother Gottfried, who was also living as a student of theology in the seminary of St. Thomas, and then we played music together well into the night.

It was Eugène Munch who accompanied in the St. William choir concerts, and came from Mulhouse for that purpose. At the rehearsals it was I who played. Later, when Ernest Munch's brother could no longer come for the concerts, I accompanied for those too. Munch had me play also as a soloist. This took place for the first time, if I remember correctly, in St. William at one of the concerts that were given regularly at this time for the ministers' conference at the beginning of the summer. The pastors from every part of Alsace, with hardly an exception, gathered for this occasion, and were grateful to Munch for these concerts.

During these years after 1894, the St. William choir began to realize the plan of its director to interpret, not only the few cantatas of Bach which were already pretty well known, but also to give little by little those that were not known. At that period the enterprise

[1] From Le Choeur de St. Guillaume de Strasbourg: un Chapitre de l'Histoire de la Musique en Alsace, compiled by Erik Jung. Strassburg: P. H. Heitz, 1947, pp. 51–62.

was a bold one, for it was necessary first of all to train the public just to understand Bach. One member of the municipal orchestra, who regularly took part in the St. William concerts, coined for Munch the sobriquet the "cantata man." It is probable that we produced in the course of those years a good many cantatas that had not been played since the death of Bach. Little by little our auditors arrived at the point where we were able to demand of them some comprehension of the serious and less accessible compositions of Bach.

The very first cantata of Bach played at Strassburg before 1870 was *Thou Shepherd of Israel, Hear* [1] (No. 104). The organist Théophile Stern of the Temple Neuf interpreted it with his choir, called, I believe, *Chant Sacré*. I know from my father, who was a student at that time, and sang in it, what difficulty the choir had in familiarizing itself with this style, which was so strange to it.

How many times during those days did Munch, his brother Gottfried, and I gather around a table in the evening to study together a volume of cantata scores in the great edition of Bach, regretting our inability to play them all at the same time! Before we separated for our vacations at the end of the summer we had chosen the four cantatas which were to be given in the concert on Reformation Sunday. It was often necessary to copy the parts, for we could not yet procure them in print.

One great difficulty arose from the arrangement of the participants. Choir and orchestra had to find places in the narrow space between the organ and the wall of the church on the St. William street side. The number of artists was therefore too limited. But the effect of the choir was marvelous from this location.

When a greater number of performers was necessary, only the space beneath the tower was available. This had one disadvantage: it was necessary to play behind the audience, and to be satisfied for the accompaniment with the little single manual organ which was there.

I remember very well the performance of the *St. Matthew Passion*, which took place about 1894. As is well known, this work requires two choirs and two orchestras. But Munch dared to separate the two

---

[1] *Du Hirte Israel, höre.* C. R. J.

choirs and the two orchestras—the first choir with its orchestra under the tower, and opposite them the second choir and orchestra beside the great organ. Gottfried Munch accompanied on the little organ under the tower, and I played on the great one. In spite of the distance we obtained a perfect ensemble. But the audience was still a bit disconcerted by listening to music coming from two opposite sides. For us the experience was very interesting.

The only satisfactory solution of the problem of arrangement involved the setting back of the organ—there was still room behind it—in order to make sufficient space for the choir and orchestra in front of the audience on the platform so enlarged. Unfortunately this solution involved the transformation of the fine old Silbermann organ. I personally regretted this very keenly. This organ, which had been maintained and finely restored by the Alsatian organ builder, had a marvelous sonority. I still remember the amazement of Pirro, a pupil of Widor, who acquired later a great reputation as a musicologist, when I had him mount the organ bench as he passed through Strassburg in 1895. He kept repeating, he who knew the splendid Cavaillé organs in Paris, "I have never heard such sonority!" Even in the *forte* the organ possessed a sweet and limpid sonority. It rendered the Bach fugues with marvelous clarity. I remember one evening going to the church when Munch was rehearsing for a concert. He was playing a *mezzoforte* passage on the flute stops. I was so entranced by the beauty of the tone that instead of going up to the organ loft, as I had intended to do, I sat down in a pew to listen in silence.

The cost of moving and changing the organ—they wished to enlarge and modernize it at the same time—was so high that the project could not be carried out without a subvention from the municipality. In the securing of this many difficulties were encountered, and it was not until 1896 that they were overcome. I can still see Munch when he brought me the long-awaited news: "Now, my little Schweitzer, it is going to be done; now we shall have the space we have needed so much."

For the first concert on the enlarged platform, the Bach *B minor Mass* was given, if I remember rightly. Munch of Mulhouse accompanied this performance (February 5, 1898).

Another difficulty in connection with our concerts arose from financial problems. In principle, the concerts had to be popular and free. But how were we to meet the expenses? How were we to cover the deficits? Therefore each concert brought discussions with Mr. Frick, the treasurer of the church. These were complicated by the fact that the consistory of the church wanted very much to have a choir to sing the church office on the festival days, but showed very much less interest in the numerous concerts the choir wanted to give. As both Munch and Frick had rather violent tempers, there were on several occasions collisions which threatened the activity, nay even the existence of the choir. Finally I was charged with the disagreeable negotiations with Mr. Frick.

I always let him talk, and then each time I would say to him, "From the point of view of the church and of the consistory you are evidently quite right. In your place I would talk exactly as you do. Nevertheless, from the point of view of the choir, Mr. Munch also has some justification. And we should take his views into account. Now we must reconcile ourselves to the fact that the choir, as Mr. Munch conceives it, is not simply a church choir, but a choir which also sings religious music apart from the church services. And St. William should be a little proud of a choir which sets such noble tasks before it. Where is there a church choir in Alsace of which the newspapers speak so often?" In this way the conversation would go on until Mr. Frick became a little more conciliatory, and with a little grumbling would agree to what we were asking. When we did not come to an agreement, we adjourned the deliberations to a more favorable moment, anticipating in this way the procedure now observed in international conferences. When a little later Robert Will was appointed to St. William, Munch found in him great understanding of the efforts of the choir, and a support so powerful that from that moment the discussions with the treasurer of the church, which continued to be my responsibility, became less difficult.

Moreover, financing the concerts became much easier, because it was decided to make a charge of one mark for the better places (about half of them), and to give free admission to the others. In this way the principle of free admission was preserved, and still an opportunity was given to those who wished to help with the expenses of the concert to assure themselves of a good seat. We continued to take a collection for expenses at the door, and the friends of our concerts had a chance to assist us with their gifts. We had at this time devoted supporters among the members of the teaching faculty at the University. The material support of the concerts was thus fairly well assured.

Naturally the means did not suffice for us to engage only soloists of the first rank. Nonetheless, even those of less reputation often gave distinguished interpretations, when they were wise enough to profit by the fact that Munch studied the scores with them. Neither did we have the means to engage only instrumentalists from the municipal orchestra, so we had to be content with the assistance of good amateurs—as was customary in the time of Bach. They were available in sufficient number.

Because our resources permitted us to pay for only two rehearsals with the orchestra—a first rehearsal and a general one—Munch arranged, on the three or four Sundays that preceded a concert, for what he called organ rehearsals between five and seven o'clock. The organ took the part of the orchestra to familiarize the choir with the instrumental accompaniment. At the same time the amateurs who were to complete the orchestra had an opportunity to practise their parts.

The members of the municipal orchestra who assisted at our concerts were full of enthusiasm. The orchestra soloists were excellent. I can still see them: Hofhansel the oboe player, Birkright the flutist, who was still playing with the wooden flute, the first violinist Benno Walter, and the violoncellist Schmidt.

What marvelous musical ardor prevailed at these rehearsals! Munch did not have to pay any attention to the choir, for the choir knew its business; he was able to concentrate exclusively on the orchestra. He conducted the rehearsals with much care and sensitiveness, and never wearied the performers. It was evident that he had prepared these rehearsals down to the last detail. He never lost time with secondary matters, but devoted all his efforts to the essential thing. This is the reason the attention of the performers never faltered, however long the rehearsals lasted.

We had a curious experience with one of the first concerts that followed the enlargement of the gallery. The performance, in our opinion, had been a great success. But the newspaper critics did not express an appreciation equal to our own; their reserve indicated that not everything had been perfect. As we thought it over we came to the conclusion that this might have been because the musical critics were all seated together, so that if one shook his head or puckered his eyebrows at some passage, none of his colleagues would risk giving a completely favorable report for fear of compromising himself. From that time on we saw to it that the critics did not sit together, and thus had their impartiality safeguarded; and this had a good result in their articles. The principle was once more proved that nothing must be left to chance.

The most important of the musical critics attached to the Strassburg newspapers at that time was Doctor Altmann. He had a mania for never expressing complete satisfaction, and for exaggerating the faults in detail, to prove that he was a connoisseur of music. This procedure irritated Munch, and more than once I had to come to Altmann's defence, when Munch became too angry with this quibbler, and proposed to tell him what he thought of him or have some one else do so. At heart Altmann was well aware of the worth of our enterprise, to which he owed after all his own excellent acquaintance with Bach. His wife, an admirable contralto, educated at the Conservatory of Strassburg, was one of the appreciated soloists at St. William.

We should not pass over in silence the excellent treatment we received from the Strassburg press. The newspapers took all the articles, even though very long, which we sent them to acquaint the public with the works we were going to play. For some years I was the accredited reporter for the St. William concerts, and many a time I sent to the papers veritable *feuilletons* upon the works of Bach. Never was one of them refused, even when it was delivered at the last moment. What this good press meant to us I did not fully appreciate until I became cognisant of the difficulties the John Sebastian Bach Society of Paris encountered in getting publicity for their concerts.

Let us render homage to Madame Munch also, who, at a time when her children were still very small and demanded all her atten-

tion, collaborated with the choir for years by taking care of the constantly growing musical library. On the days of the concerts she
undertook still another duty. After the performance the soloists and
the other participants were always invited to dinner at the Munches'.
The final chord had hardly ceased to sound before Madame Munch
hastened to return to her home to prepare for her guests. What did
she not do to permit her husband to exercise this generous hospitality,
which was for him a necessity! We, who had a chance to appreciate
her activities close at hand, were filled with admiration for her gentle
and distinguished manner in everything. Hers was a remarkable personality, with a great nobleness of soul.

The familiarity with the Bach scores and the practice in interpreting his works which I had acquired through association and collaboration with Munch, made it possible for me to accede to Widor's
wish when he begged me in 1901 to undertake a study of Bach and
his music with the French public in mind. It is to the St. William
choir and its director that I am indebted for the ability to write this
book, which appeared in French in 1904, and afterwards in German
and English. I expressed my gratitude in the preface.

When I published in 1906 my work on the German and French
organ builders, I dedicated it to Munch.

Somewhere around 1904 we journeyed together to Frankfort to get
acquainted with Siegfried Ochs, who was giving Bach's *Mass B minor*
there with the help of the Cecilia Society. Siegfried Ochs was trying
to do in Berlin and Frankfort the same thing that we were trying to
do in Strassburg, but with much superior resources. He had at his
disposal choirs, orchestras, and soloists of the very first quality. He
did not have to worry about the expenses incurred by his concerts,
and could have as many orchestra rehearsals as seemed good to him.
From one point of view, we were better off at Strassburg than he was:
for the interpretation of the religious music of Bach we had the
church which it required, while Siegfried Ochs had to interpret it in
concert halls. The hours that we spent with this man, who was a
remarkable connoisseur of Bach and shared our enthusiasms, were
all too short. During the night of the concert, which was perfect in
every respect, we had to take the train in order to be at our posts in
Strassburg the next morning.

Some years before, in the neighborhood of 1898, Munch had gone to Breslau to play Bach there. An orchestra conductor from that city had been present at a Bach concert given by the chorus of the Strassburg Conservatory. Munch was at the organ, and his manner of accompanying pleased the visitor so much that he called him to Breslau to give a Bach concert. Munch cherished a very happy memory of this journey.[1]

Among the concerts of church music which Munch directed outside of St. William, I remember more particularly the Grell *Mass* at St. Thomas, and Händel's *Israel in Egypt* at the Temple Neuf. For the Grell *Mass*, this belated masterpiece in the purely vocal style, written for sixteen voices *a cappella*, all the church choirs of Strassburg came together under the direction of Munch. On this occasion he showed himself a past master in the art of directing a great vocal ensemble. Rehearsals were not spared, since we had no orchestral expense to consider.

For the performance of the *Israel*, the choir and orchestra were placed on a platform erected around the altar of the Temple Neuf. If my memory serves me, the concert was given in this church because there was not room enough at St. William. Although the exclusive study of Bach might have interfered with our appreciation of Händel, both of us, during the preparation of this work, came under the spell of this music, much more simple and direct, but still so expressive. As Munch did not want to dispense with the organ, I had to accompany at the great organ, at the opposite end of the nave from the altar. I could see the conductor of the orchestra only in a big mirror placed very close to the organ and brilliantly lighted, and I had to try in my playing to be always a little ahead of the time beaten by Munch, in order that the organ, in spite of the distance that separated it from the choir and the orchestra, should be perfectly synchronised with the ensemble. This *tour de force* succeeded to the satisfaction of the orchestra conductor, but it took days for me to recover from the fatigue resulting from the effort.

When the post of director of the Conservatory and conductor of the municipal orchestra became vacant upon the death of Franz

[1] Performance of the *St. Matthew Passion*, March 16, 1898.

Stockhausen, Munch became a candidate for the office, and as such conducted one of the concerts of the municipal orchestra. That evening he outdid himself. The way in which he rendered a Brahms symphony remains for me unforgettable. The public was carried off its feet with admiration. The next day the newspapers said, "If the choice had depended upon last evening's audience, Munch would have been selected." But we who were in touch with Mayor Schwander in this matter knew that he had other plans. A petition covered with signatures addressed to him in favor of Munch did no good. It was in vain that some of us, among others Doctor Pfersdorff and I, spoke to him in Munch's favor. He called Hans Pfitzner to the vacant post. But at the same time he created for Munch, as he had promised, a privileged position at the Conservatory, which gave him a great deal of freedom with respect to the director. Moreover, when Munch came to know Pfitzner he felt so profound an admiration for him and his work that he forgave him for having been chosen.

As for us, we were happy that Munch had come to know, during the weeks of his candidacy, in what esteem the people of Strassburg held him.

For some years I took his place at the organ of St. William's for marriages and funerals, when he was busy at the Conservatory and at the Protestant *Gymnasium*, where he was the singing teacher. In the same way I served as a substitute for the organist Schalz and his successor at the Temple Neuf, where I greatly loved the fine organs. They had been built by the Maison Merklin of Paris, and were sacrificed unfortunately for the sake of the church heating.

The advanced courses for organists, which were given for many years in the second half of July at Strassburg, made both of us a great deal of work and gave us much satisfaction. For these courses some fifteen teachers received a vacation, which permitted them to profit from the instruction of Munch for a period of two weeks. He insisted upon hard work. They had to turn these days to account in perfecting their organ work. I collaborated with Munch in giving some of the instruction, and in interpreting the works of French and contemporary organists. The evenings were given up to friendly gatherings, in the course of which Munch became the comrade of these teacher-organists. He had a gift for friendship. That was what attached so many men to him. I have always admired his simplicity, his naturalness, his cordiality.

From the beginning of the new century, I often had to give up my place at the St. William organ. The post of accompanist which I accepted, in succession to Guilmant, with the Jean Sebastian Bach Society in Paris, and other duties, monopolized more and more of my time. When in 1905 I began my medical studies, I had to husband my time and my strength still more, and so had to renounce many of the activities which I should have loved to continue.

Moreover, I thought it my duty to give place to the younger men, that they might have, as I had had, a chance to accompany the choir at St. William's and so gain knowledge and experience. Adolphe Hamm, who later became organist at the cathedral of Basle, was the first to succeed me. I have a vivid recollection of the remarkable way in which he accompanied the *Christmas Oratorio* of Bach. He was followed by others among the younger and better pupils of Munch.

Among the students of the older generation, Niessberger, the organist at the Reformed Church, was closest to Munch. Following the example of his master, he had founded a choir and organized distinguished concerts, which lent themselves to the progressive unfolding of his natural talent as an orchestra conductor.

One of the most remarkable among the Munch pupils belonged to this same generation—Émile Rupp, who was vitally interested in the manufacture of organs and possessed extensive knowledge in this field.

As an organist and as an orchestra leader Ernest Munch established a school in Alsace. It is thanks to him above all else that the Protestant churches have gifted organists and choir leaders. Others continue faithful to his ideal, because of the impetus they received from him. He accomplished the work to which he was called.

One incident at the beginning of a concert at St. William's impressed me very much at the time—I no longer remember in just what year it was. Munch was with us before the concert, in the room under the organ gallery where we left our vestments. He gave us the signal to go up and take our places. Upstairs the choir, the orchestra, and the soloists waited for him to mount his platform and to give the signal to begin. The time came, but he did not appear. As we continued to wait, one of the members of the choir asked me to play an organ number to quiet the impatience of the audience, which we began to feel. I did so. Finally twenty minutes later, Munch arrived and began the concert. He seemed pale and exhausted. Only little by little did he recover. We learned afterwards that he had been taken by a severe colic, and that this had not been the first time he had suffered such pains. This attack heralded, some years in advance, the malady to which he was later to succumb.

III

Vocation and Avocation

ON December 1, 1899, Schweitzer was appointed a deacon at the church of St. Nicholas. His mother's half brother, Albert Schillinger, for whom he was named, had previously been minister there, but had died young. His mother had been very fond of Uncle Albert. When he died he was buried in the cemetery of Saint–Gall, and later Uncle Louis, with whom Albert Schweitzer had lived in Mulhouse, and who spent his declining years in Strassburg, was also laid to rest there.

Strassburg had been converted to Protestantism in 1559. From that time on no mass was said even in the cathedral until Louis XIV restored it to the Catholic church. The city was therefore an important evangelical center. The church of St. Thomas, with its great square tower, was just behind the theological foundation where Schweitzer had been a student, and was the most important of the Protestant churches in the city, but St. William, where Schweitzer was collaborating with Ernest Munch, was not far away, and St. Nicholas, to which Schweitzer was called as deacon, was also rather near on the other side of the River Ill. St. Nicholas was not the most important church in the city, yet it was a significant post of service. It did not conform to any particular architectural style, and one who lived beside the building said that its tower was more like a great pigeon house than the spire of a church. To this church Schweitzer went. Technically he was no longer a student.

His second theological examination was passed on July 15, 1900, but not with great credit to Schweitzer, who was too busy with other things to review his studies. Schweitzer remembers his dismal showing in hymnody. When asked about the authorship of one hymn, writ-

46

ten by Spitta, the famous poet of Psalter and Harp, Schweitzer said that he did not think the hymn was important enough for him to bother about the author. The poet's son, Professor Friedrich Spitta, was one of his examiners!

The licentiate in theology was conferred on July 21, 1900, and on September 23 he was ordained as curate of St. Nicholas. In addition to his preaching he had to conduct a confirmation class three times a week, but often he was free on Sunday, and would preach for his father back in Gunsbach. In 1901 he published an important study on the Lord's Supper; the same year he was made provisionally principal of the Theological College of St. Thomas, from which he had just graduated; in 1902 he received an appointment as Privatdozent and began lecturing at the College; and in 1903 he received a permanent appointment as principal.

With lecturing and writing and preaching the ordinary man would have been busy enough, but Schweitzer still found plenty of time for his music. There were no confirmation classes in the spring and fall, and by arranging for pulpit supplies when necessary Schweitzer could be away for three months in the year. At Easter he usually spent a month with Widor in Paris; in the fall he usually spent two months in the Munster Valley.

The Paris Bach Society was founded in 1905 by six musicians, two of them being Widor and Schweitzer. Gustave Bret, the conductor, insisted that Schweitzer should play the organ part in every concert; and from that time on he made many trips to Paris for the winter series of concerts. These were precious visits, bringing him the friendship of many distinguished people, including Romain Rolland; who was a musician as well as a writer, with notable books on Beethoven, Händel, early French music, and so on. It was he who organized the International Society of Music; and his great novel Jean–Christophe was a musical romance.

At the home of Uncle Charles and Aunt Mathilde Schweitzer most frequently met Widor and other members of Paris society; and the artificiality of that society depressed him. Its rigid conventions contrasted painfully with what was at that time the freer air of German life. His impressions he set down in an article which is included here because it gives a picture of the social conditions of that epoch.

Happily this day has largely passed, and what Schweitzer has written should be considered only as a historical socio-musical study.

❧

THE CHORUS IN PARIS [1]

WHEN my friends and I a few years ago started to organize a Bach Society in Paris to produce the Passions and cantatas, people everywhere expressed the opinion that sooner or later our enterprise would certainly go on the rocks, since it was impossible to keep a good choir together very long in Paris. When we said that what succeeded elsewhere should certainly be possible there as well, we received in reply only sympathetic shrugs of the shoulders.

The fact is that none of the choruses composed of society volunteers has enjoyed a very long existence in Paris. Usually they died with their founders, if not before. For the most part they were not purely Parisian organizations, but were undertaken by the Alsatian community resident in the capital city. This is the reason that Paris had the best mixed chorus in the middle of the eighties, when the Alsatian community and its adherents from the departments of the east, by virtue of the exodus from Germany after the year 1870, had achieved the greatest importance, and had taken a leading place in politics and intellectual culture. At that time the "Concordia," founded by the engineer Fuchs, was flourishing. Paris was indebted to it for its first acquaintance with the Bach passions and cantatas. The most distinguished musicians were interested in it and dedicated their talents to it. All at once, however, its splendor departed. The group which backed the organization was not important enough to bring to it in the long run the necessary vitality. The organization itself was not able to make the transition from the status of a personal creation to that of an independently organized society possessing objective stability. Its rich library of music was offered for sale at a ridiculously low price some years ago without finding a

[1] "*Warum es so schwer ist einen guten Chor in Paris zusammenzubringen*" [Why It Is So Difficult to Organize a Good Chorus in Paris] in *Die Musik*. Berlin: Bernhard Schuster, Bülowstrasse 107, Volume IX, No. 19.

buyer, which proves that no efficient chorus had taken the place of
the "Concordia."

Only those choruses have survived that were composed entirely, or
almost entirely, of paid professional singers. The best of them belong
to the Society of Conservatory Concerts, the Colonne Society, and
Vincent d'Indy's *Schola Cantorum*. They get their recruits from the
church singers who at the same time belong to the choruses of the
great operas.

None of those choruses has had a real success. Colonne had the
greatest success with his Berlioz' *Damnation of Faust*. That at best
they remain rather mediocre is not the fault of the voices available.
These are at times even excellent, especially in the chorus of the
Conservatory concerts. But money and time are lacking for the thorough study of the works. For each rehearsal one must count on from
three to five francs a singer. That means for a chorus of from eighty
to ninety people four to five hundred francs. Under these circumstances a profound analysis of the works is impossible. The *Messiah*
or the *St. Matthew Passion* must be produced often after three or
four rehearsals. The routine work of the professional singer is of
course superficially good; gross mistakes seldom occur even after the
hastiest study. But dynamic and depth are lacking.

The discipline is not very rigorous. It has always impressed me how
little the conductor is heeded even in the chorus of the Conservatory concerts. More than three-quarters of the singers watch their
notes from beginning to end for lack of discipline and skill. The
director must make all possible concessions to them. The rehearsals
are usually conducted with the singers seated. Men and women
often keep their hats on. Intermittent pauses are numerous. And
under no circumstances may the time agreed on be lengthened.

But it is morale more than anything else that is lacking. The sense
of unity produced by a common goal is essential in a genuine chorus.
There is no sign of this in the Parisian choruses of professional singers. Moreover, the deep emotion and inspiration that spring from
the long and devoted study of a work and give warmth and fire to
it are supremely wanting. Of the joy and pride which so often enable
mediocre choruses to rise to artistic heights in their performances
there is no trace here. In art, as in all places where the realm of the

spirit begins, there are things which only the free man is able to accomplish.

Parisians are well aware that their choruses are only relatively good, and that the ideal is not to be reached in this way. When anyone comes back from Germany he praises, along with the railways of the neighboring country, its choruses. When a foreign chorus is heard in Paris, which does not happen very frequently, the public and the critics often give rein to an uncritical enthusiasm. The feeling is very widespread that the lack of good choruses means the loss of something of enormous worth to the musical life of the capital.

The need is felt, the enthusiasm is present, but the difficulties remain the same. They lie in the nature of Parisian life.

A young girl of a good family in proper Paris circles cannot belong to any chorus. She is not permitted to go out unaccompanied. Life is frightfully complicated by this. From the day when her daughter is fourteen years old, the Paris mother no longer knows any life of her own, but sacrifices herself for her child. She plans and plans to find the time to accompany her, and to make possible numerous excursions. Only those who have lived in these circles and have got an insight into such households can know how difficult life can be made by the rigid observance of the principle that a young, unmarried woman under thirty may not go out alone. If it is a matter of an evening engagement the difficulties multiply. Ordinarily this is possible only in houses where at least two servants are present. Parisians believe that a girl should be seen in the evening only in the company of her parents; it is absolutely unthinkable that she should be found alone in any other company. This is one of the horrors of that emancipation that "Americanism" brings with it.

It is evident, then, that a mixed chorus in Paris may not count on the younger women; they are still in a dependent status. Only such women can be counted on as have won their freedom through the years or through marriage. But even in such cases, going out in the evening constitutes such a difficulty that rehearsals must be held afternoons. It follows then that the chorus must get its recruits from such circles of society as are not averse to the cost of a carriage for every rehearsal. The Paris tramway system has, because of the topography of the city, developed badly, and will remain inadequate.

A woman who does not live in the neighborhood of one of the principal streets is always compelled to use a carriage in the evening.

One of the greatest hindrances in the development of choruses arises from something one would not suspect, namely, the strongly developed family feeling of the Parisians. Widespread social intercourse, so customary among the people of German cities, is unknown here. Of the coöperative movement there is no sign. Difficulties from this source in relation to chorus attendance do not arise, in the main, as they do in Germany. But the Parisian lives for his family; it demands everything of him. One evening in the week is from the outset rigidly set aside for the members of the family who live away from home. In the winter, January and February are largely filled with invitations to dine in the wider circle of relations. It is unthinkable to the Parisian that a chorus rehearsal should take precedence over such obligations; it would do violence to his sense of ethics. Whoever, then, has a large family circle and a large number of relations cannot even contemplate the possibility of joining a chorus. This agrees with the observation made daily in romance regions that wherever the family cult flourishes the taste for public enterprises in the main is less strongly developed.

The small and middle-class bourgeoisie can also provide few members for choruses. The society from which they must get their recruits —at least so far as the women are concerned—is in the highest degree untrustworthy. It is absent from Paris from the beginning of July to the end of October, so that there are really only six months available for regular rehearsals. From this one must again subtract half of January and February. At this time the conductor may make only minimum demands upon his ladies: their time is taken up with the after-New Year calls, which the Parisians make with exemplary conscientiousness. If the days when some of their friends receive fall on the days when there are afternoon rehearsals, their appearance at the chorus is quite impossible, since the visiting hours do not begin until late afternoon. I know the story of a woman who had been singing in a chorus, had had a falling-out with the conductor, and then had made his life miserable by choosing the afternoon of the rehearsal for her receiving day. Because of her intimate friendship with many of the chorus members, the director was made very unhappy worrying about the crucial rehearsals for a performance that was to take place in February.

Recently we have had to reckon also with the many invitations to tea which are becoming more and more fashionable.

The circle from which trustworthy chorus members may be drawn is therefore remarkably narrow. Moreover, the necessity of having rehearsals in the afternoon hours brings with it a multitude of difficulties which would not be present in the evening.

For the men's voices the situation is, if possible, even more unfavorable. Those who can regularly free themselves for an afternoon rehearsal are in the minority. The man who has an office or who is in business can do this only once in a while, perhaps only for an important rehearsal. The leader of the chorus finds himself therefore compelled to rehearse the women in the afternoon and the men in the evening, which is a great disadvantage in the study of the works. The rehearsals are far less interesting when the voices are drilled separately. The members do not hear the ensemble until the final rehearsals, and until then have to be satisfied with piece-work.

To be a member of a Paris chorus, then, requires enthusiasm, will and self-sacrifice. He who commits himself must make up his mind to carry on a fight with hostile circumstances.

This is particularly difficult, since there is no tradition to sustain the individual. Whereas in Germany it is taken for granted that a man with a talent for singing should belong to a choral society, in France he must first secure the approval of his family, in which effort he encounters all possible objections. In such matters we recognize the bearing of tradition upon cultural life, and the importance of the fact that an ideal has won acceptance in its time, and now without any discussion of its wisdom or its foolishness is recognized as reasonable and self-evident. The more closely one observes the more he becomes aware that the excellence of musical life in Germany is based in the last analysis on the fact that traditions and institutions were established in the eighteenth and nineteenth centuries, which provided the foundations for the regulation of our musical organizations today. These traditions sprang out of the artistic life of the free states and the little courts. In France the monarchy degraded all the cities of the country to the status of provincial cities. They possessed no cultural life of their own, but were dependent on the stimulus that came from the capital city. In the great city of Paris, however, the growth of traditions which put the individual at the service of the musical life were from the beginning impossible. They could arise only in small degree. This is the explanation also of the fact that no French city has an orchestra, whereas the little German cities very often have really excellent orchestras, at which French artists are always so astounded.

It is disastrous that the French school that came out of the Revolution does not cultivate singing. School choruses are a novelty. What the private schools have done for the art is also as good as nothing. The educational ideal of the great republican, Plato, who considered art as a part of general culture, is still without any influence in the most modern of republics.

The love of choral singing which the German carries with him from his school is not to be found in France. The idea of belonging to a chorus, and of becoming part of a whole, is strange to the Frenchman from the beginning; he must first familiarize himself with it through reflection.

In the existing choruses one notices that that indefinable something which is called "chorus discipline" is almost lacking in the members. Everyone brings to the rehearsals his full personality; he does not become a member of the chorus, a stop that the director pulls, but remains Mr. So-and-So, or Mrs. So-and-So, who wants to be recognized as such. The modern Frenchman has an instinctive anxiety about anything that is called discipline; he sees in it nothing but a submission that is unworthy of a free being. The higher conception, that discipline means the natural expression of the individual in a society united for a purpose, is in all circumstances foreign to the French spirit. He sees first of all in discipline the sacrifice of freedom and personal worth. The forming of groups—and not alone artistic groups—is made very difficult by this mentality.

Therefore the manifold difficulties combine in France to make the organization of a mixed chorus hard and to throw every imaginable difficulty in its way. A chorus organized after the German model is not to be thought of. Above everything else one should not start to assemble great choruses. Choruses of up to a hundred members are for Paris concert halls fully adequate. The Trocadero, which offers larger dimensions, is little adapted to musical performances because of its bad acoustics.

But quality makes up for what is lacking in quantity. Those who disregard the hindrances and agree to a chorus usually find excellent and well-trained voices at their disposal.

Only that chorus can expect to endure, however, which is recruited from a particular social group. If the members are not acquainted with each other, or are not bound together by common friendships, no coherence is to be expected. Through the peculiarity of the French mentality, the idea of corporate entity is in itself incapable of shaping a community.

First of all we must consider for possible recruits the Alsatian circles and those associated with them from the departments of the east, who are somewhat influenced by the German ways and pay homage to them in matters of organization. The French–Swiss community also provides good elements. Upon the genuine Parisians one cannot count very much at the beginning. They listen with passionate eagerness to choral music, but the way from enjoyment to coöperation is not yet for them a well-trodden path.

As for men's voices, one is still compelled for the time being to secure the coöperation of professional singers, since it remains hard to get volunteers in sufficient number.

If a conductor adapts himself to these circumstances, it is possible —provided he has good relations in the circles in question—to assemble an excellent chorus. He must realize, however, that he must begin small, and resolutely train his men and women singers to discipline, while preserving all the amenities. The leader of the Bach Society has pursued his goal in this way, and worked for three years in secret; whereupon the press, amazed at the performance of the small chorus, did their best to smooth the way for him.

It is to be regretted, for more than one reason, that choral music in the life of Paris is so shockingly retarded. Above all, a splendid literature remains closed to the Parisian. Until a few years ago I knew important musicians in the French capital who had never heard Händel's *Messiah*, or Mendelssohn's oratorios, or had heard them only in a very unsatisfactory rendering; to say nothing of the choral works of Bach, Beethoven, and Brahms. Even Mozart's *Requiem* is almost unknown. In the musical experience of the French the over-powering youthful impressions which the German receives from these works have no influence.

The composers are necessarily forced by these circumstances to neglect a whole category of music, in spite of the fact that as pupils in the Conservatory they have been trained in the composing of cantatas—this is a requirement in the competition for the *Prix de Rome*.

I have been much disturbed by the embarrassment which leading Paris conductors manifested when they were called to conduct a work with a chorus. It was evident that this was something utterly foreign to them. At a major rehearsal for César Franck's *Beatitudes* one of them had particularly to practise giving the signal for the chorus to rise. I have seldom found conductors who can manage the choral attacks in a way that is a matter of course to the German. Very often the rehearsing of the chorus is done by a coach; the conductor undertakes its direction for the first time in the rehearsals with the orchestra.

Most of all, however, the general musical education suffers from the lack of choruses. Only by rehearsing together and singing to-gether can we arouse an interest in polyphony. One who has never experienced a work of art which he has helped to create, in the midst of which he stands as it passes by, which he hears from within out, never emerges from the position of mere musical feeling to that of genuine artistic perception. The educational value of choral singing, which we may assume as a matter of course in the German people— at least for much the greater part of them—is lacking in the French. The feelings of the French are probably just as elemental and vital as those of the Germans, but the power of judgment that can be gained only through artistic activity is wanting.

Recently an organization has been formed—it calls itself the "French Society of the Friends of Music"—whose chief purpose is to naturalize choral singing in France. Among the founders we find almost none but people who know and prize from their own experi-ence the German and Swiss musical life. As one of the first tasks of this organization, the statutes propose the encouragement of choral singing in the schools. The immediate founding of a model chorus of professional singers in Paris is also contemplated. This chorus is to be at the disposal of the concert societies, and will supply good substitutes for the voluntary choruses.

Jules Ecorcheville, one of the most capable French writers on music, is in charge of the business of the organization; the training of the model chorus is entrusted to Gustave Bret, the director of the Bach Society.

As much courage is required for this undertaking as for the reforestation of heights which for hundreds of years have stood barren. It is to be hoped that the energy and enthusiasm of the new organization will succeed in laying the foundation for artistic traditions which will be of inestimable value in the musical life of France.

Concerning this, however, we may not forget that choral singing in France will never come to blossom and significance until the social attitudes and customs of the people from whom volunteer choruses are recruited have experienced a change. If an emancipation occurs which will permit a greater freedom to the young, unmarried women, so that evening rehearsals can be set, the major difficulties will be removed. If not, the circumstances will continue to remain abnormal.

A great artistic problem is therefore tied in the closest way to one phase of the woman question, which in other lands has long ago been solved. In France the fight will be long and hard, for paradoxical as it is, no other citizenry in the world is for good or bad as conservative as that of the modern French Republic.

❧

ONCE, in 1900, Schweitzer had seen the Passion Play at Oberammergau. Aunt Mathilde in Paris had invited him to accompany her and some friends on a carriage drive from Bayreuth to the Tirol. He had charge of the baggage of the party; this, he says playfully, was why he was invited. He did not like the Passion Play, though he felt that the players were putting their souls into it. It was not the simple peasant play acted by simple folk for other simple folk that he felt it ought to be. The play had surrendered to the demands of an eager public, and was being given on a huge stage with distracting theatrical effects. But the scenery of the Bavarian Alps was magnificent.

Bayreuth, however, he visited again and again, and always with a thrill of pleasure. In the cemetery of the town were the graves of the German satirist and humorist, Johann Paul Friedrich Richter, usually called Jean Paul, the French pen name he adopted, and Franz Liszt, the great Hungarian musician, who became towards the end of his life an abbé. But for Schweitzer the place was a Wagner shrine; for in the garden of Wahnfried the great composer lay buried, and in the theatre his genius lived on.

Schweitzer's enthusiasm for Wagner never faltered; perhaps in small part because the controversy over pure music and pictorial music came to rage around him as it had raged around Wagner. The Bach Society had published a monumental edition of Bach's works in the middle of the nineteenth century, and his music was claimed by the anti-Wagnerites as a supreme example of pure music. So they set Bach and Mozart over against Wagner, of whom Nietzsche once said with keen discernment, "As a musician Wagner should be classed among the painters, as a poet among the musicians, as an artist in the more general sense among the actors."

But Schweitzer couched his lance against these "guardians of the Grail of pure music," and described Bach as one who had something in common with Wagner, and even more with Berlioz. Wagner was to him a dramatic lyricist, for whom he had great admiration, and a fellow feeling in the controversy that raged bitterly about him. No man has ever been more hotly attacked or ever more zealously defended. He has been called the Carlyle of music and drama, with a passionate enthusiasm for the reform of art.

Almost fifty years after Schweitzer's first visit to Bayreuth, he wrote some burning words from Africa which showed that his veneration for Wagner had not dimmed with the years: "His music is so great, so elemental, that it makes Wagner the equal of Bach and Beethoven. Such assurance in composition, such grandiose musical architecture, such richness in his themes, such consummate knowledge of the natural resources of each instrument, such poetry, dramatic life, power of suggestion. It is unique; unfathomable in its greatness, a miracle of creative power!" [1]

With Richard Wagner's second wife, Cosima Wagner, Schweitzer finally became well acquainted in Heidelberg, Strassburg, and Bayreuth. He tells the story of this colorful and dominating personality in a vivid pen picture, with a glimpse of Richard Wagner's son Siegfried and his daughters.

✤

MY RECOLLECTIONS OF COSIMA WAGNER [2]

I SAW Cosima Wagner for the first time in Bayreuth, when in 1896 The Ring of the Nibelung was taken up again, twenty years after its 1876 première, which Wagner had directed in person. The musicians of the orchestra, with whom I used to lunch, spoke of her with great respect. But they were not unanimous in their opinion that it was a real advantage to have a woman of such an imperious will as Madame Cosima directing the performances.

It was about 1904, if I am not mistaken, when I made her acquaintance. It was at Heidelberg, on the occasion of an audition of Bach's B minor Mass executed under the direction of Philippe Wolfrum. Madame Wagner was there with her son Siegfried and one of her daughters. I acted with reserve, for her manner of receiving people who came to see her after the concert was lacking in simplicity and naturalness. She did not have the gift of putting people at their ease; she liked to have them approach her with the reverence due a princess.

A little while afterwards, when I was working on my book about J. S. Bach, she stayed for a time at Strassburg with her daughter Eva. Professor Johannes Ficker, whom she knew well, gave her as a guide one of his students in the history of art, and I joined them in their walks about Strassburg. Cosima Wagner had heard something about

[1] Prophet in the Wilderness, by Hermann Hagedorn. Copyright 1947 by Hermann Hagedorn, and used with the permission of the Macmillan Company, New York; p. 50.
[2] "Mes Souvenirs sur Cosima Wagner," from L'Alsace Française, Volume XXV, No. 7 (February 12, 1933), pp. 124 ff.

the book I was preparing, and she showed some interest in my idea that some of the music of the cantor of St. Thomas was descriptive. She asked me during our promenade to explain my views, and I noticed that she knew the work of Bach thoroughly. To demonstrate my ideas to her, I played for her on the beautiful organs of the Temple Neuf some of the most significant of the chorale preludes.

During our walks we talked about other things besides music. She told with great animation of the fight Wagner had waged in support of his art, so far as she had shared the struggle with him. I was surprised to find that still in that epoch, when Wagner's work had finally triumphed, she was haunted by the idea that the master's enemies remained active and formidable. This attitude seemed to me hardly consonant with the remarkable personality of Cosima Wagner.

Since I was a theologian, she touched also on religious problems. She once spoke to me of the religious instruction she had received, and of the questions she put to her professors. She had always thought that the great problem was how to reconcile the justice of God with His love, since, she said, love cancels justice, and as an attribute of God admits of no other. Therefore, she concluded, we may represent God only as a God of love, Who desires and achieves the salvation of all His creatures. In the course of this interview, which took place one beautiful, sunny afternoon, while we were walking along beside the Ill from the St. Thomas bridge to the University, I realized what a delicate and vital soul there was in this woman, at first approach so distant.

Her daughter Eva appeared very simple and natural. I conceived for her an extraordinary esteem, and we have always remained in excellent relations.

When, some time later, I went to Bayreuth to attend the performances, I paid a visit to Cosima Wagner, who received on certain days between eleven and one o'clock. On my first visit I had occasion to admire her amiability and savoir-faire. She was conversing with a gentleman who was pretending to know her quite well, although so far as I could see she did not remember him at all. She was floundering, but her floundering was that of a virtuoso. For me it was a very diverting spectacle. Finally her daughter Eva perceived her mother's embarrassment and rescued her.

Every time I was received at the Villa Wahnfried I admired anew the accomplished art and the perfect consideration with which Madame Wagner and her children devoted themselves to the visitors, who were often just curious people.

Two days after my first visit to the Villa I was invited to have supper with the Wagner family, during the second entr'acte of *Tristan and Isolde*, in the little hall of the Festspielhaus.

Also invited were the Prince of Saxe–Meiningen and Mademoiselle Grandjean of the Paris Opera, where the latter had played brilliantly the role of Isolde. The dessert consisted of a plate of magnificent peaches, which Mademoiselle Grandjean had brought from Paris. I was amazed at the skill which Cosima Wagner displayed in sustaining an interesting conversation. Moreover, she bore almost all the burden of it. I took some satisfaction in noticing that my fellow guests were as much overawed as I by this eminent woman.

As a matter of fact I was not at all at my ease during this supper. I was too much under the influence of the masterpiece that Felix Mottl had just been directing in such a sovereign manner. I should have preferred to go out into the country to sit down by myself, as I usually did at Bayreuth during the entr'actes.

In Cosima Wagner's activities at the theatre of Bayreuth she revealed a personality without an equal. With all her heart she was trying to conserve intact the traditions of the old Bayreuth.

I was able to take note of this during my different pilgrimages there. But in spite of the perfection with which the works of the master were executed, I was not wholly satisfied with them. I had the feeling that at no time could the interpreter give way to his own inspiration, and that his singing and playing had been too strictly ordered by Cosima. At the most moving moments there were lacking that spontaneity and that naturalness which come from the fact that the actor has let himself be carried away by his playing and so surpasses himself. Frequently, it seemed to me, perfection was obtained only at the expense of life.

I was very happy to know more intimately Siegfried Wagner. Rarely have I met a man more natural and more thoroughly good. As a stage manager and animator he was marvelous. He looked out for all the details of the stage setting. And how well he knew how to instruct and inspire the singers! He forced them to do nothing that went against the grain; he urged them to perfect and deepen their own conception of their role. I cherish an ineffaceable memory of the performance of *The Flying Dutchman*, which he had arranged and directed.

When I left for Africa in 1913 I promised myself to arrange my first leave in Europe in such a way that I could attend the performances at Bayreuth in the autumn of 1915. But then came the war, and afterwards the sad and troubled years that followed it!

It was not until the winter of 1923 that I was able to return to Bayreuth, on my way back from Prague, where I had been giving some organ concerts. The journey was not as easy as I had thought it would be. A special visa was necessary at that time to stop in Bavaria. Since my passport had no such visa in it, the gendarmes at the frontier station forbade me to take any train except the express which crossed Bavaria to the west. Luckily it was evening, and the guardians of the law were not performing their duties very conscientiously. I succeeded at the last moment in sneaking into the forbidden train, with a magnificent bouquet of white roses, which the admirers of Bach's music had presented to me on my departure from Prague, and which I intended to give to Cosima Wagner.

How sad to see again these loved places! At the Villa Wahnfried what dejection! They wondered if it would ever be possible again to stage the Wagnerian dramas at the Festspielhaus. The money was lacking to put the great theatre and the machinery into condition again. Was the international Wagnerian community still in existence? Or had the war shattered it?

At that time, as I learned when I arrived at the Villa Wahnfried, Cosima Wagner could receive only on those days when she was quite calm. But the news of my arrival (though she should hardly have remembered me at all) had disturbed her so much, that she had fussed for hours in advance about the dress she would put on to receive me. Finally, because her daughter feared the excitement would be harmful to her, I gave up the idea of seeing her and sent her the bouquet of white roses, which gave her a great deal of pleasure.

Afterwards I paid a visit to the widow of Hans Richter, the orchestral leader for whom I had so much respect. Cosima Wagner died a little while afterwards.

And now it is Siegfried Wagner who has passed away. . . . The Bayreuth that we knew, we the Wagnerian enthusiasts of my generation, exists no more. . . .

IV

Bach: The Musician-Poet

*T*HE new presbytery at Gunsbach was on the main street of the village, just east of the town hall, set back a bit and separated from the street by a lovely private garden. The main entrance to the house was on the other side. Albert's room was at the left of the door that led to the garden, and faced the sunny south. He had come home for the Whitsuntide holidays in the early summer of 1896; and one morning as the bright, warm sun streamed into his room and wakened him, and the birds sang in the garden before the house, he began to think of his favored lot, the happy family in which he lived, the privilege of books and music, teachers and loyal friends; and then he realized that he must give something for all these precious things that he enjoyed.

What should he give? Simply and clearly the answer came to him. He should give himself, after he reached the age of thirty, to the immediate service of humanity. He was then twenty-one. He had, therefore, nine years more which he felt he might rightly devote to his music and his studies. After that, service.

What was the service to be? He did not know. He thought it might be for destitute and abandoned children, perhaps for tramps and discharged prisoners.

His thirtieth birthday approached. A few months before the day came he found on his table a green-covered magazine, in which Alfred Boegner, the president of the Paris Missionary Society, pleaded for workers in the Gabun. This was the call. He would go.

He was in Paris again in the fall. On October 13, 1905, he dropped into the mailbox letters announcing that at the beginning of the winter term he would start his medical studies in preparation for work as a doctor in French Equatorial Africa. His resolve had not wavered. Neither did it falter when his family and friends argued with him about his decision. Romain Rolland was eloquently silent. Widor was eloquently vocal. He thought the general was deserting his command to fight at the front like a common soldier.

Nothing made any difference. He resigned as principal of the theological college, and towards the end of October began his studies in the medical school of Strassburg University.

Meanwhile he had completed his work on Bach, and in this same year, when his momentous decision went into effect, the book was published. It was high time for such a book. Bach's death in Leipzig in 1750 had created no stir whatever; his greatness was not recognized. At the end of the eighteenth century musicians thought that the great composer of the Bach family was Emmanuel, one of the sons. To all intents and purposes Johann Sebastian had disappeared. Then came Forkel's brief biography in 1802, followed in midcentury by the publication of the complete works of Bach by the Bach Society—a frightfully difficult undertaking in the face of an indifferent musical world—and in 1874 and 1880 by the two volumes of the detailed and almost exhaustive study by Spitta. In Germany, France, England, Belgium, Italy, Bach began to come into his own. It was almost like a rising from the grave, and indeed one of the chapters in Schweitzer's later German biography of Bach is entitled "Death and Resurrection." Yet when Schweitzer began his work on Bach much still remained to be done, as is evident from the conversation with Widor already reported. To help in the larger appreciation of the cantor of St. Thomas, to make his music understood for what it is, Schweitzer wrote his book. But in his characteristic modesty he disclaimed too much credit. What is needed, he said, to make Bach known and loved is not Bach festivals and books like his own, but the unheralded devotion of thousands of humble folk who should find food for their souls in his work, and then should tell others about it. Bach speaks to such men alone.

At the close of his epoch-making book, which for some time was a storm center among musicians, because of its contention that much of Bach's music was not of that pure, classical type that Spitta had declared it to be, Schweitzer says:

"The problem of interpretation is far from being solved. The work and the efforts of an entire generation of artists will be needed to establish the elementary principles for a modern rendering of the works of Bach. How can one speak wisely today, when the most beautiful and the most modern of the cantatas have never yet been given anywhere? We think we do sufficient honor to the master in giving from time to time the St. Matthew Passion, and we do not even suspect all the riches contained in the volumes of cantatas published by the Bach Society!

"Still, it seems to us that the day of the Bach of the cantatas has come, and that Bach, the musician-poet, will cease to be venerated as an unknown man as soon as musicians are found to perform his cantatas.

"It is both the grandeur and the weakness of music that it needs interpreters. A fine old painting commands the respect of the public today by its own merits. The older music, on the contrary, will remain strange as long as it is not rendered for us in a way that resembles a bit our modern music. The character of the work is necessarily corrupted by the spirit and the opinions of the man who undertakes to give it.

"But of what importance are these divergent interpretations? Whether the principles we employ are right or wrong the future will decide. The only thing of significance at the moment is that we should make known the great music of Bach. We cannot conclude in any better way than by citing the happy observation that Monsieur Gevaërt, one of the oldest enthusiasts for the cantor of St. Thomas, made to me: 'It is with the music of Bach as it is with the gospel. The people can understand it only according to Matthew, according to Mark, according to Luke, according to John, gospels which differ much, but which are always the Gospel. One thing only is needed, one thing indispensable: to stir discerning and sensitive souls!' " [1]

This is Schweitzer's humility speaking. But when Widor from Venice wrote his introduction to Schweitzer's book, on October 20, 1904, he was lavish in his praise. Listen to Widor:

"Better than all the speeches in the world, the pages you are about

[1] From *J. S. Bach. Le Musicien–Poète*, by Albert Schweitzer. Leipzig: Breitkopf & Härtel, 1908, p. 434.

to read will show the power of Bach's extraordinary brain, for they will give you examples and proofs. From Mozart to Wagner, there is no single musician who has not considered the work of Johann Sebastian Bach as the most fruitful of teachers. All right! If this was the opinion of the masters, while it was difficult to get the full meaning of his work, with a part of it lying unknown, buried in the dust of libraries, what will be our opinion today now that everything has been published?

"Until the present moment it was this writing, this polyphony, this technique that we have admired, astonishing mixture of ability and good common sense; not a note which did not seem to be the result of long cogitation and yet did not come to the point of the pen quite naturally as the only true, the only right note. And now in addition to these astounding qualities of workmanship, we are about to discover others of a higher order. Here is a thinker, a poet, a gifted interpreter of ideas, who reveals himself suddenly as a prodigious sculptor, the father of the modern school, the moving and graphic master.

"Bach died July 28, 1750; one hundred and fifty-five years, therefore, have been needed for us to penetrate his symbolism, to discover in him a descriptive and pictorial feeling like that of the primitives, to follow his thought step by step, and to contemplate in the clear light of day the incomparable unity of his art.

"As we read Monsieur Schweitzer's book, it seems to us that we are present at the inauguration of a monument; the last scaffolds, the last veils have fallen; we walk around the statue to study its details, then we withdraw a little to a point from which our eyes can survey the whole; and then we pass our judgment upon it." [1]

The moment the book was written a demand was made for a German translation. This Schweitzer attempted at once to do, but found it impossible for him to translate his thoughts into German. Therefore he wrote an entirely new book in German, the first pages of which were written in the Black Horse Inn at Bayreuth in this same year. It took him two years to finish it, but in view of the fact that he was having a heavy course of medical studies, lecturing regu-

---

[1] From J. S. Bach. Le Musicien–Poète, by Albert Schweitzer, Leipzig: Breitkopf & Härtel, 1908, pp. xiv f.

larly, preaching at St. Nicholas, making concert tours, and writing
two other books, the marvel is that he was able to complete it at all,
especially since the new book, to the consternation of the publishers,
had 844 pages instead of 455. The German edition was published in
1908, and from this the English edition was made. The English
edition in turn was largely altered and expanded at Dr. Schweitzer's
request, so that it expresses Schweitzer's latest thought about Bach.
And now there exists at Schweitzer's Alsatian home an interleaved
edition of the German book, in preparation for that happy moment
when the whole work can be revised again, in accordance with the
latest knowledge of the great musician.

The following excerpts from the French edition include a study
of the place of the chorale in Bach's work, a complete account of
Bach's life and activities in brief compass, and an explanation of the
symbolism which Bach employs. Here, then, is the heart of Schweitzer's interpretation of Bach—though all comment on particular
works, whether instrumental or vocal, motets, Passions, oratorios and
cantatas, is omitted. Those who wish to make a detailed study of
these works are referred to the English edition.[1] It is a pity that the
French version is not better known among the lovers of music. It
has the tremendous advantage of brevity, and it is not a duplication
of material in the German and English editions. As Schweitzer has
himself said, the latter have an entirely fresh approach to the subject.
The rhythm of the French sentence, the clarity and conciseness of
the language, are qualities Schweitzer was unable to transfer to the
German. He points out that there is something finished about
French literature, in the good and the bad sense of the word, something unfinished about German literature in just the same way.

[1] *J. S. Bach*, by Albert Schweitzer. New York: The Macmillan Company, 1947.

꙳

THE CHORALE IN BACH'S WORK [1]

THERE is a fundamental difference between Bach and Händel. Bach's work is based on the chorale, Händel for his part makes no use of it. With one of them free invention is everything; with the other, the author of the cantatas and the Passions, the work springs from the chorale and effaces itself in it. The most beautiful and the most profound of Bach's works, those where the deepest aspect of his philosophic thinking is expressed in the form of music, are his organ fantasies on the chorale melodies.

Is it not a strange thing that Bach, if he was a creative genius, should use as the basis of his work melodies already composed? The reason is that external circumstances constrained him. He was an organist and chapel master. As such he composed for the service of worship. His cantatas and Passions were destined to find a place in the liturgy, and he did not imagine that one day they would be given outside the service. Writing for the church, he felt himself compelled to attach his work to the chorale, the sole principle in the sacred music of Protestantism. Händel was free; he did not write cantatas, but oratorios for spiritual concerts.

From necessity springs power, it is precisely to the chorale that the work of Bach owes its greatness. The chorale not only puts in his possession the treasury of Protestant music, but also opens to him the riches of the Middle Ages, and of the sacred Latin music from which the chorale itself came. Through the chorale his music sinks its roots deep into the twelfth century, and so establishes a vital contact with a great past. It is not solely an individual phenomenon; in it live again the aspirations, the strivings, even the soul of former generations. Bach's art represents the blossoming of the chorale under the breath of a great genius. It is not simply a generation, it is the centuries that have produced this colossal work.

If, then, it is true that genius sums up in itself an entire generation, by giving adequate expression to the idea which fashions its time, and

[1] From *J. S. Bach. Le Musicien–Poète*, by Albert Schweitzer. Leipzig: Breitkopf & Härtel, 1908, pp. 1–4.

that it is necessary, therefore, for the understanding of that genius, to examine it at work in the age from which it has come, one consequence follows: we must base the study of Bach upon an even broader foundation. His great biographer Spitta understood this very well. Before painting for us his picture, he goes back into the past and retraces for us the history of Bach's large family. We see them spread out among the little villages of Central Germany, all of them organists and cantors, all upright and a bit stubborn, all of them energetic, all modest but with some appreciation of their value. We are present at the big family reunions, where they cultivate a spirit of solidarity and a common ideal. We run through what has come down to us from their works. And from this environment and from these works we see Sebastian Bach emerge. We are presentient of him, we understand him before we become acquainted with him. We foresee that the ideas and aspirations which are manifest in this family cannot stop there, but must necessarily be realized some day in a perfect, definitive form, in some unique Bach, where the different personalities of this big family reappear and survive. Johann Sebastian Bach, to speak the language of Kant, imposes himself upon us as a kind of historic postulate.

So the biographer proceeds in relation to the man; so the musician must proceed in relation to the work itself. A history of the chorale: such is the base that the study of the work demands. The evolution of the music, and the evolution of the religious poetry of the German Middle Ages, lead to the advent of the chorale in the Reformation. But they do not stop there. The final point, towards which both evolutions converge in their complexity, is Bach. Whether one follows one or the other, at the end of the road will be found Sebastian Bach.

The most beautiful flowers of German poetry from the Middle Ages to the eighteenth century, the strophes of the chorale. adorn his cantatas and his Passions. It is Bach who reveals their beauty; it is he who takes them out of the hymn collections to make them the property of the whole world.

Likewise, the efforts to harmonize the chorale, made by the former masters, come to their climax in him. It is he who achieves the ideal harmonization.

What the Scheidts, the Buxtehudes, and the Pachhelbels proclaimed from a distance in their fantasies on the chorale, becomes a reality in those of Bach: they are organ poems.

From the motet which is attached to the chorale comes, under the influence of Italian and French orchestral music, the cantata. This great foreign impulse follows its course and finds itself in the Bach cantatas. Just one fact: the chorus of the first cantata he conducted at Leipzig in 1714 (No. 61), is a French overture. Bach himself calls it Ouverture, and uses the word "gay" to indicate the movement in the middle part.

At the end of the seventeenth century, the biblical drama, which was in favor in the Middle Ages, comes back again in the form of the passion play in music to knock on the door of the churches. The fight begins between those in favor and those opposed. It is Bach again who puts an end to the struggle. He rehabilitates the ancient Passion by idealizing it: he writes the St. Matthew Passion.

From whatever direction he is considered Bach is, then, the last word in an artistic evolution which was prepared in the Middle Ages, freed and activated by the Reformation and arrives at its full expansion in the eighteenth century. The chorale is in the center of this evolution. Its story is, therefore, necessarily the prelude to a study of Bach.

❧

THE LIFE AND CHARACTER OF BACH [1]

1. BACH AND HIS FAMILY

BACH was born at Eisenach on March 21, 1685, and died at Leipzig on July 28, 1750. There is nothing particularly striking about his life; it is the life of a bourgeois, honest and laborious. An orphan at ten years, Bach found a refuge in the home of his oldest brother at Ohrdruff. At the end of some years, as his brother Johann Christoph's family continued to grow more numerous, he felt it his duty not to remain as an expense to his brother but to provide for his own wants. Because of his fine voice he was accepted as a chorister

---

[1] From J. S. Bach. Le Musicien–Poète, by Albert Schweitzer. Leipzig: Breitkopf & Härtel, 1908, pp. 105–170.

in the boarding-school of the lycée at Lüneburg, where he followed
all the classes. Of course he could have desired nothing more than
to continue his studies at the University and to complete his general
culture; but one had to live before he began to philosophize. Bach
was forced to accept the job of violinist in the orchestra of the Prince
of Weimar. Some months later, in 1704, he was made organist in
Arnstadt, where a new organ had just been constructed. He remained
there four years. In the end, his stay was spoiled by the dissensions
that broke out between him and the municipal council concerning a
leave which had been granted him, and which he had prolonged by
more than two months without even informing his superiors. Moreover, Arnstadt was really too little for him; he felt himself crowded
there. It was therefore with real satisfaction that he accepted the
post of organist at Mulhouse in 1707. He was immediately married
there to his cousin, Maria Barbara Bach. In June 1708 he left Mulhouse for Weimar, where for nine years he fulfilled the functions of
court organist and chamber musician. To these titles he added in
1714 that of concert master, that is, assistant conductor of the orchestra. But when the post of bandmaster became vacant, the prince,
instead of offering the place to Bach, who believed he had good
reasons for counting upon it, gave it to an entirely insignificant musician, Johann Wilhelm Drese, whose only qualification was that he
was the son of his father, the former bandmaster. Under these circumstances Bach could not remain there longer. The Prince of
Cöthen offered him the position of bandmaster at his court. Bach
accepted, and continued to serve from 1717 to 1723. At length, however, his work ceased to please him, for it had little relation to the
vocation which he felt within him. As a matter of fact, he was only
the director of music in the Prince's chamber; the cantatas were not
performed at all; for the court, like that of Prussia, was not Lutheran
but Reformed; the organ of the court chapel was a small instrument
with hardly a dozen stops, and moreover Bach did not have the title
of organist. Let us add that Prince Leopold had married a woman
who was not at all interested in music, and his love for art began to
grow cold. Other reasons also decided Bach: his sons were growing
up; it was necessary to give thought to their education. But Cöthen
had hardly any educational resources to offer. Hamburg would have

been the city of his choice, but the intrigues and the thalers [1] of his rival succeeded.

Nonetheless, when the position of cantor at St. Thomas, that is, chapel master for the Leipzig churches, became vacant on the death of Kuhnau in 1722, Bach hesitated for several months before announcing his candidacy. The cantor at St. Thomas was only a simple professor, the fourth from the top in St. Thomas School; he had to give certain lessons and to direct the choirs which the boarding pupils formed in the two principal churches. For a chapel master at a ducal court this was not at all an advancement. In the end, the father of the family decided: the bandmaster agreed to become a schoolteacher. He began his new duties May 31, 1723; he was to perform them for twenty-seven years.

Bach enjoyed very robust health. Except for some indisposition which prevented him from going in 1729 to greet Händel at Halle, we do not know of any serious illness that came to interfere with his work. His eyes were his one weak spot. He was myopic from birth, and it goes without saying that it did not help his sight to write music and to engrave his compositions on copper himself. During the last two years of his life his eyes became weaker and weaker. The operation performed on him during the winter of 1749–1750 by an English oculist who was passing through Leipzig, far from helping them, brought in its train the most disastrous consequences; not only did he become completely blind, but his health was also severely shaken. On July 18, 1750, he suddenly recovered his sight, but a few hours later an attack of apoplexy struck him down. He died in the evening of July 28, and was buried on Friday, July 31, in St. Jean Cemetery.

Such, with the exception of some minor episodes and some short journeys, was the life of the master. The obituary which was drawn up by his son, Karl Philipp Emmanuel, and his pupil Agricola, and appeared in Mizler's *Musikalische Bibliothek* in 1754,[2] hardly gives more than dates. Later, Forkel, the well-known historian of German

---

[1] A thaler is a German coin, formerly worth about three marks, but no longer minted. C. R. J.

[2] The Mizler *Bibliothek* was a musical review which appeared in Leipzig. The obituary notice is found in the 4th vol., 1st part, pp. 158–176 (1754).

music, in the biography he wrote of Bach in 1802, added to these dates some information he got from the two eldest sons of the musician, Friedemann and Emmanuel. Almost all the anecdotes about Bach go back in their original form to this biography.[1]

Then interest grew dull, and the study of Bach remained stationary for nearly sixty years. The first who undertook to publish a new biography, based on more careful research, was Bitter. His work, which appeared in 1865, was soon supplanted by a more solid and vaster work, the *Bach Biography* of Philipp Spitta. This work is the fruit of fifteen years of study, study singularly attractive doubtless, but fraught with extraordinary difficulty. Let one remember that hardly any letters of Bach exist, and that the information secured from contemporaries was insignificant and inadequate. It was necessary, therefore, to make the archives and the manuscripts speak. And Spitta made them speak. He leafed through the ecclesiastical registers in the localities where Bach had lived, scanned the acts of the municipal assemblies, and found more than he had ever hoped to find. In 1873 the first part of this work appeared, which, finished in 1880, was to be for the history of music what the book of Justi on Winkelmann was for the history of art.[2]

These more recent studies permit us to determine with more precision the appearance of the master. One is involuntarily tempted to trace a parallel between his life and that of Kant. Both lived a very simple bourgeois life, broken by no striking event; but though they lived within the confines of a modest and quiet environment, they were able to keep a vital contact with the world; both had the gift of letting the numerous impressions they received from the outside world ripen within them; neither had any great doubts about the road to take, nor any great difficulty in winning the esteem of his

---

[1] *Ueber Johann Sebastian Bachs Leben, Kunst und Kunstwerke. Für patriotische Verehrer echter, musikalischer Kunst* [Concerning Johann Sebastian Bach's Life, Art and Artistic Works. For patriotic admirers of genuine, musical art], by I. R. Forkel, Leipzig. Bureau de Musique, 1802. 69 pp. This work, inspired by an ardent admiration for Bach, is precious of its kind, and must be considered as the point of departure for every study of Bach. Nevertheless, it is not exact in all its details.

[2] *Johann Sebastian Bach*, by Philipp Spitta, Leipzig, Breitkopf & Härtel, 1st vol. 1873, 855 pp.; 2d vol. 1880, 1514 pp.

contemporaries; both, one may say, were greater and happier than other gifted men, because there was a complete identity between the ideal they followed and their daily occupations: Kant wanted to teach young people, Bach wished to enrich the Protestant service.

On the contrary, what a difference there was between the life of Bach and that of Händel! Händel was already a *virtuoso* and an admired composer at the time when Bach, his equal in age, was only a simple and obscure violinist in the ducal orchestra at Weimar; Händel was heard before Buxtehude, whom Bach a year later went to listen to with the respect and the curiosity of a pupil desirous of learning from such a master; Händel was applauded in Italy, Bach was an organist in a little German village. Händel lived at the English court and had at his disposition orchestras, choirs, and soloists of distinction; Bach was a schoolteacher and had only pupils to render his works. The *Messiah* had a resounding success; no one spoke of the *St. Matthew Passion*. Händel was buried in Westminster Abbey; we are reduced to conjectures as to where the remains of the cantor of Leipzig lie. And still, of these two destinies, which do we prefer: that of Händel, who for more than twenty years was mistaken about his true vocation and sought in the opera the glory that he was to find in the oratorio, or that of Bach, who discovered the way he was to take with such certainty and security?

Unfortunately, we possess very few details about Bach's intimate life, about the husband and the father of a family. He married twice. His first wife died suddenly at Cöthen in 1720, while he was at Carlsbad, where he had had to accompany Prince Leopold. She was already buried when he returned; he could only go and weep upon the still fresh grave of the woman who for thirteen years had shared his life and his work. Philipp Emmanuel in his obituary describes in a moving way the grief and prostration of his father; he was only six when his mother died, but the poignant scenes he witnessed left upon him an indelible impression. A year later the master married Anna Magdalena Wülken, the daughter of the trumpeter (*Hof- und Feldtrompeter*) of the Weissenfels orchestra. She was then twenty-one, Bach was thirty-six. This union was perfectly happy. Anna Magdalena was able to understand her husband and to follow him in all his work. She was a musician herself, with a beautiful soprano voice.

It was at the court, where she was a singer, that Bach doubtless came to know her. Let us add that she was endowed with remarkable musical intelligence, which her husband undertook to develop. We still have two books for the harpsichord that belonged to Anna Magdalena (*Klavierbüchlein*); the first is from 1722, the second from 1725. They contain, among other compositions for the harpsichord, French suites, sacred songs, and soprano airs. The second of these *Klavierbüchlein* is particularly precious to us, for in it Bach has written the fundamental rules for playing the figured bass. Anna Magdalena was not only an economical housekeeper—and economy was certainly necessary in such a numerous family—but more than that, she rendered great service to her husband in copying music. It was she, for instance, who copied the largest part of the *St. Matthew Passion*. A curious detail: her handwriting became more and more like her husband's; it was hardly possible to distinguish them.

What a charming family scene is called up, for instance, by the second oboe part in the cantata: *Ihr, die Ihr Euch von Christo nennet* [You who take the name of Christ], (No. 164)! The heading and the clefs are in Anna Magdalena's writing, but the notes, awkward and stiff, betray a child's hand. At the bottom is a primitive little monogram, where an effort is made to combine the three letters "W.F.B.": Wilhelm Friedemann Bach! The cantata is probably from 1723; the child was then thirteen years old; it was his first fair copy. Do you see the scene? Mother and son are sitting at the same table; a step is heard on the stairs: "Hurry up!" says the mother, "father is coming in."

On the other hand, how many sad scenes are evoked by the Weimar, Cöthen, and Leipzig registers! Bach had, in all, twenty-one children; seven by his first wife, fourteen by his second. Several died young, others at a more advanced age. Only eight were still alive, four girls and four boys, when the father died.[1] How many times he had to follow the coffin of someone dear to him: June 29, 1726, Nov. 1, 1727, Sept. 21, 1728, Jan. 4, 1730, Aug. 30, 1732, April 25, 1733—there were many days of mourning in the house of the Thomas cantor! Does the profound sadness of certain cantatas surprise us, when

---

[1] In the German version Schweitzer states that Bach had twenty children, of whom nine survived him. C. R. J.

we know under what sorrowful circumstances they saw the light of day? If the cantatas could only tell us of all these tearful days, we should understand to its full extent the anguish of which the inventory prepared after the death of the master hardly gives us a hint. The eldest of the sons of Anna Magdalena—he was called Gottfried Heinrich—is represented by a guardian, for he was mentally defective. Altnikol, the son-in-law of Bach, took him into his own home before Bach's death; the son did not die until 1763. It is precisely this Gottfried Heinrich who gave rise to the legend of David Bach, the deranged *virtuoso*, whose strange playing, it was said, brought tears to the eyes of the listeners. But Bach never had a son of that name.

The happiest epoch in Bach's family life was the years before the older sons had left the paternal home. Friedemann and Emmanuel had both received a very careful musical education. Bach had a talent that is not given to all fathers: he knew how to teach his own children. In 1720, when Friedemann had reached the age of nine, he had him begin his music, and wrote in succession the pieces which make up the *Klavierbüchlein* for Wilhelm Friedemann Bach. The *Inventions* (1723), and also the six sonatas for the organ, which come from the same epoch, were intended to serve as studies for the two older boys. But while he was encouraging his sons in their music, he insisted that they should take general subjects at the University of Leipzig; a certain amount of university culture was then, we used to say, indispensable to the artist. Emmanuel was not destined for an artistic career, but for the study of law, because his father did not think he had sufficient talent for music. It was not until 1738 that he decided definitely for music.

A letter written by Bach in 1730 to Erdmann, his former schoolfellow at Lüneburg, incidentally gives us some information about the family concerts. The motive of this letter is not the most happy one: Bach, disgusted with Leipzig because of various annoyances arising from his superiors, writes to his friend, who was then filling the important post of Russian representative at Dantzig, asking him to come to his help. After having set forth all the disadvantages of his present situation, he speaks of his family, and tells him that his children, big and little, are born musicians. "With my family," he says, "I can already organize a concert, vocal and instrumental, especially since my wife sings a very lovely soprano, and my eldest daughter also sings her part very well." Many of the compositions of the master, notably the concerts for one or more harpsichords with orchestra and certain solo cantatas, were doubtless written with these family concerts in mind.

Bach lived long enough to witness the success of his sons. Friedemann became organist at Halle; Emmanuel, harpsichordist for Frederick the Great, and later, in 1767, chapel master at Hamburg, where he succeeded Telemann; Johann Christoph Friederich held the post of chamber musician for the Count of Lippe at Bückeburg; Johann Christian, who afterwards in 1769 was to succeed Händel in the post of chapel master for the Queen of England, was only fifteen at the death of his father. Bach had a high opinion of Johann Christian's gifts; he even gave him at one time three pedal harpsichords, which did not fail to arouse the jealousy of the older brothers. This same Johann Christian was at one time (1754) organist at the cathedral of Milan.

Only one of the daughters of Bach, Juliane Friederike, married: she became the wife of Altnikol (1720–1759), organist at Naumburg, one of the favorite pupils of the master. In the postscript to a letter dated October 6, 1748, Bach announced with a certain pride to his cousin Elias Bach that Emmanuel was the father of two sons, but he regretted that the elder should have been born at the time of the Prussian invasion of Saxony (1745): "*Mein Sohn in Berlin hat nun schon zwei männliche Erben, der erste ist ohngefähr um die Zeit geboren, da wir leider! die Preussische Invasion hatten; der andere ist etwa 14 Tage alt.*"

His son's compositions interested him vitally. He copied with his own hand Friedemann's fine organ concerto in D minor, and it is difficult to say to whom this copy—it is kept in the Berlin Library—does the greater honor: the father or the son.

Friedemann had always been his favorite son; his manner of writing for the harpsichord and the organ, indeed, resembles that of Johann Sebastian. But the thirty cantatas he composed at Halle do not at all resemble his father's; one would rather say that they were works composed before the time of J. S. Bach. Emmanuel was less gifted than his brother, but conscientious and assiduous in his work.

It is he who transmitted to his generation Johann Sebastian's principles of touch and style. He constitutes an epoch in the history of music, for it is with him that modern piano technique begins. In his cantatas and in his oratorios he is modern in the fashion of his time. If he had had ideas we might consider him in a certain way the hyphen between Bach and Beethoven. Johann Christian, the "Bach of London," wrote a number of commonplace little operas. To speak truth, it seems that the old stock of the Bachs was exhausted in producing Johann Sebastian; if the sons were remarkable artists it is due less to their talent than to the solid instruction they had received from their father.

As for Wilhelm Friedemann, he would have been the despair of his father if the latter had lived long enough to witness his downfall. Strange and irascible, he had, moreover, an unfortunate craving for drink. In 1764 he resigned at Halle, and afterwards led the life of a Bohemian. His friends, who picked him up drunk on the street, tried vainly to help him by paying his debts and by seeking jobs for him: he only sank deeper and deeper. He abandoned his wife and children, to drag himself around from one village cabaret to another with his violin. The precious manuscripts which had come to him as his share were lost, or sold to the first comer for ridiculous sums. Nevertheless there were times when he recalled with pride that he was the son of the great Bach. They say that one day in an inn, having heard a musician remark that the violin sonatas of J. S. Bach could not be played, he picked up his violin and played them from memory, drunk though he was. He did not die until 1784; Emmanuel lived until 1786.[1]

Anna Magdalena herself survived her husband for ten years, and this in a state of complete destitution. The sons by the first marriage abandoned her completely. The way in which they distributed among themselves their father's manuscripts before the inventory hardly testifies to a very tender regard for their stepmother. In 1752, two years after the death of Bach, in order that she and her three daugh-

[1] See *Carl Philipp Emmanuel and Wilhelm Friedemann Bach*, by C. H. Bitter. Two volumes. Berlin 1868. By the same author, *Die Söhne J. S. Bachs. Sammlung musikalischer Vorträge* [The sons of J. S. Bach. Collection of Lectures on Music]. Breitkopf & Härtel.

ters might live, she had to ask for monetary help from the municipal council. And her poverty became even worse after that. She lived by alms, and died in a miserable house in the Hainstrasse. No one knows where she is buried. Regine Suzanna, the youngest of the daughters, who was eight years old at the death of Bach, lived until 1809. Rochlitz, the great admirer of the works of Bach, learned of her misery, and made an appeal to the generosity of his contemporaries for the benefit of the last of Bach's children. The first to send a contribution was—Beethoven.

2. Bach's Situation and Duties at Leipzig

Bach lived in the left wing of St. Thomas School: it was the residence assigned to the cantor. After long hesitation he had decided to accept a situation which was in no sense an advancement for him. Doubtless it was an honor to succeed the celebrated Kuhnau; doubtless the prospect of being able to devote himself entirely to sacred music was pleasing to him; but what constraints awaited him! As the fourth professor, he was under the rector and the council; as the teacher of the choir, under the consistory of the church. One anticipates the complications and the disagreements that will inevitably arise when his independent spirit begins to crash against all these barriers. One cannot avoid a certain feeling of resentment in reading the deliberations which preceded his nomination and the contract he signed. A man of the distinction of Bach had to submit to almost humiliating conditions: he is forbidden to leave the city without the permission of the Burgomaster-regent; he has to participate in the funeral cortèges and march beside the St. Thomas choristers as they sing the chorale or the motet; besides, he is enjoined "to arrange music for the church services which shall be short and not similar to operas."

Let us not forget in fairness that the municipal council was looking only for a schoolteacher capable of directing church music; and it did not find this schoolteacher in Bach. We read, indeed, in the deliberations that preceded the nomination of his successor: "The school needs a cantor and not an orchestra leader; Herr Bach was a great musician, but he was not a schoolteacher." Their experience had been unfortunate.

At first it seemed as if everything was going for the best. Bach declared his willingness to give the five Latin lessons each week which were his responsibility in the third and fourth classes. Afterwards, however, with the consent of his superiors, he freed himself from this duty, and had his place taken by a colleague, who agreed to give the lessons in return for fifty thalers a year. When this substitute was prevented from being there, Bach himself took the class, and was content to dictate to his pupils an exercise to be worked out (*ein Exercitum zum elaborieren*), and then to monitor the class.

Unfortunately, the St. Thomas School was then in a deplorable condition. It dated from the thirteenth century, and had been founded by the Augustinians of St. Thomas. When the schools were secularized during the Reformation it became a communal school and was considerably enlarged. It counted fifty boarding scholars. It was recruited from the young people and the poor children of the city and the vicinity who wanted a schooling; they were brought up gratuitously, but were required to sing in the church choirs. Twice a week they went out singing from house to house, divided into four choruses; they shared the gifts they received as well as the money they got from marriages and burials among themselves, after the rector, the professor, and the cantor, of course, had taken out the portion that was theirs by right.

This *schola cantorum* was, one realizes, at the same time a *schola pauperum*; and its organization was very antiquated. The "Thomaner" had a bad reputation; discipline was not very strong among them. There were even some among them who roamed the streets barefoot to beg. The bad condition of the rooms in the boarding-school, and the irregular life of the choristers, led to frequent epidemics in the St. Thomas School. In short, at the beginning of the eighteenth century the establishment, once so celebrated and so prosperous, was in a state of complete decay. The good families did not send their children there any more. Of one hundred and twenty boarders which the three lower classes formerly counted, there remained in 1717 only fifty. The council in vain made surveys and issued orders for the reorganization of the studies; its efforts had no result. The rector Ernesti was a tired old man who passively resisted the reform efforts, which sought, above all, to abolish the collections. These reforms would have diminished his income and the income of the professors.

It was at this time that Bach began his work; the situation was evidently hardly brilliant, and it grew worse until the death of Ernesti (1729). In 1730 Bach presented a statement to the municipal council, in which he made it clear that it was impossible for him to give sacred music worthily in the churches of Leipzig because of the bad condition of the choirs.

Very slender, indeed, were the musical resources at his disposal. The churches were supporting only eight instrumentalists. To have a complete orchestra—Bach in his statement demanded eighteen musicians—the cantor had to depend upon students who played an instrument, and who consented to give their help regularly, either for love of the art or in the hope of pay. But in the time of Kuhnau St. Thomas had been abandoned more and more by the students. Kuhnau lacked initiative, and, moreover, was an open adversary of "modern" music in operatic style. On the contrary, Telemann, who was studying at Leipzig at the beginning of the eighteenth century, and held at the same time the post of organist at the Temple Neuf, was a representative of the new music. His concerts won great success among the students; he finally attracted them entirely to his side in founding the *Collegium musicum*, to the great loss of Kuhnau. The best of the St. Thomas choristers left to go to him, hoping to be engaged later through his help at the Leipzig opera or at the opera in Weissenfels. Telemann's departure brought no change in this state of things: his *Collegium musicum* remained the center of artistic life in Leipzig, and it was not until 1729, when Bach himself undertook to direct the society, that he was able to secure the support of the students.

Let us add, however, that the position of cantor had its advantages. The daily work was not too absorbing. Bach gave a singing lesson from noon until one o'clock every day except Thursday. Saturday afternoon he rehearsed the Sunday cantata, and on Sunday he directed the choirs either at St. Thomas or at St. Nicholas. The professor therefore had abundant leisure, by which the composer profited.

The boarding-school of St. Thomas provided choirs for four of the city churches: St. Thomas, St. Nicholas, the Temple Neuf, and St. Pierre. The fifty-five boarding pupils formed, therefore, four choirs. For St. Pierre they chose the worst. "To St. Pierre we send the rubbish, that is, those who know nothing about music and can hardly sing a chorale." This is the way Bach himself expresses it in his statement of 1730.

The choir at the Temple Neuf was numerically very small, for at least three voices for each part were needed in the choirs of the principal churches. "It would be desirable," Bach says in the same statement, "if we could take four 'subjects' for each part and have sixteen persons in each choir." The fact is that he gave the *St. Matthew Passion* with two choirs, each composed of twelve, at the most sixteen voices, soloists included, since it was the first choristers who gave the solos.

Each choir was directed by a prefect (*Praefectus*); it was the cantor's privilege to choose the prefects from among the best singers. The positions were very much desired, the prefects having a special part in the income of the choir. The cantor himself directed only the choir which rendered the cantata, the *Figuralmusik*, as they used to say. For the cantata, as for the Passions, the two churches alternated. One Sunday the cantor directed the cantata at St. Thomas and the first prefect directed the motet at St. Nicholas. The following Sunday the cantata was given at St. Nicholas and the first prefect directed the motet at St. Thomas. This alternation was scrupulously observed. One year Bach wanted to give the Passion at St. Thomas when it was the turn for St. Nicholas. The programs announcing that the Passion would take place at St. Thomas were already in the hands of the public: it could not be helped; he was forced to abandon his project.

A cantata was given each Sunday, except for the last three Sundays of Advent and the six Sundays of Lent. Let us add the cantatas for the three festivals of Mary, and those for the New Year, the Epiphany, the Ascension, St. John's Day, St. Michael's Day, and the festival of the Reformation: in all fifty-nine cantatas each year. If we suppose

that Bach composed five cycles of cantatas (*Jahrgänge*), as the obituary states and as Forkel tells us, he would have written in all two
hundred and ninety-five; about a hundred must have been lost, therefore, since we have only one hundred and ninety.

The service at the two leading Leipzig churches was perhaps, of
all the Protestant services, that which most resembled the Catholic
mass. In Saxony they were very conservative in respect to the liturgy.
The details of the service are known in part to us, thanks to the notes
that Bach wrote on the cover of the cantata "Nun komm der Heiden
Heiland" [Come now, Savior of the Gentiles] which he gave on the
first Sunday of Advent in 1714.[1] The service began at seven o'clock
and ended about eleven. It was composed of the following two parts:
prelude on the organ; motet; introit, *Kyrie*, intoning of the *Gloria*,
to which the choir replied with "*et in terra pax*"; often also in place
of the choir it was the congregation which sang in German the
chorale of the *Gloria*. Then came the Epistle, followed by the German chorale, and the Gospel, with the intoning of the *Credo*; after
the *Credo*, the organist preluded, to permit the tuning of the instruments. Upon a sign from the cantor he stopped, and then began the
rendering of the cantata, which lasted on the average twenty minutes.
The winter cantatas were in principle a little shorter than the summer
ones. After the cantata, the congregation sang the *Credo* in German;
then came the sermon, which lasted at least an hour.

The second part of the service was centered in the Holy Communion. After the close of the sermon several verses of a German
chorale were sung, then the words of Jesus instituting the Lord's
Supper were recited. During the Communion the chorales of the
Last Supper were chanted, the different verses of which were inter-
luded with long organ passages. Several of the great chorales of Bach

---

[1] Here are these interesting notes: "*Anordnung des Gottesdienstes in Leipzig am
1. Advent Sonntag frühe:* 1) *Praeludieret,* 2) *Motetta,* 3) *Praeludieret auf das
Kyrie, so ganz musiciret wird,* 4) *Intoniret vor dem Altar,* 5) *Epistola verlesen,*
6) *Wird Litaney gesungen,* 7) *Praeludieret auf den Choral,* 8) *Envangelium
verlesen,* 9) *Praeludieret auf die Hauptmusik,* 10) *Der Glaube gesungen,* 11)
Die Predigt, 12) *Nach der Predigt, wie gewöhnlich einige Verse aus einem Liede
gesungen,* 13) *Verba institutionis,* 14) *Praeludieret auf die Musik und nach
selbiger wechselweise praeludieret und Choräle gesungen, bis die Communion zu
Ende et sic porro.*"

were written to be played during the Communion, among others, the admirable, mystical chorale *"Schmücke dich, o liebe Seele"* [Adorn thyself, dear soul], (VII, No. 49).

After the main service came a shorter one, in which the music did not have an interesting part. Finally, during the vespers, which began at a quarter past one, a motet was rendered. On festival days the part played by the music was even greater. During the main service the *Kyrie* and the *Gloria* were executed by the choir, the *Sanctus* during the celebration of the Communion. At the Christmas vespers the *Magnificat* was sung, and at the Good Friday vespers a Passion. There was preaching at all the services—not only at the two morning services, but also at vespers. The passions were done in two parts, the first before, the second after the sermon in the Good Friday vespers.

The Church of St. Thomas was for a long time opposed to Passions in the modern style. We used to say that Kuhnau was the adversary of everything in the nature of theatrical music. The Passion which he finally wrote, giving way to popular taste, in the new style, and which was presented in 1721, proves to us how ill at ease he felt in a manner which did not please him; the rough draft of it which we have is very mediocre. Let us note in passing that the musical Passions disappeared from the services in Leipzig in the course of this same eighteenth century. The last of them was performed in 1766, or sixteen years after the death of Bach. He had arrived just in time to write the *St. Matthew Passion.*

On the whole, Bach found himself in the most favorable conditions for musical creation. The petty difficulties and disagreements in his work were not such as to impede his artistic activity. Unhappily the master was not the kind of person to surmount lightly the smallest difficulties. He ran headlong into them, creating in this way troubles that another, more calm and flexible than he, would have avoided. Moreover, he lacked ability to fulfill his duties to the satisfaction of himself and others; organization was the least of his talents. When he undertook something, it was with the impetuosity of genius. If those around him were not won by his enthusiasm, Bach felt himself powerless and disarmed. He had no knowledge of the means which would have permitted a deliberate and methodical spirit to arrive at a goal in spite of everything. For instance, he was unable to preserve the respect of his classes and choirs, and from this arose all the later unpleasantness. He had only the authority of genius, of the man who pursues an ideal. When this did not impress his pupils he was helpless: the authority of the simple schoolteacher was missing. Then everything went wrong and discouragement came. At Arnstadt they had already found fault with him for neglecting the choir. It was the same at Leipzig. More often than was justifiable he turned over his singing lessons to the first prefect. And more than once, also, he had to have recourse to the authority of the rector to maintain his own authority over the choristers. Under the first two rectors, Ernesti the elder (who died in 1729) and Gesner (1730–1734), everything went relatively well; they upheld him to the full extent of their power. But the third, Ernesti the younger (1734–1759), quarrelled with Bach about the nomination of a prefect. Abandoned by his superior, the master after that was in a very difficult position.

Let us not think, because of this, that his superiors were ill disposed to him. Certainly they were unable to appreciate at its true worth the greatness of their cantor; but in fairness let us remember that they did not cease to esteem Bach, and nothing could be found to bear witness to any intention on their part that was frankly malevolent. It was not possible for them to avoid the inevitable friction, given the independent spirit and aggressive temper of the cantor. Whenever he felt his right infringed upon in the slightest way in the world, he flamed up, and out of a mere bagatelle made a great fuss. It is doubtless true that he never defended anything except what was his right in the numerous quarrels which he conducted; yet one cannot justify the almost fanatical frenzy with which he fought.

He had hardly been installed before he began the battle.[1] Görner, the organist of St. Paul's Church, which was the church of the University, had profited by the weakness of Kuhnau to detach this church somehow from the authority of the cantor of St. Thomas, who was director general of sacred music for all the Leipzig churches. Formerly, cantatas were given at St. Paul's only on the festival days under the direction of the cantor of St. Thomas, who received on these occasions a special remuneration. Later, cantatas were intro-

[1] See Spitta, II, pp. 36 ff.

duced regularly; and when Bach arrived at Leipzig the custom had
been established of having the cantor direct the cantatas on the
festival days, while Görner conducted them on the ordinary Sundays,
both of them sharing in the honorarium allotted by the University.
The first thing that Bach did on his arrival was to attempt the impossible—to reëstablish the full authority of the cantor of St. Thomas,
and particularly to secure the full honorarium for himself. In September, 1725, he even addressed a petition directly to the King, who
had an investigation made and supported the request of the master,
without, however, succeeding, it appears, in ending the debate entirely in his favor; the proof of which is that Bach alternated with
his rival afterwards in composing the odes rendered at the solemn
ceremonies of the University. Later in 1730 Görner was even named
organist at St. Thomas, and vexed the master more than once by
his ignorance and his arrogance. As a matter of fact Görner did not
at all consider himself Bach's subordinate but his equal. In one
anecdote Bach during a rehearsal was so impatient with the organist
who was accompanying the cantata, that he is said to have pulled off
his peruke and hurled it in his face, shouting: "You ought to have
been a shoemaker!" If this anecdote is true, it may very well have
been Görner who received in his face Bach's peruke. After a while,
however, the two men came to understand one another; later we
shall see Görner figure as a tutor for Bach's four younger children,
which would be difficult to explain if the relations between them
had continued bad.

In 1727 the schoolmaster Gaudlitz, who filled the office of preacher
for the afternoon services, drew in his turn the wrath of the master.[1]
It was customary for the organist to choose among the chorales de
tempore the one they were to sing. In order to make them fit his
sermon the schoolmaster Gaudlitz preferred to choose them himself,
and requested the consent of Bach and the consistory. Neither of
them caused any difficulty. But a year later Bach withdrew his consent, and without warning had cantatas of his own choosing sung,
pretending to be ignorant of those the preacher had indicated. This
procedure was, of course, not correct. Gaudlitz complained to the

[1] See Spitta II, pp. 57 ff.

consistory, which took his part. Bach, on his side, sent a statement to the council defending "his rights." We do not know the issue of this affair, so typical of the tactics of the master, which consisted in arousing the council against the consistory, or the consistory against the council, and then profiting by the ensuing discussions to advance his own ideas. Even at the time of his installation jealousy had broken out between the two authorities: the council insisted that the representative of the consistory had taken upon himself an importance which did not belong to him, and they exchanged any number of notes on this subject without being able to come to an understanding.

In 1729 and in 1730 the relations between Bach and the council were very strained. Bach had to examine the pupils who were seeking admission to St. Thomas boarding-school, and it was well understood that those he did not consider to be musicians were not to be admitted. But in 1729, at the reopening after Easter, several weeks after the first rendition of the *St. Matthew Passion*, several boys whom Bach had declared too lacking in musical gifts were admitted, and others whose request he had supported by a good certificate were refused. Moreover, the council had withdrawn certain funds which until then had been at the disposal of the cantor and which had served to compensate the amateur students who were willing to give him their help. The consequences were not long in coming. The rendering of the music in the churches became worse and worse, and the council thought they were justified in complaining to Bach himself about it. It was during the session of August 2, 1730, that the general dissatisfaction against the master came to an explosion. They complained, among other things, that the colleague ·charged with giving the Latin lessons had neglected his duties, that Bach had left Leipzig without notifying the Burgomaster-regent, and that his singing lessons were very irregular. No one of the councillors took his part. The Syndic Job even added: "The cantor is incorrigible." They thereupon passed a vote of censure; and because they anticipated that this censure would leave him rather indifferent, they decided to withdraw a part of his extraordinary income originating in certain foundations in which the professors of St. Thomas shared. And the records of St. Thomas School show that in 1729 and 1730 Bach did not share at all in the extraordinary remuneration from which his colleagues benefited.

These proceedings could not fail to wound him deeply. Greedy as he was in matters of money—the Görner affair provides proof of that—he cherished for many years a rancor towards his superiors for having wished to attack him by measures of this kind. As to their reproach that he had permitted the music of the churches to fall into jeopardy, he refuted it in a curt and trenchant *mémoire* of August 23, 1730;[1] the defense followed closely the accusation. The master proves in it (with reason) that these same superiors, who set themselves up as his accusers, are themselves responsible for the bad condition of the choirs. Is it not they that admit the boarding pupils without paying any attention to their musical abilities, and is it not they also that withhold the funds intended to secure the assistance of students? "Not only," he adds, "have I a great number of incapable choristers, but worse still I have to take for the orchestra from among the capable ones those who know how to play an instrument. What then is there astonishing about the fact that the choirs should be so small and so bad? If I am deprived of the means, how can I remedy the evil?" And so seriously does he take his rôle of accuser that he even neglects the most elementary rules of politeness and respect which should be shown to superiors. His *mémoire* ends with a sharp statement: "In the present choir are seventeen capable persons, twenty who are not yet up to their task, and seventeen entirely incapable." Signed: "Bach"—no more. Certainly the council was not accustomed to read such *mémoires*. The Syndic Job was right: the cantor was incorrigible.

It was in this mood that the master wrote to his friend Erdmann the letter full of bitterness in which he begged him to find another post for him. He complains particularly of the material disadvantages of his situation. This situation had been represented to him as very advantageous, and at first sight it seemed indeed to be so: in addition to the lodging, they had offered him a fixed sum of about seven hundred thalers, and every special fee would bring him from one to two thalers. But when he arrived in Leipzig he perceived that life was

[1] "Kurtzer, jedoch höchstnöthiger Entwurf einer wohlbestellten Kirchen-Musik: nebst einigen unvorgreiflichen Bedenken von dem Verfall derselben."

extremely dear there. "In Thuringia," he said, "I go farther with four hundred thalers than here with twice that." And besides, the fees were very uncertain. In 1729, for instance, since the "air was healthy" he lost about a hundred thalers because of the small number of deaths.

With what little things the great ones are associated! This year of 1729 is for us a blessed year: it is the year which gave us the *St. Matthew Passion*. To Bach it was a year that brought only unhappiness. One feels through this whole letter that the shabby treatment given him by the council has cut him to the quick: in resentment he wants to seek his fortune elsewhere.

Yet his financial situation was not at all bad. The inventory made after his death, and the luxury he allowed himself in instruments of music prove clearly that, in spite of the family expenses, he enjoyed a certain affluence. The truth is that Bach was niggardly in matters of money. Is there any better proof of it than the following anecdote? His cousin Elias Bach from Schweinfurth, in gratitude for the hospitality he had received at Leipzig, sent him a small barrel of cider. But it happened that when it arrived at Leipzig it had lost a third of its contents. Bach, in a letter of 1748, thanks him very amiably for his kindness, but in a postscript gives a detailed account of what he had to pay for carriage, excise, and town tax, and begs him not to send any such shipment in the future, "for, in these circumstances," he adds, "the cider cost me too much to be considered a gift." [1]

Fortunately the new rector, Gesner, was an admirer of Bach's and sincere friendship soon bound the two men together. Using his influence with the members of the council, Gesner had the master liberated from his class work, and secured a restoration of his right in the distribution of the gifts. But the benevolence of the rector was in no way a sufficient guarantee in the mind of Bach. Already he had addressed himself directly to the Dresden court in the affair Görner; this time, to protect himself forever against these vexations,

[1] Here is the postscript: "*Ohnerachtet der Herr Vetter sich geneigt offerrieren fernerhin mit desgleichen liqueur zu assistiren; so muss doch wegen übermässiger hiesiger abgaben es depriciren, denn da die Fracht 16 gr., der Überbringer 2 gr., der Visitator 2 gr., die Landacise 5 gr., 3 Pf. und general accise 3 gr. gekostet hat; als können der Herr Vetter selbsten ermessen, dass mir jedes Mass fast 5 gr. zu stehen kömt, welches denn vor ein Geschenke allzu kostbar ist.*"

he sought from the King–Elector, his sovereign, the title of Court Composer. Like his compatriots in general, he attached a certain importance to titles. Though Kuhnau, for instance, had been called simply "cantor," Bach, particularly in his relations to the council, felt it a bit humiliating to bear this subordinate title. He called himself preferably *Director Musices*, or *Director Musices et Cantor*; and at the top of his compositions he never failed to signalize his titles of Bandmaster to the Cöthen Court and the Weissenfels Court. But the titles which he had from these little princes hardly impressed his superiors. The important thing for the master, therefore, was to be attached to the court of the sovereign of the country. So we find him from this moment intriguing to obtain the coveted title of Court Composer.

In the request he makes July 27, 1733, of Augustus III, King of Poland and Elector of Saxony, he frankly confesses the practical reasons that lead him to seek the title in question. He dedicates to him the *Kyrie* and the *Gloria* of the *Mass in B minor*, the only parts of the great work which were then finished, begging him to deign to accept his "poor work" and not to judge him by this "bad composition" but in accordance with his celebrated kindness, and to take the composer "under his powerful protection." "For several years now," he continues, "I have been directing the music in the two principal churches of Leipzig; several times, without any justification, I have had to submit to vexations; they have even cut the incidental income which goes with my duties; all this will stop, if your Royal Highness will grant me the favor of conferring upon me a title which will attach me to the court chapel." In 1733, that is, he still remembers with bitterness the measures they had taken against him in 1730, though these had been rescinded for two years. Futile pains! In vain he reminded his sovereigns of his ambitions by many an occasional cantata written in their honor: he had to wait three years more before he received the nomination desired. The disorders in Poland required the presence of the King–Elector, who was absent from November 3, 1734, to August 7, 1736. Finally, on November 19, 1736, Bach received the decree which made him Court Composer for the Royal Chapel. This nomination arrived just in time to strengthen his case in a new strife with his superiors.

In 1734 Gesner had been called as professor to Göttingen, and a young scholar of great distinction—called Ernesti, like Gesner's predecessor—became rector of the St. Thomas School. The reorganization of the studies which Gesner had undertaken was very much on his heart. But he lacked his predecessor's tact. Besides, having no interest in art, he considered the time the students gave to music as lost from their studies—not without reason, of course. Everything went well, however, at the beginning. The rector and the cantor even became close friends, and Bach chose Ernesti as the godfather of his son Johann Christian, born in 1735. But in 1736 Ernesti inflicted a very grave punishment on the first prefect, Gottfried Theodor Krause, because he had corrected the choristers, perhaps too severely, for misbehaving during a marriage ceremony. Bach, who held Krause in great esteem, interceded in his favor, but in vain; Krause had to leave the school before he had completed his studies. In his place the rector promoted another Krause to the post of first prefect, Johann Gottlob Krause, of whom Bach did not think very highly; a year before, when the position of fourth prefect had become vacant and Ernesti had proposed him for this post, the master had observed that he was a scamp—in his energetic manner of expression "ein leiderlicher Hund"; but since he was in good spirits that evening, coming back in a carriage with Ernesti from a wedding feast, he interposed no objection to the nomination. Neither did he have anything more to say when Krause was promoted to be third and then second prefect. He even raised no objection—as he had a right to— when Ernesti made Krause the successor to his namesake. But several weeks later Bach abruptly dismissed him; and from this point an affair began which dragged on for more than two years. Ernesti rightly said that Bach should have made his objections earlier, at the time of the nomination; moreover, he was wounded by the uncomplimentary remarks Bach had made about him in the presence of this same Krause. Bach, on his side, insisted that it was for him and not for the rector to name the prefects. This was the way Bach had behaved in the Gaudlitz affair: he let things go, and then one fine day he remembered "his rights."

The rector restored Krause to his place; but when the latter presumed to direct the motet Bach drove him away in the midst of the service. At vespers the rector mounted to the organ loft and forbade the choristers to sing under the direction of any other prefect except Krause; but Bach chased Krause away again. And this was not the end. Bach began again his old tactics, arousing the consistory against the council; but this time he did it maladroitly, and the consistory remained on its guard. The Leipzig archives have preserved the innumerable letters and mémoires which Bach and Ernesti, one after the other, addressed to the council, during the two years through which this unfortunate affair dragged.[1] In them, Bach appears as hotheaded, blinded by his prejudice, but always right. Ernesti is prudent, and remains the master of the situation; profiting, perhaps too skillfully from the point of view of loyalty, from the blunders of the cantor. We wonder how Bach could have behaved that way in a matter of such little basic importance, especially since he was the first to suffer for it. The choristers exploited the dissension between the rector and the cantor, and it became almost impossible for Bach to maintain discipline. Even several of his ecclesiastical superiors, who at bottom wished him well, were vexed at the trouble he was causing them and withdrew their sympathy; among others the superintendent and president of the consistory, Deyling, a man of remarkable personality, who up to that point had had great regard for him and had always to the best of his ability upheld him.

In spite of his title of Court Composer, Bach therefore saw himself like Ernesti causing trouble to others. Since Krause was to finish his studies by Easter 1737 they kept him in his place until that time. But after his departure the undiscouraged Bach again began the fight. He wanted to have full liberty to make nominations at his pleasure. Even more: he insisted that Ernesti make official apologies to him in order to restore his authority over the pupils. On October 18, 1737, he addressed a petition to the King, who immediately sent an order to the consistory to make an investigation. By February, 1738, it was not completed; at Easter the King came to Leipzig with the Queen, and Bach directed some evening music in the square in honor of the sovereigns. We do not have this music, but we know from an article published in 1739 that it made an excellent impres-

---

[1] Spitta has reproduced them in extenso. See Vol. II, pp. 893–912.

sion. The King doubtless intervened at that time in favor of Bach, for from this time on we do not find any further reference to this affair. Ernesti remained rector, and made all kinds of difficulties for the master. The other professors took Ernesti's part, and showed a haughty disdain for everything that pertained to music in the school. When Ernesti found a pupil studying the violin, he did not fail to make fun of him; this is reported to us in the history of the Leipzig schools by the pastor Friedrich Köhler.

Thus the moral authority of Bach was done for at the school, with the pupils as with the professors. We may say with no fear of exaggeration that this affair spoiled for him the last ten years of his life. He felt himself abandoned and isolated at Leipzig; he would have looked for another situation had he been a younger man. He was compelled to resign himself to live in the milieu of St. Thomas as a stranger. What was being done at Leipzig did not interest him any more. Therefore he remained outside the great musical movement which took place in this city at precisely this epoch. In 1743— to cite only this one fact—a new concert society was founded, which had a great success, and which later, in 1781, gave birth to the society of the *Gewandhaus* Concerts. Bach showed no interest in this enterprise, which, as it developed, was to place Leipzig in the first rank of musical centers in the entire world.

3. THE AMIABILITY AND MODESTY OF BACH

Let us not believe, however, that Bach had a mean character. The ferocious sensitiveness which he displayed the moment he felt his independence threatened did not prevent his being a very agreeable person to deal with. Of this there is unanimous testimony. He was above everything else upright, incapable of an injustice. No one, moreover, questioned his impartiality. In his organ appraisals he was severe and meticulous; no detail escaped him, and he pointed out, without deference to anyone, what seemed to him to be badly done. Forkel said very finely on this matter: "Whether it was a question of an organ appraisal or a competition of organists, he was so conscientious and impartial that the number of his friends hardly grew because of it." His strict justice, indeed, made enemies for him: Scheibe, for instance. The fact that Scheibe was the son of the celebrated organ manufacturer did not help him at all when he competed for the place of organist at St. Thomas, which had become vacant in 1729: the master, in his impartiality, was compelled to decide in favor of that same Görner with whom he had had a bone to pick in respect to the University church. Scheibe took his revenge later in a malevolent criticism which he published in the Hamburg "Kritische Musicus" in 1737. Stung though he was by the proceeding, Bach did not modify afterwards his most flattering praise for the organs of Scheibe, the father.

But Bach was more than impartial: he was benevolent. When he thought that an organ was well made, Forkel tells us, and that the profit of the constructor was not at all in proportion to his work, he sometimes requested for him a larger compensation. The certificates he gave as recommendations to young organists and to singers witness this benevolence. To this natural amenity was joined a modesty which made him sympathetic with all who approached him. If his pride made him haughty and even offensive towards people he suspected, rightly or wrongly, of considering him as some kind of subordinate, his simplicity and modesty were just as great, the moment this independence no longer seemed in jeopardy.

It was not at all that hypocritical and vain modesty which celebrated men sometimes affect, but a healthy and robust modesty, which was sustained by the knowledge of his worth. This is what gives his modesty its moral worth and grandeur. He never ceased to remain dignified even when writing to kings. The petitions he addressed to the King–Elector, his sovereign, are written in a very submissive style; but through the formulas of extreme deference which the times demanded breathes something of pride and resolution. We read between the lines: "I, J. S. Bach, have the right to make this request of you." Very different is the tone of the letter which accompanies the dispatch of the Musikalische Opfer [Musical Offering] to Frederick the Great. Bach speaks to him as to an equal, while respecting his royal dignity. He explains to him that, since his improvisation has not succeeded as he wished, he has felt the need of "elaborating the royal theme in a more profound way, and to make it known to the world with the sole purpose," he continues, "of enhancing, if only at one point, the glory of a monarch whose greatness and strength are admired by all the world, not simply in respect to the sciences of war and peace [*in allen Kriegs- und Friedenswissenschaften*], but also, and especially, in music." If we undress this sentence, and take off the refined politeness with which it is clothed, what have we left? Johann Sebastian Bach is proud to honor His Majesty Frederick the Great by publishing a fugue on a subject which he has devised.

With the exception of his pupils, he treated all artists as equals. Forkel tells us that he would not permit anyone to speak about the Marchand story before him. Here in a few words is the episode. Jean Louis Marchand (1669–1732), the "King's organist," had fallen into disgrace, and had been compelled to leave Paris temporarily. In 1717 he interrupted his travels at Dresden, where he had a great success. Some of the court persons, lovers of music, got the idea of organizing a musical competition between him and Bach. But on the appointed day they waited for Marchand in vain. Fearing defeat, he had left the city without a word, ceding the victory to his great opponent. Bach would not suffer anyone to allude to this triumph. Thus he honored himself, and at the same time respected his adversary.

When he was asked how he had attained such perfection in his art, he replied simply, "I had to apply myself; whoever applies himself in the same way will arrive at the same result."

Never, in his judgments of other people, did he depart from this kindly justice. There is no single instance of his having passed a severe criticism on the composition or the playing of a confrère, in spite of his pretentious vanity. One day he had a visit from a certain Hurlebusch of Braunschweig, a peripatetic *virtuoso* who was eager to be heard by Bach. The latter listened patiently; and when Hurlebusch left he gave a volume of sonatas, doubtless of his own composition, to the two sons of Bach, and urged them to study them well for their profit, not knowing how far advanced they already were in the art. The master must have smiled inwardly; but he never varied in the slightest from his amiability towards his visitor. Forkel lays great emphasis on all these signs of modesty. Doubtless the sons of

Bach were eager to have this side of the paternal character brought into view.

Even if these anecdotes were lacking, his attitude towards Händel alone would suffice to show how much Bach could admire all that was great and forget all personal vanity. If he never became acquainted with his great compatriot and contemporary, at least he did everything possible to meet him. Händel went from England to his native city of Halle three times, first about 1719. Bach was still at Cöthen, about four leagues from Halle. Bach immediately set out to visit him, but when he arrived Händel had just departed. The second time was in 1729; Bach was already at Leipzig, but he was ill. He sent Wilhelm Friedemann at once to invite Händel to come to see him. Händel sent his regrets that he was not able to accept the invitation. At the time of Händel's third sojourn,—in 1752 or 1753— Bach was already dead. It was one of Bach's regrets that he had never been able to make the acquaintance of his great rival. It was not that he would ever have thought of measuring himself against him; though in Germany they would like to have seen the two celebrated musicians pitted against each other, and discussed in advance Händel's chances on the organ, over the technique of which Bach had such superlative mastery.

But what better proof is there of this great modesty than the copies he made of Palestrina, Frescobaldi, Lotti, Caldara, Ludwig and Bernhard Bach, Händel, Telemann, Keiser, Grigny, Dieupart, and others—not only at the time when he considered himself still a pupil of these masters, but at the time when he had become a master himself? He disdained them so little that he took the time to copy their works; and, moreover, what has come down to us certainly represents only a small part of all that he copied. Seeing him copy the cantatas of Telemann, we wonder why he was not halted many times by his critical sense. The answer is that he was dealing with recognised masters; he respected them and copied them. A similar good fortune would not have occurred if the original score of the St. Matthew Passion had been lost; none of the contemporary masters had taken the pains to copy it.

4. CONCERT TRIPS; CRITICISMS AND FRIENDS

Modest as he was, Bach was eager to make himself known; each year as autumn came he undertook a kind of small concert trip. We have very little information about these expeditions. About 1714 we find him at Kassel, where he is heard on the organ. A pedal solo which he played before Prince Frederick so astonished the future King of Sweden that he took a precious ring from his finger and gave it to Bach as a souvenir of this occasion. The anecdote is told us by a certain Bellermann, rector at Minden, in his treatise on music (1743).

A year before, in 1713, Bach performed at Halle, with such great success that they wanted to make him accept at any price the place of Zachau (1663–1712), Händel's master, at the *Liebfrauenkirche*. Since they were constructing there a superb organ with sixty-three stops, Bach was easily persuaded to enter into negotiations with them. He even composed a cantata to show what he could do; but when the moment came to make a decision, he declined. The Halle council held a grudge against him for leaving them in suspense for more than a year; they went so far as to reproach him for having broached the matter for the sole end of obtaining a raise in salary at Weimar. We still have a letter from Bach which denies these insinuations very energetically, insisting that he had really refused, only because the information he had obtained showed that the proffered increase in salary did not seem sufficient to justify the change. Here is a new proof that Bach did not consider money questions as merely incidental in life—and did not conceal the fact either. This trait of character must have been very pronounced; for later Ernesti in a *mémoire* written about the Krause case was to go so far as to insinuate that a thaler never failed to have its effect when one wanted a certificate from Bach. The accusation, of course, had no justification; and it reacted upon the one responsible for it.

In December, 1714, Bach came to Leipzig to give his cantata *Nun komm, der Heiden Heiland* [Come now, Savior of the Gentiles] (No. 61); during the service he played the organ. We do not insist that this journey, concerning which there has been considerable discussion, actually took place. In 1717 we find him again at Halle.

The council had forgotten its grievance against him, and when at last the organ was finished they begged him to come and appraise it. Bach replied with a very polite letter, and considered it an honor to accept the invitation.[1] In 1715 or 1716 he had to appear at the court of Meiningen, but we lack precise information about this journey. We know of the journey of 1717, when he met Marchand at Dresden. Not only did this success make him famous in all of Germany, but at the Dresden court it also made a good impression which afterwards stood him in good stead at Leipzig.

The sojourn at Cöthen was interrupted by numerous journeys. His duties left him a great deal of leisure, and, moreover, his prince took him with him on his travels. In July, 1720, for instance, Bach had to accompany him to Carlsbad, and it was on his return from this journey that he learned to his sorrowful surprise of the death of his wife. Three years before, in 1717, he had been for the second time to Leipzig, having to make an appraisal of the new organ at the church of St. Paul. This organ had been constructed by Scheibe, who until then had passed as a rather ordinary organ builder; but the laudatory official report Bach wrote after the appraisal placed Scheibe at once among the first master builders of the sacred instrument. This organ at St. Paul was the most perfect and the most complete of all the Leipzig organs, and Bach used it by preference whenever strangers came to ask him to play for them.[2]

Once installed at Leipzig, Bach continued his custom of making an artistic journey at least once a year. He went on several occasions to play before the friendly courts of Cöthen and Weissenfels. In 1727 we find him at Hamburg; a little later at Erfurt.

The opera often attracted him to Dresden, where he was usually accompanied by Wilhelm Friedemann. When his favorite son was installed in his post as organist at the Ste. Sophie church in Dresden in 1733, he had one more reason for coming frequently to the "para-

[1] See this letter in Spitta, I, p. 514.
[2] Note the arrangements of the Leipzig organs in Spitta II, pp. 111–118. The great organ in St. Thomas had three manuals, with thirty-six stops; the organ at St. Nicholas also numbered thirty-six stops distributed over three manuals; but the new organ at St. Paul had fifty stops on three manuals. It had an excellent mechanical action, for Scheibe had an inventive spirit and had made several very happy discoveries.

dise of musicians," as they called Dresden, the German city where artists were the most munificently paid. Bach doubtless did not lack a certain envy of posts so generously remunerated. In one of his letters addressed to the Leipzig council he complains, among other things, about the inequality of treatment of the musicians of Leipzig and those of Dresden.

Of all his good friends among the court musicians, those who attracted him the most were Adolphe Hasse and his wife Faustina, the noted *cantatrice*. Hasse in July 1731 had been called to Venice to direct the royal opera. On the morning of the *première* of *Cléophide* (September 13), an event of which all Germany was talking, Bach, who had come to Dresden for the occasion, was heard on the organ of Ste. Sophie before the entire *Kapelle*. In 1736, after his nomination as Court Composer, he returned to Dresden and gave an organ concert at the *Liebfrauenkirche*. A select and numerous company came to hear him. How many times he must have compared the singing of the admirable soloists in the Dresden opera with the way the choristers of St. Thomas rendered his songs! We do not know whether he heard one or more of his compositions sung by Faustina; this was not impossible, in view of the friendship between them. Hasse and Faustina went several times to visit him at Leipzig.

His last journey took him to the court of Frederick the Great. The King, Forkel tells us, had on several occasions expressed to Emmanuel Bach, who had been in his service since 1738, the desire to see his father. Finally, in 1747, Bach set out with Wilhelm Friedemann. Frederick II had the habit of looking every evening through the list of the strangers who had recently arrived. One evening, when he was preparing to play a piece on the flute, he saw on the report the name of Johann Sebastian Bach. "Gentlemen," he said to the artists gathered for the chamber concert, "old Bach has arrived." He put down his flute and sent for Bach, who, without having had time even to change his costume, was forced to present himself with his greatcoat and his dusty shoes. Then began, so Forkel says, a long and lively conversation between the artist, who wanted to excuse himself, and the royal host, who wanted to cut short his excuses. The flute was not taken up again that evening. Bach had to play on all the Silbermann pianofortes, of which the

King had fifteen. After having played several improvisations, Bach asked for a fugue subject. When the royal theme had been developed, Frederick wished to hear a six-part fugue. Bach remarked that not every subject could be treated properly in six parts, and begged that he might have a free choice. The fugue he thereupon executed stunned the King. The next day he had to make a tour of all the organs in Potsdam; they had him visit Berlin also. When he got back to Leipzig, he wrote the *Musikalische Opfer* [Musical Offering] on the theme given him by the King, and dedicated it to him.

His superiors did not regard with a very favorable eye the frequent absences of the cantor. "Herr Bach," it is stated in the records of the famous session of August 2, 1730, "has gone on a journey without asking leave of the Burgomaster-regent." It was another such journey, undertaken in July 1736, which helped to provoke the conflict with Ernesti; moreover, in his reports to the council the rector did not fail to mention the frequent absences of Bach; and we learn, incidentally, that at such times the organist of the Temple Neuf conducted the cantata in his place. We may presume that these observations made no impression whatever on Bach. He needed these journeys to get his breath again, and to escape from the petty troubles and restrictions from which he suffered at Leipzig.

The modesty and amiability of the man, as well as the skill of the virtuoso, made Bach universally famous. From 1717—that is, from the time of his triumph over Marchand—he was placed among the glories of Germany, and benefited by the jealousy the German musicians felt for the French and Italian musicians, who everywhere occupied the best places.[1] The Germans were proud of being able at last to set over against them an invincible adversary. German patriotism, which had not yet appeared in the field of politics, was awake in the field of art. Until that time the superiority of foreign music, and especially of foreign *virtuosi*, had never been questioned. Frederick the Great was not even willing to admit that good German *cantatrici* could exist, any more than, even in Lessing's time, he was willing to admit that there was a German literature. Bach therefore became a kind of musical hero. There were only two heroic figures

---

[1] Read the *Musikalische Quacksalber* [Musical Charlatan] of Kuhnau (1770) to see the state of mind of German artists towards their French colleagues.

yet in the eighteenth century: Luther and he; the third, the man who was to create German philosophy, Kant, was still unknown. Frederick the Great died without suspecting the greatness of the simple Königsberg professor.

National pride even silenced personal jealousies. Mattheson, who, far from celebrating the greatness of Bach, had always taken satisfaction in criticizing certain of his works in a manner which had in it little of kindness, could not help exalting Bach after his death as a representative of the national genius, exhorting all foreign artists to risk their *louis d'or* in buying *The Art of the Fugue*, which had just then appeared.

At a time when the great minds of Germany, the Goethes and the Hegels, fascinated by the appearance of Napoleon I, were still far from conceiving the idea of a German nation such as was to be born in the course of the nineteenth century, Forkel, the first biographer of Bach, dedicates his work to the "patriotic admirers of the true art of music"; and in the preface he speaks at length about the national character of his enterprise. "The works which John Sebastian Bach has left us," he says, "are a national patrimony of incommensurable value; no other people could match it with a similar work." And farther on, "To cherish the vivid memory of this great man—let me be permitted to say it once again—is not only an artistic duty, but a national duty." The personality of Bach plays, then, an important rôle in the revival of national feeling in Germany. The moment when the remains of the ancient Germanic empire were being reduced to crumbs, like the remnants of Wotan's sword, is precisely the moment when artistic Germany is inaugurating the cult of Bach.

This means that Bach did not have to strive to win the place in German thought to which he was entitled; his fame did it for him. Let us note, however, that the composer of the cantatas and Passions hardly enjoyed at all the celebrity of a *virtuoso*. No one, not even his enemies, contested the fact that he was the prince of harpsichordists and the king of organists; but no one either, not even his intimate friends, imagined the true greatness of the composer.

The adverse criticisms he had to endure while he was alive came from ill-disposed persons whom he had wounded without knowing it.

We may suppose that the remarks of Mattheson on the cantata "*Ich hatte viel Bekümmernis*" [I suffered great affliction], No. 21, did not affect him profoundly, if indeed he had any knowledge of them. But the criticism of Scheibe, which appeared in 1737 in the *Kritische Musicus* at Hamburg, and which stirred up a polemical literature that lasted for several years, did not fail to wound him to the quick. We cannot say that this criticism, so interesting in every respect, was stupid, for Scheibe did not lack intellect. He did not attack the greatness of the *virtuoso*, but criticized the composer for lacking gracefulness and naturalness. "Bach obscures the beauty of his works by an excess of art. Moreover," the critic continues, "they are too difficult; Bach judges only by his own fingers, and wants the singers and instrumentalists to do with their voices and their instruments what he does with his fingers on the keyboard. Again, he permits no latitude to the player, because he expresses exactly in his notes all the *manières* and all the little ornaments. In short, he is bombastic; which is what leads him from the natural to the artificial, from the sublime to the obscure. We admire the difficult work, although it comes to nothing, because he fights against reason." This criticism is in music what the famous criticism formulated by the Garve–Feder against the *Critique of Pure Reason* was to be later in philosophy. Both give evidence of unusual sagacity, but both also prove in the end only how little their contemporaries were capable of judging the greatness of a Bach or a Kant.

Scheibe is perhaps the first to become aware of the radical difference between Bach and his contemporary composers. Scheibe has sensed something irrational in this art, something that remains inexplicable, as long as one judges Bach from the standpoint of the musicians of his time. This clairvoyance does him honor; the criticism of that time was putting the master in the same class as Mattheson and Telemann, thinking thus to render him the highest praise. It is still with the same meaning that a year later Scheibe expresses his ideas about the Bach cantatas in particular. Unfortunately, in what follows he lets himself be dragged into purely personal invective, and the critic finishes as a pamphleteer. But in 1730, and later still in 1745, realizing that a procedure so little worthy of the greatness of Bach was in no sense an honor to himself, he made a kind of *amende honorable* in the same *Kritische Musicus*.

As it usually turns out, these unjust criticisms were to redound to the honor of Bach, and to make the musical world unanimous in their admiration of him; Mattheson himself disapproved openly of Scheibe. A certain *Magister* Birnbaum, professor of rhetoric at the University of Leipzig, published in Bach's defense two writings which bear witness more to his good will than to his real knowledge of the subject. And it was thus with all the adulation showered on Bach at the time: it teaches us very little; it is purely eulogistic. Gesner, the former rector of St. Thomas, for example, speaking about Bach in an annotated edition of the *Institutiones oratoriae* of Quintilian which he published in 1738, pictures the master at the harpsichord, at the organ and directing his orchestra, and then ends in this way: "For the rest, I am a great admirer of antiquity, but I believe that in my friend Bach, and in those who perhaps resemble him, there are contained several artists the equal of Orpheus and twenty singers like Arion." This testimony of friendship and sincere admiration which his former rector paid him must have at least comforted Bach; it came at the time when the master was embittered by his fight with Ernesti.

A man named Friedrich Hudemann, a *docteur-en-droit* at Hamburg, and at the same time a remarkable musical dilettante, sang Bach's praises in a poem he published in 1732. It plays among the ancient allegories like the eulogies of Gesner, and like them also it is addressed particularly to the organ *virtuoso*.[1] He knew Bach personally, and Bach must have had some esteem for him, judging by the canon he dedicated to him in 1727.

Bach, then, was esteemed and fêted. Does this mean that he had many truly intimate friends?

[1] Ludwig Friedrich Hudemann: *Proben einiger Gedichte*, Hamburg, 1732. "An Herrn Kapellmeister J. S. Bach:
> Wenn vor gar langer Zeit des Orpheus Harfenklang
> Wie er die Menschen traf, sich auch in Tiere drang,
> So muss es, grosser Bach, weit schöner dir gelingen,
> Es kann nur deine Kunst vernünftge Seelen zwingen.
> Apollo hat dich längst des Lorbeers wert geschätzt;
> Du aber kannst allein, durch die beseelten Saiten,
> Dir die Unsterblichkeit, vollkommner Bach, bereiten."

He remained in constant contact with numerous people: Hasse and Faustina Hasse, Graun, Gesner, Birnbaum, Telemann, and many others; his pupils remained attached to him, and never missed an occasion to show their warm affection for him, in which was mingled pride in having been disciples of such a master; even princes, like Prince Leopold of Cöthen, the Duke Ernst August of Weimar, and the Duke of Weissenfels, treated him as a friend. Forkel, on the testimony of Bach's sons, states positively that these sovereigns showed him a cordial affection. Faithful to the traditions of the family, Bach kept in contact with all his numerous relations, and received into his home all the Bachs who came to study at Leipzig.

But these were not intimate friendships. Did Bach feel a more intense need of them? It hardly seems so. His intimates were in his family; his confidants were his wife and his elder sons. His greatness, the burden of his work, in which his thoughts were always immersed, hardly permitted him to have other friendships, and necessarily made of him a creature who was "distant" to others. His impetuous and irascible character, finally, made an intimate friendship with him somewhat dangerous. The real reason for the coolness that developed between him and Walther, as well as his rupture with Ernesti, was his cantankerousness and his stubbornness in never admitting that he was wrong. One cannot deny that the rector acted with loyalty, even with kindness, until the moment when Bach, without any apparent reason, attacked him personally.

5. The Self-Taught Man and the Professor

In the course of his polemic, Scheibe dared to say that Bach's general culture was not what one would expect of a great composer. What are we to think about this accusation?

Bach, let us say, was a cultured man. The *lycée* of Ohrdruff, where he began his studies, and even that of Lüneburg, where he finished them, had a great reputation. It is to be presumed that when he left Lüneburg he had completed the two years of rhetoric which would have opened the doors of the University to him, had it not been for the hard necessity of earning a living. Bach therefore had to rest content with what he had been able to get from the *Gymnasium*.

He was very familiar with Latin; his letters and his *mémoires* bear witness to that. Otherwise, when his appointment at Leipzig was being discussed, would he have declared himself ready to give Latin lessons to the third and fourth classes? We even get the impression that there was a certain pride in this declaration, after his rivals had admitted that they did not possess the requisite knowledge. His grasp of the vocabulary of rhetoric, to which the musical explanations he gave his students bear witness, prove that rhetoric as it was taught in those days was not at all strange to him. Moreover, *Magister* Birnbaum, himself a professor of rhetoric, taking up Bach's defence against Scheibe, insists that Bach, in his lessons and in his conversations, liked to dwell upon the analogies between rhetoric and musical theory. Therefore on the whole Bach possessed a good classical education. And like all cultured people of that time, he had a certain knowledge of French and Italian. The foreign words people were accustomed to misuse in those days when writing German are always employed by the master in the most correct way; the addresses of his letters are often written entirely in French. For example:

"A Monsieur A. Becker, Licencié en Droit, Mon très
honoré ami à Halle."

Or again:

"A Monsieur S. E. Bach, Chanteur et Inspecteur du Gym-
nase à Schweinfourth."

But even in default of such proofs, the value which scholars like Gesner and Birnbaum placed upon his society and his conversation would have sufficed to establish the fact that Bach was in no sense solely a man of his art. Would he have attached so much importance to his sons receiving a good education, if he had not had himself the taste and the respect for intellectual culture?

Unfortunately, the best way of determining what books he read is missing. Since his eldest two sons had set aside beforehand all the books having to do with sciences in general and the theory of music in particular, as they had set aside also the musical scores, in order to divide them, the inventory mentions only the books on theology. But this little catalogue in itself witnesses to the scientific turn of Bach's mind. Besides the devotional books we find all the current theological publications; Bach therefore was interested in the religious questions that were being discussed around him. Moreover, the same little catalogue mentions two big editions of the works of Luther.

Should we be astonished, knowing Bach's character, that polemical literature should be abundantly represented? But we find here even Josephus' *History of the Jews!* Imagine Bach reading attentively the classic work of the friend of Vespasian!

The criticism of Scheibe, therefore, falls as false. Yet in reproaching Bach for being too little versed in the general studies related to music, he really expressed awkwardly an idea which at bottom was correct. Bach was a self-taught man, and as such he had a horror of all superfine theories. He had had no professor of the harpsichord, nor of the organ, nor of harmony, nor of composition; it was only by incessant toil and by constantly repeated exercises that he had learned the fundamental rules of his art.

This is to say that many of the theories and much of the reasoning on the art of music, strange or even new to others, had no interest for Bach, because he had seen to the heart of things. For example, he gave no weight to all the speculation on the mathematics and mutual relations of harmonics. This indifference of the master to these alleged discoveries must have been pronounced, for Mattheson says in one of his writings that in the lessons in harmony Bach gave there was certainly never any question of mathematical speculations. And indeed the teaching of the master at this point was summary: "Two fifths and two octaves may not follow each other; that is not only a *vitium* [1] but it also sounds bad." And that is all. This phrase is found in the copy of a course on the figured bass which he gave his students in 1738; he had doubtless dictated it as it stands. "But it also sounds bad." Can you not see him walking up and down in his class, his face illuminated with a superbly ironic smile?

His indifference to all the erudite enterprises in the field of music comes out clearly in his attitude regarding the Mizler Society. Lorenz Christophe Mizler, born in 1711, had studied at the University of Leipzig at the same time that he was studying the harpsichord and composition with Bach. To obtain the degree of *Magister* he published in 1734 a dissertation, "*Quod musica ars sit pars eruditionis*

[1] *Vitium* (Latin) means "fault." C. R. J.

philosophicae," which he dedicated to four musicians, among them Mattheson and Bach. In 1736 he inaugurated courses on mathematics, philosophy, and music, and founded at the same time a historical review called *Neu eröffnete musikalische Bibliothek* (1736–1744). The *Societät der musikalischen Wissenschaften* dates from 1738.

This Society proposed to reform the art by drawing up a system of musical science. Telemann became a member in 1740; Händel was made an honorary member in 1745; but Bach was so little interested in it that in spite of Mizler's urging he did not decide to seek a membership in it until June 1747. Since it was necessary to furnish some work in order to acquire the right of membership in the Society, he presented some canon variations on the Christmas carol "*Vom Himmel hoch, da komm ich her*" [From high heaven I come down], which he had engraved after he had revised them carefully.[1] The purpose of these variations explains their abstract and strictly scientific character. It is to this circumstance also that we owe the detailed obituary of Bach which appeared in the *Musikalische Bibliothek* of 1754, and a portrait in oil made by the court painter Hausmann. This portrait represents Bach holding in his hand a paper on which is inscribed the canon he presented at his entrance. Are we then indebted to this Society? Or rather is not the Society indebted to Bach? Without him, who today would know anything about the Mizler Society?

Self-taught Bach was, then, if ever an artist was that. He belonged to no school, and no preconceived theories guided him in his studies. He was the student of all the masters, the ancients and the moderns. Every time that distance and means made it possible for him, he went to visit the contemporary artists, to hear them and to study their way of working. He used to copy the works of others. Thus, without ever having left Germany, he was familiar with French and Italian art. Among the French, he was particularly interested in Couperin. During the Weimar period he studied especially Frescobaldi (1583–1644); Legrenzi (1625–1690), who was the master of Lotti; Vivaldi (died in 1743); Albinoni (1674–1745), a contemporary of Vivaldi; and Corelli (1653–1713).

---

[1] Bach V, pp. 92–102. *Einige canonische Veränderungen über das Weihnachtslied "Vom Himmel hoch, da komm ich her."*

Vivaldi interested him particularly. His concertos for violins and orchestra amazed Bach, and he transcribed sixteen of them for the harpsichord and four for the organ. But he was not content with merely transcribing them. In arranging them for another instrument he tried in some way to make them over: he made the basses more interesting, invented new intermediary parts, and introduced imitations which the author had not foreseen. It is regrettable that we do not have all the originals; a comparison with the transcriptions would have permitted us to examine the changes made by Bach—a very interesting study in any case; the ways in which he transcribed the violin effects on the harpsichord and on the organ deserve in themselves a special analysis. One thing is certain: he used the greatest liberty with the models, and many times he keeps almost nothing of the original but the theme and the general character. This should not surprise us; we know from other examples that he was in the habit of appropriating the ideas of others, and of treating them as though they were his own. He wrote an organ fugue on a Legrenzi theme (IV, No. 6), another on a theme from a violin sonata by Corelli (IV, No. 8), and two more (a major and a minor) on themes of Albinoni—all of them compositions that have nothing in common with the originals except the borrowed themes. They are greater and more developed; and one senses the pleasure the master surely experienced in finding that when treated in the right way these themes could yield much more than his predecessors had got from them. These are the efforts of a pupil who becomes dangerous to his masters.

At Leipzig Bach was particularly busy with the masters of Italian singing; he copied Palestrina (1515–1594), Lotti (1667–1740), Caldara (1670–1736), and others. His apprenticeship never ended; like all the great self-taught men, he preserved to his death an ardent desire to learn and a surprising ability to assimilate. Here again is another resemblance to Kant, who was always eager to be correctly informed about European literature.

As a self-taught man, Bach had also the mind of an inventor. Just as theories were repugnant to him, so everything in the way of practical experience attracted him. He knew thoroughly the structure and the nature of all the instruments, and was ceaselessly reflecting on ways to perfect them. From this arose his sympathy with Scheibe, the organ builder, who also had an experimental and inventive bent; Bach must have encouraged him more than once to carry on his researches and to penetrate deeper into the secrets of his art. The least detail in the mechanical structure of instruments had in his eyes an enormous importance. He never ceased to demand that the keys for the organ manuals should be made short, and that the superimposed manuals should be as close to each other as possible, for he was aware that slurring and easy changing from one keyboard to another depended in large measure on these details.[1] These are precepts which German organ builders have not taken into account; they are still building organs with keyboards far apart, and with keys whose proportions are copied from those of the modern piano, complicating to this degree the task of the musician who wants to execute the works of Bach with the desired perfection.

Bach was not at all content to form practical observations: he also invented. When the Mulhouse organ was to be renovated, he undertook the construction of a carillon of twenty-four bells which was to be connected with the pedals; we do not know whether it was constructed, because Bach had left the city before the organ repairs were finished.

At Cöthen he invented the *viola pomposa*, an instrument which occupied a place between the viola and the violoncello; it had five strings (*do, sol, re, la, mi*), and was intended to permit the rapid rendering of passages which were difficult to play on the violincello. The son of one of his pupils, Gerber, who lived close to the master from 1724 to 1727, states that the instrument was in use in the period when he was a Bach pupil. An instrument maker of Leipzig named Hoffmann had constructed it in accordance with the master's specifications. The last of the six suites for violoncello solos was intended for the *viola pomposa*.

The problem of perfecting the harpsichord always interested Bach. He was cognizant of the beginnings of the modern piano, for from 1740 Gottfried Silbermann had been constructing the *Hammerklaviere* [harpsichord with hammers]. Frederick the Great, as we have already

<hr />

[1] See Adlung, *Musica mech. organ.*, 1763, where we find a multitude of interesting notes on Bach, the practical man.

said, had a whole collection of pianofortes from his factory. But though Bach encouraged Silbermann to pursue his experiments, he himself was not satisfied either with the mechanism or the sound of the new instrument. He dreamed of an instrument as sensitive and flexible as possible; and he had the organ builder Zacharias Hildebrand make for him in 1740 a harpsichord-lute which was to fulfil these conditions. To prolong the sound, he had planned two rows of catgut strings, and in addition one row of metallic strings an octave apart. In this way he had two sonorities at his disposal. When the metallic strings were pressed by the felt damper, he had a lute with a loud sound; without the damper, an instrument with a deeper sound. But this experiment still did not satisfy Bach; he was forced to continue to use the simple harpsichord. Forkel relates that in spite of the thinness of the tone he preferred it to all the other kinds of harpsichords, because it permitted him better than any other to get the exact shade of expression he wanted. He tuned his instruments himself; and with such skill that it never took him more than a quarter of an hour.

He was more successful in his attempt at touch reform. He was the inventor of modern fingering. Until the beginning of the eighteenth century harpsichordists did not use the thumb at all; they played with three fingers, or at most with four, which were held out straight and superposed and crossed at will. Bach told his son Philipp Emmanuel—who brings us the new proposal in his *Véritable Art de Toucher le Clavecin*—that in his youth he had heard great *virtuosi* who never used the thumb except in the last extremity, in long stretches. But growing technical complications called naturally for the use of the thumb. In France, François Couperin (1668–1733) established the theoretical necessity for it in his *Art de Toucher le Clavecin*, which appeared in 1717. But his fingering was much less modern than Bach's. Bach was the first to have the idea of normal and constant fingering of the scales.

Let us beware, however, of identifying too closely the fingering invented by Bach with modern fingering; Bach's fingering was richer in its resources—he combined the old method of fingering with the new procedures. Frequently he had recourse, for instance, to the expedient of crossing the second and third fingers, or the third and fourth, as is proved by two little fingered pieces in the *Klavierbüch-lein* of Friedemann. Our fingering does not offer these possibilities. Emmanuel Bach, the immediate author of modern fingering, simplified and modernized his father's fingering by renouncing the former procedures, that is, the crossing of the second, third, and fourth fingers.

This fingering reform proves how clairvoyantly and methodically Bach proceeded in all his researches. If true logic is the logic of induction, Bach was logical as very few artists have been. His theories and his principles always proceeded from facts; they were the quintessence of endlessly repeated experiments. He had the rare faculty that permitted him to see the ensemble in the details and to perceive all the details in the ensemble. Spitta points out, with justice, the difference between Bach's method of composing and Beethoven's. Beethoven accumulated his drafts, and experimented, so to speak, with his main idea, before finding the true form for its expression. The Bach scores, on the contrary, sprang up all at once. From the moment he began to write, the plan for the whole was already fixed, and the details began to group themselves quite naturally around the central idea. When later he happened to take up again one of his scores, he never failed to work it over, though without touching the plan itself. He did not upset the first idea, as Beethoven did: his modifications had to do only with detail. In short, he worked like a mathematician who sees clearly before him every step in a complicated operation, and is concerned only with expressing them in figures.

It was this sureness and really mathematical clairvoyance that give his official explanations their admirable clarity. Whether he is speaking about repairs to an organ, of preparing a *mémoire* on the condition of the St. Thomas choirs, or replying to an attack by Ernesti: the words and the sentences follow one another with a precision and a logic that nothing can stop. Never too much or too little; it is solid and closely packed. One cannot read Bach, even though only a short letter of recommendation, without real esthetic pleasure.

At heart Bach was an architect. The more one studies penetratingly his development, the more one becomes aware that all the progress the art of music owes to him can be gathered into a single word: a ceaselessly growing *perfection* in musical architecture. As for the fugues in particular, those of his youth are often admirable in invention and in richness, but they lack a plan; there is a superabundance of "subjective" climaxes. With time, however, his objectivity, that essential quality of architecture, seems to grow; the fugues become greater and at the same time more simple. In this respect the *G minor Fugue* for the organ is the most perfect; in spite of the abundance and interest of the details, there is nothing unexpected to shatter the unity of its great architectural lines. We stand before an ideal edifice, where strength and pliability unite to create the impression of grandeur.

There is something more here than parallelism and fortuitous harmony; Bach had a very unusual knowledge of architectural matters. During his sojourn at Potsdam he visited the opera house in Berlin, which had just been finished. When he arrived at the grand foyer, he went up into the gallery that surrounded it and looked carefully at the ceiling. "The architect," he said, "without knowing it, wanted to give us a surprise. If a person standing at the end of the room with his face turned to the wall speaks a word in a low voice, another person at the opposite end and also facing the wall will understand it perfectly; at any other spot in the room he will hear nothing at all." Just the conformation of the vault had revealed to Bach this acoustical phenomenon.

A man endowed with such clarity of thought could not fail to possess to a high degree the faculty of transmitting to others what he had acquired by his work. Bach was a remarkable teacher. His failures as a teacher at St. Thomas are to be attributed much less to a lack of teaching ability than to his inability to keep the respect of very young people. The member of the council at Leipzig who said after his death, "Herr Bach was a good musician but a bad professor," was right if by "professor" he meant schoolteacher. Kant, speaking of his long years as a tutor, loved to poke fun at himself: "Never," said he, "with the best intentions in the world was there a worse tutor." In the same way one might say of Bach: "Never with the greatest pedagogical talent has there been a worse schoolteacher." On the contrary, those who came to him to study under his direction found in him the best of guides. The distinction won by his pupils substantiates this: Johann Tobias Krebs, later court organist at Altenburg (dead in 1780); Johann Philipp Kirnberger (1721–1783), afterwards court musician for the princess Amelia of Prussia; and Kittel. It was Kittel who handed down to the nineteenth century the traditions of Bach's organ playing; he lived until 1809.

Forkel devotes a very interesting chapter to Bach as a professor. Doubtless Emmanuel had told him a great deal about this subject. Bach started his students with lessons in touch. We know that he had a peculiar method of fingering: to let the cord attacked vibrate to the full, he did not lift his finger directly from the key but drew it backwards and so performed a rapid *glissando*.[1] Forkel describes this touch without being able to explain its details. The students kept at these exercises for several months. To give them a rest, Bach had them play little pieces which he often composed during the lessons themselves. This is the origin of the *Preludes for Beginners* and the *Inventions*. Emmanuel Bach tells us that he would not let them linger too long on the easy pieces, but from the very beginning loved to inure them to difficulties. The *Klavierbüchlein* of Wilhelm Friedemann we have already mentioned offers the pupil very quickly indeed little pieces of some difficulty. For example, the master wanted to familiarize him at the beginning with all the kinds of ornaments: on the first page of the *Klavierbüchlein* of Friedemann all the indications for embellishments are illustrated with notes. It is a precious indication for us; these things show us how we must render the mannerisms and grace notes in the works of Bach.

To encourage his pupils he had the habit of playing for them, often several times, everything that he gave them to study. Gerber, who was his pupil from 1724 to 1727, tells us that Bach had played for him no less than three times the first part of the *Well-Tempered Clavichord*. "Among the happiest hours of my life," Gerber says, "I count those when Bach, pretending that he was not inclined to make me study, sat down in front of one of his admirable instruments, and so changed the hours into minutes."

But while he was teaching his disciples technique, he was instruct-

---

[1] This discription of Bach's method of touch is obviously not the modern idea of the *glissando*, which means running the finger over a number of keys in succession. C. R. J.

ing them in the elementary rules of composition. All the pieces he
had them play were presented to them at the same time as models of
composition, and he had them make an analysis of them. This double
purpose shows up clearly in the title of the *Inventions* and in the
title of the *Orgelbüchlein*. The *Inventions* are written to teach the
correct playing of two or three parts, to help the pupil to develop
for himself a fine *cantabile* style (*eine cantable Art im Spielen*")—
something that was essential in the eyes of Bach—and, finally, to give
him a "strong foretaste" of composition.

For special lessons in composition he had his own method, which
differed from every other course of lessons. Instead of beginning with
simple counterpoint, he had his pupils immediately harmonize chorales of four parts, and initiated them in composing a figured bass
correctly and interestingly. Every lesson in Harmony became at the
same time a lesson in counterpoint. His suggestions for the figured
bass have fortunately come down to us in different forms. The 1725
Klavierbüchlein of Anna Magdalena contains several brief explanations.[1] Moreover, we have a complete course on the same subject,
thanks to the copy that a certain Johann Peter Kellner made in 1738.
The original manuscript, we feel sure, was written from Bach's dicta-
tion to his class. Forkel does not mention this course, so precious for
the numerous examples it gives.[2] One cannot imagine more precise instruction. The introduction of material all by itself reveals the great
yet practical man. After having given some etymological information
and a few definitions, after having explained of what intervals the
perfect chord is composed, he immediately comes to the formulation
of a general rule: "The hands must always be made to move in contrary movements, in order to avoid successions of fifths and octaves."
Therefore from the very first lesson the pupil takes away experiments
to try.

Let us add another document no less valuable. Bach had the habit
of having his advanced pupils write out figured basses of strange

[1] They are reproduced in Spitta II, pp. 951 f.
[2] "*Des Königlichen Hof-Compositeurs und Capellmeisters in gleichen Direc-
toris musices wie auch Cantoris der Thomasschule, Herrn Johann Sebastian Bach
zu Leipzig Vorschriften und Grundsätze zum vierstimmigen Spielen des General-
Bass oder Accompagnement, für seine Scholaren in der Musik 1738.*" Spitta re-
produces this manuscript, II, pp. 913–952.

sonatas, which he afterwards corrected. So it was that Gerber, of
whom we have already spoken, had to elaborate a sonata for the
violin by Albinoni; his manuscript, with Bach's corrections, has come
down to us, thanks to his son.[1]

As soon as his pupils had become familiar with the figured bass,
they were set at the study of the fugue. Bach forbade them to com-
pose on the harpsichord; and wanted above everything else to lead
them to reason clearly.

He compared each part to a person in the act of speaking. It was
forbidden to interrupt him or to silence him until he had said everything he had to say; it was just as much forbidden to let him speak
when he had nothing to say. In correcting their essays, he urged
them above everything else to avoid all "disorder." But with the
personality of each part so respected he permitted them all kinds
of liberties. There was no audacity which he would not tolerate, on
the condition that there were reasonable ideas behind it. The pupils
who had no imagination were eliminated at the beginning. All this,
nonetheless, was in his eyes only the first apprenticeship; for genuine
progress in the art of composition he knew only one way, that which
he had followed himself: the study of the masterpieces. To become
familiar with everything that is beautiful, that was for anyone the
best way of teaching oneself; and he not only formulated the principle, he did better still—he applied it himself.

Still, among his numerous pupils, one cannot cite a single one
who became a great composer; not even Friedemann, not even Emmanuel. They were only talented men. Even Julius Krebs, of whom
Bach himself was the most proud, did not rise in his compositions
above the level of honest mediocrity. They became orchestra leaders,
cantors, or remarkable organists; but at bottom they owed their pres-
tige and their distinction to the fact that they were former pupils of
Bach.

There were only two of them in reality to whom posterity owed
something: Emmanuel Bach and Kirnberger. Again, it is not to their
compositions that they owe their celebrity—though the harpsichord
compositions of Emmanuel are truly remarkable in some respects—

[1] The manuscript is reproduced in Spitta at the end of the second volume.

but to the theoretical works in which they formulated and popularized the master's principles of teaching. Emmanuel wrote his two volumes, *Sur la Véritable Façon de Toucher du Clavecin* [The True Method of Harpsichord Playing],[1] whose importance in the history of the modern piano we know. Kirnberger wrote his great work in two volumes on the theory of composition, in which he developed Bach's idea about teaching, and urged above everything else that one should begin with four-part harmonizations and not with little exercises in counterpoint; a work which stirred up long discussions in the world of the theoretician.[2]

Bach's pupils have added nothing, then, to the glory of their master; nor have they helped to make his works known. Though they played his organ and harpsichord compositions, they allowed the cantatas and the Passions to pass into oblivion. Emmanuel performed the cantatas and the Passions well at Hamburg; but his brother and he kept for themselves all their father's scores, and their friends even had to pay for the privilege of going through them. At Leipzig there remained only a very small number of Bach cantatas. Moreover, Doles, a pupil of Bach's, who was appointed cantor of St. Thomas in 1755, was not the kind of man to administer the great heritage that had come down to him. Already during Bach's lifetime he had tried to play a rôle as composer beside the master. His insignificant and sentimental works would never lead one to suspect whose disciple he was. He rendered some of Bach's works well, but without giving a thought to the possibility of establishing a Bach cult at St. Thomas.

And yet what difference does it make to the great geniuses if their immediate pupils are mediocre? They continue to instruct by their own works. When Bach recommended to his pupils above everything else the study of classic works, he did not suspect that his real teaching would begin when posterity should rediscover his Passions and his cantatas. It is told of Brahms that he awaited with impatience the appearance of each new volume in the *Bachgesellschaft* edition, and the moment he received it dropped everything else he was doing to

---

[1] Philipp Emmanuel Bach (1714–1788): *Versuch über die wahre Art das Klavier zu spielen.* Two volumes, Leipzig, 1753–1762.

[2] Johann Philipp Kirnberger: *Die Kunst des reinen Satzes in der Musik.* First part, 1774; second part, 1776–1779. The work has not been completed.

go through it; "for," said he, "with this old Bach there are always surprises, and one always learns something new." When a new volume of the great edition of Händel's work arrived he put it on the shelf, saying, "It ought to be very interesting; I will go through it as soon as I have the time."

6. BACH'S PIETY

One trait in the character of Bach is missing in this outline—the essential trait: Bach was a pious man. It was his piety that sustained him and kept him serene in his laborious existence. His scores, without any other document, would suffice to show us this; almost all of them carry at the head: "S.D.G.," *Soli Deo Gloria*. On the cover of the *Orgelbüchlein* the following verse may be read:

> *Dem höchsten Gott allein zu Ehren,*
> *Dem Nächsten draus sich zu belehren.*
> [For the honor of the most high God alone
> And for the instruction of my neighbor.]

This deeply religious spirit is disclosed even in Friedemann's *Klavierbüchlein*; at the top of the page where the first little pieces to play begin are the words, "*In Nomine Jesu*." With anyone else these declarations of piety, scattered at every turn, and under the most insignificant circumstances, would appear exaggerated, if not affected. With Bach one feels that there is nothing there unnatural. Certainly here was a profound spirit; but profound not after the fashion of those who in a sort of jealous fear anxiously disclose to the public their internal life. There was something frank about his piety. He did not withdraw from it; it constituted an integral part of his artistic nature. If he embellished all his scores with his "S.D.G." it was because music was something essentially religious to him. It was after all the most powerful means of glorifying God; music as a secular accomplishment occupied only the second place. This fundamentally religious conception of art is completely expressed in his definition of harmony. "The figured bass," he says in his course, "is the most perfect foundation of music. It is executed with two hands; the left hand plays the prescribed notes, and the right hand adds consonances and dissonances in order that the whole shall produce an agreeable harmony for the honor of God and for the proper delight of the soul. Like all music, the figured bass has no other purpose than the glory of God and the refreshment of the spirit; otherwise it is not true music, but a diabolical and repetitious prattle [*ein teuflisches Geplerr und Geleyer*]." It was therefore wholly natural that he should speak in a somewhat disdainful fashion of secular art. Witness the proposal he made to Friedemann when he invited him to accompany him to the Dresden opera: "What do you say if we should go again to listen to the pretty little songs of Dresden (*die schönen Dresdener Liederchen*)?" But this did not prevent him from writing secular music and even burlesque cantatas! In the last analysis this activity was less a work of art for him than a pastime and a recreation for his spirit.

This pious artist had a remarkable theological knowledge. The theological works mentioned in the inventory certainly enabled him to have opinions on the numerous dogmatic questions which were then agitating Protestantism. Did he not live in that troubled epoch which followed the Reformation, in the time of that second Reformation which arose, we know, at the turn of the seventeenth and eighteenth centuries, and in time was to produce a transformation in the spirit of Protestantism? The subjectivism in religion which had been restricted within definite limits by Luther reappeared at that time in all its strength in Spener, the leader of pietism.

Spener was by birth an Alsatian—he was born at Ribeauvillé in 1635; and he occupied ecclesiastical posts of great importance in turn at Frankfort a/M., at Dresden and at Berlin. He died in this last city in 1705. Without desiring to work an injury to the fundamental dogmas of his church, the leader of the pietists insisted however on the importance of individual piety; and by that very insistence put in doubt (without wanting to) the normative worth of formulated dogma. In any case Lutheran orthodoxy, which after the death of Luther had inaugurated a kind of new scholasticism, felt itself attacked. The struggle was engaged on all fronts. To speak the truth, it was never to end; the same strained relations still exist at this very moment between Protestant subjectivism and the dogma adopted by the Reformation, between pietism and orthodoxy.

This struggle between the orthodox and the pietists had at the time of Bach reached its climax. One might believe that the individual piety of the master had carried him to the new tendency. Numerous indeed in his works are the traces of pietism. The theological reflections, the turn of his sentences, and especially his use of diminutives—in short, his sentimentalism—all these are so many indications of the influence of pietism. His Passions can not disavow the date of their birth; one feels that they were born at a time when pietism begins to take root in the spiritual poetry of Protestantism. And still Bach was a member of the orthodox clan. The Weimar registers are there to attest to this fact; they show us that he chose as godfather for his first child the pastor Georg Christian Eilmar of Mulhouse. But this pastor Eilmar was the protagonist of the orthodox party in Mulhouse; he had attacked in a brutal fashion the pietist pastor Frohne, his older colleague. At the very time when Bach was at Mulhouse the council had even to intervene, to prevent a complete schism in the parish. Frohne—his attitude during the strife is ample proof—was a man profoundly pious, distinguished, sympathetic in every respect. Eilmar himself was the exact contrary; he was not only aggressive, but also spiteful, devoid of all intelligence and of every religious sentiment. And it was with this representative of orthodoxy that Bach was bound in friendship! Otherwise would he have chosen him as the godfather of his child, especially since he had already left' Mulhouse when the baptism occurred?

How can we explain this dual religious attitude of Bach? At bottom he was a conservative spirit; quite naturally, therefore, he took his place with the orthodox, and saw in the pietists only inopportune innovators. Pietism, moreover, was antiartistic, in that it extolled the greatest simplicity in the service, was suspicious of art, and saw in its introduction in the church only a dangerous invasion of mundane pomp. The cantata and everything that closely or remotely resembled concert music was suspected by the pietists, who spared the chorale only because of its simplicity. This was why his sympathies at Mulhouse were with a man who in other respects little deserved them.

At heart Bach was neither pietistic nor orthodox: he was a mystic thinker. Mysticism was the living spring from which sprang his piety.

There are certain chorales and certain cantatas which make us feel more than elsewhere that the master has poured into them his soul. These are precisely the mystical chorales and cantatas. Like all the mystics, Bach, one may say, was obsessed by religious pessimism. This robust and healthy man, who lived surrounded by the affection of a great family, this man who was embodied energy and activity, who even had a pronounced taste for the frankly burlesque, felt at the bottom of his soul an intense desire, a *Sehnsucht*, for eternal rest. He knew, if any mortal ever did, what nostalgia for death was. Never elsewhere had this nostalgia for death been translated into music in a more impressive way. Many are the cantatas he wrote to describe the weariness of life. The moment the Gospels touch on the cherished idea, Bach seizes it and devotes to it a long description.[1] All the cantatas for bass alone are in this sense mystical cantatas. They

[1] Here are some of these cantatas:

Liebster Gott, wann werd ich sterben, No. 8
[Dearest God, when shall I die]

Liebster Jesu, mein Verlangen, No. 32
[Dearest Jesus, my desire]

Schlage doch, gewünschte Stunde, No. 53
[Strike, then, longed-for hour]

Ich will den Kreuzstab gerne tragen, No. 56
[I will gladly bear the cross]

Selig ist der Mann, No. 57
[Blessed is the man]

Ich habe genug, No. 82
[I have had enough]

Gotteszeit ist die allerbeste Zeit, No. 106
[God's time is the best time of all]

Ach lieben Christen seid getrost, No. 114
[O dear Christian, be comforted]

Ich steh mit einem Fuss im Grabe, No. 156
[I am standing with one foot in the grave]

Komm du süsse Todesstunde, No. 161
[Come, sweet hour of death]

Ach ich sehe, jetzt da ich zur Hochzeit gehe, No. 162
[Ah, I see, now that I go to the wedding].

begin with the idea of weariness of life; then, little by little, the
expectation of death quiets and illumines; in death Bach celebrates
the supreme liberation, and describes in lovely spiritual lullabies the
peace that at this thought invades his soul; or again, his happiness is
translated into joyous and exuberant themes of a supernatural gaiety.
We feel that his whole soul sings in this music, and that the believer
has written it in a sort of exaltation. How powerful, moreover, is the
impression! What a penetrating charm is in the admirable cradle
song, "*Schlummert ein ihr müden Augen*" [Fall asleep, you weary
eyes], in the cantata "*Ich habe genug*" [I have had enough] (No. 82),
or again in the simple melody "*Komm, süsser Tod!*" [Come, sweet
death!].

So desired, so awaited, death did not at all surprise him. At the
supreme moment his face must have been transfigured with that
supernatural smile that we believe we can see in his cantatas and his
mystical chorales.

7. Bach's Appearance, *Summa Vitae*

Four oil paintings have preserved for us Bach's features; one of
them, the one executed by the court painter Hausmann for the Mizler Society, is at the St. Thomas School. Moreover, there exists a
modern bust which has a very special value, having been modelled
from a skull found in the St. Johann Cemetery in Leipzig, which
without any doubt is the skull of Bach himself.[1] In 1894, when the
church of St. Johann was being rebuilt, they dug up the old cemetery
that surrounded it. We know from the registers that Bach was buried
there in a rather shallow grave and in an oak coffin—the ordinary
caskets were made of fir. Moreover, a local tradition had it that he
was buried south of the church six paces in a straight line from the
door. And indeed at this very spot they found an oak coffin containing the skeleton of an old man, whose skull had the characteristic
features of Bach's head, as the oil paintings reveal them: prominent
eyebrows, very marked nasal angle, a somewhat protruding lower
jaw, very prominent chin. A renowned sculptor, Seffner, using as a

[1] See William Cart's study of Bach, pp. 252 f.

base a cast from this skull, made a bust of Bach with the valuable assistance of Herr His, professor of anatomy in the University of Leipzig, who gave him precise indications of the proportions which the fleshy parts and the muscles of the head would present at a given age. The bust obtained from these data confirms and completes to a certain extent the contemporary portraits of Bach.

Nonetheless, in spite of these portraits and this bust, the real appearance of Bach remains an enigma. We see easily a certain energy in the forehead, between the eyebrows something severe and sombre, and in the mouth a certain kindliness. But what the artists do not picture at all is the ensemble of his physiognomy. They have tried to seize his face in a state of repose, but this state was not at all natural to him; they combine and express simultaneously the different aspects of his face, but without accentuating his characteristic expression *par excellence*. These composite portraits are therefore to some extent impersonal ones, which assemble on the same canvas the different traits of the master without even attempting to catch the personality behind his face.

Only an artist of the first rank could have made a true portrait of Bach. The portrait painters of that day, considerable as they were, have in reality supplied us with only the elements of a portrait of him; and it is only when our imagination animates the features, lending a smile to them or letting the light play on them, that we can evoke the true Bach.

In general, let us say in conclusion, Bach was a happy man. Certainly his long career was a weary one, certainly he was not spared vexations; he lived in an environment too narrow for him not to be frequently wounded; and the last years of his life went by in a certain isolation. But he did not know the supreme sadness of the artist—the indifference of his contemporaries; justice was his lot even during his lifetime. His contemporaries revered him; he was able to render all his works himself; he lived in the midst of a large family, protected from material anxieties, having as his confidants and as his artistic companions his wife and his elder sons. What more could the man and the artist desire? Compare this calm existence with the tumults and the internal discords of Beethoven, or the stormy life of Wagner, full of strife, of assaults and of despair!

✣

THE SYMBOLISM OF BACH [1]

BACH was a poet; and this poet was at the same time a painter. This is not at all a paradox. We have the habit of classifying an artist according to the means he uses to interpret his inner life: a musician if he uses sounds, a painter if he uses colors, a poet if he uses words. But we must admit that these categories, established by external criteria, are very arbitrary. The soul of an artist is a complex whole, in which mingle in proportions infinitely variable the gifts of the poet, the painter, the musician. Nothing compels us to set forth as a principle that the sort of thing that issues from a man must always express an internal dream of the same order: that, for instance, one can transcribe a dream of a musical nature with the help of sound. There is no impossibility in conceiving a poet's dream expressed in color, or a musician's dream taking the form of words, and so forth. The instances of such transcriptions abound.

Schiller was a musician. In conceiving his works he had auditive sensations. In a letter to Körner May 25, 1792, he expressed himself thus: "The music of a poem is more often present in my soul, when I sit down at my table to write, than the exact idea of the contents, about which I am often hardly in agreement with myself." Goethe himself was a painter to this extent, that he was for a long time haunted by the idea that that perhaps was his true vocation. He studied design with assiduity, and suffered from not being able to render things as he saw them. We know how he sought to consult fate, in the course of a journey on foot which took him from Wetzlar towards the Rhine, in order to put an end to these uncertainties and to decide upon his future. "I was following the right bank of the Lahn," he says in *Dichtung und Wahrheit*, "and I saw at some distance below me the river shining in the rays of the sun, and partly hidden by a lush growth of willows. Then my old desire to be able to paint such things worthily awakened in me. By chance I held in my left hand a fine pocket knife; and at the very moment I heard

---

[1] From *J. S. Bach. Le Musicien–Poète*, by Albert Schweitzer. Leipzig: Breitkopf & Härtel, 1908, pp. 325–341.

resounding in my soul an imperious command to hurl this knife immediately into the stream. If I saw it fall into the water, my artistic aspirations would be realized; if the fall of the knife were hidden by the overhanging branches, I should have to renounce my wishes and my efforts. I had hardly thought of it when this fancy was executed, for without any regard for the utility of the knife, which had a number of parts, I threw it immediately with all my strength and with my left hand into the river. Unfortunately, this time I also experienced the deceitful ambiguity of oracles, of which the ancients have already so bitterly complained. The plunge of the knife was hidden from me by the last branches of the willows, but the water was thrown up by the shock like a powerful fountain and was perfectly visible to me. I did not interpret the incident to my advantage; and the doubt it awakened in my mind had subsequently this unhappy consequence, that I applied myself to the study of design in a more desultory and negligent manner. Thus I myself gave the oracle the chance to fulfil itself."

He became a poet, therefore, while he remained a painter: his work is composed of portraits and landscapes. Visual evocation—in this lie the originality and the secret of his narrative talent. His letters from Switzerland are sketches; and in his letters from Italy he congratulates himself "on having always had the gift of seeing the world with the eyes of a painter, whose pictures were present to his mind." In his gondola trips, Venice seemed to him like a succession of pictures from the Venetian school. His characters are portraits; in Faust, it is himself that he paints. All the idyllic scenes in this vast drama, naïve, tragic, burlesque, fantastic, allegoric, are so many backdrops on which the portrait of Goethe stands out at different moments of his life. Even music he perceived in a visual form: in listening to Bach he saw tall people in their finery descending with solemn steps a great staircase.

Is there any reason for recalling the classic case of Taine, this painter in literature? Gottfried Keller, author of *Romeo and Juliet in the Village*, began in the same way with painting. Conversely, Böcklin is a poet who has gone astray among the painters. His poetic imagination carries him away to mythological distances, and calls forth before his painter's eyes, in the form of concrete images, this world of elementary forces dreamed of by the pantheistic poets. From that moment on what does the poet care for lines or colors? Pictorial composition, exactness of design—he holds them cheap; the essential thing for him is ever more and more to express his ideas. Nothing is more significant in this respect than Böcklin's last work, that formless but dramatic picture in the museum at Basel of the pestilence.

Nietzsche was a musician. He even made some attempts at musical composition, and submitted his drafts to Wagner. They are still more mediocre than the designs of Goethe. But at one time he thought he had the gifts of a composer. He did possess them, in effect: it was he who created in literature the symphonic style. His method of composing a literary work is that of a writer of symphonies; study from this point of view his *Jenseits von Gut und Böse* [Beyond Good and Evil], and you will find even little fugues like those in the symphonies of Beethoven. To read a work without rhythm was for him an ordeal. "Even our good musicians write badly," he cried peevishly. Is not this affinity strange between Nietzsche, the musician among the thinkers, and Wagner, the thinker among the musicians? Their fate was to meet only to separate, to love each other only to hate each other. Yet nevertheless, of all the Wagnerians Nietzsche is the only one who understood the soul of the master of Bayreuth. It was he who found this formula, so perfectly true, to characterize the artistic spirit of Wagner: "Wagner as a musician should be classified among the painters; as a poet among the musicians; as an artist, in a more general sense, among the actors."

It is from this coexistence of different artistic instincts in the same personality that we must start to establish those reciprocal relations which unite the arts. In esthetics we have too long delighted in formulating definitions borrowed from the nature of the different arts, and then in piling up on this arbitrary base theories and controversies. From this there have usually resulted axioms and judgments whose solidity was only illusory. What has not been said or written about descriptive music! For some it is nothing less than the final goal of all music; for others, it represents the degeneracy of pure music: affirmations diametrically opposed, neither of which may be called false, but which contain only parts of the truth. How resolve this antinomy? By studying the question, we would say, from the point of view of the psychology of history.

Every art teaches us psychology, manifesting "descriptive" tendencies in so far as it wishes to express more than its own proper medium of expression will permit. Painting wants to express the feelings of the poet; poetry wants to evoke plastic visions; music wishes to paint and to express ideas. It is as if the soul of "the other artist" wants also to speak. Pure art is only an abstraction. Every work of art, to be understood, should suggest a complex representation, in which are mingled and harmonised sensations of every kind. He who, before a picture of a landscape filled with heather, does not hear the vague music of the humming of bees, does not know how to see; just as the man for whom music evokes no vision knows not how to hear. The logic of art is the logic of the association of ideas; and the artistic impression is all the greater when the complex associations of ideas, conscious and subconscious, are communicated through the medium of the work, in a way more intense and more complete. Art is the transmission of the association of ideas.

The painters do not simply copy nature, they reproduce it; so that we may share the surprise and the emotion that they themselves, seeing her as poets, experienced in her presence. And what do they teach us, if not to look at nature everywhere with the eyes of the poet?

Descriptive music is, then, legitimate; since painting and poetry are like the unconscious elements without which the language of sounds could not be conceived. There is a painter in every musician. Listen to him, and this second nature will immediately appear to you. To express the simplest idea, the musicians could not get along without pictures and metaphors. Their language is a kind of word painting; from which arises the attraction of their writings, so original, so picturesque, often also so odd and incoherent. Nothing could be more interesting than their letters in this regard: they show their minds ceaselessly agitated by visual images.

The descriptive tendency appears already in the works of the primitives. It is a very naïve, imitative tendency; they wish to reproduce the song of the birds, laughter, lamentation, the sound of a spring or a cascade; even more, they pretend to represent entire scenes, and end with musical narrations where the climaxes in a composition are supposed to correspond to those of a story. It is precisely in the two generations before Bach that we see the simultaneous appearance in Italy, Germany and France of this rudimentary descriptive music. So it is in characteristic pieces of Froberger and the French harpsichordists, with which Bach was acquainted; in the orchestral descriptions of the Hamburg masters, the Keisers, the Matthesons and the Telemanns; and especially in the biblical sonatas of Kuhnau, which are a kind of classic expression of this tendency.[1]

This primitive descriptive music has not come to an end; on the contrary, it reappears with all its pretensions in our program music. In the hands of Liszt and his disciples, great and small, who travel in this direction, the symphony becomes a symphonic poem *(Symphonische Dichtung)*. The climaxes cannot be explained by themselves; they necessitate a commentator to announce what the music is going to represent. Make no mistake: however great the means it employs and the clarity of expression it attains, this descriptive music is nonetheless primitive and marginal in art, just because it cannot be explained by itself. And when it is practised by musicians of the second order, it is in vain that they multiply the explanations and comments on each measure; this primitive character becomes only more accentuated. Such were the old painters, who used to represent the utterance of their characters by garlands of words issuing from their mouths, instead of being content with gestures and expressions.

The story of primitive descriptive music is divided into two periods, therefore: ancient and modern. Here and there we are in the presence of normal tendencies, which in view of the way they appear and develop have resulted only in a false art.

In pictorial art we notice an analogous anomaly: biblical painting. Seduced by episodes known to everybody, the painters, ancient and modern, allow themselves to be carried beyond the natural limits of pictorial narration. They think to represent such and such an episode in sacred history by assembling on the same canvas the people who figure in it; they never think of asking if the action in the episode could be concentrated in a single scene and be interpreted in a con-

---

[1] The beginnings of descriptive music merit a special study. It would be necessary to assemble all the material in question, which has not yet been done.

crete way by the attitude of characters, as the logic of every pictorial composition requires. Like the biblical scenes in Kuhnau's cantatas, their works can be explained only by their implications. A man with a knife, a child with bound hands, a head which appears through the clouds, a ram in the bushes: all these brought together on a single canvas represent the story of Abraham's sacrifice. A woman and a man sitting beside a well, a dozen men coming two by two along the road, in the background people leaving a village: this is Jesus and the Samaritan woman.

Biblical painting provides an abundance of examples of this false pictorial narration, which in truth is only pretty imagery. However finished the execution, it does not make us forget the complete absence of composition. In reality there are only a very few biblical scenes that lend themselves to painting; the others are not such as to fulfil the desired conditions.

The only man who really showed discernment in his choice of subjects, and who never made a false biblical painting, is Michelangelo. Let us compare with his powerful evocations of sacred history the simple illustrations that Veronese has given us. Admirable and enchanting as *The Marriage at Cana* is in form, should we not think this was an ordinary banquet if it were not for a kind of tacit understanding between the painter and the public?

Biblical painting and historical painting are the two aspects of false description in the history of painting; and these two chapters in the history of plastic art have their parallel in the history of music. The two supreme representatives of the descriptive *genre* are, in plastic art Michelangelo, in music Bach.

Bach was a poet; but he lacked the gift of expression. His language was without distinction, and his poetic taste was no more developed than that of his contemporaries. Would he otherwise have accepted so gladly the libretti of Picander?

Nonetheless, he was a poet in his soul, in that he looked in a text first of all for the poetry it contained. What a difference there was between him and Mozart! Mozart is purely a musician; he takes a given text and clothes it in a beautiful melody. Bach, on the other hand, digs in it; he explores it thoroughly, until he has found the idea which in his eyes represents the heart of it and which he will have to illustrate in music. He has a horror of neutral music, super-imposed on a text with nothing in common with it except the rhythm and a wholly general feeling. Often, it is true, when he finds himself in the presence of a text which has no salient idea, he is forced to make the best of a bad situation; but before resigning himself to it he does his utmost to discover some germ of music in the text itself. The musical phrase he applies to it is already born from the natural rhythm of the words. In this he goes beyond Wagner. In Händel we often perceive a latent antagonism between the words of the poetic text and the musical phrase superimposed on it. For instance, he sometimes divides long periods into several phrases, which cease from that point to form a whole. In Bach, on the other hand, the musical period is modelled on the phrasing of the text; it springs from it naturally. The longest phrase is rendered by one of those magnificent musical periods of which he has the secret. From passages without any structure, which at first sight seem un-suited to any declamation, he draws the most beautiful musical phrases, and with such a natural skill that one is surprised he did not suspect this phrasing before.[1]

His greatest concern was to give the text the lustre that music requires. It does not matter much to him that he amplifies the feeling expressed by these words; contentment readily becomes exuberant joy, and sadness extreme anguish. Often he seizes upon a single word which for him gathers up all the musical substance of the text, and in his composition gives it an importance it actually does not have. This is evident in the text of the cantata *Es ist ein trotzig und versagtes Ding* [It is an insolent and discouraging thing], No. 176, where he has given musical expression only to the word "trotzig" [in-solent], though the whole passage has rather to do with contrition. Often he presents the text in a false light; but he always brings into

---

[1] Let us cite, for instance, the first chorus in the cantata *Die Himmel erzählen die Ehre Gottes* [The heavens declare the glory of God] (Psalm 19:2, 4), No. 76, and the cantata *Nach dir Herr verlanget mich* [I long for thee, Lord], No. 150. One appreciates this art particularly wherever Bach has set to music biblical verses. These are the ones, indeed, which present the most difficulty in musical declamation, never having been intended for music, and characterized, because of the various translations to which they have been subjected, by a strange and incoherent style.

the foreground the idea that lends itself to musical expression. The composition brings this out, as in repoussé work.

His dramatic instinct is not less developed. The plan of the *St. Matthew Passion*, so admirably conceived from the dramatic point of view, is his own invention. In every text he seeks the contrasts, the opposing elements, the gradations, to be brought out by the music. In the little collection of chorales (*Orgelbüchlein*) he brings out most clearly the importance he attaches to the contrasts: he arranges the chorales there in such a way that one sets another in relief. In the same way, in the mystical cantatas he opposes the fear of death (*Todesfurcht*) to the joyous nostalgia for death (*Freudige Todessehnsucht*). He often enriches a text by commenting upon it with a chorale theme which one hears in the orchestra. To the text "*Ich steh mit einem Fuss im Grabe*" [I am standing with one foot in the grave] is added the chorale, "Lord, deal with me according to Thy mercy" (Cantata No. 156); in a recitative from the cantata "*Wachet, betet*" [Watch and pray], No. 70, the trumpet suddenly sounds the chorale of the last judgment, "*Es ist gewisslich an der Zeit*" [Surely it is the time]; in the cantata "*Sehet, wir gehen hinauf nach Jerusalem*" [Come, we are going up to Jerusalem], No. 159, rises the passion chorale, "*O Haupt voll Blut und Wunden*" [O Head, covered with blood and wounds].[1][2]

But that which occupies the most prominent place in his work is pictorial poetry. Above everything else he seeks the picture, and in this respect he is very different from Wagner, who is rather a lyric dramatist. Bach himself is nearer to Berlioz, and nearer still to Michelangelo. If it had been possible for him to see a picture by Michelangelo, doubtless he would have found in him something of his own soul.

But his contemporaries remained unaware of his painter's soul. His pupils and his sons did not perceive his pictorial instincts, any more than they suspected that his true greatness was as a musical poet. So too with Forkel, Mossevius, von Winterfeld, Bitter, and Spitta. Spitta, whose profound acquaintance with the works of Bach

[1] Usually translated "O sacred Head, now wounded." C. R. J.
[2] For other examples of texts illustrated with chorale melodies see cantatas Nos. 14, 23, 25, 48, 75, 106, 127, 161.

put him in a position to see things clearly, has a fear of carrying his researches in that direction. When he cannot do otherwise, he confesses that such and such a page contains descriptive music; and is always sure to add that it is there purely by accident, to which one would be wrong to attach any importance. These examples are curiosities for him, nothing more. On every occasion he insists that the music of Bach is above such puerilities, that it is pure music, the only kind that is classic. This apprehension leads him astray. The fear that one day someone would find descriptive music in Bach, and that this discovery would injure his reputation as a classic writer, prevents Spitta from recognising the rôle which it plays in his compositions.

Let us watch Bach at his work. However bad the text, he is satisfied with it if it contains a picture. When he discovers a pictorial idea it takes the place of the whole text; he seizes on it even at the risk of going contrary to the dominant idea of the text. Preoccupied as he is exclusively with the pictorial element, he does not perceive the weakness and the flaws in the libretto.

Nature itself he perceives, so to speak, in a pictorial fashion. The poetry of nature in his work is not at all lyrical, as it is with Wagner: it is seen rather than felt; it is the tornadoes, the clouds that advance along the horizon, the falling leaves, the restless waves.

His symbolism also is visual, like that of a painter; that is how he expresses ideas that are completely abstract. In the cantata No. 77, for the thirteenth Sunday after Trinity, he deals with the verse from the Gospels, "Thou shalt love the Lord thy God with all thy heart, and with all thy soul, and with all thy strength, and with all thy mind, and thou shalt love thy neighbor as thyself" (Lk. 10:27), Christ's reply to the scribe who asked him what was the greatest of all the commandments. These commandments, great and little, are then represented by the melody from the chorale *Dies sind die heilgen zehn Gebote* [These are the holy ten commandments], which the organ basses sound forth in minims and the trumpets in crotchets, while the choir renders the words of the Savior, who proclaims the new law of love.

Was Bach clearly conscious of this pictorial instinct? He hardly seems to have been. We have not found among his confidences to

his pupils any allusion that allows us to say so. The title of the
Orgelbüchlein announces that the pieces contained there are model
chorales; but he does not say that they are typical just because they
are descriptive. And besides, are not all the parodies he made of his
own works, that suppress in this way the pictorial intent of his music,
there to show that his descriptive instinct was unconscious? Then
where in the genius is the dividing line between the conscious and
the unconscious? Is he not one and the other at the same time? This
is true of Bach: he is not conscious of the importance in his work of
descriptive music; but in his way of seeing the subjects to be treated,
and in his choice of the means, he is thoroughly clairvoyant.

The great mistake of all the primitives consists in wishing to translate into music everything they find in a text. Bach avoids this danger.
He is well aware that the climaxes of a text should be, if one is to
risk retracing them with sound, both simple and strongly accented.
Hence the times when he uses this means are very rare.

Moreover, when he follows the indications of a text he does not
insist upon it in the pretentious fashion of the primitives. We must
admire the way in which, in the recitatives of the *St. Matthew Passion*, he underlines one word in this way, and another word in that.
These are light musical inflections, destined to pass unobserved. It
is the same with the cantatas and with the chorales. On the other
hand, when a new motif appears in the text the music changes immediately, since for Bach a new picture requires a new theme. In
some choruses two or even three themes occur successively, because
the text demands them. So in the cantata *"Siehe, ich will viel Fischer
aussenden"* [Behold, I will send out many fishermen], No. 88, based
on the text in Jeremiah: "Behold, I will send for many fishers, saith
the Lord, and they shall fish them; and after will I send for many
hunters, and they shall hunt them." The music of the first part paints
a picture of waves, because the word "fisher" brings to Bach's mind a
lake; in the second half (*Allegro quasi presto*), it is hunters climbing
over the mountains: we hear fanfares. Many of the airs show the
same peculiarity: the theme of the middle part corresponds to another image than that of the principal part.

What is there to say except that the music of Bach is descriptive
only as far as its themes are always determined by an association of

pictorial ideas? This association is sometimes energetically asserted, and sometimes is almost unconscious. There are themes whose pictorial origin would not at first be suspected, if it were not for the fact that in other works is to be found an entire series of analogous themes whose origin is not at all doubtful. There are then more accented themes that explain the origin of the others. When one brings together the Bach themes, one discovers a series of associations of pictorial ideas that are regularly repeated when the text requires them. This regularity in the association of ideas will not be found in Beethoven, or in Berlioz, or in Wagner. The only one who could be compared with Bach is Schubert. The accompaniment to his *Songs* depends on a descriptive language whose elements are identical with the language of Bach—without, however, attaining to his precision. Schubert hardly knew the works of the Leipzig cantor; but desiring to translate into music the poetry of the *Songs*, he had to agree with the man who had translated into music the poetry of the chorales.

The musical language of Bach is the most elaborate and most precise in existence. It has, after a fashion, its roots and derivations like any other language.

There is an entire series of elementary themes proceeding from visual images, each of which produces a whole family of diversified themes, in accordance with the different shades of the idea to be translated into music. From the same root we often find in the different works twenty or twenty-five variants; for to express the same idea Bach returns constantly to the same fundamental formula. Thus we encounter the walking themes *(Schrittmotive)*, expressing firmness and hesitation; the syncopated themes of weariness, themes of quiet, represented by calm undulations; Satan themes, expressed in a sort of fantastic violence; themes of serene peace; themes consisting of two slurred notes, expressing suffering nobly borne; chromatic themes in five or six notes, which express acute pain; and finally the great category of themes of joy.

There exist fifteen or twenty of these categories, in which one can catalogue all the expressive motifs characteristic of Bach. The richness of his language consists not in the abundance of different themes, but in the different inflections which the same theme takes in accordance with the occasion. Without this variety of *nuances*, one might even find fault with his language because of a certain monotony. It is indeed the linguistic monotony of all great thinkers, who find only one expression for the same idea because it is the only true one.

But Bach's language permits him to define his ideas in a surprising fashion. He has a variety of *nuances* at his disposal to describe pain or joy, which one would seek in vain among other musicians. When the elements of his language are once known, even the compositions that are not associated with any text, like the preludes and the fugues of *The Well-Tempered Clavichord*, become vocal, and announce, after a fashion, a concrete idea. If we have to do with music written for words, we can, without looking at the text, and with the help of the themes alone, define the characteristic ideas.

But the strangest fact of all is that the language of Bach is in no way the fruit of a long experience. The different motifs that express pain are already found in the *Lamento* of the *Cappricio*, which he wrote between the ages of eighteen and twenty. When he composed the *Orgelbüchlein*, which dates from the Weimar epoch, he was about thirty. But at this time all his typically expressive motifs are already formed and fixed, and are not afterwards subjected to any change. While trying to represent in music a whole series of chorales, he found himself forced to seek ways of expressing himself simply and clearly. He gives up description through musical development, and adopts the procedure of expressing everything by the theme. At the same time he fixes the principal formulas of his musical language.

These little chorales are therefore Bach's musical dictionary. One has to begin with them if one is to understand what he wants to say in the cantatas and the Passions.

But in his effort for precision in language he sometimes transgresses the natural limits of music. It is not to be denied that we find in his works many disappointing pages. It is because a goodly number of his themes proceed from vision rather than from musical imagination, properly so called. In trying to reproduce a visual image he permits himself to be carried away into the creation of themes which are admirably characteristic, but which have nothing left of the musical phrase. In his youthful works such examples were rare, because his melodic instinct was still stronger than his descriptive instinct. But later the instances of this ultra-pictorial music become frequent. Among the great chorales of 1736, some, like the chorales about the Last Supper (VI, No. 30) and about the baptism (VI, No. 17), have already passed beyond the limits of music. It is the same with all the airs constructed on the theme which pictures the steps of a stumbling man. It is so with the cantata *Ich glaube Herr, hilf meinem Unglauben* [Lord, I believe, help thou mine unbelief], No. 109, which is almost impossible to listen to, because it describes a faith that swoons with themes of this kind. Did Bach, when he played or directed these pieces himself, know how to make them agreeable by the perfection of his execution? Did he have some secret of interpretation that we have not yet discovered?

However that may be, the fact is indisputable: his pictorial interest sometimes overbalanced his musical interest. Bach then exceeded the limits of pure music. But his mistake is not comparable to that of the great and little primitives in descriptive music, who sinned through ignorance of the technical resources of the art; his error has its source in the unusual loftiness of his inspiration. Goethe in composing *Faust* thought he was writing a piece appropriate for presentation in the theatre; but the work became so great and so profound that it can hardly stand dramatic representation. With Bach, also, the intensity of a thought he desires to express without reticence and in all sincerity is sometimes so great that it injures the purely musical beauty. Mistakes were possible for him; but his errors were those which only a genius is capable of making.

V

Organs and Organ Building

*T*HE two Bach books, for there were two, were a stupendous undertaking for this young man, Albert Schweitzer. Once in later years he picked up the German edition and turned the pages thoughtfully. "Did I really write this?" he asked, with a look of bewildered wonder on his face.

But this achievement was no greater than the stupendous labor of the next eight years: student of medicine and intern, professor at the University, settled pastor of a church, organist in demand for concerts in many places, and writer of extraordinary books on medical, theological, and musical subjects. The story of these years is an amazing record of endurance and erudition.

Immediately after the French Bach, and while he was working on the German Bach, he published in 1906 his first important book in the field of religion. It was a history of research into the life of Jesus, called Von Reimarus zu Wrede. The ink of the printing presses was hardly dry before his book on organ construction appeared. The book on Jesus was the fruit of long thought and study, which had begun when he was a soldier in the Kaiser's army in 1894 and carried a Greek New Testament around with him in his knapsack. The second book was also the fruit of long study and research, which had begun in 1896 when he stopped at Stuttgart on the way back from Bayreuth to hear the new modern organ in the Liederhalle. From that moment he began to say that the new organs were not as good as the old ones.

He was not contending for the organ of Bach's day. That organ was only a kind of forerunner of the wonderful instruments built between 1850 and 1880, and best exemplified by Aristide Cavaillé–Coll's organs in St. Sulpice and Notre Dame. The organ at Notre

Dame had been exposed to the weather during the First World War, when the stained glass was removed from the church; but the organ at St. Sulpice, Widor's organ, was functioning as well when Schweitzer became acquainted with it as when it was completed in 1862, and Schweitzer felt confident that if it were properly maintained it would be equally good two centuries hence. Indeed, he thought that Gabriel might still find it useful in the last days for the "wakeful trump of doom."

Often in the years before 1899—when the venerable Cavaillé-Coll died—Schweitzer used to meet him. On many a Sunday the two would climb the high flight of steps to the great organ and watch Widor play. Cavaillé-Coll would sit on the organ bench and run his hands affectionately over the console of this, the most beautiful creation of his musical genius. Then they would go with Widor into the organist's little room with the wonderful gravures and talk.

But not always was Schweitzer in such sympathetic company. Most organists and organ builders scoffed at his strange ideas, and thought him prematurely senile. And the mad destruction of the old instruments went on. For thirty years Schweitzer carried on the fight, until he felt at last that the principles for which he contended had conquered. But what sacrifice in time and energy, what incessant travel, and unending correspondence, and ceaseless argument it cost! A few of the old organs he was able to save, in France and Denmark and Holland, the first being Silbermann's magnificent instrument in St. Thomas at Strassburg. Later, when he was working in the jungles of Africa, his friends used to say of him, "In Africa he saves old Negroes, in Europe old organs." But there were many he could not save, sacrificed because of their mechanical defects, though with the proper restoration the defects could have been removed and the beauty of tone retained. All over Europe there was a craze for size and modernity, the largest number of stops, the greatest number of gadgets, the most imposing organ case. To a Swedish organist who was much more interested in the external adornment of his instrument than in its intrinsic beauty, Schweitzer once remarked, "An organ is like a cow; one does not look at its horns so much as at its milk."

As one climbs the staircase in Schweitzer's home in Gunsbach he is reminded of Schweitzer's passionate concern for the organs of Europe. For the walls are lined with framed pictures of fine old instruments. It is no accident that some twenty-five of these pictures are of Dutch organs, while only ten or so are of organs in other countries. For Holland as a whole was never tempted by the product of the modern factory; it preferred the marvelous tone of the old organs. It is not strange that Schweitzer has gone back to Holland again and again for concert tours, and that he has a host of friends and admirers in that country.

That modern organs can be built with the lovely tone of the old instruments has been proved by the Alsatian builder, Fritz Härpfer, of Boulay; and the little organ in the Gunsbach church, restored by his artistic ability, gives forth today under the inspired fingers of Albert Schweitzer as beautiful organ music as can be heard in the greatest of cathedrals. Not the biggest instrument for the available money, but the best one; that is the ideal.

The reader should remember that these writings on organ construction and organ playing were written a good many years ago, and do not reflect Dr. Schweitzer's present opinions concerning these matters. They are included here because of their importance in the history of the organ during the past forty-five years. Dr. Schweitzer intends to comment in the near future upon recent tendencies in organ construction.

The book which follows was dedicated to "Professor Ernest Munch, teacher of Alsatian organists, in heartfelt friendship."

❦

THE ART OF ORGAN BUILDING AND ORGAN PLAYING IN GERMANY AND FRANCE [1]

EVEN if it be true that the signature of our time is travel, it must still be conceded that this travel has not brought equal benefit to all domains of art, and that certain indications might almost make one doubt whether art had entered the sign of travel at all. One may ask himself candidly whether a kind of itinerant virtuosity has not profited almost exclusively from it, and whether the art of learning,

[1] From *Deutsche und französische Orgelbaukunst und Orgelkunst*, by Albert Schweitzer. Leipzig: Breitkopf & Härtel, 1906.

which seeks to appropriate the best in the lands of all the masters, has not rather gone backwards because of it. It almost seems as if art in the time of Bach was in a certain sense more artistic in its internationalism than it is today, in so far as people used to travel at that time to learn and to teach, whereas today they travel more often to perform.

That artistic ramparts exist, in spite of the sign of travel, to a greater extent than one might suppose, becomes clear to me each time I talk with a French organist about German organs and the German art of organ playing, and with a German organist about French organs and the French art of organ playing. It is something more than total ignorance about conditions on the other side that comes to light; it is almost an impossibility to understand one another even with the best will imaginable. It does not help to intercede in Paris for Reger and others among our promising young organists, and in Germany to call attention to Widor's organ symphonies. What purpose does this serve? Reger's works cannot be performed on the organ of Notre Dame or on the organ of St. Sulpice, and Widor's symphonies can be rendered on German organs only by doing a kind of violence to the nature and arrangement of the instruments.

"Therefore," each party says, "the other organ is no good." This shows that neither side knows the other organ. In order to bring this judgment, from which nothing of value issues, into a field of intelligent discussion that can be advantageous to the organ and to organ playing, and in order to acquaint the quarreling parties with each other, I take the floor as one who has had the advantage of both the German and the French schools, as one who by force of circumstances has felt for more than twelve years at home with both German and French organs, as one who defends the German art of organ playing in Paris and the French art of organ playing in Germany, and as one who is convinced that an agreement between the two types of organs and the two different conceptions must be reached; and that with such an understanding, with such an interpenetration of the German and French arts, a new period, rich in ideas and mastery of forms, will dawn in the history of organ playing. If the signs of the times do not deceive, the moment has come to learn from one another.

The rather sharp differentiation between the German and French organs began about a generation ago. When old Hesse played upon the new organ of St. Clothilde, he felt at once at home on it, and declared that it was his conception of the ideal organ. Today no German organist would find himself immediately at home on a French organ, and no French organist would ever give a recital on a German organ without rather long practice and intelligent assistance in registration.

The differentiation springs from the ways in which organ building in the two countries has been influenced by the new factors of electricity and pneumatics. French organ building remained more conservative. The organ of St. Sulpice, which will soon be fifty years old, remained the type of all French organs. German organ building followed the inventive path, utilized fully every technical advantage of pneumatics, and used electricity for the generation of unlimited wind volume and wind pressure.

There is in addition a purely superficial difference. In French organs the couplers and composition stops are arranged exclusively for the feet. The development in Germany led to the almost exclusive use of pistons.

But even the inner artistic principle is different. The artistic quality of an organ, and still more the whole nature of organ music, is determined by the way in which one proceeds from *piano* to *forte*, and from *forte* to *fortissimo*, and then back again to the initial tone color. In the German organ the revolving drum or cylinder prevails. It dominates the organ, as the playing of our *virtuosi* shows. It rules organ literature and composition, as a glance at any new work for the organ makes sufficiently clear. In other words, we [1] produce a *crescendo* by bringing all the stops into play one after the other without a break, so that they all operate in the same way upon the great organ; we sacrifice in this *crescendo* the artistic individuality of the stops; we take it for granted that every increase means at the same time a change in tone color; we reconcile ourselves to the mo-

[1] Albert Schweitzer was until the end of the First World War a German citizen. C. R. J.

Eugène Munch was Dr. Schweitzer's first important music teacher.
This photograph hangs on the walls of Schweitzer's Alsatian home and
shows Munch just before his untimely death. On the photograph Schweitzer has written: "Eugène Munch, my revered piano and organ teacher at
Mulhouse from the autumn of 1885 to August 1893. What a debt of
gratitude I owe to him! Albert Schweitzer."

Here is the magnificent Silbermann organ in the Church of St. Thomas, which rose behind the theological seminary where Schweitzer was a student and where he became afterwards the principal. St. Thomas was the most important Protestant church in Strassburg, and on its organ Schweitzer was often invited to play.

The Church of St. Nicholas in Strassburg was very familiar with the name of Schweitzer before Albert Schweitzer was called to be its minister, for his uncle had been pastor there before him. The church had no particular distinction architecturally, but under Schweitzer's ministry it was thronged with eager worshipers, who found that he spoke to their hearts.

Schweitzer was as much at home at the console of the St. Nicholas organ as he was in the pulpit of the church. Unfortunately the church was badly damaged during the second World War.

Because of his birth in Alsace when that little country was under German rule, Schweitzer was regarded as an enemy alien during the first World War. He was interned in Africa and then transferred to France as a war prisoner. But at Garaison in the Pyrenees he still managed to keep up with his organ technique, playing on a rude table and on the floor. One of his fellow prisoners made this amusing silhouette of him.

Dr. Schweitzer plays the famous zinc-lined piano presented to him in
1913 by the Paris Missionary Society. In the evening, when the heavy
work of the day is done he sits here for a half hour and plays the majestic
music of Bach and Mendelssohn, and Widor and Saint-Saëns. Here he
finds solace for his soul as he fills the African night with music. A shaded
oil lamp stands above the piano, and beyond him is the small pen where
he sometimes keeps his baby antelopes.

Here Dr. Schweitzer plays at his piano in his loved Alsatian home at Gunsbach in the Munster Valley. Like his Lambarene piano it has pedal attachment, and the doctor is able to keep his feet in practice as well as his hands.

He is constantly slipping off to the village church, where a lovely little organ of beautiful tone, which has been rebuilt under his direction, responds to his skilled fingers. He likes to have friends sit beside him on the bench as he plays. Here Ruth Anne Oppenheimer, the great-granddaughter of one of his two god-mothers, and the granddaughter of one of his early piano teachers, sits beside him.

M. Georges Frey, director of the Conservatory of Music at Mulhouse, plays a Bach fugue for Dr. Schweitzer in the latter's home at Gunsbach, with the round violin bow similar to those used in Bach's time. With this bow all four strings can be played at once, and Bach's violin solos can be rendered as he intended.

notony which necessarily results from the fact that the sequence of the stops is always the same; we resign ourselves to the fact that we cannot determine when to introduce into the tone blend the sixteen-foot pipes, when the eight-foot, when the four-foot, when the two-foot, when the mixtures, when the reeds; we become the eternal slaves of the organ builder who designed the revolving drum, and give up all our independence in the execution of the *crescendo*, at the very moment when freedom is so closely allied to artistry: and all this in order to be in a position to achieve a *crescendo* by the simple movement of a wheel or a pedal.

It is otherwise with the French organ. It chooses the second alternative. It gives up the possibility of a *crescendo* executed with a single movement, and is reconciled to the necessity of a number of motions. In this way, however, it preserves at all times its freedom to introduce the stops in just the way indicated by the character of the particular *crescendo*.

The *crescendo* in a French organ depends upon the use of the couplers. In this way, the three persons which constitute the divine trinity of the organ are fully appreciated. If this, however, is to be really accomplished, the player must not be limited to the coupling of his second and third organ (choir and swell) to his first, but must be left absolutely free to start with any organ at all and couple the others to it. So in all the French instruments the first organ is called the great organ, as well as the neutral, nonspeaking, coupling organ. Its stops, that is, the stops that are pulled on the first manual, sound only when the pedal marked "G. O." (that is, great organ) is pressed. One can therefore couple to the nonspeaking manual (great organ), first the swell organ, then the choir organ, then by the use of the G. O. pedal the great organ, following at will the sequence II I III, II III I, I III II, or the one familiar to us, I II III.[1] All possibilities are provided.

It is the same way with the retiring of stops. It lies within the power of the player to keep till the end the I, the II, or the III organ without leaving the great organ.

There is for each organ a ventil for reeds and mixtures, that is, a

[1] I II III designate great, choir, swell organs. C. R. J.

pedal by which the mixtures and reeds arranged for that organ are made to speak at the discretion of the player, so that the player has it in his hands—or rather in his feet—to introduce into the tone color of the foundation stops the mixtures from the three organs in any sequence he chooses, before, during, or after their coupling, or in alternation with it.

The three couplers and the three combination pedals represent a multitude of crescendo possibilities; and at the same time offer the advantage that one can bring in the necessary crescendo at a designated climax, on its characteristic strong accent—which is not possible with the revolving drum, inasmuch as the drum introduces one register after the other, never a whole group of them, and therefore requires a certain period of time.

A third method of producing the crescendo and supplementing the other stops is the swell organ of the III manual. The III manual of the French organ is more significant than the II. The swell box encloses not only the soft-toned little stops, but also a mass of sound as important in number of registers as in intensity. The tone characters are represented in it in all pitches as completely as—almost more completely than—in the I organ. That means that crescendi can be produced with such a III organ, its shutters serving not only to make certain nuances possible upon the III organ, but also to develop the crescendo of the entire instrument up to a certain point. I remember an organ of Cavaillé–Coll's where one could alter the character of the full, coupled instrument by the swell box of the III organ.

The crescendo in the French organ depends, then, upon the couplers, the introduction of mixtures and reeds, and the use of the swell shutters.

For instance, we have the III organ, its shutters closed, coupled to the nonspeaking I. We have drawn the foundation stops on all three, sixteen-foot, eighteen-foot, four-foot, two-foot; we have prepared the mixtures and the reeds. The same in the pedal. We couple the II organ to the III; at the next climax we bring in the foundation stops of the I, while we play on the G. O. Thereupon we couple the pedal organ to the other organs when we need it. How, then, shall we proceed without a jolt from the foundation stop character to the tone color of the mixtures and reeds? By bringing in the mixtures and reeds first in the III organ. With closed shutters this can be done almost unnoticed. Now we open the shutters slowly. The tones of mixtures and reeds float along above the tones of the foundation stops in long, delicate waves, and blend with them. This introduction of the tone color of mixtures and reeds, previously only virtually present behind the closed shutters, is the climactic moment of the *crescendo*. Since in the III organ all tone qualities are represented, the full power of the whole instrument is felt from the moment of the introduction of the mixtures and reeds, which had been muffled in the swell box of the III organ. From this point on there is only the question of its unfolding. The subsequent introduction of the mixtures and the reeds of the II organ, of the I organ, and of the pedal organ, and the introduction of the suboctave coupler and the superoctave coupler (*octave grave* and *octave acute*) do not alter this tone color in any way; they make it only more intensive.

The dynamic indications in French compositions are to be explained accordingly. The sign for *crescendo* or *decrescendo* refers only to the handling of the swell box, even when the musician is playing on the first organ. At the top of the piece it is expressly indicated whether in addition to the foundation stops (*jeux de fonds*, or for short *fonds*) the reeds and the mixtures also, and which of them, should be prepared on the different organs. Their introduction is then definitely indicated, as well as the coupling and uncoupling. *Crescendo poco a poco* in an increase leading in a short line to *fortissimo* means that the player, when he has permitted the full III organ to develop with the foundation stops of the first two, should introduce at the climactic strong accents the mixtures and reeds of the other organs and of the pedals. Only this last *crescendo* corresponds to the increase we get with German organs with the register cylinder. The signs < >, no matter how many measures they stretch over, refer always to the swell box only.

I point out this fundamental difference in dynamic indications, because I have found that almost all German organists, when they are playing on the first organ, produce their *crescendi* and *decrescendi* by habit with the register cylinder, and so destroy completely the effect desired by the composer, who was not reckoning on a change in tone color.

The basic principle of the French system is the arrangement of all the resources of the instrument in the pedals. The French organs have no pistons under the keyboards. What system shall we decide upon?

I do not sit for five minutes beside Father Guilmant on the bench of his beautiful house organ at Meudon without his asking me, as if he had just remembered where we left off the last time: "And in Germany do they still build pistons? That I can't understand. See how simple it is when one has everything under his feet," . . . and the short, agile feet press couplers and combination pedals silently, then in a trice let them up again.

On another day Widor, for the twenty-fifth time, begins on the same subject. "Tell my friend Professor Munch at Strassburg that he must point out for me a single place in a Bach prelude or fugue when he has a hand free for a moment to reach for a piston! He must name someone for me who can play on the manual and at the same time press the piston on the key strip with his thumb."

I keep my silence, for the first German organist into whose hands I fall a few weeks later, and to whom I put this controversial question, answers me invariably, "The French are very backward. Formerly we too had all this in the feet; now, however, we have our beautiful pistons."

It is first of all a matter of habit. The French organist sits helplessly before the pistons; the German organist finds the pedals awkward. The question is nonetheless one of principle. Should one rather have a hand free or a foot free?

In principle one must concede the case to the French. One seldom has a free hand, but often a free foot. And experience corroborates the principle. I am always hearing on German organs the hesitations, the unrhythmical dislocations, which result from the fact that the player at the particular climax can not find the right moment to press his pistons. I know *virtuosi* who to avoid this sit between two helpers who push the pistons for them. But that means to sacrifice one's independence. And who has ever played with helpers without some untoward thing happening? And besides, when one has a chance to observe the pedal system one becomes conscious of the great complexity of the system of pistons. Let one see Guilmant, Widor, Gigout, or Vierne at their organs! They need no helpers. Quietly, serenely, and infallibly they do everything themselves. Whoever has observed this will cherish no more doubt as to which system is better.

I myself, though I am at home on both organs and have become familiar with both systems, must testify to the fact that the resources of the French system are simpler and therefore better. First of all, because all French organs are the same. Under the left side are the three pedal couplers; in the middle the manual couplers; close to that the octave couplers; then usually comes the swell shoe; at the right of that, the combination stops for the introduction of the mixtures and the trumpets—everything always in the order I, II, III. When Saint-Saëns was commanded by the President of the Republic to take his place at the organ of Notre Dame on official occasions, which used to happen before Vierne was made organist of the cathedral, he did not need five minutes to feel as much at home there as he was on the organ of St. Séverin, where he used to improvise so wonderfully.

With us every organ differs from every other in the arrangement of its resources. In order to play successfully on one of them, one must spend at least a few days in familiarizing himself with it. One could still be partly content with this situation if this were merely a chaotic condition out of which the perfected organ type might come. But such a hope would be vain, for in these differences is neither rhyme nor reason, but only chance, habit, caprice. There can be only one really perfect organ type. Yet instead of moving in this direction we remain stuck in this formless multiplicity, and even believe that this must be.

Now German art, and particularly German music, are greatly—yes, infinitely indebted to the little German states; a fact one realizes first of all when he lives in lands that have never known these conditions. But the effect on organ building has been bad. May France be here the unifying power for good, as she once was in history for bad.

The advantage that a player on the French instrument is most vividly conscious of is his ability to regulate the tone strength and tone color of the basses at any time by coupling or uncoupling the pedal organ without changing anything in the manuals. He finds this almost more agreeable than the possibility which always exists of coupling the manuals together; though the greatest reproach of our new organ devices is exactly this, that they make the coupling and uncoupling of the organs—the regulation of the blending of the three personalities which constitute the unity of the instrument—the exception rather than the rule.

Which of us has not regretted with almost every Bach number his inability on our organs to make the bass speak now more softly, now more strongly? To which of us are not certain prolonged bass notes, especially when the left hand is busy in the lower register, a torture? This difficulty does not exist in the French organ. One should hear Widor increase the volume of the great pedal organ notes in the Bach *F major Toccata* without changing the manual tone color! One should hear him command the basses in the *G minor Prelude!* Before the held bass note begins, all his pedal couplers are released in five short, successive movements. Then, towards the end of the held note, each coupler at the proper time enters again on the strong accent, strengthening the stress: the V, IV, III, II, I organs! This procedure is repeated six or seven times. But, I assert, I have never yet anywhere else heard the *G minor Prelude* without "Bach troubles."

The control of the foot couplers and the combination pedals requires, of course, a very special technique, which is almost more difficult to learn than the pedal technique. How often under the inexorable eyes of Guilmant, Gigout, or Widor, the pupil practises a transition, until he finally gets it, exact to the hundredth part of a second, quietly, without contortion, with infallible assurance, pressing down a coupler or a combination pedal and at once in readiness for the next one! For almost every piece one has to practise the climaxes, where the sequence of movements attains a certain complexity. I stood beside Widor when he was studying his last symphony, the *Symphonie Romane.* How many times did he return to certain places, before the couplers and the combination pedals obeyed him as he wished!

But when the particular movements are once learned, one is completely free, and master of the *crescendi* he wants to produce. Let one take his place beside Vierne, the young organist of Notre Dame who has hardly a gleam of eyesight, and follow him as he brings his wonderful instrument from *pianissimo* to *fortissimo* with no help of any kind except that of his feet, now endowed with sight!

An organist once objected to me that only the more talented pupils could learn this second "pedal technique." But Guilmant and Gigout, the teachers of the modern generation of French organists, have proved that any pupil, even though but moderately gifted, can overcome these difficulties by means of diligence.

But what prevents us from uniting the French and German arrangements in a single instrument, introducing the main couplers and combinations as pistons as well as pedal levers in such a way that pistons and pedals should always correspond? Then one would be in a position to use at any time the particular member that was free. One could, for instance, set a coupler with the hand, and then, since it would be set automatically at the same time in the feet, be in a position to shut it off either with the hand, or, if more convenient, with the foot. We boast, and rightly, that there are no technical impossibilities for our pneumatics. The organ builder who would undertake to provide the player with the main resources in this double fashion would in the right way cut through this knot which no amount of discussion can untie. This double arrangement can be installed, moreover, on any organ, by a simple, unpneumatic, purely mechanical device.

In the same way can be solved the question of whether we should have a cylinder *crescendo*. I myself know very well the advantages of a revolving drum when, for example, accompanying oratorios with great choruses to consider; and I admit that in certain cases one can produce unique effects. But I do not like its exclusive domination, especially in an organ with fewer than thirty stops, where it operates in a barbaric fashion. I am afraid, too, that it has not had the best influence upon the artistic sensitivity of our younger organists, and especially of our organ composers, since it has led both away from the true, simple, selective registration, and into the temptation to regard the organ as an instrument on which one played "strong and weak," not as a manifold unity in which every *crescendo* must come from the blending of certain tone units. I believe that if one should institute a general inquiry among experienced organists, many of them would testify that for artistic reasons they had lost their exaggerated appreciation of the revolving drum.

Here again it is a matter of doing one thing without leaving the other undone. Let them leave us the revolving drum, but give us at the same time the French resources, so that we shall not be confined exclusively to it. Then the harmful influence the revolving drum has exerted on the ideas of our young organists and on modern literature will of itself disappear.

It is surprising that our German organs lack the thing we most need. We have the revolving drum, the blind combinations, the synthetic stops, the *tutti (sforzando)*, and so on—that is, all the resources in which one *ensemble* of stops replaces another. But while we hold an actual organ registration we are not able to introduce new stops at our pleasure. This most elementary of resources, the very first requirement of composers, actually does not exist.

It is really unfortunate that very often the organs are never once independent of each other, because the stop that activates the blind combinations, or the one that brings in the *tutti (sforzando)* and *mezzoforti*, works for the sake of simplicity on the three organs and pedals at the same time—otherwise we should each time have to have four movements instead of one! Our apparent wealth is really a frightful poverty. It is impossible, when *tutti (sforzando)* is on, to use the pedals with the third organ, since the pedals also are on *tutti (sforzando)*. One could write a book about the pedal emergency in these modern organs of ours, which smile at one with their numberless, glittering little stops so rich in promise; a façadal wealth that is really only a glittering poverty, since it lacks the simplest and therefore most artistic of all the resources needed.

And to meet this need, the organ builders offer us today a weaker pedal introduced automatically, a pedal which replaces the other as soon as one passes over to the II or III organ by putting off the *tutti (sforzando)*; but this is only a lamentable makeshift, more adapted to reveal the need than to bring it relief; for a genuine organist wants the particular pedal that he needs, not any pedal that the organ builder prescribes as good for him in the full II or III organ.

We must also find a way of adding and retiring new tone *ensembles*. Here too I believe a compromise between the French and German types will commend itself, namely, a compromise between our blind combinations and the French introduction of mixtures and reeds. The French arrangement has the disadvantage of providing only for the introduction of the mixtures and the reeds; the German, that the entrance of the blind combinations retires the chosen registration. Since anything is possible in pneumatics, the registration provided by the blind combinations should be arranged to replace the registration chosen by the organist, or to complement it (the blind combinations to be withdrawn again by the same action of piston or pedal), in accordance with whether the musician, before beginning to play, has pressed a pedal or pulled a stop to activate or annul the main registration.

We should have, then, as resources for a medium-sized organ: pedal couplers, manual couplers, super- and suboctave couplers, doubly available blind combinations of the kind described above for each organ and for the pedals, and along with them all the revolving drum. With the couplers, the stops of the first organ would be introduced in the manner of the French G. O.

The idea of this type of organ has been forced upon me by a year of reflection about French and German organs and by a continuous striving for a useful compromise between them. Stimulating conversations with organ builders here and there have given me valuable hints. If one reflects on these simple resources, he will find that their riches stand in inverse proportion to their simplicity.[1] Whatever is

[1] The organ just finished for St. Nicholas in Strassburg [Schweitzer's own church at the time—C. R. J.], the work of two young Alsatian organ builders, Dalstein and Härpfer at Boulay in Lorraine, is of this type.

All the couplers and composition stops are doubled, in the form of pedals or pistons, in such a way that the piston and the pedal are connected with each other by a simple mechanism invented by Mr. Dalstein. The cost of each coupler or composition has been raised about twenty marks by the addition of this device. The double availability of the blind combinations, which enhance or complete at will the hand registration, makes all other resources actually superfluous; and even those organists who at the beginning distrusted the modernization that did away with the *piano*, *mezzoforte* and *tutti* (*sforzando*) became convinced of this. The advantage of using the first organ as a coupling organ

possible on a French or German organ is possible on this one also. Bach, César Franck, Guilmant, Widor, and Reger might all play on it with equal success.

Indeed, one might perhaps take exception to this organ on the ground that it is too simple; for in spite of warning voices the complexity of our organs has gradually become a mania with us. If an organ does not look like the central signal room of a great railway station, it is from the very start worthless to a certain category of our organists. They want half a dozen blind combinations spread out one over the other, even though they must be arranged on a panel behind their backs with pistons for synthetic stops, *tutti (sforzando)*, and composition stops—all of them in the greatest possible number. I am sure that I have never heard better playing on such complicated organs than on others, and have usually noted that these instruments, though rich in interrelated resources, are equally poor in other respects.

Of our echo organs I may not speak; for they have nothing to do with the organ itself, and are dangerous playthings, which destroy the taste of the listeners, and, even worse, of the organists.

The Organola represents in our modern organ building "the fall of man." When will enough voices be raised publicly to characterize the production of such an apparatus for mechanical playing as what it is, an insult to the art of organ playing! For me the Organola has only a social meaning: in the future cripples and war invalids may hold organists' positions.

How far good taste has already strayed is evident in the fact that our organ builders dare to offer us meaningless things like echo organs and Organolas!

Then, too, it is almost laughable to see how people seek modernity even for little organs by overloading them with pistons. On organs with ten or twelve registers we find composition stops for *piano*,

---

was evident after the first practical demonstration. The whole console cost about 200 marks more than usual.

For a two-manual organ of twenty stops, with two doubly connected pedal couplers, two doubly connected manual couplers, and three doubly available blind combinations (organ I, II, and pedals), the difference in cost might be only a hundred marks!

mezzoforte, forte, and fortissimo! In thoughtless indolence our organists are getting away entirely from planned hand registration.

It almost seems to me as if we were all being deceived by the phantom of the "concert organ." What, then, is a concert organ? Are there two kinds of organs? Or is there not simply a best organ, and is not this good enough for a church organ? What would old Bach say of our distinctions? What, indeed, would he say if he knew that we distinguish between organists and organ virtuosi? Can there be anything better than a "good organist," one who does not consciously seek his own fame, but tries to hide behind the objectivity of the holy instrument and let it speak as if it spoke for itself, ad majorem Dei gloriam?

"Just think," said Widor to me once, "I have been insulted. I have been called in a magazine an organ virtuoso. But I am a genuine organist. An organ virtuoso is only a savage among organists."

That the concert organ and the "organ virtuoso" are almost unknown in France is due to the organ builder Aristide Cavaillé–Coll, the creator of the simple, and, in its artistry, the perfect type of French organ. He was more than a great organ builder: he was, like Silbermann, a genius in organ building. I can never forget him; I can still see him today with his little cap, and with the good, true eyes in which so much of art and intelligence lay, sitting every Sunday beside Widor on the organ bench at St. Sulpice, and caressing with his hand the console of his darling organ.

In German organ circles it has been repeatedly taken amiss that in my French book on Bach I maintained that Bach would have found his ideal organ once more in the model created by Cavaillé–Coll, rather than in our own instruments. Since I reaffirmed this position in the German and English editions that followed the French, I should like to raise the subject for discussion here and give the reasons for my assertion.

The test of every organ, the best and only test, is Bach's organ music. Let one apply this test artistically to organ building, instead of trying to imagine how Bach would throw his peruke in the air for joy over our pistons, and then after catching it again, set off to find out from one of our modern organ *virtuosi* how on the modern organ one can bring everything out of his music.

As a mind always prying insistently into the nature of things, he would immediately ask about the mechanics of our organ.

At once the practical advantages of our organ pneumatics would appear: ease and rapidity of touch, simplicity of arrangement, the unlimited possibilities in all the resources. Are these, however, as great esthetic advantages?

No. Our organ pneumatics is a dead precision. It consists in the transmission of power solely through wind pressure. It lacks the vital and elastic quality of the lever. Not all the springs can replace this direct, elastic transmission. The player must exert himself to cover this dead precision. It requires an artist to play well on a good pneumatic organ. And the pneumatic systems of our Walcker and Sauer, to name only two of the most outstanding, are true masterpieces.

If one, then, considers the average of the many kinds of pneumatic organs, with badly regulated keys, without depth, without free play, without a contact point that can be felt, where the slightest finger substitution is a hazard because the adjacent keys speak with the slightest touch, with pedals on which it is impossible for the best of organists to play correctly and cleanly—if one considers this average pneumatic organ, which one leaves in a high state of nervous despair, one may well wonder if we have not gone far astray with our pneumatics. No organist wants any longer a mechanism.[1] And yet many who played well and cleanly on their old mechanical organs now smear on the new ones of which they are so proud, and play without precision; though they do not notice this, because they have not become accustomed to the demands of the pneumatic organ.

I believe that we in Germany have abandoned our blind enthusiasm for the pneumatic organ, and are beginning to realize that from

---

[1] I dare not speak of the pneumatic organs built by houses of second rank in the transition period. What sums would be necessary to redeem these victims of the first experiments, which shriek every Sunday to high heaven, and to give them a new and positive spirit!

And how many of our modest organ builders, who once constructed simple and beautifully sounding instruments, sometimes even artistically toned, have failed, because they had to participate in the inventions!

an artistic point of view pneumatics is only a makeshift in situations where the tracker is no longer feasible.

With the tracker the finger feels a certain tension exactly when the tone comes; it feels the contact point. And the depressed key pushes up under the finger, in order that, when the finger shows the slightest impulse to leave it, it may immediately rise with its own strength and lift the finger up with it. The strength of the keys coöperates with the will! With the tracker even the mediocre organist cannot smear. With pneumatics there is no such coöperation on the part of the keys. It makes the playing worse instead of better, and brings to light the slightest fault.

Only with the tracker does one come into really intimate relationship with his organ. In pneumatics one communicates with his instrument by telegraph—for even the Morse apparatus depends on a key with a spring. The tracker system of the organ in St. Thomas's in Strassburg is well over a hundred years old; but it is a marvel to play a Bach fugue on. I know no other organ on which everything would come forth so clearly and so precisely.

Besides all this, the pneumatic organ is affected by the smallest thing. Once, between a final rehearsal and a performance, the organ builder had to be summoned by telegraph, because something had gone wrong with the pneumatic system. The trouble was found. Triumphantly he showed me the mischief maker: a little grain of sand fallen from the ceiling. "Just a little grain of sand!" . . . "It's a bad thing," I replied, "that a little grain of sand should cause such a disturbance. If it had been an earthquake I would say nothing. As for that, you will see that the old tracker organs will not suffer even when the world comes to an end, but will remain standing there for the angels at the last judgment to play the *Gloria* on." He was so perplexed over this upsetting of values that he even forgot the speech about the hot summer, which one usually brings into the discussion in opposition to the tracker.

"But the pneumatic organ operates so easily!" The man who threw in this comment was a giant, who might have appeared as the strong man at any yearly fair.

That a good tracker organ is better in small ways than a pneumatic organ our organ builders know very well, and even admit. But a pneumatic organ is simpler and cheaper to build. And conditions compel them to favor the cheaper thing.

The French pneumatic organ, which depends upon the principle of the almost sixty-year-old Barcker chest, does not have even this advantage. It is almost half again as expensive as our pipe pneumatic system. But it is more artistic and more elastic, since it operates with the pneumatic lever, and so has carried over into the pneumatic organ to a certain extent all the artistic advantages of the pure tracker organ. When I play in Paris an organ of Cavaillé–Coll, or a beautiful Merklin organ, I am each time delighted anew with the elastic and certain precision of this action, and afterwards I always have trouble in accustoming myself once more to our pneumatic organs. But among us the question of cost is final.

In general we could learn a great deal about the details of arrangement from the French organ. Its keys are somewhat shorter than ours; the black keys cunningly rounded off; the manuals closer together than ours as they rise above each other. Everything is provided for the most exact blending, and for the easy and sure changing from one manual to another, on which, as is well known, Bach laid a great deal of stress. And as for the French pedals, they cost, indeed, about double ours. But what perfection! All arranged concave and radiating, recently reaching to g^1, and with a really ideal spring. Our demands are much more modest.

The concave pedal has not yet won its way among us, in spite of its apparent advantages, and in spite of the fact that everyone who has reflected upon the radiating movement of the foot in pedal work must mark it as the only one that makes sense. I might almost have made an enemy not long ago of an organist friend upon whom I forced concave pedals when his organ was being rebuilt, had I not promised to replace the concave pedals after the space of a year with straight ones if he were not convinced of the utility of the innovation.

When I was talking to one of our most distinguished organ builders about this matter, and said to him that he constructed beautiful concave pedals only for other lands, while almost always he built straight ones for Germany, he answered, "In foreign lands I have to build these pedals. In Germany they are not wanted, and since many inspectors have never had concave pedals under their feet, I get nowhere with them."

In a word, it is easier to play well on a French organ than on a German organ. Because of the simple, practical refinement of the arrangements, one there is not exposed to many things that can happen to us. We think more of external refinements installed to please the eye. Instead of drawknobs we are beginning to favor tilting tablets; we introduced elegant pistons, and find them entrancing to touch, instead of pulling real drawstops or couplers.

I had just ended a Bach fugue on a wonderful old Silbermann organ, and was still completely captivated by the magic tone of the old mixtures, when someone next to me, who had his modern organ for two years, remarked, "You know, it must be disagreeable to play on an organ that does not have a single tilting tablet." In his irritation over the old drawstops he had not heard the organ.

I should like to raise the question whether in general we have not paid more attention to the visible changes in our consoles, and less to the important thing, the effect upon the tone. Are the advances in organ building beneficial to the tonal quality?

No! Not at all! Our organs are indeed more powerful than the old ones, but no longer as beautiful. Our old organs, even those built twenty years ago, are more beautifully and more artistically voiced than those of today.

It is remarkable to me that the laity have noticed this before the organists have. Musical laymen have often remarked to me timidly, when an old organ has been replaced by a new one, "that the old one was still almost more beautiful." This recognition makes but slow headway with the organists. We must first of all arouse ourselves from this intoxication with inventions before we can get our hearing back again.

That the tone has not profited by the modern inventions results in part from the fact that one of the principal inventions, the possibility of getting unlimited wind production by the electrically driven bellows, quite naturally set us off on the wrong track—even the most thoughtful among us. We began to exchange tone richness for tone power. In the old organs we had to be economical with our supply of wind. When this was no longer necessary, we laughed over the narrow wind ducts of our fathers, and began to intone strongly and vigorously, ever more strongly, ever more vigorously, rejoicing in the roaring and blustering. The high point of our enthusiasm was reached with the introduction of high-pressure flue stops.[1] A distinguished organist wrote at that time, "We have succeeded now in making an organ of fifteen stops that produces the full effect that formerly an organ of thirty stops produced." The aberration could not describe itself better.

The disenchantment arrived; it grows stronger. But how long a time must still elapse before we strive once more for tone richness alone, renouncing the tone power which the electrical bellows offers us as a gift from the Greeks, and going back once more within the boundaries of art, where the difficulty of producing the desired volume of wind formerly kept us.

A fat person is neither beautiful nor strong. To be artistically beautiful and strong is only to have a figure with a perfect play of muscles. So in time we shall desert the modern organ inflated by wind pressure, seek the full, rich, and beautiful organ only through the collaboration of the normal, differentiated, and artistically toned stops, and give up trying to assemble a full organ by craftiness. Craftiness does not belong with art, for art is truth.

But even if we had had artistic insight, so that the mounting possibility of wind pressure would not have tempted us in the wrong direction, nonetheless our organ building would have been forced along this road. It is all a financial question. Our organ builders found themselves in the embarrassing position of having to accept those inventions which made possible a reduction in prices, and therefore success in competition. Everything else, the purely artistic, was compelled to stand aside. The past forty years, the age of invention in organ building, will not appear some day on the pages of history as the great years of artistic progress, as many among us believe, but rather will they be described in this way: "Battle between the commercial and the artistic; victory of the commercial over the artistic."

---

[1] In a very large church two or three artistically built, high-pressure stops may be added for a grandiose effect, and have a place therefore in the perfection of the instrument. In middle-sized rooms, however, they can only disfigure the organ tone, and must therefore remain the exception in organ building.

Any concern that placed the artistic above the commercial was from the beginning lost. The invention intoxication that gripped us organists in this period demanded external, epoch-making, cost-reducing discoveries. Our organ builders had to bow to this spirit; many of them, as I know, inwardly furious.

So we have come to the factory organ—the good old factory organ. For what is artistic in it we are indebted to the sacrificial spirit of our organ builders, who even for these reduced prices still did the best work they could, and were satisfied if generally they could "get by." In the righteous judgment of history they will some day be honored, in spite of the fact that their organs are only good factory instruments; but we, who decided what organs should be built, and supposed that art could profit from this undercutting competition, shall be dishonored, because we did not sufficiently comprehend, what as pupils of the old Bach we should have comprehended, that an organ builder can be an artist only when he is engaged as an artist by an artist. If this support is lacking, then circumstances force him to become a dealer in objects of art.

Of course there have been exceptions. But in general we organists cannot deny that we have followed the tendency of the times towards cheapness; and that we often gave the contract to that man who for the same price offered one or two more stops, even though they were only a little aeolina or a little piston, and that we did not ask if at the same time artistic work, that is, work that does not need to take either time or pay into consideration, was still possible.

A happy fate protected Cavaillé–Coll from being forced at the same time along this road. His principal activity fell in the last decade of the Empire, when money for ecclesiastical purpose was plentiful. Afterwards Guilmant and Widor, his artistic advisers, gave him such a reputation by their support that he did not have to lower his prices to meet competition. "Yes, the old Cavaillé," one of our sympathetic organs builders said to me not long ago, "when one of his men worked on something for three weeks and it did not please him entirely, he had him start again at the beginning; and if again it did not satisfy him, still another time. Who among us can do that? We should not last three months."

At last, however, fate overtook even him. In his last years he had to contend with financial difficulties. The firm itself in its venerable house, 15 Avenue du Maine, in the business district of the Gare Montparnasse, was, indeed, saved; Cavaillé, however, died poor, leaving nothing behind him for his family. But for this very reason the organs of St. Sulpice and Notre Dame will sing his praise as long as one stone rests upon another. Until some day Paris has become a heap of rubble like Babel, those who are susceptible to the magic beauty of his organs will leave Notre Dame and St. Sulpice thinking with deep feeling of the man who dared in spite of the times to remain a pure artist.

Cavaillé–Coll was convinced that he had found in the Barcker chest, which he employed for the first time in the Basilica of St. Denis, the ideal action to connect the keys with the pipes. For resources he was satisfied with couplers, and the ventil for mixtures and reeds. For large organs he provided a simple series of blind combinations; this is the way it is on the organs of St. Sulpice and Notre Dame. No efforts to go farther in this direction interested him: all his inventiveness and endeavor were directed towards the perfecting of the voicing and timbre of the tone, precisely that which in German organs had been neglected.

In the strength of tone he gave to a single stop he remained conservative. It is true that he constructed high-pressure reeds (*trompettes en chamade*) [1] for the swell organ; for the other stops he sought only beauty. Even his flutes—not simply his principals and gambas—are wonderfully beautiful; though they perhaps lack the interesting variety that certain German organ builders have achieved in the flute family.

In order to make clear the difference between German and French organs, let us draw on both of them all the foundation stops, sixteen-foot, eight-foot, four-foot and two-foot, in all the manuals. In the German organ the *ensemble* often sounds harsh, at times intolerable. I know modern organs on which even all the eight-foot foundation stops of the I manual produce an effect that is intolerable. Let us not speak of our double flutes. An organ builder confessed to me that he shuddered at the double flutes people forced him to build; and I

---

[1] *Trompettes en chamade* were originally horizontal pipes outside the case. Cavaillé–Coll revived them and put them inside the case. C. R. J.

myself in certain instruments hear the double flutes plainly even when the whole organ is sounding.

All the foundation stops are the basis of the entire organ. When the basis itself has no lovely unity of tone, what becomes of the whole instrument?

It is quite different with Cavaillé. The foundation stops are voiced with reference to the tonal unity they should form. Not only those in each manual alone, but also all of them together, form a well-balanced, harmonious whole, and indeed in such a way that the individuality of each of the three organs is fully brought out. The foundation stops of the great organ provide the groundwork. They are exceedingly weak, but have a full, round tone; those of the II organ introduce to some extent the brightness; those of the III furnish the intensity. The tone of the swell is much more intense than the tone of the great organ. With us the coupling of the third organ, when all the foundation stops are pulled, is not noticed. With Cavaillé, on the contrary, it is as if at every instant light—white, streaming light—came flooding into the mass of tone from the foundation stops.

And there is no harshness, not even in the highest registers. Since French compositions are prepared for such organs, they are intolerable on our organs. "How can Widor set down such sustained dissonances?" said a Berlin organist to whom I owe a great deal. Indeed they were unbearable on the organ in question, a torment . . . but not on the organ of St. Sulpice!

In order to avoid this, I take for French compositions on German organs only half the foundation stops, almost no four-foot and two-foot stops on the first organ, for the sake of the upper registers. In principle I draw only as many foundation stops on the I and II organs as will permit all the coupled foundation stops of the III to be plainly heard, and the swell to influence the ensemble. Only when one observes this practice can one make César Franck, Widor, Guilmant, Saint–Saëns, Gigout, and the others sound on our organs as they sound on their own.

The voicing of our foundation stops, which is not concerned with the ensemble, is such, then, that the mixtures do not blend with them, but only make them strong by adding their own overpowerful voicing. When one hears a modern organ, he hears the foundation stops and the mixtures rolling along unblended; whereas the mixtures are designed to enter into the tone color of the foundation stops to make them light and transparent, that is, adapted to polyphonic playing.

On our organs it is simply impossible to play a Bach fugue and prelude with foundation stops and mixtures, the latter now added and now retired; impossible, too, to bring out the climaxes by coupling and uncoupling the manuals or by changing them; impossible, in other words, to make the fugues and preludes stand forth as architectonic, vitalized musical creations. On Cavaillé's organ this is possible, because everything is based on the beautiful tonal unity of the foundation stops and the mixtures. Therefore the French organists play the Bach fugues in many respects more simply, clearly, and appropriately than we; because their organs are nearer to the Bach organ than ours.

We, however, have to adapt the Bach fugues to our organ. Our interpretations spring in part from necessity, which does not prevent most people from considering these interpretations as evidence of artistic progress. Since we cannot play them as simply as was intended, our registration and treatment are orchestral. We pour them into a new form, and introduce *crescendi* and *diminuendi* where none is foreseen in the fugue plan, because on our organ we cannot create the clear and satisfying tone color which Bach intended.

But in the end nothing helps at all, for on our organs one can hear only treble and bass; it is impossible to follow the figures of the middle voices. I will not speak of the bad taste which is current in the registration. I once heard the theme of the great G minor *Fugue* interpreted with the flutes of the III organ, in such a way that the whole fugue swelled up like the body of a fish. But whether the registration is in good taste or bad, fugues played in this way are untrue and unnatural, as though one wished for greater effectiveness to publish the Dürer engravings as colored chalk drawings.[1]

---

[1] Even our modern grand piano is unsuitable for Bach's music. The recognition of this fact begins to be felt everywhere. See concerning this matter, *Sur l'Interpretation des Oeuvres de Clavecin de J. S. Bach* [Interpretation of Bach's Harpsichord Works], by Wanda Landowska, Mercure de France, 1905.

I can still see today the surprised countenance of one of our most famous Bach singers, when not long ago she heard the G *minor* *Fantasy* take shape on the organ of St. Sulpice under Widor's fingers in its simple, tone-satisfying, and transparent form.

Back to the polyphonic organs desired by Bach; away with the orchestral organs! More delicate foundation stops! The harmonious unity of the foundation stops! Away with our few shrieking mixtures! Many soft mixtures!

Where is the mixture family adequately represented, even in some measure, on any manual of our instruments? Our II and III organs were for a long time denuded of mixtures. Slowly we are coming to the point of again adding a mixture even to small organs. But how long will it be before we shall have secured the right proportion of mixtures in all organs, before it shall become a dogma that an instrument is the richer, truer, and more beautiful the more lovely mixtures it has, that in general it can never have too many of them, and that even our swell organs must be filled with them? For the Bach fugue requires homogeneity in tone color on all three manuals! It is designed as a monochrome, like a copper plate engraving.

But this again is a question of money. An organ of forty stops with the right mixtures is at least as expensive as our present organ of fifty stops, if not more so. But there will surely come a time when we shall again think not of the number but of the tonal richness of the stops, when we shall prefer the true expensive organ of forty stops to the false one of fifty; when we shall look back on these instruments of ours, with their few, small, brutal mixtures in unresolved conflict with the gigantic, formless body of our foundation stops, as on something we have overcome.

Then, and not before, the problem of the pedals will be solved. Our pedals are at once so strong and so weak because the tone is not characteristic and not clear. When one listens to a pedal solo on one of our organs, he begins to think that the body of some dragon is twisting around in the background of the church in wild, ponderous writhings. When the manual is added to the pedal, however, one asks immediately, what has become of the pedals? Our whole organ stands on feet of clay, for in comparison with the full body of our coupled manuals our pedals are always too weak, especially since our greedy manual foundation stops, quicker to snap up the wind than the big, cautious sixteen-foot animals, take it away from them.

The adding of lovely mixtures to the pedals is the only answer to the pedal problem for the entire instrument. Now, however, we find hardly any mixtures in our pedal organs. Even the four-foot ones are usually lacking. And the one or two mixtures sometimes found there are unusable because they do not blend with the tones of the foundation stops, but make blurred figures with them in unresolved discord, sometimes even with acoustical distortion. On the other hand, in the increase of tone volume in our pedal foundation stops we are already far beyond the limits of artistic tolerance. Listen once to the *F major Toccata* on our organs. Who could think this rumbling forth of excessive tones beautiful? Who could find in it the wonderful Bach lines?

We must build pedals that are not excessively strong, but rich, intensive, and flexible, with tones that carry alone and carry also when the foundation stops and mixtures of all the manuals are coupled to them. That means sixteen- and eight-foot foundation stops, not excessively powerful and not too many, and almost as many beautiful and softly voiced mixtures. Such a pedal organ is never too weak and never too strong; it does not obscure or cover the middle stops of the manual.

This realization that we must go back to many and lovely mixtures made more and more headway with Cavaillé–Coll in the last period of his creative work. His pupil Mutin, who now directs the concern, follows in his master's footsteps, and accomplishes this purpose. I shall never forget when I first heard the ideal pedal of which I had dreamed. It was on the model organ that embellishes Cavaillé's studio, an instrument of about seventy stops rich in mixtures. In the pedal organ almost all the mixtures, even the *septième*, are represented. I played Bach's *A minor Fugue* with coupled manuals, all the eight-foot, four-foot, and two-foot foundation stops and mixtures drawn. The lines of the pedal figures stood forth clearly without any obtrusiveness, with intensive plasticity. "Play it once more," said Mutin, "without the mixtures." As I started to push in the pedal mixtures he said, "Stop, let them stay." And the same pedal that previously had been everywhere strong enough for the whole instrument without the reeds . . . was for the new registration, though unchanged, not too strong. Finally I made use of the same full pedal organ, and left in the manuals only the eight-foot and four-foot principals . . . and again it was not too strong. . . . Then I felt like one who had been permitted to look into the future; and I stepped down from the bench completely convinced that the time for the organ powerful in tone was passing, and that the time for the organ rich in tone, the organ of Bach, the old organ arising in new glory, was coming.

An organ rich in tone presupposes that the waves of the single tones should come to the ears of the hearer unmixed, not intermingled to any extent with the others, and that only there should they blend as independent personalities in the richest variety with the artistic unity.[1] Cavaillé–Coll had already turned his attention to the phenomenon of fusion (entrainements harmoniques), and had reflected on the means of preventing one pipe in the full instrument from devouring the same tone in other pipes—as the lean cattle of Pharaoh devoured the fat ones—so that when all fifty stops of an instrument were sounding we could really hear only twenty-five, the others only strengthening to a certain extent instead of enriching, because as physical individualities they no longer existed.

Mutin has carried his experiments to a practical conclusion, and turns them to good account on all his organs. Pipes with the slightest difference in dimensions never destroy each other's effect, but each stands forth as a personality whatever its volume of tone. If the diameters are the same, or if the difference is greater, then the entrainement is within the bounds of toleration. In installing an arrangement Cavaillé–Mutin always sees to it that the richest minimal differences in dimensions are observed throughout.

[1] From the first it has impressed me that certain splendid Silbermann organs sound rather bad near by, because the individuality of the different registers persists unbrokenly. All the more splendid, however, is their tone in the nave of the church.

It has been observed also that such old organs, even when they are weakly voiced, can be heard through the walls of the church! Every tone in the polyphony arrives clearly at the ears of the listener in the square before the church. How is it with the modern organ? With all its power it is able to send through the stones only a muffled howling and moaning. Thus even the stones bear witness against it, and furnish the proof that its tone does not carry.

Is the tone of our organs appealing, however? Yes . . . if one considers prompt speech of the pipe the same thing as good speech. Let one play rapid trills in the lower register of the manual, and quick passages with the sixteen-foot pipes in the pedal!

But prompt speech of the pipe is not necessarily good speech, for good speech means promptness plus quality,[1] that is, that the tone of the pipes is properly adjusted and to a certain extent articulate. On our organs the tone often blusters forth—is not adjusted. The right blending of the separate tones is therefore impossible. When one listens closely, one always hears an interval between two tones, or, on the contrary, they sound together for a small fraction of a second. There is no vital relationship between them; rather do they roll after each other like cannon balls. The organ is the ideal choir, to which only words are denied. Is it then comprehensible that so little value is attached at times to the artistic expression of the stops?

Here also, it seems to me, Cavaillé's pupil Mutin is on the right track. He proceeds from the observation that a wooden bellows gives a different wind pressure in his instrument to the different registers: below, a good deal of wind but with restraint; in the middle, moderately strong but in quantity less than below; above, very little pressure but intense—the quantity always therefore in inverse proportion to the intensity. If now the volume of tone in a wind instrument is very small in relation to that of an organ stop, and yet requires this difference for a proper tone, how much more is this true for an organ stop! Therefore the wind chest of the stop is divided into three or four parts, and each part receives the supply and pressure of wind that makes for the best tone in that register. The great model organ in the studio of Cavaillé–Mutin operates with wind chests divided into three parts, which are fed with wind of different pressures. Of course the construction is much more complicated and the costs appreciably higher; but listen to the result! Such a stop is worth three others; to say nothing of the fact that now the whole instrument also receives for its lower registers their proper amount of wind. Let one listen sometime to the middle voices in a Bach fugue played on organs so constructed! Not a tone, not one, is lost, since each has a

---

[1] *Ansprechen heisst eben An-Sprechen.*

different individuality from that above and below. I do not venture
to assert that this organ in the Mutin studio—with which the builder
will not part—is technically and artistically the most perfect one
ever built. But it certainly is an instrument that suits Bach's works,
in so far as it meets the requirements his organ music makes of the
ideal organ.

When will the time come when this most elementary esthetic requirement of differentiation in wind pressure is met on all organs?
Now, if all goes well, each organ has its wind—the first the strongest,
the second not quite so strong, and the third the weakest; which
means that the first is much too strong, because about the same pressure is provided for it as is required for the supply of the pneumatic
system. One should listen to the sounds produced in this way by the
principals and the flutes! How richly sounds, on the contrary, the
instrument in which the stops of the same manual are supplied with
two or three different wind pressures, in such a way that each one
receives the wind required for the most perfect tone, without having
to take into consideration whether it is in front or in back, high or
low! What a wealth of perfect tone individuality in such an instrument!

Instead of this we find among us excessively strong-toned mixtures, placed above in the very first rank, which seem to be particularly designed to destroy the beauty of the whole instrument. And
many organists—incredible as this seems—think they can accomplish
through a differentiation in the wind supply the same thing that is
accomplished by a differentiation in the wind pressure, though these
have to do with entirely different things. The collaboration of both
differentiations is required to give an organ a beautiful wealth of tone.

And the reeds? They are pleasing on neither the German nor the
French organs, because on both they are too strong and dominant.
When once I said to Widor that I considered the French reed, in
other respects so beautiful, as an artistic handicap, he admitted to me
that he had been carrying around with him for years the same conviction, and was of the opinion that we must go back to the building
of reeds which do not dominate the whole instrument, but harmonise
with the foundation stops and the mixtures, and to a certain extent
only beautify them. Gigout holds the same opinion. But what work,

what trouble, to build reeds that are at once beautiful, soft, and good sounding!

When we once have them, the other question of whether we should play Bach with reeds will be solved. With our reeds, of course not. But it seems to me certain that Bach was dependent on his eight- and four-foot reeds. And who would deny that a pedal organ, with delicate reeds which lead to the mixtures, is the perfect ideal? Yet let us not forget the four-foot pipes. Four-foot flutes, four-foot principals, and four-foot trumpets, not coarsely voiced, should be on any comparatively perfect pedal organ. No coupler can replace them in the entire ensemble. Without them the pedal figures roll to the ground, instead of standing upright in the range of the stops.

And this is all a question of money! With today's prices the technical, artistic problem, which constitutes the problem of the rich-toned organ—that is, the beautifully toned organ—cannot be put in the foreground. Instead, the builder has to offer the most stops for the least money, and sometimes against his better judgment deliver what the customer wants instead of what the builder knows is the best; he has to build for the eye and not for the ear—the useless instead of the useful!

If only the highly gifted inventiveness of our German organ builders, who in recent decades have had to go in almost exclusively for cheapness, could be turned loose upon purely artistic questions! But that will happen only when we no longer give thoughtless consideration to the number of stops, and reconcile ourselves to the fact that prices are going up a good third higher! Until then we shall live in the period of the good factory organs.

But even with these prices, who can get really first-class quality? How is artistic tuning possible under these circumstances? A tuning appropriate for the locale, done with conscientious art, takes four times as much time as is now customary, when each day's tuning expense must be anxiously reckoned; and even the effort to tune artistically would eat up all the profits.

Good tuners should be paid like ministers, and should occupy such a place in the rank of artists that one artistic tuner should be considered equal to six average *virtuosi*, since a half dozen of the latter are easier to find than one artistic tuner. Only the mistakes of ministers concern posterity; of the *virtuosi* it cherishes perhaps the names; the work of the tuners, however, just as it leaves their hand, edifies generation after generation.

Where at present-day prices is the organ builder to find the means for research, without which there is no progress? They say that we are about to become a wealthy land. The future will not know that from our organs, for the poor Germany of earlier days built better ones.

Let no one deceive himself: as the organs, so the organists. No other instrument exercises such an influence upon artists. Perfect organs train organists in perfection; imperfect ones train them in imperfection and in false virtuosity. No talent and no genius can prevent this. The art of organ playing is always the product of the art of organ building. Without the art of organ building, which for his time and in its way was perfect, the Bach art of organ playing would never have arisen.

So, too, the modern French school of the organ is the result of this perfected organ construction. We in Germany are unquestionably richer in talent. But we do not possess such a circle of extraordinary artists as that which is represented in France by the names of Saint–Saëns, Guilmant, Widor, Gigout and Vierne.

The French organist differs from the German in the simplicity of his playing. The virtuosity that is found among our leading organists is much less prevalent there. Above everything else they seek a quiet plasticity, which brings the tone pattern to the listener in all its greatness. It seems to me as if the French organist even sits more quietly on his organ bench than we do. With all of them one finds an absolute precision in pressing and releasing the keys, which results in blending and clear, natural phrasing. Of course there are many organists among us who have these qualities in the same measure; but in France they seem to be the product of the school itself. All, even the otherwise mediocre players, possess them; whereas we have outstanding players who lack perfect precision, whose hands and feet do not work together with mathematical exactness, so that the other qualities in their playing are spoiled for the listener who really listens. To be sure, it is even more difficult to play with perfect precision on our organs than on the French organs with their mechanical action. What always surprises me particularly in the French organists is the quietness and infallibility of their pedal playing.

I cannot express my feeling better than by saying that the French organist plays more objectively, the German more personally. This, too, comes from the school. We have no school, hence each man goes his own way: so many organists, so many conceptions. To a certain extent that is an advantage we have over the French. I often rejoice in the vital individuality of our German organists—when they are men of taste. But we go much too far; and out of sheer "personality" playing and composition introduce emotion into the organ —natural human emotion, but not the wonderfully luminous, objective emotion of the last great preludes and fugues of Bach; and thus spoil the works of our great master by trying to animate them with our personal feelings. The organ itself should speak. The organist and his idea should vanish behind it—*s'effacer*, as the French say. He is, with all his thoughts, too little for the quiet majesty of his instrument, which is evident even in its outward appearance, and which, as Bach teaches us, expresses gloriously all feelings.[1]

Perhaps the French, on their side, at times carry too far the objectivity of their playing. But the repose and greatness that lie in it are so beneficial that one does not profit by the appearance of any outspoken personal feeling. "Organ playing," Widor once said to me on the organ bench at Notre Dame [2] as the rays of the setting sun streamed through the dusk of the nave in transfigured peace, "is the manifestation of a will filled with a vision of eternity. All organ instruction, both technical and artistic, has as its aim only to educate a man to this pure manifestation of the higher will. This will, expressed by the organist in the objectivity of his organ, should overwhelm the

---

[1] For this it is also important that the organist should be invisible, which often is not the case in our newer Protestant churches. For me it spoils the most beautiful Bach fugue, when from the nave of the church I can see the organist moving convulsively about at his console, as if he wanted to prove to the believers *ad oculos* how hard organ playing is. A little man can be only grotesque in his playing before a great instrument. Let us be protected from this sight by a screen from the organ housing around the visible console.

[2] In the early period, after the nomination of Vierne to be organist of Notre Dame, Widor often played on the cathedral organ. At the time in question he was practising his latest organ symphony.

hearer. He who cannot master the great, concentrated will in the theme of a Bach fugue—so that even the thoughtless hearer cannot escape from it, but even after the second measure grasps and comprehends it whether he will or not—he who cannot command this concentrated, peaceful will imparting itself so powerfully, may be a great artist in spite of this but is not a born organist. He has mistaken his instrument; for the organ represents the rapprochement of the human spirit to the eternal, imperishable spirit, and it is estranged from its nature and its place as soon as it becomes the expression of the subjective spirit."

The same conception of the nature of the organ lies at the basis of Guilmant's playing, except that with him the objectivity is interestingly and peculiarly animated by a certain lyrical experience.

We may say that in the French art of organ playing the feeling for architecture, which is to some extent the basis of all French art, comes to light. The swell box has therefore an entirely different significance from what it has with us. Instead of expressing feeling, it serves an architectonic purpose. The swell organs are so important on all French instruments that one can model the foundation stop tones of the whole organ with the volume of sound shut up in them. Says Gigout to his pupils, "A player handles his swell organ rightly, if his hearers do not suspect that the swell is functioning at all, but only feel as necessary the unnoticeable opening and shutting of the box." Guilmant presents the same principle to his pupils.

In the French art of organ playing, the noble and the simple in the use of the swell box come ever more clearly to light. In César Franck, and in the earlier compositions of Saint-Saëns, one still finds the small but frequent use of the swell, where this device to a certain extent takes the place of the emotional expressiveness which is lacking in the organ. This is the handling of the swell box which is still current among us. As time goes on, however, the simple, economical use of the swell box, used only in a general way, prevails; as it triumphs in the last works of Guilmant and Widor. To their pupils, and no less to the pupils of Gigout, it has become flesh and blood. Let us read through with this in mind the first organ symphony of Vierne, and compare it with the indications in our modern organ compositions. It will be easy then to shed the prejudice that the French are foolishly seeking effects with the swell box, and admit that right here we can learn from them.[1]

But when shall we have such proper swell boxes? It was not very long ago that leading organists among us held the opinion that a small organ needed no swell box, any more than it was necessary to have the pedal organ extend to f[1]. But the swell and the complete pedal belong to the nature of the organ itself, just as much as four feet belong to the horse. Rather have two or three fewer stops, for with the right kind of a swell box one can make two stops out of each single one. It is in these small organs in particular that certain advantages possessed by the French instruments appear much more conspicuously than in the great ones.

In registration also the French are much simpler than we. Almost twice as many registration changes are prescribed in a German organ composition as in a French one. Saint-Saëns is a master of gifted registration. Guilmant's registration is extremely skilful and in very good taste. Widor gives up registration almost completely, and increasingly so. "I can no longer comprehend very well a registration which is intended only to change the tone color," he said to me once, "and I find only that change in tone color right which is unmistakably required by the climax of the piece. The simpler our registration is, the closer we come to Bach." In his *Symphonie Romane*—the only registration in the first ten pages consists in adding the mixtures and reeds from time to time to the coupled foundation stops. Of course one should not forget that the French swell, in its

[1] I cannot imagine what automatic swell boxes can be. They open and close automatically at times determined in advance once and for all, and thus under certain circumstances produce a *pianissimo* where the composer intends the climax of the *crescendo* to stand. This "epoch-making" invention will be practical only when it succeeds in setting in operation the same clock work in the brains of the organ composers, so that they cannot do otherwise than imagine their periods of *crescendo* and *diminuendo* in the manner of the automatic swell box. Until then the automatic *crescendo* must remain the prerogative of the harmonium, where it succeeds admirably in giving "expression."

One of the best known instruments in Berlin has an automatic swell in the echo organ.

We already have even automatically operating roller *crescendi*. This is the final consequence of our mechanical slavery.

effect on the entire instrument, makes a great deal possible which can be accomplished on our organs only through registration.

Among the formal advantages of French organ compositions I should like to include also the wisely considered, effective use of the pedals, and the avoidance of every unnecessary octave doubling, whether in the manuals or in the pedals. It seems to me that our younger composers have not sufficiently studied the use of the pedals in the preludes and fugues of Bach, otherwise they would themselves have become aware of the mistake of incessantly bringing in the pedals. Over eighty percent of the octaves prescribed so frequently in modern compositions are usually meaningless, cause loose playing, and are ineffective. One should study Widor's works for his use of the pedals both in single line and in octaves!

Close observation discloses really two French schools: an old one, not directly influenced by German art, and a younger one, which shows German influence. As specifically French I would count in the older generation Boëly (died 1858), Chauvet and César Franck. The younger generation is represented by Saint–Saëns and Gigout. Gabriel Pierné and Boëllmann—so prematurely dead (born at Ensisheim in 1862, died as organist of St. Vincent de Paul at Paris in 1897)—also belong here.[1]

This older school had to strive with difficulty after an organ style, without ever quite attaining it even in its best representatives. César

[1] The works of Boëly and Chauvet have hardly any enduring significance; César Franck's early compositions, Six Pièces d'Orgue [Six Organ Pieces], published by Durand, also have really none. But his Trois Pièces pour Grand–Orgue [Three Pieces for the Organ], and his great fantasies which he calls chorales, will endure as something peerless (published by Edouard Durand). These three chorales are Franck's final work. They come from the year 1890. When he could no longer walk, he still managed to drag himself to St. Clothilde's to complete the registration indications.

To prevent misunderstandings, let me remark that the chorale in modern French organ literature means simply a fantasy on a formal, noble theme, which, however, is freely conceived. This designation arose because certain organists of the older generation thought that the chorale themes in the chorale fantasies of Bach come from Bach himself.

Among Boëllmann's compositions I cite: Douze Pièces en Recueil. 2e Suite; Fantaisie [Twelve Selected Pieces. Second Suite; Fantasy] (Leduc); Suite Gothique; Fantaisie Dialoguée [Gothic Suite; Fantasy in Dialogue] (organ and orchestra; arranged for organ alone by Eugène Gigout) (Durand). Gabriel Pierné: Trois Pièces pour Orgue [Three Organ Pieces] (Durand).

Franck's and Saint-Saëns' works [1] are the improvisations of gifted musicians on the organ, rather than organ works, even though the content in the later works of César Franck makes one overlook certain violences done to the organ style. Boëllmann's compositions are interesting youthful efforts, which certainly would have led to something significant.

Gigout [2] stands all alone in this school. He is the classicist, who has attained a pure organ style. He has something of Händel's manner. His influence as a teacher is outstanding, and his playing marvelous.

This specifically French school cultivates the art of improvising—though not so much, of course, as that old organist of Notre Dame (may his name not be cherished by posterity) who boasted that he had never played anything on his organ from notes—but still to the extent of laying very special stress upon it. Saint-Saëns is first fully appreciated when his improvisation is heard at St. Séverin, where occasionally he substitutes for the gifted Perilhou. Gigout's strength also lies, above everything else, in this very domain.

Vincent d'Indy tells, in the masterly book which has just appeared about his teacher (ed. Alcan, Paris, 1906), of César Franck's improvising. As Franz Liszt was leaving St. Clothilde on April 3, 1866, he was so moved that he said to those around him that no one else since Bach had so improvised on the organ.

Guilmant likes to improvise. Widor not so much, "only when he feels forced to say something." Vierne's improvisations at Notre Dame excel by their perfection of form. Schmidt, also, belongs

---

[1] Among the works of Saint-Saëns should be mentioned *Trois Rhapsodies sur des Cantiques Bretons* [Three Rhapsodies on Breton Songs] (Op. 7, Ed. Durand), of which the first and the third are really wonder works, and have also the unusual advantage of pleasing the listener immediately; *Trois Préludes et Fugues pour Orgue* [Three Preludes and Fugues for the Organ] (Op. 99, Durand); *Fantaisie pour Grand-Orgue* [Fantasy for the Organ] (Op. 101, Durand). The last two *opera* are ingenious and substantial, but do not completely please in their organ style.

[2] Of Gigout's works let us name *Six Pièces*. [Six Pieces] (Durand); *Trois Pièces* [Three Pieces] (Durand); *Prélude et Fugue en Mi* [Prelude and Fugue in E] (Durand); *Méditation* [Meditation] (Landy, London); *Dix Pièces en Recueil* [Ten Selected Pieces] (Leduc); *Suite de Pièces* [Suite of Pieces] (Richault); *Suite de Trois Morceaux* [Suite of Three Pieces] (Rosenberg); *Poèmes Mystiques* [Mystical Poems] (Durand).

among the leading improvisers. He is one of the most talented of the younger generation, who, unfortunately, because of his appointment as Chapel Master at St. Philipp du Roule, is for the present lost to the organ.

In general, improvising and even playing from memory have a bigger place in French organ instruction, as Widor, Guilmant, Vierne (his assistant at the Conservatory), and Gigout have imparted it, than among us. In the competition for the organ posts at Notre Dame are required the improvisation of a fugue on a given theme, a free improvisation, and twenty modern or classic works for the organ played from memory. The pedagogical value of playing from memory on the organ is in fact extraordinarily great, because the pupil is compelled thereby to take account of everything. It may be that we too much neglect playing from memory on the organ.

The other French school, represented by Guilmant, formerly at the Trinity, and Widor, at St. Sulpice, had its origin in Belgium. Guilmant and Widor were pupils of Lemmens, who in turn in his time was a pupil of Hesse. From the very beginning, therefore, as their early works show, Guilmant[1] and Widor were acquainted with the organ style which emanated from Bach, and did not need to seek gropingly for it.

Guilmant is now not only one of the leading musicians, but at the same time the most universal teacher, with outstanding pedagogical talent and musical historical culture. He is the one who has made known in France the old organ music from the era preceding Bach. How much German organ music can learn from his works concerning form and construction has been constantly emphasized for years in German critical circles.

[1] Alexandre Guilmant: *Sieben Sonaten* [Seven Sonatas] (Durand–Schott) (Op. 42, 50, 56, 61, 80, 86, 89); *Pièces dans Differents Styles* [Pieces in Different Styles] (18th Volume, Op. 15, 16, 17, 18, 19, 20, 24, 25, 33, 40, 44, 45, 69, 70, 71, 72, 74, 75) (Durand–Schott); *L'Organiste Pratique*; 12 Lieferungen [The Practical Organist; 12 books] (Durand–Schott); *Noëls, Offertoires Elévations*; 4 Lieferungen [Carols, Offertory Elevations; 4 books] (Durand–Schott); *L'Organiste Liturgiste*; 10 Lieferungen [The Liturgical Organist; 10 books]; *Concert Historique d'Orgue* [Historical Organ Recital]. Guilmant deserves special credit for his edition of the French organ masters of the 16th, 17th, and 18th centuries. Up to date six annual volumes have appeared.

Widor is more of an introversive spirit. His ten symphonies [1] reveal the development of the art of organ playing as he himself has experienced it. The first are creations perfect in form, permeated by a lyric, melodic, sometimes even a sentimental spirit, which show however in the wonderful structure of their themes the peculiar endowment of the creator. With the fifth symphony he deserts this road; the lyric withdraws; something else strives to take form, first in the fifth and sixth symphonies, which are among his best known, and which are still in melodic form. The seventh and eighth are transition works; they are of the organ, and yet conceived in a boldly orchestral manner. What a marvel is the first movement of the eighth symphony! At the same time the austere appears ever more clearly—the austere that Widor brings back to sacred art in his last two symphonies. "It is noteworthy," he said to me in that period, "that except for Bach's preludes and fugues—or, rather, except for certain preludes and fugues of Bach—I can no longer think of any organ art as holy which is not consecrated to the church through its themes, whether it be from the chorale or from the Gregorian chant." Thus the ninth symphony (*Symphonie Gothique*) on the theme "*Puer natus est*" [A boy is born] is written as a Christmas symphony, and the tenth (*Symphonie Romane*), on the wonderful motif of the "*Haec dies*" [This is the day], is conceived as an Easter symphony. And when one May Sunday, still striving with technical problems, he played for the first time in St. Sulpice the *Symphonie Romane*, I felt with him that in this work the French art of organ playing had entered sacred art, and had experienced that death and that resurrection that every art of organ playing must experience when it wishes to create something enduring.

Louis Vierne, who was called in 1900 to the Church of Notre Dame while still hardly thirty years old, is the pupil of César Franck, Widor, and Guilmant. His two great and important organ symphonies have very much promise.[2]

I should not want to forget the good Dallier, a pupil of Franck,

---

[1] Charles Marie Widor: *Symphonies pour Orgue* (Hamelle), Nos. 1–4, Op. 13; Nos. 5–8, Op. 42 (2d edition 1900); No. 9, *Symphonie Gothique* (Op. 70); No. 10, *Symphonie Romane* (Op. 73).

[2] Ed. Hamelle.

formerly at St. Eustache, now at the Madeleine, where he became the successor of Gabriel Faurés, the wonderfully gifted improviser and student of Bach, who himself was the successor of Dubois. A rendering of Bach's *E flat major Triple Fugue*, during a musical festival at St. Eustache, I shall never forget.

Among the young men we should name are Quef, the successor of Guilmant at the Trinity; Tournemire at St. Clothilde; Jacob, a very outstanding player, at St. Louis d'Antin; Marti at St. François-Xavier; Libert at the Basilica of St. Denis; Marquaire, the substitute for Widor at St. Sulpice, whose very interesting organ symphony has been published by Hamelle; Bret, who as the director of the Bach Society now places all his gifts exclusively at the service of the works of the old master; Mahaut, an accomplished player, and at the same time an enthusiastic interpreter of the works of his teacher César Franck; and Bonnet, the successor of Dallier at St. Eustache.

Common to both schools, and to the old as well as the young, is their reverence for Bach. Even among us Bach is hardly played more frequently and exclusively than in many a Paris church. During the offering at Notre Dame, Bach's choral prelude on *"O Mensch bewein' dein' Sünde gross"* [O man, mourn for thy great sins] flows through the mighty halls of the cathedral.

Of the future of the French school I cannot speak. *L'Orgue Moderne* [The Modern Organ], a collection of the more modern and most modern efforts, which appears periodically under the patronage of Widor, does not please me at all. In form everything in it is good, and much more mature than the first works of our young German organists. But the resourcefulness, the storm and stress, the fermentation, that could give wisdom to this clever young generation, in order that from it something more than cleverness, something great and enduring, might come—these are lacking. The contemporary works of the young German organists display less ability in form, sometimes less organ style, less reflection and clarity; but in place of these many of them have a very promising wealth of ideas.

But what in general will become of French organ construction and the French art of organ playing? What will the separation of church and state bring? Already the churches are preparing for the separation, and are cutting the already small salaries as far as they can be cut. Most organists have already been notified that a fourth of their pay will be taken away. Dallier first lost a third of his income at St. Eustache and then a half. Thereupon he applied for the post at the Madeleine, which was just becoming vacant. The position of organist at Notre Dame may in the future pay hardly more than 1000 francs. Organ building stagnates. Splendid organs which once stood in the churches are to be bought for ridiculous prices. Often one asks himself if the most certain result of the separation will not be first of all the ruin of organ building and organ art. The crisis which both will pass through will in any case be very severe.

But let us leave the future alone. At the moment the point is that the partition between the French art of organ playing and the German should be razed, and each should learn from the other. German and French talents are destined to stimulate each other. In the art of organ playing especially, just as we Germans can learn a limitless amount in technique and form from the French, they on the other hand can be shielded by the spirit of German art from impoverishment in their pure and perfect forms. By the interpenetration of both spiritual tendencies, new life will arise on both sides. Up to this time only the American organists have really profited from the advantage of passing through the German and the French schools, inasmuch as they usually passed half of their period of learning in Germany, and the other half in Paris. In the future may it be that both the German and the French, in order to enjoy the same benefits, may be seized by that urge to travel and learn which characterized the old organists. Perhaps when that time comes a French organist will acquaint his colleagues with the art of Reger, Wolfrum, Lang, Franke, De Lange, Reimann, Egidi, Irrgang, Sittard, Homeyer, Otto Reubke, Straube, Beckmann, Radecke, G. A. Brandt, and the rest; even as I have tried herein to make better known to the German organists the nature of the French organ and the French art of organ playing.[1]

[1] This treatise first appeared in *Musik*, Volumes 13 and 14, 1906. Fifth Year.

❧

*T*HUS Albert Schweitzer launched the campaign for the new organ; an organ which should preserve the lovely tone of the old instruments, but somehow avoid their mechanical defects. The factory organ was not the answer; another answer had to be found. The publication of Schweitzer's small book brought down on him an avalanche of correspondence—mingled praise and blame; bitter criticism; constructive suggestions. The following years were filled with many things, but his interest in this question never wavered.

The great opportunity to advance his cause came with the invitation to address the Third Congress of the International Society of Music at Vienna in 1909. In preparation for his appearance there Schweitzer wrote a questionnaire which was sent out to organ players and organ builders in half a dozen European countries. Some hundred and fifty detailed answers were received. The labor involved in analyzing the replies was enormous; Schweitzer states that he spent on each report an average of six hours. Months were consumed by the study; but the report made to the organ section of the International Congress was an important milestone on the road to the better organ. In the previous booklet we have Schweitzer's own ideas; in the report to the Congress we have a cross section of informed opinion in Europe at the beginning of the twentieth century concerning this burning question of organ construction. The questionnaire and report form an appendix to this book. (See pages 253–289.)

After hearing Schweitzer's report the organ section went to work through days of intensive application to draw up the International Regulations for Organ Building, which were later sent to organ players and organ builders throughout Europe. These detailed and elaborate specifications, containing at great length the recommendations of the organ section, are sometimes attributed to Schweitzer himself. He had a major hand in framing them, but of course they are the work of all the faithful members of the organ section. Because they are too technical, and because they are not exclusively the work of Albert Schweitzer, they are not included in this book.

VI

Medicine, Theology and Music

SCHWEITZER describes these early years of the century as a "continual struggle with fatigue." No wonder! His medical studies were exacting enough, but there were all the other things too. He loved his preaching, and he had not been able to make up his mind to resign from his pastorate at St. Nicholas. He kept on, moreover, with his lectures at the University, made still more burdensome because he was giving new lectures on Pauline problems. He was trying to follow the development in Paul's thinking, as he passed from primitive Christianity, with its extreme eschatological emphases, to a new and strange mysticism, characterized by the central idea of dying and being born again in Jesus Christ; a mysticism which prepared the way for the hellenization of Christianity with its doctrine of the Logos. He had hoped to finish this study before the end of his medical course; he succeeded only in completing the introduction. But what Schweitzer called his "introduction" was a large volume in which he had surveyed all important previous interpretations of the writings of St. Paul from the Reformation on. The book was published in 1911. It was almost twenty years later before the rest of his study was ready for publication.

The delay was in part caused by the fact that he was working on the greatly enlarged second edition of his history of research into the life of Jesus, which was published just after his departure for Africa in 1913. It was delayed also by the enormous amount of work he had to do in preparing his thesis for the doctorate in medicine—a study of the mentality of Jesus from the point of view of psychiatry. And lastly it was delayed by his music.

He was going to Paris regularly now for the concerts given by the

Bach Society. That meant three days of absence each time. The Bach Society, founded in 1905, had already taken an important place in the musical life of Paris. It was composed largely of professional singers, and was led by Gustave Bret. The competence of conductor and chorus made it possible for them to render each season a goodly number of Bach's choral works.

Dr. Archibald T. Davison, professor of music at Harvard University, gives an interesting glimpse of Albert Schweitzer as organist for the Bach Society. In contrast to what he calls the mechanical and heartless perfection of the chorus and orchestra, Schweitzer's work at the organ was easily the most distinguished of all.

"I was struck, first of all, by Schweitzer's indifference to any 'effectiveness' in registration or manner of playing, the entire process being concentrated in the presentation of the music in its proper setting without the slightest effort to make it 'telling' of itself. And it must be remembered that the question was not of the great organ compositions; it was solely of the organ background to, let us say, one of the cantatas. My early studies had centered about the instrument as a vehicle of display, and from Widor I was discovering that the organ and the organist were the servants; the music, especially that of Bach—the master. The unpretentious accompanimental parts must always be a pretty routine affair to the organist who loves his playing better than the music he plays. Schweitzer, however, never once obtruding himself, lavished upon them all the scrupulous attention they deserve but all too seldom receive. I realize now that my feeling about his skilful and appropriate support was primarily a technical one, albeit an as yet undiscovered clue to the impulse that converted these stylistic marvels into an almost biographical record of Bach himself.

"As far as I can remember, Schweitzer, in spite of his authoritative knowledge, was never consulted—publicly, at least—regarding any of the questions involved in the performance of Bach's music. In fact the only occasion upon which I remember his forsaking the near-anonymity of the organ bench was at a rehearsal when the conductor, wishing to judge an effect from the rear of the hall, put his baton in Schweitzer's hand, and asked him to direct the chorus and orchestra. At that time, at least, Albert Schweitzer was in no sense a conductor, and it is significant that he made no pretense of being one. Turning his back squarely upon both orchestra and chorus, one hand thrust in his trousers' pocket, his head back, staring up into the dark of the Salle Gaveau, his arm moving in awkward sweeps and unorthodox directions, it was quite obvious that if he gave himself a thought—which I doubt—it was only to consider himself the agent who should bring the music to life. Beyond that he had no responsibility. It was for the conductor to judge whether the balance of tone or the seating of the participants was satisfactory. Above all, there was complete detachment; entire absorption in the sound of the music. To this day I can remember the intense admiration I felt for Schweitzer's indifference to externals. How I swelled with indignation at the pitying smirks of the orchestral players as they condescendingly shrugged their shoulders and ostentatiously disregarded the vague gestures of the conductor pro tem. It was then, I feel sure, that I first sensed the stature of the man." [1]

In addition to his regular appearance as organist for the Bach Society in Paris, Schweitzer was traveling also to Barcelona to play for the Bach concerts given by the Orféo Català. He liked and admired the conductor, Luis Millet, and greatly enjoyed these engagements, though they were very exhausting.

On one occasion an organ and orchestra concert was given for the king and queen. After the rehearsal Señor Millet insisted that Schweitzer leave his music book on the organ. "No one will touch it," he said. Very reluctantly, Schweitzer did so. An hour before the concert they came back again; the book was gone. The director and the assistant director hunted everywhere for it in vain. The time for the concert came; the king and queen arrived; and still there was no book. Schweitzer was in despair. Finally someone suggested that they look in the room where the cleaning-woman kept her things. And there they found it.

After the concert the king and queen expressed their deep appreciation to Schweitzer. "Is it difficult to play the organ?" asked the king. "Almost as difficult," replied Schweitzer, "as to rule Spain." "Then you must be a man of courage," laughed the king.

[1] The Albert Schweitzer Jubilee Book, edited by A. A. Roback. Cambridge, Mass.: Sci-Art Publishers, 1945, pp. 200 f.

Other concerts called him away from Strassburg frequently. They had become a financial necessity, for the loss of income resulting from his resignation as principal of the theological faculty had to be offset somehow. But they were often delightful occasions. There was, for instance, the autumn week in 1911 when he went to Munich with Widor to play at the Festival of French Music. A certain wealthy count who had a great champagne plant and sold to all the big hotels went to Widor and said, "I have to eat at these hotels and I cannot eat alone. I must have a little company with me. Do you know one or two French students who would have lunch and dinner with me regularly?" Of course Widor suggested Schweitzer, and of course Schweitzer accepted. For reasons of economy he had been eating in small restaurants, and now to his surprise he found himself for the remaining six days having lunch and dinner in the big hotels. The count naturally had to honor his own product, and always ordered champagne. Other distinguished guests were there. In this way Schweitzer came to know the old French organist and composer, Charles Camille Saint-Saëns, who was also an occasional guest at the table.

Widor and Schweitzer had come particularly to give Widor's Second Symphony for Organ and Orchestra. The day it was to be given both were invited to dinner. Schweitzer declined with thanks. He wanted to be fresh for the symphony, which is very difficult. But Widor went. At eight o'clock, when they were to begin, Widor was not there. At five minutes past he had not arrived. At ten minutes past he appeared, rushed to the rostrum, and began at once to conduct the orchestra with one hand while he searched for his glasses with the other. He was unable to conduct the symphony without the score, and neither he nor the orchestra was thoroughly familiar with it. With his baton first in his right hand and then in his left he searched in his pockets, one after the other. They were a quarter of the way through before he found them. Had not Schweitzer been so sure of himself and supported so well with the organ, the whole thing would have been disastrous. Said Schweitzer afterwards, "You see, I was right in not accepting the invitation."

Towards the end of his medical course Schweitzer began to prepare, in collaboration with Widor, an edition of Bach's organ works.

Five volumes were completed before his departure, and published later. This too meant many days in Paris, and occasional visits of Widor to Gunsbach. It was not an easy enterprise. Bach had left in his organ works no suggestions for registration or changes of manuals. The organs of his day were so constructed that automatically the pieces were rendered as he intended. When, after a long period of oblivion, Bach's organ works again became known in the middle of the nineteenth century, organs had changed, and even those in Germany who knew the old traditions in organ playing were abandoning them. But by a queer paradox the French organists remained loyal to the old German traditions, which they had learned from the Belgium organist Lemmens, who had been a pupil of Adolph Friedrich Hesse of Breslau. And the splendid tone of the great French organs made it possible to render Bach as Bach had intended.

The new edition was intended for those who knew only the modern organs. Schweitzer and Widor tried first to show what the registration and manual changes had to be on Bach's instruments, and second to suggest how the variations in volume and tone possible on the modern organ might be used without injuring the work. All these suggestions, however, were contained in the introduction, and not attached to the pieces themselves. To both men the important thing was the architecture of the piece. Tone was secondary to lines of melody, which must always move along side by side with perfect distinctness. Perfect plasticity in phrasing, loveliness of tone, a moderate tempo—these were the authentic marks of Bach's organ works.

These were all rich years for Albert Schweitzer, rich in the variety of their activity, rich in the many friends who gathered around his brilliant and charming personality. It was at this time that he came to know well Marie-Joseph Erb, the pianist who had so thrilled the small boy at his first concert in Mulhouse. About the same time—perhaps a few years earlier—Schweitzer had journeyed with Ernest Munch, as already related, to Frankfort to hear Siegfried Ochs, the director of the Philharmonic Chorus of Berlin, perform, with the help of the Cecilia Society, Bach's B minor Mass, and he also came to admire greatly this fine musician. His tributes to these men should not be forgotten.

❦

MARIE-JOSEPH ERB [1]

WHEN I first became acquainted with the organist Marie-Joseph Erb, I immediately felt admiration and sympathy for him. That which struck me in him was the flexibility of his playing and his profound acquaintance with all the resources of the sacred instrument. He did not seek to produce effects with his registration, yet his execution, so simple in appearance, brought out the meaning of the work he was interpreting by means of the sonorities he employed. In many respects his playing resembled that of Alexandre Guilmant.

The opportunity to know Erb better came in 1908, when the Silbermann organ in the St. Thomas church in Strassburg was being restored. The church council, on my request, charged Erb, together with myself, with the responsibility of deciding the character of this restoration—which was entrusted to the organ builder Frédéric Härpfer of Boulay—and of supervising the work.

It was the first time, so far as my knowledge goes, that an old organ was restored instead of being replaced. I had secured from the church council approval for my plan of preserving the ancient instrument, while replacing all its defective or worn-out parts, and adding modern diapason pipes. I was greatly relieved when Erb said he was ready to share the responsibility with me. How many hours we passed together at the organ as the work progressed, trying with the builder, Frédéric Härpfer, whom Erb valued as highly as I did, to find the best solution of our problems! In these conferences I was able to appreciate the profundity and extent of the knowledge of organ building that Erb possessed.

When the restored instrument was dedicated, Erb was the first to play on it, using an organ concerto of Bach's. The rendering of this concerto showed the musicians who were present at the dedication that the task of conserving this ancient instrument was fully justified and had been well carried out. For the first time we learned

[1] From *Un Grand Musicien Français: Marie-Joseph Erb*. Strassburg–Paris: Editions F.-X, Le Roux & Cie., 1948, pp. 84–88.

how Bach's music must have sounded when executed by a great builder of his age; and we were able to imagine the effects which could be produced with the resources offered by the sonority and the arrangement of keyboards in these ancient instruments. How many times since, while playing on the St. Thomas organ, have I been reminded of the splendid rendering of Bach given us by M.-J. Erb at this dedication!

Some years afterwards, Erb and I had to do with the construction by Mr. Härpfer of the organ in the *Salle des Fêtes*, then called the *Sängerhaus*. In order that I might judge the sonorities, as we planned the slight changes necessary for the harmonization of the stops, Erb improvised while I listened at the back of the hall. But many times these improvisations were so interesting that as I followed them I forgot to make the comments and indications which were to help us secure the perfect harmonization of the various stops in the new instrument.

The new organ in the *Salle des Fêtes* was first played by Widor. At the inaugural concert two symphonies for organ and orchestra were played, one composed by Widor and one by Erb; the second had been composed expressly for this occasion. I played the organ for both works.

In studying the Erb composition, I became aware of its worth. The themes were rich, the structure of the work ingenious, and the organ and orchestra complemented each other and blended with each other admirably. Widor also admired the score. All of us who were friends of Marie–Joseph Erb hoped it would be published, and take rank among the most beautiful compositions for organ and orchestra. For various reasons, Erb, in spite of our begging, could not make up his mind to undertake its publication. I have always regretted it.

His lovely piece for the violin and organ, based on Gregorian motifs, I have included a number of times in my church concerts in foreign lands. Each time the violinists have expressed their delight in making the acquaintance of a work so profoundly inspiring, where organ and violin are handled with equal mastery.

The compositions written by Erb for the theatre have always surprised me by the quality of their dramatic sentiments. We are all inclined to class Erb as a composer only of pure music, but in listening to his works for the theatre I have been struck from the first by the variety and the flexibility of his talent. His dramatic music shows an admirable comprehension of those exigencies of music which must develop in conformity to the events and movements of the stage; and also an elevation of style that is often lacking among those composers who think they are ordained to write for the theatre. The dramatic music of M.-J. Erb is lyrical, and at the same time picturesque in the best sense of the word.

In a conversation with him one day, in the course of which I congratulated him on the remarkable theatrical qualities of his dramatic music, I said to him, "Some day you must find a libretto of distinction which will permit you to express the full measure of your talent. Then you will create a work which will attract attention and place you among the masters of music for the contemporary theatre."

Before my departure for Africa, I tried for several years to find an operatic subject suitable for the quality of Erb's gifts. To no purpose, however; then Erb wrote himself excellent librettos for *The Iron Man* and *Saxophone and Company*.[1] Unfortunately I was not able to be present at the theatrical presentation in Strassburg of these two lyrical works.

I was able, however, in each of my European sojourns, to note the influence Erb exerted on the musicians of the new Alsatian generation. He devoted himself completely to his pupils; they knew what they owed him, and they worshipped him.

A close friendship existed between Erb and myself. He knew the interest I took in his creations. Between 1920 and 1923, when I stayed often in Alsace, I had the pleasure of seeing him many times and of keeping in touch with his activities. I remember particularly some charming afternoons Widor and I passed at the home of Mr. and Mrs. Erb. Widor, when passing through Alsace, always stopped to visit the Strassburg master. I had the opportunity then of listening to some very interesting conversations about music and musicians.

What impressed especially those who had the privilege of coming close to Erb were his simplicity and his modesty. His very nature

[1] *L'Homme de Fer* and *Saxophone et Cie.*

made it impossible for him to assert himself. He interested himself without prejudice in the musical creations of various schools and personalities, trying to judge them only in accordance with their innate worth. His criticism was never harsh. He believed that what was destined to endure would endure, and that the rest would of itself pass quietly into oblivion. He had a calm and wholesome wisdom from which he never swerved.

Such was Marie–Joseph Erb, as I knew him, and admired and loved him. I am sure that his memory and his works will always give him a place in the history of Alsatian art and in the hearts of the Alsatian people. As for me, I consider him the most remarkable of all the composers Alsace has produced.

❧

SIEGFRIED OCHS [1]

A CERTAIN performance of the Bach *B minor Mass* by the Cecilia Society of Frankfort, under the direction of Siegfried Ochs, was for me unforgettable. It was about 1908, I believe. It was the first time I had heard him direct it. The impression I then received remained decisive in my judgment of his reading of Bach, and was only strengthened by everything I heard of him later.

What impressed me again and again in Siegfried Ochs was his profound and unique study of the composition. One could tell from the chorus that he was the master of his subject. He had completely immersed himself in the tone-lines he was rendering, and made them resound as vital wholes. Moreover, the stress he put on enunciation always struck me as exceedingly pleasant.

But he required a technically perfect rendering not only of the chorus but also of the orchestra. And this was something new in those days. Siegfried Ochs was one of the first to understand the meaning of the phrasing and accents in Bach; and he worked accordingly. Heretofore it had not been felt as self-evident that the Bach tone-lines for the strings could be properly rendered only if all the players

[1] From the *Fest–Programm des Berliner Philharmonischen Chors*, Berlin, December 5, 1932, pp. 11–13.

phrased and accented in the same fashion; but for Ochs this was axiomatic. Therefore he made with the greatest care every necessary notation in the parts before he laid them on the music rack. With what conscientiousness he did this work I was able to see for myself, when, about 1911, he placed at my disposal for the *première* in Barcelona his manuscript of the parts of the *B minor Mass*. And the pains he had taken were well repaid by the results. With Siegfried Ochs one was again and again surprised by the plastic and vital way in which the orchestral parts were brought out. How splendidly flowed along the accompaniment of a Bach aria under his leadership, because the tone-line had been fashioned in accordance with a clear and well-considered conception!

If today much more care is given to phrasing and accenting in Bach than one even dreamed of in an earlier day, this is in large measure due to the influence of the standards Siegfried Ochs left behind him for those who undertake to conduct Bach's music.

Furthermore, everyone who values Bach's work must take satisfaction in the great appeal of Ochs' rendering of it. Siegfried Ochs had made a clean sweep of the ideal which had been accepted as classic for the playing of Bach, as only a person as full of feeling as he was could have done. He had attacked the widespread opinion, accepted even in the circle of excellent musicians, that Bach must be played in rigid time and generally in the most objective manner possible— in their words, "played down and sung down." He was conscious of the elementary vitality that makes itself felt in this perfected form. And he tried to do equal justice to the life and the form. Great architecture in colossally vital lines: this hovered before him as his ideal for the rendition. And even when one was not inclined to agree with his tempi (which he liked to make too lively), and his dynamics (which he liked to elaborate too richly), and in general with his inclination to virtuosity, one still found his rendition a genuine experience. For Bach's music as he performed it always took shape before the hearer in its mighty lines and in its rich individuality. This interpreter, who was always striving for the most refined result, possessed at the same time by nature the gift of great simplicity. This has always appeared to me to be the secret of his music.

That Siegfried Ochs accomplished so much in his rendering of

Bach is to be explained in the end not simply by his musical sensitivity and ability, but also by the fact that Bach was for him a spiritual experience. Siegfried Ochs had a nature that drew him to the creator of the Passions and Cantatas. Whoever had the good fortune to get more closely acquainted with him learned that this eminent director was a man of great depths, and lived in the works of the master of St. Thomas not simply as a musician but also as a great soul. To him the piety embedded in the texts meant something.

And this comprehension of the spiritual in Bach's work made itself felt in his renderings. It was imparted during the rehearsals to those who worked with him; in the performance to those hearers who had ears to hear.

Hearing the *B minor Mass* directed by Siegfried Ochs, and *Tristan and Isolde* directed by Felix Mottl, were for me two equally unforgettable experiences.

May the Philharmonic Chorus of Berlin, which gave us under Siegfried Ochs such perfect performances of Bach, and which now under Otto Klemperer celebrates its jubilee with the *B minor Mass*, continue to fulfil its mission of bringing us close to Bach in the spirit of its great and never-to-be-forgotten director.

※

*T*HE *time for Albert Schweitzer's departure to Africa had come very near. To a crowded congregation in St. Nicholas one spring Sunday in 1912 he preached from the high pulpit his last sermon there. "May the peace of God which passeth all understanding keep your hearts and minds in Christ Jesus." He had used those words to end every service at St. Nicholas all through the years. On this closing Sunday the benediction had become his sermon text.*

His last course of lectures at the University in the winter of 1911–1912 had been on the reconciliation of religious truth with comparative religion and natural science. In the spring he gave his last lecture, and with a feeling of deep sorrow he stepped down from the platform in that second lecture room at the east of the main entrance of the University building, knowing that the world that had been his was to be his no more.

That spring he spent in Paris studying tropical medicine. He had passed his medical examinations the previous December, paying for them with the fee he received at Munich with Widor, but he did not receive his degree until February, 1913, when he had completed his year as an intern, and had submitted his doctoral thesis. This was his Psychiatric Study of Jesus. Seldom has so small a book resulted from such voluminous reading and research.[1]

On June 18, 1912, he married Helene Bresslau, who had been born in Berlin. Her father was a distinguished professor of history there, later moving to the University of Strassburg. She had been a social worker in Strassburg, and had been of great assistance to Schweitzer in various ways, finally studying nursing that she might be the better equipped to work with him. She, too, had a brilliant mind.

They spent the following months, as much of them as they could, in Gunsbach. But the funds had to be collected for the proposed African hospital, the supplies had to be purchased and packed, and the manuscript for the second edition of the book on Jesus had to be completed.

In February, 1913, seventy packing cases were sent off to Bordeaux, and on March 26, Helene and Albert Schweitzer embarked for Africa.

[1] The Psychiatric Study of Jesus, by Albert Schweitzer. Boston: The Beacon Press, second edition, 1949.

VII

Africa

QUICKLY, by stream and jungle ways, by dugout and river boat, the news spread through the forest that a white doctor had come to the mission station at Andende. The natives and officials carried the word, the beat of the tam-tam spread it abroad. And the sick came in large numbers to be healed. There was no time to prepare for them. The little bungalow on the hillside, surrounded by its broad verandas, was filled with white patients. An old henhouse became the consulting room, and bamboo huts with palm-leaf tiles began to shelter the native patients. In the fall of 1913 a small building of corrugated iron was built, with an operating room, dispensary, and consulting room; and there the ill were treated. There was a surprising amount of lung trouble, and heart trouble, and urinary diseases. And there were of course the tropical maladies: malaria, leprosy, sleeping sickness, dysentery and ulcers. The operations were mostly for hernia and elephantiasis tumors. It was hard to secure good orderlies and interpreters; but Mrs. Schweitzer proved to be a tower of strength. She took care of the dressings and the linen, prepared the operating room, administered the anesthetics, nursed those who were gravely ill, and still somehow found time to look out for the household.

At the end of a few weeks there were at the hospital forty patients and their attendants.

In the late afternoons of those early days, before the sudden coming of the tropical night, Schweitzer used to sit for a few moments on the veranda of his house and look out upon the peaceful scene with a sense of joy and satisfaction in his heart. It was a beautiful country. He could look far up the broad river to the low line of far-off mountains. At the right was the large island where was located the administrative center of Lambarene. At the left was the primeval forest, dipping its roots into the waters of the Ogowe, losing itself in the uncharted distance. River and sky and forest seemed blended in some kind of mystic unity; and as he sat there he could forget the cruel tragedies of the jungle, the strange superstitions that shackled the native mind, and for a brief moment even the sick stretched out on their raffia mats below him there in the bamboo huts.

Soon he found that the sacrifices he had been prepared to make were not demanded of him. At the very outset he realised that he would not have to sacrifice his music. The Paris Missionary Society had given him a zinc-lined piano with pedal attachment, specially designed for the tropics. And now he knew that in the solitude of the forest, against the background of the chanting of crickets and toads and the mysterious noises of the jungle, he had such an opportunity to perfect his technique as he had never had in Europe. He set to work to learn by heart the great music of Bach, Mendelssohn, Mozart, Widor, Max Reger and César Franck. Even though he could find each day but half an hour for this practice, he could still go on with his music. Indeed, during the first three months he got three more volumes of Bach's choral compositions ready for the publisher—though unfortunately they have not even yet been published.

He found, of course, difficulties he had not known in Europe. There was the terrible humidity of the climate; the voracious termites with an appetite for wood and paper; even the petty thieving of the very people he had come to help. One day he found that someone had stolen his edition of Wagner's Meistersinger, and, what was even more serious, Bach's St. Matthew Passion, to which he had added his carefully worked out organ accompaniment.

He had agreed to give up his preaching, but to his great joy the prohibition was quickly removed by the missionaries in Africa, so much broader minded than the mission board in Europe. To preach to the natives of the jungle, most of whom had never heard of Christianity before, became to him a thrilling delight and an inexpressible privilege.

The dry season gave way to the wet season. The second dry season came, with its overcast skies and its cooler temperatures. Then, suddenly, in August 1914, came the ominous word that there was war in Europe. The Schweitzers, by the accident of their birth, were German citizens. A stupid French government ordered the hospital closed. The Schweitzers were to consider themselves prisoners of war. The day after this news had been brought him Schweitzer began work on a new book, The Philosophy of Civilization. The coming of war had made that subject much more important than the completion of his book on Paul. And even when the hospital was reopened after a few months, largely because of Widor's influence back in Paris, he continued to work on this book that was to engross his attention for the next thirty-five years. His writing was another of the possible sacrifices he had not been called on to make.

Civilization was falling to pieces, he thought, because our traditional attitude of ethical affirmation had been weakened. But how can this attitude be demonstrated in thought? For long months Schweitzer vainly sought the answer to this problem. Then, one bright day, in September 1915, while he was making a long river journey, the answer suddenly came to him in the phrase "Reverence for life." Perhaps it was the playful disporting of a herd of hippopotamuses in the water about his boat that brought him this revelation. At any rate, it was a turning point in his intellectual life. Undoubtedly life was as precious to these ugly, vicious creatures in the river as it was to us. If we are life that wills to live in the midst of other life that wills to live, then we must respect this other life, whatever its nature, just as we demand respect for our own life. This became the central thought in the ethical and philosophical system he began at that time to build.

After spending the hot, rainy season of 1916–17 on the coast because of his wife's poor health, Schweitzer returned to his work at the hospital; only to be almost immediately informed that they were to be transferred as prisoners of war to an internment camp in France. Saddened by the forced closing of his hospital, which he was not to see again for seven years, but still reveling in the unexpected leisure that came as a boon to his writing and music, he spent the time on the steamer learning by heart Widor's Sixth Organ Symphony and a number of Bach's fugues.

Their first internment camp was at Garaison, an old monastery under the shadow of the Pyrenees. The name of the camp, significantly enough, was the Provençal form of the French word for "healing" (guérison), and soon Schweitzer was permitted to practise as a doctor among his fellow internees. But he still had plenty of time for his writing and his music. On a simple wooden table, made for him by a friend in the camp, he began once more to "play the organ"—the table-top his manuals, the floor his pedals. Another prisoner drew an amusing silhouette, showing the doctor practising at his "organ" with such vehemence that the dishes on the table went flying into the air.

There were gypsy prisoners at the camp also, who had played their music in the cafés of Paris, and when they heard that Albert Schweitzer was also a musician they accepted him as one of themselves and welcomed him to their loft concerts. Mrs. Schweitzer was awakened on her birthday by a serenade the gypsies played outside her door, the waltz from Tales of Hoffmann.

Thus passed the winter at Garaison. In the spring they were transferred to St. Rémy de Provence. This institution had belonged to the Catholic Church, and had been set aside as an asylum for the insane. Here it was that Van Gogh had been for a time imprisoned. Schweitzer became once again a doctor, not simply for the camp but for people living at some distance from it. On Sunday there were Catholic and Protestant services. Schweitzer played the harmonium for the Catholic service, and because everyone liked to hear Schweitzer play the whole camp became Catholic. Then came the Protestant service, when again Schweitzer played the harmonium, and alternated with Pastor G. A. Liebrich, another Protestant clergyman, in preaching the sermon. His writing continued. Even in these internment camps Schweitzer found it possible to carry on all his activities: he was still a preacher, a musician, a philosopher, a physician.

At the end of July 1918 he was back again in Gunsbach; an exchange of prisoners had made this possible. Gunsbach was close to the front. The roads were camouflaged; the people carried gas masks. But his father was there to greet him, and it was home. In November the war ended.

Then followed six years of uncertainty. At the beginning of that period his health was bad. Two operations were necessary, the result of the dysentery from which he had suffered after his return from Africa. He did not know whether he should ever be able to return to Africa; and he knew that his neglected hospital at Lambarene was reverting to the jungle. The immediate problem of his living was solved by the offer of a post as physician at the city hospital in Strassburg. He returned also to his old pulpit at St. Nicholas.

His leisure was spent on Bach's choral preludes, but the American publisher seemed to have lost interest in the work; so this chore was put aside for continuing work on the Philosophy of Civilization. There were at this time changes in his family. Towards the end of the war his mother had been killed in a tragic accident at Gunsbach. On January 14, 1919, his own birthday, a daughter Rhena was born to him. "One generation passeth away, and another generation cometh."

His confidence in his musical skill was restored when once again, in October 1919, he played for his friends at the Orféo Català in Barcelona. He knew then that his work on his pedal piano at Lambarene, his wooden table at Garaison, his harmonium at St. Rémy, had been worth while. He had not returned to Europe an amateur. His Christmas that year was gladdened by an unexpected invitation from Archbishop Söderblom of Sweden to deliver the next spring a series of lectures at the University of Upsala. He accepted; and then the kindly archbishop suggested a series of other lectures and recitals in Sweden; these enabled him to pay off the greater part of the hospital debts. He returned to Alsace with health restored and mind at peace. Now again he knew it would be possible to return to Africa.

But not at once. At home once more, he set at work to write an account of his African experiences, in a book that an Upsala publishing house had commissioned him to write. On the Edge of the Primeval Forest was published in 1921. That spring he was back again playing Bach's St. Matthew Passion at the Orféo Català, the first time it had ever been given in Spain. When he returned, he resigned from St. Nicholas in Strassburg, and from his post at the city hospital. He knew now that he could support himself as a writer and organist. He retired with his wife and daughter to Gunsbach, where he could continue to work in quiet on his Philosophy of Civilization.

In the summer of 1921 Professor Archibald T. Davison was again

in Europe with the Harvard Glee Club. As already recounted, he
had been associated with Widor and Schweitzer earlier in Paris.
Now he met Schweitzer again in Strassburg; and many years afterwards wrote an entrancing account of Schweitzer the organist in
his middle forties.

"On July fifteenth," he wrote, "Schweitzer took us to St. Thomas
Church for organ music and singing. The church was dark except
for the necessary lights around the organ, and a single candle in the
church itself, so placed as to make my motions visible to the Glee
Club, which sang unaccompanied church pieces in the intervals
between the organ numbers. Finally Schweitzer invited me to the
organ loft to inspect and to try the organ.

"There it was, very much as it was in Bach's day, devoid of all
the labor-saving devices of the modern instrument, cumbersome, and,
from the point of view of one who had been used to the mechanically
effortless instruments of America, calculated to set up for the player
almost every conceivable impediment to easy and comfortable manipulation. That was my first experience with the type of organ which
had served Bach; and like many another, I found myself soberly
pondering the manner in which the average 'concert' organist deals
with Bach's music. When Schweitzer sat down to play the G minor
Fantasia and Fugue as a crown to a memorable evening, one was
literally transported back into another St. Thomas's, and there came
vividly to mind all of Widor's admonitions concerning speed, clarity,
legato, rhythm, and dissonance in the performance of eighteenth
century organ music; admonitions born not of what one might think
Bach would have liked had he had at his disposal the instrument of
to-day, but born, rather, of a knowledge of the organ for which Bach
actually composed, and, of equal importance, the organ on which
he played. . . .

"Before Schweitzer began to play, he made sure that all was in
readiness for the performance. Two assistants were to draw the stops;
one at his right hand, the other directly behind him, posted at that
section of the organ located in the rear. Even such stops as Schweitzer
could himself reach, were in the care of a helper, as, with proper and
characteristic conscientiousness he would not allow himself for any
reason to interrupt the contrapuntal lines. The omission of a brief

phrase, even of a single note, was unthinkable. The music began. The 'machinery' of the old organ was plainly audible, but it was clear that Schweitzer was not aware of it. Lost in the music, only the eloquence of Bach concerned him; and soon, for his hearers who were standing about the organ, all the mechanical intrusions disappeared in the superb playing of transcendent music. Only once, indeed, after the beginning, did any physical element make itself felt. That was at a climactic point when a considerable dynamic addition became necessary. As the music swelled up towards its peak, the assistants looked hurriedly at the music and placed their hands near the group of stops to be drawn. Suddenly the player threw back his head and shouted 'jetzt!' whereupon, with a sudden and well-synchronized stroke, the assistants pulled forth the required handful of stops with a terrific clatter. Amazingly, these diversions, not to be imagined in the 'organ recital,' were but dimly realized by the listener; so overpowering was the effect of the music and its registration. That was the miracle. One forgot everything for the moment, the awkward manipulation of the stops, the noise of the shrunken mechanism, even the player himself. Only Bach was there. It was the complete relegation of all agencies of performance to a position of total unimportance, with a corresponding glorification of the music itself. Modern virtuosity of every type has too often created a barrier between the composer and the listener. Too often, indeed, is the music no more than a vehicle for the self-expression of the interpreter. Of all that there was nothing on that evening in Strassburg. For once there was the realization of that so-oft-dreamed ideal, the artist at one with the composer." [1]

Doctor Schweitzer adds a little sequel to this lovely evening at St. Thomas. The Glee Club was staying at the Hotel Terminus near the station. It was a hot evening in July, and they walked back from the church together. Doctor Schweitzer said good-night. The others went to their rooms and he started back to his house. Then Doctor Schweitzer realized how warm and tired he was, and decided he would return to the sidewalk café for a refreshing drink. As he sat down at a table he heard familiar voices behind him. There were

[1] The Albert Schweitzer Jubilee Book. Edited by A. A. Roback. Cambridge, Massachusetts: Sci-Art Publishers, 1945.

all the students, with Professor Davison, sitting at the tables having beer. "Well," said Doctor Schweitzer, "it seems that we all had the same idea." Then they passed a delightful hour of relaxation together.

There were many journeys for lectures and concerts during the next two and a half years. In the autumn of 1921 he was in Switzerland. In November he was back again in Sweden. He had made many friends there, and had come to love the country. The Swedish organs pleased him; they were not large, but some of them had very beautiful tone. The next year, 1922, he was lecturing and playing in England; in Sweden and Switzerland again; and in Denmark. In 1923 he went to Czechoslovakia on the invitation of Professor Oscar Kraus of the University of Prague.

So the months passed swiftly away, with music, study, writing, speaking. In the spring of 1923 the years of work on his Philosophy of Civilization came to fruit, and the first two volumes were published. This same year too his book on Christianity and the World Religions was published; and soon after his Memoirs of Childhood and Youth, the vivid memories of his early days in Alsace.

He was now ready to return to Africa. The evening before he was to leave he dedicated a new organ at Mühlbach, an organ which had been planned by him and built by the organ builder Härpfer, a small but remarkably beautiful instrument. Refreshments were served in the parsonage, and a delegation from the historic Münstertalvereins surprised him with an artistic diploma that made him an honorary member. The bells of the new church were rung, and the church was crowded with people from far and near. After a little Schweitzer spoke to the loved people of his severely tried valley. Said he:

"I first played in this church as a nine-year-old boy. My Grandfather Schillinger had built a fine organ under the direction of the organ builder Stier. How happy I was before my first journey to Africa to restore it! Then in the primeval forest I read in a Swiss paper that not merely the organ but the church and the pastor's house, indeed the whole village, had been destroyed in a barrage. It seemed as if my heart would break. The next day I met a Negro king, who lived across the river from me in Lambarene, and he said to me: 'Oganga, why are you so sad?' I said, 'In my homeland they have destroyed things that are beautiful and dear to me. There was an organ among them.' And the king asked, 'What is that, an organ?' I had difficulty in explaining to him what an organ was. (You know I also have frequent trouble in explaining this to Europeans.) Then I asked him, 'King, will you give me the beautiful mahogany tree that stands there on the bank of the river, spreading out in such majesty?' 'Yes,' said he, 'I will give this to you for the organ in your homeland.' How I thanked him, when I thought of you, dear homeless people! I had men come to fell the tree and saw it up into boards by hand—there is no other way of doing this in Lambarene; and had the boards placed under a roof, and planned to sell them for you when they were dry. But soon after that I was made a prisoner. When I came back a few years afterwards the great pile of beautiful boards had rotted, the roof I had put over them along with the rest. Then again I grieved for your organ. But when I was in London after my return, a leading churchman there permitted me to give a concert for you in his church. Then I laid the foundation for your instrument. Now it is finished. It has a lovely tone, and you should learn from it of that world where there is no more war, a world which is stronger than all wars. Gott mit Euch!"

Then Schweitzer played on the organ, an hour of lovely music: Bach's overtures and preludes, Mendelssohn's choral sonatas, Widor's Christmas Music, and Luther's Ein feste Burg. It was as if a great cathedral organ were unfolding its fullness and splendor. Here was the model for all village organs—seventeen registers, rich enough to play all worthwhile compositions.

Late that evening he drove in a car to Colmar, and his friends of Mühlbach bade him a last farewell. The next day he left Strassburg, and a few days later he was at sea, bound for Africa.

VIII

The Revolution in Organ Building

*I*T was at dawn on the day before Easter that Doctor Schweitzer
arrived once more at Lambarene, after an absence of almost seven
years. The hospital buildings were in a sorry state of neglect. It was
symbolic, perhaps, that he had arrived at the Christian season of
resurrection, for the hospital had died and the time was come for its
resurrection. For more than a year he labored to reconstruct it.
Everything was sacrificed to it except his music. At evening time his
tired body found relaxation and his weary mind found refreshment
at his piano. Even in the heart of the jungle his reputation as a
musician spread, though sometimes a bit distorted. A certain timber
merchant, passing by the hospital, said to him, "Doctor, I am told
that you play the harmonium beautifully. I wish I did not have to
hurry to get home before the tornado strikes, for I like music too,
and I should like to have you play one of Goethe's fugues for me."

Hardly had the hospital been rebuilt, when famine and dysentery
struck simultaneously, and it was immediately evident that the hospital would have to be enlarged. That meant moving the whole
institution, for there was no room for expansion at Andende, shut
in as it was by the river in front, the hill at the back, and the swamps
on either side. A new site was found a little way upstream, and immediately began the laborious work of clearing the virgin growth of
the forest, bringing land into cultivation, and erecting a whole set
of new buildings. Again Doctor Schweitzer found himself a lumber-
man, a mason, and a carpenter, as well as a physician; but by the
summer of 1927 the "doctor's village" at Adolinanongo had been
established, and the doctor felt free to return again to Europe, though
a year and a half later than he had planned.

His return, in July 1927, was preceded by two more articles on organ construction. It was now twenty-one years since he had written The Art of Organ Building and Organ Playing in Germany and France. It was time to pause and take stock, to see what had happened in these two decades since he had challenged the organists and organ builders of that day to halt and see where they were going, and to return to the lovely organs of the years between 1860 and 1880. So he wrote an epilogue to the 1906 book, in which, while modifying two or three of his earlier recommendations, he nonetheless reëmphasized his central conviction and rejoiced in the victories already won. In addition to the epilogue, an article upon reform in organ building appeared in the Monatschrift für Gottesdienst und kirchliche Kunst. The revolution in organ building, for which he had labored so hard, had begun.

❧

THE 1927 EPILOGUE [1]

A LITTLE more than twenty years ago the cry was raised in this book: Back from the modern factory organ, produced by the devil of invention, to the true organ with its beautiful tone! Strangely enough, until then there had been no one to ask organists and organ builders where organ building and organ playing were really going. It was accepted as self-evident that the booming factory organ was the instrument of the future, and that as soon as possible all earlier organs would fall to the axe and the furnace.

That I myself was not deluded by the modern factory organ, I owe to the circumstance that I grew up among beautifully toned organs. As a boy I played on the Walcker organ, which had been built in the best days of this concern, in the sixties and seventies of the past century. One of these, with sixty-two stops, stood in the evangelical church of St. Stephen at Mulhouse in Alsace. Towards the end of the century it was so renovated and modernized by the house that had installed it that nothing was left of the old, lovely tone. The

---

[1] From *Deutsche und Französische Orgelbaukunst und Orgelkunst*, by Albert Schweitzer, Leipzig: Breitkopf & Härtel, 1927, pp. 49–70.

other, with about forty stops, in the evangelical church at Munster in Alsace, I was able to save from that fate. But it later fell a victim to the war. As an eighteen-year-old lad I came to know the Paris organs of Cavaillé–Coll, with their wonderful foundation stops and mixtures. As a student in Strassburg I was intoxicated with the sound of the Silbermann organs in St. William and St. Thomas, and with their delightful sister in the Evangelical state church in Colmar. The St. William organ had to give way towards the end of the century to a modern factory organ; both the others were saved.

For long years I ventured to bring my heretical belief in the beauty of the old organs and the inferiority of the modern factory organs, with their consoles studded with push buttons, to the ears of friendly organists. What I heard from them on the subject did not encourage me to carry my old-fashioned ideas any farther. When, however, the praise of the factory organs that had taken the place of the older, more beautiful ones became ever more exuberant in the newspapers as they were dedicated, I overcame all my scruples, and in 1906 came out publicly with my heresies. I owe it to the intelligent reception of the editorial staff of *Musik* that I found a publication that would print such foolishness. The friendship of the house of Breitkopf & Härtel made it possible for my treatise to live on as an independent book.

At first the only result was that many organists gave up their former friendly associations with me. There was no lack of sarcastic letters. A well-known Berlin organ *virtuoso* said that I was ready for the insane asylum.

The slaughter of the old organs went on. With great difficulty I was able to save the organ at St. Thomas in Strassburg; its death sentence had been already drawn up in the form of a cost estimate from a powerful organ factory. That the necessary number of votes in the chapter of St. Thomas was found to preserve it was due to two intelligent pastors and to the teacher of constitutional law, Laband, who as legal counsellor had in this corporation a place and a voice.

This first victory came in 1909. Guido Adler, who was responsible for the preparation of the third congress of the International Music Society, which had been invited to Vienna, got in touch with me,

and requested that I should give an address at the congress about
organ construction. In preparing for this address I sent a questionnaire in German or French about the problem of organ construction
to organ builders and organists in all European countries; principally,
however, to the German, Austrian, Swedish, and French, because
with these I had the closest relations. The answers that came in were
to provide the material for the work of the organ section of the
Vienna Congress. This effort revealed how little sympathy there was
for raising the question of organ construction at all. Instead of answering to the point, many of those addressed came out with threats
against those who would encroach upon the freedom of the organ
builder, and, as one man wrote, "would like to make all organs on
one last." Worst of all were the answers of many organ builders and
many organ inspectors. There were organ builders who did not understand what it would mean to them to have minimum prices set
which would permit them to do artistic work. They saw only that a
movement was on foot that would make it impossible for them to
drive their rivals from the field by underbidding or by means of the
newest inventions. Very many of them had at that time not the
slightest comprehension of the whole matter.

Many official organ inspectors were unsympathetic to the enterprise, because many unofficial persons were presuming to meddle
in these organ matters, and wished to leave the responsibility for
ordering and examining organs in a particular region not to the
discretion of a single expert, always one and the same, but to the
consensus of opinion of several experts.

Along with the uncoöperative and suspicious answers there arrived,
however, an imposing number of others that went to the heart of the
matter, and expressed the opinion that a discussion of organ building was to be desired.

This congress of the International Music Society in Vienna, from
May 25 to 29, 1909, elaborated the *International Regulations for
Organ Building*.

In the very first hours of the assembly the members of the section
on organ building found themselves of the opinion that something
should be undertaken to restore the organ builders to the position
where they could build in accordance with artistic principles, without

destroying themselves in the effort. To us it seemed most urgent to work to this end. Therefore we formed a plan for drawing up regulations for organ building to which every organ builder could refer when confronted by purchasers and experts, in order not to be underbidden or eliminated by competitors peddling the most modern inventions.

The material for such regulations lay in my lecture about the state of organ building at that time, printed in the annals of the congress, and in my report on the answers received from the questionnaire.

In four days these regulations for organ building were drawn up and issued! We renounced the congress festivities; our section sat, so to speak, permanently; we took hardly time to eat or sleep.

Dr. Xavier Matthias, the representative of church music on the Catholic theological faculty at Strassburg, and I presided alternately over the sessions. The Austrian organ builders Rieger and Ullmann, the organ builder Härpfer from Boulay in Alsace, the Viennese organ inspector Walter Ehrenhofer, and the Viennese engineer Friedrich Drechsler, were specially helpful with their technical knowledge. The last two named deserve great credit in the fulfilment of our task.

The *Regulations*, about fifty pages long, were issued, at the expense of the International Society of Music, in German and French; and were sent without charge to the experts in organ construction, the organ builders and the organists, to whom the questionnaire had previously gone. An Italian edition was later added, which the organist Carmelo Songiorgio (Mazara de Valle, Sicily) took charge of.

Thus for the first time were set forth the conclusions emerging from a thorough discussion of the ideal to be sought in organ building. The *Regulations* offered standards for keyboards and pedals, and specified in what way the pedals should lie under the manuals, and what distance was to be kept between the manuals. Size, form, free play, depth, strength of resistance, elasticity of the keys for the best playing—all these were determined.

It was set forth as a necessity that every organ, no matter what the number of its stops, had to be complete in external arrangements, that is, it must have at least two keyboards, stretching from G to g ^{3}, pedals stretching from C to f ^{1}, and a swell box.

The complicated console, with its many blind and fixed installations, was stripped of its repute, and the utmost simplicity was suggested as the solution. Instead of many different kinds of registration helps, it should have that one in particular which the artistic logic of organ playing demands, but which is not found in the consoles of the factory organs because it is more difficult to build and more expensive than many of the impractical inventions. This significant and valuable registration help is the one that makes it possible, on each separate manual and on the pedal, to add as desired to the stops drawn other stops prepared in advance, or to substitute these stops for the stops drawn and then retire them again. In addition, a *sforzando* and a register *crescendo*, which by means of a balance lever bring all the stops of the organ into play or silence them, and in such a way that the successively introduced stops, at the discretion of the musician, permit the drawn registration to remain or to be retired.

A three-manual organ with hardly more than a half-dozen registration helps, in place of the fantastic console of the modern factory organ provided with some dozens of them! A two-manual organ with fewer than a half-dozen!

And on every organ about the same registration helps and the same arrangement of the console. On the left side, the couplers of the pedals to the manuals and those that couple the manuals together; on the right side, registration helps arranged as stops and pistons for the hands as well as pedals for the feet, with the pistons and pedals working together or independently of one another.

In respect to the stops, the *Regulations* expressed the opinion unheard of at that time, that it was not a matter of their number but of their quality. What a feat the reëstablishment of this self-evident truth was, the present generation can no longer appreciate. How often did I have the experience of seeing in those days construction estimates offering many cheap little stops gain a victory over those that dared to offer excellent stops in smaller number! And whenever the organ expert had the exceptional wisdom to recommend the more excellent proposal, the congregation opposed it and ordered the organ with the greater number of stops! The organ builders, if they wished to receive any orders, had to submit to this stupid tyranny! The opposition to this madness took final form in these regulations for organ construction.

By what means, however, were the artistic fullness and beauty of tone produced in the pipes? On this there was excited discussion in the section on organ construction. Everyone agreed that the increased wind pressure was to a large extent responsible for the unpleasant sound of the modern factory organ. But long deliberations were necessary before we dared to draw up in the *Regulations* the statement that the foundation stops and the mixtures should be fed with wind of only 70 to 85 mm. [2.76 to 3.35 inches] pressure. It was readily agreed that generous dimensions and thick walls in the pipes had great influence on the beauty and fullness of the tone. But to many it seemed too bold to state that the modern technically perfect wind chest was equally responsible for the unpleasant sound of the factory organ. The defenders of the old chest did not at that time know how to prove this from a physical point of view. On the other hand, it had to be admitted that when, in rebuilding, old pipes were set on new chests they fell far short of giving forth the same full, round tones as before. On this subject we extremists in the section on organ building were able to get approval for a sentence in the *Regulations*, very carefully framed, which laid down the advantages in tone production of the slider wind chest. After we had accomplished this we breathed easily again.

It was also difficult to push through the opinion that mechanical action from the keys to the wind chest was artistically the most perfect; and that in smaller and middle-sized instruments, where there were no technical objections, it had an unquestionable advantage.

So in the 1909 *Regulations for Organ Building* we favoured the old, simple, tone-beautiful organ. The timid ones were carried along by the courageous.

By its thoroughly unbiassed declarations the *Regulations for Organ Building* made an impression even on those who at first were not receptive to this idea of "Back to the old organ." In the following years there began to appear a critical attitude towards the modern factory organ, even though the murder of old organs went on almost without slackening. People began to concern themselves scientifically and experimentally with the problem of the wind chests and the dimensions and tones of the pipes. All this led one to anticipate that the problem of getting the true organ might be nearer solution at coming congresses of the International Music Society, where greater participation and more valuable material might be expected.

The World War put an end to such congresses for the time being. But the idea went on its way even without congresses, and even in the midst of the anguish of the time. On concert trips, which after the war took me into almost every country in Europe, I was able to see that the idea was making headway. Everywhere organists gave their support to it. The science of organ building was once again honored. Where the old organs still remained they were genuinely valued. News was bruited about of astounding conversions: organ manufacturers and organ virtuosi began to idolize what they had formerly burned.

But recently the depreciated currency of Middle Europe almost proved disastrous to the old organs of the north. I passed through this crisis in Sweden and Denmark. Because the factory organs of Middle Europe could be had very cheaply in these lands with hard valuta, and because up there they still had their former attraction, people began to do away with the old organs in order to provide themselves at the favorable moment with modern wares. I was able to coöperate with Bangert, the cathedral cantor from Roskilde (Denmark), and with other northern experts, in the saving of a few specially threatened old masterpieces.

Today the fight is won. Scientific experts in organ building and old organs, like Ernst Schiess of Solothurn and Hans Henny Jahnn of Hamburg, are actively rebuilding old organs. In the Institute of Musical Knowledge at the University of Freiburg in Baden, Professor Willibald Gurlitt and his pupils are engaged in research into old music and old organs. Societies have arisen for the preservation of old organs.

We had not dared to hope that a young generation would carry on so soon and so strongly what we had undertaken in Vienna against the spirit of the time. With deep emotion I think of those who shared with us the work of those wonderful days but were not permitted to see the triumph of the idea.

At the wish of the publishers, the book about *The Art of Organ Building and Organ Playing in Germany and France* was republished in its 1906 form, as a kind of document from the beginning of the fight for the true organ. Only a mistake on page 20 concerning the Mecklin organ in the *Oratoire* at Paris was corrected.

To the ideal that I set forth in that book I am still loyal today; only in details have I departed from my views of that time, or gone beyond them. For instance, I have become convinced that the divided wind chest with different pressures, advocated by the successors of Cavaillé–Coll, does not in reality fulfil what it promised in theory. The organs provided with it have a less rounded tone than the old organs of Cavaillé–Coll with their simple slider wind chests; hence I consider the slider wind chest to be the one that produces the more beautiful tone. Here I leave the question open; whether for acoustical reasons we must go back to the slider wind chest, or whether in the end the inventive spirit of our organ builders, working on the relevant problems, will succeed in building modern wind chests that will equal in acoustical merit the slider wind chest.

I have become ever more certain that the mechanical tracker is from an artistic point of view the ideal action between keys and wind chest, as more organs with pnuematic and electric action have come under my hands in different lands since that time. I plead, then, that all the smaller and middle-sized organs should be furnished with good mechanical trackers. In the larger instruments, where pneumatic or electric action seems to be technically required, a mechanical tracker, however short, should be added to the pneumatic or electric action, in order that the keys may retain the ideal elasticity indispensable for good blending and good phrasing.

In one important respect I go beyond the 1906 book and the *Regulations* for organ building. More and more there is borne in upon me the artistic significance of the *rückpositiv*. That a group of stops is not contained in the main case, but sings out freely in the church, has an influence on the total sound of the organ. The complete instrument consists of three personalities: the main organ, with its round, full tones; the rückpositiv, with its bright, free tones; and the swell organ, with its intense and sustained tones. The character of the perfect organ depends upon this trinity. The old instrument had only two tone individualities: the main organ and the rückpositiv. The third organ, housed in the main case, was so undeveloped and so set up that it played no individual rôle in the total harmony. The modern instrument, which has no rückpositiv organ, has again therefore only two tone qualities: the main organ and the swell. The second organ (the rückpositiv), spoiled by being placed within the main case, has no tone individuality of its own, but is only an addition to the first. It is not the number of manuals that determines the quality of the organ, but the number of tone individualities. Since Cavaillé–Coll took the rückpositiv away from the five-manual instruments at St. Sulpice, Widor plays—as I am accustomed to charge him—on a two-manual organ with five keyboards. In spite of its hundred stops, the St. Sulpice instrument has only two tone individualities: the main organ divided among four keyboards and the swell organ. The organ at Notre Dame is the same. We must once more build instruments with rückpositivs.

That will be hard, of course. The arrangement of a rückpositiv involves a heavy additional expense. But it is better to have fewer stops and a rückpositiv than more stops and only two tone individualities. Without a rückpositiv there is no ideal, complete instrument. A second organ of eight stops, arranged as a rückpositiv, is superior to one of fifteen stops that stands in the main case.

Artistically it is not sensible to build organs with more than two manuals, unless it be for very large rooms which demand an exceedingly great number of stops. In this case one may separate the main organ into two manuals. One gets along well, however, with three manuals up to eighty stops.

On the other hand, three manuals should be provided wherever possible for even thirty stops, in order that the instrument may have a rückpositiv. No one should be influenced by the consideration that the instrument could have, with the money spent for the rückpositiv, many more stops. The instrument with the rückpositiv is always better, regardless of the number of stops.

The bigger the room, the more necessary is the rückpositiv. In small churches an organ with two tone qualities is pleasing, because here the instrument is not far away and is not placed high, and the great organ itself sounds out directly in the church. The farther and the higher the instrument is moved away, the more necessary it is that a group of stops should be moved out below.

An objection to the *rückpositiv* besides its cost is usually advanced; namely, that the accurate pitch of the instrument becomes impossible, especially in heated churches, since the *rückpositiv* stands in cooler air than the parts higher up. I have never found such a disadvantage really noticeable, except for a few Sundays and in relatively small, overheated churches. The larger the room, of course, the more equable the temperature in the region of the organ loft.

To equip an instrument with two swell organs is not reasonable. The large quantity of wood in the organ casing injures the production of the tone.

Echo organs continue to be sentimental toys which have nothing to do with the true organ.

In many places the solution "Back to the old, tone-beautiful organ" has been misunderstood to mean that the organ of the eighteenth century should be exalted as an ideal. This is not the case. By "old" organs is meant those organs made before the era of the modern factory organ, at a time when the masters of organ building were still free to work as artists; that is, the organs of the seventeenth century and those of the eighteenth century into the seventh decade.

Certainly we must preserve the still existing old organs of the seventeenth and eighteenth centuries as historic treasures; and as far as possible restore them reverently even with their failures and weaknesses, in accordance with their nature. Certainly we must learn to know the organs of that time much better than we know them now. What precious things, still unrecognized, may be the old organs of Spain, and particularly of Catalonia! We will once more take over many of the manifold pipes of the earlier organs, as we are beginning again to honor the slider wind chest for its acoustical qualities.

Our ideal for the organ has also been shaped by the achievements of the great masters of organ building in the first seven decades of the nineteenth century. Moreover, we must make allowances for the demands which the leading organ composers—César Franck, Widor, Reger, and the others—make of the organ in their writings.

All these were responsible for the enrichment of the organ in the nineteenth century through the development of the swell. Out of the meagre echo organ with its small Venetian blind swell came the well-furnished, intensively working modern swell organ, which enriches the sound of the instrument with a new tone personality, and at the same time endows it with a hitherto unsuspected flexibility.

In the arrangement of the instrument a swell must be provided that is suited to it. It should have the most stops of all the manuals. In a two-manual instrument of fifteen stops I would allot five to the first organ, seven to the second, and three to the pedal. With a two-manual organ of twenty, twenty-five, or thirty stops, I would dispose them about like this: 7, 9, 4; 8, 12, 5; 10, 14, 6.

In a three-manual instrument with a *rückpositiv*, of thirty stops about nine would be placed in the great organ, five in the *rückpositiv*, eleven in the swell, and five in the pedal. With forty stops the arrangement would be: 12, 7, 14, 7; with fifty stops: 15, 8, 18, 9; with sixty stops: 20, 11, 25, 14.

The *rückpositiv* can remain rudimentary, for its stops are most expressive. If it is set opposite the great organ as a second organ, it is in a position to be coupled with the swell chest. In the older organs, where its keyboard lay under that of the great organ, and with the coupling technique of the time could not be connected directly with the third organ, this did not work. Therefore the *rückpositiv* had to be at that time as complete as possible; today it can remain incomplete.

The difficulty of getting enough stops within the case of the *rückpositiv*, and the impossibility of connecting the *rückpositiv* directly with the third organ by the couplers of that day, led builders to neglect the acoustical and artistic significance of the *rückpositiv*, and to spoil it by placing it as a second organ within the casing of the great organ.

If the second organ in the three-manual instrument is not constructed as a *rückpositiv*, but is placed within the great organ case, it can remain, in spite of this, incomplete. It is then of course not an independent sound personality, but only an addition to the great organ.

Under all circumstances, we must hold fast to the principle that the swell must be the most complete. If the number of stops in the organ permit only one mixture and one reed, these should then be placed in the swell.

It is important in the disposition to take into consideration the registration plans of the leading organ composers. César Franck, Widor, and the other Romantic masters, assume that the swell organ is supplied with an intense gamba stop; a *voix celeste*, no less intense and of not too narrow scale; an oboe 8'; and a trumpet *(clarion) 4'*. They expect to find a clarinet 8' in the *rückpositiv*. If through some whim of the builder these stops are not found in their places on an organ, then in order to render the works of these masters and all the composers influenced by them the entire registration must be upset.

Moreover, the arrangement must take into consideration the demands made on the organ for the accompaniment of Bach cantatas and Passions. Besides a soft, open flute the swell should contain a soft and not too narrow salicional and a pleasant principal-flute. If these three stops in this quality are not available, the proper accompaniment of the recitatives and arias is not achievable.

If a *rückpositiv* is constructed, it has the immediate advantage that the solos in Bach's works may be accompanied by stops which are near the singers and the instruments. This is in the tradition of Bach's time. In this case the bright, mild *musikgedackt*, which played the principal rôle in accompaniments of that age, should not be forgotten. An 8' gemshorn should be provided for accompaniments on the *rückpositiv*. Wherever possible a mild bourdon 16' should also be provided for it. If there is a bourdon 16' in the second organ, one can use this with the left hand for the playing of the bass in the recitatives and the arias, while the right hand plays the chords in the swell organ.

Under all circumstances a beautiful, broad salicional 8' must be had along with a bourdon 8' and a flauto major 8' in the great organ. It makes no sense to forsake these old traditions. Salicional 8' cannot be replaced here by any other stop. A gamba 8' also belongs traditionally to the first organ. One should not be afraid of having the gamba 8′ and the salicional 8′ in different dimensions in the great organ and the swell organ at the same time.

The English custom of giving two or three different principals to the great organ on the larger instruments has much to say for itself.

In the swell organ of Swedish instruments built between 1850 and 1890 there is usually a waldflute 2′. This broad-dimensioned open flute is much more expressive than all other 2′ stops in the swell, and is of supreme importance.

The question of the reeds is still unsolved. The most beautiful reed stops are found on the organs of the great German organ builders of the sixties and seventies of the past century, and on English organs of that same time. They speak with a wind pressure of 80 mm. [3.15 inches]. Their tone blends most beautifully with the foundation stops and mixtures, and with them builds up to a splendid *fortissimo*. When will these reeds, which have the advantages without the imperfections of those of the eighteenth century, be built again?

They fell into disuse because they did not speak so promptly as those of Cavaillé–Coll, and had less brilliancy, and because reeds with high wind pressures did not cause the same trouble in voicing as the others. If the choice lies between a prompt entrance and tone, one should always choose tone. The time is gone when uneducated experts in organ construction could terrorize the organ builders by finding fault with every slow onset of tone as a failure. A beautifully toned reed stop will never speak promptly. A beautiful salicional and a gamba also need some time before they speak. But this makes no difference in playing. In the full organ the delayed speaking of the reeds does not disturb; hardly, even, with the lazy reeds of the eighteenth century. The speaking is improved to the degree that other stops sound at the same time. The reeds are carried along by the others. Not the most precise speaking, but the utmost beauty, is to be sought; not only in the reeds, but in all other stops.

The intensive reeds of the French organ, speaking under high wind pressure, do not blend with the other stops, but kill them. Moreover, they make impossible the *legato*. In the full French organ the tone line emerges hacked into pieces. Cavaillé–Coll's reeds cannot be used, therefore, for a Bach *fortissimo*. Hence there arose among French organists the extraordinary opinion that Bach himself, in his preludes and fugues, had disregarded the reeds. In the Paris Conservatory this was accepted in his day as dogma.

One of the chief tasks for modern organ construction, therefore, is to build again the beautiful reeds of the time of 1860.

There is no reason to take exception to the single reed stop with high wind pressure which is found in English organs as a solo tuba beside the usual reed stops, or to several of them. The mistake is only in furnishing an organ exclusively with intense reed stops.

Concerning the problem of the console, I stand on the ground of the *Regulations* for organ construction. Cavaillé–Coll, with his ventil for mixtures and reeds, offered as registration aids the device by which mixtures and reeds chosen in advance could be brought in or retired on every manual and on the pedal. In this way he in principle blazed the right trail. But he limited the introduction of the previously prepared stops to the two ranks of pipes named.

Yet, even when extended to all stops, the device for introducing the chosen stops gets its full value only when it is so laid out that the previously drawn stops may be retained or retired at will. To add new stops to those already drawn and to retire them again, to bring in new stops in place of those already drawn, and when the latter are introduced again, to retire them: this, as you know, is the twofold action—which is what all registration amounts to. The ideal is to accomplish both with a single device. Then a pedal or a draw-stop (piston), at a selected time in advance, has to secure or release the drawn stops at the moment when the prepared stops are introduced. This may be accomplished technically without difficulty.

When in 1909 the doubly available introduction of stops chosen in advance was demanded by the *Regulations for Organ Construction*, it was already realised on several Alsatian organs, as well as the similar doubly available stop crescendo.

Many organists and organ builders find it at first difficult to believe that with this simplified console the introduction of the stops already chosen for each separate manual should be more advantageous than the usual blind combination by which a piston or a pedal changes the registration for the whole instrument. They think they can accomplish more with half a dozen such general blind combinations than with the arrangement suggested by the *Regulations* for organ construction. But the advantage of a series of such general blind combinations, working on the whole organ, and each time retiring the entire drawn registration, is only apparent. These combinations would be useful if their registration remained, continuing to alter the whole registration and to carry over from one tone color into the other. But usually the logic of the composition requires that stops should be added to those already drawn, now on this manual and now on that, or should replace them, only to be withdrawn at a later moment and leave the former alone speaking. It is also more to the purpose that the console should make possible the introduction of selected stops on each separate manual. For three-manual instruments the *Regulations* for organ construction provide in addition another pedal or piston, which adds or takes away together all the prepared stops of the organ.

In time the normal console will win the day because of its simple utility. The important thing is that in the future every console should be equipped with the doubly available introduction of prepared stops for the separate manuals. Over and above that, the organ makers may offer us whatever they wish in the way of registration helps from the console of the old factory organ, in order to modulate in economical fashion from the earlier complexity to the coming simplicity.

It should be accepted as self-evident today that the couplers and registration helps should be arranged both as draw stops and pistons for the hand and as pedals for the foot. It may remain a question whether there is any real need to tie the two together so that they operate every time as a unit and permit the musician to release with either the foot or the hand, at his pleasure, the stops brought into play by the foot, and to release with the hand or the foot, at his pleasure, the stops brought into play by the hand. Formerly I was for this tie, since it offered great advantages. My observation has taught me, however, that most musicians, in accordance with their custom, use exclusively either hand or foot for these playing aids. In the face of this fact the work and the significant costs involved in installing this connection of draw-stop (piston) and pedal do not any longer seem to me justified.

The principal thing is that the playing helps should no longer be arranged exclusively for the hand, but also for the foot. Before the coming of the factory organ console they were invariably built, even in Central Europe, as pedals. For the operation of the playing helps it is easier to free a foot than a hand.

It is a very practical thing on the English organ that the manual and pedal couplers should stand together on the left as draw-stops for the hand, next to the lowest keyboard and under the lowest row of stops. There they are actually more easily and more securely reached than farther to the right under the left half of the front board of the lowest keyboard, to which the *Regulations* for organ construction assigned them. On the basis of this experience I should now be in favor of the English arrangement of the draw-stops or pistons for the couplers. On the place left free below the left half of the key strip of the lowest keyboard would then be found space for draw-stops or pistons for the introduction of the selected registers; they would be better situated there than at the left above the top keyboard.

We Central Europeans, too much occupied with registration helps, have neglected many things in the arrangement of our consoles which would make direct hand registration easier. Formerly the registration stops were on both sides of the keyboards and over the upper keyboard. With the left hand—which one can free incomparably more often than the right—the player could not only manipulate the stops placed at the left but also the stops above the top keyboard. Since the stops are no longer placed above the upper keyboard, the very valuable hand registration can stretch over only one-third of the stops instead of two-thirds. This is a great disadvantage.

On the old Walcker instrument at Mulhouse, where the draw-stops were still arranged in the earlier manner, I was able to manipulate all the stops of the great organ and of the second organ—and the couplers too, which lay at the left next to the lowest keyboard—with the left hand; and also even some of the stops for the third organ which lay at the right of the manuals, but so high that the left hand could reach them comfortably. Only the pedal registers, whose stops lay at the very bottom at the right of the manuals, could not be operated by hand registration.

Compelling reasons for abandoning this comfortable arrangement cannot be adduced. In England it has been retained. One should see what the English organists accomplish entirely by direct hand registration!

Therefore one should not forget the most important matter in relation to playing helps: the most comfortable arrangement possible of draw-stops for hand operation. Away with all considerations of symmetry. The supreme law in the arrangement of the stops must be that the largest possible number of them should be made accessible to the left hand in the most comfortable way possible. So let them be placed at the left next to the manuals and above the top keyboard. The space at the right next to the keyboards, which can be reached only with such difficulty, may be left entirely free, circumstances permitting, or may hold the pedal stops, if these cannot be arranged anywhere else—or even the name plate of the firm of organ builders, which usually claims the best place of all above the highest manual. As many as forty draw-stops can easily be arranged next the manuals at the left and above the top one.

I firmly believe that draw-stops are more comfortable than pistons or keys; the hand can seize them better. Moreover, it is a much more natural motion to pull or to push with the whole hand than to manipulate a key or a piston with one finger.

The idea for which I prepared the way twenty years ago has conquered. In my rejoicing over it there is mingled sadness. The victory came unexpectedly early, yet still too late. When we lived in prosperity and disposed of great wealth for the purposes of art, we built commonplace organs. Today, when the ideal of the organ has advanced, we are so impoverished that we can spend very little for organ construction. For a long time to come we may not think of replacing the common organ. Every Sunday the sins committed in the past shriek in our ears.

Who will bring back again the old, beautiful organs, which in our blindness we destroyed?

Who will again produce for us the masters of organ construction, who in that senseless period when the manufacturers were industrializing organ building were ruined by the dozens and had to give up their calling?

Lao-tse's word is fitting here, "He who conquers should demean himself as at a funeral."

Therefore we must carry on in little ways what then we could have accomplished in big ways. Only a future generation will richly benefit by the knowledge to which we have returned.

We work for the future. We pray that it may come to pass.

❧

REFORM IN ORGAN BUILDING [1]

IN a valuable treatise, "The Organ as an Artistic Memorial," in the *Monthly for Divine Worship and Ecclesiastical Art*," [2] Peter Epstein of Breslau pleads for the preservation of the old organs. In it he names me as one of the first to call attention to the significance of the older instruments. It is somewhat misleading that in his exposition he makes me demand a return to the organ of the eighteenth century for the proper rendering of Bach's organ works, inasmuch as others demand the harpsichord for the piano works of the master. To avoid misunderstandings I should like to set forth briefly the case against the modern organ.

Neither in my treatise on the art of organ building in Germany and France (1906), nor in my book about Bach (1906), nor in the deliberations on organ building at the Vienna Congress of the International Society of Music (1909), which led to the setting up of *The International Regulations for Organ Building* (Leipzig, Breitkopf & Härtel, 1909), nor in the American edition of Bach's organ works (Schirmer, New York, 1913), have I advocated such archaic ideas. Those who know the old organs are aware that, along with their tone excellence, they have defects that make a simple return to them impossible. It would never occur to us, I hope, to propose as ideal the primitive bellows, the too narrow wind chests, and the generally scant pedal organs of the eighteenth century!

The solution proposed in my 1906 book was: back from the booming factory organ to the organs of the master builders so rich and beautiful in tone.

[1] "Zur Reform des Orgelbaues," in *Monatschrift für Gottesdienst und kirchliche Kunst*, Vol. XXXII, No. 6 (June 1927), pp. 148–54.

[2] *Monatschrift für Gottesdienst und kirchliche Kunst*, No. 12, 1926.

The most perfect organs were built between 1860 and 1880 approximately. At that time the master organ builders created instruments which had in perfection the tonal excellence of Bach's age but without its technical defects.

Why was this skill in building abandoned later? Because the trend of the time was to factories and manufactured goods. The man who was producing organs of the fine old quality failed; he delivered too slowly and was too expensive. When he came with his cost estimate for thirty stops, the builder of the factory organ offered thirty-five stops or even more for the same price. On paper the second organ was superior to the first; that it was inferior to the other and would not equal it in tone production, in spite of the larger number of registers, could not be made clear to the customer. So the producer of the factory organs received the order.

Why could the latter deliver more stops than the organ builder for the same price? He economised in wood, by making the pipes as narrow as possible and giving them the thinnest possible walls. Moreover, he limited the variety of pipes. He standardised and tried to get along with the smallest possible number of pipe types, in order to simplify the manufacture of the organ. Instead of every register having its special pipes, of well-considered dimensions, the same kind of pipes had to serve for several registers. In this way handwork was displaced by factory work. These pipes, made to scale, too narrow and thin-walled, were much cheaper than the others, but could not produce the same tone.

Moreover, the tone of the factory organ was injured by increased wind pressure, in order to extort a tone from these unnatural pipes. Instead of the pipe speaking, the tone blustered through it. And thus, because artistic traditions were abandoned, came the organ with the roaring basses, the shrill treble, and the subdued middle tones—the overvoiced organ.

In order to manufacture as much and as cheaply as possible, the organ builders went on to make other inventions. They sought to substitute pneumatic or electric devices for the mechanical connection between the keys and the wind chest. This had a certain justification for the bigger organs, since their keys were too stiff with mechanical leverage. But with the usual two-manual church organ,

THE REVOLUTION IN ORGAN BUILDING

this was not a problem, since it could also be played without exertion by mechanical leverage. Yet for the sake of cheapness all church organs were equipped with pneumatic or electric actions. Again the unnatural displaced the natural: a good mechanical action is much more durable than a pneumatic or electric one. Above all else, however, it is much easier to play precisely, to blend properly, and to phrase well on a mechanical organ than on the other. But such professional and artistic qualities could not be considered, because the times called for the cheapest possible manufactured work.

The pneumatic action was fatal for the poor organs also because of the higher wind pressure necessary. Since it had now become too dear, especially in the smaller organs, to construct the bellows in such a way that it could produce wind of different pressures—strong to supply the pneumatic action, somewhat weaker for the pipes—the strong wind necessary for the pneumatic action was also forced through the pipes. In this way the already booming, shrill, and over-voiced organ became still more booming, shrill, and overvoiced.

The wind chest, which so greatly determines the quality of the tone, was also "improved." The slider wind chest used by the earlier organ builders was abandoned and others were built. But none of these modern wind chests is acoustically equal to the old. When in the reconstruction of an organ the old pipes are kept and set in a modern wind box, they no longer have the beautiful tone they had before; the tone becomes dry, loses its roundness, and no longer carries.

In just what the acoustical quality of the slider wind chest consists cannot yet be surely proved—as indeed so much else in the speaking of the pipes remains still acoustically unexplained. For the time being we must be satisfied with knowing that the pipes and wind boxes formerly built produced a more beautiful tone than the present ones. Next to the slider wind chest comes the cone chest (ventil wind chest).

The many registration devices in the console helped very much to carry the factory organ on to victory. Towards the end of the century there appeared an orchestral conception of the organ. It was believed that one could not do enough in varying the tone color. Hence organs were called for with many contrivances for changing the stops. Three-quarters of these registration devices were unnecessary and served no purpose. In order to obtain these modern consoles organists sacrificed their beautiful organs, and exchanged them for instruments with mediocre tones. They valued the cow for the horns rather than for the milk.

Towards the end of the century, twenty years after this unwholesome development in organ building had set in, matters had already progressed to such a point that the builders of the factory organs could no longer produce worthy organs even if they wanted to. They no longer had the facilities to build in the former manner; moreover, they no longer had the workmen who knew how to install the mechanical action and make pipes artistically. In general, their workers were so specialized that they were no longer accomplished craftsmen in the whole field of organ handcraft.

Therefore the process of replacing the beautiful old works with ugly and unstable factory organs continued. This instability was even exalted into a principle. Organists and organ builders persuaded each other that the organs installed would have to be rebuilt every twenty or twenty-five years: first, because they would no longer be functioning well, and second, in order that in the modernised form they might benefit by all the discoveries that had meanwhile appeared.

How did it happen that the organists paid so little attention to the tonal qualities of these organs? They had lost their sensitivity to tonal beauty and tonal richness. A great deal in the history of mankind is to be explained in the end only by the inexplicable—that a generation has lost its comprehension of something.

Today has come the desire to work our way out of this decline. Those who have so long been considered backward because they were prejudiced against the modern factory organ, now find listeners. The old, beautiful organs that remain are again valued; though, unfortunately, there are now left only poor remnants of the splendor that was still there a generation ago.

The program for the future is simple: that we should again build with artistic principles, starting once more with the fine traditions of the earlier organists.

A prerequisite for this is that when an order is given for an organ, our concern should be not just for the number of its stops, but for its quality. This basic principle must become axiomatic to congregations and church authorities. Until this happens organ building will not improve.

But when we shall have accomplished this, everything else will come of itself. No witchcraft is required to build a good organ. When we cease demanding of our organ builders more stops than excellent and artistic workmanship can furnish for the designated sum, and when we allow them the necessary time to build, they will again become genuine organ builders. An outstanding musician, a conservatory director, some years ago wanted an organ ordered for a concert hall at the end of July to be ready for the opening of the fall concerts!

In studying an estimate, one should see that it is not the largest number of stops cheapest in material and work that are advocated, but rather those necessary for the perfected quality of the organ. A good sixteen-foot violone in the pedal is much more expensive than two or three other stops, but it is essential. Twenty excellent stops are more expressive than thirty mediocre ones.

For the form, the dimensions, and the mouths of the pipes, we shall once more be guided by the treasured models of the old organ builders. Naturally we shall strive to improve upon them; but our efforts must be genuinely artistic, and not efforts to serve the factory business.

The return to normal pipes carries with it the return to normal wind pressure. In this way we shall get pipes that speak in a natural way, that is, pipes that let the tone take shape instead of forcing it out.

The question of the wind chest will bring difficulties. We can get tones that carry in their perfect beauty only from the slider wind chest. But the organ builders will be on the defensive against it; they will have to sacrifice many technical advantages offered by the modern chests. It is to be hoped that they will try to build modern boxes which are equal to the slider wind chest in tone production. If they succeed, much will be gained; if they fail, there is nothing for them to do but to return to the slider wind chest, which the *International Regulations for Organ Building* (1909) declared to be acoustically more advantageous.

In the smaller and medium-sized organs we shall surely come in time, if the striving for the artistic organ continues, to the mechanical trackers from the keys to the wind chest. That the keys in this method of organ construction work a little harder than in the usual keyboard is of little consequence, compared with the great advantages this method offers in precision and clarity of playing, and in the durability of the organ. Perfected mechanical trackers are now offered that function noiselessly and that load the keys as little as possible.

It is true that mechanical action costs a good deal more than pneumatic. But it is better to dispense with one or two stops and have the mechanical action.

With the larger organs, where significant distances between the keys and the wind chest must be overcome, we shall have to enlist the aid of pneumatics and electricity in such a way as to keep as far as possible the mechanical action. In this manner the keys will retain the qualities of mechanical action.

In the console we can dispense with a good part of what is supposed to be necessary for good playing. The generally complicated and sensitive consoles with their innumerable registration devices belong to a time already past. A pedal that brings in all the stops one after the other, a register crescendo, a mezzoforte, a forte, a tutti (sforzando)—a pedal that permits the stops pulled out in advance to reinforce the registration already drawn or to retire it, available for each separate manual or for the whole organ (the doubly available blind combination of the International Regulations for Organ Building): these are the playing aids that make possible all the registration required for classical or modern organ music, as far as the player himself can undertake it. If one permits the organ builders some day to build the simplified console recommended for all organs in the Regulations, a great deal of money will be saved which can be used to good purpose on the stops!

In church instruments of three divisions we should try wherever possible to have the second organ project out into the church from the gallery as a rückpositiv; this is what the older builders did. It was a serious mistake to house the three divisions together in the main case, as they did from 1850 on. The stops in the rückpositiv, sounding out freely and directly in the body of the church, produce an effect not otherwise possible—to say nothing of the fact that the *rückpositiv* belongs to the architecture of the instrument.

Of course the *rückpositiv* costs a good deal more than a second organ placed within the main casing; but a *rückpositiv* of seven stops produces a better effect than a second organ of twelve stops enclosed in the main case.

In all this harking back to the prized, artistic traditions of earlier organ building we shall still, however, build modern organs, in so far as we equip them with strong swell boxes. The Venetian swell, as it was developed by Cavaillé–Coll in the sixties of the last century, is the only revolutionary advance over the older masters.

With Cavaillé–Coll the meagre echo organ, enclosed in wooden shutters, became the well-furnished swell organ, which gave to the tone of the entire instrument an expressiveness and a flexibility it had not previously possessed. Every instrument, therefore, should have a good swell organ. To accomplish this, the shutters must leave enough space for the required number of stops, they should be made of thick boards, and they should be so constructed that they close tightly. How far the factory organs fall short of these requirements, because they economize on their swell boxes!

The swell organ should have at least as many stops as the great organ. In the smaller instruments with only one reed stop and one mixture it is well to put these in the swell organ.

The organ of the future is, then, an organ which has all the excellent and precious tone quality of the organs of earlier generations, which preserves as far as possible the *rückpositiv*, and which is enriched by the possibilities for expression to be had from a well-furnished swell.

We shall then of ourselves go back to the practice of supplying the organs in the earlier manner with mixtures, that is, with stops with harmonic ranks of pipes. The unified stops are intolerable in the modern harmonic organ; they enhance only the shrillness, which the tone already has to a certain extent. Even a fifth will not blend with the foundation stops in a way pleasing to the ear. But if we once again have normal pipes, speaking under normal pressure—which means an organ poor in harmonics—then beautiful mixtures will be necessary to add artistic overtones.

In order to judge the tone of an organ, one first pulls out all the eight-foot stops and plays a polyphonic movement. In the midst of the web of tone the alto and the tenor must come through well; and the tone, even when the stops are played in the upper register, should never be unpleasant. Thereupon one lets the four-foot and two-foot stops enter, and repeats the test. Finally, one plays Bach fugues for a half-hour without interruption on the full organ. If the hearer is able to follow the voices clearly, and if he finds the sustained fullness of tone is not exhausting, then the organ is good. The full organ from a modern factory, in this test with Bach fugues, produces a chaotic uproar which cannot be endured for five minutes.

This, for our time, is the way back to an organ that is rich and beautiful in tone. It is a matter of getting for the available money that organ which sounds best, instead of that one which in the bid makes the most grandiose appearance. When artistic competition shall have taken the place of commercial rivalry, organ building will of itself find the right path, because organ builders will arise who will build in the excellent and artistic manner of the old masters, and produce organs on which not only Bach but the moderns will sound as they ought to sound.

❦

*B*Y 1927 the pendulum in organ building had already begun to swing to the other extreme; and again Albert Schweitzer quickly saw the danger. The rapid development of the organ made possible by the introduction of electricity at the beginning of the century produced its own reaction. In the effort to imitate the orchestra a huge variety of new stops had been added. The passion for size, against which Schweitzer had raised his cry of warning, had gone to an absurd degree; people began to talk about the world's biggest organ. For a time it was the one set up at the World's Fair at St. Louis in 1904. Then the distinction—if it were that—went to Philadelphia, where a five-manual organ with 232 stops and 18,000 pipes was installed at Wanamaker's. But in 1932 the giant of them all was built for the convention hall at Atlantic City; incredible as it may be, this organ had seven manuals, 1,233 stops, and 32,882 pipes!

It is to be hoped that no further efforts will be made to build "organ skyscrapers." These organs were marvels of technical ingenuity, with a multiplicity of gadgets and devices; the stops ranged from the merest whisper to the most frightful roar; there were often fine solo voices, and an appeal to sentimentality. But most of these organs were overpowering and dull, lacking the pure, clear, transparent tones of the organs for which Schweitzer was contending.

Hence the reaction began, and organs of the Bach type began to be favored. But compositions of the romantic and modern periods could not be satisfactorily rendered on these organs; Schweitzer himself had not considered the organs of the seventeenth century as ideal, but only as the predecessors of the ideal organ. Today, however, some of our modern organs have successfully combined the tonal beauty of the older organs with the register riches and mechanical excellence of the modern period. This was exactly what Schweitzer had hoped for and worked for. In some unimportant respects the evolution of the organ had proved him unduly pessimistic about the future; but in the main he was right, and the better organs of today are in considerable measure the gift to the world of Albert Schweitzer. Even in 1927 he believed that in all essential matters the fight had been won.

The two and a half years he was now to spend in Europe were filled once more with his manifold activities and interests. Lectures and concerts in Sweden, Denmark, Holland, Germany, Czechoslovakia, Switzerland, and England; in his spare time constant work on his book The Mysticism of Paul the Apostle. In 1923 he had built a house at Königsfeld in the Black Forest, and there during this period he did much of his writing.

On August 28, 1928, on the invitation of the city of Frankfort, he delivered his famous address on Goethe, and in recognition of his service to humanity in the spirit of Goethe, received the Goethe Prize.[1] The money he received was used to build his present house

[1] See "The Goethe Prize Address," in Goethe, Four Studies, by Albert Schweitzer. Boston: The Beacon Press, 1949, pp. 103–113.

at Gunsbach in the Munster Valley of Alsace, but it is characteristic of Schweitzer that in the next few years he gave to German charities an equivalent sum which he had earned from concerts and lectures.

We have from this period of his life four fascinating glimpses of Schweitzer the musician. In December 1928 he was in Prague for lectures and recitals. One day he lunched with President Masaryk, practised on the organ at the Smetana Saal until 7.30 P.M., listened to a concert, ate a few sandwiches, returned to the organ until almost midnight, and then went off for a pleasant supper with some friends until 2 A.M. The next day he gave an organ concert in the afternoon, and then played on the organ of the Evangelical Church until almost midnight; when, to his great amusement, the police informed him that he was disturbing the peace and keeping the citizens of the neighborhood awake.

Doctor Alice Ehlers, now professor of music in the University of Southern California, first met Doctor Schweitzer in 1928, when she was giving a series of harpsichord recitals in Europe. After one of Schweitzer's lectures he had invited any who wished to join him to a nearby restaurant. Doctor Ehlers was sitting quietly at one table with some friends, when one of Doctor Schweitzer's assistants came over and asked, "Are you Doctor Ehlers?" Too surprised to answer, she only nodded. The assistant said, "Doctor Schweitzer would like to meet you."

"It is hard to describe my feelings," writes Doctor Ehlers, "as I approached Doctor Schweitzer. I remember that I felt like a little schoolgirl, and I am afraid that I behaved like one. Doctor Schweitzer must have understood my puzzled expression. He took out his African diary, a most interesting book he always carries with him; it contains hundreds of pages of very thin paper, unbound, but held together in such a manner that new pages may at any time be added. In this diary he showed me a remark he had written while in Africa: 'When in Europe, I want to meet Alice Ehlers; interesting programs; unusual.'

"Then he explained that his friends kept him informed of what was going on in Europe by sending him magazines and programs. In this way he had followed my concerts, and, as he expressed it, the quality and the outspoken tendency of my programs had awakened his interest. No great applause or enthusiastic critic could have given me such happiness as did these words coming from Doctor Schweitzer. I told him that it was his book on Bach which had been my main guide. Amidst all his many friends and admirers, we were able to exchange a few thoughts on Bach; and when he said he should very much like to hear me play, I enthusiastically thanked him. The very next day one of my harpsichords was sent to his residence, where I played for him and Mrs. Schweitzer for a full hour. I started with the C minor Fantasy by Bach, one of the Doctor's favorite pieces, and also one of mine. His encouraging remarks helped me to overcome my first shyness, and I played on and on.

"When I left the Schweitzers, he thanked me, and said: 'Go on the way you started out, and never allow virtuosity to guide you. Always listen to the inner voices in Bach's music; each voice lives its own life, dependently and independently at the same time. If you will look at Bach's music that way, if each voice is allowed to sing out its own beauty, I am sure you cannot fail.' Those words I have remembered all my life."

From that time on Doctor Ehlers used to spend a little time at Gunsbach each summer. "When there were no visitors," she reports, "Doctor Schweitzer would very seldom come out of his study—usually only for meals; after meals he loved to sit with us for a while. He did not speak much, yet we went on talking without making conversation with him; we all knew that these were his hours of relaxation. Doctor Schweitzer is not a voluble talker; he is a great thinker, possessing the magnificent gift of complete concentration. Though the room in which I used to practise was next to his study, it never disturbed the Doctor to hear me practise; he admitted he missed it when I stopped. Often he would come in, sit down, listen to my playing, make his remarks about the music, and sometimes ask for one of his favorite pieces. When I played the piano, he almost always asked for Mozart; he loves Mozart.

"After dinner, when his day's work was done, Doctor Schweitzer would go to the church to practise on the organ. This organ was built after his own design and wishes, resembling the old organs as much as possible. Those hours with him at the organ are unforgettable. I would sit with him on the organ bench listening, and he would ask my opinion, and we would discuss phrasing, tempo, dynamics. It was in those hours that I received my best musical education. The Doctor also loved these evenings; for he was always in his happiest mood when playing the organ. All responsibilities, the whole world, disappeared for him; there was only music—the organ, nothing else. He loves music and needs it. Even in Africa, when working very hard, the day is not ended before he has his one hour of practice on his piano with organ pedals." [1]

Doctor J. S. Bixler, President of Colby College, recalls his visit at this time to Doctor Schweitzer's home in the Black Forest. He was very much puzzled when Doctor Schweitzer smilingly asked him if he would not like to hear a little "Yotz." This was a German word which Doctor Bixler did not understand until Doctor Schweitzer sat down at the piano to play in syncopated time; then he knew that the good Doctor was speaking not German but English—he was talking about jazz.

There is a fine old organ in Ottobeuren in southern Germany, built in the eighteenth century by Master Karl Riepp in Dijon, and restored in 1914 by Steinmeyer of Oettingen. One lovely day in Whitsuntide Schweitzer found himself in that vicinity, and visited the church with a few of his friends. On this instrument he played Bach toccatas, preludes, and fugues; Mendelssohn, Franck, Widor. He ended with the choral prelude "Wenn ich einmal soll scheiden" [When some day I must part]. The prior of the Benedictine cloister came in the exquisitely beautiful baroque church to shake hands with this evangelical pastor and organist; and Schweitzer was very happy to meet him. He knew of the prior's efforts to save the old organ from destruction. Schweitzer said, "Whoever does that is my brother or my sister."

[1] The Albert Schweitzer Jubilee Book. Edited by A. A. Roback. Cambridge, Mass.: Sci-Art Publishers, 1945, pp. 230 f., 234.

IX

The Round Violin Bow

*S*CHWEITZER'S third sojourn in Africa began at the end of 1929 and lasted two years. This was the period when he published The Mysticism of Paul the Apostle; wrote his autobiography Out of My Life and Thought; the sequel to his book, On the Edge of the Primeval Forest, which bore in English the title, More from the Primeval Forest; [1] and his address for the one hundredth anniversary of Goethe's death, which was delivered in March 1932, after his return to Europe.[2] He worked also on the third volume of his Philosophy of Civilization.

Miss Margaret Deneke, the choir master of Lady Margaret Hall in Oxford, who spent a few months at Lambarene towards the end of 1931, tells of Schweitzer's half hour with Bach every evening when the pressure of his enormous correspondence and his hospital work made it possible. She tells also of the voyage back to Bordeaux, of the marvelous improvisations on the boat, and of the organ recital in the Bordeaux church, given for the four nurses who accompanied him, when he played from memory Bach's Passacaglia and the Little E minor Prelude and Fugue. How happy he was to have again, after more than two years, a real organ under his fingers! [3]

In February 1932 he was back in Europe, for a little more than a year of lectures and concerts in Holland, England, Sweden, Germany, and Switzerland. His energy was inexhaustible. He rose early

---

[1] On the Edge of the Primeval Forest & More from the Primeval Forest, by Albert Schweitzer. Recently republished in America as a single volume. New York: The Macmillan Company, 1948.

[2] See Goethe: Four Studies, by Albert Schweitzer, Boston: The Beacon Press, 1949, pp. 29–60.

[3] Seaver, pp. 125–127.

and worked late, and rushed from place to place to fill his heavy schedule of engagements. He somehow found time to see all the organs worth seeing, but he saw almost nothing else. He said with a grin, "I shall not begin sightseeing until I am seventy-five!" While in England and Scotland he received four honorary degrees: an LL.D. from St. Andrews, a D.D. from Oxford, a D.D. and a Mus.D. from the University of Edinburgh. He greatly valued this recognition from these institutions of learning; yet the honors themselves meant so little to him that later in writing an autobiographical record of this period of his life, he forgot to mention them.[1]

Pierre van Paassen gives a characteristic glimpse of his activities. "I recall," he says, "how Doctor Schweitzer once came to Zutphen (Holland) to preach the Christmas sermon when I was a guest at the manse. He arrived on a Monday, and Christmas fell on a Saturday. We did not see the great man all week, until finally, passing by the cathedral and hearing the organ, we found Dr. Schweitzer covered with dust and sweat, up in the loft busy cleaning the pipes. On Christmas he not only preached the sermon, but also played the organ to the astonishment of the churchgoers, who upon entering the cathedral, looked up in amazement when they heard the prelude and said: 'Is that our old organ?' Archbishop Söderblom told me that Schweitzer did the same thing once in Upsala. But there he worked for two months before he had the organ back to what it should have been." [2]

On January 24, 1933, Concert Master Rolph Schroeder gave a memorable Bach recital for the Strassburg Association of Professional Musicians, and Schweitzer published in the Schweizerische Musikzeitung an essay on the round violin bow which Schroeder had invented, and with which he played. This was the kind of bow that Bach himself had used. With it he had been able to play as chords what with our customary bow can be played only as arpeggios. Schweitzer had seen pictures of this bow in his early boyhood; the angels in the

---

[1] For most interesting accounts of Dr. Schweitzer's journeys see Seaver, chapters VI, VIII, and XI.

[2] From *That Day Alone*, by Pierre van Paassen. New York: The Dial Press, Inc., 1941.

Grünewald paintings in the museum at Colmar all have these round bows.

❦

THE ROUND VIOLIN BOW [1]

EVERY ONE of us has already suffered from the fact that we never hear the splendid polyphonic parts from Bach's *Chaconne*, or from his other works for the violin alone, as they stand on paper and as we hear them in our minds. They are executed for us in such a way that the chords do not sound as such but are rendered as arpeggios. Since the bass notes are not prolonged, the harmony has no foundation. And whenever the polyphonic parts appear, the violinist must always play *forte* even when the logic of the piece demands *piano* for that particular place. For he can play the polyphonic parts, as far as he can play them at all, only by pressing the bow sideways on the strings. The sounds that necessarily accompany these arpeggios played *forte* are disagreeable. Great violin *virtuosi* by their technical skill can make this imperfect rendering somewhat less imperfect; but they fall far short of executing the Bach works for the solo violin in such a way as to give the hearer unalloyed enjoyment.

The question now arises whether Bach, that great connoisseur of string instruments, really wrote something for the violin which can be rendered on it only very imperfectly. As a matter of fact, he did not do that. How then? Were he and the players of his time more skillful than our greatest *virtuosi*? No. But they used a bow different from ours.

The difficulty with the playing of several parts lies only in the modern bow, with its straight stick and its hair tightly stretched by the screw. With this bow it is simply impossible to play all four strings at the same time; the straight violin stick and the narrow distance between the hair and the stick (the stick of the modern bow is even bent inward towards the hair in order to secure the desired tautness) do not permit. The stick, along with the hair, would of course touch the strings.

[1] *Der runde Violinbogen. Schweitzerische Musikzeitung*, No. 6, 1933.

These difficulties do not exist for the round violin bow—which, of course, is really a bow. All of us are acquainted with this bow; it is the one the angels hold in their hands in the old paintings. By slackening the tension sufficiently, one can draw the hair of the round bow over all four strings at the same time without the slightest hindrance from the stick, which is arched outward. Under these conditions nothing stands in the way of polyphonic playing.

The masters of the Bach era and of the era that preceded Bach—not alone the German masters but the Italian and others—wrote in polyphonic style for the violin alone, because they were accustomed to play polyphonic pieces on this instrument with the round bow, and had brought to perfection the technique of this method of playing.

We learn from Nicolaus Bruhns, one of the most gifted musicians of the generation that preceded Bach (he was an organist at Husum in Schleswig, and died at the end of the 17th century before he was thirty), that he was accustomed to sit on the organ bench and improvise polyphonically upon the violin, while playing at the same time one or two parts on the organ pedals.

Whether the round violin was in common use in Bach's days we do not know. It is, of course, exceedingly difficult to reach any definite conclusion on this—as on other questions that have to do with the technique of playing.

Arnold Schering, in a study which dated from the year 1904, is the first to deal with the problem of the violin bow in Bach's time.

The "modern" bow, with its more or less straight stick and its mechanical contrivance to secure tension, originated in Italy and appeared in Germany at the end of the 17th century. In Bach's days —that is, in the first half of the 18th century—it must already have been generally used. But the old round bow, the hair of which was kept taut only by the natural elasticity of the bent stick, was still known, and still used for polyphonic playing.

In the older models of the "modern" bow the mechanical tension was secured by a movable handle with a wire ring hooked to teeth on the back of the stick. Such a bow is found, for example, in the Bach House at Eisenach. In Bach's time, however, bows with the present screw tension were already common.

Until the end of the 18th century these modern bows still had a stick arched slightly outward, which can be seen in the illustrations Leopold Mozart furnished for his book *Die grundliche Violinschule* [The Fundamental Violin School] that appeared in 1770. It was not until the 19th century that a stick perfectly straight or arched inward toward the hair was constructed to offer the greatest possible resistance and to provide a correspondingly greater tension.

The advantages of the straight, mechanically tightened bow are that it is easier to manipulate than the round one, since it is not so high; that its greater tension permits spring bowing and staccato technique; and especially that the tone produced by the stroke with the tauter hair is more intense than that produced by the slackened hair.

Because of these advantages for one-part playing, the straight bow gradually prevailed over the round one during the course of the 18th century. Indeed, it supplanted the round bow so completely that very few round ones have been preserved for us, as anyone who searches the museums will find to his regret.

But in the 19th century Ole Bull, the Norwegian violinist, brought the round bow back into esteem—though only temporarily. Ole Bull's life was like a romance. He was born in the vicinity of Bergen, and got his first instruction from Spohr, whom he then left for Paganini,—then residing in Paris. In Paris all his belongings, including his precious violin, were stolen. In despair he threw himself into the Seine; but he was fished out. A wealthy woman took him under her protection, and gave him a Guarneri violin. The money he earned in his concert journeys in Europe and America he lost in founding a theatre in Bergen and in land speculation in Pennsylvania for the benefit of Norwegian emigrants. He died in Norway in 1880.

As an artist he was a very controversial figure. To some he was a magician with the violin, to others only a clown. But most were fascinated by his playing, because it was different from anything they had heard. In what was it different? In this: that Ole Bull played polyphonically.

How did this happen? He used a bow, like the old round one. For his knowledge of the round bow he was indebted to the circumstance that in the conservative lands of the north it had remained in use well into the 19th century. And this artist whose aim was mastery of his instrument took note of the possibilities this old bow offered him and went to work to realize them. In this he succeeded. Ole Bull's bow was not arched quite like the old one; it had an almost straight stick, but at the point it was bent sharply downwards, and thus achieved the separation of the hair from the stick that was necessary for polyphonic playing.

It is interesting to note that Ole Bull always maintained that he had not introduced anything new with his polyphonic playing, but was pleading only for the true old violin art.

It would have been quite natural for Ole Bull to devote himself to the Bach compositions for violin alone, which offered him such a splendid opportunity for the development of his polyphonic playing. He did not do this, however, but expressed himself mainly in his own works, so far as he did not improvise—which he knew how to do in a masterly fashion. Bach's creations were first becoming really known when Ole Bull's life span ended.

But though Ole Bull did not dedicate himself to the works of Bach which required polyphonic playing, others could have done this, after he had reintroduced the technique of the round bow.

This, however, they failed to do.

How was that possible? There on paper, in their unique splendor, were Bach's works for the violin alone. They could be rendered properly only with the round bow. But the violinists continued to maltreat them with the straight bow: simply because no one wished to undertake—a very simple matter—to have a bow constructed like the old pictures, and with this bow to undertake this interpretation.

I had been long convinced of the need of going back to the old bow for Bach's solo violin works. While I was studying Bach's compositions at the beginning of this century, I begged my friend, the Alsatian violinist Ernst Hahnemann, an excellent Bach player, to let me hear at any price the polyphonic parts of the *Chaconne* with a bow that would make possible polyphonic playing. We took an old bow and altered it as well as we could, to make the distance between the stick and the hairs enough to permit the playing of the four strings at the same time without too much difficulty from the stick. Naturally we lessened in the required manner the tension of the hairs.

What I then heard from the playing with this very imperfect Bach bow was enough to produce in me complete conviction that the Bach works for the violin alone, as well as the works of the other old masters, required the round bow. Thereupon in my book about Bach I demanded that the instrument makers should again furnish us with round bows for the proper rendition of these works, and that the *virtuosi* should again learn the technique of the round bow.

Wherever I could, after the appearance of my Bach book, I talked about this matter with violinists of reputation and sought to win them to this project. But they were all averse to it. Why? They were all convinced that the tone that would be produced by the moderately stretched bow would not please our ears, accustomed as they are to the intensive tone of the violin. To justify this conviction they usually referred to the tone that one gets if one loosens the hairs on an ordinary straight bow, puts the stick under the violin, lays the hairs on the strings, and holding them and the stick with the right hand draws the hairs over the strings with the reversed and completely relaxed bow. They forget that the hairs of the round bow are never as completely relaxed as they are in this violinist's trick.

They also added that Ole Bull, in playing with the round, imperfectly stretched bow, was able to produce only a small tone, which those who criticised his playing always reproached him for. Granted; yet in spite of this smaller tone he delighted his hearers.

Often I heard also from the masters of the violin that a great deal in Bach's polyphonic passages for the solo violin cannot be played as it stands on paper—that is, in sustained chords. Those who expressed this opinion forgot to take into consideration that Bach's fingering, and especially that of the old masters who were accustomed to play polyphonically and were at the same time masters of the fingering technique of the lute (something that one must indeed remember), was probably much more perfect than ours, accustomed as we are to the playing of only one or two parts.

More than anything else, however, it was the fear of not being able to play the single part with a bow inadequately stretched which kept the great violinists of the 19th century and of recent times from venturing to try the round bow. But unknown violinists began to interest themselves in the problem, and went courageously to work on it.

The problem is not simply a matter of returning to the old round bow. The player stretched the old bow by pressing the hair towards the stick from below with the thumb; and held it in this way when he played monophonically. When the polyphonic passages came he relaxed his thumb, so that the set of hairs could be loosened and drawn over all four strings at the same time; for the pieces in which the polyphonic parts appeared the players used specially slack bows.

When in this or that study of the old bows it is maintained that the player also relaxed the bow in order to play a single part *piano*, that is not true. The moment he relaxed with a specially slack bow he could no longer play a single part, since the slack hair played other strings as well. Therefore he relaxed only for the polyphonic playing.

The tightening of the hairs with the thumb was of course limited by the strength of the thumb; therefore this method always remained unsatisfactory. But why not build into the bow a mechanical device, to be manipulated by the thumb, which would make possible a much greater tension or a much greater loosening than the thumb alone could provide? In this way might be created a bow which would unite the advantages of both old and new.

This, then, quite properly became the objective of those who worked on the problem of the Bach bow as it confronts us today.

The first bow equipped with such a mechanism was brought to me by Dr. Hans Baumgart of Rastatt, who had conceived it, and had had it constructed for him by a bow maker at the beginning of the year 1929. It was satisfactory in many respects except that it was rather heavy, and that the tightening and loosening mechanism made much demand on the thumb. What could actually be accomplished with it, I was unable to imagine rightly, since no outstanding violinist was at hand to go to the trouble of making himself familiar with its technique.

Let us not forget also the bow of Berkowski in Berlin.

Now someone has appeared, in the person of Concert Master Rolph Schroeder of Kassel, who has improved the round bow and at the same time is an eminent violinist. His bow and the perfection with which he uses it permit us to say that the problem is in the main solved.

In Rolph Schroeder's bow the loosening and tightening of the hair is accomplished by a lever that takes the place of the handle. The tension possible with this bow is almost as much as that we are accustomed to; in monophonic playing, then, the performer is hardly hindered with this bow. Moreover, the tone produced in single-part playing is almost as great in intensity as that to which we are accustomed with the straight bow. On the other hand, a much greater slackening of tension is possible with the bow of Rolph Schroeder than with the old round bow. Without any noticeable pressure by the hand the hair stretches over the four strings at the same time. Polyphonic playing is therefore even significantly easier than it was for Bach and the old masters.

In order that the stick may not be in the way when the hair is most relaxed for polyphonic playing, it has a very marked arch. Though rather high, this bow is nonetheless not unwieldy, and it is as light as the modern one.

With the fully loosened bow, then, the performer can play in the polyphonic passages as loudly as is generally possible on the violin; he has only to put necessary pressure on the bow.

Its manipulation is the simplest imaginable. During the single-part playing the thumb is pressed against the lever from below, and without any great exertion produces a strong tension. During the polyphonic playing the thumb rests only very lightly against the lever, which, yielding to the resistance of the hair on the strings, gives of itself, as far as the thumb (which always remains on it) will permit. Therefore the bow is not like the old round one, either taut or loose; but instead the player can use a whole series of degrees of tension and relaxation lying in between.

On Tuesday, January 24, of this year (1933), Concert Master Rolph Schroeder played with this bow, after two years of practice with it, the G minor Sonata, which contains the famous fugue, and the Partita, which has the Chaconne for a finale, before the members of the Association of Professional Musicians (Society of the Friends of the Conservatory) in the great hall of the Strassburg Conservatory. At last, chords whose bass notes resounded—chords not only in *fortissimo* and *forte* but also in *piano* and *pianissimo!* And what marvelous *crescendo* and *diminuendo* in the sequence of the chords!

Everything that had been adduced to characterize the experiments with the round bow as hopeless was demonstrated in five minutes of this performance to be untenable! The tone produced with this round bow is a bit less intense than with the modern bow, but nonetheless is always full and wonderfully beautiful; in fact it seems·even better. In any case, it meets a great need. It is remarkable that with this bow overtones are far less noticeable than with the ordinary one; this is particularly evident in *pianissimo* playing.

And what has also been said about impossible fingering was contradicted by Rolph Schroeder's playing. It is true that the difficulties of mastering the fingering technique required for sustained polyphonic playing are great, greater than those of the round bow and the thumb lever; but they are not unconquerable. Bach asks nothing really impossible of the violin or of the organ—however great his demands on the performer.

Since the bow of the old masters could be relaxed only to a limited degree, they may have used for their polyphonic playing a somewhat flattened bridge. It is certain that Ole Bull did this.

When the round bow is provided with a lever, however, the slackening is possible to such a degree that without the slightest difficulty the hairs can bend over the four strings of the usual rounded bridge. The flattened bridge, which constitutes a difficulty for one-part playing, is therefore not needed.

Henry Joachim, in an article in the *Musical Times* devoted to the question of the bow for Bach violin solo pieces, expressed the hope that some day a gifted violinist may appear who would play Bach's music with courage and idealism in Bach's spirit and mood, and thus force all concert violinists to do the same.[1]

We who heard Rolph Schroeder know that this hope has been fulfilled. The time has passed when the lovers of Bach had to be satisfied with a wholly inadequate rendition of the polyphonic parts of the violin pieces of Bach and the other old masters because violinists stubbornly insisted on using only the straight modern bow.

---

[1] This article in German translation has also appeared in the *Schweizerische Musikzeitung*, March 1, 1932.

Henceforth those who would play these works for us must use the round bow which they demand.

❦

IN 1950, in connection with the Strassburg Music Festival, Dr. Schweitzer republished the foregoing article on "The Round Violin Bow" in the official program of the festival and simultaneously in the Strassburg monthly Saisons d'Alsace. This article was subsequently published in English translation in Musical America. It is identical with the 1933 article with the exception of the concluding paragraphs, which are added here.

❦

IT looked for a time after 1934 as if the round violin bow had conquered. Guests from Paris who heard Rolf Schroeder play in Strassburg invited him to perform in Paris, where he had a great success. Thibaud became interested in the bow. In Brussels and Berlin this manner of polyphonic playing evoked a great deal of enthusiasm. In 1939, on the invitation of Professor Stein, Rolf Schroeder was asked to give a course in Berlin on playing with the round bow. But then the war broke out.

Impressed by Rolf Schroeder's playing at Strassburg, Georges Frey, violinist at Mulhouse, decided to devote himself to the round bow. With the help of a Swiss bowmaker he had a round bow built, somewhat like Schroeder's bow, and began to perform Bach's violin solo works in Alsace and elsewhere in France. In this way Mr. Frey initiated many a musician into the correct way of rendering Bach's violin solos.

After the war I heard nothing of Rolf Schroeder for some time. Not until June 1949 did I have any news about him. Then I learned that for some time after the war he had been concertmaster with the Dresden Philharmonic Orchestra, and then had gone back to Kassel, where he had lost all his property, to build himself a new bow, which he considers better than the former one.

During 1949 I became acquainted with the attempts made by Rudolf Gutman of Constance to make a straight bow, the hair of which is at a greater distance from the stick than usual. A continuous row of celluloid rings between hair and stick made the tightening or slackening of the hair possible. Mr. Gutman is not only an excellent instrument maker but also a genuine musician, and has himself demonstrated this bow on the gamba. He told me he thought it possible to perfect this bow by replacing the celluloid rings with a flat sack between hair and stick, filled with air under a certain pressure.[1]

For the time being we have no opinion about the possibility of a future straight bow superior to the perfect round bow of Bach's time. The latter is adequate for the rendering of Bach's violin works as he conceived them and as they should sound, and we do have artists who know how to perform them correctly for us with this bow.

May the coming months, dedicated particularly to the memory of Bach and his works, bring us on the programs of Bach festivals such performances of his violin solo compositions. Thus the correct manner of rendering them will become known, and an increasing number of violinists may be influenced to familiarize themselves with the perfected round bow and the technique of sustained polyphonic playing. Once such a bow for polyphonic playing comes again into use, modern composers will doubtless be stimulated to write once more solos for violin, cello and gamba, and to give new life to a kind of musical composition which has seemed to belong wholly to the past.

[1] In America the violinst Roman Totenberg and the California bowmaker John Bolander have together constructed and demonstrated a bow suitable for the playing of Bach's violin solos. The Bolander bow is convex, and has the screw and head and some of the other structural peculiarities of the Tourte bow.

❦

*I*N 1940 Mr. Georges Frey, who had already begun to give concerts with the round violin bow, was driven out of Mulhouse by the German army. He was afraid he would have to leave his bow behind, but at the last minute he managed to put it into a case with two violins. He escaped to the unoccupied zone in southern France, and continued to give his concerts, at Vichy, Lyons and elsewhere. The conventional musicians were all opposed to the round bow, but he persisted. He found it wonderful on three or four strings, satisfactory on two strings, but not so good on one.

In May 1949 Mr. Frey came to Gunsbach on Dr. Schweitzer's invitation to play for him. It was the writer's great privilege to be there when Mr. Frey arrived. It was an unforgettable occasion. Again there were distinguished guests in the house—A. Haedrich from Guebwiller, deputy Joseph Wasmer from Mulhouse, Auguste Dubois, the famous Alsatian artist. Monsieur Frey began to play in the upstairs study. Miss Gloria Coolidge, the American nurse from Lambarene, came into the room, and Monsieur Frey began to clear the music from a chair he was using as a kind of music rack so that she might sit there. Dr Schweitzer playfully protested, "An artist should not trouble himself about anyone else," he said. Miss Coolidge sat on a stool beside the stove.

Monsieur Frey began to play a Bach fugue. He had not practised it, and did not know it by heart. He tried to follow the score lying on the seat of the chair. He could not see it very well, and in the middle of the piece lost his place and stopped. Dr. Schweitzer jumped up and made a music rack of himself, sitting on the chair and holding the music in front of his face. After a few moments Monsieur Frey said, "It is necessary to turn the page." Someone tried to help, but Dr. Schweitzer turned the page himself, and continued to hold his exhausting pose until the fugue ended. The fingering was very difficult; at times the player had to use his thumb as well as his fingers, and not only the tip of his little finger but the base of it as well.

The picture is etched deeply on my memory: Madame Martin in

front of Dr. Schweitzer's table, Monsieur Dubois on a chair with closed eyes and folded hands, Miss Coolidge on the stool by the stove, the other guests on the sofa in rapt attention; and Albert Schweitzer sitting with bowed head and holding the music in front of him with both hands.

So Bach came to life again at Gunsbach.

X

Records for the World

ALBERT Schweitzer spent the years from 1933 to 1950 in repeated sojourns in Africa and repeated visits to Europe. From April 1933 to January 1934 he was at Lambarene for the fourth time. He gave much time to the preparation of the Gifford Lectures, which he had promised to deliver in 1934 and 1935. From February 1934 until February 1935 he was back in Europe. He gave a series of lectures at Manchester College, Oxford, on "Religion in Modern Civilization," which he repeated at London University College. The Gifford Lectures at Edinburgh were on the great thinkers of India, China, Greece, and Persia. The lecture on the Indian thinkers grew later into a book, which was published under the title of Indian Thought and Its Development.

On February 26, 1935, he reached Africa for a stay of six months, during which he prepared a second series of Gifford Lectures. Then for a year and a half he was in Europe, from September 1935 to February 1937. He gave his lectures, and was busy with many organ recitals. Just at this time he was asked by Columbia Records in London to make a series of recordings, which he finally completed on the fine organ of St. Aurelia's, Strassburg, in October 1936. Louis-Edouard Schaeffer has written an interesting newspaper story of the making of these records on the wonderful Silbermann organ there.[1]

"The organ stops. In the frame of the door that leads from the interior of the church into the sacristy Albert Schweitzer appears. I have surprised him in the midst of his work, in shirt sleeves. He has even taken off his vest here in the late autumn in the cold church. I see again the imposing head that reminds one of Nietzsche, the

[1] Neueste Nachrichten, Strassburg, November 11, 1936.

243

powerful form with the broad shoulders which seems to me today even heavier and more crammed with energy than ever. We know of the lofty spirit that drives this man to ever new undertakings. We know especially about the iron, almost mysterious will that disciplines and steels body and soul in an astonishing vital effort. The task he has been mastering for some days now in St. Aurelia is in accordance with his character—nothing less than filling thirty records with Bach and César Franck. He is completely absorbed in his work. The theologian, the preacher, comparative religion, the significance of the Apostle Paul and his mission, the burial and resurrection of Christ, the doctor and surgeon, the jungle hospital—all this has passed into the background. It is now the master of the organ who speaks, the interpreter of Bach.

"Before the organ over the church pews hangs the microphone; it carries the tones of the organ to the receiving apparatus in the sacristy. Here the wax disk turns, and here the needle scratches the organ tones in the surface of what looks like a thick, deep yellow honey cake. 'You are arriving just at one of the most difficult places,' said Albert Schweitzer to me, as he took me up to the choir loft with him. About half of the piece he is about to play is exclusively in the pedals. He supports himself on the organ bench with both hands, and plays with assurance and energy the difficult foot pedals once or twice through. Then he telephones the sacristy that he is ready. The man in charge of the reception there puts on a new disk and lowers the needle. Now a muffled bell beside the console gives the signal, and then beside the organ, exactly as in the theatre, a red light goes on. The organ begins. Once more Schweitzer props himself up with his hands on the organ bench; and while I watch the amazing touch of his feet on the pedals, I am struck by the elegant, close-fitting low shoes which I have never seen on Schweitzer at other times. He puts them on only for his organ playing, and on his concert trips carries them with him in a linen bag to the organ lofts.

"Another muffled signal comes from the sacristy; the transcription is finished. Schweitzer does not seem completely satisfied, and we go down to listen to it. He notes a couple of minor changes he wants to make, then goes up to the organ for a second rendition, which finally satisfies him.

"After a short pause for rest Albert Schweitzer begins a Bach Adagio. How smoothly the notes of the Silbermann organ flow! When one hears the warm, swelling basses the instrument seems to be mysteriously enraptured in technical purity and freed from the bonds of mechanics. To the 'elegant slowness' of the Adagio, as he himself expresses it, Schweitzer lends the last measure of maturity, and gives each sound wave its full resonance, soft splendor, and resounding luminosity. Because of this the transcription is a couple of minutes too long. What I felt only vaguely and without any total impression while I was beside the organ becomes a certainty when we go down in the sacristy to hear the record. The tender and spacious motifs of the Adagio, its magic lustre and restrained fire, flow happily into the soul. 'How beautifully the basses sound!' 'Yes,' nods the doctor, 'it turns out well.'

"At a long bench in the sacristy sits a music critic from London. With the music before him he follows the transcription. He points to one place and asks, 'Why do you play a trill just here?' 'Look,' exclaims Schweitzer eagerly, 'here is a trill, and here is one; therefore there must also be one here. Bach was too indolent to draw it in. You must remember that Bach wrote everything just for himself. When Bach played the Adagio he put in a couple of trills right at this place.'

"Meanwhile it has grown late, and the church has become very cold. The organ builder Härpfer from Boulay is testing the organ. It is as temperamental as a woman, and the organ builder says, while he tries the reeds: 'What do you want to do? The colder it gets in the church now, the more easily it gets out of tune.' 'Then we will quickly make two more records,' Schweitzer decides, and rises from his reclining chair near the organ.

"At half past nine in the morning he is already practising again. While they are making arrangements for the first transcription, and an organist from Berne is having a look at the pedals and stops, he tells me how it happens that he is making records in St. Aurelia. He has already played Bach for 'His Master's Voice,' but the trials made at that time in the London concert hall, Queen's Hall, did not turn out to his satisfaction—the organ was too harsh. For the Columbia Records he sought in London for an appropriate instrument, and played next on the organ of Tower All-Hallows, the All Saints Church in the Tower. Finally he suggested the possibility of transferring the transcribing to the St. Aurelia Church in Strassburg. The experts from Columbia found conditions ideal in this church, located in an out-of-the-way corner behind the Weissturmstrasse. In a medium-sized room with excellent acoustics the beauties of the organ are kept. The organ itself does not have to be a mighty instrument, fitted out with all the technical novelties—it is sufficient that it has all the stops. The Silbermann organ in St. Aurelia is specially fitted for Schweitzer's interpretation of Bach. Shortly before the war, and a year after the organ at St. Thomas, it was restored by the Lorraine organ builder Frédéric Härpfer. In the course of the conversation Schweitzer asserted repeatedly that he considered Härpfer the most noteworthy artist among the organ builders of our time. Schweitzer has now played in St. Aurelia for the wax records, in addition to works of César Franck the great organ works from Bach's later years. In some two weeks of incessant toil he has filled altogether twenty-five records with Bach and eight records with César Franck.

"Schweitzer's work is filled with unusual harmony. Is it not an evidence of an even deeper and special accord to give Bach's work anew to the world on an organ that comes from the middle of the eighteenth century, originating in the time of Bach and erected by Johann Andreas Silbermann, a Strassburg organ builder whom Bach so greatly prized and revered?"

In 1935 the city of Leipzig invited Schweitzer to speak at the great Bach festival there; but Schweitzer politely refused. He did not set foot in Germany all the time that Hitler was in power

In February 1937 he was back again in Africa for his sixth sojourn there. He hoped this time to be able to finish his Philosophy of Civilization, on which he had been working steadily since 1923; but the pressure of work at the hospital made it impossible. He had accumulated a large amount of material, and had planned to publish two additional volumes to complete the two already issued. In the end, however, he resolved to complete his Philosophy in a single volume, and to publish in a separate work the chapters on the Chinese thinkers, in whom he had become profoundly interested.

In 1938 he published a little volume of anecdotes about the natives of Africa called From My African Notebook. In February 1939 he arrived in Europe once again; but this time, his stay was to be of the briefest. On the way back from Africa he had become convinced that war was imminent; and if it were to come he knew that his place was at his hospital. Suddenly he changed all his plans, and went back to Africa on the return trip of the steamer that had taken him to Europe, arriving March 3. Then came the terrible war years; the activities of the hospital seriously curtailed for lack of funds and supplies, yet still maintained by the sacrificial devotion of the little staff, who wore themselves out without respite or relief. Even after the war was over Dr. Schweitzer was not able to return to Europe, for the hospital had to be reorganized and new doctors and nurses recruited and trained.

Finally, in October 1948, Dr. Schweitzer was back again in Europe after an absence of almost twelve years—broken only by the few days in Europe in February 1939—back again with his loved organs, with his circle of close friends, in the great world where his life and thought had become increasingly known and respected. There was no rest for him in Europe; requests for lectures, recitals, and other services came streaming in to the "house that Goethe built" in every mail. Friends and admirers came to call on him; groups of people from schools and churches made pilgrimages to his door. Most of the requests for lectures and recitals had to be declined; the burden had become too heavy for one man to carry.

Twice he declined the cabled invitation to give the principal speech at the Goethe Festival at Aspen, Colorado; but when Dr. Schweitzer realized how much he could do for his hospital with the generous fee offered, he finally accepted, "for the sake of his lepers." And so in the summer of 1949 Albert Schweitzer found himself for the first time in America, for a few brief and crowded weeks. He delivered the address at Aspen—at some risk to his health because of the unexpectedly high altitude—received an honorary LL.D. from the University of Chicago, visited organs and friends and pharmaceutical houses in Cleveland, New York, and Boston, and then sailed back to Europe for a few feverish weeks of preparation for his return to Africa. More than ever his previous return to Europe and his visit to America had been a triumphal journey, crowded with recognition by the communities with which he had been associated—Gunsbach, Kaysersberg, Mulhouse, Strassburg. The French Government bestowed on him the Legion of Honor. In America he was hailed as one of the truly great men of the world.

But all this failed to divert him in the slightest from his course of duty. He made a hurried journey to Sweden and Denmark. Unable to write letters in the shaky third class carriage, he memorized something from César Franck, his fingers playing on his knees, his feet tapping the floor. In October of 1949 he was once more on his way back to Africa for more months of arduous work on the equator. These months proved to be among the hardest he had ever known; sometimes he felt like a drowning man, gasping for breath. For again the hospital was understaffed, and much of the work he usually turned over to others he again had to do himself. He even had to operate again, and at the age of seventy-five painstakingly learned new surgical stitches. The meeting of the International Bach Society occurred in April, but its president was unable to attend. He could not leave his hospital.

XI

The Musician at Seventy-Five

SOONER or later many of the world's distinguished musicians find their way to the little village of Gunsbach, which will be remembered in history only because it was the home of Albert Schweitzer. On one memorable day in 1949, Mr. Valentyn Schoonderbeck, professor of organ at the Lyceum of Music in Amsterdam; Mr. Bangert, director of the Conservatory of Copenhagen and Domkantor at the great Roskilde Cathedral where the Danish kings are buried; and Doctor Antonia Brico, orchestra director from Denver on her way to Finland to give a series of concerts, were all there; and on special invitation the Hutt Double Quartet had come from Colmar. The founder and leader of this quartet had been Professor Edouard Hutt, a close friend of Doctor Schweitzer's and a very competent musician, and Doctor Schweitzer had invited the men of the double quartet to visit him in appreciation of a concert they had given in the Evangelical Stadtkirche of Colmar for the benefit of his hospital work.

After pleasant fellowship at the house they all went to the church, for Doctor Schweitzer wished them to see and hear the organ there, of which he was very proud. The organ had been repaired and renovated in 1928 according to the specifications he had drawn up. In the course of the Second World War the tower of the church had been blown down, and dirt, plaster, and water had got into the organ, so that in 1949 it had to be thoroughly overhauled, cleaned, and tuned by the firm of Härpfer from Boulay in the Moselle—again under the constant supervision of Doctor Schweitzer. Now it was in excellent condition, and the Doctor's guests must hear it.

Doctor Schweitzer sat at the organ in the high balcony at the rear of the church. One by one he played for them the various stops—first the flue stops, then the mixtures—which he humorously called the vitamins of the organ—and finally the pedals. Then he said: "Now I want to show you what is possible with such an organ," and he played from memory Bach's Toccata in D minor, the chorale prelude to "Herzlich tut mich verlangen" [With all my heart I long], and a part of the lovely 6th Organ Sonata by Mendelssohn.

Then he slid off the organ bench, bowed, and said, "Now it is your turn." He walked over to the steep stairs in the corner of the balcony and descended to the floor of the church, where he went forward and took his place in an empty pew alone. The Hutt Double Quartet sang Bortnianski's Doxology. Professor Bangert played one of the variations which Johann Pachelbel wrote on Schob's chorale "Werde munter mein Gemüte" [Be gay, my spirit], and a Prelude and Fugue in D by Dietrich Buxtehude. The Double Quartet sang again. Finally Professor Schoonderbeck threw open the chorale book and improvised beautifully on "Was Gott tut, das ist wohlgetan" [What God does is well done], and ended with Bach's "Wie wohl ist mir, O Freund der Seelen" [How well it is with me, O Friend of souls].

The next morning Schweitzer was busy again in his study, and the villagers passing on the street could see his graying head bowed over his writing table, his lively eyes intent upon his work, his fingers grasping the old-fashioned fluted glass fountain pen with which he writes laboriously. "What a head!" said one. "What knowledge!" said another. "He has done wonderful things!" said a third. "He sits at the window there, writing, writing, writing, until far into the night," said a fourth with awe.

Every day offerings were laid on the window sill, as tributes of love and respect: mirabelles or radishes, apples or grapes. Doctor Schweitzer smiled, and remembered the old seigneurs of the Middle Ages, whose retainers descended from their high, strong castle at the mouth of the valley and levied tribute on all who passed by.

Thus it was in the summer of 1949. Thus it was to be in the summer of 1950. He was to come back again from Africa, back to Gunsbach, back to the loved routine of his Alsatian home. To play the piano with pedal attachment across the hall while the maid cleaned his room and made his bed after breakfast; to greet the visitors who would come in endless numbers to this house by the side of the road as to a shrine; to make an excursion to Strassburg on the business of the hospital; perhaps to play the organ in the Evangelical church at Munster; perhaps to advise about organ construction with the organist at Turckheim; perhaps to play for the Catholic mass at Colmar, where the beauty of his music would find at the other end of the church an echo in the exquisite loveliness of Schöngauer's "Madonna of the Rose Bush."

He might have preached in the village church; he might have played the organ for the simple service there; he might have sat down in some gay mood to improvise the lilting measures of a waltz at the piano upstairs in his home; he would have walked through the village streets with his old felt hat pulled down, his small black bow tie (the only one he has) tied around the white wing collar (a size too large), his hands clasped behind his back, stooped a bit, but still vigorous, with no outward sign of the fatigue that is his constant companion; in the evening he would have strolled along the road towards Munster to sit quietly for a little while on the bench he has erected there beside the highway.

This would have been his routine at Gunsbach, had he returned for the summer of 1950, as he planned to return. But he did not come. Until the last moment it was hoped that he would be in Europe to participate in the various Bach festivals, commemorating the two hundredth anniversary of the death of Bach, but it was impossible. He still planned to arrive in the middle of the summer, but just before he was expected to take the boat from French Equatorial Africa a cablegram arrived in Europe saying that he could not leave. The work in Africa was paramount in his life. If his presence there was needed that was where he had to be.

Thus at seventy-five he continues his work in Africa—laughing at the idea of retirement, making of each day a ministry of mercy as he works in his hospital and of each night a ministry of music as he sits at his loved piano.

The last of the many times I heard him play at Gunsbach I shall always remember. It was evening when we found our way to the little darkened church, Doctor Schweitzer with his organ shoes in their little white bag under his arm. There were only five of us: Madame Martin, his secretary and representative in Europe; Miss Gloria Coolidge, the American nurse on leave from Lambarene; her mother, Mrs. Coolidge; Doctor Schweitzer's sister, Madame Woytt; and myself. Quietly we entered the church, and Doctor Schweitzer took his place on the organ bench. He turned on the light above the console, selected the registration he wished, and began to play, with not a note of music before him. First it was the great, monumental works of Bach, as only he can play them, with stately, expressive dignity. Then it was César Franck, pater seraphicus; then Mendelssohn, so important in the evolution of modern organ music. Schweitzer gave himself to the music, oblivious to everything around him, his head bowed over the manuals, molding the music, endowing it with the transforming magic of his own superb execution. It was like the evenings when he used to play at St. Thomas and St. Aurelia in Strassburg.

After a while I slipped down from the organ loft and picked my way silently down the center aisle of the church to one of the front pews. From this place Doctor Schweitzer was invisible—as he would wish to be: it was not for the organist to intrude; the radiance of the music was most beautiful if the window through which it streamed was invisible.

The little church was full of memories even for me; how full it must have been for him! There in the high pulpit his father had preached. There on the other side from the pulpit his mother had had her place among the women. He and his brother and sisters had sat with the other children in the front pews, where he could see through the chancel screen the angels of the Catholic altar. Up where he now sat he had begun as a small boy of nine to play the organ. And now he was there again, alone with his music and his memories, his heart singing forth its paeans of praise and prayer, in this little village church as in a great cathedral.

It is thus that I want to remember him. There were those who remembered Bach in just that way.

Appendix

THE QUESTIONNAIRE ON ORGAN CONSTRUCTION [1]

1. From a purely artistic standpoint what is the best action from the key to the wind chest: mechanical (tracker), the Barcker lever (Cavaillé–Coll), or pneumatics?

Is the size of the organ determinative in the choice of the action? What do you think of the opinion that little organs up to fifteen stops should still be built mechanically? What pipe pneumatic system do you consider the best? What electric system has in your experience proved to be the best? Over how many years does your experience extend?

2. What do you think of the slider wind chest and the ventil wind chest in their influence on the forming of the tone? Have you had experience with the favorable tone-producing qualities of the slider wind chest on well-maintained old organs?

3. What is your judgment of the arrangements in the organs built during the past thirty years?

Please sketch on the accompanying sheet No. 1 the model arrangement of an organ of ten registers, of fifteen registers, of thirty registers, of forty-five registers, of sixty registers.

In these arrangements count only the original, speaking stops. What do you think of the use of borrowed registers, of unifying?

4. What do you think of the tone and the expression of the modern organ? What is to be praised in modern intonation, what to

---

[1] *Die allgemeine Umfrage bei Orgelspielern und Orgelbauern in deutschen und romanischen Ländern,"* in III. *Kongress der Internationalen Musikgesellschaft,* Wien, 25. bis 29. Mai 1909. ("The general questionnaire sent to organ-players and organ-builders in German and Romance Countries," in the *III Congress of the International Society of Music,* Vienna, May 25–29, 1909.) Vienna: Artaria & Co., Leipzig: Breitkopf & Härtel, 1909; pp. 581–583.

be criticized? With what wind pressure should foundation stops be intoned? What is the best wind pressure for the mixtures? What for the reeds? With what pressure should organs which can be supplied with only one wind pressure be intoned? With 70, 80, 90, 100, or 110 water mm. [2.76, 3.15, 3.55, 3.94, or 4.33 inches]? What is your opinion of differentiations in wind pressure in middle-sized and larger organs? What comments would you make regarding the commonly chosen dimensions and mouths?

5. What dimensions do you consider the best for manuals and pedals? Are you for little or big keys, for keyboards near one another or rather far apart? Do you prefer the straight or the curved pedals? How should the pedal lie under the console? What range of notes should it have?

6. Do you consider it wise to have the dimensions of the console prescribed by the authorities?

7. What do you consider to be the simplest and at the same time the most advantageous arrangement for the normal console? Are you in favor of fixed combinations, synthetic stops, cylinder crescendo, or blind combinations? What do you think of the various blind combinations being offered today even on middle-sized organs?

Should the couplers and registration helps be arranged as drawstops (the German way) or as pedals (the French way)? Are you acquainted with organs where these are arranged both as drawstops or as pedals, either independent of each other or connected with each other, so that the pedal draws the stop at the same time or releases it, and vice versa? Are you familiar with devices which add a new registration to the drawn registration without retiring the drawn registration? What do you think of the practical value of such stops?

How would you arrange super- and suboctave couplers?

Please sketch on the accompanying sheet No. 2 what is in your opinion the simplest and most practical console arrangement for two manuals and for three.

8. What do you think of the tone, the position and the outward appearance of the organs in concert halls which you know?

9. Are you in sympathy with the architectural design of the organs now being supplied? What do you think of the usual plans in respect to the architectural appearance? Do you not believe that the rück-

positiv that projects from the choir loft of the church and hangs down below it should be favored more than previously for its architectural appearance and its tone effect?

10. What do you think of present organ prices, on the basis of the arrangements of the organs known to you? Do you believe that truly durable and artistic work can be had at such prices?

11. What do you think of echo organs?

12. Other remarks, experiences, or suggestions.

❦

THE ORGAN THAT EUROPE WANTS [1]

IT is fitting that our gratitude should first of all be here expressed to the Committee of the Third Congress of the International Music Society, gratitude it richly deserves. Through the initiative of Professor Guido Adler of Vienna, *Lektor* Bagster of the same place,[2] and Mr. Thomas Casson of London, the means for printing and circulating the questionnaire on organ building, the results of which will be reported here, were provided; and through the creation of a section of the Congress on organ construction the opportunity has been given to organ builders and organ players to discuss on an interconfessional and international basis the problems with which all friends of church music and organ playing are concerned. This is the first time this has happened.

It was high time that it happened. In recent speeches and remarks about organ building it has been difficult to distinguish between personal opinion and generally current conviction, for the two have usually been inextricably intermingled. Moreover, the publications about organ building have frequently been mistrusted, because they seemed to conceal a recommendation of this or that house—a mistrust often unfair, yet sometimes just.

[1] "*Die Reform unseres Orgelbaues auf Grund einer allgemeinen Umfrage bei Orgelspielern und Orgelbauern in deutschen und romanishen Ländern,*" in *III. Kongress der Internationalen Musikgesellschaft, Wien,* 25. bis 29. Mai 1909. Vienna: Artaria & Co.; Leipzig: Breitkopf & Härtel, 1909; pp. 581–607.

[2] A *Lektor* was a foreign teacher of his mother tongue appointed for a time by German universities. C. R. J.

The time had come, therefore, for a large amount of material to be assembled, from which general tendencies and general convictions could be clearly deduced. To this end the questionnaire about organ construction, with its twelve groups of questions, was sent out. The result has exceeded our expectations. The survey given here is based upon approximately 150 questionnaires answered in detail, most of them from Germany, Austria, France, Italy, Switzerland, and the Netherlands. Many of the answers were large treatises worthy of being printed. How much labor is represented by this material may be judged from the fact that the study of each answer took an average of six to ten hours, because it had to be examined from many sides. I trust that those who have thought with us, worked with us, and now speak to us from a distance may be aware of our appreciation.

In our analysis of the returns no names will be mentioned—difficult though it is for me to be unable to recognize personally those whose opinions are reported. The reason for this is that all personal factors should be minimized, to remove all grounds for suspicion that this or that individual, this or that firm, is being favored. The answers will be given in the order of the questions on the sheet that was sent out.

The Connection between Keys and Chest

The answers to the question about the connection between keys and chest were anticipated. The French and the representatives of the Romance countries favor mechanics and the Barcker lever; the Germans, Austrians and Swiss favor pneumatics. In this connection it should be said that German organists who are acquainted with the Barcker pneumatic lever favor it almost without exception, and that some French organists for practical reasons favor pipe pneumatics.

It is interesting to see that the artistic advantages of mechanics and the disadvantages of pipe pneumatics are recognized even in the camp of the supporters of pipe pneumatics. In about two-thirds of the answers from the German experts and organ players this stereotyped phrase occurs again and again: "The artistic ideal for clear and plastic playing and for elastic precision is mechanics." And in more than half these answers the opinion is sympathetically upheld that organs up to fifteen stops should once more be built with mechanical action.

Thus is expressed a critical appraisal of pipe pneumatics, which has taken shape only within the past ten years. Until that time pneumatics had been preferred to the tracker because of its *alleged* absolute precision; this prejudice accounted for its rapid victory.

More precisely, the critics of pipe pneumatics mention its slowness for distances over twenty meters, as well as the fingering difficulties it causes within the boundaries where it functions well. The expression "dead precision" often occurs. "Even the better pneumatic systems are always somewhat disconcerting to me when I play," writes a competent artist. "I retard, I hurry, as though at every moment I had to struggle with the instrument to make it obey my rhythmic intention." Another expresses his feeling in these words: "With many pneumatic organs the expression is extremely precise. A pressure of the keys—and the tone is already there. And yet when I play a composition in a quick tempo I feel betrayed and sold out; I drag, I hasten, I play incorrectly, and it is as if I were kneading dough. Experience has taught me that the pneumatics itself is not to blame, but rather the spring pressure under the keys, in contrast to the pull of the tracker."

In the face of such universal observations by the artists, it signifies little that many organ builders are astounded that any objections at all should be raised against pneumatics; and that one of them disinters the ancient anecdote about a player who complained that he could not play Bach well on a pneumatic organ and received the well-merited answer that he should learn.

It is significant, however, that in the circle of the critics the conviction is almost universal that none of these complaints could have prevented the victory of the pneumatic system in those countries where it has prevailed. "The future is no longer with mechanics," is the word on all sides; even the supporters of the Barcker lever admit that it will hardly conquer those countries in which it is not already domesticated.

The following advantages are attributed to pneumatics:
1. simplicity of the arrangements;
2. cheapness;

3. noiselessness in good systems;
4. independence of temperature;
5. its advantages in the arrangement of playing helps.

It is the last fact that brings even Romance organ builders into the camp of the pneumatics.

The general judgment is then as follows: on the whole the victory is conceded to pneumatics, but its artistic improvement is desired. Those who study the nature of playing severely criticize the false assumption, so widespread among organ builders and organ players, that that organ speaks precisely whose keys release the sound at the slightest touch. That is a deception. Our pneumatic systems work badly because, in order to simulate precision, no free play is provided; without such free play no artistic playing is possible; artistry demands that before the tone comes the finger should feel the key.

As a second disadvantage, the excessive lightness of pressure the finger has to exert upon the key is generally recognized.

As a third, the kind of springs used are objected to; the simple down-pressure of a spring will always be unpleasant to the finger; it does not suffice to give the feeling of elastic resistance, which in the mechanical action controls the rising and falling of the keys, so that the result is a clearly integrated playing.

In the fourth place, it is argued that when one has to supply the pipes also with the wind from the pneumatic system, the pressure in the pipes in small and middle-sized organs must be greater than usual.

The solution, then, is the improvement of the pneumatic system; and not by any means the pipe pneumatics only, but the pneumatics of the keys as well. The triumph of the "primitive key" is clear. The proper fall and the proper free play of the key must be provided; and an elastic manner of playing suitable to the finger must be sought. One task is here indicated.

Among the solutions which lead to the ideal, that one only will be named here which provides a mechanical leverage in the console, which then in turn operates the pipe pneumatics. This opinion would be supported by a good many of those who answered, even among the Germans. They want, in place of the spring, a "weighted lever for the finger," which would also be a kind of mechanical transmission.

This union of mechanics and pipe pneumatics would perhaps have the additional advantage that one could employ pneumatics without hindrance for distances of more than twenty meters by lengthening the mechanical action accordingly.

More than once the thought was expressed that in small and middle-sized organs the connection between the keys and the chest should be mechanical while the controlling devices should be pneumatic.

The chest which utilizes the outgoing wind is generally considered the best system; though the utilization of the incoming wind has also its intelligent defenders.

The enthusiasm for electricity is not great. Isolated voices are indeed heard from those who think that even the smallest organs should be electric; but in general the attitude towards electricity is cool and somewhat skeptical. "How far can we depend upon it?" is the recurrent, stereotyped question. The French are almost without exception opposed to it. Among the others are those who recognize electricity as a necessity to overcome distances that are beyond the capacity of pneumatics, though even here some champions of electricity think the Barcker mechanism the best. Concerning the advantages and the durability of a particular system the judgments are often diametrically opposed, and this often in relation to the same instruments. One hails the electrical action in question as precise, another is not pleased with it; one praises it as very durable, another says of the same instrument that he has continual trouble with it.

Whether the wholly electric or the electro-pneumatic system is preferable cannot be decided from the answers.

The Germans who answered believe that the future belongs to the electric systems that have proved their worth in very big organs. On the other hand, the same circles must admit that the keys, as they are now constructed on electric organs, are almost beyond imagining unsatisfactory and primitive for playing.

The Chest

In the answers to the second question, concerning the slider wind chest and the ventil wind chest, one is as much surprised as in the answers to the first question about mechanical and pneumatic actions. The majority defend the artistic advantages of the slider wind chest for promptness of speech and tone formation. The effect of the slider wind chest on the reeds is especially emphasized; the statement is often made that the total effect of an organ is appreciably better with the slider wind chest than with the ventil wind chest. A competent German organist states "that with the slider wind chest one can get a delicate and sustained tone without any hissing aspiration," which is not characteristic of the ventil wind chest; another goes so far as to make the ventil wind chest responsible for the concertina-like tone of the modern organ. In several answers one reads of the impression that the tone production of the Silbermann organs makes on attentive observers. It is interesting to note that even German and Swiss organ builders, who work with ventil wind chests, recognize the advantages of the slider wind chest. What is adduced against the slider wind chest often goes back to the fact that the writers have in mind the poor slider wind chests of the old village organs, and are not aware of the existence of good old slider wind chests and improved modern wind chests, as the French build them. Otherwise they would not state that a slider wind chest can never furnish sufficient wind for a considerable number of stops.

Justly, however, the remark is made in various quarters that the modern defenders of the slider wind chest credit it with more merit than it deserves; and that an objective judgment of its effect upon tone formation can be formed only on the basis of an experiment in which one hears the same pipes in the same room first on the slider wind chest and then on the ventil wind chest, since it can never be determined otherwise whether the tonal advantages are really to be attributed to the slider wind chest. It is therefore highly significant that one organist who answers, and who is at the same time an accomplished organ builder, has with great care carried out this experiment. He used for the same pipes first the slider wind chest, then the ventil wind chest, then the diaphragm chest; and pronounced in favor of the slider wind chest, which he could identify by its sound even blindfolded and therefore not knowing which wind chest was to be used.

Various things are mentioned to explain the favorable effect of the slider wind chest. One of its defenders remarks, "The thinning of the air in the slider wind chest channels, along with the lessened wind pressure, is the cause of the prompt, elastic, and beautiful expression of the Silbermann and French instruments." Others think that the direct admission of the wind is responsible; still others believe that the slider wind chest has a certain capacity for vibration and resonance which the other chests lack.

In spite of the artistic recognition the slider wind chest receives, it appears from the questionnaire that people in countries where it is not current will never go back to it. "From the artistic standpoint I am for the slider wind chest, from the practical standpoint I am for the ventil wind chest, or the diaphragm chest"—dozens of times this opinion appears in the answers. Most organ builders are no longer equipped for the construction of slider wind chests; they are more expensive to build, and to be good demand very careful construction; moreover, the ventil wind chest offers advantages for a cheap and convenient arrangement of the controlling mechanism that the slider wind chest does not have.

Therefore the solution here also appears to be this: to keep the modern, but in such a way that the artistic advantages of the old may as far as possible be united with it. Let the ventil and pneumatic wind chests be built in any manner desired; but arranged in such a way that they permit to the greatest degree possible the direct admission of the wind to the pipes. This is the way pointed out by several German builders. One remarks that if the pipes are not placed too closely together any chest will finally give good results.

The Disposition of Registers

The judgment in general is pretty uniform concerning the arrangement. It is asserted that the arrangements of the past thirty years are no longer suitable to the nature of the organ, but that for some years past a noticeable improvement has been evident. On all sides more mixed stops are demanded; fewer thick, eight-foot pipes should be built, and sixteen-foot stops in the manuals should be used more sparingly. An organ richer in lovely overtones is once more desired. At the same time there is a demand for the enrichment of the manuals with good reeds. Several times the remark is made that more four-foot stops than formerly must be built for the proper blending of the eight-foot foundation stops with the mixtures. These principles should be applied not simply to the big and middle-sized organs but also to the smaller ones. Even for organs of ten stops a mixture and a reed should be provided. By and large we have then a reversion to the old ideal of the organ; it has been realised that an organ equipped only with foundation stops is incomplete.

Concerning the distribution of the stops on the manuals, two somewhat confused conceptions arise together. For some, the second and third manuals are simply miniatures of the great organ; for others, each manual should present a distinct individuality, in which the numerical gradation of the organs has no importance whatever. In general, however, the enrichment of the other organs is advocated. In this respect northern Germany is most backward.

Of the greatest value are the arrangements sent in; for here each man could draw up his plan without any reference to its cost, and solely to express his dominant ideal. The French prefer the reeds at the expense of the mixtures and foundation stops; the arrangements of organ builders from the south of France are typical in this respect. The Italians lay great stress upon the mixtures, the ripieni, and thus greatly if not completely neglect the reeds; the Germans permit the reeds and mixtures to disappear almost entirely—even when their expressed principles might have led us to expect something else. In the arrangements of the pedal the Germans call for an excessive number of sixteen-foot and eight-foot foundation stops, while in contrast the French and English pedals are poorly equipped with them.

In principle it is generally agreed that the smallest organs—even those with fewer than ten stops—should have two manuals; though some voices call for at least ten stops in each manual. The three-manual organ usually begins with thirty registers. One cannot clearly discern from the answers whether four or five manuals are generally considered useful for the bigger organs. Outstanding organists are of the opinion that three manuals—all three representing distinct tone personalities—suffice for as many as seventy stops, and that four or five manuals are often misused.

The Swell

Concerning the swell box many voices are heard expressing the old opinion that a little organ, and particularly a church organ, does not need a swell box; one of the answers characterizes the introduction of a swell box in little organs as "a nuisance." But in general the principle still prevails that every organ should have a well-constructed and well-furnished swell box. Different opinions are still to be found as to whether, of three organs, two belong in the swell box. Prominent musicians in general think one swell box organ sufficient, especially when the organ is placed in a church auditorium; some organ builders point to the danger of marring the tone by too much wood inside an organ. The question whether an entire instrument should be encased in the swell box is not at the moment being seriously discussed; the question arises mainly for very little organs, and for big organs in concert halls.

The divergence of opinion about principles of arrangement is naturally most noticeable in connection with small organs. The sketches sent in for ten, fifteen, and twenty stops are farthest apart. In the German arrangements the second organ becomes far less important than the first; whereas the French usually furnish it more completely, and always provide either a reed or a reed and a mixture. In German organs the two-foot stops, the reeds, and the mixtures are first placed in the great organ, and the second organ is provided with such stops only as the number of stops increases.

The French and British arrangements for three-manual organs are concerned with the completeness of the first and third organs, and let the second remain by comparison imperfect, so that it often numbers only half the stops of the third organ; they do this because of their conviction that the second organ is supplemented by coupling the third to it. In the German, Austrian, and Swiss plans the organs shade off in the order of first, second and third, so that neither of the two supplementary organs is complete, and the third, the swell-box organ, is often greatly stunted. The principle ever gaining more headway in Germany, that the full instrument should be clearly affected by the swell box of the coupled third or second organ, is practically negated by these arrangements.

The Octave Couplers

With reference to the octave coupling, most of those who answer are of the opinion that this is not to be dispensed with, particularly in small and middle-sized organs; but only that superoctave coupler is designated as artistically defensible which really brings in an upper octave. It is interesting to note that the earlier octave coupling, which was generally bad, and which brought in the upper octaves of the first organ, is severely attacked because of its crude effect; and in the same way the pedal superoctave coupler, which brings in the upper octaves of the pedal, is rejected as inartistic and of little use. The opinion is often expressed that the sub- and superoctave couplers should be limited to the supplementary organs, where they are less conspicuous. It is desired then to play the upper and lower octaves of the supplementary organs from the great organ. One organ builder proposes that the octave coupling should be so arranged that it would work the same when one plays on the supplementary organ itself as when one couples the great organ to that particular secondary organ; furthermore, the superoctave coupling of the third organ, or of the second and third organs, would be activated also by the coupling of the pedal to the particular organ or organs, whereby the bass would get an excellent touch, and attain a wonderful clarity. Organists who have tried such octave coupling have spoken appreciatively of its effect, and have recognised its great importance, particularly for the smaller church organs. We must not fail to say that many artists entirely reject octave coupling.

Borrowing

With reference to borrowing, the following distinctions, according to the answers which have come in, are to be made. Borrowing in the usual sense means that to supplement one organ arrangements are made to add to it one or more stops of another, or that the pedal should be enriched in the same way by stops from the manuals. To be distinguished from this is the combination of stops by which the series of octaves in one register is used in other pitches for the production of new registers, by which at times a three- and fourfold use of the same series of pipes is provided.

The principle of composition stops is defended in different ways. Its enthusiastic supporters see in it the revolutionizing of all organ building, and want to see it used on all organs, great and small. Others see in it only an emergency device to give a greater number of stops to small organs and to organs installed in small rooms. In general there is no great enthusiasm for composition stops. The opinion persists that this road is a deviation from true art, and results in sham organs, in which the distinctive character of a single stop cannot appear because the same rank of pipes must serve in different registers.

Borrowing by which the stop as a whole may still be played from another keyboard is, by and large, neither approved nor tolerated as an aid in small organs. It is believed that borrowing can be used in small organs to solve the pedal problem. But again and again we are made aware that the toleration of borrowing must be kept within the narrowest limits, because in the end it would result in the falsification of the entire organ. It is desired that in the arrangements the borrowed stops should not be counted twice, but only once; in order to prevent the unfair competition formerly carried on in this domain.

That borrowing which has as its purpose to make every stop usable from every manual is something very different. It would completely destroy the arrangement of an organ. The organist disposes of so many stops, which every time he divides among the different keyboards at his discretion and in accordance with his need. This ideal, called the "free keyboard," is vehemently defended by some organ players. Others do not go so far, and want only to play certain solo stops from each keyboard.

The Organ Tone

In the judging of the tone of the modern organ there is a unanimity of praise and blame which appears nowhere else. The praise—to take the good first of all—is for the voicing of the single stops, which is much more characteristically formed than on the old organ. The blame is directed at the *ensemble*; this criticism is particularly pronounced among the German and Austrian experts. There is hardly one among them who does not complain about the *forte* and the full modern organ. Always the same expressions are used: too strong; too dull; too flat; too blustery; too plethoric; too coarse. One of the Romance organists very well says, "Most organ builders confuse noise with fullness of tone." It is important that the organ builders themselves express this opinion.

The unpleasant cloudiness in the *ensemble* of the stops is explained by different circumstances, one emphasizing one thing and one another. Very often the domination of the shrill strings is held responsible; also the sharpness and the bad composition of the mixtures are blamed for the lack of rich and beautiful overtones. "Our mixtures have no brilliancy and no silver tones," writes a well-known organist. The poor quality of our diapasons is also pointed out. It is easy to convince oneself of this by pulling out together the diapason eight, the octave four, and the octave two, and listening to the result.

If, accordingly, the general judgment is that we have lost the true brilliancy of the organ to the orchestral effects, it must still be remarked that not everyone complains in the same manner of this change. From the answers we may conclude that today there are two conceptions of the organ, not one: the first, which abhors the orchestral in itself; and the second, which sees therein an evolution towards another type of organ. The alternative is church organ or concert organ.

Some organists express themselves in favor of the separation. One writes: "I do not hesitate to state that a complete separation of the church organ and the concert organ must and will come, so that the two instruments will hardly resemble each other any longer." Others desire to see the separation, but not in such an extreme form. Most, however, condemn the distinction, and find fault with any organ when the domination of characteristic stops, intoned without reference to the total sound effect, becomes too marked. They admit only one ideal for the organ: an instrument which contains indeed characteristic modern stops, but so shaded as not to injure the fullness and tone beauty of the entire instrument. It is generally admitted that it is for us to effect a reconciliation between the old organ and the modern one. One organist proposes that the great organ and the pedal should be kept with the old soft tone color, but that the other manuals should be modernized.

Wind Pressure and Dimensions

General unanimity rules, moreover, in the opinion that the unpleasant total sound effect is indeed partly a result of modern arrangements, but that wind pressure and scales are in incomparably greater measure responsible for it. Too strong wind pressure, too narrow scales, too high mouth: these comments recur again and again, so that the comparative reading of answers in this section becomes extremely monotonous.

These complaints are not unjustified. It appears from the statements of the organists that the average wind pressure that produces the tone equals about 100 mm. [3.94 inches] water column, whereas Silbermann worked with 65 and 70 mm. [2.56 and 2.76 inches]. The narrow scales and the high mouths are only the consequence of the high pressure, since the construction of the pipes must be adapted to the wind pressure. Thus we have come to the narrow, high-mouthed pipes, which are the cause of the harsh, unbearable tone in the upper register; the old measurements, with the exception of the diapasons, are considerably broader, and all have lower mouths. Abnormal wind pressure, abnormal pipes—this is what ails our art of organ building. It is a comfort to note that at last it is being generally recognized.

How did we come to get this wind pressure? Because we wanted strong-toned organs, and because we were looking for precision in the form of an unnaturally prompt speech in the pipes. "The inspector," one organ builder writes, "sat down at the organ, and the moment he stretched his finger over the key the tone had to be there already." In order to satisfy such demands, nothing remained but to overpower the pipes and to tear the tone from them with a high wind pressure, instead of permitting it to produce the tone naturally; which always takes a small fraction of time, whether we are dealing with a pipe blown by a human mouth, or with one that stands on a chest. "It is the high wind pressure that is responsible for the unnatural, unarticulated, thundering entrance of the tone," writes one well-known musician, "and the hissing noises that accompany it are also attributable to it."

A second temptation to high wind pressure came from the use of pneumatics for the pipes. In small organs, particularly when one has to think of economy, the most important thing is to get along with one and the same wind pressure, and to make the pipes function with the same pressure as the pneumatics. It happens, therefore, that many small and middle-sized organs have a wind pressure of up to 110 mm. [4.33 inches].

The generally expressed verdict is: back to the lower pressure, to the broader scales, to the lower mouths. With reference to the scales, many informed persons think that not only the scales themselves are false, but also the interval at which the scales are halved.

A normal pressure of 80–85 mm. [3.15–3.35 inches] for the foundation stops and of 70–75 mm. [2.76–2.96 inches] for the mixed stops is suggested. For the reeds the most favorable pressure proposed is 100–120 mm. [4.33–4.73 inches]; many, however, would go as high as 150 mm. [5.91 inches] for single reeds. A few Italian organ builders work today with the lowest wind pressure. One of them gives for the foundation stops 45–50 mm. [1.77–1.97 inches] and for the solo stops and the reeds 60–80 mm. [2.36–3.15 inches].

A reasonable difference in wind pressure is in general favored, because it is also of course the most natural thing for each kind of pipe to receive its most favorable wind. But the additional cost of these differences in bellows, wind channels, and chests always cause some discouragement. It is a cause of rejoicing to find the conviction that it is a crime to voice small organs with high wind pressure. A medium wind pressure of 80–85 mm. [3.15–3.35 inches] is suggested, with which, when only one pressure is available, foundation stops, mixtures, and reeds sound well; yet one will commonly usually use in organs with pneumatic action the pressure of the pipe pneumatics for the reeds. It is interesting to see that those acquainted with reed stops propose that in the larger organs should be installed not only modern reeds with high wind pressure, but also those which sound with only 85–90 mm. [3.35–3.55 inches] and give the soft tone of the old trumpets. Especially favored are the soft English trumpets.

In general, the principle is upheld that the wider and bigger the pipes, the more moderate the pressure. In this connection, it seems remarkable that in spite of this many answers propose that the pedal should receive a stronger wind than the manuals. On the other hand, some want for the foundation stops of the pedal not more than 80 mm. [3.15 inches], and report that with this they have got specially clear and full pedals.

A French organ builder employs a special differentiation in wind pressure by dividing his wind chests into three parts, so that the lower register of the stop gets a great deal of wind at moderate pressure, the middle register a moderate amount of wind at a higher pressure, and the upper register very little wind at a high pressure. The results of this differentiation are very good, especially for beautiful expression; but the expense is correspondingly high.

The answers often bring out that the wind pressure must be adapted to the size of the room, so that to achieve an adequate tone we may have a high pressure for big rooms. Others are of the opinion that the size of the room has nothing to do with the pressure to be applied to the foundation stops and mixtures, but that we get a much more beautiful effect if somewhat larger scales are used for big rooms and a richer supply of wind is provided.

From the answers this fact in any case emerges, that when we are concerned with wind pressure and scales we are in the center of the problem, and that the time is past when we may leave the decision in these matters to the organ builders; yet it is also evident that a number of experts are wholly uninformed about this subject. There are a few who think that the experts do not need to concern themselves with wind pressure and dimensions.

Concerning the question of scales, the complaint is made in various quarters that many organ builders no longer make their own pipes but get them from the factories, and therefore accept the scales and mouths which happen to be in vogue at the time, instead of making their own artistic experiments and copying old and tested scales. In the end, the question of scales is not a problem in higher mathematics and physics, as it sometimes might seem, but a problem of simple artistic experimentation and imitation.

"To bring scales, wind pressure, and tone into harmony," therein lies, in the opinion of one of those answering, the task which confronts organ builders if they wish once again to create tuneful and beautiful instruments.

The Pedal

On the question of the pedal the opinions are very diverse, above all concerning the range. England, France, Switzerland, and the south German provinces are generally in favor of having the same pedal board for every organ, small or great, with thirty notes, extending to C-f[1], and a few even want it to go to C-g[1]. The North will be satisfied with a pedal for middle-sized and smaller organs of twenty-seven keys reaching to C-d[1], and wants a pedal to C-f[1] only for big instruments. It has been often remarked that this difference does not make sense, since modern compositions all presuppose a pedal extending to f[1], and are not to be played exclusively on big organs. The higher costs for a pedal with thirty keys are so slight that opposition from this point of view is not understandable.

The range is much more conditioned by the presupposed dimensions of the pedals. "How can anyone expect me to compass a pedal of C-f[1]?" an angry Northern organist asks. We can understand his irritation if we remember that he accepts as correct the old royal Prussian measurements of 1876, which are so great that acrobatics were required to reach the f[1]. On these pedals 112 cm. [3 feet, 8 inches] were necessary for C-d[1]. The new Prussian arrangement of 1904 has 104 cm. [3 feet, 5 inches] for the same range of keys; the Mecheln dimension—shown on Catholic Day [1] at Mecheln in 1864 —provides 97½ cm. [3 feet, 2 inches] for twenty-seven keys; the modern French pedals are still narrower.

Those who go farther into this question of pedal dimensions express themselves in favor of the Mecheln measurements. From the North, however, rises the anxious cry that the pedals might be too narrow and the keys too small. That the pedals of Bach's time were even narrower and smaller than the Mecheln pedals, and that nevertheless he had no objection to them but played tolerably well on them even by modern standards, seems not to have come to the mind of many an excellent respondent to the questionnaire.

[1] The German Catholic Day was first observed in 1848. Since 1880 it has been an annual observance. C. R. J.

The solution of the problem of scales is closely tied to the decision concerning another alternative: the straight or the concave pedal. If the concave pedal is accepted in principle, then the large proportions no longer play as significant a rôle, since the foot can easily cover an even longer span because of the concavity. The answers inform us that even in those countries where this pedal is not well known the opinion in favor of it has greatly advanced in recent times. Even those who are not acquainted with such a pedal in practice say candidly that it commends itself to natural reflection. Therefore a majority have come to favor the concave pedal, which only a few years ago was not thought of.

As for the position of the pedal in relation to the manual, most people still hold fast to the dogma that c must lie under c^1; the ardent advocates of the pedal of thirty keys remark, however, that the abandonment of this principle can be justified, and that it is indeed feasible to let the middle of the manual be over the middle of the pedal, since otherwise the upper half of the pedal keyboard would be wider than the lower.

In relation to moving the pedal farther under the manuals, voices are heard to the effect that a somewhat deeper position—something like that which the French use—would be an advantage for comfortable playing.

The Manuals

In the answers to the question of the manual dimensions, it is emphasized without exception that the manuals should be brought as close together as possible, so that changing from one manual to another may be expedited to the highest degree. It is well known that Bach expressed himself in favor of this principle. But very few draw from this demand the consequence that we must then build somewhat shorter keys, as we did forty years ago.

Concerning the range of the keyboard and the breadth of the keys, some demand a close imitation of the dimensions of the modern concert piano; others point to the fact that *legato* playing on the organ, with its sustained notes and finger substitutions, would be greatly facilitated if the keys were shortened, and in this they refer to the measurements of the old keyboard. At any rate, there is more conviction here than in the demand that we should accept the keyboard dimensions of the concert piano. It is axiomatic that the dimensions of a keyboard should be adapted to the necessities of the kind of playing practised on it. The pretext that familiarity with the dimensions of the piano keyboard would constitute hindrance for playing on a somewhat narrower organ keyboard is contradicted by wide experience, and would collapse of itself at the slightest trial.

The Striving for Unity

Complete unity in the measurements of the console have not been achieved, then, even though the proper lines for a future unity are much more clearly revealed than we might have expected. What is the opinion about letting the authorities regulate the dimensions of the console? Affirmative and negative answers clash rudely and in equal numbers. There is nowhere, however, much faith in the possibility of achieving unity in this way. Often a middle way is sought. It is to be desired that the experts should first come to an agreement, and then that what is recognized to be good may of itself in time be everywhere realized; therefore only one thing needs to be desired of the authorities, namely, that they should place no difficulties in the way of what the wide circle of experts recommends as simple and practical, but should permit it to find acceptance alongside the arrangements existing at the time.

What many have to say concerning the extent of the unity to be sought after is well worth taking to heart. They believe that we should not exaggerate the notion of unity, and seek to create circumstances shaped for the benefit of the traveling musician, to the extent that these shall everywhere find the same measurements and arrangements to relieve them of the necessity of familiarizing themselves with strange instruments. The striving for unity has nothing to do with such demands; it desires only that whatever is generally recognized to be practical should everywhere prevail. That a genuine artist should quickly find himself at home on any organ constructed with a certain amount of intelligence, even though it has other keyboards and pedals than the one to which he is accustomed—this must be considered as axiomatic.

The result of the answers, then, is that the authorities in countries and districts where official specifications exist should modify these in the interests of a desired unity to such an extent that an opportunity is given to experiment with that which elsewhere is recognized to be practical, and if it really proves to be so, to let it prevail.

The Playing Aids

In classifying the answers to the question about the arrangement of the console, we have to distinguish between what is wanted in the way of playing aids and what their arrangement should be.

A simplification of the console is everywhere desired. It is found that the middle-sized and smaller organs are particularly overburdened with all possible draw-knobs and pistons, sometimes quite useless, which are often in striking contrast to the number and quality of the stops.

The synthetic stops, on which a few years ago we used to place so much emphasis, have fallen completely into discredit.

The same fate has befallen the fixed composition stops. "It is not the organ builder, but I, that determine the registration," says one energetic gentleman; others are less drastic in their words, though just as decisive.

The register crescendo is attacked by many as the work of the devil, by others regarded as a necessary evil; by most, however, it is considered a useful aid, when it is properly placed and intelligently used. It is thought to have special advantages in the accompanying of cantatas, passions, and oratorios, when the steps in the changing tone color and tone strength are concealed by the singing voices and the orchestra.

The blind combinations are generally approved, and make the fixed ones wholly superfluous. Even the French and the Italians recognize the worth of this device. In German lands, on the contrary, an opinion is expressed in favor of a pedal to bring in the mixtures and reeds, especially in the larger organs.

The situation is therefore much clearer than one might have expected. As constituent helps in the organ of the future, only blind combinations and crescendo register are envisaged; in large organs something should be considered in the way of pedals to bring in the mixtures and reeds. Everything else is more or less superfluous trimming.

There are different opinions about the number of general blind combinations. Some would get along with one, or on larger organs with two; others want from four to six. This latter demand is to be explained by the fact that the draw-stop which brings in the blind combination is usually so arranged that it works on all the manuals and the pedal at the same time, so that several blind combinations are of course necessary for repeated changes in tone.

Most of those who answer consider this kind of arrangement so necessary that they do not take into consideration how much more useful a blind combination would be if it were so arranged that it could be restricted to each single manual or to the pedal, and then at will, by the use of another draw-stop, all the keyboards could be brought in together. Only a minority consider the advantages of this arrangement, by which each manual and the pedal would have its own blind combination stop, and at the same time another stop would be provided to place the whole organ on a blind combination.

The question whether from the artistic standpoint those playing aids are most advantageous which add new stops to a drawn registration or retire them, without cancelling the drawn registration, is generally recognized in principle as most important, in so far as it makes a change in tone color possible without an interruption, as is usually desired in the masterpieces; since these much oftener have in view the modification of the tone color and the return to the first registration than the continuing change of the tone colors.

It should be mentioned that only very few among the organ builders have seen the significance of this question; a considerable number of them reply that they cannot imagine the usefulness of such an arrangement. It is clear from this how unwise it is to turn over the arrangement of the console to those who often have room in their thinking only for technical considerations and none for artistic ones.

Concerning the kind of playing helps, two proposals, which have been tested practically and artistically, are made. One is that we should have two sets of blind combinations: one that cancels the drawn registration, another that adds the stops prepared to the drawn stops. The second proposal anticipates the double use of the same set of blind combinations; by a previously drawn stop, which either fixes the hand registration or makes it unstable, a device operates which either adds the prepared registration to the existing registration, when one introduces the blind combination, or detaches it from it—depending on whether one has given a fixed or fluid character to the drawn registration by the draw-stop.

As to the arrangement of the register crescendo, the observation is made that it has value when it is connected with a stop or tablet movement which permits it to work so that it either annuls or supplements the drawn registration and the blind combination.

It is desired, moreover, that the sequence in which the stops are introduced should not be determined by the organ builder alone but by the artist in coöperation with him, so that the crescendo would be beautifully and effectively planned.

Among the artists themselves, however, there is no unanimity about the arrangement of the register crescendo. Some think of it as exhausting itself upon a single keyboard, whereby, however, the possibility of an unbroken crescendo is given up. For the others the ideal lies in an unbroken crescendo on the whole organ; they want to bring in the stops on the coupled manuals, without regard to their progression on the single keyboard, so as to produce the most beautiful total crescendo of which the organ is capable. Both arrangements can be defended; the second is more commendable because it usually is concerned with the total crescendo through the use of the register crescendo.

Worthy of much consideration is a proposal which brings into the foreground these opposing principles. It is that over the draw-knobs other knobs should be placed with which the player can determine each time at his own discretion the crescendo that he wants to realize with the register crescendo, not only in the sequence of stops but also in the use of the couplers. If this can be carried out—and our organ builders assure us that it is technically possible—then with one stroke the register swell has become something very different from what it was, and offers an artistic help of the first rank.

The tendency that comes to light in the desired playing aids may be expressed in two sentences. The first is: away from the principle of rigid, unchangeable combinations, even for the register crescendo.

The second aims at such an arrangement of the blind combinations and register *crescendo* that they can either keep or replace the drawn registration. A supplementary demand is that the blind combinations have draw-stops for each separate organ, and at the same time a stop that brings them all into play together. If this is accomplished, then we are freed from the motley organ which has been built for the past thirty years, in which there is a clash of the most diverse principles.

The Arrangement of the Playing Aids

As to the arrangement of the playing aids desired, the answers show sharply divergent opinions. The group influenced by the French desire pedals for the feet, the Germans want draw-stops for the hands. With conviction the defenders of the first theory assert that one usually has a foot free in playing, never a hand; with the same conviction the others maintain that the feet already have too much trouble with the playing pedals to be further bothered with couplers and combinations. If one goes to the bottom of the answers, one notices that we are really dealing with two different artistic ideals. In accordance with one, the player wishes to manipulate the couplers and combinations himself; in accordance with the other, he turns this responsibility over to one or two helpers. The second is plainly favored by German musicians in their answers, and is set down as the rule for concert playing. Thereby we should arrive again at the distinction between the concert organ and the church organ, between concert playing and playing for divine worship, and therefore any general conception of the organ and of organ playing would be impossible.

But the way is open for an agreement: in that even many musicians with German tendencies are outspoken for the practical worth of pedals, consider the technical demands which the utilization of them raises no longer as insuperable as it seemed a short time ago, and have come to value an independence from assistants in playing. On the other side, the players with French ideals have had to admit that the ideal of self-sufficiency is not always possible when one has to do with a rather complicated registration, so that draw-stops which make possible the assistance of others are in any case an advantage.

Thus the majority envisage the outcome of this conflict in a double arrangement of playing helps, and want the most important resources made available both as pedals and as draw-stops, so connected that what has been introduced or cut off by the foot may be at the same time introduced or cut off by the hand, and vice versa.

No technical difficulties stand in the way of satisfying this demand; and the costs involved are very moderate for the advantages secured, particularly when the organ builders are prepared for it. The support won for the idea of the double availability of the playing helps—a fairly recent idea—is surprisingly large. About four-fifths of the answers are in favor of it.

As for further details of console construction, it is to be noticed that the recently customary method of arranging a playing help in such a way that it offered two adjacent draw-stops—one for the introduction and the other for the release—has more and more been given up, because this method needlessly doubles the number of stops. It is desired that the same stop should serve for the introduction or the release, as one pushes it in or lets it return to its original position.

There is no agreement yet about the movement of the pedals. Some want the same movement for bringing in and cutting off the stop, following the English model. To introduce the stop one presses the pedal, which rises again of itself; when one presses it a second time the stop is cut off. The French principle is that the pedal when pressed down automatically catches at the side; to release it one needs only to detach it from this catch by a slight pressure, whereupon it comes quickly up again. This has the advantage that one can always see whether a coupler or a combination is on, and that one can release several depressed pedals at one time by gliding the foot lightly over them and letting them rise again. It is to be supposed that this method will triumph. The direction of the hooking should be always towards the outside in the movement of the foot; the pedals lying at the right should hook to the right, those lying at the left should hook to the left.

Deserving of every consideration is the advice in a number of answers that the pistons should not be placed in the middle under the manuals, where they are hidden by the hands and sleeves of the player, not only from his controlling eye but also from his assistant, but in disregard of symmetry should be shoved over to the left, where they are more accessible to the eye of both the assistant and the player: to the player because he much oftener has his left hand free—thanks to the pedal, or can make it free at need—than his right. The use of the thumb to press the pistons while the fingers play quietly on is not to be thought of, no matter how often it is proposed.

The Arrangement of the Stops

The remaining opinions concerning the console have to do with either self-evident or unimportant things. Concerning the distribution of the stops beside or above the manuals, no single idea emerges; in this thing only everyone is agreed, that we must put an end to the absence of planning. Foundation stops, mixtures, and reeds must no longer be all mixed together like cabbages and rape. The French like to arrange foundation stops at the left of the keyboard and the mixtures and reeds at the right. This arrangement has its advantages; the disadvantages are that one never has an organ as a whole before him, and that this distribution is often very difficult to effect. The Germans want to keep all the stops of a single organ together; this is very clear in many respects, but it has still the disadvantage that one has to find the reeds and mixtures under the foundation stops. A compromise proposal suggests that the stops be arranged in the German fashion by organs at the side of the manuals, but that the mixtures and reeds be placed at the outer edge, whereby the control of the draw-stops is greatly facilitated.

The preference for register knobs or tilting tablets remains undecided. German organists have become accustomed to the tablet; but already voices are lifted there again to praise the beauty, the solidity, and the other advantages of the simple register draw-knob.

Questions of Detail

There is a good deal of wrangling in the German camp as to whether the register *crescendo* should be installed as a cylinder pushed by the foot, or as a balanced pedal. There are mutual recriminations. The stubborn defenders of the cylinder in the north greatly outnumber the defenders of the balanced pedal. The latter object principally to the jolting movement which is unavoidable in the use of the cylinder.

It should of course be taken for granted that the apertures for the balanced pedal are generous, that the balance has the proper breadth, that the balancing movement is even and comfortable for the foot, and that it can be stopped in any position. How seldom this may be taken for granted in actual construction is evident from the answers; almost all the players complain, particularly—as one of them expresses it—because the balanced pedal seems to be better adapted to the foot of a little ballet dancer than to the masculine boot. Complaints are also voiced that many organ builders reverse the motion, so that the descrescendo is produced by pressing down the pedal and the crescendo follows when it is brought back.

Thus may be summed up the most important results of the questionnaire concerning playing helps and console arrangements. The interesting point is that even here the proposed solutions show one and the same tendency, the "simplication of the console."

The Concert Organ

The answers to the question, "What do you think of our concert organ?" has turned out to be really classic. Almost without exception the organists answer, "Not much," underlining both words; and the organ builders declare that it would not be becoming to them to pass judgment on the work of their colleagues. We have to do here mainly with the answers from German lands, since in the Romance countries there are very few organs in concert halls. The Romance organists express themselves, however, as little edified by German concert organs.

It is the unanimous judgment that the architects are primarily responsible for the undeniably artistic failure in the construction of concert organs. They are to blame for the fact that these organs have been set in holes where they cannot be played effectively; and where, in addition, distance makes almost impossible any good collaboration by organ and chorus and orchestra.

It is also emphasized that these organs sound bad because they all speak with too high a wind pressure. The mistakes in modern mensuration and intonation come out in the dry acoustics of these halls—dry in comparison with the acoustics of vaulted stone churches —two and three times more conspicuously than in the auditoriums consecrated to the service of God. Therefore these instruments have about them something harsh and shrill, which is the general complaint. As for the problem the concert organ has set for modern acoustical art, it is crystal clear that the latter is not equal to such problems because it does not even recognize them.

The Question of Appearance

The appearance of the modern concert organ is also criticized. The words "miserable, devoid of taste," and their synonyms are heaped upon it in an almost alarming manner. A number of respondents go into a rage over the fact that these organs lose all external similarity to the ecclesiastical instrument by the concealment of their pipes. On the other hand, a few justify from an artistic point of view this fault, due to a lack of money. They seek to prove that the appearance of pipes is not appropriate for a hall, and that the exterior of the organ in these rooms should be a painted surface, which hides the pipe work. A few would like to see the sight of pipes banished even from the church, and one proposes for the front of the organ pictures from Bible history.

The opinion is unanimous that the design and the construction cannot please because there is too much emphasis on economy. Furthermore, the haste with which the work must proceed in view of the short time allowed for delivery makes genuine and excellent wood carving impossible. Therefore modern organs cannot compare in appearance with the old.

Several organ builders remind us of the dangers to the sound which arise from such a crowded case. For smaller instruments the simple English arrangement of external pipes with no wood at all is often to be recommended for esthetic and practical reasons.

The Rückpositiv

The rückpositiv projecting out into the church has both friends and enemies. The enemies find it ugly and do not think much of the acoustical effect. Further, they would have us remember that such a projection prevents the proper disposition of the choir, and hides from the organist the view of the church. The defenders are in an impressive majority. They not only mention the architectural significance derived from interrupting the bare balcony rail we now see before the organ, but they speak also of an interesting acoustical effect. In the disposition of a choir before the organ they emphasize the fact that the *rückpositiv* can be set so low that we need not be concerned about its concealing anything. A number of those who answer want to have the *positiv* just for the sake of the singing, because only in this way is it possible to bring the pipe stops so close to the singers and the orchestra that we can properly speak of an accompaniment. Whoever has heard the Bach Passions accompanied by organs with the *rückpositivs*, which form with singers and orchestra a compact mass, knows how to prize them as they deserve. The organ builders as a body are against the *rückpositiv* because it is difficult to set up and costly to construct. When they assert, however, that the small size of the case will permit them to install only three or four stops, we may be permitted to reply that it should be easy to build a projecting structure for as many as ten. Of course, for the *rückpositiv* there may be considered only rather narrow eight-foot stops, a disproportionately large number of four-foot stops, and delicate mixtures.

Prices

In answer to the tenth question, about prices, organ builders and organists alike agree that prices are far too low for good and artistic work. A single organ builder had the effrontery to say that they were sufficient, but had nothing to say about the quality of the work. Most of those who answer are of the opinion that even the usual factory wares cannot in the long run be delivered at these prices. Among the experts there are groups who have not yet taken this question seriously enough; otherwise it would not be conceivable that a number should declare themselves incompetent to speak on this point—though it is easy to get informed—and that others think this something that concerns only the organ builders. But those who hold such views are a diminishing minority compared to those who appreciate the seriousness of the situation.

That the artistic ability of the organ builder is in question needs no proof. But prices are too low, as trustworthy organ builders assert, even for stereotyped factory work. The question raised on many sides, "What will some day become of the organs built under such circumstances?" is alarming in its significance. It is often said that we are approaching a period of repairs and renovations—a period that will startlingly prove that the cheap organ is in the end more expensive. Nothing can be said for the durability of the organs now being built. In many ways the era of repairs and renovations has already begun.

The little firms most clearly see the critical situation into which organ construction has been brought by the conscienceless, mutual underbidding of the organ builders, by the false economy and the shortsightedness of buyers and organ inspectors. But even the bigger firms, which for a while thought lower prices would cause the downfall of the medium-sized and smaller organ builders and leave them untouched, are beginning to be worried lest they themselves be involved. One of the foremost German organ builders writes, as characteristic of the shocking situation, that recently he lost an order for a 5000-mark organ because another underbid him by 400 marks, though he himself had set the lowest price possible, and sacrificed all profit. It is also characteristic of the situation that the representative of a still larger firm remarks that it is able to continue only through its large sales and through the most farreaching utilization of machine work; and also because the organ maker has invested in the business only his own money. Thereby, however, he is admitting that organ building has ceased to be artistic handwork. In the complete use of machine work lies a great danger: the machine can never produce anything but the same work—always the same; it is the negation of that individualism in the little things that is the essence of artistic work. Most desolating is the remark of an organist who has also worked as an organ builder and can appraise the situation exactly. "If the cheaper zinc did not more and more take the place of tin, there would be hardly any profit left in the business."

And if it is asked why our organs are so badly toned, one familiar with the situation knows it is because the man who tones it is so poorly paid and has to work so rapidly that an artistic tone is not to be expected.

The Echo Organ

In the answers to the question of the justification for the echo organ, yes and no, conditional and unconditional, arise incoherently. Many reject it unconditionally as an inartistic plaything. "Angel song which drips down from a hole in the roof of the church," one calls it; another characterizes it as "the greatest of all wonders for old women, but an agony for musically sensitive ears." One group thinks it has some value as an appurtenance for the concert organ; as a concession to those who want such sensations—but protests immediately against its all too frequent misuse.

Others go farther, and consider the echo organ indispensable for concert use but not to be tolerated in the churches. A further group, which we may call the extreme right wing, thinks that the echo organ is particularly appropriate for the church. One member of this group asks, "Is it not exactly in accordance with the supernatural, to which we have to give expression in the service of worship and in the playing of the organ, that we should have sounds which float down upon us as if from the heights of heaven?"

On the technical side of the question, it is remarked that an echo organ can never be in tune with the main organ, because it is placed in another, higher part of the room, and accordingly has another temperature. Because of the distance it is impossible for it to work in harmony with the second and third organ, even with the use of electricity.

In numbers the judgments divide as follows: two-thirds of the respondents deny any justification at all for the echo organ; a quarter would permit its use, with certain precautions, in concert organs; the remainder assert that it has real justification either in the church or the concert hall.

It is interesting to note that in regions where good swell organs are built, only flat "no's" are given the echo organ question. Usually it is added that everything really musical which one tries to secure with an echo organ can be had with a beautiful, elevated, and well-furnished swell box.

Special Remarks

The twelfth question asked the respondents to make remarks, to share experiences, and to make suggestions they considered important; and the most valuable of these remarks are mentioned here, beginning with the technical matters.

That organist who is also an accomplished organ builder, and who has already been quoted several times, tells how, in pursuing and amplifying the ideas of the well-known Abt Vogler, one can get, in rooms which will not permit the installation of an open sixteen-foot pipe, the same effect by having a covered eight-foot pipe of quintadena quality speak with an open eight-foot one.

An organ expert pleads for the manufacture once more of beautiful metal gedackts and flutes; and urges us to replace the sixteen-foot violone, which speaks with difficulty and makes the whole pedal lazy, with a broad-scaled sixteen-foot contrabass speaking under lower pressure, or with a salicet bass, which would give the bass in fact the same volume.

A number of times the thought was expressed that the organ builder should be considered once more with greater interest from the scientific side, and that a part of the work and strength that are now devoted to purely historical studies in the domain of musical science should be devoted to the old and new organ construction. A few good doctoral theses on organ construction would surely not be a bad idea.

Several organ builders and players speak for a good tremolo stop. Others call our attention to the fact that it would be a good thing to introduce some day a unified list of stop names, so that the same thing would not appear under so many different names—one of the evils of the culinary art.

Another suggestion was made that each organ should be provided with a thermometer, and an indicator to show at what temperature the instrument, and particularly the reeds, were tuned.

A proposal aroused our sympathy that the few remaining beautiful organs from the eighteenth century should be adopted and classified as historic monuments, in order that they should not fall victims to the vandalism of modern times like so many of their beautiful sisters, but should be intelligently and worthily restored so that they might outlive our modern instruments.

It has also been suggested that we form a collection of old and beautiful organ cases, and make them known, so that architects and organ builders can cultivate good taste by studying them.

We are warned by organists who love the old cases not to force new and enlarged organs into them. A number of other respondents who have seen this repeatedly happen take the opportunity to speak out passionately against the current widespread craze for enlargement. They do not think it fitting, that an instrument of forty stops should be installed in a room once comfortably filled by an instrument of twenty-five. The complaint is general that in the planning and ordering of organs too much attention is given to the number of stops and too little to their quality.

It should be remembered that many of the answers preach a crusade against architects who dare to assign the organ even in the churches to a completely inadequate and unsuitable position; and never take the trouble to inquire in authoritative quarters whether an organ can properly be placed in the room assigned to it.

The Problem of the Organ Inspector

Along with these technical questions the problem of the inspectors is often discussed. People point to the ignorance, the conceit of infallibility, and the instincts of a *pasha*, which not infrequently are found in government inspectors. It is asserted on all sides that one root of evil lies in the system of inspection as we now have it. The answers make clear that there are many intelligent and excellent inspectors. It would be a great mistake to generalize too much from the outspoken complaints, even though they come from many sides.

The evil lies not so much in the persons as in the institution. For a reform two roads are suggested. On one side, a different training of inspectors is desired. They should work for a year as practical organ builders and then pass an examination; their number should be decreased, and they should be better paid, in order that they may devote themselves entirely to their duties.

Others see the principal evil, not so much in the inadequate professional training of the inspectors, as in the fact that the incumbent rules without restraint in a particular area, making it impossible for any opinion but his own to be heard, and therefore putting on all the organs in that area the stamp of any erroneous ideas he may have. There is a known case of an inspector who considered the pedal C-f^1 superfluous, and never would permit the construction of a complete pedal, even when the organ builder added the three notes at his own expense. There is no need to emphasize the disadvantage that accumulates when a whole generation is allowed to have only those arrangements that conform to a particular scheme.

Certain proposals, therefore, are directed against the sole authority of the official inspectors, so that any organist interested in organ construction might have opportunity to be active in that field, and upon the invitation of the congregations to serve them as an inspector. No one person alone should decide the plan and building of an organ, but a commission of several should be appointed, so that every peculiarity in the plan of the organ and every personal prejudice in the choice of a builder may be avoided.

One comprehends the bearing of these remarks only when he reflects that in countries and regions where the institution of official inspectors exists it is often impossible for experts to secure any currency for their ideas or to render any service. If in the past decades there has been little constructive criticism on the art of organ building, one major reason is that many useful resources, both younger and older, have been paralyzed. It is to be noticed that not even in the Germany of the eighteenth century was there any privileged system of inspection; instead, the congregations called experts of their own choice. And it should also be mentioned that in countries which have no official inspectors organ building is in no worse condition than in the others; on the contrary, it has been advantaged by the freedom it has enjoyed, for this freedom has directly benefited the art. How far the authority of the official inspectors goes in many districts is evident in the demand made by one inspector that even private organ building should come under his jurisdiction. In this way organ building would fall entirely under official control.

The natural consequence of requisitioning a group of experts for the building of an organ would be that the office of inspector would cease to be an appointment for life, and would become an honor, with very modest compensation for travel and time. It is taken for granted that such a reform would take place only with full consideration for the present incumbents of the official posts, which they should be permitted to occupy for life.

Into the same category fall the remarks which characterize as unsuitable the custom of calling in the inspector only at the beginning and at the end of the installation of an organ. Usually he has the estimate to approve and the complete work to examine, but is wholly eliminated from the construction. "The organ examinations," remarks an inspector, "have only a conditional value, if the expert is brought in only when everything is finished. At that time he has usually nothing more to do than to inspect the damage." The proper thing would be for him to supervise the installation and the intonation. What might result from this, those who have been permitted to take part in the construction of an organ under these circumstances can testify.

If, however, such work were expected from the inspectors, it is clear that where previously one sufficed at least six or ten would then be necessary. It is pointed out at the same time that the inspector would get technical experience in organ building by this method. What he really needs to know he would learn on the spot by questions, observations, and common trials and tests with the organ builder.

The Organist and the Organ Builder

A number of observations have already been made upon the relations between the artists and the organ builders. Our artists, it is said on all sides, have nothing to do with the organ builders, or the builders with them; from this comes the often astonishing technical ignorance of the organists and their lack of intelligence in what they demand artistically of the builders; so that both are to blame for the stagnation in modern organ building. Improvement can come only when, by a gradual reform in the ways mentioned above, the construction of each organ becomes for the builder and several organists an opportunity for fruitful discussion and intensive collaboration.

The Economic Situation of the Organ Builder

A last group of remarks has to do with the economic situation of the organ builder and improvement in his standing. It is emphasized above everything else that the maintenance of the middle-sized and smaller organ builders is indispensable for the art. Of course there must be big concerns; they are required for the international market, and are created for it. But the smaller and middle-sized builders are equipped to produce worthy instruments for the church, and to watch over them with loving care. The big organ firm cannot fulfil these tasks as can the local master of organ building resident in a particular region. The big builder makes his own way; but to intercede for the support of the master of organ building, in the old excellent sense of the word, and with the idealism that surrounds it—this is the task of the church and of art, to both of which he belongs.

It is not only the low price that endangers the middle-sized and smaller builders; other things enter the situation. First mentioned is the short time allowed for delivery. Hardly has an organ been ordered when it is expected that it will be finished. One instance is known in which the builder was requested to install an instrument of over forty speaking stops in the space of three months. The reports on these questions are hair-raising. The smaller and middle-sized builders must divide the work among themselves. If one of them has to postpone delivery for a year he may not get the contract. The big firm can take a chance on a much shorter period. This almost childish conduct on the part of the buyer is to blame for much suffering among the masters of organ building, and often puts their very lives in jeopardy. One year they may have to let a number of good orders go by, because they are more than completely occupied; the next year they may have hardly anything to do. With a little understanding and a little coöperation on the part of the buyer both sides would be served.

The sense of almost all the answers is that the master of organ building must be so placed that he can serve his art without worry about his living, and with the assurance of a modest income; without having to wear himself out in a price war, and without having to submit himself unconditionally to the whims of an expert. If things go on as they are, in twenty to forty years organ building in most countries will be so ruined, artistically and economically, that it will have ceased to exist as an artistic handcraft.

But it is everywhere emphasised that only the capable ones should be maintained. When master joiners set themselves up as organ builders they ought to go quietly under; and when workers in the construction of organs make themselves independent without a penny of capital there is also nothing we need do to help them.

These, then, are the most important conclusions from the answers to the questionnaire. These answers have given all of us the impression of a clear conviction everywhere that ways and means must be found to help organ building out of the intolerable artistic and economic position in which at the moment it finds itself, and that, by and large, there is agreement in the minds of all earnest observers as to the means that must be taken. It is expected, however, that we who are here assembled should after mature consideration express these convictions clearly, and help to shape a common opinion which in time shall triumph over thoughtlessness. From this expectation we shall derive the fervor of our work and its joy.

Index

13. When you have finished praying through the hurts you have suffered, pray this prayer of faith:

Lord Jesus, by faith, I receive Your unconditional love and acceptance in the place of this hurt, and I trust You to meet all my needs. I take authority over the Enemy, and in the name of Jesus, I take back the ground I have allowed Satan to gain in my life because of my attitude toward _____.

Right now I give this ground back to the Lord Jesus Christ to whom it rightfully belongs.